DARKMAGE

A PORTION OF
THE EMPIRE
OF FERRYTH

DARKMAGE

THE SILENT TOWER
THE SILICON MAGE

Barbara Hambly

Nelson Doubleday, Inc.
Garden City, New York

Published by arrangement with
Del Rey/Ballantine Books
201 East 50th Street
New York, New York 10022

Printed in the United States of America

Quality Printing and Binding by:
Berryville Graphics
P.O. Box 272
Berryville, VA 22611 U.S.A.

CONTENTS

THE SILENT TOWER

TO THE MEMORY OF
JUDY-LYNN

CHAPTER I

"HAS THE ARCHMAGE RETURNED?"

The wizard Thirle looked up sharply at Caris' question, strongly reminding the young man of a fat gray field rabbit at the crack of a twig. Then he relaxed a little. "Not yet." He picked up the garden trowel he'd dropped when Caris' shadow had fallen over him on the brick steps of his house, where he had been kneeling. He got to his feet with the awkward care of the very fat and dusted off his black robe. "Can I help you?"

Caris hesitated, his right hand resting loosely around the hilt of the sword thrust through his frayed silk sash. He cast a quick glance at the doorway of the house next door. Like all the houses on the Mages' Yard, it rose tall, narrow, and cramped-looking from the flagstones of the little court, dingy with age and factory soot. Two or three of the other sasenna, the archaic order of sworn warriors, lingered, waiting for him on the steps. Like him, they were clothed in the loose black garments of their order, crisscrossed with sword sashes and weapons belts; and like him, they were sweaty, bruised, and exhausted from the afternoon's session with the swordmaster. He shook his head, and they passed into the shadows of the carved slot of the doorway.

"I don't know." He turned back to Thirle, noting automatically, as a sasennan must, the tiny details—the sweat on his brow, the twitch of his earth-stained fingers—and wondered what it was that troubled him. "That is . . ."

The look of preoccupied nervousness faded from the fat man's eyes, replaced by genuine concern. "What is it, lad?"

For a moment, Caris debated about simply shrugging the problem off, pushing it aside as he had pushed it aside last night, and returning to the only matters which should concern the sasennan—serving his masters the mages and bettering his own skills in the arts of war. "I don't know whether I should be asking this or not," he began diffidently. "I know it isn't the Way of the Sasenna to ask—a weapon asks no questions of the hand that wields it. But . . ."

Thirle smiled and shook his head. "My dear Caris, how do we know what the dagger thinks when it's sheathed, or what swords fear in the armory when the lights are out? You know I've never approved of this business of the sasenna being—being like those machines that weave cloth and spin thread in the mills, that do one job only and don't care what it is."

Under the warm twinkle in his eyes Caris relaxed a little and managed a grin at Thirle's heresy.

Of the dozen or more houses around that small cobblestoned court on the edge of the ghetto of the Old Believers, only eight actually belonged to the Council of Wizards; of those, three were rented out to those— mostly Old Believers—who were willing to live near wizards. Few mages cared to live in the city of Angelshand. Of those few, Caris had always liked Thirle.

The Archmage, Caris' grandfather, had been absent since Caris had come out of the morning's training. If he did not return before dinner, there was little chance Caris would be able to speak with him until to-morrow.

It was not the Way of the Sasenna to fear, and Caris did not think he could endure another unsleeping night with the secret of his fear gnawing his heart.

But having spent the last five years in rigorous training of muscle and nerves, he was uncertain how to speak of fear. Nervously, he ran his scarred fingers through his short-cropped blond hair, now stiff with the drying sweat of training. "I don't know whether I should speak of this," he said hesitantly. "It's just that—A weapon wasn't always what I was." He struggled with himself for a moment, then asked, "Is there any way that a mage can lose his magic?"

Thirle's reaction was as unexpected as it was violent. A flush of anger mottled the fat cheeks and layers of chin. "No!" He almost shouted the word. "We are born with powers, some greater, some lesser. They are like our flesh, like our souls."

Confused at this rage, Caris began, "Not even . . ."

"Be silent!" Thirle's face had gone yellow as tallow now with fury. "You might have been mageborn to begin with boy, but your powers never amounted to anything. There's no way you could know about power. You are forbidden to speak of it. Forbidden!" he added furiously, as Caris opened his mouth to explain.

To be sasenna is first to serve; when, after three years' grueling training in the arts of war and the sneakier deaths of peacetime, Caris had made the last decision of his life, he had sworn his warrior's vows to the Council of Wizards. The vows held good. He closed his mouth, willing himself not to feel the scathe of astonished hurt, and made himself incline his head.

His hands shaking, Thirle picked up his trowel and watering can and hurried through the door of the house, slamming it behind him. Standing on the step, Caris observed that the little mage had been so agitated that he'd left half his beloved pot-plants, which clustered the step and every windowsill within reach, unwatered. Across the city, the big clock on the St. Cyr fortress began striking five. Caris would have less than an hour for dinner before going on duty in the refectory when the mages ate.

Confused, Caris moved down the step with the sasennan's lithe walk. He felt shocked and stung, as if he had been unexpectedly bitten by a loved old dog; but then, he reflected a little bitterly, it was not the Way of the Sasenna to pat even a loved and toothless old dog without one hand on one's knife. He made his way to the house next door that was shared by the novice mages and the sasenna of the Council with the frightening chill that lay in his heart unassuaged.

It was years since Caris had even thought of himself as mageborn. He was nineteen, and for five years he had given himself, heart and soul, to the Way of the Sasenna. But he had originally entered it, as many mageborn did, only as the gateway to greater learning which had never materialized.

His powers, he knew, had never been much—a sharpness of sight in the dark and a certain facility for finding lost objects. In his childhood he had desperately wanted to become a mage and to take the vows of the Council of Wizards in order to serve and be with his grandfather, who even then had been the Archmage. From studying the Way of the Sasenna as a means to an end, it had become an end in itself; when he had realized, as he eventually had, that his powers were insufficient to permit him to become a wizard, he had remained as a sasennan. When it had come time to take his warrior's vows, it was to the Council that he had taken them.

Was that why Thirle had refused to reply? he wondered. Because Caris, having what he had, had turned from it?

It might have explained his refusal to answer, but, thought Caris uneasily, it did not explain the note of fear in his voice.

At dinner that night Thirle was absent—odd, for though the wizards in general ate plainly, the little botanist was still very fond of the pleasures of the table.

There were seven wizards and two novices who lived in the Court. The fourteen sasenna who served them regularly traded off dinner duty, some serving, some standing guard, as there were always sasenna standing guard somewhere in the Yard—a few still sleeping, or just waked and ready to go on night watch. Though few of the thieves and cutpurses that swarmed the dark slums of Angelshand would go near the Yard, the mageborn had long ago learned that it never paid to be completely unguarded.

A little uneasily, Caris noted that the Archmage had not yet returned. His place at the high table had been taken by the Lady Rosamund, a beautiful woman of about forty, who had been born Lady Rosamund Kentacre. Her father, the Earl Maritime, had disowned her when she had sworn the vows of the Council of Wizards—not, Caris had heard rumored, because in doing so she had revealed herself to be mageborn in the first place, but because the vows precluded using her powers to benefit the Kentacre family's political ambitions. Undoubtedly the Earl had known—his daughter had been nearly twenty when she had sought out the Council—and had probably arranged to have her secretly taught in the arts of magic by one of the quacks or dog wizards who abounded in such numbers in any major city of the Empire. But for Lady Rosamund, the half-understood jumble of piesog, hearsay, and garbled spells used for fees by the dog wizards had not been enough. To obtain true teaching, she must take the Council Vows, the first of which was that she must never use what she had learned either to harm or to help any living thing.

"He should never have gone without a guard," she was saying, as Caris bore a tray of duck and braided breads up to the high table.

Beside her, the thin, tired-looking Whitwell Simm protested, "The Regent wouldn't dare . . ."

"Wouldn't he?" Cold fire sparked in her green glance. "The Prince Regent hates the mageborn, and always has hated us. I'm told that the other night, after a ball in the city, he was getting into his carriage when an old man, a shabby old dog wizard, accidentally brushed up against him on the flagway. Prince Pharos had two of his sasenna hold the old man while he almost beat the poor wretch to death with his cane. The rumors of what goes on in the dungeons of the old Summer Palace, which he has taken for his own, are a scandal. He is as mad as his father."

"The difference being," remarked Issay Bel-Caire on her other side, "that his father is not dangerous, except perhaps to himself."

At the foot of the table, the two novices—a short, redhaired girl of seventeen or so and a creamily dark, thin girl a few years older—said nothing, but listened with uneasy avidity, knowing that this was not merely gossip, but something which could easily affect their lives. Near them old Aunt Min, the most ancient of the mages who dwelt in the Yard, sat slumped like a little black bag of laundry in her chair, snoring softly. With a smile of affection for the old lady, Caris woke her gently up; she lifted her head with a start and fumbled at the tangle of her eternal knitting with hands as tiny and fragile as a finch's claws, muttering to herself all the while.

Whitwell Simm said, "Even if the Prince hates us, even if he believes our magic is nothing but charlatanry, like that of the dog wizards, you know he'd never dare to harm the Archmage. Neither the Council nor, as a matter of fact, the Church, would permit it. And we don't know that Salteris has gone to the Palace . . ."

"With the Regent's sasenna everywhere in the city," retorted Lady Rosamund coolly, "it scarcely matters where he goes. Prince Pharos is a madman and should have been barred from the succession long ago in favor of his cousin."

Issay laughed. "Cerdic? Maybe, if you want quacks and dog wizards like Magister Magus ruling the Empire."

Her ladyship's aristocratic lip curled at the mention of the most popular charlatan in Angelshand, but she turned her attention to her plate with her usual air of arctic self-righteousness, as if secure in the knowledge that all opposing arguments were specious and deliberately obstructive.

Caris, clearing up the plates afterwards and getting ready for the one last training session with the other sasenna which the incredible length of the midsummer evenings permitted, felt none of the wizards' qualms for his grandfather's safety. This was not so much because he did not believe the mad Regent capable of anything—by all accounts he was—but because Caris did not truly think anyone or anything capable of trapping or harming his grandfather.

Since Caris was a child, he had known Salteris Solaris as his grandfather, a mysterious man who visited his grandmother's farm beyond the bounds of their Wheatlands village, sometimes twice in a summer, sometimes for the length of a winter's storm. He had known that afterwards his mother's mother would sing at her household tasks for weeks. The old man's hair had been dark then, like that of Caris' mother—Caris took after the striking blond beauty of his slow-moving, good-natured father. But Caris had the Archmage's eyes, deep brown, like the dark earth of the Wheatlands, the color of the very old leaves seen under clear water, tilted up slightly at their outer ends. For a time, it had seemed that he had inherited something else from him besides. When he had taken his vows as sasennan to the Council, it had been with the aim of serving the old man as a warrior, if he did not have the power to do so as a wizard. Only lately had it come to him that there would be a time when it would not be the old man who was its head.

Caris was too much a sasennan even to think about his grandfather, or the secret fear which he had carried within him, during that evening's training. With the endless, tepid twilight of midsummer filtering through the long windows of the training floor on the upper storey of the novices' house, the swordmaster put the small class through endless rounds of practice sparring with split bamboo training swords. Ducking, parrying, leaping, pressing, and retreating under the continuous raking of barked instruction and jeers, in spite of five years of hard training Caris was still sodden with sweat and bruised all over by the time he was done, convinced he'd never be able to pick up a sword again. He was familiar with the sensation. In that kind of training, there was no room for any other thought in the mind; indeed, that was part of the training—to inculate the single-mindedness critical to a warrior, the hair-trigger watching for the flick of an opponent's eyelid, the twitch of the lip or the finger, that presaged a killing blow . . . or sometimes the sense of danger in the absence of any physical sign at all.

By the time it was too dark to see, it was past ten o'clock, and Caris, exhausted, stumbled with the other sasenna back downstairs to bathe and collapse into bed. It wasn't until he was awakened by he knew not what in the tar-black deeps of the night that he remembered his grandfather and what he had wanted to ask of him, and by then it was too late.

His magic was gone.

Long before, Caris had given up his belief in his magic. Only now, lying in the warm, gluey blackness, did he understand how deeply its roots had run and how magic had made the skeleton of his very soul. Without it, life was nothing, a hollow, gray world, not even bitter. It was as if all things had decayed to the color and texture of dust—as if the color had been bled even from his dreams.

He had heard the mages speak in whispers of those things by which a mage's power could be bound—spell-cord and the sigils made of iron, gold, or cut jewels, imbued with signs that crippled and drained a wizard's powers, leaving him helpless against his foes. But there was nothing of that in this terrible emptiness. His soul was a mold with the wax melted out, into which no bronze would ever be poured—only dust, filling all the spaces where the magic had been.

He would have wept, had the Way of the Sasenna not forbidden tears.

Unable to bear the hot, close darkness of the sasenna's dormitory another moment, he pulled on his breeches and shirt and stumbled downstairs to the door. The Way of the Sasenna whispered to him that he ought also to put on his boots and his sword belt; but with the loss of his magic, all things else seemed equally trivial and not worth the doing. The fresher air out on the brick steps revived him a little. Across the narrow, cobblestoned Yard, he could hear the sleepy twittering of birds under the eaves of the houses opposite. Among the squalid alleyways of the Old Believers' ghetto, a cock crowed.

Thirle had said that it could not happen—ever. But it had happened to him last night, a few moments' sickening waning that had wakened him, his heart pounding with cold terror. It was something he knew even then should not happen, as Thirle had said . . . And now magic was gone completely.

He leaned against the carved doorframe, hugging himself wretchedly, wondering why he could feel almost nothing, not even real grief—just a kind of hollowness that nothing, throughout the length of his life, would ever again fill. Looking across to the tall, narrow windows of his grandfather's little house, he wondered if the old man had returned. The windows were dark, but that would not necessarily mean he was asleep—he often sat up reading without light, as the mageborn could do. Perhaps he would know something Thirle did not.

But at the same time, it seemed pointless to speak of it now. Gone was gone. Like his long-departed virginity, it was something, he told himself, that he would never recover. To the west, a drift of noise floated from the more populous streets of Angelshand, from the bawdy theaters on Angel's Island near the St. Cyr fortress, and from the more elegant gaming halls near the Imperial Palace quarter. Carriage wheels rattled distantly on granite pavement; voices yelled in all-night taverns.

Almost without thinking of it, Caris found himself descending the brick steps, feeling for the purse in his breeches pocket, knowing he was going to go over to the Standing Stallion and get drunk.

Get drunk? He stopped, surprised and disgusted with himself. There was no stricture against the sasenna drinking. If need arose, Caris could hold his own against most of his mates when they went to the taverns;

but on the whole, he preferred to remain sober. It was the Way of the Sasenna to be ready to fight at all times, and Caris had never believed in blurring that edge.

But now none of it seemed to matter. He was dimly aware that what he wanted was not the wine, but the numbing of his awareness of grief, and he knew also that it would do him more harm than good. But, after a moment's hesitation, he sighed, not even caring that he was unarmed and hadn't put on his boots, and continued down the stairs.

As his bare foot touched the uneven cobbles of the court, he heard Thirle's voice cry desperately. "NO!"

Five years of training had inculcated into Caris the automatic reaction of drop and roll for cover until it was instinct. But now he stood, paralyzed like a stupid peasant, in the waxy moonlight at the foot of the step as the fat black shape of the wizard came stumbling out of a nearby alley, aptly named Stinking Lane. He saw the man's round moonface clearly and the shocked panic in his eyes as Thirle began to run clumsily across the court, arms outspread like a bird's wings for balance.

From the darkness on the opposite side of the Yard, Caris heard the crack of a pistol.

Thirle rocked back sharply at the impact of the bullet, his feet flying out from under him as he flopped grotesquely on the stones. A dark shape broke cover from the shadows on the opposite side of the court, running toward Thirle, toward the mouth of Stinking Lane behind him, a black cloak covering him like a wing of shadows. All this Caris watched, but all of it, including the fact that he knew Thirle was dead, was less to him than his grief for the loss of his magic. None of it mattered—none of it had anything to do with him. But deep within him shock and horror stirred—at what was happening and at himself.

In a daze of anger, he forced himself to run, to intercept that fleeing black figure. He'd gone two steps when the digging bite of the cobbles on his bare feet reminded him belatedly that he had neither boots nor weapons. Cursing the carelessness and stupidity that seemed to be upon him tonight, he flung himself to one side into the black pocket of shadow between the novices' house and Thirle's. From across the court, he caught the flash of a pistol shot.

Splinters of brick exploded from the corner of the house, so close to his face that they tore his cheek. He knew it would take his man some moments to reload and knew he should dart out and take him then—but he hesitated, panic he had never known clutching at his belly. He heard feet pounding the cobbles and forced himself to stumble upright, to race in pursuit, but his legs dragged as if tangled in wet rope. It meant nothing to him. His soul had turned as sterile and cold as the magicless world around him. It would be easier to stop now, shrug, and go back to bed—Thirle's body would still be there in the morning. Dully angry at himself, he made himself run. For five years, in spite of exhaustion, occasional illness, and injuries, he had made himself pick up the sword for training, but forcing himself now was more difficult than it had ever been. In some oblique corner of his mind, he wondered if this were a spell of some kind, but it was unlike any spell he had ever known.

His steps slowed. The fugitive leaped over Thirle's body and vanished into the utter blackness of Stinking Lane. Caris dodged sideways, pressing against the house wall and slipping forward to the corner, knees flexed, ready to drop if that hand with its pistol appeared around the edge. The two shots had been so close together that the killer must have had two weapons—both empty now—and possibly he had a third. Through Caris' thin shirt, he felt the roughness of the coarse-plastered wall and the dampness that stuck the thin fabric to his ribs with sweat. He found he was exhausted, panting as if he had run miles.

He reached the mouth of the lane and looked around.

He saw nothing. No light—no walls—no sky. There was only a black and endless hollow, an abyss that seemed to swallow time itself, as if not only the world, but the universe, ended beyond the narrow band of pallid moonlight that lay on the cobbles beneath his feet.

Terror tightened like a garrote around his throat. He had not felt that hideous, nightmare fear since he had waked in the night as a small child to see the gleam of rats' eyes winking at him in the utter dark of the loft where he slept. Staring into that emptiness of endless nothing, he felt horror pressing upon him, horror of he knew not what—the whisper of the winds of eternity along his uncovered bones. He pressed his face to the stone of the wall, squeezing his eyes shut, unable to breathe. He felt in danger, but his training, like his magic, had deserted him; he wanted to run, but knew not in which direction safety would lie. It was not death he feared—he did not know what it was.

Then the feeling was gone. Like a man dreaming, who feels even in sleep the refreshing storm break the lour of summer heat, he felt the hideous weight of hopelessness lift from him. Still pressed to the chill stone of the wall, Caris felt as if he had waked suddenly, his heart pounding and his breathing erratic, but his mind clear. His magic—that trace of intense awareness that all his life had colored his perceptions—had returned. With it came a moment's blinding fury at himself for being so child-simple as to wander abroad unarmed and barefoot.

His knees felt weak at the thought of what he knew he must do. It took all his will to force himself to move forward again, crouching below eye level though he knew that the man with the pistols was gone. It was the Way of the Sasenna never to take chances.

Cautiously, he peered around the corner into the alley.

Filtered moonlight showed him the moss-furred cobbles, the battered walls of the houses, and the glitter of noisome gutter-water in the canyon of dark. There was a puddle right across the mouth of the lane, too wide to jump, but there were no prints on the other side.

Caris turned back to where Thirle lay like a beached and dying whale in the silver wash of the faint starlight. Lights were going up in the houses around the Yard, and voices and footsteps made a muffled clamor on the edges of the darkness. As he reached Thirle's side, Caris saw the dark glitter that covered all the breast of his robe. With a gutteral gasp, the fat man's body twitched, lungs sucking air desperately. Caris fell to his knees beside him, and for one moment the dark, frantic eyes met his.

Then Thirle whispered, "Antryg," and died.

"The police must be fetched."

The Archmage Salteris Solaris, kneeling beside Thirle's body, made no reply to the words of the skinny old swordmaster, who stood in the little cluster of men and women, Old Believers and novices, all clutching bed-clothes about them and looking down at the body with the wild eyes of those startled by gunshots from sleep. Caris, kneeling beside him, looked from the corpse's eyes, staring blindly now at the faint pearliness of false dawn visible between the crowding black angles of the roofs, to the thin, aquiline features of his grandfather. The old man's white brows were pinched down over the bridge of his nose, and there was grief in his eyes for the loss of one he had known for so many years—grief and something else Caris could not understand. The old man glanced up at the crowd behind them and said "Yes—perhaps."

The Lady Rosamund, standing fully dressed even to the hyacinth stole of a Council member—a mark of rank that the Archmage seldom wore—sneered. As the scion of one of the noblest houses in the land, she had little use for such bourgeois institutions as the Metropolitan Police. "The constables will find some reason to wait until light to come."

Salteris' thin mouth twitched in a faint smile. "Very likely." He looked back down at the plump heap of black robes. In the soft glow of bluish witchlight that illuminated the scene, hanging like St. Elmo's fire above his high, balding forehead and flowing white hair, the muscles of his lean jaw tightened.

Something twisted inside Caris, and he put out a hand to touch the old man's square, slender shoulder in comfort, but he remembered that he was sasenna and stopped himself with the gesture unmade. He was used to death, as the sasenna must be. He had killed his first man at fifteen; the schools of the sasenna were given prisoners condemned to die by the Emperor or the Church, for even in peacetime, they said, the sword blade must learn the taste of flesh. As the sworn weapon of the Council of Wizards, he would have cut Thirle's throat himself, had they ordered it. But still, it had been many years since anyone he had known personally had died. A little to his shame, he found that the training had not changed that shocked grief of loss, and anger stirred in him that anyone would cause the Archmage pain.

Salteris stood up, his black robes falling straight and heavy around his thin form. For all his snow-white hair, for all the worn fragility that had begun to come over him in the last few years, he took no hand to help him. "We should get him inside," he said softly. He looked over at the two sasenna who had been on patrol duty that night. When they opened their mouths to protest that they had been in the alleys on the far side of the Yard, he waved them quiet. "It was no one's fault," he said gently. "I believe Thirle was killed only because he was in the man's way as he fled —perhaps because Thirle saw him and would give the alarm."

"No," a cracked, thin old voice said from the darkness of Stinking Lane. "You forgot about the Gate—the Gate into the Darkness—the Gate of the Void . . ."

Salteris' head turned sharply. Caris stepped forward in a half-second of reflex, readying himself to defend his grandfather, then relaxed once more as he recognized the voice. "Aunt Min?"

From the shadows of Stinking Lane, the bent form of the old lady who had once been known throughout the Council as Minhyrdin the Fair hobbled determinedly, her black robes coming untucked from her belt and dragging in the puddles, her workbasket with its everlasting knitting dangling haphazardly at her side. Half-exasperated, half-concerned for the old lady, Caris hurried forward to take her fragile arm.

"You shouldn't be up and about, Aunt Min. Not tonight . . ."

She waved the remark fussily away and twisted her head on her bent spine to look up at Salteris and Lady Rosamund, who had also come to her side. "There is evil abroad," she piped. "Evil from other worlds than this. Only a curtain of gauze separates us from them. The Dark Mage knew . . ."

Salteris held up his hand quickly against that name, his silky white brows plunging together. Caris glanced quickly from him to Aunt Min, who had returned to fussing with the trailing strands of her knitting, and then back. "Other worlds?" he asked worriedly. His eyes went unwillingly to the dark maw of the alley, an uneven agglomerate of dim stone angles, with the gutter picking up the quicksilver light of the sky like a broken sword blade. "But—but this *is* the world. There is no other. The Sun and Moon go around us . . ."

Salteris shook his head. "No, my son," he said. "They've known for years now that it is we who go around the Sun, and not the Sun around us, though the Church hasn't admitted it yet. But that is not what Aunt Min means." He frowned unseeing for a moment into the distance. "Yes, the Dark Mage knew." His voice sank to a whisper. "As do I." He put his arm around the old lady's stooped shoulders. "Come. Before all else, we must get him inside."

They sent one of the night-watch sasenna—the only two sasenna to be dressed—for a physician. Rather to Caris' surprise, it was less than a half-hour before he arrived. In the low-roofed closeness of the Archmage's narrow study, Caris was telling Salteris, Lady Rosamund, and old Aunt Min of what he had seen—the pistol-shots, the chase, the terrible Gate of Darkness—when he heard the swift *tap-tap* of hooves in the Yard and the brisk rattle of what sounded like a gig. He was surprised that any citizen of Angelshand would come to the Mages' Yard during the dark hours, and even more so when the man entered the study. He had expected Salteris to send for a healer of the Old Believers, whose archaic faith was still more than a little mixed with wizardry. But the man who entered wore the dapper blue knee breeches and full-skirted coat of a professional of the city.

"Dr. Narwahl Skipfrag." Salteris rose from the carved ebony chair in which he had been sitting, extending a strong, slender hand. The physician took it and inclined his head, his bright blue eyes taking in every detail of that small room, with its dark ranks of books, its embryos bottled in honey or brandy, and its geometric models and crystal prisms.

"I came as quickly as I could."

"There was no need for haste." Salteris gestured him to the chair that Caris brought silently up. "The man was killed almost at once."

One of Skipfrag's sparse, sandy eyebrows tilted sharply up. He was a tall man, stoutish and snuff-colored, with his hair tied back in an old-fashioned queue. In spite of the fact that he must have been wakened by Salteris' messenger, his broad linen cravat was neatly tied and his shirt-ruffles unrumpled.

"Dr. Narwahl Skipfrag," Salteris introduced. "Lady Minhyrdin—Lady Rosamund—my grandson Caris, sasennan of the Council, who witnessed the shooting. Dr. Narwahl Skipfrag, Royal Physician to the Emperor and my good friend."

As a sasennan should, Caris concealed his surprise. Few professionals believed in the power of wizards anymore, and certainly no one associated with the Court would admit to the belief these days, much less to friendship with the Archmage. But Dr. Skipfrag smiled, and nodded to Lady Rosamund. "We have met, I think, in another life."

As if against her will a slight answering smile warmed her ladyship's mouth.

Slumped in her chair, without raising her eyes from her knitting, Aunt Min inquired, "And how does his Majesty?"

Skipfrag's face clouded a little. "His health is good." He spoke as one who remarks the salvage of an heirloom gravy boat from the wreck of a house.

Lady Rosamund's full mouth tightened. "A pity, in a way." Salteris gave her a questioning look, but Skipfrag merely gazed down at his own broad white hands. She shrugged. "Good health is no gift to him. Without a mind, the man is better dead. After four years, it is scarcely likely he will reawaken one morning sane."

"He may surprise us all one day," Skipfrag remarked. "I daresay his son thinks as you do."

At the mention of the Prince Regent, Lady Rosamund's chilly green eyes narrowed.

"It is about his son, in a way," Salteris cut in softly, "that I asked you here, Narwahl. The man who was killed was a mage."

The physician was silent. Salteris leaned back in his chair, the glow of the witchlight gleaming above his head and haloing the silver flow of his long hair. For a time he, too, said nothing, his folded hands propped before his mouth, forefingers extended and resting against his lips. "My grandson says that he heard Thirle cry 'No!' at the sight of a man standing in the shadows on this side of the court—the man who shot him, fleeing to the alley across the yard. Caris did not see which house the killer stood near, but I suspect it was this one."

The bright blue eyes turned grave. "Sent by the Regent Pharos, you mean?"

"Pharos has never made any secret of his hatred for the mageborn."

"No," Dr. Skipfrag agreed and thoughtfully stared into the witchlight that hung above the tabletop for a moment. He reached out absentmindedly toward it and pinched it, like a man pinching out a candle—his forefinger and thumb went straight through the white seed of light in the glowing ball's heart, the black shadows of his fingers swinging in vast, dark bars across the low rafters of the ceiling and the book-lined walls. "Interesting," he murmured. "Not even a change in temperature." His blue eyes returned to Salteris. "And that's odd in itself, isn't it?" Salteris nodded, understanding. Caris, standing quietly in a corner, as was the place of a sasennan, was very glad when Lady Rosamund demanded, "Why? Few believe in our powers these days." There was bitter contempt in her voice. "They work in their factories or their shops and they would rather believe that magic did not exist, if they can't use it to tamper with the workings of the universe for their personal convenience."

Softly, the Archmage murmured, "That is as it should be."

The deep lines around Skipfrag's eyes darkened and moved with his smile. "No," he said. "Most of them don't even believe in the dog wizards, you know. Or they half believe them, or go to them in secret—the dog wizards, the charlatans, the quacks, who never learned true magic because they would not take Council vows, so all they can do is brew love-philters and cast runes in some crowded shop that stinks of incense, or at most be like Magister Magus, hanging around the fringes of the Court and hoping to get funding to turn lead into gold. Why do you think the Church's Witchfinders don't arrest them for working magic outside the Council vows? They only serve to feed the people's disbelief, and that is what the Witchfinders want.

"But the Regent . . ." He shook his head.

Through the tall, narrow windows at the far end of the room, standing open in the murky summer heat, the sounds of the awakening city could now be heard. Caris identified automatically the brisk tap of butchers' and poulterers' wagons hastening to their early rounds, the dismal singsong of an itinerant noodle vendor, and the clatter of farm carts coming to the city markets with the morning's produce. Dawn was coming, high and far off over the massive granite city; the smell of the river and the salt scent of the harbor came to him, with the distant mewing of the harbor birds. At the other end of the table, Salteris was listening in ophidian silence. Aunt Min had every appearance of having fallen asleep.

Skipfrag sighed, and his oak chair creaked a little as he stirred his bulk. "I was his Majesty's friend for many years," he said quietly. "You know, Salteris, that he was always a friend to the mages, for all he held them at an arm's length for political reasons. He believed—else he would never have raised the army that helped you defeat the Dark Mage Suraklin."

Salteris did not move, but the witchlight flickered with the movement of his dark eyes, and something of his attitude reminded Caris of a dozing hound waked at an unfamiliar footfall.

"Pharos' hatred of you is more than disbelief," Skipfrag went on quietly. "He blames you for his father's madness."

Lady Rosamund waved a dismissive hand. "He was hateful from his boyhood and suspicious of everything."

"Perhaps so," Salteris murmured. "But it is also true that, of late, the Regent's antipathy toward us has grown to a mania. He may fear me too much to move against me openly—but it is possible that he would send an assassin." His dark eyes went to Skipfrag. "Can you find out for me at Court?"

The physician thought for a moment, then nodded. "I think so. I still have Pharos' ear and many other friends there as well. I think I can learn something."

"Good." Salteris got to his feet and clapped Skipfrag lightly on the arm as the big man rose, dwarfing the Archmage's slenderness against his blue-coated bulk. Caris, hurrying before them to open the outer door, saw in the watery dawnlight outside that Thirle's blood had already been washed from the cobbles in front of Stinking Lane; the puddles of water left by it were slimy and dismal-looking. The swordmaster and the two novices still stood on the brick steps of the novices' house, talking quietly, all three wrapped in bedgowns, though, Caris noticed, the swordmaster had her scabbarded blade still in hand, ready for action.

It occurred to him suddenly to wonder, as he watched Salteris usher the physician over to his waiting gig, what Thirle had been doing abroad at that hour of the night at all? For that matter, what had Rosamund been doing up; she had been fully dressed, her hair not even crumpled from the pillow, so she must have been so for some time. He glanced back into the room behind him. Aunt Min, too, was dressed, though her thin, straggly white hair was mussed—but of course, reflected Caris, with rueful affection for the old lady, it always was.

Had they all, like himself, been restless with the damp warmth of the night?

Tepid dawn air stirred in his close-cropped, fair hair and stung the tender cuts on his cheek, where the assassin's bullet had driven brick-chips into his face. The day was beginning to blush color into the houses opposite, the black half-timbering of their shabby fronts taking on their daytime variation of browns and grays. The jungly riot of Thirle's pot plants was wakening to green in daylight their owner would never see.

Down in the Yard, Skipfrag was climbing into his gig, adjusting his voluminous coat skirts and gathering the reins of the smart bay hack that stood between the shafts. Salteris stood beside the horse's quarters, talking quietly to him. The physician's voice came clearly to Caris where he stood on the steps. "It's best I was gone. My reputation as a physician might carry off experiments with electricity, but it would never recover, if word got around I believed in magic. I'll learn for you what I can—do what I can, at Court. Until then, watch yourself, my friend."

Salteris stepped back as Skipfrag turned the gig. The iron wheels clattered sharply on the stones. Then the Emperor's physician was gone.

The Archmage stood still for some time after Skipfrag was gone. The brick steps were cool under Caris' bare feet, and the dawn air stirred his torn and muddied shirt. He looked down at his grandfather in the paling light of the Yard and noted again how the old man had aged in the eighteen months since Caris had taken his vows and come to live at the Mages' Yard. When he had last seen the Archmage before that time— before he had gone into training in the Way of the Sasenna—the old man had had a kind of wiry strength for all his age. Now he seemed like antique ivory worn to the snapping-point. With a sigh, the old man turned back, stopped, and looked up when he saw Caris on the steps.

"What did Aunt Min mean?" Caris asked softly. "About other worlds? About the Void and the Gate in the Void?" He came down the steps and offered the old man his steadying hand. "*Are* there worlds, besides this?"

This time Salteris took the hand. The cold, thin fingers felt delicate as bird bone. Not a big man, Caris was conscious as he had never been before that he stood slightly taller than the Archmage, this gentle old grandfather who had once lifted him up in childhood. Though it was not his way to think much about the passage of time, he felt its fleeting shadow brush his thoughts. He was silent as he helped the old man to the top of the steps.

As they stood there together, the Archmage was quiet, too, considering, as he often seemed to do, what he could say to one who did not have the training in magic ever to understand fully.

Then he nodded. "Yes," he said quietly. "And I very much fear that what you saw, my son, was a Gate such as Aunt Min described—a Gate through the Void that separates world from world."

Caris stammered, "I—I've never heard of such a thing."

A faint smile flicked those thin lips. "Few have," the Archmage said softly. "And fewer still have crossed that Void, as I have—once—and walked in a world on its other side." For a moment, the dark eyes seemed to gaze beyond him, as if they saw past the stones of the Yard, past the dawn sky, past the cosmos itself. "As far as I know, only two men in this world have ever had an understanding of what the Void itself is, how it works, and how to touch and feel it, to see across it to its other side. One of them is dead . . ." He hesitated, then sighed again. "The other one is Antryg Windrose."

"Antryg?" Caris murmured. "Thirle said that name . . ."

Salteris glanced at him quickly, and the long white eyebrows quirked up. "Did he?" A moment's doubt crossed the dark eyes, then he smiled. "He would have, if he thought—as I do—that some danger might be coming to us from across the Void. Antryg," he repeated, and Caris felt a stirring in his memory, like an old story overheard in childhood.

"Antryg," Lady Rosamund's derisive voice echoed behind them.

Caris turned. Darkly beautiful, she stood in the doorway of the house behind them, her slender white hands folded around the buckle of her belt, her dark curls lying thick on her shoulders like a careless glory of raven flowers.

Memory seemed to filter back to him of things spoken across him, without his understanding, by the mages. "He was a wizard, wasn't he?"

"Is," the Archmage said. He shifted his dark robes up on his thin shoulders, and his eyes, again, seemed to look out across time.

"A dog wizard." Lady Rosamund's voice could have laid frost-flowers on glass. "Forsworn of his vows and no more than the dog wizards who peer into treacle and asses' dung for the secrets of gold and immortality at the bidding of any who'll pay."

"Maybe," Salteris said softly. "Except that he is, beyond a doubt, the most powerful mage now living. Thirteen years ago, he was the youngest member ever elected to the Council of Wizards—three years later he was expelled from the Council, stripped of his rank, and banished for meddling in the quarrel between the Lords of the Wheatlands and the Emperor. Since that time, he has been reinstated and banished again, and I and the other mages have had occasion to hunt him half across the face of the world."

Caris frowned. Half-recalled childhood memories ghosted into his mind, framed in amber hearthlight—the Archmage sitting beside the brick chimney oven of Caris' grandmother's house, and beside him the tall, thin young man he'd brought with him, gravely constructing a pinwheel by the light of the kitchen fire, or telling horrific ghost stories in a deep, extraordinary voice that was beautiful and flamboyant as embroidered brocade.

"Is he evil?" Caris did not remember evil.

Salteris thought for a moment, then shook his head. "I don't think so. But his motives have always been obscure. No one has ever, as far as I know, been able to tell what he would do, or why. He is, as I said, more powerful than any mage now living, including myself. But his mind is like a murky and bottomless well, into which all the wisdom of the ages and all the accumulated trivia of several universes have been indiscriminately dumped. He is both wise and innocent, incredibly devious and hopelessly scatterbrained, and by this time, I fear, quite mad."

Lady Rosamund shrugged with the grace that only years with a deportment master could impart. "He has always been mad."

"True." A smile flicked across the old man's face. "But the problem with Antryg is that no one has ever been able to tell just how mad." Then the lightness died from his eyes. "And for the past seven years he has been a prisoner in the Silent Tower, whose very stones are spelled against the working of magic. After that long, held prisoner by the Church and separated from the magic that is the core of any wizard's being, I can only hope that Antryg Windrose is still sane enough to help us. For I fear that, if we are dealing with some threat from another world than our own, we may need his help very badly."

CHAPTER II

**ERROR: UNRECOGNIZED CONDITION IN BINARY
TREE STRUCTURE
**CORRECT AND RE-TRY:
OK>

"Binary tree?" Joanna Sheraton groaned. "I just corrected the goddam binary tree."

Patiently, she typed:

>SEARCH: TREE. DATA.0
OK>
>EXECUTE TIGER.REV8

A moment later, green letters materialized on the gray of the screen:

**ERROR: UNRECOGNIZED CONDITION IN BINARY TREE STRUCTURE
**CORRECT AND RE-TRY:
OK>

"I'll give you an unrecognized condition," she muttered. She scanned up the screen, looking for anything else in the miles of data that could conceivably be preventing the running of the program. "Well, what's wrong with it? You didn't like my tone of voice? I didn't say 'Mother, may I'?" She tried again:

```
>SEARCH: TREE.DATA.0
OK>
>EXECUTE TIGER.REV8
**ERROR. UNRECOGNIZED CONDITION IN BINARY TREE STRUCTURE
**CORRECT AND RE-TRY:
OK>
```

"You know, I'm getting very tired of your OK." She pushed the soft tangle of her shoulder-length, too-curly blond hair from her eyes and reached for the much-thumbed program that rested on top of the precarious stacks of printouts, manuals, schematic drawings of Tiger missiles, and scrawly handwritten ads for the in-plant newspaper, the *San Serano Spectrum,* that heaped the desk on all sides of the keyboard. "And I'm also getting very tired of you," she added, scanning the long, cryptic columns on the screen. "You're supposed to be the hottest mainframe west of Houston, you know. We shouldn't have to play Twenty Questions in binary every time I want to run a . . ."

Her hand froze in mid-gesture.

There was someone out in the hall.

But when she listened, she heard nothing but the faint hum of air conditioning. Even the massive radios of the janitorial staff, which generally drove her to take long walks to the coffee machines in the far corners of Building Six, had ceased, she realized, some time ago.

It occurred to her that it must be very late.

Security, she told herself and turned back to the monitor.

She didn't believe it.

She'd worked enough overtime, running analyses of missile test-flight results, to know well the sounds of the security staff as they patrolled the corridors. That swift, breathing rush of light footfalls outside her cubicle had nothing in common with the familiar hobnailed tread and jingle of keys.

With reflex reassurance, part of her said, *If it isn't Security, Security will take care of it.* Another part, with equally reflex dismissal, added, *Don't be silly.* It was probably some poor technician wandering around looking for the john or for a coffee machine that still had coffee—or what passed, at San Serano, for coffee—in it at this hour, whatever this hour was.

It was nothing to worry about.

Nevertheless, Joanna worried.

She was a small girl, with an air of compact sturdiness to her despite her rather delicate build. Ruth, the artist who lived downstairs from her, was of the often-expressed opinion that Joanna could be beautiful if she'd take the time, but Joanna had never seen the point of taking the time—or anyway not the hours a day Ruth put into it. Now she soundlessly hooked the toe of her sneaker under the pull of the desk drawer and slid the metal bin open far enough to allow her to dip into her mailsack of a purse and produce a hammer.

Then she sat still and listened again. This time she heard nothing.

It occurred to her that she had a throbbing headache. It must be after ten, she thought—there had still been people around when she'd started working on the program for analyzing the Tiger missile test results for next week's Navy review. There was no telling how much longer she'd . . .

Her eyes sought the green luminosity of the clock.

2:00 A.M.

Two! She could have sworn it wasn't later than ten—well, eleven, since the janitors had gone home.

No wonder I have a headache, she thought, and ran her hands through the feathery tangle of her hair. She recalled vaguely that she'd been too busy to eat dinner; in any case, she'd long ago given up buying the overpriced slumgullion doled out by the junk machines in the break-room to those who worked on after regular hours. That was the tricky thing about the whole San Serano Aerospace Complex she had learned. The cool, even, white lights never varied; the unscented air never altered its temperature; and as a result no one ever had a very clear idea of what time it was.

But two in the morning . . .

Without warning, a wave of despair crept over her, filling the farthest corners of her tired soul like cold and greasy dishwater. The uselessness of it all suddenly overpowered her—not only getting the program to run, or the tedious documentation that would have to follow, or the fact that the data was going to have to be altered tomorrow in any case. Her whole life seemed suddenly to open before her in a vista of uselessness, an empty freeway leading nowhere.

It was strange to her, for she had, since she left her mother's house, been pretty content with her solitary life. Maybe that was one of the things wrong with her, she reflected. She knew herself to be far less good with people than she was with machines—no matter what you looked like, a computer would never laugh at you behind your back. Computers never expected you to be capable of things you had not been taught to do, or cared one way or the other what you did in your spare time.

She was familiar with the vague sense of an obligation to be other than she was—to be more like her bright and sociable co-workers—but she had never experienced this hollow, gray feeling of the futility of either staying as she was or changing to what she ought to be.

The image of Gary Fairchild returned to her mind—handsome, smiling, and enamored. Her loneliness seemed suddenly overwhelming, her vacillations over his constant request for her to move in with him suddenly petty and futile. *Why not?* she thought. *If this is all there is ever going to be . . . Maybe everybody's right about living with someone, and I'm wrong . . .*

Yet the thought of giving up what she had filled her with the dread of some inevitable doom.

Within her, a small voice struggled to insist, *In any case there isn't anything you can do about it at two in the morning. Tomorrow I'll see him. . . .*

As swiftly as it had come, the dull sense of hopeless grief ebbed away. Joanna blinked, rubbed her eyes, and wondered with the calm detachment that had gotten her into trouble in the past, *What the hell was that all about?*

The thought that she had, for one second, seriously been planning to accede to Gary's next demand that she live with him made her shudder. She might, she knew, be the sort of mousy little woman men never went out with, sealed like an anchoress in a chapel with a pile of books, computers, and cats, but it was preferable to the struggle between her conscientious efforts to please Gary, her boredom with watching TV in his enormous, gray-upholstered party room, and her sneaky sense that she'd rather be by herself, reading. It was not, she knew, the way she ought to act or feel about the man who loved her. But shame her though it did, it *was* how she felt, despite all her efforts to convince herself otherwise.

I must be hungrier than I thought, she reflected. *They say low blood sugar can make you depressed—they didn't mention it could make you suicidal.* With a sigh, she began backup procedures, to save what she'd done for tomorrow. At this point, she knew, she would make more errors through sheer exhaustion than she would correct. She chucked the floppies on top of the general heap. Her co-workers never believed her when she said that she located things in the heaps of printouts, programs, floppies, data, reports, management bulletins, journals, and ads on her desk by the oil company principle of geological stratification. They were all mystified by it—Joanna herself would scarcely have been surprised to find trilobites in the bottom layer.

It was only when she stood up that she remembered the stealthy footfalls outside her cubicle.

Don't be silly, she told herself again. *San Serano is a security installation. The idea that anyone could get in without being checked out by the guards is ridiculous.*

But somehow, she felt unconvinced.

She patted the pockets of her faded jeans for her car keys, dug her purse—an enormous accessory of Hopiweave and rabbit skins bulging with rolled-up printouts, computer journals, and an incredible quantity of miscellaneous junk—out of the desk drawer, and made a move to slip the hammer back into it. Then she hesitated. She'd feel awfully silly if she met a guard or a co-worker—*what co-worker's going to be around at 2:00 a.m.?*—walking down the corridor with a hammer in her hand. But still . . .

You are twenty-six years old, she told herself sharply. *The odds against your meeting the boogieman in the corridors of the San Serano Bomb and Novelty Shop are astronomical.*

So were the odds against meeting a mocking and judgmental co-worker, but she compromised by sliding the hammer into her purse with the handle sticking out. Then, soundlessly, she pushed open the cubicle door and stepped into the corridor.

Somehow, the bright lighting of the corridors made her uneasiness worse. The doors of the other cubicles she passed and the typing bullpen were wells of eerie, charcoal half-light, the machines all sleeping in unearthly silence. Corridors leading to the test labs on the other side of the building made ominous echo tunnels which picked up the padded *swish-swish* of Joanna's sneakers on the dark-blue carpet, incredibly loud in that brilliantly lit silence. Once or twice she glimpsed the industrial-strength cockroaches who lived in such numbers in the warm mazes of the backs of the equipment in the test labs, but that was the only other life she saw.

Then light caught her eye.

She stopped. Not the even white illumination of the fluorescents . . . *Candlelight?* No more than a finger-smudge of gold reflection against the metal molding of the half-open door of the main computer room.

Fire? she thought, her pace quickening. The main computer room contained a lot of printout bins. The mainframe, a Cray the size of a Cadillac, the biggest defense computer west of Houston, could be tapped into by any of the desk stations, but there was a lot of work in the computer room itself. There was no smoking in the room, but one of the yobos on the janitorial staff might have dropped a cigarette into a trash bin, though the light looked too small and too steady for a fire.

It was, as she had thought, a candle. An old-fashioned tin candle holder, rested on a corner of the monitor desk. A gold edge of light danced over the dark edges of the three massive monoliths of the Cray, over the huge six-foot graphics projection monitor screens and the smaller CRTs and keyboards. As she came up the slight ramp which raised the level of the room above the subfloor wiring, the single red eye of the power-light regarded her somberly beside that seed of anachronistic brightness.

Now what the hell was a candle . . . ?

It was her natural nervous timidity which saved her. She knew she hadn't heard the man behind her, but it was as if, half-ready, she felt the dark shape loom up behind her a moment before hands closed around her throat. Certainly her hands were there, clutching at the long, cold fingers as they tightened; she cow-kicked back and up, half-conscious of her foot tangling with fabric.

The grip loosened and fumbled; the gray, buzzing roar which had filled her ears and the terrible clouded feeling in her head abated for one instant, and she whipped her right hand down to the hammer ready in her purse. There was breath, hot against her temple, and the smell of woodsmoke, old wool, and herbs in her nostrils. She struck back over her left shoulder with all her strength.

Then she was falling. Her head struck the floor, hard under the thin, coarse nylon of the rug. She had a last, confused glimpse of the candle propped before the monitor, of a shadow bending over her—of something else on the wall . . .

She came to choking on ammonia. Her flailing fist was caught in a large, black hand, her scream was nothing more than a wheezing croak.

The face bending over hers focused—worried, black, and middle-aged. "You all right, miss?"

She blinked, her heart hammering and her whole body shaking with an adrenaline rush that nearly turned her sick. The upside-down beam of a flashlight at floor level gleamed brassily off a security badge and made dark lines along the regulation creases of the guard's light-blue shirt as he helped her to sit up.

"Did you get him?" she asked confusedly.

"Who?"

Her hands fumbled under the tangle of her blond hair, to feel the bruises on her throat. She swallowed, and it hurt. Her head ached—she realized she was lucky she'd hit the slight give of the raised floor and not the cement subfloor beneath. "Somebody was in here. He grabbed me from behind . . ." She looked back at the desk. The candle was gone.

The guard removed a walkie-talkie from his belt. "Ken? Art here.

We've got a report of an intruder in Building Six, near the main computer room." He turned back to her. "Did you get a look at him?"

She shook her head. "He was taller than me . . ." She stopped herself ruefully. Everyone was taller than she. "But I think I heard him walking in the hallways earlier."

"What time?" he asked.

"About two. I—I saw a light in here."

"And he attacked you with this?" The guard held up the hammer, protected from his hand by a handkerchief and gripped by the very end of the handle.

Joanna blushed. "No," she said, feeling very foolish. "I had that in my purse."

The guard cast a startled glance at her purse, then saw the size of it and nodded at least partial understanding.

"I sometimes carry one when I know I'm going to be working overtime," she hastened to fib, because she generally carried one as a matter of course. "For walking across the parking lot." This wasn't as odd as it sounded—San Serano was situated in the dry chaparral hills beyond Agoura, as deserted an area as you could get that close to L.A. Though parking lot crime was generally limited to the more ostentatious vehicles—'Vettes, Porsches, and four-wheelers—being looted or stolen outright, it was still a spooky walk across the enormous paved emptiness late at night.

The guard's walkie-talkie crackled. He listened, then said, "We've called on extra people. They'll be here to search the plant in about twenty minutes. He's not going to get away."

But that was, in point of fact, precisely what he did do. Joanna sat in the guard shack—actually a modest cement-block building near the plant's main gate on Lost Canyon Road—drinking tea and feeling conspicuous and hideously embarrassed, listening to the reports come in and answering questions put to her by the guard. Every door and entrance to Building Six was checked, and found to be inviolate. The building itself was methodically quartered by teams of security officers, and nothing was found.

At four, Joanna went home. She'd toyed with the notion of calling Gary, because the idea of returning to her apartment in Van Nuys alone tonight was somehow frightening, but she discarded it. This late, Gary would argue that she should come and spend the night with him, since his house was just over the hill, and she was in no mood for the "But *why* don't you want to?" argument that she knew would follow. Why she didn't want to was a question she'd never been able to answer to either

Gary's satisfaction or her own—it was too often easier to consent than to explain.

In the end, the guards walked her out to her solitary old blue Pinto sitting in the parking lot, and she drove down the dark canyons to the freeway and the brighter lights of the Valley. She wasn't sure just why the thought of going home alone would frighten her. When she reached it, the place was quiet and normal as ever; but when she finally slept, toward six, it was not restful sleep.

No trace of an intruder was ever found.

CHAPTER III

THE SILENT TOWER STOOD TEN MILES FROM THE ANCIENT ROYAL city of Kymil, separated from it by the sheet-steel curve of the River Pon, and by the silver-and-green patch-work of the Ponmarish, where sheep and pigs foraged among the boggy pools and town children hunted frogs in the long summer evenings. As Caris and his grandfather crossed the long causeway toward the old city gates of Kymil in the hush of the endless dusk, farmers and the river-trade merchants who made the money of the town drew aside from the sight of the old man's long black robes, making the sign against evil. The folk of Kymil had long memories and reason to fear the mageborn, even Salteris Solaris.

From the causeway, Caris could see the Tower, lonely on its hill; a finger raised in warning.

A warning, certainly, that no mage ever forgot.

A stage line ran between Angelshand and Kymil; though, like the Old Believers, the mages did not travel by stage, it meant that the roads were good. Two nights on the road, Caris and his grandfather had lodged in peasant huts, and once in the self-consciously rustic country villa of a wealthy merchant from Angelshand who had conversed with earnest condescension all through dinner about "the hidden strength of these ancient beliefs," and whose daughters had stolen downstairs after the household had gone to bed to ask Salteris to read their fortunes in the cards. Two nights they had slept under the stars. Caris worried that, in spite of the warmth of the fading summer, a chill might have settled into the old man's bones. Still, Salteris was tough. Like most sasenna, Caris slept only lightly, and when he had wakened in the night, it had always been to see Salteris sitting in silent meditation, gazing at the stars.

At the highest point of the causeway, Caris paused to shift his knapsack across his shoulders. Around the feet of the raised roadway and along the walls, just out of reach of the marshpools, were the hovels of the poor, built each spring when the waters went down and abandoned with their winter rising. Now children in rags were playing in between the sorry little huts, shouting and throwing pebbles at one another; a religious procession appeared, en route from one of the numerous shrines which dotted the marshes, and a whiff of incense and the sweetness of chanting rose to where he and his grandfather stood. People in the shantytown below paused to bend a knee to the gray-robed priests, as did half-naked boatmen from the river and a scarf vendor decorated like a Yule tree with his wares; a merchant crossing the causeway behind them, in his sober blue broadcloth coat and breeches, did likewise, and Caris felt the man's eyes on his back when neither he nor Salteris made this sign of subservience to the Church's will.

"We can stay at the House of the Mages in the city tonight," Salteris remarked, looking out past the marshes to the silence of the pale hills beyond. The hills marked the edge of the Sykerst, the empty lands that stretched eastward two thousand miles, an eternal, rolling plain of grass. "Nandiharrow runs it—the Old Faith has always been strong in this city, and many of those who came here twenty-five years ago for the trial of Suraklin found welcome enough among them to make it their home."

A touch of wind moved across the hills, murmuring among the willows at the level of their feet and bringing the wild scents of distance and hay. "Suraklin was tried here?"

"Indeed, my son." The old man sighed. "Tried and executed." The breeze flicked at his white hair, he gazed into those undefinable distances, with no elation for the memory of his ancient triumph.

"I didn't know," Caris said softly. "I thought, since the Emperor presided over it—the Prince, then—it must have taken place in Angelshand."

A wry expression pulled at the corner of the old man's mouth. "It is difficult to try someone for the misuse of his wizardry in a city where few believe in it," he said. "Suraklin was known in Kymil. Even those who did not think that his powers stemmed from magic dared not cross him." He nodded out towards the silent hills. "His Citadel stood out there. They have thrown down the standing-stones that marked the road that led there, at least those that were visible from the city; the Citadel itself was razed, and its very stones we calcined with fire. The Tower . . ."

In the blue-gray softness of the dusk, Caris saw the old man's white brows draw down, bringing with them a whole laddering of wrinkles along his high forehead.

"The Silent Tower had stood there of old, but we strengthened its walls —I and the other members of the Council. We put our spells into its stones, spells of nullification, of void. We fashioned the Sigil of Darkness from the signs of the stars and the Seal of the Dead God, which binds and cripples a mage's power, and that we placed upon the doors, so that no mage could pass. In the Silent Tower Suraklin awaited his trial. From it he was taken to his death."

He turned away. "Come," he said quietly. "It is not good to talk of such things." And he led the way along the dusty causeway toward the square, gray gates of the city.

They passed the night in the House of the Mages, a big, rambling structure in the heart of Kymil down near the river. Like most buildings in Kymil, it was built of wood; unlike most, it was fancifully decorated, with odd carvings and archways, small turrets and little stairways leading nowhere, balconies whose railings were carved into intricate openwork filigrees of flowers and leaves overlooking miniature gardens no larger than a single flowerbed, but so thick with vines that their small central fountains could scarcely be seen. Most of the buildings in Kymil, Caris noticed, were rather plainly built, and often garishly painted, pink or daffodil or a hard phthalo blue. One, near the gates as they entered the town, was illustrated in a wealth of architectural detail that the building itself did not possess—colonnades, friezes, facades, balconies, and marble statuary in niches, all painted in careful detail upon its flat wood sides. None of them appeared to be much more than twenty years old.

"That wasn't Suraklin's doing, was it?" he asked later that night of Le, second-in-command of the small troop of sasenna attached to the House of the Mages.

The dark, blade-slim woman nodded. "There was a deal of destruction wreaked in the town when the mages broke his power," she said. "Other houses were destroyed later and were found to have the Dark Mage's mark in them, drawn on a wall or a doorpost." She glanced across at him out of jet-bead eyes under her short crop of dark hair, then up at the head of the hall, where the mages of the house were talking quietly over their after-dinner wine. The four or five sasenna who had table service that night were moving quietly about in the dim candlelight, clearing up. There was rumored to be a poker game starting up in the barrack-quarters, but, like those they had sworn to serve, Caris and Le had lingered over a last cup of wine to talk before going to investigate.

"But what would it matter, after Suraklin was dead?" Caris was familiar with the principle of wizards' marks, though to make one was far beyond his rudimentary powers.

Le shook her head. "They say they weren't only to guide him there and let him enter where he'd been before. They say that, through the marks, he could influence the minds of those who were much near them; sway them to his thoughts from afar; sense things through them, even, in his dreams. It might be only stories, for folk feared him enough to believe anything of him, but then again . . ."

"Did you ever see him?"

The full mouth curved, but the expression could hardly be termed a smile. They were sitting at one of the long refectory tables in the lower part of the hall, the last of the sasenna to leave; at the other low table, parallel to theirs like the arms of a U below the main board where the mages sat, and nearer the vast, empty darkness of the fireplace, a couple of novices discussed spells with the earnestness of new explorers in some strange and wonderful world. The novices' table would be the more comfortable in the winter, but in the summer, with the diamond-paned casements that punctuated the length of the room thrown open to let in the milky warmth of the hay-smelling night, there was no comparison.

"I only saw him the once," Le said. "I was eight. I saw him die and saw what was left of his body strung up and burned. The Church's Witchfinders wanted to have him burned alive, but your friend the Archmage . . ." She nodded towards the head table, where Salteris sat, slender hands folded, fingers extended against his lips, nodding gravely to something the big, stout, graying mage Nandiharrow was saying. ". . . wouldn't have it. The Church has no jurisdiction over those that have sworn their vows to the Council and, though they needed the Church's might to subdue him, the Church would not be given the right to kill a mage—any mage." She pushed the sleeves of her loose black jacket up on her arms, and Caris saw, with some envy, the scars of half a dozen fights in a white zigzag over the fine, hard muscle of her forearms. "But as for Suraklin, I doubt it made any difference to him by that time. I don't know what the Council and the Witchfinders and the Prince did to him, but I remember he came to the block broken, stumbling, and silent. He never so much as raised a hand against the headsman's sword."

Her words returned to Caris' mind the next morning as he and the Archmage left the city by the Stone Road Gate and took the track that wound toward the hills. In the marshes near the town, the road was well-repaired and used; down in the lowlands, all around them, men and women were cutting hay from the common lands of the city corporation, carting it in wheelbarrows or on their backs to the higher ground to dry, their voices and laughter rising from all around like the cries of unusually noisy marsh birds. But away from the town, the road quickly dwindled to a narrow track; though it saw some use, Caris could tell that it had been long since much traffic had passed over it. As they passed into the green, silent folds of those treeless hills, he saw where huge standing-stones had once lined its sides, but had been thrown down and were now half-buried in the long summer grass.

"This was the road to Suraklin's Citadel?" he asked softly, unwilling to break the hush of the hills.

The old man seemed to wake from some private meditation at the sound of Caris' voice. "Yes, it led to his fortress. But the road was older than he—these stones were cracked with a thousand winters before ever he made people curse them as his."

Caris frowned, looking at the fallen menhirs. Another such line ran near Angelshand, mile after mile of ancient stones, standing like sentries in the deep grass, guarding what had long been forgotten. The Devil's Road, they called it. "What were they?" he asked, but his grandfather, relapsing into thoughts of his own, only shook his head.

On the hill to their left, the Silent Tower rose, dark-gray against the wind-combed emerald silk of the grass that lapped against them on all sides.

Caris saw now that it was more than the single finger of stone he had seen from the causeway. A curtain wall surrounded it, pierced by a single gate; the portcullis was down, unusual for daytime; through it, he saw what looked like a small monastic barracks. People were moving about inside, some in the black uniforms of sasenna, others, with the shaven heads of priests, in white. Near the gate, he got a glimpse of someone robed like a monk, but in flame-red rather than gray, the staff of a wizard in his hand. One of the Church Wizards, the Red Dogs. For the first time he felt uneasy at the thought of entering those walls.

"It's all right," Salteris said softly. "They don't see us yet."

They stood within full view of the gate, but Caris knew better than to question the Archmage's statement. From his robes the old man drew a small wash-leather bag and, opening it, tipped a little ball of what looked like hard-baked dough onto his palm.

"This is a *lipa,*" he said. Looking more closely, Caris saw that it was, in fact, made out of dough. Runes had been scratched into it with a pin or a fine stylus, covering its surface with an almost invisible net of tracery. "Keep it where you can get to it. Should any harm befall me, or should you and I be separated for more than three hours, burn it. The other mages will come." He pulled shut the strings of the bag again and handed it to Caris, never taking his eyes from the gates of the Silent Tower.

He started to move off again, but Caris held him back, troubled. "If Antryg's a prisoner, he can't work magic against you, surely?"

Salteris smiled. "Antryg is the least of my worries at the moment. No, he cannot work magic in the Silent Tower—but then, neither can I. Once within its walls, I will be only an old man, alone among people whose relations with the mageborn have always been at best a guarded truce. There has been no trouble between the Church and the Council of Wizards since Isar Challadin's time—but the Church is old. They watch and they wait." His dark eyes warmed with wry amusement. "I should not like to be the first one to hear of a surprise attack."

Caris looked back along the deserted, perfectly straight road and felt again how isolated the Silent Tower was in these empty hills. Le's words of last night returned to him—how the Church Witchfinders had wanted to burn the Dark Mage alive, and how Salteris had refused to give them the power of life and death over any mage, even the most evil. The Church might say that it forgave, but he knew that it never forgot.

He tucked the *lipa* into the purse at his belt, and they resumed their walk up the narrow track to the Tower compound. As they approached the gatehouse with its shut portcullis, Caris mentally reviewed the location of every weapon from his sword and the garrote in his sleeve to the hideout dagger in his boot. Glancing back, he saw that, beyond the turning where that track left the straight, ancient path, the old road was almost completely eradicated by grass. Where it passed over the crest of the next hill, he could see that the stones along its verges still stood.

His eyes went to the old man who walked at his side, trying to picture him as he had been twenty-five years ago, when he had led the Council against the Dark Mage. He had been Archmage even then, for he had come young to his power and to the leadership of the Council. His hair would have been black, Caris thought, and the silence that coiled like a serpent within him not so deep. The lightness in him that Caris remembered from before his grandmother's death five years ago would still have been there; the capacity for teasing and jokes that he had loved so well had not yet been replaced by that glint of irony in his eye.

The Bishop of Kymil met them at the gate. She was a tall woman in her fifties who had never been pretty. Her head was shaved, after the fashion of the Church. Heavier than she appeared at first glance, she was robed in velvet of ecclesiastical gray with the many-handed Sun of the Sole God like a splash of blood on her shoulder. As she held out a hand in greeting to the Archmage, she looked him over with a fishy, blue-gray eye. "My lord Archmage."

Looking past her into the court as the gates were opened, Caris wondered how many of the Church's sworn sasenna were stationed there. Le had said that five of the sasenna from the House of Mages were on Tower duty at a time—Caris guessed there were at least twenty sasenna in and around the small, dreary yard now. The two Red Dogs he had glimpsed stood quietly behind their ecclesiastical mistress, observing him and Salteris with cool, fanatic eyes. The Church called them hasu, the Bought Ones—bought from Hell by the blood of the saints and the Sole God. The less refined among the mages used the feminine form of the word—hasur—which had its own connotations.

"My lady Bishop." Salteris bowed. They touched hands, a formal contact of two fingers quickly withdrawn.

"You wrote that you wished to see the man Antryg Windrose?"

The warriors fell in around them as they crossed toward the tower itself. The place stank of a trap, of the crosscurrents of formality covering the resentments and envy the Church held against the only group ever successfully to defy their law; Caris was conscious in his bones of the portcullis sliding shut behind them. A quick look around showed him that escape from the compound would be difficult; no building was close enough to the curtain wall to allow a jump from roof to battlement, and in any case the drop on the other side was far enough to make breaking a leg a virtual certainty. The air here felt hot and still between high walls of parched gray stone, a bleak and cheerless place in contrast to the hills beyond. The sasenna moved about with somber faces, like most Church sasenna only one step from becoming monks. It was not the Way of the Sasenna to feel pity, but Caris felt it now for anyone who would be held prisoner here for the rest of his life.

At a sign from the Bishop, the captain of the Tower unlocked the massive iron fastenings of the Tower door. It swung open to reveal a dense mouth of shadow, cold even in summer. On the door's inner side, just above the lock, Caris could see an iron plate fastened. Affixed to it was a round plaque of lead, about the size of an Imperial eagle coin and incised and inlaid in some design that lifted the hair from his neck. In spite of himself, he turned his head away, abhorrence clutching at his belly, as if a rat had crawled over his flesh. As his head turned, he saw his grandfather flinch from it also, averting his eyes. The two Church wizards did not even come near.

He did not need to be told what it was. It was the Sigil of Darkness of which his grandfather had spoken, the Seal of the Dead God, which bound a wizard's power like a chain of despair. As the guard carried it away from the door to allow the Archmage to enter, Caris felt for the first time the true power that lay in the walls of the Silent Tower. He knew in himself that not all the harsh discipline of the sasenna could have induced him to touch that Sigil or any door that it sealed, no matter what was at stake. His own powers of magic were small and, he suspected miserably, failing; but through them he felt its influence as they entered those cold blue shadows, with an oppressive sense of horror lurking in the smoke-stained, windowless stone walls. What they must be to his grandfather's greater powers he loathed to think. He understood then why his grandfather had said that he hoped that, after seven years of it, Antryg would still be sane.

At the end of a cold, bare passage was a large guardroom, smoky, dark, and close-feeling in the smoldering glare of torches. The tower was windowless, the air freshened by some hidden system of ventilation that did not work particularly efficiently. They ascended an enclosed stone stair, the treads worn into a long hollow runnel in their center, slippery and treacherous. The two Church sasenna who followed them bore torches. Looking up, his hands pressed to the walls for support on the age-slicked stone steps, Caris could see the low roof entirely crusted with soot.

Owing to the tapering of the Tower, the room above was smaller; but though cluttered and untidy, it was clean, lacking even the stench of the guardroom. All around the walls, boxes had been piled to form crude shelves for the books that filled the place; more books were heaped on the floor in the corners and along the back of the small table that stood against the wall. The tops of these barely cleared the disordered piles of papers burying most of the table's surface; among them Caris could see a pot of ink and a vast number of broken quills, magnifying glasses, yellowing scientific journals, an armillary sphere, two astrolabes and the pieces of three more mingled with the component parts of elaborate mechanical toys. About a dozen cups, scattered through the colossal litter, contained the moldering remains of cold tea. Among the papers, he saw scribbled mathematical formulae and the complicated patterns of the Magic Circles, drawn as if the artist had been memorizing them by rote, although he could use none of them; with them were sketches—a leaf, a bone, the Bishop, the stars at certain times of winter nights, or simply the single many-branched candlestick that reared itself amid the confusion with its long stalactites of guttered wax.

The Bishop stood for a moment in the doorway, looking around the appallingly untidy room with pinched disapproval on her flat, potatolike face. Then she said to her guards, "Fetch him down."

They turned towards a door that would lead, Caris guessed, to another dark seam of stair and a yet smaller, windowless room above. Almost against his will, he felt a twinge of anger at this final violation of the prisoner's privacy. But before the guards could reach it, the door was flung open from the other side, and Antryg Windrose strode into the room in a tattered swirl of mismatched robes.

"My dear Herthe!" Passing between the startled guards as if they had been invisible, he seized and shook the Bishop's hand with old-fashioned cordiality and genuine delight. "How good of you to call! It's been—what? Six months? Seven months? How's your rheumatism? Did you take the herbs I prescribed?"

"No!" The Bishop pulled her hand away irritably. "And no, it's no better. I've brought . . ."

"You really ought to, before it comes on to rain tonight. Salteris!" He turned and checked his stride for a moment, looking into Salteris' face with startled gray eyes behind his thick-lensed spectacles. Then he stepped forward and clasped the Archmage's hand. "I haven't seen you in—oh, five years?"

Tall, thin, no longer young, Antryg Windrose had a beaky face in which all the individual features seemed slightly too large for the delicate bone structure, surrounded by a loose mane of graying brown hair and a straggly beard like frost-shot weeds that had been trailed in ink. Crystal earrings glinted in it like the snagged fragments of broken stars; half a dozen necklaces of cheap glass beads flashed tawdrily over the open collars of an assortment of ragged, scarecrow robes and a faded shirt. Behind the thick spectacle lenses, his wide gray eyes were bright, singularly gentle, and not sane. It must have been months, if not years, since he had seen anyone but the Tower guards, but there was neither reproach nor self-pity in the deep, extravagant voice Caris remembered so vividly. It was as if, for him, time had ceased to have meaning.

"Quite that," agreed Salteris with a gentle smile, though Caris, watching him, thought he glimpsed a kind of wary scrutiny as the Archmage met the mad wizard's eyes.

Antryg cocked his head to one side like a stork's as he returned the old man's gaze; then he turned away. For all his gawkiness, he moved with the light, random swiftness of a water strider on a hot day.

"And—Caris, isn't it? Stonne Caris, your daughter Thelida's boy? You probably won't remember me. You were only about six at the time."

Caris found himself saying, "No, as a matter of fact, I remember you very well."

The disconcerting gray eyes flared a little wider, suspicion and wariness that could have been real or feigned in their demented depths. "Indeed? The last time someone said that to me, I ended up having to leave Angelshand in a hurry." He glanced over at Salteris. "Will you stay to tea? and you, too, my dear Herthe . . ." The Bishop stiffened, evidently not liking being called so casually by her first name by a man who was her prisoner. ". . . and these gentlemen too, of course." He gestured toward the guards and moved over to the hearth where a kettle bubbled on the small fire. In spite of the fact that it was still summer, the fire was not uncomfortable. The tower was damp, and its shadows cold—little of the sun's warmth penetrated from the outside.

"Is this purely a social call, Salteris?" Steam rose in a mephitic veil around his face as he tipped the kettle into a chipped earthenware teapot on one corner of the raised brick hearth. "Or is there something I can do for you? Within the limits imposed by circumstances, that is." There wasn't a trace of sarcasm in his voice—he might have been speaking of a prior engagement rather than imprisonment for life. He stood up again, all his tawdry beads rattling. "I'm afraid all I can offer you is bread and butter. I keep ordering caviar, and it never comes."

The prelate looked affronted, but Caris saw the corners of his grandfather's mouth tuck up in an effort to suppress a smile; at the same time, he was aware that the Archmage had relaxed. "Bread and butter will be quite acceptable, Antryg."

Antryg turned to extend the invitation to the Bishop's guards; but, at a signal from her, they had stepped into the black slot of the doorway. With a shrug, he took a piece of paper at random from the mess on the table, lighted a corner of it in the fire, and proceeded to kindle the half-burned candles in their holder to augment the sooty torch- and firelight of the dim room.

"My lady," Salteris said quietly, "may I have your leave to speak to this man alone?"

The Bishop's pale, protuberant eyes grew hard. "I would rather not, my lord. Too often there has been collusion between the mageborn. And my predecessor told me that this man was once your pupil—that it was only through your intercession that he was placed here at all and not executed. As chief prelate of the Empire I cannot . . ."

"She doesn't trust you, Salteris." Antryg sighed, shaking his head. He blew out the half-burned paper and dropped it back onto the table. "Well, never mind."

The Archmage had already taken one of the two chairs at the cluttered table; Antryg offered the other one first to the Bishop, who refused it indignantly, then to Caris, as if he had been a visitor in his own right and not merely the sasennan of the Archmage. Refused on both counts, he took it himself, setting his teacup precariously on top of a pile of papers. "What did you want to see me about?"

"The Void," Salteris said softly.

The candlelight flashed sharply across Antryg's spectacles with his sudden start, his hand arrested mid-motion. "What about the Void?"

"Can you sense it? Feel it?"

"No." Antryg set his cup down.

"You used to be able to."

"Outside, yes. In here, I can no more sense the Void than I can feel the weather. Why do you ask?"

Salteris folded his hands and rested his extended forefingers against his lips. "I have reason to believe that someone from another universe passed through it and killed Thirle in the Mages' Yard. Shot him," he went on, as Antryg's look of grieved shock reminded Caris that he, too, must have known and liked the little herbalist, "Though, when the ball was drawn, it was unlike any pistol ball any of us have seen."

Caris frowned suddenly in the reddish, springing shadows. "And there was no smell of powder," he said. "No smoke, though it was a still night."

"Curious," Antryg remarked softly.

"Caris here saw something that sounds like the Gates that Suraklin used to open in the Void," the Archmage went on. "Aunt Min thought so, too. Are there mages in other worlds beyond the Void, Antryg, who could open the Void and come here to work mischief?"

"Oh, I should think so." Antryg looked down into his tea. Salteris was watching that strange, expressive face as the steam laid a film over the thick rounds of the spectacle lenses; but Caris, watching the long fingers where they rested on the teacup's chipped pottery side, saw them shake. "It doesn't necessarily mean he—"

He broke off suddenly, and Salteris frowned, his white eyebrows plunging down sharply over his nose. "He what?"

"He what?" Antryg looked up at him inquiringly.

"The fact that the intruder came through the Void doesn't necessarily mean what?"

Antryg frowned back, gazing for a long moment into Salteris' eyes. Then he said, "I haven't the slightest idea. Did you know that all the wisdom in the cosmos can be found written in magical signs on the shells of tortoises? One has to collect and read an enormous number of tortoises in order to figure it out, of course, and they have to be read in the correct order, but somewhere here I have a collection of tortoise-rubbings . . ."

"Antryg," Salteris said reprovingly, as his erratic host made a move to search the jumble of shelves behind him. The madman turned back to regard him with unnerving intentness.

"They don't like to have rubbings taken, you know."

"Quite understandable," Salteris agreed soothingly. "You were saying about the Void?"

"I wasn't saying anything about the Void," Antryg protested. "Only that, yes, some of the worlds one can reach by passing through it are worlds wherein magic can exist. In others it does not. And there is continual drift, toward the centers of power or away from them. So, yes, a mage from another world could have opened a Gate in the Void last week and come through for purposes of his own."

"I thought you claimed you could not feel the Void." Caris stepped forward, into the circle of the candelabra's light. "How do you know it was last week?"

Antryg regarded him with the mild, startled aspect of a melancholy stork. "Obviously you came here as soon as you knew the problem involved the Void. It's a week's walk from Angelshand to Kymil—unless you took the stage?" He glanced inquiringly at Salteris, who sighed patiently and shook his head.

"Purposes of his own," the Bishop said suddenly. Like Caris, she had remained in the denser shadows at the edges of the room. Now she came forward, her thick face congealing with suspicion. "What purposes?"

"What purposes did you have in mind?" Antryg dug a long loop of string from beneath the general litter on the table; the multiple shadows of the candle flame danced over his long, bony fingers as he began constructing a cat's cradle.

The Bishop's wary glance slid from him to the Archmage. "To bring abominations into this world?"

Salteris looked up sharply. "Abominations?"

"Had you not heard of them, my lord Archmage?" Her gruff voice grew silky. "All this summer there has been a murmuring among the villages of strange things seen and heard and felt. In Voronwe in the south a man was seen to go into his own house in daylight and was found there an hour later, torn to pieces; in Skepcraw west of here there has been something like a sickness, where the hay has been left to rot in the fields while the people of the town huddle weeping in the Church or else drink in the tavern, not troubling to feed either themselves or their stock. We have sent out the Witchfinders, but they have found nothing. . . ."

Salteris frowned. "I had heard rumor of this. But it has nothing to do with Thirle's murder or the opening of the Void."

"Hasn't it?" the Bishop asked.

"I scarcely find it surprising that you've found nothing," Antryg remarked, most of his attention still absorbed by the patterns of the string between his hands. "Old Sergius Peelbone, your Witchfinder Extraordinary, is looking for some*one* rather than some*thing*— if he can't try it for witchcraft and burn it, it doesn't exist. Besides, Nandiharrow and the others at the House of the Mages would have known if unauthorized power were being worked in the land—and in any case, there are sufficient evils and wonders in this world, without importing them from others. Could I trouble you . . . ?" He held out his entangled hands to her and waggled his thumb illustratively.

Irritated, she yanked the string from his fingers and hurled it to the floor. "You are frivolous!"

"Of course I'm frivolous," he replied mildly. "You yourself must know how boring gravity is to oneself and everyone else. And I really haven't much opportunity to be anything else, have I?" He bent to pick up the string, and the Bishop, goaded, seized him by the shoulder and thrust him back into his chair.

"I warn you," she said grimly. "I can have you . . ."

"You can not!" cut in Salteris sharply. "He is the Church's prisoner, but his person is under the jurisdiction of the Council of Wizards to which he made his vows."

"Vows that he foreswore!"

"Does a priest who sins pass from the governance and judgment of the Church?" Salteris demanded. For an instant their gazes locked. The wizard was like an old, white fox, slender and sharp as a knife blade against the Bishop's piglike bulk. But like a pig, Caris knew, the Bishop was more intelligent and more dangerous than she seemed; here in the Tower, Salteris, like Antryg, was at her mercy.

"A priest's sins concern a priest alone," the Bishop said softly. "A wizard who foreswears his vows not to meddle in the affairs of humankind endangers not only all those he touches, but all those he encourages to follow his example. He can not only be a danger, but he can teach others to be a danger, and if we cannot trust the mageborn to govern their own . . ."

"Can you not?" Salteris replied in a voice equally low. Deep amber glints shone catlike in his eyes as they bored into hers. "Were it not for the mageborn on the Council, it would be Suraklin who rules this city, and not yourself."

"Suraklin was defeated by the army led by the Prince."

"Without us, his precious army would not so much as have found the Citadel. Suraklin would have led them like sheep through the hills and, in the end, summoned the elemental forces of the earth to swallow them up. By our dead that day, by this . . ." With a swift move Salteris flung back the long sleeve of his robe. Age-whitened scars blotched his arms, beginning like a sleeve, four inches below his elbow and, Caris knew, covering half his chest. ". . . I have earned the right to say what shall be done with a man who has taken Council vows."

He turned suddenly back to where Antryg was calmly drinking his tea and taking no further interest in the discussion of those by whose whim he would live or die. "Antryg," he said. "Has there been movement through the Void in these last weeks?"

"There must have been, mustn't there, if you've seen an intruder," Antryg said reasonably. He swirled his cup in his hand and gazed down into its dregs. "Do you realize the spells on this tower affect even the tea-leaves?"

"I think you're lying," the Archmage said softly.

Antryg raised his head, startled. "I swear to you I haven't gotten a decent reading in seven years."

Salteris rested his slender hands among the junk on the table and looked for a long moment down into the madman's wide, bespectacled, gray eyes. "I think you're lying, Antryg," he repeated. "I don't know why . . ."

"Don't you?" Their gazes held, Salteris' wary and speculative, Antryg's, suddenly stripped of the mask of amiable lunacy, vulnerable and very frightened. The Archmage's glance slid to the Bishop, then away, and something relaxed in the set of his mouth. He straightened up and stood for a moment looking down at the seated man. Light from the candles in their holder, clotted with stalactites of years' worth of dribbled wax, glinted on the round lenses of Antryg's spectacles and caught like droplets of yellow sunlight in the crystal of his earrings.

Then abruptly Antryg got to his feet. "Well, it's been very pleasant chatting with you, but I'm sure we all have things to do." With manic briskness he collected teapot and cups, stacked them neatly in one corner of the table, and piled papers on top of them. "Herthe, why don't you put a division of your guards at the Archmage's disposal? I'm sure they'll come in handy. Salteris . . ." He looked away from the Bishop's gog-gling indignation to his former master, and the madness died again from his eyes. In a sober voice he said, "I think the first place you should look should be Suraklin's Citadel. You know as well as I do that it was built on a node of the lines. If there is some sort of power abroad in the land, signs of it will show up there."

Salteris nodded. "I think so, too."

For a moment the two wizards faced one another; in the silence between them, Caris was again made conscious of how quiet the Tower was. No sound penetrated from the outside, save a soft, plaintive moaning of wind in the complex ventilation; no light, no warmth, no change. Antryg was not a young man, but he was not old, and Caris was aware that mages could live to fantastic ages. Was this room and the one above it all the world he could look forward to for the next fifty years? In spite of himself, in spite of what he now knew about Antryg, he felt again a stab of pity for that tall scarecrow, with his mad, mild eyes.

Salteris said, "Thank you, Antryg. I shall be back to see you, before I leave Kymil."

Antryg smiled like a mad elf. "I shall see what I can do about getting us caviar by then. Come any day—I'm generally at home between two and four." He thought about it for a moment, then added, "And at any other time, of course."

"Are you?" asked Salteris, in a voice so low that Caris, startled, was barely sure he heard the words. Then the old man turned and, followed by the Bishop and his sasennan, descended the blackness of the narrow stair to the guardroom below.

It wasn't until they were again on the ancient road, shadowed now by the gray, unseasonable clouds that were riding up from the river to cover the town with the soft smell of coming rain, that Caris said, "He was lying."

The Archmage glanced over at him and raised one white brow.

Caris jerked his head upward, toward the clouds. "He said that he could no more sense the Void than he could the weather. But the first thing he said to the Bishop was that it would rain tonight."

With a brisk jingling of harness, shockingly loud in the wind-murmuring quiet, the Bishop's carriage passed them by, returning to her palace in Kymil. Counting her outriders, Caris noticed that Herthe had left the two Red Dogs back at the Tower. Through the thick glass of the windows, he caught a glimpse of the lady herself, fretfully rubbing her aching joints as the badly sprung vehicle jolted over the unpaved way. The Bishop did not even spare a glance to the old mage and his sasennan walking in the long grass at the road's verge.

Salteris sighed and nodded. "Yes. I feared it was so. He's hiding something, Caris; he knows something, or there is something he will not speak." The wind made its soft, thrumming thunder in their ears and lifted the long white hair from his shoulders. The waning daylight glinted in the sepia depths of his eyes.

Caris was silent for a time as they walked on through the dusk. He thought about the practiced ease with which the mad wizard had sparked the tensions between Bishop and Archmage, to make them turn upon one another and cease questioning him. Antryg had said it had been five years since they'd met—Caris wondered how he had known the suspicion would be so easy to arouse, for that touchiness of temper was something which had grown in the old man more recently, he thought, than that. But then, Antryg had known Salteris well.

He glanced back at the windowless tower, its surrounding buildings hidden again by the hills, a single warning finger lifted against the twilight milkiness of the sky. Then he dug in his purse for the *lipa* and returned it to the Archmage. He was plagued by the odd sixth sense that the sasenna develop, the feeling that there was coming a time when the old man was going to need it badly.

CHAPTER IV

THE SILENCE AFTER THE PRINT-RUN FINISHED WAS LIKE THE DROP OF a cleaver. Joanna looked up, startled as if by a noise.

But the only noise in the cubicle now was the faint, self-satisfied hum of the air conditioner.

Around her, Systems felt suddenly, terrible empty.

In something like panic her eyes jerked to the clock.

6:45.

Her breath leaked away in a small sigh. Not so very late.

You can't keep doing this, she told herself, shoving off with one sneakered foot against the filing cabinet and coasting in her wheeled swivel chair to the printer to tear off the long accordion of green-and-white paper. *The data's going to come in from the SPECTER tests this week, and everybody in the plant is going to be working insane overtime. You can't refuse to do the same on the grounds that you're afraid of the boogieman.*

She didn't even look at the graph as she folded it and stashed it on top of the stratified layers of junk on her desk. Her small hands were perfectly steady as she punched through backup and shut down, but she was wryly conscious that she performed the activity in record time.

You can't keep doing this, she repeated to herself. *It's been almost two weeks. Even if they didn't find him, nobody could live in hiding in this building for that long. And they've been over it a dozen times.*

But as she stashed her copy of *Byte* and the massive roll of printout from one of her own programs that she'd sneaked in to run on the Cray, her fingers touched the smooth handle of the hammer that she always carried with her these days. Once or twice in the last ten days, particularly when she was working late, she had had the feeling of being watched, and it came unbidden to her mind that there were a vast number of places in Building Six where someone could hide. The Analysis and Testing building was two stories high, but in most places it had only one floor. Above the labs and test bays loomed a vast loft of space crossed by catwalks where someone could lurk for hours unseen. Joanna knew it well—she had been tempted, over and over, to go there during the periods of gray and causeless depression that had come to her in the last few days, and only her fear of what she might meet there had kept her away. But Digby Clayton, the Programming Department's resident crazy, frequently went there to meditate—and have visions, so he said—and a number of people in the Art Department claimed to have gone up there and made love at ten-thirty on a Tuesday morning unnoticed.

It wasn't the only place, either, she thought, stepping resolutely into the well-lit blankness of the empty hall. The garage where they kept the fork lifts and electric trucks was accessible from a door near the supply offices. With a pocketful of change, you could live indefinitely from the junk machines—until malnutrition caught up with you, anyway, she added with an inner grin, in spite of her fears. And in the teeth of the much-vaunted security system, thefts had, as the guard said, proceeded regularly—everything from paper clips to computer components to telephone equipment by the metric ton. It would be easy to hide out there and wait. . . .

For what? Joanna demanded sensibly of herself and, with some effort, prevented her step from quickening. *If the man was a thief, he'd have gotten himself out the same way he got in—never mind what it was—and be long gone. Nobody in his right mind would hide out in San Serano for a week just to jump out and strangle people.*

But nobody in his right mind would climb to the top of a University bell tower to take potshots with a scope-sighted rifle at passers-by, either, her mind retorted, or murder perfectly innocent, semiretired rock'n'roll stars just to say they'd done it, or do any of the other gruesome things that had made the headlines within her memory.

You're paranoid, Joanna.

Who told you I was, and why? she retorted jokingly, and glanced once again over her shoulder.

It was like scratching a mosquito bite, she thought—something that didn't help, that you shouldn't do, but you couldn't stop.

Uneasiness stalked her, like the faint sound of her sneakers on the carpet. She found herself increasingly loath to pass the darkened openings of rooms and hallways on both sides of the lighted corridor, though she was not certain what it was that she feared to see.

At the junction of the main corridor she stopped, hiking her heavy purse up onto her shoulder and pushing her soft, unruly hair out of her face. Around her, the plain pastel walls were decorated with walnut-framed blowups of some of the more scenic photographs of the San Serano plant, dramatic in its barren backdrop of chaparral hills and clumps of twisted live oak, the grass either the white-champagne of summer or the exquisite emerald velvet of winter rains. The shots, Joanna was always amused to notice, were carefully set up to exclude the parking lots, the barbed wire, and the bluish blanket of Los Angeles smog in the background.

Down the dim hallway to her right was the main computer room.

The lights there were still on, though she could hear no voices. No shadow moved across them to blot the sheen of them on the metal of the doorframe. She'd been in the room almost daily since the assault, but there had always been people at the monitors and graphics printers connected to the enormous mainframe, and she had had deadlines prodding at her back. A half-memory from that night tugged at the back of her mind like a temptation she could not quite define—some unchecked incongruity that she had not spoken of to the guards because it was too absurd, and she had feared their laughter, but she wanted to verify it in her own mind.

It took more determination than she thought it would to make herself walk down the unlit hall toward the glow of the doorway. Knowing herself to be timid and passive by nature, her very reluctance made her go on.

The trouble is, she thought wryly, stepping up the slight ramp and into the clean-lit, cold vastness of the room, *you can't always tell what fears are irrational and what are only improbable. It would certainly help if this were a movie—I could listen for the creepy music on the sound-track to warn me whether I'm making a stupid mistake or not.*

The computer was still up. In good lighting it was beautiful, its tricolored bulk looming like the Great Wall of China amid a tasteful selection of add-ons, which included four input desks, several banks of additional memory, and two six-by-six-foot color monitors capable of forming the most exacting of projections. Digby Clayton assured her that Pac-Man played on such a monitor was a truly visceral experience.

A blue-gray polyester blazer hung neatly over the back one of the chairs, and Joanna identified it, with a slight sinking of the stomach, as Gary Fairchild's. Better, she thought, to get this over quickly before he returned and asked her what she was doing here. She did not precisely know herself and she was never good at explaining things to people, particularly to Gary.

She walked a little ways into the room, and knelt on the floor in approximately the place she'd been thrown. Her memory of what she was seeking was a little clearer from down here, as if she'd left it like a contact lens on the carpet. She'd seen the candle in its anachronistic holder, the candle of which the guards had found no sign, sitting in front of the nearest monitor. A precaution, they'd said, against turning on the lights and possibly alerting a passing guard—but a flashlight would have served better, she thought, as she had thought then. There had been a black shadow descending upon her as her own mind darkened and, at the last moment, that glimpse of something on the wall.

From her angle near the floor she narrowed her eyes, finding the place. Of course there was nothing there now.

She got to her feet again, feeling a bit silly. Brushing off the knees of her jeans, she walked to the spot. It had been a mark, she remembered, like a Japanese pictograph, but definitely not Japanese, about eight inches about her own eye-level and a foot to the left of the doorframe. It had been clear and sharply defined, but somehow unreal, like a spot of light thrown from a stray reflector rather than anything actually written there. She'd only had a glimpse of it, a sidelong flicker from the corner of her eye as she fell, and the memory of it was fogged by panic and terror. In any case, there was certainly no sign of it now.

She put the side of her face to the wall and peered sidelong at the spot, hoping to see something from the different angle, as sometimes could be seen with glass.

Still nothing.

Mentally she shook herself. The janitors would have washed the wall since then, if nothing else, she told herself, or—*did* the janitors wash the walls here? Probably—the computer room was a favorite showplace of the front-office boys. Or maybe there had never been anything in the first place.

Alfred Hitchcock's profile? she wondered frivolously. George Lucas' signature of THX1138? The footprint of a giant hound?

When someone yelled "Boo!" behind her, she nearly jumped out of her skin. A week of the jitters had, however, schooled her reflexes—her hand was in her purse and gripping the handle of the hammer before she had completely swung around enough to recognize Gary Fairchild.

"Hey, calm down," he said, with his deprecating smile. "Did I scare you?"

She was trembling all over, but, rather to her surprise, her voice came out level and very angry. "Why? Wasn't that the idea?"

He looked confused and taken aback. "I—uh—Don't get mad. I mean —you know." That explained, he hastily changed the subject. "Were you looking for me?"

It was in her mind to say, *Why would I look for someone who'd play juvenile tricks like that?* but there was no point in getting into a fight with Gary. He'd only hang onto her, apologizing like hell for days, until she got tired enough to forgive him. Instead she said, "No, I came back in the hopes of catching the criminal when he returned to the scene of the crime."

Nonplussed, Gary said, "But that was days ago, babe. You don't think he's lurked around here all this time?"

With a mental *Oi, veh,* Joanna said, "Joke, Gary."

Obediently, he gave a hearty laugh. Regarding him—white jeans, Hawaiian shirt bulging just slightly over conscientiously built-up muscles and an equally conscientious tan—Joanna wondered if she'd even like him, if she met him for the first time now.

In spite of two years of dating him, she had her own suspicions about that.

"Besides," she added, surreptitiously sliding the handle of her hammer back into her purse under the heavy wads of printouts, a brush, a mirror, pens, notebooks, screw-cap boxes, and a collapsible cup, "he might have come back. Whatever he was out to steal . . ."

"Babe," said Gary patiently, "what could he have stolen from here that he couldn't have gotten easier from the storage bays? Computer stuff is easier to rip off from there, before it's been dedicated—safer, too, because if it hasn't been logged in, nobody would even know it's gone."

This, Joanna knew, was true. She had her own theories about how Gary would know it. In her idle moments she had a habit of thumbing through the mainframe, breaking into files which the management of San Serano confidently assumed were hidden under their secret passwords; and she knew that, as a result of switching over to a new computerized system, the invoices were in a hopeless tangle. It was one of the things that had troubled her from the first about the guard's glib theory that she'd surprised and been surprised by a thief.

Her own alternative theories weren't particularly pleasant ones.

"I'll be done here in a few minutes, Joanna," Gary said after a few moments. "I can walk you out. Maybe we can stop someplace . . ."

She shook her head. "Thank you, but that's okay." She might be nervous about walking those empty corridors alone; but in her present uneasy mood, she knew Gary would be no improvement on imaginary maniacs. "I'll see you tomorrow, okay?"

He stepped forward and put his hands on her waist in the confident expectation of a kiss which, after a microsecond's hesitation for no particular reason other than that she simply didn't feel like kissing him, she gave him. As usual, he overdid it. "You are coming out to my place this weekend, aren't you?" he asked. "Everybody from the department will be there."

Reason enough to avoid it, she thought and vacillated, "I don't know, Gary . . ."

"I've got four new games for the computer, some good beer—even wine if you like that stuff—plus the new jet system in the jacuzzi, and some real nice . . ." He mimed blowing smoke in an elaborately silly euphemism for smoking pot.

Joanna sighed. So in addition to the boring middle-management types Gary hung around with, there would be drunk, stoned, boring middle-management types. On the other hand, she never went to parties, but she knew parties were the sort of thing people were supposed to enjoy. "It's a long drive," she began.

"Only ten minutes past here," he pointed out. "Most of the folks are coming up in the afternoon. We can sit by the pool, catch some rays, turn the speakers up full-blast. . . . What's the point of living clear the hell out here if you can't make a little noise now and then?" He repeated what Joanna had always guessed was the line fed to him by the real estate man who'd sold him the place. Since she knew Gary's taste in music ran to heavy-metal bands like Havoc and Fallen Angel, the prospect was getting less and less appealing all the time.

"The new graphics system I've got on the games computer is fabulous," he urged. "Please," he added, seeing her unmoved even by this. He flashed her a nervous grin that she had never liked and that had increasingly begun to irritate her. "Hey, you're my sweetheart, remember? The love of my life . . ." He drew her to him for another kiss. "I just wish we could be together. . . ."

"Gary." With sudden firmness that was less determination than simple weariness, she wriggled free of his indecisive embrace. "If you ask me to live with you one more time I really will quit speaking to you. I told you I don't know . . ."

"But why not, babe?" he asked, reproach in his big brown eyes and a suspicion of a whine creeping into his voice. "It isn't like your apartment is great or anything. You'd be closer to work here and not have to drive all that way; and you'd save on rent money. You know I'll always love you, babe . . ." She suspected he'd heard that line on TV. "Come Saturday, anyhow—see the place now that I've got the new computer stuff in. Are you doing anything else on Saturday?"

She wasn't, but hemmed, not sure how she should be reacting. "I don't know, Gary. I may be going out with some friends . . ."

"Invite 'em along," he offered. "Who are they? Anyone from here?"

Not feeling up to more flights of invention, Joanna sighed, "All right, I'll be there." His brown eyes warmed and his smile returned full-wattage.

"That's great, babe," he beamed. "Hey, are you doing anything else right now? I'll be done with this program in about fifteen minutes. . . ."

Joanna hesitated for a moment, wondering if she'd indulged in enough selfish behavior and ought to keep him company, even though it would probably involve dinner afterwards . . . and dinner at some coffee shop, at that. For all the money he made, Gary didn't believe in spending more than he had to on anyone but himself. But there was no guaranteeing how long any program would take to run—she was used to playing "Another five minutes" for up to an hour and a half at a time. "I don't think so," she said. "I'm going to go home, take a very long bath, and go to bed. I'll see you tomorrow." Ignoring his protesting, "Aw, babe . . ." she hiked her monstrous purse up over her shoulder and reciprocated his rather wet and amorous farewell kiss, more out of a sense of duty than enjoyment. Duty, she reflected later, walking down the dim hallway toward the bright rectangle of the main corridor ahead, not so much to Gary as to all those years of being pointed at as the School Nerd. She was conscious, as she walked, of a feeling of relief and wondered how she could ever have been in love with Gary Fairchild.

If it *had* been love, she thought, and not just the sexual glitter that surrounds the passage from virgin to nonvirgin. He had been, almost literally, the first man who had ever taken notice of her in her shy and bookish life. When she had first come to work at San Serano two years ago, Gary had asked her out, first to lunch and later to dinner, and had taken her home one night to the high tech Westwood apartment he'd been staying in that year.

He had always wanted her to live with him. Lately, he had begun to pester her about it, Joanna suspected, because he was thirty-four and reaching the age when he felt he ought to be living with somebody. He had bought the house in the expectation of it—or anyway, that was what he'd told her. But then, Gary was seldom completely honest, particularly if he thought he could drum up pity.

She sighed again, turning along the bright expanse of corridor. Twice in the last week, she had been plagued by the same queer, terrible feelings of hopeless depression which had come upon her on the night of the assault; at those times, she had found herself considering marriage to Gary, not because she loved him or even cared very much about him, but because she felt hopeless about her future to the extent that she did not much care what she did. Those depressions frightened her, chiefly because some small, sane part of herself realized that, in the grip of one, she had no real concern whether she lived or died—that if one came upon her while driving down the freeway, she would literally not bother to get out of the way of the other cars. The thought of living with Gary, she knew, was a little like that.

The rest of the time, she wondered what her life would be like now if she had moved in with him when first he had asked.

Well, for starters, she thought, you wouldn't be working here. And the reason you wouldn't be working here is because pool, jacuzzi, video room, an IBM-AT with 60 megabytes and $200,000 house in the hills notwithstanding, Gary would have driven you to leave him within two months by his assumption that he could interrupt whatever you were doing to keep him company, and you'd have quit your job and moved to another town.

Or else, she thought with a shiver, you'd be so chicken of change you'd still be with him.

And abruptly, the corridor lights went out.

Joanna stopped and swung around, feeling that the blood in her veins had turned to water. In brownish gloom, the corridor stretched empty behind her. Far back at the rear of the building, she could see the yellow glow of crossing hallway lights—ahead of her, the corridor stretched for another twenty yards or so, to the dim illumination around the corner that led toward the hall to the main lobby. *Just this section,* she thought. *Just a fuse . . .*

Terror breathed over her, like the wind from a half-open door that looked into the pits of eternity, unreasonable, shocking; she had to fight it to keep from breaking into a panic run. *It's just the lights going out,* she told herself, it's stupid to be afraid. . . .

Down some hallway to her left, she heard the stealthy slip of footfalls. *Gary,* she thought, hoping against hope, but knew that Gary never walked with that effort at silence. She hastened forward, her heart pounding, her hand sliding down to the handle of the hammer again, knowing it would do her no good. There was something else here, something past ordinary fear, a terrible knowledge that hummed over her screaming nerves.

Do I run? she wondered. *Or is this just what it's like to go insane? Were the depressions just a foreshadowing?*

But now the end of the corridor lay in darkness. The next section of cross-corridor must have gone out as well, she thought; but even as the idea went through her mind, she knew that no fuse failure could have produced a darkness like that. There was nothing beyond that darkness. She could not see the crossing wall with its bland photos of San Serano, only a shadow that seemed to have no end, as if she were looking into a starless night sky through a tube. Her reason told her it was a trick of the shadows, but her whole soul cried out against taking a further step toward that darkness.

Don't be silly, she told herself, sweat suddenly chilling her throat and clammy on her temples. *There's nothing to be afraid of in the dark.*

But there was. Was that movement, far off—farther off that could possibly be real, at the end of that corridor of darkness that could not actually exist? The glance of shadow along the fold of a robe, like a stirring of wind in the darkness—a breath of a smell she could not identify, but which shot her with an adrenaline injection of unthinking horror.

She turned right down a corridor, trying to remember how the other halls joined up to the one that would get her to the main lobby. . . . *This is silly,* she told herself, hastening her steps as much as she could while trying to keep them soundless. *Why am I having a nightmare when I don't remember falling asleep?*

The corridor plunged on, dim and uncrossed, to the far reaches of the test bays.

Without even questioning what she did or why, she opened the only door on that whole unbroken length, slipped inside and shut it behind her. It was a janitor's closet, smelling of ammonia and mildewing mopheads; as she shut herself in, the diffuse glow from the one-sixth-power lamps in the hall glanced briefly off a black, chitinous shape that retreated with offended haste beneath the baseboard. Even her old hysterical terror of roaches didn't trouble her now. She pulled the door shut and held fast to the inner knob in the darkness.

She could hear something in the hall.

It was hard to analyze, though she'd gotten good at identifying the minutest sounds from her months of living alone. Waking at night, she could track her way through her apartment with her ears—that was the refrigerator, that was the television antenna wire moving across the roof in the wind.

That soft, slurring sound outside now was like a stealthy footstep, but

subtly different from those she knew. Fabric, she thought, remembering
the heavy tangle of robe as she'd kicked at her assailant last week. . . .
In the silence she wondered about the ears listening out there, and if they
could hear the wild hammering of her heart.

Evil surrounded her, breathing and waiting, and she had backed herself into this corner in the stupid hope that it would pass. She heard the
padding tread—walk, walk, halt. Walk, halt.

Does it know that I'm here?

There was a louvered grille in the lower part of the door to let in air
and a feeble bit of light. Something blocked the louvers, some shadow.
Under her hands, the doorknob moved testingly.

Her teeth and hands shut so tightly her bones ached. Terror jammed
like a knot of unscreamed sounds in her throat, and she thought she
could smell through the grille the faint, familiar odor of her earlier terror;
the pungency of woodsmoke-permeated wool and the lingering cold scent
or feeling that she could not define. The knob moved again, and she held
tight to it, willing whatever was outside to think it was locked. Later she
would find the gray plaid of her shirt soaked with sweat, but she had no
consciousness of it now, nor of anything but a hideous dread. She knew if
she had any courage at all, she should fling open the door, face what was
outside, and see the intruder. What, after all, could he do to her in a
public place like San Serano with help within easy call? But her resolve
drained from her and a small, sane voice at the back of her mind whispered to her, *If you do that you will die.*

She wondered how she knew that, or if it was a common delusion. But
her knowledge of it was so strong that she knew that nothing could have
induced her willingly to open that door.

Filtered yellow light returned to the louvers. Whatever had blotted
them was gone.

It is still in the hall, she thought—waiting for me. Waiting for me to
think it's safe, to put my head out and look.

What?

What?

How long she stood in the smelly darkness she didn't know. Her legs
began to shake, and dizziness swept over her. *There's a fifty-foot walk
down this hall, around the corner to the next big corridor, and up along
that to the lobby,* she thought. Her knees were trembling so badly she
wondered if she'd be able to run.

Of course you won't run, the cool part of her mind said. *You've already
made your reputation with the Man Who Wasn't There—not a fingerprint
in sight and nothing but a few bruises which could have come from any-*

*where to prove there ever was such an intruder. They never found the place
where he got in. What are you going to tell them if you go pelting into the
lobby full-tilt and screaming?*

> *Yesterday upon the stair*
> *I met a man who wasn't there.*
> *He wasn't there again today.*
> *I wish that man would stay away. . . .*

It took all the courage she had to open the door. The corridor was dim,
innocuous, and totally empty. A few yards away the main hall crossed it,
brightly lit as always and ordinary as only an aerospace building can be.

She managed to walk to the lobby. But she did it very swiftly and
drove down the hill toward Van Nuys at breakneck speed through the
darkness, to stare uncomprehendingly at the television set until it was
dawn and she finally dared to turn out the bedroom lights.

CHAPTER V

STONNE CARIS REMAINED AMONG THE SASENNA AT THE HOUSE OF the Mages for nearly a week. He trained with them, morning and afternoon, and enjoyed the chance to hone his skills with a new master's teaching and fresh opponents. One summer evening, all of the sasenna of the town, whether of the Mages, the Church, or the few nobles who kept permanent seats in the district and were wealthy enough to retain their own troops, went on a training hunt in the marshes. Caris had drawn to run with the wolves and dodged in and out among the boggy pools, accounting for four of his pursuers from ambush before Le struck him down from behind. They all returned to the city bruised, battered, and plastered with mud, to celebrate with much beer their joint funeral.

In that week he had a casual affair with a tavern girl, one of the few who did not open wide, kitten eyes at him and breathe, "You serve the *mages?* Is it true that . . ." and produce some fantastic piece of sexual practice rumor ascribed to wizards. It was short-lived, though he was fond of her; they quarreled during one of those strange, aching episodes of depression, when his magic deserted him, quarreled stupidly, as if they could not help it. Coming down from her rooms, he heard her crying behind her shut door; but in the strange colorlessness of the world, he saw no reason to go back to comfort her. Afterward, ashamed of the senselessly cruel way he had acted toward her, he felt it was too late.

His grandfather he rarely saw. He knew the Archmage was frequently at the episcopal palace, far grander than the one attached to the St. Cyr fortress in Angelshand, for the Bishop of Kymil was the chief prelate of the Empire. At other times he knew the old man was simply abroad in

the countryside, tracing the stories of strange happenings and abominations which seemed to haunt the surrounding villages like restless ghosts.
One night by the fire in the small sasenna barracks of the House, Le
spoke of things seen, heard, or rumored seen and heard—flopping white
shapes glimpsed between the birches of the woods by a home-going
farmer or the herd of sheep found slaughtered with marks upon them no
dog could have made or the three people who went mad in the bright
sunlight of an open field near Poncross.

"Could that be connected with Suraklin's Citadel?" Caris asked her
the next morning, while they wandered off-duty under the vast brick
arches of the town's grimy central market.

Around them a hundred stalls sent up a conflicting cacophony of smell
and noise, the heavy scents of violets and roses vying with the half-
spoiled meat and cheese of the vianders and the overwhelming stink of
fish. Chocolate candy from Angelshand, fine cottons from the mills of
Felleringham and Kymil itself, daggers, shoebuckles, cheap tin or porcelain pots of cosmetics, something advertised as Electrical Hair Cream,
clocks the size of a child's hand, silk and delicately fragranced tea
brought on caravans and ships at huge cost from distant Saarieque—
anything could be had in that huge and gloomy emporium. They had
bought rolls hot from the baker with primrose-yellow summer butter
dripping from them and ate them as they roved among the stalls.

Le shrugged and took another bite of her roll. "Not that I ever heard,"
she said. With her short-cropped black hair and broken nose, she looked
like a skinny teenage boy in her black jacket, trousers, and deadly, curving sword. "The fortress was razed by the wizards and the Emperor's
Heir. All that's left are a few crumbled walls and a hole in the earth, far
out in the hills."

"Will you ride out there with me?"

The lieutenant hesitated, as everyone, Caris had noticed, hesitated
when it came to mention of the Dark Mage or anything he had touched.
Then she nodded. "As long as we're back by four." They had duty that
night, and Le, Caris knew, had a girlfriend of her own.

Once it passed the feet of the Silent Tower, the road to Suraklin's
Citadel was lined once more with the standing-stones so hateful to the
memories of those who dwelled in Kymil; it lacked even the pale traces of
occasional commerce. Once or twice Caris, simply to test his own skills,
tried to find signs that his grandfather had passed that way—as he knew
that at some time in the last few days he had—but saw nothing. It took a
powerful sasennan indeed to track a wizard. The road itself, overgrown
to little more than a notch running through the round-backed green hills

that crowded so close on all sides, ran perfectly straight, scaling the flanks of hills it could easily have gone around, or, on one occasion, climbing to the crest of a green tor from which Caris could see all the rolling, silent land beneath and the faint arrow of the road pointing inexorably away to vanish into the green wastes of the Sykerst, the empty lands to the east.

Wind thrummed in his ears and stirred his soft, fair hair and the mane of his horse; cloud shadows moved like torpid and amorphous ghosts across the land. The silence oppressed him. "It can't be this far, surely." For aside from the perfectly straight track of the old road, there was no sign that habitation had ever touched these bleak lands.

"It's a few hills over." Le, usually as calmly matter-of-fact as a pistol ball, did not raise her voice against that windswept hush. "You can't see it until you're nearly on top of it."

Caris shivered. He was conscious of how small he and the woman were in these hills, two black-clad forms in that empty silence. He looked around him for he knew not what. Old spells still clung to the land, the Dark Mage's might lingering in the stones. Squinting into the wind, he could see where another line of standing-stones crossed the far hills. Antryg had said to the Archmage that the Citadel was a node in the lines. The rudimentary stumps of Caris' own slight magic could sense the movement of power along this ancient road, and he realized that the Citadel had been built by some people far earlier than Suraklin along one of the energy-tracks that crisscrossed the earth.

The mages called them paths or lines or leys. Few understood what they were, and none knew why they existed. But exist they did—straight lines of energy along which magic could move, linked in some vast, unknowable grid. All magic—and all life, in some ways, the Archmage had told him once, back in the days when he had hoped to be a mage himself—was connected through them. The House of the Mages in Kymil lay in the line of this one—undoubtedly the Mages' Yard in Angelshand did the same with the line of stones called the Devil's Road. He felt, like a brush of wind, the touch of that moving power in his soul as he clucked to his horse and rode on.

The Citadel of Suraklin lay in the midst of a cup-shaped valley among the hills. Judging by the extent of the ruined walls, Caris could see that in its day it had been a great place indeed, yet he completely believed what Salteris had said—that without the help of the wizards, the troops of the Emperor's Heir, twenty-five years ago, would have wandered helplessly around the hills, unable to locate it, until the dark and nameless magic of that evil wizard had overtaken them. Though Suraklin had been dead these twenty-five years, some terrible spell of concealment clung about the place, and Caris literally was unaware that he was near it until Le called out, "Caris, watch out!" He woke from some momentary private daydream to find himself a yard from the vine-covered brink of an enormous pit, in the midst of a sprawling network of fallen stones that covered half a square mile of ground.

"It takes me that way sometimes, too." She rode up beside him as he cautiously kneed his horse to the very edge of the chasm. "Be careful—the ground isn't too good here." She glanced around her, her hand straying instinctively to the hilt of her sword.

The horses, knee-deep in the tangle of vines that cloaked much of the ruins of the Citadel like a rotting shroud, were clearly nervous as well. Caris felt a good deal of sympathy for the beasts' sentiments as he listened for some sound in the windless hush or scanned the skeleton outlines of stone walls still visible—hall, tower, workrooms outlined like the broken bones of a half-eaten carcass. Weeds forced apart broken paving-stones in what had been a vast court and lay in traceried circles of stringers. But mostly the ground had been torn open by the cumulative wrath of the wizards of the earth, and the pits which had underlain the Citadel gaped bare.

"They must have feared him," he said softly, "to leave no place where one course of stones stands upon another."

Le's curving mouth tightened. "You didn't live in these parts when his power covered the land," she said. "They said his ears were everywhere, and there was no telling who might be his agent; I know for a fact my uncle Welliger was involved in one of the attempts to contact the Archmage, with men he trusted—his own kinsfolk and his wife's, all men who'd had their goods taken or some member of whose family disappeared. But Welliger went blind before he could set out for Angelshand."

An odd gust belled in Caris' black jacket, flattened the thin shirt beneath against his ribs, then dropped to stillness again. Cloud shadows walked over the sun. Looking down into the pits, he could see down a number of levels, with shattered doorways with ivy and weeds. A tumble of white stones lay at the bottom like knocked-out teeth. It had been his grandfather's wrath that had called down the lightning to blast this pit—his might which had turned the tide against the cold evil that had so long festered here. It was hard to imagine it of the slender, quiet man who was his grandfather.

Like the final echo of the Dark Mage's decaying spells, wind sighed again in the nodding weeds. And without knowing quite how, Caris knew that someone was coming.

He glanced sideways at Le. She started to speak of something else, oblivious, and he signaled her silent. Though she was the elder and higher ranked, she obeyed his sign. They dismounted and led their horses down a crumbled ramp to what had been a shallow cellar, the only cover in that blasted ruin. After a few moments, Caris heard what had only whispered in his mind—the soft *swish-swish* of hooves in the tangling vines and voices which, in spite of their involuntary hush, sounded loud in the still air that hung over the Citadel.

A man's said, "Our men have followed him here thrice this week, my lord."

"So." That, too, was a man's, though higher and cold as the touch of metal on bare flesh. Caris was aware of Le's quick glance. Silent as a cat, he slipped forward, up the half-ruined ramp to the edge of the cellar pit. Lying flat in the wiry brambles, he could look along the ground to where the newcomers sat their horses at the edge of the ruins. "One may ask for what purposes. Abominations multiply in the lands . . ."

Somewhat diffidently, the first speaker, a middle-aged man in the plain gray breeches and narrow-cut gray coat that Caris recognized with sinking heart as the uniform of the Witchfinders, said, "The abominations have been seen for weeks, my lord; since long before the Archmage came to Kymil."

"He is a mage," the second man said. He turned his head. Against the summer sky, Caris recognized the ascetic profile and scant gray wisps of hair under the widebrimmed shadow of the hat. It was Sergius Peelbone, Witchfinder Extraordinary to the Church. He felt something chill along his veins.

Peelbone went on, almost disinterestedly, "They say that the mages could move along the energy-lines at their will, traveling hundreds of miles in a day, to do a deed in Kymil when they had been seen that morning in Angelshand. And certainly it will be difficult for him to prove that he has not done so, particularly if it can be shown that he has been to this place." He scanned the desolation which lay about him. A scud of wind flicked the standing weed stalks by the broken stones, and his horse flung up its head with a nervous start. The Witchfinder's powerful hand twisted, dragging cruelly on the heavy bridle bit to force the beast to stillness. Even at that distance, Caris could see the smudge of blood that dripped to the grass.

"My lord," ventured the other Witchfinder, "it was the Archmage himself who brought about the ruin of this place and brought the Dark Mage down in defeat. It could be argued . . ."

"Anything can be argued," Peelbone said. "The old legends speak of the power of this place, before the Dark Mage raised his walls here; the old spells that linger are themselves enough to tempt in his dotage the mage who battled them in his youth. That, and the growing number of abominations in the land, should be enough to convince the Regent to give us the power we need, Tarolus—the power to put them all under arrest and to extirpate the heresy of witchcraft from the Empire."

The two horses moved off through the ruins. Caris slid cautiously down to where Le waited, her hand over her mare's muzzle, her dark eyes hard. Caris found himself chilled all over with rage, both at the slandering of Salteris and at the calm deliberation with which Peelbone had spoken. As sasennan of the Council, he was powerless to do anything, for a weapon does not strike in anger, but he said softly, "Let's go. The Archmage should know about this."

They moved silently through the trenches of the broken cellars, leading their horses as far as the nearest ridge before mounting. Even so, as Caris glanced back at the silent ruins of the Dark Mage's Citadel, he could have sworn that the taller of the two mounted figures below turned to watch them as they disappeared over the hill.

"My lord! My lady! Please stop!"

Caris drew rein at the cries, looking down at the three or four men and women who came scrambling up the weedy, overgrown side of the marsh causeway from below. His horse, even before these people appeared, threw up its head with a snort, and Caris saw the white rim of fear around its eyeball. He cast a quick, semi-automatic glance down the other side of the raised roadbed, making sure it was not an ambush of some kind. There was no reason for it, but it was not the Way of the Sasenna to take chances. Then he and Le reined a step nearer to the panting farmers who came stumbling to their side.

"You are sasenna," the man gasped—little more than a boy of sixteen, stripped to his breeches for the haying, without stockings or shoes, his bare calves plastered in bog mud. "You must help us! Please! There's a thing—a thing in the marsh . . ."

"We can't stop," Le said coldly. "We are sasenna—we cannot strike without the command of our masters. . . ."

Caris held up his hand and leaned from the saddle. "What is it?"

"An evil—an abomination . . ." One of the women, stout and forty-ish, with her voluminous skirts tucked up to reveal legs as muddy as the boy's, grabbed at the bridle of Caris' horse. The gesture made him nervous, even though he knew there was no ambush planned. "Oh, dear God, it's got Shebna!"

"Caris . . ." Le said warningly as Caris dropped from the saddle and pulled his sword sheath from his sash. "It is not for us . . ."

"My grandfather would command me to help them," Caris said. "I know it. He's the head of the Council. . . ."

Le's voice was sharp, "That decision is not yours to make!" Technically, he knew she was right; the anger in her voice stemmed from her own indecision. "Your sword is not your own to draw."

One of the women sobbed, "Oh, please!"

An older man shouted, "Look, you heartless bitch . . ."

Caris caught that man by his bony shoulder. "No," he said. "She's right, but I'm coming anyway. Le—get the Archmage or Nandiharrow— or anyone." Hands were tugging at his sleeves, the faces all around him tallowy with terror and panic under the smearing of mud. He felt his own heart begin to pound with the rising lift toward battle. "Go on," he added as Le hesitated, her instincts to help warring with a lifetime of discipline in her sharp-boned face. He was turning back to the farmers before she had even lashed her horse to gallop away. "Where is it?"

It interested him to see how well his own training held. In spite of the cold excitement that surged through him, he found himself able to think clearly as they led him to the edge of the road and down the steep bank to the watery tangle of willows in the marshes below. For five years he had trained to become sasennan, yet now he was aware, with knife-blade clarity of thought, that, for all his training, he had never yet truly fought for his own life. The Empire was at peace; unlike many sasenna, he didn't seek brawls in taverns. Beside him, one of the women was sobbing, "It's the curse of the Dark Mage! He's left his curse upon the land! His devils are buried in the pools. . . ."

The smell of the marsh and the thick humming of the gnats that swarmed where the sunlight struck the scattered pools brought back to Caris his own childhood days of slogging after his parents at haying. His sword-sheath carried loose in his left hand, he cursed the head-high grasses that forced him to continually occupy his right hand in pushing a path—if there was an abomination here, the instants occupied in grabbing for his sword hilt might cost him or one of the people with him their lives.

"It's a devil," gasped the older man who had cursed at Le, his breath rasping with the effort of keeping up. "It's the Bishop we must be sending for, and the Witchfinders. . . ."

"Tell her to bring a sword, then," Caris snapped, still annoyed with him. "I may need . . ." His words ended in a gasp, as he stepped into the open shade of the willows.

The rank, standing sweet-hay had been cut for a little way along one side of a broad pool whose clouded brown waters showed how vast a thing had heaved itself up from their depths. The stubble, the felled hay —even the leaves of the willows above—were all dappled with the crimson brightness of splattered blood; it lay in little swirls in the water around the crushed skulls of the two men who sprawled on its verge. The thing on the far bank of the pool was holding a third person—a girl of thirteen or so—between its pad-fingered paws, her cracked skull still between its dripping mandibles. Blood overlay the reddish, tripy folds of its massive body like a glittering slime. At the sound of Caris' sword sliding from the sheath, it raised its crayfish head, rubbery, semitransparent pendules swinging his way for an instant; then, before Caris' shocked mind had a chance to do more than stare, it struck.

For all its size, it moved hideously fast. The water of the pool erupted in a surge of mud on both sides as it plowed through; Caris, used to the onrush of a man, had only time to gauge the paws and the stumpy, squamous, green-blotched tail before it was on him. Though his mind screamed to know what it was and from what obscene depth of insane horror it had risen, as sasennan his business and his training were simply to deal with it as an objective threat, a challenge like any other. That training saved him, letting him time the thing's incredible rush and spring aside, cutting down at the slender neck that connected that sagging, squidlike head to the rugose mass of body. The thing was turning even as he sprang, and the sword sliced through the dangling, stumpy tentacles that surrounded the mouth—or what might have been the mouth. Clear slime burst over him from the wounds, and the putrid fetor of the thing nearly made him gag as he twisted aside again and cut at the paddy, grasping, knotted paws.

His feet skidded in the mud. He was peripherally aware that, save for himself and the creature, whatever it was, the glade was deserted—the peasants had very sensibly fled. *They're unarmed,* he thought, desperately evading another lurching lunge, *and God knows, even armed and trained, how can I touch this thing?* Its long arms outreached him, and it moved with a horrible speed. His sword came down on the thin wrist and jarred on the bone—the blade that could cut off a man's leg with a single swipe. He felt the vibration of it through the bones of his arms to his shoulders, as if he had struck an iron bar; it crossed his mind to wonder if it had bones as he leaped aside. He splashed knee-deep in the muddy water and wondered, with sudden horror as the tepid liquid slopped over the tops of his boots, if there were more like this, buried in the immemorial black mud of the pool.

Something turned and rolled underfoot, and he staggered, hacking at the thing and trying to splash back to firmer ground. It was before him, churning in the shallows like an enormous cow, throwing filthy water up over his face, and he realized he was being driven. The water slowed his movements; his wet garments tangled stickily to his limbs. He cut at the grabbing paws again and opened one of them to the bone, but the sword jarred, unable to sever, and stinking, ochre slime leaked down the striated arm to pool like oil on top of the water. He sprang back and stumbled; something underfoot held for an instant, then shattered. His foot dropped into some cavity below and broken branches gouged his ankle through the boot leather. The next second, mud covered, slime-dripping paws closed bone-breakingly around his shoulders.

Waist-deep in water, pinned and nearly suffocated by the thing's stench, his hand fumbled for a dagger, even as he knew his own short life was over. He felt the massive strength of the thing tearing him free of the pool's bottom, lifting him toward the dripping beak, the slime running hotly down over his face as he tried to strike upward. . . . Then with a lurch the thing staggered, and the hideous vise of its grip slackened. Caris twisted and fell; mud half blinded him, but he saw the haft of one of the haymakers' pitchforks standing upright in the thing's back, flung at the last second by someone on the bank. As the creature tried to paw it loose, Caris rolled clear, scrambling desperately through the heaving waters that were now tobacco-colored with a mixture of blood and mud. There were people on the shore, many people. . . . He had a clouded impression of Le, of the Bishop Herthe standing in open-mouthed shock, and of the Archmage.

Salteris' voice cut like cold acid through his thickening senses. "Get out of the water!" The creature whirled and came slavering after him once more. Brown ooze streamed from it; the pitchfork bobbed and jerked in its back. Caris, still somehow clutching his sword, half crawled, half threw himself up on the bank among the damp, rank pads of the bloody hay. There was no time to get to his feet to run—he rolled over and over, inland, until he fetched up with a bruising wallop against the roots of a tree.

Thus he saw Salteris stride forward, his empty hand upraised. In the frame of silver hair, the thin features were very white, the dark eyes wide and somehow inhuman, calling down power as he had called it down against Suraklin. There was a leap and a crackle from the clear sky overhead, the harsh sizzle and stink of ozone, and thunder like a hand slamming Caris' ears. Blue in the daylight, lightning struck the brown waters of the pool. The creature was still knee-deep in them. For an instant, it seemed that the bolts crawled up over the whole of that hunched, hideous form. Then the thing convulsed, bending backwards, all the remaining, pendulous tentacles round its head stiffening out for an instant in a hideous corona around the flabby, desperately working mouth. The stench clutched Caris' throat and belly, even as the thing sprang and twisted, the pool waters heaving up around it in a brown and filthy wall.

Then it was rolling slightly, like a foundered boat, the muddy blobs of its feet sticking up above the slopping water and the tentacles of its head slowly relaxing in death. The pool was filled with crawling currents of nameless fluids and stank like a cesspit.

Caris buried his face in his arms, fighting the desperate sear of nausea in his throat. The frog-smelling hay scratched his face, and his wet clothes and dripping hair were suddenly cold on his clammy flesh as the battle-rush ebbed from him like blood from a severed artery. He was aware of the aching bruises on his shoulders, the sting of air through his torn shirt and jacket, and the excruciating ache of his right ankle. It was only gradually that it sank in upon him that he was still alive.

Footsteps approached. His every sinew protested as he did it, but as a sasennan must, he rolled over to meet what might be another attack with a drawn sword.

It was Le, as he had known it would be, and with her the boy who had guided him to the place and who, he suspected, had thrown the pitchfork which had distracted the monster's attention and saved his life. They helped him to his feet, Caris almost unable to stand with the violence of the reaction. He freed himself from their grip and picked up his sword, which was covered, like his clothes, with an unspeakable coating of mud and slime. Dripping like a halfdrowned sewer rat, he somehow walked by himself to the edge of the pool.

The Bishop Herthe stood there in the midst of her sasenna, still openmouthed with horror. Against the gray of her velvet robes, her potatolike face looked pallid and boiled with shock.

On the churned and muddy brink, the Archmage Salteris gazed at the obscene thing still bobbing and wallowing in the pool. His white brows were drawn over his nose, his dark eyes not only baffled, but deeply troubled. Their expression changed to one of concern as Caris came near him. "Are you all right, my son?"

Caris nodded. He looked for some moments at the thing in the pool, thinking unbelievingly, *I fought that,* and wondering how he had dared. It was over twice the size of a horse. His whole body was one vast pain— his soul, too, with the shaken reaction to that single second when he had looked down the thing's pulsating throat and had known he would die. Shakily, he started to draw another deep breath. But this close, the stench was enough to make him change his mind.

"What *was* it?"

The old man shook his head. "I don't know, my son," he said softly. And then, even more quietly, he added, "But I have a suspicion who might."

CHAPTER VI

THEY FOUND ANTRYG IN THE GUARDROOM ON THE LOWEST LEVEL OF the Tower, sparring with the captain of the Tower guards with split bamboo training swords.

The journey to the Tower from the marsh had restored the Bishop to her usual equilibrium—she had begun quarreling with Salteris before they were halfway there. As he leaned against the stone arch that led into the guardroom from the passage, Caris could hear them at it still. Before him, in the jumpy light of a dozen torches, shadows looming huge on the fire-dyed wall, he could see the forms of Antryg and the captain circling like cats. The captain's loose black jacket and the shirt beneath and Antryg's trailing robes and beard were blotched with dark patches of sweat; their wet faces caught the yellow glare of the light as if they'd just doused themselves in a rain barrel.

The mad wizard, Caris was interested to note, didn't wear his spectacles for the bout, but he moved unerringly and with a dancer's grace. Caris had worked with the captain of the Tower once in the previous week; he was a huge Church sasennan, taller even than Antryg, fat and flexible and capable of crushing an opponent beneath the weight of his rush. Perhaps because of Antryg's madness, Caris had not expected the skill with which the wizard sidestepped and returned.

Looking at that odd face in its streaming tangle of hair, the gray eyes wide and intent with calm madness, Caris had the suspicion that, on the training floor, the mad wizard would be his master.

Behind him, he was aware of the Bishop's harsh whisper, "I cannot permit it," and the impatience in Salteris' voice.

"You needn't fear I will abet his escape."

"Needn't I?" Without turning his head, Caris could almost see the slitting of those shallow blue eyes. "He was your pupil, Salteris Solaris. It was only through your intercession that he was not killed, as he should have been, for meddling in the affairs of men at the time of the uprising in Mellidane. The Council of Wizards exist solely on the sufferance of the Church, a sufferance which depends upon our trust in you to regulate the teaching and practice of your arts and to keep those arts from ever touching the general life of humankind—*ever*. Look that you do not find the Church's might turned against you, as it turned five hundred years ago at the Field of Stellith."

"You *dare* . . ."

There was a note in his grandfather's voice Caris had never heard before. He swung around with such sharpness that every pulled muscle of his back twisted with a red stab of pain. The old man's eyes blazed with wrath and infuriated pride, looking amber as a wolf's in the firelight. His anger was like the molten core of a star sinking inward upon itself, swallowing both light and time. The Bishop fell back a pace before that sudden fury, her heavy face yellow with fear. In almost a whisper, the Archmage said, "You *dare* to threaten *me?*"

Her own anger kindling, the Bishop snapped, "I dare to threaten any who would break the vows that hold all things in order!"

Salteris opened his mouth in rage to reply, but Antryg's voice cut in reasonably, "In that case, we'll let you handle things the next time an abomination appears in the hay marsh." He had materialized without a sound at Caris' elbow, still holding his bamboo training sword. Sweat dripped from the end of his long nose and shone on his bare forearms as he drew the remains of a red Church wizard's cloak over his shabby robes.

The Bishop turned furiously on him. "What do you know of it?" she demanded, catching a tattered handful of his robe. Her face was scarlet with anger, as happened when one had been publicly driven to fear. Antryg shook back his sleek-matted hair and put on his spectacles, blinking at her from behind them in mild surprise.

"There must have been an abomination, mustn't there, for you to come in force like this to see me, and so urgently that Caris wasn't even able to change his clothes," he said. Caris, a little surprised, looked down at his dark clothes, still caked with the residue of mud and slime, though he had washed it from his face and hair and hands. "Whatever Caris did battle with, it was certainly in a marsh, and that marsh must be one of the hay marshes around the town. I'm surprised at you, Herthe—you're usually so good at the obvious."

He started to turn away. With angry violence, the Bishop seized his scarecrow robes and pulled him back to face her. The torchlight gleamed on her shaven skull and in her small, porcine eyes. "Beware, Antryg," she warned.

"Beware of what?" he asked reasonably. "I'm safe behind the walls of this Tower. It's you who have to deal with the things. Would you hold this?" He offered her the long hilt of the bamboo sword still in his hand. Surprised, she took it, releasing her hold on his robes to do so. He said, "Thank you," and vanished into the darkness of the narrow stair.

Her face flushed, the Bishop moved to follow, but Salteris laid a staying hand on her beefy shoulder. "No," he said softly. "It would do little good, with you there."

"We can compel him . . ."

The Archmage's voice was suddenly harsh. "No member of the Church—*none*—has the right to lay hands upon one who has sworn the vows to the Council of Wizards."

"The case is different!" the Bishop declared furiously. "The abominations . . ."

"The case is not different!"

For a long moment they stood, staring into one another's eyes. Caris felt the heat of the old man's pride and wrath again, as if he stood near the door of a stove, but hidden now, heat without light. The Bishop's heavy mouth set. Then, as if he realized where they were, without magic in the Church's power, the old man turned suddenly away. "Come, Caris. There is little to be learned here. But I tell you this, Herthe of Kymil. Should you or Peelbone and his Witchfinders or anyone else move against Antryg Windrose or any Council mage without my leave, I shall learn of it, and then . . ." His voice sank, and the dark brown of his eyes seemed to glint again with an amber flame, ". . . you will have to deal with me."

It was only when they were walking down the hill in the lingering blueness of the summer dusk that Caris dared to speak. The Archmage was walking very swiftly, his black robes billowing about him. Caris' hurt ankle jabbed him at every step; but, after five years of training, neither that nor the bone-weariness of stiffening muscles troubled him as much as that terrible silence that still hung about Salteris like the darkness of stormclouds.

As they reached the foot of the tower hill, Caris asked, "Why?"

The old man glanced testily at him. Then, seeming to see him for the first time, he slowed his steps. "Are you all right, my son? I'd forgotten—you were hurt. . . ."

Caris shook his head impatiently. "Why did you defend him? He knows more than he's telling. If they can compel him to speak . . ."

Salteris sighed. "No. For one thing, he's tougher than he looks, our madman, and far more clever. We could never be sure we were getting the truth, if in fact he is even aware of it himself. For another . . ." He paused, staring back at the darkness of the Tower against the milky twilight sky. "They are only waiting for that. The Bishop and Peelbone—it is their chance, to establish their jurisdiction over us, to gain a precedent. That is why, above all other things, I must be careful with Antryg."

As in another life, Caris remembered the sharp noon sunlight on the desolation of the Citadel and the Witchfinder Peelbone's thin cold voice in the silence. "*Could* Antryg be responsible for the abominations?" he asked.

Salteris walked on in silence for a few moments more, his white brows drawn together, and the look on his face was one of utter bafflement such as Caris had not seen him wear in years. "I don't know," he said at last. His soft boots scuffed the long grass that overgrew the edges of the broken pavement of the ancient road. "I don't see how he could, and I . . ." He hesitated, then shook his head. "But I am unfamiliar with these things. Though I have crossed the Void, I—I have not the sense of it that Antryg has—or had." His thin mouth hardened for a moment with something like annoyance. "It might be that they come through the Void—and then again, he could be creating them in some fashion. But in either case, he can neither work magic nor touch the Void from within the Tower. Else he would have escaped long ago."

"Would he?" Caris asked suddenly. He halted, hooking his hands through his sword belt, and looked at the old man doubtfully. "A room with an open door is not a cell."

There was a long silence. In the old man's face was the nearest thing Caris had ever seen to surprised enlightenment. Then he nodded slowly to himself. "Trust a sasennan," he said softly after a moment. "The best place to hide is in plain sight—I had almost forgotten that Antryg was always a genius at that. If he has found some way of working magic from within the Tower, its walls would prevent any other mage from knowing it." As if another thought crossed his mind, he frowned again and shook his head. "No—it is impossible."

"Is it?" Caris persisted. The discipline of the Way of the Sasenna made him unwilling to contradict the Archmage, but something about the dusk and his own stretched weariness lessened between them the barrier raised by years and his vows. As a child, he had trailed gamely after the old man while his grandfather searched for yarrow in the marshes, and had asked whatever he thought. In a curious way, he felt the echo of that old intimacy. "You said yourself there are things about the Void you don't understand. Perhaps he does. Could he be creating these things, instead of summoning them through?"

As they walked on, the old man said thoughtfully, "They say Suraklin could summon the elemental spirits and bend them to his bidding—could clothe them in flesh of his own devising, so that they could tear and hurt with their uncontrolled anger, instead of just knocking on walls or throwing pots as they usually do. But if that were the case," he continued, as Caris offered him his hand to help him down a stream cut which gouged the road, "I would not have been able to slay the thing as I did."

"How *did* you slay it?" His grandfather's scarred arm felt strangely light and fragile in his grip as he helped the old man up the broken stones and cracked hunks of old pavement. Now at the end of summer, the stream which had cut the road had long since dried—the mud at the bottom bore the marks of the constant trickle of feet, coming and going to the Tower.

The memory of the old man's dark, inhuman eyes as he summoned the lightning seemed as impossible to him as the white heat of his pride and anger against the Bishop had been—as, indeed, was the knowledge that it had been he who had led the assault on the Citadel.

The old man smiled. "With electricity."

"Electricity?" Caris' dark brows dove down over his nose.

His grandfather's smile widened. "This looks like a good place," he remarked, and led the way off the road, between two of the fallen menhirs, his robe slurring softly in the open grass beyond. Limping a little, Caris followed, as he used to follow in his childhood, not asking where they went or why. They passed along a little gully between the round backs of the hills. The dusk closed around them like veils of smoke-colored silk.

"Dr. Narwahl Skipfrag has been experimenting for some years with electricity," Salteris continued, as he picked his way along some unseen track in the deep grass. "It was his experiments, in fact, which first led him to speak with me—though of course we had met at the Imperial Palace in Angelshand. During the conflict with Suraklin, the Prince Hieraldus and I became friends. When he succeeded his father and became Emperor he patronized us as much as the Church and his reputation would allow, and I came to know a good many of the Court. Narwahl was the Emperor's physician, then as now, but he's also a scientist. At first, he thought magic might be some type of electricity, and it was thus that he and I came to speak."

They crossed the stream bed again—or perhaps a different one; this one had water in it, nearly choked in a brambly tangle of wild roses, around which the last bees of the evening swarmed drunkenly. As he helped the Archmage up the far bank, Caris reflected that he must have picked up his minute knowledge of the countryside around Kymil during the days of the war against Suraklin—he certainly seemed to know every dip and gully of these silent hills. Following along in the old man's tireless footsteps, Caris felt ashamed, not only of his stiff and aching muscles, but of the queer dread he felt in this haunted land. With the starry darkness, the memory of the abomination returned disturbingly to his mind. It had come from nowhere, and he was too aware that there was nothing to prevent the coming of another.

For five years, Caris had trained as a sasennan, a strenuous life, but uncomplicated. Now, moving through the dreamlike landscape of the summer dusk, he felt as if he trod the borders of a land he did not know, fighting unknown things with weapons which would have as little effect upon them as his sword had had upon the swamp thing's iron bones. Ashamed of his uneasiness he might be, but nevertheless he felt glad the Archmage was with him in the blue and trackless emptiness through which they passed.

Salteris moved his fingers, seeming to pluck a raveled thread of light from the air, and cast it before him to float like a glow worm along the ground a little ahead of their feet. "According to Narwahl, electricity can be conducted by water, in the same way that it is conducted by metal; and, moreover, metal or water will prevent the possibility of electricity grounding harmlessly away into the earth. Lightning, he says, is only electricity in its natural form." The same wry, astringent smile touched his lips. "I shall have to write to him and tell him of the successful demonstration. He will be pleased."

"And the abomination?" Caris asked.

The old man sighed, the smile fading from his face like the last fading of the daylight.

"Yes," he said softly. "The abomination."

For a time they walked in silence, Caris thinking again of that tall, gawky lunatic in his tattered robes and ink-stained beard and of the bright gray gaze behind those heavy lenses. Would a man who had been a prisoner for seven years retain that odd, buoyant calm? The scant experience of his own nineteen years gave him little help. Smelling now the late-summer headiness of the night, feeling the touch of straying breezes on his face, he doubted it. Like the breath of a ghost, the memory of the fading of his powers brushed him, the dust-colored uncaring and the terror he felt, knowing that those spells of fading would recur, as they were recurring more and more often. In the end, his powers would never return. Could one whom his grandfather had called the most powerful mage in the world have endured that loss?

Could that, in its turn, have driven him mad?

Or had he never suffered it?

Caris turned to look back over the hills, where the dark shape of the windowless Tower bulked against the sky.

"Here we are." Salteris gestured, and a clinging frost of light momentarily edged the deep blueness of a little hollow among the hills. A standing-stone had once been planted there, but had fallen long ago and now lay cocooned in wild ivy and bramble. In the lee side of one crowding hill a thicket of laurel and hawthorn rustled with the quick nervousness of birds' wings; on the opposite hillslope, gentler and stretching off into a vague space of dusk that rose toward the deeper twilight of the sky, rabbits paused in their grazing to look down at the brief network of diamonds that the Archmage had cast. Then the swift glow faded, and with it the ravelly blue phosphorescence that had guided their feet. Caris made his way carefully to the fallen stone and sat on the bare place at its end.

"We will wait here," Salteris' voice said out of the shadows, "until full darkness covers the land."

His shape melted from the gloom; his face and the silky white mane of his hair were one large blur, his hands, two small ones at his dark sides. "And then, my son, we will return to the Silent Tower, and I will speak to Antryg Windrose myself."

He settled quietly at Caris' side. From somewhere about his person, he drew his worn black gloves, stitched with shabby bullion on their backs, a present from the Emperor, before imbecility had claimed the man. He began to put them on, then changed his mind and tucked them instead into his belt.

"Are you cold?" Caris asked, and the old man shook his head.

"Only tired." He undid the small satchel at his belt and took from it bread, cheese, and two small green apples, which he divided with his grandson. Though it was not the Way of the Sasenna to eat on duty—and Caris considered himself on duty—he accepted the food gratefully.

Ruefully, the Archmage went on, "And you must be in far worse case than I, my son. I apologize, but I must speak to Antryg alone, without the Bishop present, and it must be soon. If he knows something about the abominations, I must learn it, before the Witchfinders take it for their excuse to destroy us all. You heard them today. . . ."

Caris paused in wolfing down his supper to stare at him in surprise. "I did," he said, "but I had no idea *you* were there."

"I wasn't." The old man smiled. "But a mage can listen along the energy-trails—and I have been particularly watchful of Peelbone lately." He sighed and stroked the velvet-soft leather of the gloves at his belt. "It is an old trouble." He sighed. "And the reason, indeed, for the Council vows—the underpinning of the Church's whole attitude toward magic and toward the dog wizards. No society, they say, can exist with both magic and industry—technology—the use of tools and machines. It takes so little magic to ruin the balance of a machine, my son; and magic can be worked by so few. For thousands of years, power lay in the hands of those who were powerful mages themselves, or who could afford to hire them. It was in those years that the Silent Tower was built, and for that reason. It was then that all the binding-spells were wrought, great and small—from the Sigil of Darkness and other things like it which are utterly abominable to the mageborn, down to the little ones which make this or that thing na-aar—metaphysically dead and impervious to magic —like the pistols and crossbows of the Witchfinders, so that no mage can fox their aim or cause them to misfire, and such things as spell-cord and spancels. But it was all politics. The people were no better for it."

He sighed again. "The Sole God of the Church is not the god of the mageborn, Caris. As sasennan of the Council, you do not make the signs of obeisance in the presence of holy things. In time, the Church raised its own corps of wizards—the *hasu*—and used their magic to defeat the wizards in a long war which ended on the Field of Stellith, five hundred years ago. And they were aided by other mages, not of the Church, but who could see that, in that, the Church was right; the privileges of the few had to be curtailed for the rights of the many. That is the reason for the Council Vows.

"And since that time . . ." He shrugged. "I fear they were right. Humankind now has great new looms and gins to weave its cloth, in the factory towns of Kymil and Parchasten and Angelshand. They talk about making engines that will go from the power of steam to work them one day. There are new sorts of farm machines to sow the seed better than a man scattering it broad-cast from a sack, and engines to harvest and thrash the grain—who knows, one day they may find a way to power them by steam as well. They have ships built light and strong enough to race the wind that can make the voyage to Saarieque and the East in sixty days, to make men's fortunes in silk and tea and the emeralds of the Isles."

"But that isn't all!" Caris broke in, distressed at the sadness in the old man's voice. "There is more in the world than—than money in the pockets of the merchants and machines to make things to sell! Isn't there?"

And for a time, only the sweet hush of the long evening answered him —the sleepy twilight cry of whippoorwills from the boggy ground near the stream, the strange, half-hurtful stirring of the earth-magic whispering up out of the ground beneath the grass. He felt, even with his own small and, he suspected, fading resources, the magic all around him, alive and vibrant, and wondered how, even for the good of everyone in the world, it could be for a moment denied. The knowledge that one day soon he would lose it was like the knowledge that he would one day die.

"There is," the old man said finally. "The will—the fire—the striving. They deny it and claim that it does not exist, until all those who listen come to believe it and do not know how to name it once they feel it quicken in themselves, except by such names as 'foolishness,' and 'insanity,' and 'badness.'"

"And Suraklin?"

Caris spoke the name softly, within these hills that had been Suraklin's; within sight of the Tower where the Dark Mage had once been chained to await his death. Salteris, an almost invisible shape in the dusk, sighed again, and the last light caught one thread of silver in his hair. It was a long time before he replied.

"Suraklin was the last of the great ones," he said, "the last of the wizard-kings, born long after his time with the will and the strength to dominate. So much of his power came from the fact that most of those who obeyed him, through fear and, yes, through love, refused to believe that this magic truly existed. And his magic was the greatest—truly the greatest. I knew it. He would have been Archmage, were it not that the others in the Council distrusted the depthless darkness of his soul."

He turned and faced Caris in the intense, phthalo darkness of the summer night, his eyes nothing but shadows under the star-edged dome of his bald forehead. "That is why I fear now," he said softly. "Antryg Windrose was Suraklin's student."

For a time Caris could only stare at him, aghast and silent. For a week he had lived close to the legends that surrounded the Dark Mage; the memory of Suraklin clung to the land like a decaying ghost. It was hard enough to believe there were people alive who had known him, though Caris knew his grandfather must have. That the mad, oddly charming prisoner in the Silent Tower had been his pupil. . . . He stammered, "But—the Bishop said he was yours."

"I found him two years after the breaking of Suraklin's Citadel," Salteris said. "He was hiding in a monastery in the Sykerst. Nineteen years old; no older than you are now, my son, and already a little mad. I taught him, yes, though he had very little to learn. We traveled together for many years, both then and after he was elected to the Council, but always I had the sense in him of hidden pockets of darkness, buried so deep maybe he was unaware of them himself. There was a time when I loved him as a son. But I never underestimated him."

"Then don't do so now," Caris said, looking over at the old man's dim shape in the gloom with a sudden qualm of fear. "Don't meet him alone."

Salteris shook his head. "In the Tower he is not dangerous."

"You can't know that."

"Caris . . ." The gentle voice was at once amused and reproving, as it had been when Caris was a child. "Are you now going to protect me? Even if Antryg is the cause of the abominations—even if it was he who shot Thirle as he fled back through the Void—I doubt he would harm me. In either case, I do need to speak to him alone."

"The guards won't let you in."

White teeth caught the gleam of the stars as Salteris grinned. "The guards won't see me. No magic is possible within the walls of the Tower itself, but I can still weave illusions in the court." He got to his feet and shook the bread crumbs from his robe. "Come and watch me."

Even two years of service to the Council of Mages had not quite prepared Caris for the Archmage's entry into the Silent Tower. The guards who raised the portcullis greeted them respectfully as they stepped from the darkness. Salteris apologized to the captain and said that he had discovered something while crossing the hills which made it imperative that he speak with Antryg Windrose once again. The captain twisted the spiked ends of his red mustache, his eyes glinting like agate in the uneasy saffron torchlight beneath the gate.

"I'm sorry, m'lord," he said at last. "It's forbidden to speak to him without the Bishop present, and those are my orders."

"Very well," said Salteris quietly. "Be so good as to send for her."

The captain opened his mouth to speak, but something about the frail old man before him made him close it again. He turned abruptly and bellowed into the watch chamber just within the portcullis, "Gorn! Get out and get a horse saddled." He turned back to Salteris. "It'll be a time —she's had a good hour's start."

"I understand," replied the old man, inclining his head. "Believe me, captain, if it were a matter which could wait until morning I would certainly not put her Grace to this inconvenience."

The captain grunted and scratched his huge paunch through his loose, dark jacket. For all his faintly sloven air, Caris noted the polish of the captain's well-worn sword belt and the oiled gleam of the scabbard thrust through it. The blade within, he guessed, would not be one dulled with neglect. "Well, it's a nuisance all around. There's wine in the guard-house . . ."

"Perhaps." Salteris favored him with a chilly smile. "But there is also tobacco smoke, for which I wouldn't trade the smell of the summer night. We shall do well here, until it gets too cool." He took his seat on a stone bench just within the heavy portcullis, where the watchroom door threw a luminous bar of shifting apricot torchlight across the intense blue gloom under the gatehouse.

"As you please," the big man said. "If there's anything you want— wine or food or tea or whatever—just give a shout for it. And you—" he added to the young man who appeared in the passage, leading a rat-tailed roan gelding, "—make it smart, hear? If you catch her Grace on the road, it'll be one thing; but if she's sat down to her dinner already, we're all of us going to be what she eats for dessert. Now off you go."

The hooves thudded on the road, and a faint whiff of dust blew back from the darkness. Then, with a rattle of weight, chain, and counterwheel, the portcullis rumbled slowly down. The gate was dragged shut behind it and the small bar put into its slots; the captain's huge back blotted the rosy watchroom light for a moment, and then was gone into the smoke and frowst within. In the resulting pocket of utter darkness under the gatehouse, Caris took a seat beside his grandfather on the bench. Through the lighted door, he could see the big man settle himself at one end of the rough wooden table and pull a quart tankard to him, grumbling as someone shoved him his cards.

He was changing his seat, Caris realized, to watch them unobtrusively through the door.

"Very good," Salteris' voice murmured, pitched for Caris' ears alone. "We should have over an hour until the Bishop arrives." He folded his slender hands and settled his back against the stones of the wall behind him, like a man making himself comfortable for a long siege. In the guardroom, someone threw down his cards and cursed richly—there was laughter and profanity-sprinkled banter. The captain threw back his head to join in, but Caris was aware of the tiny glint of his sidelong glance.

He pulled a bit of chamois and an oilcloth wrapped in a rag from his belt purse and set to work getting the mud and dried slime out of the crannies of his sword hilt. Beside him, his grandfather murmured, "How are you at the courtly art of conversation, my son?"

Caris glanced over at him, startled, and again caught the quick glint of the old man's smile in the gloom.

"Do you think you could carry on half of a conversation, as if I were here?"

"You mean, just talk to the air?"

"That's right. It needn't be animated—just do as you are doing and, every now and again, address a remark my way or reply to one that I might make if I were here. Don't look into the guardroom," he added, sensing that the young man was about to cast a glance at the captain; Caris looked quickly down again, concentrating his attention upon the brasswork of the pommel instead.

"Will that serve?" Caris asked softly. "You're in the light . . ."

"And he shall see me in the light," Salteris replied, his voice equally low. "It's one of the dead giveaways of illusions, if the person next to one takes no notice of it. I shouldn't be long."

"But—"

"I'll be all right," he said softly. "I need you to cover my tracks while I'm gone. I should be able to handle Antryg, even if, as I suspect, he is not quite so powerless within the Tower as he would have us believe."

"But the Sigil? The Sign of Darkness?"

Salteris smiled. "I shall be able to deal with the Sigil of Darkness. Just stay here, my son, and talk—don't chatter, it looks unnatural—and I shall be back within half an hour. If I am not . . ." He hesitated.

"What?"

"If I am not," he went on, his voice suddenly deadly serious, "don't risk trying to deal with Antryg yourself. Get the other mages and *get them at once.*" He moved to rise.

Caris had to prevent himself from calling attention to them by catching his sleeve. Instead he breathed, "Wait." The Archmage stood poised, like a dark ghost just beyond the edge of the light. "Will you leave me the *lipa?*"

Salteris thought about it for a moment, then shook his head. "I fear I cannot. For if my worst fears are realized, I may need it myself."

Then he was gone.

Caris sat in silence for a time, belatedly aware that, with his usual ease, Salteris had duped him into staying out of danger. Perhaps, for some reason, he really had wanted to meet Antryg with no witnesses present— perhaps it was only out of consideration for Caris' weariness and injuries, though, Caris told himself stubbornly, they weren't much. In any case there was no way he could follow now without giving the game away; he had to fight the impulse even to look, knowing the captain would be watching him from the door. In the soft twilight of the hills, the Archmage had made light of the peril into which he walked; it was only now that Caris understood that his grandfather, too, knew it for what it was.

But having seen the abomination in the marsh, the old man considered the knowledge Antryg might hold worth the risk of—what?

Caris did not know.

He realized he had been silent too long. No conversationalist even with someone who *was* present, he stammered, "Uh—did I ever tell you about the time cousin Tresta and I stole the town bull?" and turned with what he hoped was naturalness to the empty place at his side. Beyond, the small square of the yard lay under a thin wash of starlight, the cracks between the flagstones like a thin pattern of spiderweb shadow. He could see the door of the Tower clearly, with its two black-clothed sasenna side-by-side. His small magical powers permitted him to see in the dark after a fashion; he glimpsed a drift of shadow that must be Salteris near the wall. One of the guards at the Tower door sneezed violently as the old man's shadow passed before him; the other, startled, jumped. Caris was not sure, but thought he saw the heavy door open a crack. In the utter darkness of the slit; white hair gleamed like a slip of quicksilver—then nothing. He did not even see the door close, but when he blinked, he saw that it *was* closed.

He recalled the Sigil of Darkness and shivered. Evidently, he thought, there *was* some way of dealing with it—at least of getting in. If Salteris knew, there was the possibility that Antryg Windrose might, also.

Remembering what he was supposed to be about, he said quickly, "That's very interesting—uh—grandfather. How did Narwahl Skipfrag get interested in electricity?"

Yet his apprehension did not fade. It ebbed for a few moments, then grew again—not his own fear of detection, but something else, something he did not understand that prickled along his nerves, a sudden uneasy fear that brushed his neck like wind from a door which ought to be locked. It was something he had felt before, somewhere—some evil. . . . He was aware of an odd stirring in the back of his mind, neither nervousness nor fear, but akin to both, a sense of magic and a danger that could not be met with a sword. . . .

Something moved in the archway of lapis darkness that led into the court. Lines of shadow from the stretched ropes of the counterweights brushed blackly across the red robes of one of the hasu as he entered the dark gatehouse at a rapid walk.

Caris bit his tongue, forcing himself to remain still. Being mageborn, the hasu would see that he was alone on the bench; but then, the hasu did not know that there was supposed to be anyone else there. Caris knew he teetered on the edge of discovery—in his finger-ends he was ready to explain or to fight. Robes crimson in the gold glare of the watchroom torches, shaven head catching an edge of the sherry-colored light, the young hasu stood beside the captain's chair, speaking rapidly, worriedly, to the captain, glancing about him, as if he scented danger but knew not where to look for it.

He feels it, too, Caris thought suddenly. The foretaste of unknown fear blossomed within him. The darkness in the corners of the court seemed to ripple, like sunlight on the open plains in burning heat. He felt again the cold touch of the unreasoning terror that had come over him in the Mages' Yard, as he had gazed into the black eternities that lay beyond the threshold of the world as he knew it, as if those abysses lay suddenly within reach of his hand.

He realized, suddenly, what was happening within the Tower.

It was as if the ground had opened beneath him, plunging him into an icy stream. He was on his feet, rage and fury igniting in him. *"No!"*

The captain swung around, and in his eyes Caris saw the Archmage's carefully wrought illusion fail and crumble. The big man lunged to the door, brushing aside the slighter form of the hasu—"Where . . ."

Caris was already running across the court, his sword in his hand. "It's a trap! Antryg trapped him!"

Wolf-swift for all his great bulk, the captain of the Tower overtook him even as the guards seized him at the Tower door. Heedless, Caris twisted against their grasp.

"Let me in! The Archmage went in there, he tricked you . . ." Close to the door the feeling was stronger, the cold breath of the Void like a death-spell whispering in his heart. The stupid, stubborn look on the guards' faces infuriated him. "Don't you understand? He thought Antryg was lying out of fear of the Bishop. Can't you feel it? Antryg wanted him alone!"

The hasu came panting up beside him, sweat glittering like a film of diamonds on his shaven forehead. "The strangeness in the air . . ." he began uncertainly, too young to trust in his own judgment.

"Let me into the Tower!"

For an instant the captain glared at him, gauging him with eyes like dark pebbles of onyx. Then abruptly he snapped at the guards, "Open it."

"But . . ."

"Open it, you fools!" he bellowed. "He's the Archmage—you wouldn't have seen him if he'd kicked you in passing!"

The breath of the Void seemed everywhere now, stirring and whispering in the night as one man removed the dark Sigil from the door and the other twisted the iron key in the lock. Looking back over his shoulder at the courtyard, Caris seemed to see flickering patches of darkness where no shadow should lie, swimming in the air of the court; the guards in the circular chamber at the Tower's base were clamoring with the edginess and anger of frightened men as Caris plunged impatiently through. Terror of the blackness of the Void and terror of what he would find pressed upon him, thicker than the darkness, as he plunged up the narrow, tenebrous spiral of the stair. He shouted, "Grandfather!" and his voice roared back at him in the strait of the walls. "Grandfather . . ."

A hideous darkness filled Antryg's study, like a wavering cloud. Like a cloud, Caris could see through its edges and make out, as if through moving gauze, the shapes of the book-littered table, the overturned chair, and his grandfather's bullion-embroidered glove lying on the corner of the small hearth. Through that darkness, the candles still burned, but the flame was a bleached and sickly white that shed no illumination into the heart of that well of black space that stretched into a falling eternity of nowhere. Far, far along the darkness, he thought he saw a dim figure fleeing, a stir of movement in those terrible depths. The darkness was already beginning to dissipate at its edges, clearing like smoke into the air; the black eye of its center retreated, farther and farther along that distance that never seemed, in all its endless plunge of miles, to reach the opposite wall.

Caris cried again, *"No!"*

His sword was in his hand as he plunged after that retreating shape into the darkness, and the cold abyss swallowed him up.

CHAPTER VII

THE NIGHT WAS SOFT AS SILK AND WARM AS BATH WATER. THE stars, Caris saw, were the ones he knew. The brilliant Phoenix-star lay on the edge of the dark circle of hills, calling to its mate a quarter of the way up the sky. The tip of the Scythe still pointed to the inner and unmoving heart of the heavens. The air was dry and sweet with the scent of warm dust, underlain by some metallic tang that caught his throat.

He, at least, was safe.

For a long time, his awareness consisted of only that. Kneeling in the thin, dry grass, he fought the wave of shakiness that threatened to wring his meager supper from his guts. It was more than just the utter terror of that long, half-falling run through cold and sightless chasms and that terrible disorientation and the horror of knowing that he could well be lost forever, without even hope of dying, more than the sickening aftermath of fear-induced exertion that had spurred his final, desperate run toward the retreating starlight at the end of the closing tunnel of eternity. He was more weary than he had ever been in his life. His exhaustion after fighting the abomination—had that only been this morning?—seemed petty and laughable now, for then he had been in a world he knew, surrounded by people of whose reactions he could be sure. Then the Archmage had been with him.

He wanted nothing more than to lie where he was and sleep for a week.

But it is the Way of the Sasenna to rise and go on.

He managed to raise his head.

The crest of the hill upon which he lay cast a black semicircle of shadow in the dell beneath. Beyond its edge, the smudgy light of a newly risen three-quarter moon lay upon the thin grass of the opposite hillslope, turning it the color of pewter, and illuminated the bizarre figure of Antryg Windrose, standing above the body of a young man sprawled at his feet.

Aware that he himself lay just below the crest of the hill, and therefore in its concealing shadow, Caris very slowly rolled a few turns down the hill to the cover of a prickly leaved bush whose scent told him it was a kind of sage. As his eyes grew accustomed to the denser shadows, he saw that the hill slope was dotted with such plants.

The climate was warm enough, he thought, for spices of this kind to grow wild, as they did in the deserts far to the south-east of Kymil, on the road to Saarieque. By the stars, they were further south from Kymil. The Archmage had spoken of other worlds lying beyond the Void. Would they have the same stars?

It didn't matter. The Way of the Sasenna was not to ask questions, but to perform one's task. His sword, miraculously, was still in his hand. Keeping his head down, he crawled downslope to the next sage bush, as Antryg knelt beside the young man's body and passed his hand gently over the dirty, twig-entangled mop of fair hair, feeling the temples and then the pulses of the throat. The young man was nearly naked, but for a pair of extremely short drawers—natural enough, in a climate as warm as this—and sandals on his feet.

The young man stirred and flailed with one hand, which Antryg caught by the wrist. The wizard's voice was clearly audible to Caris in the stillness of the night. "Are you all right?"

Are we in our own world after all? Caris wondered confusedly. *Surely the inhabitants of another would not speak our tongue?* But in his heart he knew they were no longer where they had been. Perhaps Antryg only expected a reply because he was mad. But when the young man spoke, it was not in the language of Ferr, but in some other whose meaning Caris heard in his mind, as one hears the voices of people in dreams; and he understood that Antryg was using some kind of spell of understanding, whose field extended far enough to touch him here.

The young man said, "Hunh? Sweet Holy Christ, who the hell are you?"

"Are you all right?" Antryg repeated.

"Jesus, no." The young man made an unsuccessful effort to sit up, and Antryg put a hand under his arm to assist him. The stranger's voice was slurred, as if with drink or drugs—small wonder, Caris thought, that he does not notice that Antryg is not speaking his tongue. "Somebody must have spiked hell out of that punch." He blinked dazedly up at the wizard, taking in the long, unruly mane and straggly beard, the ragged robes and crystal earrings. Then he giggled. "Hell, I must be stoneder than I thought. You come out of the punchbowl like all the rest of the stuff I been seeing?"

"No," admitted Antryg. "I'm a wizard from another universe, and I'm here to save your world—and mine, I hope—from a terrible fate. Can you sit up?"

The young man laughed again and shook his head. "Crazy."

"Yes, I am crazy, too." Antryg helped him to his unsteady feet, the young man hanging on the wizard's shoulder, still giggling vapidly.

"Man, you're about the solidest hallucination. . . . That must be some dope." He threw a friendly arm around Antryg's shoulders. "My name's Digby—Digby Clayton. C'mon back to the party, man, have a drink."

Silently, Caris followed them.

From the shadows of the higher ground, he watched them as they found a pale track of dust, which broadened quickly as it turned around the side of the hill to join a dark, smooth roadbed. At some distance along the road, he could see a house, an L-shaped building lying in a pool of brilliance in the darkness, illuminated with blazing light—far too bright and far too steady for firelight. It was like the brilliance of magic, but Caris sensed it could not be. Stunted and rudimentary as his own small powers were, he knew that there was no magic in this world. This sensation was not like the prickling weight of the spells that deadened the enclave of the Tower or the hollow, gnawing grief of those times in which his powers faded. Here it simply did not exist.

Yet magic would have been the only way to explain the house that lay before him in the island of yellow-white glare. In a courtyard behind it lay a huge pool of water, its turquoise reflections playing over the stone and glass of the house walls and the dark plants that grew around the low wall surrounding the court. People moved about on the sides of the water or swam in it like seals—men and women, naked save for bits of glaringly bright-colored cloth, drinking and eating and shouting at one another to be heard over the raucous, pounding music which seemed to come from no source, but which hung over the house and grounds and hills around like the pall of carrion stench.

From the hillside, Caris calculated his cover as his quarry and his drunken host passed through a little iron gate in the low wall to the court. The wall was stone block to half its insignificant height, and iron spindles the rest. The unkempt juniper hedge surrounding it on the out-side offered unpromising protection; but, by the look of it, most of the people in the court were far too drunk to pay much attention. The brightness of those lights would blind them to movement in the surrounding darkness.

He had sheathed his sword, but carried the sheath loose in his hand in preparation for battle. He now hooked it to the back strap of his harness and, flattening to his belly, crept down the hill.

Down near the house, the noise was incredible; the heavy, thumping rhythm of the music vibrated in his bones. The air was rank with the sickly odor of spilled beer and the queer, sweetish scent of burning marijuana, such as peasants in the villages smoked when they couldn't get gin. But there was gin—or liquor of some kind—in appalling abundance here; and by the way everyone laughingly accepted what Digby was saying, they had all evidently taken advantage of that fact to the fullest. "This is a hallucination, a genuine, *bona fide* hallucination," he was announcing over and over at the top of his voice to those few interested enough to come over and listen. Antryg, Caris could see, was looking about him in fascinated delight.

But for the lack of magic, Caris would have thought the mad wizard had somehow led him through into the Realms of Faërie. The courtyard was an unreal paradise of brilliant light and velvet shadow, of glaring colors, sparkling water, and smooth, bare, golden flesh. Clouds of steam rose from a smaller pool, which bubbled like a cauldron where a man and two women sat dreaming in its warmth. Now that he was closer, Caris could smell the odd, almost metallic tang of the waters, and see the clumps of clothing strewn at random all around the inside limits of the court. He could hear scraps of conversation as well; but, though Antryg's spell of languages gave him understanding of what he heard, it made no sense, even taking into account the thoroughgoing insobriety of the speakers—software and graphics, special effects and video, carburetors, microwaves, and Republicans. Through an enormous wall of glass, Caris could see into the dimness of the house, where people sat clumped around square, dark screens upon which images moved, some of them the shadows of people, like living paintings, others mere collections of swiftly flowing colored dots. Abandoned drinks, bits of food, and the spilled ruin of liquor were everywhere, along with discarded shoes and boots and clothing; and over all was the sourceless, screaming throb of music.

A woman was hanging onto Antryg's arm, her billowy red robe falling open to reveal great amounts of seal-sleek charms. "So you're a friend of Digby's?" she giggled.

"No, actually, I'm a wizard from another universe." Antryg pushed his spectacles up a little more firmly on the bridge of his beaky nose and regarded her with polite interest.

"You mean like Middle Earth and all that?"

Caris had never heard of Middle Earth. By the look in his eyes, neither had Antryg, but he smiled widely, his teeth gleaming in the tangle of his beard, and agreed, "Yes."

She moved nearer to him, molding her ample form to his bony one. "Far out."

He considered the remark for a moment and informed her factually, "Well, in terms of the ultimate centers of power, less far out than this one."

"Is he friend of yours, Digby?" A woman's voice, speaking close to where Caris crouched, was so quiet it was only because of its nearness that he heard at all. It took his attention, because it was the only sober one he had so far heard. Moving his head a little, Caris could see the speaker standing in an opening formed by a sliding panel in the glass wall, next to Digby, who was supporting himself valiantly against it. A small girl with fair, brushy curls framing the thin bones of her face, she held a thick roll of greenish papers in one hand. Unlike anyone else in the court, she was watching Antryg with wary suspicion in her brown eyes.

"No, Joanna," Digby slurred happily. "Like I said, he's a hallucination. He just walked right out of this big hole in the air." He took a long swig from a glass in his hand, throwing his whole body into the gesture; the rippling reflections from the pool shone damply on the bulge of his soft little paunch. "You know Gary's looking for you."

"I know," the girl said tiredly. "That's why I'm down here talking to you. My program has an hour and a half to run yet, and he's gone to look for me in the computer room."

"Oh," Digby vaguely said, clearly not even hearing the sharp fragment of buried anger in the girl Joanna's voice. Across the court, the woman in red was leading the bemused-looking Antryg into the darkness of the other wing of the house, laughing and saying, "Come show me some magic . . ."

Antryg paused in the doorway, looking around at that garish and noisy scene with his usual expression of pleased interest, like some mad saint with his ink-stained beard and tattered robes. Near him, Caris was aware of the girl Joanna watching Antryg with the same wariness that he himself felt, sensing, as none of the others seemed to, that something was amiss. But it was his own eyes, across the teeming chiaroscuro of the courtyard, that Antryg, for one instant, met. Then a hand reached out from the darkened room behind him and drew him inside.

Caris knew he had been seen.

Perhaps, he thought, Antryg had known all along that he had been followed; perhaps, in that chaotic darkness, he had heard Caris' stumbling steps at his heels. Perhaps this was the reason he had let himself be led to this strange place—so that going inside, he would leave his watch-dog to guard the front entrance, while he glided out the back.

Lying in the heavy scents of the prickling juniper, with the dried slime that crusted his torn jacket scratching the wounds on his arms, Caris felt a sudden chill in spite of the evening's warmth. The nightmare run through darkness had terrified him; the echoing depths of nothingness had seemed populated by vast presences and by chaotic horrors, beside which the abomination in the swamp seemed friendly, solid, and familiar; but it came to him now that the dark figure of the wizard whom he had followed was, in fact, his only link with his own world. To lose him would not only mean losing all chance of finding his grandfather—it would mean being stranded in this insane, magicless, noisy world forever, with no way to return to that which he knew.

Cautiously, Caris moved to circle the house, counting exits.

Of these there were appallingly many. There were dozens of windows, some of which he tested and found impossible to open sufficiently to pass a body, while others would have admitted a horse. There were outbuildings, smelling of strange things, and a vast number of big, metal machines which were obviously conveyances and whose wheels had left tracks on the soft dust of the drive, though there was neither sign nor smell of a horse anywhere. *More magic?* thought Caris, puzzled, *in this magicless world?* To the south, over the hills, there was a glare in the sky, filling the whole southeastern quarter of the horizon with its reddish reflection, like a mechanical dawn.

Silent as the drift of shadow, he returned to the house, testing, checking. Garden doors led out onto a path that trailed through the straggly dust of the hills toward the dim shape of a shed, far up the nearest rise; pausing beside them, Caris heard voices raised in argument, the blond-haired woman Joanna's and a man's, slurred with liquor and self-pity.

"I'm sorry about what I said, Joanna, okay? I didn't mean it. . . ."

"Didn't you? You may be the only man who's ever wanted me and you may very well be the only man who ever will, but I don't really care to have that pointed out in front of people that I work with."

"I mean—you know . . ." Although, looking through the half-open doors, at the young woman's rather plain face, with its awkward nose and the first fine scratches of crow's-feet around the brown eyes, Caris could believe that was true, still he felt a stab of the uncomfortable feeling that he was seeing injustice done. It didn't help to recall his own stupid and meaningless cruelty to the girl from the tavern, earlier in the week.

"Hey, I'm sorry, babe. How many times do I got to say it?"

The dim lights of the room picked out the man's shape, nearly nude, like most of the people there, his muscular body speckled with droplets of water from the courtyard pool. The woman, as he had seen in the court-yard earlier, was one of the few people clothed—unbecomingly, Caris thought—in the faded blue trousers that seemed to be uniform for such men and women who wore anything beyond a few bright bits of cloth and a close-fitting white upper garment, which showed off the figure of a diminutive houri.

Her voice was cool and precise, "You can say it as many times as you need to in order to feel that you've made some kind of amends. But it will all be entirely for your own benefit."

"What's that supposed to mean? You're my sweetheart, babe, I love you."

"If you didn't keep making fun of me to your other friends, I'd find that a whole lot more convincing."

It was strange, thought Caris as he moved soundlessly on through the dust-smelling night, that the quarrels and griefs of those who peopled this alien world should be so similar to those he knew in his own.

The house was two storeys tall in its main portion, one storey at the wing into which Antryg had gone. Most of its windows, Caris had ascertained, looked inward toward the court, and the doors leading outside could all, he estimated, be seen from the roof of the farthest eastward end —if the stars were right it was east, anyway—of the low wing. Judging by their reactions to Antryg's alien garments, none of the revelers should comment, even if they did see Caris sitting on the roof; in any case the projecting cornices of the house should hide him.

One of the metal vehicles stood near enough the wall to give him footing. Its springs gave slightly with his leap, and his back muscles and bruised ankle cried out against the jarring scramble for footing. The roof itself had only a shallow slope, like the houses in Mellidane that knew no snow. In the dark, he felt its surfaces to be some kind of granulose shingle, firm and silent beneath his boots. Crouching, he moved along the edge, where the walls would take his weight and keep the beams from creaking within. Just below the spine of the roof crest, he stretched him-self out, achingly glad to be able to rest and chiding himself for that unsasennanlike gratitude. On one side lay the darkness of the hills, the few windows throwing small squares of yellow light to gleam on the shiny metal of the vehicles or pick threads of sherry-colored grass through the soft haze of the dust. On the other lay the court, the music rising up like the blaze of colored light to the watching stars, and drifts of conversation floating above it like isolated wafts of perfume:

". . . so you could boot it warm, but every time you booted it cold you got a B—DOS error . . ."

"Hell, you think that's bad? They had the whole fiberoptic Cray mainframe disappear in pieces from Alta Clara . . ."

"I swear to God the guy swings both ways . . ."

". . . working until two in the morning. You'll never get *her* to believe it, but she's the sharpest programmer at San Serano."

"You expect *Gary* to know the difference between *auslese* and Thunderbird?"

". . . superhero and a mercenary, but in his secret identity he writes children's books . . ."

"Digby might be right about there being a Bermuda Triangle in Building Six. Sometimes that place feels so *creepy.*"

"I never found it creepy, but there are times there when I get just about suicidal."

"If I worked for Eraserhead Brown, I'd be suicidal, too. . . ."

Exhausted, Caris felt himself slipping into the trap of relaxing and knew he must not yield to the weariness of his body. He toyed with the idea of trying to steal some of the food that was in such abundance down there, but knew it was too dangerous. Antryg, he thought, might be waiting for just such a distraction.

Occasionally, the vehicles would arrive or depart, powered, it seemed, by some internal force. Growling with throaty violence, with their yellow headlamps blazing like eyes and a thin cloud of stinking smoke puffing from their tails, they reminded him of flatulent, metallic beasts. Several times he saw red lights moving in the starry darkness of the sky, accompanied by a far-off bass roar that shook his bones, but no one in the court paid the slightest heed. Such matters, then, must be commonplace in this universe. But he flinched every time such a creature passed.

And above the pain of his wounds, the ache of his muscles, the weary confusion held at bay only by the years of discipline in the Way of the Sasenna, and his growing fear, was the single thought: *I must not let him escape.*

A dim light appeared in the large window of the second-storey room in the main wing. It had been cast not by any light in the room, but by the reflection of a hallway light when the door was opened. Caris froze into stillness, for the window was directly opposite where he lay; with the room in darkness, he would be perfectly visible to anyone who came to the window.

But it was only one of the revelers, looking vaguely about him as he polished his spectacles—Caris was amused to see that with all their wonders, these people still wore spectacles, some of them no different than Antryg's—on the hem of the close-fitting, short-sleeved black shirt that he wore. The light from the door picked up strange silver runes written across the chest as he replaced the light frame of wire and metal on his long nose.

The man gazed around him for a moment at the darkened room, with its banks of metal boxes with tiny red eyes glowing in their blank faces; their small, dark screens looked like polished beryl. Then he turned back, not to the door itself, but to the doorframe. With a gesture that reminded Caris curiously of the mages, he brushed the narrow molding of wood with his fingertips. . . .

A woman's voice said softly, "It was you. . . ."

He swung sharply around as a second shadow in the doorway appeared, and Caris recognized the woman Joanna.

A glimpse of crimson down in the court drew Caris' eye. It was, he saw, the woman in the red robe again, but of Antryg there was no sign. Cursing his inattention, Caris waited until the two people in the semidarkness of the upper room were both turned from the window, then slid soundlessly down the rough shingles and dropped, catlike, to the nose of the metal vehicle below and thence to the ground.

There was no one, now, in any of the rooms of that low wing.

The uninitiated imputed to the sasenna fearsome powers of profanity when they are in their rage. But the sasenna did not curse in true rage—oaths, like complaints and tears, wasted time and only served to cloud the mind.

There was no time for them now, if he was not going to be left in this world forever.

That afternoon, he recalled, he had thought that he had never had to fight for his life before. He realized now, that he had never had to track, hunt, and watch for his life, and he stood in danger of failing, with consequences beyond his power to imagine.

With painstaking care, he cast for sign all around the house. Even with his slight abilities to see in darkness, it was not easy, and he found nothing—no track, no sign, beyond the circle of the house-lights' glow, to mark the mad wizard's passing. Antryg was a mage and had, like all those who took Council vows, been trained as sasenna. Having watched him fight, Caris knew that, unlike many mages, he had not let that training sleep.

Caris moved as close to the house as he dared and began a second cast. The track of Antryg's soft boots would be distinctive among the sharp, bizarre patterns of the shoes of this world; all around the hard black pavement where the vehicles stood was a belt of dust and weeds. A long drive ran out toward the main road, but Caris had watched it from the roof and had seen nothing on it but the coming and going of vehicles.

There was a path, leading out into the hills, toward what looked like a deserted stable or shed, nearly a mile away. Surrounded by the moldering remains of fallen fences, it stood dark and untenanted at the crest of a hill overlooking the house itself. But by the dust at the head of the path, he saw that it was regularly used by a single type of footprint—someone ran there and back, wearing cleated shoes, almost daily. But there was no mark in the starlit dust of the wizard's boots, nor of the faint slurring that the hem of a robe would cause.

Caris was beginning to feel frightened.

Once, close to the road, a vehicle leaving the house in a great jerking roar of wheels and smoke nearly ran him over, its yellow headlights sweeping him as he ducked into the coarse sagebrush for cover. Casting for sign on the hillslope near the iron courtyard gate through which Digby Clayton and Antryg had originally passed, he heard the stifled giggles of a courting couple in the weeds, and a girl's voice called out, "Is somebody there?" After that Caris moved back farther from the house again, his unease increasing with the latening movement of the stars. Detection now would mean questions and delay, and delay was what he could not afford. Weariness was closing in on him, the ache in his body exacerbated by a longing for sleep; soon it would begin to impair his survival instincts. If Antryg passed through the Void again before he found him . . .

And suddenly, he felt it again—the queer terror, the sense, almost the smell, of worlds beyond worlds, the vibration of abyssal winds in his bones. The Void had been opened.

Panic touched him, with the knowledge that this was his last chance and he hadn't the slightest clue what to do. . . .

Where? he thought desperately, his frantic gaze sweeping the hills in the thin moonlight.

There was a man, walking swiftly along the path to that distant shed.

It was the bespectacled reveler from the upper room—the one who had been speaking to Joanna in the half-dark. The moonlight caught faintly on the strange metallic runes that marked his garment and on his spectacle lenses as he paused and looked back at the house with an attitude of bemused delight.

And as he moved on, with that gawky walk that was somehow light and graceful as a dancer's, Caris realized who he was.

What had Salteris said? The sasenna knew that the best place to hide was in plain sight, and Antryg had always been a genius at it. There had been enough stray clothing lying around the house for him to find garments that fitted his tall skinny frame; without the beard and with his long hair cut, Caris had not recognized him among the others, and had gone off searching the hills, as Antryg had intended.

Anger surged through him, fed by fears, by his shame at feeling fear, and by his rage at having been duped. It drowned his weariness and his dread of passing through the Void once more, drowned everything but his determination for revenge.

Starlight flashed on glass as Antryg turned his head. He quickened his long stride, and Caris, knowing he had been seen, threw caution to the winds and flung himself forward, summoning the reserves of his strength. The wrenched and stiffened muscles of his ankle screamed at him as he crashed through the dry sage and dust of the unfamiliar ground.

Antryg, instead of running away, turned and headed for the shed. Caris knew it then—the shed itself contained the gate into the Void. Antryg was closer to it than he, with longer legs and fresher strength. Battle rage flooded Caris as he ran. With a sweep he drew his sword from where it hung upon his back. . . .

The inside of the shed was an echoing well of darkness. The night was too deep for him to see even a little of the place as it should have been— broken partitions, fallen beams, the dismantled metal bones of the strange self-moving machines, and the stinks of oil and dust. But the crumbling lintels framed a hollow, a chasm in which there was neither light nor time—only the endless, amorphous stirrings of the winds that drifted between universes.

With a yell of rage that did not quite succeed in purging the terror from his heart, Caris flung himself once again into the dark.

CHAPTER VIII

JOANNA WOKE UP IN DARKNESS.

For an instant she remembered nothing, except that she was cold, sore, and terrified of something she could not recall. The surface she lay upon was unfamiliar, narrow, and hard; under her bare arms she felt tight-stretched, satiny upholstery. She drew a breath and choked with the bruised ache in her throat.

Terror returned with an almost physical nausea.

She thought illogically, *The marks on the wall!*

There had been one in the computer room in Building Six, when she'd been assaulted by the Man Who Wasn't There.

He wasn't there again today. . . . The tall, thin, bespectacled form, the brush of long fingers over the doorframe of the upstairs room at Gary's—the sign that had appeared beneath that butterfly touch, like light shining onto the wood rather than any mark—

She had known him, of course—Digby's mysterious hallucination, defrocked and debearded. It had been the robe that had touched her memory at the party. Was that why he'd changed his clothes?

Joanna didn't know what was going on, but she wanted no part of it.

Had he left, after she'd spoken to him in Gary's upstairs room? She had the impression that he had, but her memory was clouded, events telescoping and confused. She'd come up to collect her program and leave, not wanting to put up with Gary whining at her heels for the rest of the evening, resolving even to unplug her phone when she got home, as Gary made up in persistence what he lacked in tact. . . .

He'd been there when she'd come in, she remembered, and she had known him then as Digby's hallucination. *Stepped out of a hole in the air.* . . .

The same black hole of darkness she had seen in San Serano?

She thought that he'd left, that she'd been sitting alone in front of Gary's big IBM, waiting for the modem buffers to spit the last information out from the Cray at San Serano. Had he come back later, or . . . ? She couldn't remember. Only the sudden, terrible grip of hands around her throat, the hideous gray roaring in her ears, the drowning terror . . .

And here.

Cautiously, she moved her legs. She was still dressed as she had been at Gary's, in jeans, a white tank-top, and sneakers. The idea that she had been unconscious in someone else's power made her shudder with loathing, but she could detect no bruises anywhere other than on her neck. Shrinking with inner dread, she put her hand carefully down over the edge of the narrow cot upon which she lay—like a child, she realized ruefully, who *knows* the boogieman waits under the bed. . . .

But she only encountered the floor—stone, and very cold.

Stone? she thought. She sat up, fighting a slight qualm of sickness as she did so, and groped at the sides of what she thought was a cot and which turned out to be a daybed, the eighteenth-century ancestor of the chaise lounge. At one end was a chairlike back, heavily carved; there was more carving on the tops of the thing's cabriole legs. Feeling along the floor beside it, she reached the familiar, enormous lumpiness of her purse and breathed a sigh of relief.

Although whoever had brought her here could have gone through it. . . .

Her digging fingers came in contact with her miniature flashlight. She switched it on, and the yellow light wavered wildly over the room with the shaking of her hand.

She thought, *Oh, Christ,* in a kind of frightened despair. The room was stone, small and windowless, like the turret chamber of a castle—or like somebody's idea of one. The daybed with its frivolous gilded scrollwork and rose-colored cushions struck her as a sinister incongruity, and she muttered, "Kinky," to herself as she got to her feet. She sat down again, quickly, a little surprised at the weakness and nausea that the heroines of movies never seemed to suffer after a violent assault.

The room had one door. It was only a few steps away and, not very surprisingly, bolted from the outside.

Joanna went back to the daybed and sat down again. Her knees felt weak.

Don't panic, she told herself. *Whatever you do, if you panic, you won't be able to do anything.* But her mind kept screaming at her, *Why me?*

Figure that out later, she told herself firmly, fighting not to think about the implications that she had been stalked. She dug through the contents of her purse, and her hand closed around the reassuring smoothness of her hammer. She set it beside her and checked out the rest—Swiss Army knife, several tin and plastic boxes, a measuring tape, scissors, calculator, wallet, checkbook, keys, notebook, mirror, spare toothbrush, tube of sunscreen, collapsible drinking cup, Granola bars, rubber bands, safety pins, a lipstick that she'd never used, a package of Kleenex, a sewing kit, a bundle of plastic-coated wires she'd gotten from plant maintenance, three and a half pairs of earrings, and two floppy disks.

She selected the hammer and the Swiss Army knife, opened the screwdriver blade, and returned once more to the door.

It was designed to open inward. The hinges were the pin type, though massive and, by the look of them, forged of iron rather than steel. Joanna frowned as she shined the beam of the flashlight over them, recognizing the anachronism but unable to account for it. She knew the recreational medievalists of her acquaintance made their own chain mail, but their own door hinges?

Doubtfully, she cast the light around the room once more. Of course, Southern California was rife with old stone buildings, if you knew where to look for them, but . . .

Later, she told herself again. *Right now the object is to get the hell out of here.* Carefully, she began to work the knife's screwdriver blade in beneath the hinge pin . . .

And stopped, at the soft snick of the door bolt being slid back.

She had heard no footfall; but then, she had no idea how thick the walls or door might be. Thick, she thought, for she had heard nothing at all—no traffic sound, not even the subsonic vibration of trucks, no airplane roar, and no tread of footfalls elsewhere in the building. Adrenaline surging through her like fire, she stepped back to where the door would hide her, hammer in hand, heart pounding, but feeling queerly calm. Her last thought was, *He's very tall, I'll have to strike high.*

The door opened.

He was ready for her, catching her wrist on the downswing and ducking aside, though she heard him gasp as the hammer glanced off his bony shoulder. Like most women who have had little to do with men, she was shocked at the strength of his hands. He knew the tricks too; his arms moved and twisted with hers as she tried to drive her wrist against the weak joint of the thumb to break his hold, and he turned his body to block the knee she drove at his groin. The struggle lasted only seconds. Then something drove into his back from the dark door like a striking puma. A slamming foot behind his knee made his legs buckle. She heard him gasp again and looked up as the newcomer to the fray seized a handful of his hair, pulled his head back, and laid the edge of a knife to his throat.

Joanna pulled away from the suddenly opened grip.

"Are you all right?" The young man barely glanced at her as he spoke. In the skewed glare of the flashlight, his startlingly handsome face looked drawn with strain and exhaustion, lead-colored smudges of weariness around the tip-tilted dark eyes.

"I think so," gasped Joanna.

He jerked the knife roughly against the thin skin above his prisoner's jugular. His voice was thick with rage. "What have you done with the Archmage?"

The kneeling man remained immobile between them, sweat shining on his face and trickling along his exposed throat. "Nothing," he whispered. "Caris, listen . . ." His breath stopped with a quick, faint draw; a thread of blood started from under the blade.

"I've listened to you enough, Antryg Windrose." To Joanna, the young man said, "There's a silk cord tied around under my belt. Take it and bind his hands."

"Caris, no." The older man's lips barely moved as he spoke. "You have to get out of here. There's danger . . ."

Joanna's hands were moving quickly, picking apart the knots of the cord. The young man's clothing was black, oddly reminiscent, like the curved sword stuck through his sash, of samurai or martial arts gear, though creased, torn in places, and stained with caked mud and slime. Her first thought that she had somehow been caught up in some kind of role-playing event faded when she saw that, under the torn jacket and shirt, Caris' biceps and pectorals bore a collection of really shocking abrasions and bruises.

She pulled the silk cord free from the crossed sword sash and leather dagger belt. "Look," she said shakily, "thank you and all that—really, thank you very much—but could you please tell me what the hell is going on?"

Caris' knee dug viciously into Antryg's back. "This man is a renegade wizard," he said. "He has caused evils and abominations to appear; for what he has done I should kill him here and now."

Joanna, pausing in the act of tying Antryg's hands, said, "HUNH?"

"Caris, I had nothing to do with your grandfather's disappearance."

"Then how do you know he disappeared?"

"Look," Antryg said, turning his head a little against the grip on his hair to meet his captor's eyes. "There isn't time for this. There is danger coming, an abomination beside which the thing you fought in the swamp is as nothing."

"How do you . . ."

"*I know it!*" he insisted furiously. Then, more quietly, "Please believe me." His long hands caught Joanna's as she tried to put the cord around them, staying her, but without force. "I surrender to you, I'll be your prisoner, do with me whatever you want to—but *get out of here!*"

Joanna could feel his hands, where they touched hers, shaking. It didn't prove anything; hers were still trembling from the exertion of the fight, and she didn't currently have a knife at her throat. But in the silence that followed his words, she could feel a strange, louring threat, a dread that she had known before in the too-silent corridors of Building Six—a sense of evil, beyond anything she had encountered or could imagine. Beside that amorphous darkness, mere human kinkiness and even quasi-medieval murder cults seemed oddly petty.

She said softly, "Look, I don't know what's going on but—I think he's right."

Caris glanced sharply at her, but only said, "Draw my sword."

Joanna obeyed. Whatever the scenario was, it was pretty clearly being played for keeps. There was something living and hateful in the silence that kept her from simply saying, "Count me out of this dungeon thanks," and walking out the door. As she had at San Serano, she felt again that outside the room lay, not death, but something worse whose nature she could scarcely even conceive.

Caris made sure the sword was ready to hand before he took the knife from his prisoner's throat. "Get up. If you try any tricks, I swear I will feed you your own heart."

Antryg got to his feet, wiping the trickle of blood from his neck. The tension in him was palpable; fear, thought Joanna, yet she had no sense that he was afraid of Caris, in spite of the fact that the younger man had come within a millimeter of slitting his throat. He whispered, "Stay here," and made a move towards the door, as if to check the corridor. Caris' swift, small gesture with the sword halted him again, and he regarded the young warrior in irritated frustration.

Knowing there was only one way out of this fox-goose-corn conundrum, Joanna said, "I'll look," though her stomach curled with dread at the thought of facing whatever might be in the corridor. Part of her insisted that this was absurd, but some deeper part, the part that had cowered in fear in the janitor's closet at San Serano, knew that Antryg was right and that Caris was a stubborn fool not to flee from the darkness that she could sense was gathering somewhere nearby.

Hefting the hammer that she knew would be utterly useless, she peeked around the doorframe.

The corridor stretched away in darkness to her right, unbroken, impenetrable, and hideously ominous. To her left, she thought there were doors, and beyond them, some sense of openness, of moving air. The fear was to her right—abomination, Antryg had said. There was no sound, and she felt she would have preferred anything to that unspeakable, waiting silence.

She ducked swiftly back into what had become a haven of safety. By the flashlight-glare, Antryg looked deathly white and Caris, his fair hair falling into his eyes, like a man grimly fighting his instinct to flee. She swallowed hard. "There's nothing moving out there."

"Good," Antryg murmured. In spite of the fact that he was officially a prisoner, he seemed to have effortlessly taken over the expedition. "Joanna, I'm going to have to ask you to douse that light, if you can."

Joanna, who had picked up her flashlight from where it lay on the floor behind the door, looked up at him, startled, and met only grave inquiry in his gray eyes.

"There is a way of putting it out, isn't there?"

Verisimilitude? she wondered. But he was frightened—she knew it, could feel it—frightened beyond the point where any role player would forget the bounds of a non-industrial persona and simply say, *Shut off the flashlight.*

Seeing the doubt in her eyes, he added, "I can see in the dark—so can Caris a little, can't you?"

Caris nodded—it was clearly not something that he even thought much about.

For the first time in that bizarre sequence of events, Joanna felt that she had just stepped off an edge somewhere, into waters deeper than she knew. Up until that moment, she had been sure, not of what was happening, but of the *kind* of thing it must be. Now for the first time, she doubted, and the doubts opened an abyss of possibilities whose mere existence would have been terrifying, had she believed in them. *Later,* she told herself again. Shouldering her heavy purse, she took a hesitant grip on the belt loop of Antryg's jeans and switched off the light.

Darkness swooped down upon her like a terror-bird. Her instinct was to shrink against someone for the reassurance that she was not alone, but Antryg had twice tried to strangle her, had kidnapped her from Gary's house, and brought her to this place. She knew she could not afford to tie up Caris' sword arm, even if he'd be chivalrous enough to let her, which she was pretty sure he wouldn't. So she only tightened her hold on the narrow loop of denim and tried to keep her breathing steady.

Antryg's hand touched hers and gave it a quick, comforting pat in the darkness, as if he sensed her fear; then he led the way forward, out into the haunted hall.

To Joanna's infinite relief, they turned left, moving swiftly and surely. Once, putting out her left hand, she felt the cold, uneven stone of a wall and guessed that, see-in-the-dark or not, Antryg was probably using the wall as a guide. Caris' shoulder brushed her bare arm, and the coarse, quilted, black cotton of the jacket was warm against her skin; she could hear the soft rustle of cloth and the creak of leather as that gorgeous young man turned periodically to look back. Once she herself risked such a glance and wished she hadn't.

It's only darkness, she told herself, *the same as the darkness in front of you. Nothing is nothing.* But it wasn't. Why it should seem so dense and terrifying she did not know, nor why, seeing nothing, she should have the sense that it stirred, as if with some passing form that even light would not have unmasked. *When I get out of this,* she thought, *wherever the hell I am, I'm taking the first bus back to Van Nuys, I am finding a new apartment, changing my telephone number, and looking for another job, if necessary. . . .*

But Antryg knew her now. And Antryg was one of them, whoever *they* were. Was this, she wondered suddenly, just a put-up part of the game? Was he leading her through darkness to something worse, phase two of some elaborately choreographed nightmare?

It was more logical than what she feared, in some far-back corner of her heart, might be going on.

Something stirred in the darkness. A wind touched her hair, blowing from behind them—a queer, cold smell that she vaguely recognized and which filled her with unnamed terror. She glanced back over her shoulder again and thought she saw, far back in the black depths behind them, some blur of luminosity which illuminated nothing. At the same moment Caris whispered, "Antryg . . ."

Antryg's bare, sinewy arm went around her shoulders, drawing her against him, and she felt by the movement of his body that he had shoved Caris ahead of them. He whispered, *"Run!"* There was a frantic fear in his voice that could not have been counterfeited; she felt, rather than saw, Caris start to run.

She had no idea how long they ran, nor when the ground beneath her feet changed from stone to earth, and from earth to the silky drag of grass. She stumbled and was hauled forward by main force, gasping for breath and exhausted, her mind blurred by panic of whatever it was that lay behind them. Sometime in that darkness, she was aware that the graveyard fetor that had so unreasonably terrified her had changed to wind and the thick headiness of cut hay; she stumbled repeatedly on the uneven slopes of the ground, trying to match her stride with the much longer one of the man whose powerful arm pushed her inexorably on. Through her terror, she became dimly aware of a dividing horizon between dark earth and dark sky. Then she stumbled, and fell into a final and deeper darkness.

It was just before dawn when she woke. She stirred, and sneezed. The air was thick with the fragrance of hay, with the smell of water and cows, with the twitter of whippoorwills, and with the incessant, peeping chorus of small frogs. For a blank moment, she wondered where she was. Her throat ached with bruises, and her body was stiff with the last, desperate run of the night. She was starvingly hungry.

Looking up, she could see Antryg sitting with his back to a haystack— an object which Joanna had never seen in her life outside of pictures, but which was indubitably a haystack. His long legs were drawn up, his arms rested across his bony knees, and he contemplated the glowing eastward sky with a look of meditative calm. Beyond him, Caris lay asleep, like an exhausted god, his sword still under his limp hand.

All around them, the world was bathed in the unearthly blue glow of predawn. Joanna sat up, scratching the straw from her hair. She felt a little cold, shaken, and very unreal. The hills behind them were still shrouded with the clear, purple darkness of the last of the night, but the waters of the marsh that lay in a series of crisscrossed hollows below them and to their left were already picking up the quicksilver brightness of the sky. There was no freeway roar, no growl of jets, not even the far-off moan of a train whistle. The sky was uncrossed by powerlines and, though it was late August, untainted by smog.

"Are you cold?" Antryg asked her, and she shook her head.

"Not very."

He smiled and touched the t-shirt he wore—black, with the silver-foil logo of last year's Havoc concert inscribed blazing across the chest. She recognized it as belonging to Tom Bentley, the department's would-be heavy-metal rocker. "If I'd known I might have to share, I'd have picked up something more substantial," he apologized. Then, following her glance to the sleeping Caris, he added, "It hardly seemed fair to escape while he was asleep, at least this time. He would have stayed awake to stand over me if he could; the last twenty-four hours haven't been his fault. In any case I wanted to see the sun rise. I haven't seen that in a long time."

Without the beard that had hidden most of his face when she'd first seen him at the party, he looked, not precisely younger, but more ageless. Joanna guessed his age at about forty, though his hair—an unruly mop, even when whacked off to less than half of its former length—was faded and streaked with gray, like frost-killed weeds. Behind the spectacles, his gray eyes were intelligent, a little daft, and at the same time very gentle. In spite of the bruises on her wrists left by his grip in last night's struggle and the crushed ache of her windpipe, Joanna felt her fear of him subside.

"Look," she said, sitting up cross-legged and shaking the last of the hay out of her hair. "Would it be too much to ask what the hell is going on?"

He regarded her for a moment with wary suspicion in those wide, oddly intent eyes. "Don't you know?"

She sighed. "If I knew, I wouldn't have been scared as spitless as I was last night."

He folded his long hands and looked down at the twined fingers for a moment—mottled with ink, she saw, and, in the slowly growing dawn-light, very white, as if he had spent years without seeing sun. "I suspect you would have been even more so," he said gently. "But it doesn't matter."

"Where are we?" She looked around her at the silent fields and dove-colored pools. "And why have you been stalking me? What kind of crazy game was all that supposed to be last night?"

He tilted his head to one side. "Have you been stalked?"

"I don't know what else to call your—your hunting me in the halls at San Serano."

"It is no game." Stiffly, Caris sat up and threw a quick, resentful glance at Antryg. Sullenly, he wiped his sword on his jacket and then sheathed it with a vicious snick. Pushing his blond, rumpled hair out of his eyes, he looked over at Joanna. "It is hard for you to understand, since there is no magic in your world. But you have been brought over into our world, into the Empire of Ferryth, for what purposes I don't know, by this man. He is Antryg Windrose, a renegade wizard, and I am sworn by my vows to the Council of Wizards to bring him to justice for the evil he has done."

Joanna stared at him for a long moment. "You're crazy," she said.

"No, I'm crazy," Antryg disagreed mildly. "Caris is only confused. And I'm afraid he's right about your not being any longer in your own world. Doesn't the mere smell of the air convince you?"

Joanna hesitated. There were plenty of places in the San Joaquin Valley, for instance, or up north, where smog was seldom smelled—but not, she had to admit, in the summer. And in any case, if she'd been out long enough to be taken there . . . She dug in her purse and found her watch. The readout flashed to the touch of a button—August 30, the day after Gary's party. She dropped it back into the general confusion of the purse and tried to make the times fit. Unless it was like one of those *Mission Impossible* stories in which dates had been meticulously rejiggered to convince someone it was last week or next week . . .

The countryside might have been somewhere in California's Central Valley, from what she could see of it—marshy hayfields before them, silent green hills behind, and the long brown curve of a river in the distance—except there were no mountains, not even as a far-off blue line against the sky.

Beside her, her kidnapper and her rescuer were talking softly. The younger, in spite of his dark and battle-shabby warrior's outfit, was handsome with the Nordic gorgeousness of a prince of fairy tales, save for a straight scar about an inch and a half long that marked a cheekbone straight out of a TV commercial for designer jeans. The scar disturbed Joanna, partly because it was the kind of thing that anyone could have had corrected by plastic surgery—and partly because, in spite of her guess at Caris' age as being less than twenty-one, it looked to be several years old. The jocks she had met had given Joanna a deep distrust of young men that good-looking, but Caris lacked the egocentricity she had so often encountered in the self-proclaimed hunks. It was as if his appearance was entirely peripheral to some greater force that dominated his life.

He was saying, "Why did you bring her to this world?"

Antryg, folding his long arms comfortably around his drawn-up knees, considered the matter gravely for some moments and replied, "I can't imagine. Perhaps Joanna could tell us? Joanna . . . ?"

Annoyed, Caris caught the wizard's shoulder as he started to turn toward her and pulled him back. "Don't play innocent. First you murder Thirle—then you kidnap the Archmage—now this woman. I want to know why."

"I must admit to some curiosity about that myself," Antryg remarked, disengaging his arm from the younger man's crushing grip with no apparent effort. "I should imagine poor Thirle was murdered simply because he had seen the Gate through the Void—or perhaps because he saw who it was who came out."

"Others saw the Gate," said Caris. "I, for one."

"You didn't know what it was, nor its implications."

"Aunt Min did. My grandfather did."

"But by that time, there were other witnesses. It was not simply a matter of silencing one. Joanna my dear, why would someone—let's call it me for talking purposes—have kidnapped you?" He turned those gentle, luminous eyes upon her. "Who and what are you?"

"Be careful," Caris cautioned, as Joanna drew breath to reply. "He's completely mad, but he's clever. He may have brought you here to learn something from you."

"I don't know what," Joanna said, looking in puzzlement from the young man's onyx-dark eyes to the inquiring, bespectacled gray ones. "Even if he wanted a computer programmer for some reason, the woods are full of better ones than I am. But I've been stalked for a week or more . . ." She turned back to Antryg. "What were the marks you made on the walls? You made one at the house, and there was one at San Serano, the night you tried to strangle me there."

"I assure you, my dear," Antryg protested, "It wasn't me."

"And it wasn't you who has been causing the abominations to appear?" Caris demanded sarcastically. "Or who spirited my grandfather away?"

"Of course not."

"His glove was in your room. I saw it there."

"He left it when he visited me earlier in the week."

"He had them with him that evening! I saw them!"

"Both of them?"

"You are lying," Caris said, and his dark-brown eyes were narrow with suspicion and anger. "As you have been lying all along."

"Well, of course I've been lying all along," the wizard argued reasonably. "If the Bishop or anyone else had suspected what happens when the Void is breached . . ."

"What happens?"

Antryg sighed. "It is where the abominations come from," he said. "When a gap is opened in the Void, the whole fabric of it weakens, sometimes for miles around. Yes, I knew that someone was moving back and forth across the Void for months before Thirle was killed. Not every time, but sometimes, when it was breached, a hole would open through to some other world, neither yours nor mine, and something would—wander through. Sometimes to die, without its proper food or protection against unfamiliar enemies, sometimes to find what food it could. I was aware of it, but could do nothing about it, since I could not touch the Void from within the Tower."

"Ha!" Caris said scornfully.

Unperturbed, Antryg went on. "I knew that eventually such a weakening had to take place within the walls of the Tower itself. I could only wait . . . I suppose, if I hadn't been mad already, the waiting would have driven me so."

"You knew this," Caris said softly. "You knew where the abominations came from and yet you did not tell the Archmage of it?"

"What could he have done about it?" Antryg demanded with a sudden, desperate sweep of his arm. "He couldn't have stopped it. And they would only have chained me, to prevent my escape. I'd been in that Tower seven years, Caris. I haven't seen sunlight since before you were sasennan."

Joanna looked up sharply, hearing it then. The word *sasennan* came to her mind as *weapon,* but with a suffix connoting humanness. She understood, for the first time, that the words that she had heard in her mind were not the words that they spoke. She knew, then, that she had passed into some other world, alien to her own.

The brightness of the sunlight of which he had spoken suffused the sky and all the lands around them with pastel glory, flashing like sheet glass on the waters of the meres below. Gray and black geese rose from the rushes in a wimmering flurry of wings. Joanna wasn't sure, but they looked an awful lot like the pictures she'd seen of the extinct Canada goose.

For a long moment she wanted to do nothing except curl up in a fetal position and hide. She felt bleak, sick, and frightened, as hopeless as she had felt when, as a child, she had walked for the first time into a new classroom filled with strangers. She cried, "Why did you bring me here?"

Caris and Antryg fell silent, hearing in her words the frantic demand, not for information, but for comfort.

It was Antryg who spoke, gently, without the indignant protest with which he had answered the sasennan. "I'm sorry, my dear. But truly, it was someone else."

"Can you take me back?"

He was silent for a long time. Then he said, "I'm afraid not. Even as Caris knows that I can't work magic here, because the other mages will know I've escaped and be listening for me, feeling for me along the lines of power that cover the whole of the earth in their net, so I cannot touch the Void now. The—the one who did kidnap you knows you're gone.

That one will be waiting for me to touch the Void again, to find me—to destroy me and you and all of us."

Joanna looked up miserably into the odd, beaky face in its mane of graying hair and noticed for the first time how deep the lines were that webbed around the enormous gray eyes, running down onto the delicate cheekbones like careless chisel scratches and back into the tangled hair.

Sarcastically, Caris said, "Very plausible. Except that, if you did not kidnap her, who did? Even my grandfather, the Archmage, knew little about the Void and its workings; according to him, there *was* no one else." He got to his feet, and walked around to where Joanna huddled in the hay, feeling empty and suddenly chilled. His hand was warm on her bare shoulder. "Don't worry. We'll take him to the House of Mages in Kymil. If necessary Nandiharrow, the Head of the House, will send for the Witchfinders. What he has done has put him outside all protection of the Council. We'll make him tell what he has done with the Archmage—and when we find him, the Archmage will send you home."

CHAPTER IX

IT TOOK THEM UNTIL AFTER DARK TO REACH THE CITY OF KYMIL.

It was one of the longest days Joanna had ever spent—literally; she guessed that Kymil lay well to the north of Los Angeles, but, even though the summer solstice was passed, the days were still very long. Well before the sun was in the sky, they began walking through the luminous world of predawn to which Joanna had always preferred another two hours' communion with her pillow. It had been considerably longer than seven years, she realized somewhat shamefacedly, since she had seen the sun rise.

Antryg was like a child taken into the country for the first time, stopping to contemplate cattails in the marshes below the road or to watch the men and women at work cutting hay. If nothing else could have convinced her that she had truly fallen through a hole in the space-time continuum, Joanna thought with a strange sense of despair, the sight of those peasants at work did. No role player, no matter how dedicated, was going to get out of bed at the crack of dawn and do hard labor in the coarse, awkward, bundly clothes they wore.

But in her heart she needed no convincing. She knew where she was.

"Do you want some sunscreen?" she asked Antryg as they stopped on a wooden bridge over the shining counterpane of marsh and hay meadow to watch the first hard lances of sunlight smite the water beneath them like a sounding of trumpets. "Something to keep you from sunburn?" She dug in the capacious depths of her bottomless bag.

"Thank you." He studied the crumpled tube gravely. "After seven years of living in the dark like a mushroom, right now I'd welcome any kind of natural sensation, but I'm sure I won't feel that way at the end of the day."

Oddly enough, Joanna felt more at ease and able to talk to Antryg, her kidnapper, than to her rescuer. Part of this stemmed from her distrust of extremely good-looking men, part from the fact that Antryg was sublimely relaxed about being a prisoner, far more so than Caris was about having one. Possibly, she thought frivolously, that was simply because he'd had years of practice at it. As she replaced the tube in her bag, Joanna found several Granola bars and offered them to her companions. Caris devoured his like a wolf, but Antryg divided his with the sasennan. "After yesterday, I'm sure he needs it more than I do," he said, as Caris suspiciously took the solidified mass of nuts and raisins from his hand.

"Why?" Joanna asked, glancing curiously from the wizard to the warrior. "What happened yesterday?"

"There was an abomination in the marsh," Caris replied, almost grudgingly. He touched the rip in the shoulder of his jacket and shirt, under which the bruised flesh had turned almost as black as the torn fabric. He glanced across at Antryg as they resumed their walking, the bridge sounding hollowly with their footfalls. "He knew it was there."

"Of course I knew it was there," Antryg responded. "I'd felt the opening of the Void, and you could hardly have gotten bruised that way brawling in a pothouse."

Caris' dark eyes narrowed. "You have an explanation for everything."

Antryg shrugged. "It's been my misfortune to be a good guesser. Would it alleviate your suspicions any if I didn't have an explanation?" He gravely handed the crumpled Granola wrapper back to Joanna. "Tell me one thing, Caris. Who were the other mages abroad the night Thirle was killed?"

The young warrior shifted the scabbard that he held loose and ready in his left hand. "How do you know there were any, if it wasn't you who . . . ?"

"Another guess. Was your grandfather one of them?"

"No." Caris glanced sidelong at the wizard, his eyes filled with suspicion. After a moment, he said, "Lady Rosamund . . ." and paused, with a sudden frown.

"What is it?"

He hesitated a moment, then shook his head. "Nothing. Just that . . . She was up and dressed, literally moments after the shots were fired. Aunt Min's hair was flattened and mussed, as if she'd just risen from her bed. It was as if Lady Rosamund had been up some time before."

"Even as you were," Antryg remarked softly, and Joanna saw the young man look swiftly away. "What wakened you?"

"Nothing," Caris said, his voice curt. "Dreams. Nothing that has to do with Thirle's death."

"Oh, everything has to do with everything." Antryg smiled, shoving his big hands into the pockets of his jeans and kicking at a pebble with one booted foot. "It's one of the first principles of magic."

Joanna looked doubtfully up at him. "By magic, do you mean like pouf-you're-gone magic?"

He grinned. "Yes—in fact, pouf-you're-gone is precisely the question of the moment."

"Then why . . ." She hesitated, then went on. "This is going to sound really stupid, but why don't you use magic to escape?"

Caris looked indignant at the question and started to gesture with his sword; Antryg's grin, like that of a slightly deranged elf, widened.

"Well, two reasons. I believe I can convince Nandiharrow and some of the other mages of the Council to believe my side of the story and, at the moment, I feel I'd be safer as a prisoner of the Council than a fugitive from the Church, which has its own mages. At least the Council will listen to me. And then," he added, more gravely, "if I used magic to escape, the other mages, be they Church or Council, would be able to track me through it eventually."

"You're forgetting the third reason," Caris said grimly. "If you try to escape I will kill you."

"No," Antryg said mildly, "I wasn't forgetting," and Joanna had to turn away to smother a grin.

In contrast to the silent and preoccupied Caris, Antryg had a voracious interest in everything and anything and was, for all his talkativeness, a good listener. Joanna had never been at ease with men; but as they walked along the highroad that ran above the marsh, she found herself telling him, not only about computers and soap operas and the Los Angeles freeway system, but about her mother, Ruth, the cats, and Gary.

"Ah, Gary," he said. "The one with the cruel streak."

She shrugged, guessing he'd been one of the large number of people who'd overheard Gary's remarks about her. "He probably just thought he was being funny."

"I'm sure he did," the wizard said, polishing the spectacles on the hem of his t-shirt. "And that is the worst thing which can be said about him."

It was, but it surprised her a little that anyone, particularly any man, would see it as she did.

The sun rose to noon, and Caris negotiated with some of the hay cutters to buy a portion of their bread and ale, which the three ate sitting on a half-rotted willow log beside one of the gnat-swarming meres. Joanna found the bread harsh and strong-tasting and sprinkled through with grain hulls and specks of dirt. *So much,* she thought, picking a morsel of grit from between her teeth, *for the good old days of the old mill by the stream.* "Can't you do anything about this?" she inquired, glancing up at Antryg, who was contentedly downing his share of the ale. "I mean, you're a wizard—you should be able to turn this into quiche lorraine."

"It doesn't work that way." Antryg half turned to offer the flask to Caris, who, even when eating, stood behind him, one hand never far from the hilt of his sword. Caris shook his head, and the wizard passed it to Joanna. The ale was sweeter than the beer she was used to and considerably above the California limitations on alcohol content. "I could use magic to convince you that you were eating quiche; but when all was said and done, it would be bread in your stomach; and when the spell wore off, you'd still have sand in your teeth. There are wizards and spells which can convert one thing to another—real bread into actual quiche or into gold, for that matter—but they require so much power and take so much strength from the one who casts them that it's really simpler just to change millers."

"Not to mention," Caris said quietly from behind them, "that such meddling in even the smallest of human affairs is forbidden."

"Well," Antryg agreed blithely, "there is that."

Caris' face darkened with disapproval, and Joanna, glancing sideways at Antryg, caught the flicker of his smile and wondered suddenly how much of what he said he believed—and how much was simply to get a rise out of his captor.

They had come, Caris said at one point during the long afternoon, from the far southeastern corner of the Ponmarish, where it touched the hills of the Sykerst. It was a long walk up the southward road to the gates of the city. There were few peasants in this portion of the marsh, and what few there were, Joanna noticed, worked hard and closer together than their tasks warranted. They appeared nervous, glancing over their shoulders. Poaching hay illegally? she wondered. On the lookout for the hay police? But by that time she was too exhausted and footsore to ask. The daylong walk, though it was not fast, was extremely tiring. She was a thin girl, but she had done no more strenuous walking in the last several years than was necessary to get from her car in the San Serano parking lot to her office, and by the end of the afternoon she felt a kind of wondering resentment about Caris' tireless, changeless stride. Antryg, she noticed, was more considerate—perhaps because it had been years since he, too, had done any great amount of travel. Caris only fretted and muttered that they would not reach the city before dark.

And it was, in fact, long after darkness had settled on the land that they walked through the sleeping streets of the warm, flat, mosquito-humming city, with its carved wooden balconies and brick-paved alleys that smelled of sewage and fish. The city was walled on its land side, though, in the flickering red torchlight of the enormous gateway, Joanna had gotten the impression that the gates themselves hadn't been closed in years. Caris roused a sleepy gatekeeper and rented a torch, which illuminated the tepid darkness of the narrow streets along which they passed. Down a side lane Joanna glimpsed the bent form of an old man, whose elaborately braided hair and beard would have trailed to his knees had the complicated loops of braid been undone, pushing a cart while he shoveled up the copious by-products of what was obviously a horse-dependent civilization. For the rest, the streets were quiet at this hour—Kymil, thought Joanna, scarcely qualifying as the Las Vegas of the Empire of Ferryth.

The House of the Mages lay a moonlit chiaroscuro of ice-gray and velvet black, gargoyle-decorated balconies and windows unlighted and silent, like an anesthetized dragon. Under the carved wooden turrets of the main door, a bonfire had been kindled on the flagway, and four sasenna sat around it, muttering amongst themselves and glancing worriedly about them at the dark.

In the mouth of the narrow lane, Caris stopped and swiftly doused his torch in a convenient rain barrel. Antryg, too, had flattened into the shadows along the wall. For a long moment, they looked out into the dim and mingled glows of moonlight and firelight in the square. Then Caris said softly, "Those are Church sasenna."

Antryg nodded, his spectacles gleaming dimly with the reflected brightness. With a slight gesture, he signaled them back into the alley; Joanna, mystified, followed him and Caris as they wove through a noisome alley where pigs grunted down below the cellar gratings of the narrow houses and around to another side of the square.

There was a smaller side door there. In that, too, armed men sat waiting, huddled more closely about the brazier of coals than the balmy night demanded. Caris glanced up at the tall wizard, his eyes suddenly filled with concern. In an undervoice softer than the murmur of the winds from the marshes, he breathed, "There are no lights in the house."

"Not even in the sasenna's quarters," Antryg murmured in reply.

Moonlight touched the tip of his long nose and made a fragile halo of the ends of his hair as he put his head a little beyond the dense shadows in which they stood, then drew it back. Beside them, Joanna could feel, as if she touched the two men, the tension that went through them as they found their common enemy guarding the doors of the house.

Caris said, "It's a good guess there aren't guards inside, then." He glanced around at the black cutouts of oddly shaped roofs against the velvet sky. "No wonder the neighborhood's so silent. They can't have . . ." He hesitated.

"You yourself said that the danger of the abominations abrogated my right to protection by the Council," Antryg murmured, leaning one hand against the coarse, dirty plaster of the nearest wall and looking out into the silent square. "Perhaps the Church came to the same conclusion?"

"Come on," the sasennan said quietly. "We can get over the wall of the garden court—it backs onto the next alley."

That, Joanna thought wryly a few moments later, had to be one of the Great Traditions of literature and cinema: "We can get in over the wall." Staring up, appalled, at the seven-foot paling of reinforced cedar and pine, she felt the sensation of having been cheated by three generations of fictional heroes and heroines who could effortlessly scramble up and over eight-foot, barbed wire fences without breaking sweat or scraping off their shirt buttons as they bellied over the top.

And more than that, she felt weak and stupid, as she had all the way through high school, laboring wretchedly along in the distant wake of the class jocks and wishing she were dead.

"There's a footing shelf on the inside where the beam holds the palings," Antryg whispered. "Caris, you go up first and I'll lift her to you."

Caris, no more than an indistinct shape in the revolting darkness of the alley, turned his head sharply, and Joanna saw the silvery glint of narrowed eyes.

"I'm not going to run from you the minute you're occupied going up the wall," the mage added impatiently. "As much as you do, I've got to find out what's happened."

Caris started to make a reply to this, then let out his breath unused. Without a word, he turned, took a running start at the wall, and used it as a momentum to spring for the top and carry himself over.

"How did you know there was a footing on the beam?" Joanna asked as she approached the base of the wall and saw the sasennan's catlike silhouette crouched against the slightly paler darkness of trees and roofs. "Another lucky guess?"

"No. Up until seven years ago I was a—well, not perfectly respected—

member of the community of wizards." The moonlight checkered through the trees beyond the garden wall and silvered the lenses of his specs and the foil HAVOC on his t-shirt. His hands on her waist were large and warm and, as she recalled them on her wrists when they'd struggled, surprisingly strong for his rather gawky appearance. "Up you get."

Joanna had always hated heights, hated exercise, and hated having to do things she couldn't do. Her hands scraped and riven through with splinters, she hauled herself gasping to the top of the wall, half-expecting Caris' mockery, even as the young man steadied her over. But he simply helped her down, following like a stalking cat into the pungent, laurel-scented darkness of the tiny garden. A moment later, the wall vibrated softly under Antryg's weight, and he dropped like a spider at their side.

"Can we risk a light?" he breathed as they entered the dark arches of a very short wooden colonnade that bounded the garden. "The nearest door's around the corner. That should be the barracks in through there."

Caris nodded. Joanna was about to dig into her purse to proffer a match when Antryg made a slight movement with his hand and opened it, releasing a tiny ball of bluish light which rose from his palm and floated a few feet in front of him, about the level of his chest. His grin at the look on her face in the faint phosphorescence was like that of a pleased imp.

Joanna said softly, "I'm not even going to ask." She had, she realized, just seen magic.

"That's just as well. Nobody's ever come up with a satisfactory answer, except the obvious one."

"In here," Caris murmured from the blackness of a small, half-open door.

Through an open archway to her right, Joanna had a glimpse of a vast room, with moonlight flooding through long windows to lie like sheets of white silk over a disorder of upended trestle tables and fallen benches. In the room to which Caris beckoned them the disorder was worse. All along its narrow length, furniture had been tipped over, books pulled from the shelves that lined one wall, and strange brass instruments— sextants, astrolabes, celestial globes—had been hurled to the floor and lay like twisted skeletons, glinting faintly in the moonlight. The line of wooden pillars that bisected the narrow room and supported an even narrower gallery above it threw bizarre shadows on the intricate inlay of the cabinets that shared with the bookcases the long inner wall.

"It's the Church, all right," Caris muttered soundlessly as he tiptoed the length of the disordered room, opening and closing cabinets as he went. "Only they would have destroyed like this."

The ball of witchlight drifting along before his feet, Antryg picked his way after the sasennan through the mess, turning over the torn and scattered volumes. "They were in a hurry," he murmured. He paused to stoop, and Joanna saw, by the dim pallor of the witchlight, the black stains of tacky-dry blood on his fingers. "Nandiharrow," he whispered. "Now I wonder why . . . ?"

Caris turned from one of the cabinets, a pistol in his hand pointed at Antryg's chest. "Come over here," he said.

Antryg stood perfectly still for one moment, and Joanna prudently moved to Caris's side to be out of any possible line of fire.

"And don't think you can fix the aim on it, or cause it to misfire," the sasennan went on. "It's na-aar. Joanna, there are chains in the cabinet behind me—get them out."

Joanna's liking for the mad wizard caused her to hesitate for only a moment before obeying. The chains were light, iron rather than steel, and equipped with bracelets and locks.

"Look," Antryg argued, "this isn't necessary."

"Put your arms around the pillar there. Joanna . . ."

Keeping warily out of firing line, she fitted the heavy manacles around Antryg's wrists and pushed them shut. They locked with a cold click. Caris came over and checked them briefly, then nodded to himself, satisfied.

"Caris, don't be a fool. . . ."

"I'm not being a fool." The sasennan stepped quietly away from him, his pistol still trained on Antryg's chest. "And I am not sure whether my duty does not lie in killing you here and now. I don't know what happened, but the mages in Angelshand and other places have to be warned. . . ."

"You are being a fool if you think that, even traveling by fast horse, you could warn them in time," Antryg retorted. "The Church has mages who may swear they don't communicate by scrying-stones, but we all know they do. If the Bishop has gotten permission from the Regent to order the arrest of the mages, it's because she has convinced him that your grandfather somehow spirited me away from the Tower for sinister plots of his own. That order will apply everywhere in Ferryth. You know Herthe. You know she'll have no compunction about violating every Church rule about the use of magic for what she considers a righteous cause."

"Little suspecting," Caris said softly, "that it is the other way around."

He stepped forward and put the pistol barrel to Antryg's temple. "Was that your intention all along? To use the Bishop as cat's-paw to dispose of the other wizards, once you had made sure my grandfather wouldn't be there to stop her? Or was that only fortuitous circumstance? Was that why you were so unconcerned about being my prisoner? Why you wanted so desperately to get us away from where I found Joanna—from where you were holding the Archmage . . . ?"

Antryg, his head trapped between the gun muzzle and the turned wood of the pillar to which he was chained, gazed straight ahead of him; but in the faint witchlight Joanna could see the sweat that suddenly beaded his face. "I had nothing to do with it."

The gun lock clicked, loud in the darkness, as Caris thumbed back the hammer. "Where is my grandfather?"

"They'll be in here in a minute asking you that," the wizard said calmly, "if you pull that trigger. And I'm certainly not going to be able to tell them."

For a long, frozen second Joanna held her breath, knowing that, frustrated, furious, and at sea in a wholly unprecedented situation, Caris would have liked nothing better than simply to pull the trigger in revenge for Antryg's having put him in such a position. Under the film of sweat, moonlight, and travel grime, she saw the young sasennan's jaw muscles harden and heard the deep rasping draw of his breath. Then he lowered the pistol, still breathing hard, and looked uncertainly towards the window, where the reflected firelight from the gates outside stained the bull's-eye glass.

Only Joanna saw Antryg briefly close his eyes with relief.

"Look, Caris," she said diffidently. "I don't know whether I get a vote in this or not, but if all the wizards have been arrested, and if your grandfather's gone, he *is* my only way of getting back home." Caris turned towards her, his agate-brown eyes glinting with the intolerant impatience of a strong man listening to the specious arguments of the weak, but Joanna took a deep breath and went on, "I don't know too much about the Church here, but I think, if the Church gets its hands on him, you may never locate your grandfather, either. I mean, if I were the Church and I'd just busted every wizard in the country, I wouldn't try too hard to get the Archmage back into action."

There was a long silence while Caris thought about that, and then something changed in his eyes. "No," he said quietly. "You're right, Joanna—however it came about, it's an opportunity the Church won't let pass by." He was quiet for a moment more. Joanna guessed that, for all his skill as a line fighter, he had never been required to think out the larger strategies for himself. He sighed and rubbed the inner corners of his eyes with his free hand, and some of the desperate tension relaxed from his broad shoulders.

"I'm sorry," he added quietly. "This world must be almost as bad for you to be stranded in as yours was for me."

Almost! thought Joanna, with indignant astonishment. *It isn't my world that has the Inquisition and ankledeep horse manure in the streets! Of course,* she added ruefully, *we do have the bomb and the 405 Freeway.* . . .

"It's just that . . ." he began—and stopped himself abruptly from admitting to an exhaustion that it was not the Way of the Sasenna to take into consideration and a love for the old Archmage that it was not the Way of the Sasenna to feel. After a moment he said, "I think the best thing we can do now is to go to Angelshand. The other members of the Council . . ."

"Have either been arrested or are hiding in the deepest holes they can find," Antryg finished. The hammered iron of the chainlinks made a soft clinking against the wood of the pillar as he clasped his big hands around it, almost encircling it with the span of his fingers. "The Bishop will have sent word to the Bishop of Angelshand. They'll have the Regent's consent to the arrests by the first post."

"Then we shall go to the Regent," Caris said stubbornly. "Narwahl Skipfrag is a friend of Grandfather's. He can get the Regent's ear long enough for me to explain the truth of what happened. And after that, the Witchfinders may have you, for all of me."

"Ah," murmured the mage, leaning against the pillar. "But what is the truth?"

Caris' face hardened in the zebra moonlight. "The truth," he returned, equally quietly, "is what the Witchfinders will have out of you." He turned to Joanna and handed her the pistol. "Watch him," he said. "I'm going to have a look around before we leave." Turning, he strode away down the long moonlit room and out into the darkness of the refectory beyond.

Antryg sighed and rested his forehead against the pillar, rubbing his long fingers, as if to banish the ghost of some old pain.

As well as she could, keeping the pistol in hand, Joanna righted one of the chairs, heavy black oak with waffle-crossed straps of leather nailed for a seat, and found a cushion in a corner to put on it to sit down. Her legs were immediately enveloped in a vast rush of pins and needles, and she felt she never wanted to stand up again. After a moment, she asked curiously, "If you're a wizard, can't you just break the locks?"

He looked up at her with a tired smile. "I could," he said. "That is, I could open them—they aren't na-aar, metaphysically dead, like the pistol. But the Church has its wizards, too. By this time, they will know I am free and they will be listening, smelling the air for magic, like the terwed-weeds beneath the sea that scent the tiniest ripple of the passing fish that are their prey. They would know and they would come. And then, too . . ." He paused, thought about it, and let the sentence go unfinished.

Very gingerly, Joanna folded her legs up under her—at five-feet-almost tall, no chair was particularly comfortable without an accompanying footstool. "But weren't you their prisoner before?"

"I was the Council's prisoner, in the custodianship of the Church. The Archmage . . ." He hesitated on the title, then went on, "The Archmage fought for my life."

"Caris' grandfather?"

He nodded. "Salteris Solaris, yes."

She frowned a little, her dark, feathery brows pulling together over her nose. "The one you made away with?"

"I did not make away with him," Antryg insisted doggedly. "I never saw him. He never came there." But he looked away from her as he spoke.

There followed a long silence. In the balmy warmth of the night, she wasn't cold, but all the cumulative aches of the day were beginning to stiffen her unaccustomed muscles, and she had a headache from hunger —bread, cheese, and beer ten hours ago didn't, she reflected, have a great deal of staying power. It was Sunday night. *Well,* she sighed inwardly, *you didn't want to go to work on Monday and here you are.* But even as she smiled to herself, she shivered.

She hadn't wanted to go to work Monday because she had known that she was being stalked. And here she was, with the stalker—where? And more than that . . .

"Why?" she asked softly. "Why me? I've asked you that before. . . ."

Antryg looked over at her again and smiled gently. "My dear Joanna," he said, "if I knew that, I would feel a good deal happier."

Then suddenly he raised his head, listening to the silence of that hushed and darkened house. "What . . ." Joanna began, and he raised his fingers for silence. Strain her ears as she would, she could hear nothing but the faint sough of the leaves of the courtyard trees beyond the arched door and, from somewhere far-off over the wall, the dismal singsong of a kindling-seller's cry. The faint, bluish gleam of Antryg's witchlight died, and, like nocturnal hunters encouraged by the death of the light, the shadows seemed to creep forward around them.

In a voice no louder than the brush of a scrap of silk over footworn stone, Antryg whispered, "The Witchfinders."

Joanna knew better than to try projecting a sound that soft—she slid from her chair as noiselessly as she could and stood near enough to him that she could smell the lingering scents of hay and last night's cigarette smoke in his clothes. "I don't hear anything." She did not even vocalize the sounds, but he breathed a reply.

"At the far side of the house. They have Caris. There will be a key in the top drawer of the desk—Nandiharrow always kept it there."

Joanna hesitated. She had, after all, heard nothing herself. Caris would kill her if she let herself be tricked, particularly by something this simple. Presumably, someone like Sam Spade could just narrow his eyes and snarl confidently, "You're lying, Merlin," but Joanna had never figured out how to intuit that accurately. Trying to pitch her voice as soundlessly as she could, she asked, "Why would the Witchfinders want Caris?"

He closed his eyes and rested his forehead against the wooden pillar, listening to sounds that, try as she would, she could not hear. "They want the Archmage. They think he knows . . . Get the key!" he urged, with soundless urgency, his gray eyes opening wide, and added, when Joanna wavered, "I swear it isn't a trick! Caris . . ."

She held up her hand for silence, as he had done, and whispered, "I'll see."

He opened his mouth protestingly, but she had already turned away, and he knew better than to make any further sound.

It was perhaps that which half convinced her, even before she slipped into the darkness of the refectory across the court and heard the soft voices there. An inveterate reader of spy novels, she followed every half-remembered precept, moving along the wall so that floorboards would not creak, not to mention there being less chance of tripping over miscellaneous furniture along the wall. A nervous, orange reflection of firelight outlined a door behind what must have been the high table and picked out the shining lip of a turned-wood bowl and the metal edge of a tankard, fallen amid a great red stain of dried wine. She caught an indistinct murmur of sound, fought back her instincts to hurry and tested every step. By the time she reached the doorway she could make out the voices.

"My grandfather had nothing to do with his escape! He would have prevented it if he could!"

"Either the Sigil of Darkness works or it doesn't, boy," a thin, cold voice said, chill and poisonous as crimes committed for righteousness' sake. "If Antryg Windrose had the ability to spirit the Archmage away, the Archmage would have been able to prevent him from doing so."

Very cautiously, Joanna lowered herself to her hands and knees, so as to be below eye level, carefully keeping the pistol she held from knocking against the floor, and peeked around the edge of the door. After the soft, moony radiance in the refectory, the low redness of the hearth fire seemed bright. The room had clearly been the library; its half-emptied shelves were littered with torn and fallen books, and others lay thrown in the corners or had been heaped in the fireplace to provide such dim illumination as the room had. Caris was tied to a high-backed chair of spindled wood before the low blaze. Even in the wickering light, Joanna could see the fresh bruise livid on his cheek and the blood on his lip. His sword and three daggers glinted on the table behind them. Beyond, in the shadows, stood three sasenna in somber variations of Caris' torn and stained black uniform. Like a shadow himself against the firelight, a thin man stood in a narrow-cut gray suit, his lank gray hair falling down over a turned-over collar of white linen. His hands were behind his back— small, hard, lean hands, white as the bands of his cuffs and, like them, dyed red with the gory light of the flame. When he turned his face sidelong to the fire, Joanna caught a glimpse of lean, regular features that indicated he had probably been handsome in his youth, before the habit of self-righteousness had bracketed the thin lips with lines of perpetual disapproval. Another man in a similar suit of close-fitting gray stood beside him; it was to him that first one said softly, "When he tells us where the man Antryg is, take two of the sasenna and kill him. We can't afford these waters muddied."

The other man nodded, as if agreeing that, yes, mad dogs ought to be killed; an agreement that was self-evident. "And him?"

The Witchfinder glanced casually back at Caris. "Oh, him too, of course—but after we've learned where Salteris might be. We have most of the great ones, save that one alone—if this boy is his grandson, we may be able to use him as bait."

It was not so much the words he said that affected Joanna, but the way they were spoken, the soft, insidious voice calmly matter-of-fact, as if it were not people at all of whom he spoke. As soundlessly as she could, she backed away, more afraid of being detected and of having that voice speak to her than she had been of anything, even of waking up in the darkness with the print of the strangler's hands on her throat.

Antryg was watching the door with concern in his eyes when she glided back in. The tension relaxed from his shoulders when he saw it was she, but he neither sighed nor, she noticed, moved his hands from where they had been, lest the links of the chain make even the slightest noise. If he, a wizard, could hear the voices on the other side of the refectory, it stood to reason he feared that there were Church wizards there, too, listening for any untoward sounds. After a moment's debate, she shoved the heavy pistol into her purse and slung the unwieldy bag up onto her shoulder again. As she gentled the drawer from the desk, she wondered whether Caris would tell them—or would he realize that, once that soft-voiced man got his hands on Antryg, Caris would never have the chance to find out where the Archmage was or what, if anything, Antryg had done with him?

She came back, key in hand, and touched her finger to her lips for silence. Then she pulled Antryg's t-shirt up over his head and down his arms, to muffle the iron of the lock as she twisted the key. She gestured toward the door and looked a question.

"Peelbone," he breathed, with almost telepathic quiet. "Witchfinder Extraordinary—special branch of the Church." His hands freed, he pulled the t-shirt into place and shook his hair back, crystal earrings glinting in the moonlight, and straightened his specs. "An ideal man for his job but gets invited to very few dinner parties—not that he would ever accept, mind you. I wonder why it is that dyspepsia and righteousness go so often hand-in-hand?"

"Perhaps it's what they mean when they say that virtue is its own punishment?" returned Joanna, equally soundlessly, following Antryg through a small door partially shielded by a torn curtain and into a ransacked workroom.

The room faced opposite the direction of the moon and was almost completely lightless; a droplet of luminescence no bigger than an apple seed floated like a firefly behind Antryg's shoulder, edging his long, nervous hands and preposterous nose in a thin slip of silver as he moved from cupboard to cupboard.

"As I thought," he whispered. "The Bishop's guards came through and sacked the place but didn't take anything away. Afraid to, probably. I wonder the Witchfinders had the nerve to enter the place when they heard Caris moving about." As he spoke, he was drawing things from cupboards—two packets of powders, a mechanical implement that looked like a wind-up toy, and a small box tied tightly shut. Joanna, nervously aware that the small room constituted a cul-de-sac and the one window was far too narrow to admit even her, kept glancing over her shoulder into the barred and dappled shadows of the study beyond.

"We have to help him," she whispered, forgetting entirely that Antryg had every reason not to do so.

"If he's in the hands of the Witchfinders that goes without saying," he replied, the seed of light warming infinitesimally as he bent over the clockwork mechanism, disconnecting a gear and rod arrangement.

Joanna peered worriedly past his shoulder at it. "What is it? It looks like the innards of a clock."

"It is. Like most mages, Nandiharrow was interested in other things besides pure magic—whatever that may be. This is actually a musicbox mechanism run by a clock spring. . . . You didn't happen to bring along my chains, did you, my dear?"

Joanna shook her head, mystified; he *tch*ed under his breath as if she'd forgotten to bring money on a shopping trip and handed her a rag from a corner of the bench. She paused for a moment, hating the silent checkerwork of moonlight and shadow in the room outside and sensing through her skin the shortness of time. Having come in and found Caris, the Witchfinders would be fanning out through the building; it was only a matter of time until she and Antryg were discovered. Moving as quickly as she could without making any noise, she stepped over to the chair where she'd been sitting and where she had put the chains, covered them with the rag, and brought them in, cushion and all. As she did so, she felt, more than heard, the muffled tread of approaching feet on the refectory floor, and it was all she could do to keep from breaking into a run back to the workroom.

"They're coming," she breathed.

He nodded and moved soundlessly to the far wall, passing his hand swiftly down it as she had seen him do in Gary's computer room when the wizard's mark swam into brief, silvery life under his sensitive fingers. This time it was no mark that appeared, but a slit of still deeper black in the shadows. He pushed gently, and a segment of the wall fell back; the tiny light that burned above his head drifted forward to illuminate a very narrow flight of worn and mended steps. He paused, then handed her the clockwork, packets, and box; and to her speechless horror, he turned swiftly and vanished back into the darkness of the study. A moment later he was back beside her, shoving a small wash-leather bag into the pocket of his jeans.

"What is it?" she whispered as he led her into the secret stair.

"Money," he breathed. "Nandiharrow always cached the House funds under the bottom shelf of the bookcase. We'll need it come morning."

"For what?" They were ascending the stairs—wood, like everything else in that rambling house, and so narrow there was not even enough slack to creak under their weight.

"Breakfast, of course. I'm starving. Do you have anything like thread or string about you, my dear?"

Silently, Joanna fished into her purse and produced her sewing kit; Antryg swiftly unraveled about five feet of thread and tied one end to the middle of the chain, the other to some projection of the clockwork mechanism he had taken. Very carefully he cranked it tight. Joanna could hear the swift firm stride somewhere below now; she shivered.

"Right," he whispered. "Would you take the chains down a few steps, my dear? Thank you. Just set them down on the step." He made an adjustment on the clockwork, stood up, and held out his hand to her. She came back to him, careful not to step on the taut thread, and picked up her purse where she'd left it beside him. The weight of it reminded her of the pistol—he could have easily taken it and used it against her, but the thought didn't seem to have crossed his mind. He pushed open another panel in the blackness, and then they were in a long upstairs colonnade, with moonlight slanting through a series of windows that barred the wall to their right in molten silver and lay like pearl stepping-stones along the worn oak of the pegged floor.

Antryg shut the panel behind them; Joanna thought it blended invisibly with the linenfold of the walls, but in the uncertain light, it was difficult to tell where even unhidden doors lay. Taking her hand, he led her with that same catfooted tread along close to the wall. They were halfway down the hall when Joanna heard, faint but audible, the soft bump and clink of the chain.

"The secret stair's like a sound tunnel," Antryg whispered as they reached the far end of the gallery. "You can't tell where the noise is coming from. The music box pegs should pluck at the taut thread intermittently enough to keep them looking awhile yet."

"How do you know about all this?" Shifting the weight of her purse, always considerable and now aggravated by five pounds of metaphysically dead iron, Joanna followed him down a broad flight of steps at the end of the hall, toward a darkness like a velvet well beneath.

"I told you, I used to stay in this house all the time. There are few enough of the mageborn in the world these days—whatever we think of one another, we are all acquainted." He halted again, this time in the embrasure of one of the stairway windows; for a moment Joanna could see him, like a gangly black spider against the light that picked a steely line along his spectacle-frames and made the lenses gleam like opal when he turned his head. She saw the glint of something in his hands and realized it was the box he'd taken from the workroom.

"It's fortunate for us," he went on, still in that soft, subvocal whisper, "that since I cannot use my own magic, I can borrow someone else's. There." He pocketed something—Joanna could see that it was the string that had tied the lid shut. "Whatever you think is happening," he went on softly, "don't turn aside—just follow me. All right?"

She nodded and took a deep breath. "All right."

He smiled at her in the moonlight in a way that made her remind herself firmly that he was the villain of the piece. "Good girl." Turning, he hurled the box outside into the darkness of the garden. Then he caught her hand and started to hasten silently down the stairs.

They had gone three steps when Joanna heard it, and her heart caught and twisted within her. Shocking in the alien night, Gary's voice had a frantic note to it that would have brought her up short but for the insistent drag of that powerful hand on her wrist. "Joanna! *Joanna!*"

There was some kind of commotion below—she heard Caris' voice cry *"No!"* and the scuffling crash of something falling. Antryg halted short, forcing her to stop, as two men in the black uniforms of sasenna raced past the foot of the stairs. A second later, she heard the crashing of their feet in the garden outside; already Antryg was dragging her down the stairs, and she was stumbling to keep up with his longer stride.

In the ransacked library, Caris was struggling wildly against his bonds, desperation and fury in his face. "Grandfather's out there!" he shouted, as Antryg scooped one of the daggers from the table. "I have to . . . !"

"It's a Crier." Red light slipped along the blade as the wizard slashed the bonds; he caught Caris by his torn jacket and sword belt as the young man lunged for the garden doors. "An illusion of summoning—Come on!"

"But . . ." Shaken Caris might have been, but not so shaken that he forgot to snatch his weapons from the table as they passed.

"It's true, I heard Gary's voice," Joanna panted. They were already on the run for the window. Footfalls pounded behind them on the oak of the corridor floors. Antryg kicked open the leaded casement of the window and swung through; Joanna scrambled next, still hanging onto her purse, and dropping a surprising distance into a pair of strong hands.

Antryg was already hauling her back into the shiny, green-black thicket of a camellia bush as Caris dropped from the window; in the tepid night air, the scent of the waxy white blossoms hung thick around them. Caris ducked back to join them, still shoving a last dagger into his boot, the bruise on his face showing up horribly against the exhausted grayness of his skin. Joanna thought about going over the fence again, and her every stiff and aching muscle whined in protest, but the thought of the cool, self-righteous voice of the Witchfinder brought the cold sweat of fear to her face. Remembering it and those chilled and empty eyes, she no longer questioned how an animal could bite off a foot to escape a trap.

Caris whispered, "They're outside, waiting for us to come over." Indeed, beyond the garden wall, she could hear men shouting in the street. With his teeth, Antryg ripped a corner from one of the sacks of powder and dumped a little into his palm, then did the same with the other. Shoving the sacks into the pocket of his jeans, he pulled a camellia from the dark shrubs around them and ground the white blossom into the mixture.

With a quick glance back at the window above them, he threw the blossom over the fence. Just as it crested the top of the wood, it burst into violent flame. Shouting rose beyond the palings and from the room they had just left. As Antryg dragged her away Joanna could see the sasenna who had run past the base of the stairs leaning from the window, pointing excitedly at the fireball. Running feet pounded the pavement outside the fence.

Very calmly, Antryg opened a small door that led back into the house and led the way at a swift walk down a short, darkened hall, across the ghostly moonlight of a rather bare reception room, and out one of the great doors and into the street outside.

There were no guards. Their abandoned brazier still flickered on the pavement, but Joanna could see them pelting around the corner towards the smoldering glare, their huge, jumping shadows thrown on the tall primrose and blue fronts of the houses opposite. His arm protectively around Joanna's shoulders, Antryg walked unhurriedly across the cobbled square and on into the concealing darkness of the nearest lane, with Caris trailing silently at his heels.

CHAPTER X

"YOU'RE A FOOL." CARIS CAST A NERVOUS GLANCE AROUND THE EAT-
ing house of the Bashful Unicorn as a stout, red-faced serving-woman in
a greasy apron brought a platter of stew and breads to the table. "We
could have been long on the road by this time."

"No matter how quickly we'd gotten on the road, the patrols looking
for us would have been mounted." Antryg gravely poured ale from the
earthenware jug for the three of them, the grimy, orange glow of the
solitary lamp overhead glancing along his spectacles. "Even the ones who
remained behind to search the quarter of the Old Believers, under the
impression that they'd be likelier to shelter fugitive mages, would never
dare risk being caught in a tavern, should their captain ride by." He
raised his dented tankard in a toast. "Confusion to our common foe."

Caris paused, tankard in hand. "Have we one?"

"I'm sure we do, if we look hard enough." The mage smiled. "Or
should we say, 'To the Emperor's good health'?"

Across the dining room, a well-heeled young man in a mint-green satin
court coat slumped forward across the table amid empty bottles and
glasses; the two painted strumpets with him instantly ceased their up-
roarious appreciation of his jokes and got down to the serious business of
relieving him of his valuables. In the street outside, the first clattering of
the market carts and the crowing of cocks in a thousand backyard hen
coops could be heard.

Caris drained his mug in silent disapproval. Joanna, sitting between
the two men on the hard, backless bench, mopped her bread in the stew.
Worried as she was about remaining in Kymil after daybreak, she could

not help being glad Antryg had vetoed immediate flight on the grounds that they wouldn't get any breakfast.

From their escape from the House of the Mages, Antryg had led them, illogically enough, to an all-night public bathhouse. "Who'd think of looking for fugitives from the Witchfinders in the public baths?"—an argument Joanna found cogent and Caris dismissed as utterly frivolous. Emerging clean, shampooed, and gasping from the cedar-lined sweatbox with its bubbling tub, Joanna found a bundle of secondhand petticoats, blue skirt, pink bodice, and shift that Antryg had acquired from an old clothes dealer next door. "There must be more old clothes dealers in the quarter of the Old Believers than in the rest of the city put together," Caris had told her, when they'd met Antryg in the tavern, the sasennan looking uncomfortable and not very convincing in a peasant's knee breeches, woolen stockings, and coarse smock. "They all go into the trade and stay open till all hours."

Antryg had been waiting for them, his graying hair close-curled with dampness, resplendent in a much-mended shirt of ruffled lawn that was far too big for him and a rusty black court coat whose silver bullion embroidery had long since been picked out. He'd retained the jeans and harness boots he'd picked up at the party and had added to his crystal earrings an assortment of gimcrack bead necklaces and a cracked quizzing glass. "You might be prepared to take the road like a wolf in winter," he added, gesturing with his tankard at Caris, "but I'm not, and Joanna certainly isn't. By daybreak, the men who have been out combing the roads will be tired, and there will be enough people about so that we won't draw too much attention to ourselves."

Caris glanced at Antryg's attire, sniffed, and said nothing. Joanna had the distinct impression that Caris knew very well he was no longer the leader of the expedition, but wasn't entirely sure either how this had come to pass or what to do about it. Antryg was, nominally at least, still his prisoner—only with the Council of Wizards gone or in hiding, there was nowhere Caris could take his prisoner for the moment. There was a good deal of dour frustration in his mien as he watched the wizard spooning honey onto bread.

"Very useful stuff, honey," Antryg was saying. "Did you know the Mellidane scholars make a decoction of it to preserve embryos for study, as well as use it as a base for poultices?" He cocked his head a little, considering the thick, liquid-amber stream dripping from the spoon. "The ancient Saariens said it was the tears of the goddess Helibitare and mixed it with myrrh and gold and offerings—and it has other uses as well. You're aware, of course, that the guards at the city gates will be looking for the Archmage's sasennan who slew the abomination in the swamp? And they'll certainly be looking for that."

Caris shied back from the touch of Antryg's finger as the mage flicked the purpling bruise on his cheek. "My cloak has a hood."

"And terribly convincing in midsummer it is, too." The mage sighed, sliding a few spare rolls into the capacious pockets of his coat.

"Did you really?" Joanna looked a little shyly up at Caris, remembering the mottled, hideous bruises she had seen on his chest and arms through the torn cloth of his jacket. "Slay it?" It felt strange to say. Nobody she had ever known had ever killed anything larger than a cockroach—or admitted to doing so, anyway.

"Not really," the sasennan said, pausing in his rapid and efficient consumption of a hunk of beef. "My grandfather slew it. He caused lightning to strike the water of the swamp—lightning that is in truth electricity. . . . Do you have electricity, in your world?" he added.

"Sure." Joanna dished herself out a second platter of stew and picked the trailing ends of her bodice lacings out of the gravy. The food made her feel much better, as had the bath. She had been twenty-four hours without sleep, much of it on her feet, either running or walking. It occurred to her suddenly to wonder whether Antryg had taken that into account in his erratic choice of a hiding place. "Our whole world runs on electricity—everything's powered by it, just about. Lights, radio, television, computers, you name it."

"That music?" Caris asked, a little sourly.

"Particularly music—although, mind you, I think it's an insult to Johann Sebastian Bach to call that stuff music. But we won't go into that. The instruments are electric; they're electronically synthesized and electronically recorded and played back. The only human things involved are the group who plays and the guy who wrote it, and even those are being computerized these days."

Across the room the two sluts rose and departed, leaving their incapacitated Romeo amid the beer mugs. The moving gust of air from the opening door made the brownish shadows jump over Caris' elegant cheekbones and nose as he glanced automatically up to make sure no one else entered. It was gray dawn outside, lightening towards day. Though reeking of garbage and horses, the air smelled fresher than the dark and beery frowst inside.

"Record . . ." He looked back at her dubiously. "So that it can be reproduced at any time, you mean?"

Joanna nodded. "But you have the same thing. The—Crier, did you call it?" She glanced across at Antryg in time to see him cache the squat black bottle of gin he'd ordered in one of his copious coat pockets.

"Not really," the wizard said. "The Crier doesn't record a sound, but an emotional reaction which you associate with sound, in much the same way the spell of tongues allows you to understand what I'm saying now. There are other spells which reproduce sound—Screamer and terror-spells—fairly simple, really. Have you a screw-cap jar with a wide mouth in that bag of yours, my dear?"

Joanna wordlessly produced one. Antryg cast a quick glance to make sure the proprietress wasn't looking, then began spooning honey into it. He went on, "Caris heard his grandfather's voice calling for help, didn't you, Caris? Whereas you, Joanna, heard—your lover's?"

The word took her by surprise; her reaction to it, even more so. She had always subconsciously thought of Gary as "boyfriend"—a somewhat childish word never adequately replaced in adult parlance. She wondered, a moment later, why her first impulse had been to shy away from the use of the word *lover*—in the physical sense, that was what he had been. But she understood for the first time that she did make the distinction, and the distinction was a critical one.

Gary, she thought, a little sadly, would never be anything but a "boyfriend."

He probably wouldn't even realize yet that she was gone, she reflected later, as they left the inn with the first brightness of the day dispersing the gloom in the lanes. Her car would still be at his place. Possibly he'd deduced—although privately she didn't consider Gary capable of deductive reasoning—that she'd gone home with someone else.

As she remembered his words about his being the only man who'd want her, the thought pleased some small, vindictive corner of her heart. Thus he might not find it odd she didn't answer her telephone all day yesterday, which was Sunday. It was only when he went to work today, smugly counting on meeting her at the office and offering her a ride to his place to pick up her car—with the obligatory *Let's have dinner* and *Why don't you spend the night* thrown in—would he realize she was, in fact, missing. He might spend another day or two trying to reach Ruth before that jet-propelled, stainless steel butterfly remembered to listen to her answering machine, called him back, and they figured out that nobody had seen Joanna since Saturday night.

It was a slightly unnerving thought.

The air outside was fresher, reviving her and chasing the insistent cobwebs of sleepiness from her brain. The night had never really cooled off; the morning, already sticky-warm, though the sun was not yet in the sky, promised hot. It was in her mind that now would be the ideal time to make her escape from Antryg—except that, in this world, there was nowhere for her to go. It was rather like trying to escape from a rowboat in the middle of an ocean—her options were limited. The best she could do, she thought, was stay with the wizard and his captor and hope they could locate the Council—or, at worst, talk Antryg into sending her back himself.

Once outside the inn, Antryg turned, not toward the lane upon which it stood, but into the smelly little alleyway which ran between it and the bathhouse. Caris followed, clearly uneasy, because, in his peasant clothes, he couldn't openly have a weapon in hand. The pistol was concealed under his smock, available, but awkward to get at. Joanna, holding up her skirts from the mud, brought up the rear, reflecting that all the swashbuckler films she'd seen had apparently forgotten to mention certain facts of life, like pig dung in the lanes and the general awkardness of petticoats.

In the alley, Antryg unscrewed the cap from his jar of pilfered honey, tore pellets from the bread he'd pocketed, and, with the assistance of a little of the mud and offal liberally available underfoot, created half a dozen disgustingly convincing pustules to cover the bruise on Caris' face. "I don't suppose you could manage to drool and stagger a bit?" he asked judiciously, producing the gin bottle from another pocket. Its reeking contents, dumped over the sasennan's clothes, totally drowned the smell of the honey. Caris only looked indignant. "I didn't think so. Pity the rag shop didn't have sasennan's gear to fit Joanna—then she could have carried your sword openly instead of bundling it up as it is."

Joanna glanced at the big, sloppy bundle which contained her own clothes, sneakers, and bulging purse, Caris' torn and shabby black uniform and boots, and a couple of hooded cloaks which could double as light blankets, should the weather turn cool. It was tied loosely onto a pole, which concealed the long, hard-edged shape of Caris' sword, but it still didn't look particularly convincing. "We could always say they belonged to my brother," she pointed out. "The Witchfinders only think they're looking for one person, or at most two, or . . . Could *you* pass yourself off as a free sasennan?"

"A free sasennan is a contradiction," Caris said, turning away from trying to catch a glimpse of his reflection in a nearby rain barrel. "There are no free sasenna. The Way of the Sasenna is to serve. We are the weapons, no more, of those who hold our vows."

Joanna shouldered the long bundle and followed the two of them from the alley and into the lane once more. Flies were already beginning to buzz around the greenish scum in the gutters; Caris waved furiously at them as they hummed around the fake sores on his face.

"But what about you?" she asked.

His back stiffened. Momentarily he forgot that he was supposed to be a pox-ridden drunk. "My masters are and always will be the Council of Wizards," he said. Under the dirty slime, his face was cold and proud as Athenian marble. "My grandfather is not dead. . . ."

"Isn't he?" Antryg asked softly.

Caris halted and turned to face the wizard in the lead-colored shadows of the lane. "If he were," he said with equal quiet, "there is only one way that you could know it, Antryg Windrose."

"Is there?" The mage tipped his head on one side, his gray eyes suddenly very weary behind their heavy specs. "He was my master, Caris; we traveled together for many years. Don't you think I would know?"

The sasennan's voice had an edge to it like chipped flint. "He was not your master," he said softly. "Suraklin was your master."

"So he was." Antryg signed, turning back to the lane. "So he was."

They moved out into the main street. Though it was fully light now, the sun had not yet risen above the roofs of the houses; the gold brilliance of it flashed from the slates of the roofs, but the lanes themselves were like canals of still, blue shade. Rather to Joanna's surprise, since it couldn't have been more than five in the morning, the lanes were crowded, men, women, and small children jostling along the herringbone brick cobbles between the wooden houses. Some, in the dark livery of servants, carried market-baskets; tiny children and old men in rags held out skinny hands to them and whined for alms. A few of the women were better dressed, strolling with their maids and looking about them, as Joanna was doing, savoring the glory of sun flashing from the wings of the pigeons that circled overhead and the sweet, wild scent of the hay marsh that blew in over the stinks of the waking town. But most of those abroad on the street, roughly dressed and still-faced, hurried drearily along with the stride of those whose sleep has been insufficient and who care nothing for the beauty of a day which will not be theirs.

They turned a corner into the main thoroughfare of Kymil. The clattering of wheels and hooves which Joanna had heard far-off grew louder, and the slanting sunlight sparkled on the broad street before her, the tepid air redolent with the smell of horses. Carts in incredible numbers clattered by, laden with produce or rickety coops of chickens; butchers' wagons darted between them, as if trying to outpace pursuing swarms of flies; drays of sand or beer barrels rumbled heavily on the cobbles. Just ahead of them, Joanna saw a little boy with a broom dart out into the street to sweep a path through the accumulated muck for a couple of well-dressed ladies. One of them flung the boy a coin, which he caught like a Cubs outfielder jumping for a pop fly.

Joanna stood still upon the flagway, the bundle forgotten on her shoulder, staring around her in a kind of amazement. Yesterday's walk through the countryside and last night's brush with Church authorities and magic had not prepared her for the thoroughly prosaic scene before her. Antryg paused beside her, causing Caris to turn back toward them suspiciously, but the wizard only asked, slightly amused, "What is it?"

She shook her head. The truth sounded silly, but she said, "I sort of expected it to be . . . more medieval."

Antryg grinned, comprehending her surprise and appreciating her rueful self-amusement at her assumptions. "Not the sort of place you expected to find wizards in, is it?"

Joanna looked around her again. Down the lane to their left, massive, dreary brick factories crouched against the shining gold of the sun-shot river; a group of little girls in patched dresses moved past like a school of fish and, with unwilling haste, joined the throng of men and women milling toward the factory gates. Beside her, Caris said, "It is why wizards are forbidden to touch human affairs—so that we can have such a world." He shrugged, clearly ill at ease in his peasant clothes without a weapon in his hand. "Come."

As they moved down the street, Joanna cast a last glance back at the tired-looking children shuffling toward the factory gates.

"Flax mills," Antryg said softly, falling into step at her side. "They'll work till seven or eight tonight, to take advantage of the daylight. At twopence a week, the owners find it cheaper than hiring men. And then, running a machine doesn't require strength."

Looking up, she saw in his face the tired bitterness of one who sees suffering which he cannot alleviate and from which he has, by fate, been exempted. Thinking of those hurrying, tiny forms, she knew exactly how he felt.

He went on, "This is their technology, their industry for the betterment of all. To have no magic in politics, in industry, or in trade, to make no exceptions for the few at the expense of the many . . . For this world, we have forfeited what we are and could be."

"What you could be," Caris cut in frostily, "is what your master was—a despot who ruled this town by fear for years and who instilled in you the power to do the same."

Antryg sighed, his hands buried in the pockets of his preposterous coat, the lines of his face settling into an expression that aged him—the weight of too great a knowledge of human sorrow. "Yes," he agreed, his voice quiet. "But I've never seen that technology or this progress they keep talking about has helped those who must feed its machines. Yours is a world of technology, Joanna; it lies on the other side of a night of time which our eyes can't pierce from here. Is it worth it?"

Joanna was silent for a time, her skirt-entangled steps quick to keep pace with the longer strides of the men, fishing through the dim memories of a period in history which had always bored her. "If you mean, does it get better," she said slowly, "yes. But that's six, seven generations down the line. And it gets worse."

"Much worse?" His voice was the voice of a man asking after the fate of his own children, not the sons of men and women three generations away whom he would never know.

"I think so."

The long, sensitive mouth twisted; he walked along in silence, while the morning brightened and bells all over the city began to ring for the first church services of the day. A couple of country girls passed them, their skirts hiked up to reveal tattered petticoats underneath. One carried a bucket of milk on her head, the other a tray of fish that could be smelled across the street; neither girl looked particularly well-fed. At the end of the broad street, Joanna could see the glint of sunlight on the gray, bulky towers of the city gates and the flash of steel pikes and helmets in their deep arched shadow.

"I suppose there's a certain economy to it," said Antryg at last. "To sacrifice seven or eight generations for the betterment of ten, or twelve, or a hundred."

The children of the last generations of downtrodden factory fodder, Joanna thought, had invented the atomic bomb. She said quietly, "Maybe not even that."

His glance was puzzled and worried—not understanding how, she thought, but understanding what. They were entering the jostling crowds of the square, where half a dozen streets and alleys met before the gate. The din of hawkers, wagon wheels, crossing sweepers, and soldiers calling back and forth was tremendous and masked the soft, deep richness of his voice from any but her ears alone.

"Sometimes I think it would have been better had I not been born with the powers of a mage," he said quietly. "I see what is happening and I know I am neither intellectually nor thaumaturgically equipped to remedy it. I know that those great, awful laws should apply to all, without exception. And yet, in individual cases—it seems different then."

Without warning, the strange despair that Joanna had felt two or three

times in the last weeks washed over her heart. He was right, she thought
—not only about his world, but about her own. She felt suddenly isolated
by the pointlessness of it all. This world, working to become what hers
suddenly seemed to her to be—colorless, alienated, so impersonal that
she herself could disappear and it would be days before her closest friend
and her boyfriend—she shied again from thinking of him as her lover—
knew she was even gone. . . .

Though the warm brilliance of the daylight did not fade, it seemed as if
all color, all animation had been drained from it, turning it into a tawdry
carnival of pointless despair. Ahead of them, the city gates reared up at
the end of the street, a clumsy monolith of dingy stone surmounted by a
tarnished clock and cones of moldering slate. All the weariness of the last
twenty-four hours descended crushingly on her shoulders. She could see
the sasenna standing in the gatehouse shadows now, their black uniforms
bearing the red sun-seal of the Church; with them were men in the gray,
straitlaced clothing of the Witchfinders. She remembered the man Peelbone, and sudden panic clutched her heart.

But before she could speak, Caris balked and drew back suddenly into
the mouth of a narrow lane. Under the grime and faked sores, she saw his
handsome face had turned pale. His voice was breathless, "I don't like
it."

Joanna shook her head, glad her own terrors were vindicated by the
instincts of the warrior.

"We can hide in the quarter of the Old Believers," Caris went on
hoarsely. "They'll know who I am."

"Don't be silly." Antryg ducked into the lane at his side. Joanna could
see his face, like the younger man's, suddenly clammy with moisture.
"Not finding us on the roads, they'll concentrate on the ghetto now."
There was something else in his voice, something that she didn't bother
to identify through that queer feeling of panic.

Caris went on, his voice stumbling, "We can't escape. They have the
Council; they're destroying all the wizards. We could have gotten out—I
was going to use a spell to make them ignore us—it was one of the few
magics I could do. But now . . ." He paused, his breath coming fast, as
if he fought a panic of his own. "Let's go back." He started to move
down the lane, and Antryg caught his arm in that surprising grip.

"No," the mage said.

Furious, Caris dragged at his smock for his pistol; Antryg caught his
other hand.

"It's left you, hasn't it?" he said softly. "Your magic."

Caris' eyes shifted. "No. Now move or I'll . . ."

"You'll what? Shoot me? Fifty feet from the guards at the city gate?"

They stood nearly breast to breast, the warrior in his filthy smock staring into the mage's bespectacled eyes in baffled, unreasoning rage. Then his mouth twisted, and his hand plunged for the knife in his boot. Joanna, watching, felt queerly distant from both of them, as if it were all happening to strangers and there would be no consequences. She wondered if the stew at the inn had given her dysentery and these were its opening stages, wondered if she would die of it and, if she died, if she would care. But even as Antryg caught Caris's knife hand, a cry in the street behind them snagged at her attention, though it, like everything else, seemed unimportant now.

Looking out, she saw that a lady, in a spell of crooked humor, had flung a halfpenny for one of the little crossing sweepers under the hooves of an oncoming dray. The boy had made an ill-timed dive for the coin and was now sitting on the edge of the flagway, clutching his bleeding leg and screaming while the drayman shouted at him and passersby turned aside unheeding.

Something within her told Joanna that she should feel something, do something, but it was as unreal as a scene on television. Her head felt strange, as if with hunger, though she had a weird sense that she could eat for hours without filling the gray emptiness of her soul.

At the gates, the sasenna had closed around a young man in the long black gown and braided hair of an Old Believer.

Caris, looking dully past Antryg's shoulder, said, "It's Treman. One of the mages . . . It'll never work! We'll be taken. . . ."

"We won't," said Antryg quietly, seizing the young sasennan by the shoulder and steering him out of the alleyway, "because we're not using magic to get by the guards. Don't you understand? *You're not the only one whose magic has left you.* You're not the only one who feels this despair."

Caris blinked at him, struggling in his mind. "What?"

Antryg hauled the young man's arm around his shoulder. "Lean on me," he said softly. "You're drunk."

"It'll never . . ."

"I'll knock you over the head and carry you if you don't do as I say."

Caris made one indignant move to struggle, then shook his head, as if he suddenly realized the perilous stupidity of such a display of temper. He slumped against the taller man's shoulder, his head lolling. "I—I don't know what's come over me," he whispered. Joanna, clutching the bundle that now looked more than ever unmistakably sword-shaped, fell into step on his other side. "It's as if . . ."

"I don't either," said the mage softly, "but whatever it is, it has come over the guards, too."

"It can't have." Caris managed a convincing stagger, and clutched at the mage's arm. "It's only because my magic is fading. It's been fading for weeks. It hasn't anything to do with anyone else."

As they approached the shadows of the gate, Joanna felt almost ill with despair, knowing they would be searched. Even if the Inquisition did not take her, it would certainly take her companions. She would be left stranded in this world, with its filth and peril, unable to make her living, unable to return home . . . Tears of fright and misery blurred her vision. She felt an almost uncontrollable urge to break away and bolt back to the sheltering shadows of the alleyways, and only some small, illogical corner of her that trusted Antryg's judgment kept her moving toward the massed sasenna in the echoing, stony darkness of the gate.

They were still gathered around the man Treman, who was looking terrified and at the same time in the grip of listless apathy. With a sudden oath, one of the guards struck him across the face. The other guards, watching this scene, paid scant attention to the cart and foot traffic clattering in and out of the gates behind them. The shadows were cold; by contrast, the sun on the causeway beyond, when the three fugitives reached it, was oppressively hot. Gnats hummed drearily over the marshes; the sun was blinding on the water. Joanna, Antryg, and Caris were some hundred feet beyond the gates before Joanna even realized they had successfully escaped the town.

"You feel it, too, don't you, Joanna?" Antryg asked quietly, as they lost themselves among the shuffling crowd of the city's poor who came and went on the marsh road, to cut hay or fish for their food among the pools. "And have done so for the last several weeks."

Joanna nodded, puzzled that he should know. Caris, the gates safely past, removed his arm from Antryg's shoulders and took the bundle of weapons from Joanna. He remained walking between them, looking baffled and strained.

Antryg went on, "I don't suppose that woman back there would ever have thrown a coin under the horses' feet that way—even if the thought had crossed her mind; either inherent decency or, at the very least, fear of what her friends would think of her would have stayed her hand. Ordinarily the boy would have had more sense than to go after it and more skill than to get trampled." He looked from one to the other of them, his head cocked to one side, like a gray stork's. "Don't you see?"

A passing troop of mounted sasenna kicked dust over them; it clung like flour to their sweaty faces. Joanna saw one tired-looking old farm woman who barely raised her head as the riders bore down on her; and the boy who was with her saw them coming for some moments before rousing himself to pull his mother out of the way. Joanna shook her head, feeling strangely isolated and uncaring.

"It eats life," the wizard said softly. "It eats magic. It leeches the life-force, the energy that holds all life together, from every living thing and leaves in its place only the weary wondering of where it has gone."

"What does?" Caris asked, a kind of fear struggling against the uncaring dullness in his eyes.

"That," Antryg said, "is what I mean to find out."

CHAPTER XI

THEY TRAVELED FOR THREE DAYS, THROUGH THE GREEN AND EMPTY hill country that Caris called the Sykerst, and into the farmlands beyond.

The queer, terrible sense of deadness did not pass off until sometime after noon of the first day. Joanna, asleep in the shelter of the last haystack of the lowlands before the high ground began, felt the fading in her confused dream of being married to Gary, of protesting, *But it was all a mistake! I don't want to be married to anybody,* and of Gary's smug expression as he said, *I'm sorry, babe, but you did marry me. . . .* As if a fever had been lifted from her, she wept. She felt a hand, large but very light of touch, brush her hair comfortingly as she sank into deeper sleep.

Later, as they resumed their walk through the stuffy, clinging heat of the last of the day, she asked Antryg, "Did it affect your magic, as it did that of Caris?"

"I felt it," he admitted, producing three apples from the pockets of his trailing coat-skirts and tossing two of them to his companions as they walked. "It didn't bleed all the hope from the—madness has certain advantages."

Joanna frowned up at him. "You mean magic is—is predicated on hope? Because I felt, more than anything, that was what was taken from me—the hope of anything."

He regarded her with quirked eyebrows for a moment, surprised by her understanding. "Hope," he said, "and belief in life. We move blindly from second to second through time. Hope, and magic, both involve the casting forward of the soul. In a way, both magic and hope are a kind of madness."

"Madness also has the advantage," Caris said, shifting the set of the pistol belted under his faded peasant smock, "of cloaking things which you find it more convenient not to explain—like the fact that you knew of the coming of the abominations, and why you, of all wizards, don't lose your powers to this . . . whatever it is."

"Handy, isn't it?" Antryg grinned, pleased. He finished devouring the core of his apple and flicked the stem into the nodding weeds of the roadside ditch. "Couldn't have happened better if I'd caused it myself."

Caris' coffee-brown eyes narrowed, and Joanna had to look away and purse her lips tightly against an involuntary smile.

"The thing that worries me," the wizard went on after a moment, "or one of the things that worry me about that, is that it happens everywhere. What about the children in the factories? There are enough accidents without that—uncaringness."

Joanna, who had lived all her life in a world poised a button push away from destruction, shivered. "Come to think of it," she said after a moment, "where I work—if they don't can me for being absent without calling in—on the days this whatever-it-is happened, there would always be zillions of stupid errors in documentation and programs."

"Documentation?"

Joanna hesitated, wondering how she could best explain computers to a wizard, much less to one from a world that had only begun connecting electricity with lightning. But no one, she reasoned, who wasn't interested in everything would have become a wizard in the first place; so she launched ahead and for several miles expounded upon the intricacies of programming, languages, CP/M pixels, ROM, RAM, mainframes, micros, hard disks, and floppies, while the dove-colored summer evening darkened to ultramarine and the dry-grass sweetness of the hill winds tugged at her hair.

"You are saying, then, that these—these computers—think?" Caris asked doubtfully. He had abandoned his guarding position at Antryg's back and walked now at Joanna's side, the bundle of their possessions still over his shoulder and the butt of the pistol visible against his hard-muscled belly through the half-open smock. He sounded worried.

Joanna shook her head. "They can be programmed to reproduce many of the processes of linear thinking," she said, kicking aside an encumbering fold of her petticoat which persisted in tangling around her ankles. "That is, any chain of thought can be broken down into a hundred tiny yes-or-no decisions—if A, then go to B, if not A, then go to C, and C will tell you what to do from there."

Caris frowned, puzzled, but Antryg said, "Rather like a music box—

either a key is struck or it's silent—or the punched cards they rig in automatic series to change the weft patterns in jacquard looms."

"Since computers work very fast—and we're talking a hundredth or thousandth of a second here—" She shied from explaining nanoseconds to people who, she was fairly sure, didn't work habitually in units smaller than hours. "—it has the appearance of operating like thought. But for the most part, they'll do exactly what you tell them to. It's both the advantage and the disadvantage of computers. You always know where you are with a computer, unlike a person—but they don't care what they do. They'll sit there printing out gibberish for hours, if you make the wrong request, give away state secrets to anyone who asks, or help you steal, if you know the right entry code—and any good hacker can break an entry code."

"Steal?" The sasennan's frown deepened. As soon as it had begun to grow dark, he had paused by one of the thin streams that trickled down from the hills, had washed the counterfeit sores from his face, and had rid himself of the faint, pale stubble of his beard with a razor from his belt purse. In the lingering dusk, the dark circles around his eyes had deepened almost to bruises. Joanna wondered if he had slept when they had taken refuge in the haystack for a few hours' rest or if he thought it behooved him still to keep an eye on Antryg.

"I thought you said those things were only boxes that did not move."

She shrugged. "They don't have to. It's all done over the telephone. Everything in our civilization is. A friend of mine at San Serano broke the ordering and shipping codes on the San Serano mainframe; I suspect he also used telephone modems to break the shipping codes on some of the companies that use computerized ordering systems where we get our supplies. Now and then I'll be thumbing through the mainframe and find somebody's put through an order from San Serano for some kind of equipment—like extra disk drives—and then later find that the order has been pulled from the file. When an order's pulled from a computer file, it's gone; it's as if it never existed. It's only light, after all—and when light's gone it leaves no tracks. Presumably, using modems, the record of the transaction can be removed from the shipper's files as well. That way Gary can walk off with an extra disk drive—or a whole computer, if he wanted to—and nobody's the wiser, because there's no record of the thing ever having existed."

The affronted morality of years of warrior discipline was in Caris' voice. "He is a thief without even the courage of a common burglar," he said.

Joanna nodded in agreement. They stepped down into the weed-grown roadside ditch to let a shepherd and his flock pass them, a bleating, jostling confusion of wool and dust. "Except that he'd say that the companies have a profit margin for theft included in their annual budgets, so nobody's really losing anything."

"Except Gary himself." Hands in his pockets, shirt ruffles like a shabby flower in the evening gloom, Antryg turned away from his delighted contemplation of the interplay between sheep and dogs to regard his companions. "And what he loses is the part of himself that honors the rights of others and honors his own integrity."

"Gary," Joanna said after a moment, "wouldn't really understand that integrity—which is free, and therefore cheap—isn't worth a two-thousand-dollar disk drive." She stepped back into the smelly dust cloud that hung over the road, kilting up her skirts into her belt as she had seen the farm women do, and resumed her tired walk north.

Much later, when Joanna looked back on those few days, it was with a kind of mild surprise at herself for the ease with which she slipped into companionship with both captor and captive. Timid by nature, she had always harbored an uneasy distrust of men, regarding them as an alien species who dealt with women in the relationship of users and used. But neither of the two men seemed to regard her as anything other than a comrade on the road, Caris because he was too single-mindedly intent on watching Antryg, and Antryg because it would never have occurred to him to deal with anyone except on that person's own terms.

"I don't know what game he's playing," Caris said, as he and Joanna shared a bucket of wash water drawn from the horse trough of the posting house stable where the three of them had slept the night. "He could perfectly well have escaped last night." He folded up his shaving razor and returned it to his belt purse, then doused the water angrily over his face and head and shook out his wet, fair hair. Joanna, at Caris' instructions, had gamely taken a shift at watch the previous night and had fallen asleep ten minutes into it; Caris, she knew, had waked, sat in the dark hayloft for half an hour in pistol-clutching surveillance on the sleeping Antryg, and had dropped off as well. Antryg had waked both of them at dawn.

Joanna tried but failed to stifle her grin. "But he would have missed breakfast," she said, providing what Antryg's explanation would surely be. All she got from the disgruntled Caris was a sour look.

"He has his own reasons for wanting to go to Angelshand." His glowering eyes sought the tall, loose-limbed form of the wizard as it emerged from the back door of the posting inn, half a loaf of rye bread and a hunk of cheese in hand. Then he wiped his hands on the coarse linsey-woolsey of his peasant smock, its sleeves turned up to reveal the old, white scars which criss-crossed his muscular forearms, and brushed away a stray bit of hay. Joanna had quickly discovered that hay was surprisingly persistent stuff. "It's easy to believe in his innocence," he said after a moment. "I did, myself, if for no other reason than that he seems too scatter-brained to be devious. But he brought you here for a reason, Joanna, and it may be that he only appears so docile because he hasn't had the opportunity to carry you off."

As Antryg came up to them, Joanna was obliged to press her hand over her mouth to keep from laughing at the mental picture of the be-spectacled wizard in his billowing, too-large black coat dashing away on foot across the hills with her thrown like a movie heroine over his shoulder. Caris, to judge by his expression, did not share her amusement.

In the dry warmth of the morning, the smell of the new-baked bread the wizard carried was almost painful and the drift of scent from the doors of the posting house kitchen like a glimpse of heaven. Caris had relieved him of what little money was left of Nandiharrow's small hoard, but it only amounted to a few coppers; Antryg had earned supper last night, breakfast this morning, and a bed in the hayloft of the stables by telling fortunes in the posting house, to Caris' considerable disgust.

"Lady Rosamund was right," he had said bitterly, watching the wizard bent over the fat palm of a merchant who had come in on the mailcoach. "A dog wizard!"

Dog wizard or not, Joanna thought the following evening, it did pay for supper, and she privately considered that it ill-behooved Caris to complain about it.

The day had been an exhausting one. Though she was gradually getting used to walking all day, she still felt stiff and tired and miserably footsore. Her face, arms, and shoulders were sunburned. The situation was not helped by sleeping in hay for the past two nights. Thank God, she thought, with a twinge of amusement at herself, I don't have allergies —that's probably something selected against in the evolution of heroines. Though the hills of the Sykerst were empty, tenanted only by sheep, the road was fairly well-traveled, with pack trains carrying clay down to the pottery works in Kymil and farm carts from the lowlands beyond. At long intervals, the mailcoach would clatter past in a huge cloud of choking dust, an enormous vehicle drawn by a six-horse hitch, rattling with brass and glass windows and crammed with passengers—farmers in serge, black-clothed clerks in wide-brimmed hats, or harassed-looking women of the poorer classes in faded print gowns and bonnets. Sometimes a carriage would pass them, with a coachman on the box and a couple of footmen hanging on behind, or small, lightly slung chaises, with postillions riding the horses instead of driving them.

Only once had they left the road, when a company of sasenna had ridden by, clothed in smart black uniforms braided in gold and heavily armed. As they'd climbed back onto the road again, Caris said, "The Prince Regent's men."

"Are you surprised?" Antryg asked, dusting off his velvet coat skirts. They had taken refuge in the shadows of one of the spindly clumps of birches which were beginning to grow with greater and greater frequency beside the road as it came down off the bare backbone of the hills and wended its way toward the farming and woodland country closer to Angelshand. "He has always hated the mages; it shouldn't come as a shock that he's sent his private bodyguard to join the hunt."

Caris' beautiful lips set into a grim line, and he felt for the reassurance of the pistol in his smock. Further down the road, a farmer and his young wife were trying to coax their donkey out of the ditch into which they'd scrambled for safety at the troop's approach. Joanna was interested to notice that others beside the mageborn had reason to fear the Regent's men.

Seated now with her back to the stone chimney breast of the posting house, she watched Antryg peer with his cracked old quizzing glass at the dregs of a dowager's tea. The smoky shadows of the lamplight played unsteadily over his features and put a flickering embroidery of shadow on the woman's round cheeks from the lace flaps of her cap. Behind them, the other passengers of the mail coach crowded in an interested knot, drinking their evening ale and listening with the surreptitious fascination that even nonbelievers have in the words of oracles. Joanna couldn't hear what Antryg was telling the woman, but a stout man in a suit of dark-blue superfine who seemed to be her husband laughed and said, "Mind, Emmie, you're not believing all that wizardy twiddle, are you?"

" 'Tisn't twiddle." The woman took the teacup from Antryg and held it defensively to her pouter-pigeon bosom, as if the future itself, and not merely its reflection, were held within its leaves.

Another man in a farmer's rough smock laughed. "Pshaw!" Joanna had seen the word written in novels of the British variety but had never actually heard anyone say it. "I went to one of them wizard fellows once . . ."

"What?" a red-cheeked girl teased him. "For a love-drop?"

The man blushed. "As happens, yes," he admitted and then grinned, showing broken and yellow teeth. "And damned if the girl didn't throw her cap after some other fellow."

"Perhaps the other fellow'd been to a better wizard?" Antryg suggested.

"That's what they all say."

"Suraklin . . ." began a thin, middle-aged clerk.

The first man, Emmie's husband, snorted, his round jowls pouching out over a high muslin cravat. "Suraklin wasn't more than a clever businessman who poisoned where he couldn't bribe or scare. He made the most of a few pieces of luck that fell his way, that's all, and fools called it magic. If you'll look into all those cases of people going blind or falling down the stairs or whatever they were supposed to have done, you'll find that none of it could be proved."

"And that," Antryg said quietly, coming over to Joanna with a tankard of beer in each hand, "was his strength, you know. For the most part, people didn't believe in his powers—and it was never anything you could lay hand to."

"Like this whatever-it-is," Joanna agreed. She looked up at him in the sooty shadows outside the circle of lamplight around the table, her brow puckering with frustration. "There isn't even a *name* for it."

"Which makes it all the harder to believe that something is actually happening." He settled on the bench at her side. Caris had already retired to the stables to sleep.

The casement windows of the post house were open to the azure deeps of the night, and suicidal swarms of moths, millers, and gnats hovered around each of the room's dozen or so smoky and stinking lamps. Joanna added a few more notes to her mental list of items left out of swashbuckler movies. It crossed her mind to be glad, if she had to be kidnapped for reasons unknown and haled all over the countryside in a parallel universe, she was there in the summer when the windows could be open to let the smoke and the smells escape.

"Which is perhaps," Antryg went on, handing her the tankard, "precisely what someone is counting on."

"Hunh?"

"Both you and Caris assumed it was some problem of your own—doubtless each of these people did as well." He gestured towards the fat squire and his wife, the farmer couple, and the two or three laborers, like a Hogarth print in sepia and gold, laughing over some joke in the chiaroscuro of the lamplight. "It's another dubious advantage of being mad," he added. "I understand that what is in my head *is* real, at least to me."

Joanna considered him for a moment, watching the jump of shadows over the extravagant curves of his lips, nose, and hair. "Are you mad?" she asked after a moment. "Everyone says so, but—I haven't seen it."

"Haven't you?" His gray eyes sparkled appreciatively. "All the experts have said so for the last twenty-five years—but I was always unbalanced. Light-minded, Suraklin used to say, as though gravity were some kind of virtue. And for years I believed it was. I did try to take it all seriously, to become what I thought he wanted me to be . . ."

It was the first time Joanna had heard the Dark Mage spoken of with something other than loathing and fear. Curious, she asked, "Did you love him?"

Antryg turned his head a little to regard her with something like surprise at her understanding. "Oh, yes. I was halfway between being his slave and his son, from the time I was nine and my powers began to come. They came early. I understand now that he would have taken me by force had seduction not served, but it did. There was nothing I would not have done for him, except give up what I was . . . and for a time I did my best to do even that." His eyes were not on her now, nor on the cavernous gloom of the big room, with its bumbling shadows and the half-seen glint of the copper pan bottoms on the walls. He seemed to be gazing into some private seeing-glass of memory and, she thought, observing the sudden dip of wrinkles across his brow, not much liking what he saw.

"What finally turned you against him?"

He shook his head, and there was distant sadness in his voice. "I never turned against him." He leaned back against the stone of the chimney breast behind them; the shadows obscured his odd, craggy-boned face, save for the spark on one corner of his spectacles and the star-glint of an earring. "I fled from him and hid, but there was not a night that I did not feel him seeking me through my dreams. Even after Salteris found me, years later, and told me he was dead . . ." He paused, then sighed heavily. "I'm told he had that effect on many people. But I did love him. I suppose that's what made it all the worse."

Joanna was silent. As if that brown-velvet voice, with its flamboyant richness, could weave for her the smoke-visions that he himself saw, she had a momentary glimpse of a skinny and overgrown boy moving hesitantly in the old man's terrible shadow, trying to kill what he was in order to be what he was told he ought to be. Like a glass sliver caught in a garment, she felt the unexpected stab of her own years of torn striving to conform to the fashions and morals of a peer group she despised.

Not knowing quite why, she asked, "Was he good to you?"

The fulvid edge of the light outlined the arched nose as he turned to look at her and gleamed opaque on a circle of glass. "Not really. Obsessive people seldom are. And his obsessions grew with the years, until every instance in which I could not be what he wanted me to be, every mistake I made, every day I played truant to go running to the hills or read poetry, was an insult to him."

The squire and his lady were making their way up the creaky wooden stairs to bed, their shapes wobbling huge in the reflection of a bedroom candle. The little clerk called for a final round of beer. A beefy young laborer with curly hair looked up and waved to Antryg to come back to them. The mage smiled ruefully at Joanna.

"Funny," he said, "if you're a mage, they always ask you to read the future, as if knowing it will help. I think three-fourths of all prayers prayed are for two and two not to equal four." He set his empty tankard on the hearth and got to his feet. Joanna rose to stand beside him, her head, as usual, barely coming up to the topmost tarnished silver button on his threadbare coat.

She glanced up at him curiously, remembering her own fears, doubts, and half-conviction at San Serano that she was either insane or in terrible trouble. Why she felt concerned for him or felt this strange kinship with him, she wasn't sure; he was, she reminded herself, the storm center of terrible and inexplicable events, the man who had brought her to this place, who had twice tried to strangle her, and who wanted her for some strange purposes of his own—the only man, at the moment, who could return her to the world she knew. Yet she found herself asking, "Have you ever prayed that?"

"Oh, frequently," he murmured, half to himself, she thought, as much as to her. "Frequently. Would you like me to tell your fortune?"

Joanna hesitated, knowing she was already too taken in by the daft warmth of his charm. Then from the yard came the swift clatter of hooves and the jingle of accoutrements, and Antryg turned swiftly, gray eyes wary, as the first of the sasenna entered the posting house.

They wore the gold-trimmed black livery of the Prince Regent, the braid glittering in the darkness like ropes of fire. Joanna had already identified the sounds in the yard as that of a coach, and a fairly substantial one, and was fading as inconspicuously as she could toward the rear door of the posting house. It was only as she reached it that she realized that Antryg had moved back again to the shadows of the bench by the hearth, unable to call her back to him. She got a glimpse of his wide, warning eyes as her hand pressed the latch.

Gloved fingers closed like a metal clamp over her wrist. She whirled, fighting a gasp of shock as a big, iron-faced woman in the black clothes of the Prince's sasenna pushed her back into the room. She stumbled and spun around in time to see among the black-and-gold sasenna and the cluster of crimson-liveried servants at the post-house door a man who could only be the Prince.

"She was sneaking out the back," her captor said briefly.

The Prince's queer, pale-blue eyes glistened in the shadow. "Was she, indeed?" His voice was soft and rather shrill; none of those at the tables dared move or call to themselves that odd, flickering gaze. The silence that had fallen was absolute, save for the desperate burr of a moth's wings against the hot glass of the lamp.

"A guilty conscience, child?"

Joanna tried to back away and met the hard-muscled shape of the female guard. The ebony satin of the Prince's coat was so heavily laced with gold that it seemed to glitter like black flame as he minced forward over the dirty straw of the floor. For all his diminutive prettiness, as he came close and put one small, moist hand under her chin, Joanna could see that, beneath the layer of cosmetics, his skin was coarse, pale with the pallor of one who has been weeks without sunlight or change of air. The carefully curled golden hair was limp and thin; the skin around the sky-blue eyes was painted to cover not only the fact that he was on the wrong side of thirty, but the ravages of sleeplessness and debauchery. In spite of the rouge that coated them, she could see his lips were chapped with nervous biting.

Any other man so dressed and so affected would have appeared ridiculous, but for those eyes.

She became aware that she was trembling.

His thumb and crooked forefinger tightened on her chin. Beneath their curled lashes, his eyes never touched hers. "Answer me, sweetheart."

Sweat crawling down her back beneath her peasant bodice, Joanna said, "I wasn't trying to run away, your—" What was the proper title for a prince? "—your Grace. Not from you, anyway. I—I'd had a quarrel with someone here, that's all, and wanted to get out." Not a very good story, she knew, nor, she was afraid, very convincingly told, but it was the best she could do on the spur of the moment. One of the sasenna sniggered. The Prince smiled, and his hand stole like a slug down the side of her neck.

"A quarrel? With a pretty wench like you? How very tasteless of them."

Instinctively she stepped back, loathing his touch, and his small hand snatched with the nervous quickness of a child playing jacks, seizing a handful of her shift and bodice at the shoulder. Joanna wondered desperately how far she should let this go and how much trouble they'd all be in if she struck him; but at that instant Antryg rose from his seat in the corner and drawled, "Oh, come, Pharos, you know you haven't any use for a woman."

There was a half beat of shocked, utter silence, as if someone had switched off the sound. Then the Prince threw Joanna from him, his indrawn breath of rage like the hiss of a snake. In a swooping flurry of gold-laced coat skirts and a blazing galaxy of diamond buttons, he strode across the room to where two of his men had already sprung to seize the wizard by the arms. Completely forgotten, Joanna faded back at once into the shadows. But though she knew that Antryg had bought her escape-time at who knew what cost, she could not bring herself to flee.

Had it not been for the utter silence, the Prince's voice would not have been heard, a hoarse whisper that shook with rage. "You *dare* . . ."

His arms pinned by the Prince's guards, Antryg did not struggle, but Joanna saw in the firelight the gleam of sweat along his jaw. For an instant the Prince stood, speechless—then he reached out and, with a hideous, gentle deliberateness, removed the spectacles from Antryg's face. The glass and wire rattled sharply as he flung them to the stone of the hearth. Then he held out his hand, and a crimson-liveried servant put into it a leather riding-whip.

No one in the inn so much as breathed.

The Prince struck twice, with vicious deliberation, across his defense-less victim's face. On the second blow, Joanna heard the Prince make a little sound in his throat, a whimper of satisfaction or some private, inner pain which sickened her. His hand came back for a third blow. She glimpsed in his eyes the lusting flicker of madness and knew he would go on with the flogging until he lost his already-slipping hold over himself. The candlelight caught the dark ruby gleam of blood on the leather and pouring down Antryg's still face. She thought blindly, *I should run . . . he's doing this so I can run. . . .* But when she did take a step, it was forward, not back. . . .

The third blow never fell. In the midst of his backswing, the Prince gasped, and his body convulsed as if he had been kicked in the stomach. The whip clattered on the hearthstones as the slender black form doubled over, hands clutching at the barley-gold curls as if to root out an invisible axe blade sunk in his skull. One of the sasenna holding Antryg's arm released his grip to catch his master before he toppled. Chaos erupted as the others crowded forward. To the man on his other side, Antryg said sharply, "Fetch a basin! He's going to be sick in a minute!" and the man made a dash for the kitchen.

Antryg scooped up his cracked spectacles and was fitting them back to his nose as he crossed the room, unnoticed in the fearful hullabaloo.

"Let's go," he said softly. Taking Joanna's arm, he led her through the unguarded back door and out into the moonlight of the yard.

"What did you *do?*"

"Migraine headache. Psychotics often suffer from them." The greenish eyes of the horses flashed at them in the darkness of the stables as Antryg scrambled halfway up the ladder to the loft. "Caris!"

"Here."

Joanna spun around, her heart in her throat—the sasennan faded from the blackness of a nearby stall. Antryg jumped from the ladder, landing with light springiness on the ground; the wan moonlight turned black the blood running down from the opened flesh of his face and caught in the fracture of his left spectacle lens like a skeleton star.

Caris, Joanna saw, was armed, not only with the pistol, but had his sheathed sword grasped lightly in his left hand, ready to draw and fight. The small bundle of their belongings was strapped to his back. He must have been ready, she realized, from the moment the Prince's sasenna rode into the inn yard.

"Was it the Regent?" he demanded softly, as Antryg led them down the nearly dry stream bed that ran behind the inn. Shouts and neighs and the rattle of gear were already rising into the dark stillness of the hills. Antryg nodded.

"He took a fancy to our Jo—he might have anyway, even had she not tried to slip out the back. She couldn't have known he'd have the place surrounded before going in. He's suspicious of everyone and sees plots in everything and, as Emperor in all but name, he can do pretty much as he pleases. My only fear was that he'd recognize me when he took my specs off." He paused and raised his head over the edge of the stream-bank, ridiculously like a lanky, nervous setter dog in long grass. "Ah, good."

Encouraged, Joanna stood up beside him. Down in its nook in the hills beside the road, the posting house was still visible, but the moving lights that had begun to circle away from it were returning, like indecisive fireflies.

"They're turning back?" Joanna whispered disbelievingly.

"For the moment. There, look . . ." A single horseman went streaking away down the road toward Kymil; a moment later, a second thundered westward toward where Parchasten lay in the fertile valley of the Glidden beyond. "Now what we've got to do is get as far away from this place as we can, as fast as we can, and keep away from the road."

"I don't understand." Caris scrambled after him up the stony bank of the stream, giving a hand to Joanna, who followed, cursing the custom of the country that decreed that all women should burden themselves with trailing masses of skirts. "Why aren't they pursuing tonight?"

"Because Pharos suspects a trap—some plot to lure his men away into the countryside while he's attacked at the post house. I suspect the Bishop summoned him with a claim that there's a plot of wizards afoot. He won't be terribly surprised to have stumbled into one."

"It's what I'd suspect," Joanna added thoughtfully, "from the way you deliberately baited him at the inn. But—*would* he have recognized you without your specs?"

"He might have." Joanna had retrieved her purse from Caris' pack, and Antryg accepted the handful of Kleenex she dug from it, mopping gingerly at the blood on his face. They were moving down through the dense shadows of the hills, where the starlight glittered faintly on stream water only deep enough to soak Joanna's cowhide peasant boots and make the hem of her skirts slap wetly against her ankles, no matter how much she tried to hold it clear. "Wizards don't wear specs—we work our healing spells on ourselves from a very early age. My eyes started to go within weeks of being put in the Tower. I have no doubt, if I hadn't been mageborn, I'd have been blind as a mole from the age of ten."

He paused, looking back. A fold of hillside hid them now from the inn, but faintly Joanna could hear the commotion that drifted on the darkness. "By morning he'll have reinforcements from Kymil and Angelshand both combing the countryside. I know these hills."

"As Suraklin's student," Caris said dryly, "you would."

"Perhaps," Antryg agreed equably. "But as with fortunetelling, it's just as well for all of us that I do. Be careful here, Joanna—the rock is slippery."

Balancing carefully, her purse heavy on her shoulder and her bunched skirts held in her hand, Joanna stepped forward, and the strong, light hand from the darkness steadied her. "By the way," she said softly, "thank you."

Behind her, Caris said, "He went to the trouble of bringing you to this world, Joanna—he wasn't about to risk losing you to the Prince Regent."

In the utter gloom of the hill shadows, Antryg's grin sparkled as brightly as the starlight on his earrings. "That's my Caris," he remarked affectionately and led the way once more into the darkness of the hills.

They fled like foxes in hunting country, through a nightmare of blind exhaustion deeper than anything Joanna had yet known. From the sheep pens and roadside ditches of the hills, Antryg led them, doubling on their tracks and changing direction frequently, down to the woodlands and thickly settled farms of the valley of the Glidden. Her body ached for sleep and her ankles and shins stabbed with pain at every step, but Joanna struggled to keep up with her two companions, miserable with the guilty conviction that she was slowing them down and terrified that, losing them, she would be stranded in this world forever. Having walked all day, they kept moving through the night hours and on into morning, dodging, hiding, and listening for the quick rattle of hooves or the thrashing of bodies through the hedgerows.

At mid-morning, that strange, bleak emptiness struck again, bleeding what little energy was left from Joanna's soul. In her despair, she toyed with the notion of leaving Caris and his mad prisoner and seeking some way home on her own, but her saner self knew it was folly. Fear of the Regent and the memory of the cold-voiced Peelbone kept her moving. They were in the farm country then, hiding among the hedgerows and fields of standing crops, and even Joanna was aware that, during that time of gray sickliness, the hay makers they glimpsed in the meadows slacked their efforts and fell to quarreling over the whetstones and tools, while the storm clouds gathered in louring masses in the sky. The spell lasted until noon. By that time, Joanna suspected, the damage had been done. She wondered about what the effects of such a spell would be in her own world, on trigger-happy street-punks, on politicians, or on the men responsible for the thousand dull and niggling safety regulations concerning nuclear power plants and chemical waste.

Late in the day, they rested, exhausted and oppressed by the breathless heat of the coming storm, on an islet in a sluggish stream that Caris identified as the Shan. Antryg had gathered herbs from the waterside to make a poultice for the whip cut on his face and had fallen asleep between the roots of a willow tree, his head on his rolled-up coat. Caris slumped against the tree trunk beside him, leaning his face in his hands; by the time Joanna came back from the edge of the water, where she'd gone to dash a handful of it on her face, the sasennan, too, was asleep.

For a moment she stood looking at the both of them, elder and younger. Caris had to be at the end of his rope physically, she thought, studying his drawn young face in the watered-silk dappling of the willow's green shade, to conquer his nervousness about sleeping in the open. Antryg . . .

Under the poultice, she could see that the whole side of Antryg's face was a swollen and gruesome bruise. Oddly enough, though she was normally squeamish, this didn't sicken her or make her look away. She felt only compassion for the pain he must be in, guilt that he'd taken it for her sake, and . . .

. . . And something, she told herself, that kidnapped damsels had no business feeling for the villain of the piece.

He knows more than he's telling, she reminded herself. He's going to Angelshand for some reason of his own. It had not escaped her that, for all his lightweight chatter, Antryg had never again mentioned the place in the hills near Kymil in which Caris had found her. He had, as Caris had pointed out, led them away from it as quickly as he could. Was that out of fear of what lurked there or simply fear of what Caris, if he investigated the place, would find?

With a sigh, Joanna walked to Caris and gently removed the pistol from his slack hand. He didn't stir; only his breathing and the warmth of his flushed face told her he was still alive at all. Weary as she was, she couldn't bring herself to break that sleep.

I can stay awake for a little while, anyway, she thought, sitting down cross-legged in a tangle of skirts and feeling the now-familiar agony of pins and needles through her thighs and calves. Somewhere upstream, the moving water clucked a little against the overhanging weeds and cresses of the bank. Sunlight lay like scattered pennies over her tattered blue skirt and damp, rumpled hair. She looked down again at Antryg, curled up like a child beside her, his long, straggly, gray-brown hair hanging in his eyes.

Why had he said to Digby, . . . *to save my world, and yours, too, I hope, from a terrible fate?* What fate?

This emptiness, this vampiric draining of life?

The Industrial Revolution that was rapidly overtaking these people like a sooty and impersonal flood?

Some mad notion of his straying wits?

Or something else?

Upstream there was the sharp, startled flurry of a frightened bird, and a horse's indignant snort.

Joanna felt her insides shrivel.

As quietly as she could, she tightened her grip on the pistol and sank to her belly, to crawl under the tangle of vines along the top of the bank. Brambles scratched her elbows and snagged her skirts and hair, and she hoped to hell she hadn't just taken refuge in a giant thicket of poison ivy. Angling her eye to a break in the bushes, she saw him—a black-clothed sasennan bearing the crimson sunburst of the Church. He and his horse were nearly invisible in the sun-splattered shade of the opposite bank.

Behind her, she heard a man say softly, "That's them."

Turning her head slowly as little as she could for fear of rustling the vines which covered her, she looked back. A sasennan and another man in the close-cut gray coat of the Witchfinders emerged on foot from the green laurel thickets of the little island; the sasennan was leading two horses. As they stood for a moment looking down at the sleepers, the Witchfinder murmured, "It's the Archmage's sasennan. He escaped from Kymil by magic three days ago. Whatever plot is afoot, the Archmage is in it, all right. Peelbone will be pleased."

He took a pistol from the holster on his saddle tree.

Two thoughts chased one another very quickly through Joanna's mind: *This isn't any of my business! I was kidnapped and I don't want to play;* and immediately thereafter, cold and calm, *The man in gray has only a pistol.* His shoulders were broad over a slim waist. They made an ideal target as he turned to fetch something from his saddlebags. Joanna heard the jingle of chain.

You'll have to break cover a second before you pull the trigger, she thought, as if it were something she was only reading about. Another part of her was wailing in panic, *What if I miss?*

The adrenaline pumping in her veins almost made her sick. *Just lie here quiet and they might overlook you. . . .*

And they might not.

The sasennan walked to the bank of the stream, saying back over his shoulder, "So will his Grace." He signaled. Joanna heard the quick splash of hooves in the stony stream bed as the mounted sasennan on the other side began to cross.

"There was a girl with him, wasn't there?"

The heat in the thicket clung on her sweating face like glue, the green, musty smell of the brambles smothering. She felt queerly estranged from herself, aware of the five pounds of dead iron in her aching hand and ridiculously conscious that having it meant there was no excuse she could give herself later for not using it. *Why does it have to be me?*

She rose to her knees in the tangle of the vines, held the pistol in both hands, straightened her elbows and took long enough, as every Western she had ever read recommended, to be sure of her aim, and fired at a range of less than a dozen feet.

The kick of the gun jarred slammingly in her wrists and shoulders; the huge cloud of black smoke coughed forth from the muzzle burned in her lungs and eyes. The coppery stink of new blood exploded over the still air as the man in the gray coat was flung forward against his horse, the beast plunging in wild panic. At the same instant, Caris rolled, swinging his sword free of the scabbard which had lain, even in sleep, under his hand, and was on the unmounted sasennan before Joanna could have sworn he was even awake.

The sasennan crossing the stream was down off his own terrified horse with trained and deadly speed. Joanna, her pistol discharged, saw him coming for her with drawn sword and knew his intent was to kill. As in a nightmare, she feinted a lunge for one tree and dove to the cover of another. The man pursued, sword upraised and bright. Her unaccustomed skirts tangled in her legs, and brambles caught her ankles as she plunged across the small clearing toward the slumped form of the Witchfinder, her heart hammering with frenzy. *I must succeed—I can't let him touch me—I must finish this.* . . . His grabbing hand pinched the flesh of her arm, then fell away. She threw herself on the sprawled body of her first victim, thrusting it aside to fumble the pistol with its blood-sticky butt from underneath, just as the sasennan's shadow covered her.

She swung around, rising to her knees, pistol in hands. Mottled sun seared along the downswinging arc of the sword. There wasn't time to duck—every second of time felt queerly compressed. . . .

She pulled the trigger. Blood spouted out onto her face as the ball plowed upwards through the man's body, only feet away. She flung herself aside to avoid the body as it collapsed on top of her, and fell over the Witchfinder's body. She raised herself on one numbed arm in time to see Caris pull his dripping blade from his dead assailant's still-standing corpse.

Start to finish, the whole fight couldn't have taken eight seconds.

The smell of blood was everywhere. Joanna wiped at the hot, thick stream of it on her chin and felt the sticky gouts of it in her hair. Both wrists felt numbed and broken; so did some part of her within.

As a gray wave of dimness blurred her sight, she wondered detachedly which she would do first—throw up or faint.

"Joanna?" A deep voice penetrated blurrily through the grayness; strong, light hands pulled her to her feet, lifting her with effortless strength. There was the scratching slash of a passing branch against her bare arm, then the sudden coolness of river water flowing all around her.

She started to say, "What . . . ?" A hand pinched her nose shut and she was thrust bodily under the water, then dragged up again, gasping and dripping, her head suddenly clear.

She shoved back her soaked hair and saw Antryg standing waist-deep in the water beside her. His soaked shirt was stuck to his body, his eyes worried behind the cracked lenses of his specs. "Are you all right?"

Joanna nodded. The water had rinsed away the blood on her face and hair. She felt breathless, as if she had been awakened suddenly from sleep. Shakily, she managed a reassuring grin and asked, "Does this mean I'm now a member of the Church?"

The worry dissolved into a sparkle of humor in his eyes. Solemnly, he dipped a handful of water and dumped it over her head. Not jesting, he said softly, "I'm afraid it does mean that you've been baptized, Joanna. Naturally, I can't say I'm sorry you did it—but I'm sorry that you had to."

"It's okay." Her voice sounded weak and thready to her own ear.

From the bank, she heard Caris say harshly, "Come on!"

Antryg laid a gentle hand against her dripping hair, anxiously studying her face. She would have liked to hold him—to hold someone—and cry with the sudden, sick confusion in her, but the calm part of her mind knew Caris was right. The shots would have roused the whole woods. So she only nodded in answer to Antryg's unspoken question and said, "Thank you."

He helped her to the bank. Caris, both reloaded pistols in his belt and his sword in his hand, stood scanning the woods around him, remote and beautiful and inscrutable as ever.

It was only that night, after a nightmare day of stumbling flight and of hiding from patrols that seemed suddenly everywhere, that what had happened on the island became truly real to her. For a long time she lay awake in the half-filled hayloft where they had taken refuge, listening to the approaching rumble of thunder and the restless, gusty unevenness of the rain. Her wrists ached, but it was nothing to the hideous memory of panic and the kinetic recollection of that first jet of blood dousing her face. On television, she had casually watched hundreds of people allegedly die. None of it was anything like this.

She thought, *I have killed a man,* and only belatedly remembered that she had killed two.

She knew Antryg was asleep. She cringed from waking him, partly because she knew he was exhausted, partly . . . She did not know why, save that she had never shared grief and fear with anyone, and didn't know how to go about it. Caris was awake, and she stifled her sobs as best she could, lest he hear.

But after a long time his voice said softly from the utter blackness, "Joanna?"

There was the crunch of hay, and its warm smell as it shifted. Then the warm, dry touch of the sasennan's hand on her shoulder.

"Are you all right?"

That Caris would have been concerned came as a surprise to her. She sniffled, swallowed, and hoped her tears wouldn't be apparent in her voice. "You probably think this is stupid," she began and cursed the betraying tremor of her vocal chords. "But—how old were you, the first time you killed somebody?"

There was a long silence, filled only with darkness, rain, and the green smell of the hay.

"Fifteen," Caris said at last. "It's the first thing you do in training, you know. The man's tied up. They don't start you on criminals free to fight back until your second or third year of training. But, they say, a weapon must know the taste of blood from the first."

"Oh," Joanna whispered soundlessly.

She thought it was all Caris would say. It was no wonder, she thought wretchedly, that her own inarticulate scruples sounded ridiculous to that beautiful young man. But when Caris spoke again, she realized the long delay had been because the sasennan was inept with words; not wanting to hurt her, he had paused long to choose what he would say with care.

"But I had never killed a man before in a true fight—a fight for my life, one that was not in training. We're trained to be ready for it, but . . . it really seldom happens." There was another long silence. Then he said, "Do you know what the Witchfinders would have done—to me and to Antryg, and probably to you as our accomplice?"

Joanna shook her head.

Caris told her, in a wealth of clinical detail that made her almost physically sick.

"A weapon that thinks is a flawed weapon, Joanna," he said softly. "You had to do what you did. You didn't take two lives, you saved two, probably three—probably a lot more. I have to get Antryg alive to the Regent, not as his accomplice in some plot the Witchfinders are accusing us of, but free and on my own terms, as proof of the truth. Sometimes you can't think too much. Only do what you need to do."

And in those words Joanna took a certain amount of comfort, at least for as long as she remained awake.

CHAPTER XII

THE LOWING OF A COW WOKE CARIS, TO THE CLINGING, TEPID HEAT of morning. Last night's storm had cooled the air enough to permit sleep after the killing exhaustion of the last twenty-four hours; but with the new sun, the rain was evaporating in clammy dampness which made his rough peasant clothes and coarse stockings stick to his body like an evil fairy's garment of itches.

He lay in the hay for a few moments, looking at his two companions in flight.

He had never expected the girl Joanna to be still with them after four days. What he had seen of her world and what she had told him and Antryg during the first day's walk to Kymil had made him doubt her abilities to keep up with them. Caris had been raised in the Way of the Sasenna, and, from what he had seen and heard, hers was a world in which machines, like the cars and computers of which she had spoken, had taken over both the work that strengthened the body and the entertainment that sharpened the wits. She was shy and, he suspected, more used to speaking to these computers than to people; but it had surprised him that she had not panicked yesterday. If asked beforehand, he would have laid money against her having the nerve to pull the trigger.

And, he reflected ruefully, lost it.

Curled up on the hay, she looked thin and even smaller than usual. They had gotten rid of her bloodstained peasant clothing, and she looked like a little boy in her scruffy blue jeans and creased and filthy tank-top, with hay caught in her feathery blond curls. Her arms and shoulders were brown and sunburned, covered with scratches and insect bites. For all her small size, weariness had printed lines on her face that even sleep couldn't erase, and she looked older than her age, which she had said was twenty-six, and very alone.

A little ways from her, Antryg lay with his head on his rolled-up coat. His cracked spectacles rested in the hay nearby and the strings of cheap glass beads around his throat caught slivers of hurtfully bright gold sunlight that streamed through the cracks in the barn walls. Under the unruly tousle of his hay-flecked hair, the bruises on his face already looked less swollen than they had. They were turning black; Caris had spent the last five years of his life training to be sasennan and had an intimate acquaintance with bruises; he knew they must hurt like the devil. He'd taken a swordcut on the cheek in his first year of training and he remembered that the pain had dogged even his sleep.

And well served, too, he thought bitterly. He sat up and shook as much hay as he could out of his smock. Like the pain of a burn, his anger returned to fuel his strength. *For what he has done to my grandfather— for what that disappearance did to all the mages . . .*

Outside, the cow lowed again. Raised to the rhythms of farm and village life, Caris recognized the pain in the sound. The beast was stray, he thought, and needed to be milked. The gray deadness that had gripped the countryside yesterday morning had left its effects; not a cowman between here and Parchasten had remembered to close his gates. All afternoon and evening, they had been seeing strayed beasts in the half-cut hay meadows and standing corn. Now that he thought about it, Caris looked around the barn. The storm, he thought, would have ruined the best part of the haying. It was late enough in the summer that this barn should have been full-stocked. He frowned to himself at the recollection of something the Bishop of Kymil had said regarding farms let fall to rot.

But a cow in milk is a cow in milk, and the bread that he and Antryg had variously pocketed during the last, distant supper at the roadhouse had long since been eaten. Casting a glance behind him at the sleepers, Caris slipped his scabbarded sword into his sash, ready to draw and fight, and moved cautiously to the door.

His first glance around, as he opened it a crack, showed him that the woods onto which the barn faced were deserted. His trained mind toyed with the idea of a trap, with the cow as bait, then dismissed it. Anyone who knew they were there could simply have come in and overpowered them, exhausted as they were, or simply burned the barn over their heads.

It was only at his second glance that he truly saw the cow.

She was standing a few yards from the rickety doors of the barn, and

Caris did not even need his farm background to know there was something terribly wrong with her. She stood broadside to him, weaving on her feet; her white and cream hide was sunk over her broad pelvis and barrel ribs as if with long sickness, but the green stains of grass smudged her legs. She had been out to pasture. Caris pushed the door gently open and walked toward her. There was no sign of ambush or threat from the woods, but the sixth sense of a sasennan screamed at him of danger. . . .

Then she turned her head and forequarters toward him. Caris felt the vomit rise to burn his throat and the sudden chill of sweat stick his coarse clothing to his back.

There was an abomination fastened leechlike to the cow.

It was unlike the one he had seen in the marsh, but he knew it for nothing that existed in this world. It dangled, swollen, from the beast's shoulder like a monstrous tick, mottled green-black and purple and longer than a man's forearm. By the swelling under the hide where it was attached, Caris knew there was at least four inches of head buried under the skin.

The cow lowed again and stared at him with sunken and pain-glazed eyes. Caris gritted his teeth—sick as the thought made him, he knew he could never leave an animal to suffer in that fashion.

He looked quickly about. It was broad daylight now—early, by the elongated indigo shadows. The patrols would be checking every building they found. In a little pile of rubbish by the door, he found some old tools, including a couple of broken scythe handles and half-rotted leather straps. With one of the straps, he tied a bunch of hay onto the end of a handle; with the flint and steel no sasennan is ever without, he lighted this makeshift torch and advanced, rather queasily, upon the cow and its horrible parasite. The poor beast flinched a little from the pale brightness of the fire, but was too exhausted to flee. Caris gingerly gripped her horn and brought the burning end of the torch to the parasite's slimy back.

Like a tick, it twitched revoltingly; then it backed slowly out of the wound and dropped to the ground with a horrible squishing sound.

Clotted with blood and flesh, its head was almost indistinguishable—equipped, Caris thought, with at least three mouths, mandibled like an ant's, but infinitely more hideous. For an instant, the mouths worked with an unspeakable chewing motion. Then the head swung around, and Caris leaped back as the thing writhed like a snake on the trampled grass and launched itself, with incredible speed for something so puffed, at Caris' groin.

As with the thing in the marsh, Caris' body thought for him. He struck at the thing with all the force of his arm, using the side of the torch like a bat. The mandibled mouth clamped around the wood; the tiny, lobster like claws grappled, and the thing lunged up the handle toward his chest. Horror-sickened, Caris flung the torch from him and ran; he heard the thing's body thump soddenly against the door as he slammed it shut.

"Antryg!" Renegade, devious, and student of Suraklin he might be, but he had spoken of the abominations as if he knew them. At least he would know what to do.

The wizard sat up, blinking, already fumbling his spectacles onto his lacerated face. He took one look at Caris and asked, "Where?" without bothering to ask what. Like a gawky heron, he unfolded to his feet and strode past Caris to the door to peer through the cracks. After a long pause, he held up a cautionary hand and pushed open the door slightly. Through it, Caris could see the cow lying on her chest, too exhausted to flee or even to stand. The parasite had returned to her, now hanging from her throat. Flies were already swarming over the first gaping wound its exit had left.

Caris was aware that he was shaking.

Antryg's voice was deep and oddly comforting in the hot, umber gloom of the barn. "There's nothing we can do for her now, except put her out of her pain, and I'm not sure it would be safe to get close enough to do that silently."

Quietly, Joanna joined them at the door. She made a small noise of utter revulsion in her throat at the sight of the parasite, but nothing more. "It's an abomination," Antryg murmured to her, "a thing that has come through a weakening in the Void when a gateway was opened. Or, more likely, it was a parasite on something that came through."

She took another cautious look, around him at the cow. "The original host could have died almost immediately," she said thoughtfully. "Who knows—maybe its parasites started off small and something in this universe made them grow."

The remark baffled Caris, but Antryg nodded as if he understood. There was a fleeting appearance of kinship between them, with their blue jeans and white shirts, their tangled, curly hair, and their sunburned faces. After a moment, the wizard walked back into the darkness of the barn, his white shirt a blur in the gloom. Caris saw what had not been apparent last night; the building had two doors, one facing toward the woods, through which they had come the previous night, and the other facing out into a lowland hay meadow. Green sweetness and a sharp square of primrose light breathed into the dim barn in a rush as Antryg pushed open one leaf of the vast portal. The meadow had only been partly cut; cows stood in the long, lush grass that ran down to a stream deep in cresses and ferns. When the wind shifted, Caris could hear another cow groan in feeble agony.

Antryg murmured, "As I thought."

Past the stream, the dark tangle of a quickset hedge marked the road; Caris shivered. He had not thought it so close, and wondered how obvious the barn was from it. Quietly he joined the wizard by the door. "We haven't time for this," he said softly. "We have to leave this place."

"Don't be silly." Antryg drew him back into the protective shade of the barn. He pushed his specs a little further up the bridge of his long nose with one bony forefinger, wincing where the metal of the earpiece touched the bruised mess of his temple. "We have to know at least a little of how to deal with the things. Look at how those cows are moving. They're all infected. It's more than likely the things are in the woods as well." He walked back to the piled hay where he had slept, unrolled his coat, and put it on, the worn velvet rumpled and covered with shreds of hay.

Joanna had remained by the door to the meadow. She was looking out with what might have been nauseated fascination or what might have been simple watchfulness, for it was only by close scrutiny that someone might be seen on the road on the other side of the hedgerow. Caris followed Antryg back toward the door to the woods, but caught him by the sleeve when he made to go through it. For once, he did not fear the wizard making a break for it. Indeed, he suspected that, unless Antryg was playing a very deep game, Antryg would not try to escape until they reached Angelshand itself. But the thought of stepping outside, where the dying cow and her hideous vampire still lay joined in the brightness of the morning sunlight, made his nape crawl.

Gently, Antryg shook loose the grip. He slipped through the open door, stepped quickly to where the torch lay guttered out in the dust, retrieved it, and returned. Neither cow nor parasite moved. His hair shadowing his eyes in the early light, Antryg undid the strap, shoved a little more hay under it, and cinched it tight again. He looked up at Caris. "Either come with me or lend me your sword."

The descent into the hay meadow was closer to the hell of the Church's Sole God than anything Caris had yet experienced in his life. He had been trained in the Way of the Sasenna, taught to face and fight and kill any man or woman living. But in the last weeks, he had faced, not man or woman, but things he had never prepared for: the mewing abomination in the marsh; the hideous, icy fall through the blowing darkness that lies between universes; and the ghastly uncertainties of trying to operate by the Way of the Sasenna without a master to command him. To fight even a monster was one thing; to walk through a plague of lethal and filthy parasites was something for which neither he nor his masters had ever thought to prepare him.

The meadow was full of the abominations.

What little wind there was set from the woods; it was only when he and Antryg were in the long grasses of the meadow itself that the smell of blood came to Caris' nostrils. With it came a foul, half-familiar pungency he did not know, but which nauseated him. There were half a dozen cows in the meadow, drawn there to drink at the spring. Every one bore at least one parasite; some poor beasts had two or three, hanging like swollen, slimily gleaming bolsters from their sides or throats or lying draped over them, if they lay in the grass. The parasites themselves were anywhere above a foot in length; one, twitching over the heaving side of a yearling calf, was nearly four feet long.

In his rough smock and coarse canvas breeches, Caris had never felt so unprotected in his life. Horror and revulsion made him queasy, but he heard Antryg, peering through the quizzing glass at that sunken body with its hideous burden, murmur, "Fascinating."

Around the stream, the long, rank grasses thrashed with their squirmings. Antryg raised his head, curious. "There seem to be a lot of them down there."

A sharp rustle in the meadow to their left made Caris swing around, his sword in his hand; his mouth felt dry with fear. "Let's go back. . . ."

Antryg, torch in hand, advanced, wading through the deep ferns toward the stream.

Caris had only an instant's glimpse of the abomination in the ferns before it struck. It was three feet long and launched itself at Antryg like a striking cobra; Caris' sword was whining through the fetid air while his mind was still identifying what it was that he struck. His blade caught the thing in the middle of its swollen body, checking the strike as it fell in two pieces; Antryg stepped lightly back as the head and struck at him again, bouncing short, like a hellish ball, its spined mouth snapping. Grayish slime from the split abdomen stank as it pooled in the grass; Caris whirled in horror as the whole meadow around them erupted suddenly into a sea of frantic thrashings.

It seemed as if every filthy creature in that abominable meadow was galvanized into abrupt and greedy life. From every point of the compass, there were wallowing and lunging toward the two humans. From the hay barn at the top of the meadow, Caris heard Joanna's entirely unnecessary warning scream.

The abomination feeding on the calf pulled its filthy, purpuric head from the wound and struck at Caris in a streaming splatter of blood and fluid from a distance of only feet. Caris moved his sword to strike but the thing caught the blade itself, wrapping tiny, hideous claws around it, dragging it down with its huge weight. Reflex made Caris drop the blade and spring back, remembering how its fellow had lunged up along the torch; an instant later he cursed himself for dropping the weapon. Antryg's powerful hand closed around his arm and the two of them fled through the long grass of the meadow, both knowing it was only a question of instants before that wallowing circle of creatures closed around them. . . .

But they did not. They fell to feeding, instead, on the split carcass of the dead parasite. Halfway back to the barn, Antryg and Caris stopped, panting, to look back and saw nothing of the dead abomination and the stinking pool of slime around it but a writhing, struggling mass of slimy purple backs.

Something brushed Caris' ankle, and he sprang aside with a shuddering gasp. It was a foot-long abomination, plowing through the grass like a determined maggot toward the others. Caris' whole body was shaking with something more terrible than cold, but Antryg stood, his head a little on one side, watching.

"Caris, I think we've been snubbed," he remarked. Swinging the burnt-out torch, he walked back up towards the barn.

It was only when they were very near it that Caris realized that Joanna was not alone.

There was a wagon and team tied up at one side of the barn. A man in the green livery of a coachman was on the box; a footman, carrying a long, old-fashioned pike, stood beside it, nervously watching the meadow. Caris stopped in his tracks, feeling for his missing sword and cursing himself again for dropping it. But in any case, fighting would be hopeless. From the shadows of the barn, he saw Joanna wave, beckoning. In the gloom behind her, steel flashed.

Antryg laughed suddenly, and said, "Well done!" He strode forward, leaving Caris either to abandon his captive or follow. He had to run to catch up.

The man standing beside Joanna in the dense shade of the barn was wearing armor of the sort not seen in centuries—a suit of plate that covered the wearer from head to foot. The steel was ornamented with scallop and millefleur, bright with gilding, and every inch overwritten with spells and proofs against the workings of the rival champion's wizard. It was, in fact, the product of the last days before the battle of the

Field of Stellith—massive, proof against both crossbow and heat-spell, and weighing well over a hundred pounds.

Only the helm of this archaic marvel was missing. From the enormous shoulders, with their cresting and giltwork, rose a head of startling modernity. The young man's round cheeks and a slight double-chin gave an indication of what sort of form lay beneath all that ensorcelled steel. His hazel eyes were bright with interest and meticulously painted; the soft, dark-brown curls clustering around his face showed an expert's assiduous hand in their arrangement.

The emblem on the massive breastplate was that of the royal house of the Emperors of Ferryth.

It was not the Way of the Sasenna to acknowledge lordship, other than of one's own master, not even the highest, but Caris bent his head respectfully and said, "Lord Cerdic."

The young man waved away the gesture of respect with one massively mailed hand. "That was brave—incredibly brave." He looked from the desperately thrashing meadow to Caris and then to Antryg. "Do I guess correctly that you are the mage my cousin's men have been combing the countryside for?"

Caris frowned disapprovingly, but Antryg nodded. "At your humble service," he said, with a glint in his gray eyes. "If it please your Grace, I shall keep my name to myself."

"Of course," Prince Cerdic said hastily. "Of course. I would never dream of asking such a thing of the mageborn." His painted hazel eyes returned to the field again, and concern creased his open brow. "What have you decided about them, my lord? My peasants came to me begging my help. I put this thing on—it's been standing in a corner of Devilsgate Hall for centuries—and came down to have a look at them, though deuce knows what I'd have done if I'd fallen over out there in it."

"When were they first seen?" Antryg asked.

Cerdic shook his head. "Three, four days ago one of my cowmen reported finding one—a little one, no bigger than a sausage—on a heifer up in the high pastures near the Devil's Road. He got it to back out with a torch, then it struck at him, and he ran away; fire didn't seem to bother it. When they started showing up on the herds, we tried poison, and that doesn't slow them down, either. Perhaps, if your lordship used magic . . ."

Caris glanced sidelong at his so-called prisoner, with spiteful satisfaction. Antryg pushed up his spectacles, like a man who is stalling for time to explain why he has appeared at an evening function in a morning coat.

"Well, there is a reason I can't use magic," he said apologetically. "And in any case, it would take—"

Still leaning against the jamb of the barn door, Joanna turned her head from the thrashing grasses of the meadow to ask, "What kind of fire did you use?"

Cerdic raised his plucked brows. "What other kinds of fire are there, my dear? Fire is fire."

"If fire was fire," Joanna pointed out, a little diffidently, "you'd be able to temper sword steel in the kitchen stove. Have you tried destroying them with condensed fire, as in a kiln? The hottest kind of kiln you have . . ."

"That would be a limekiln," provided Antryg thoughtfully. "They have steel hearths hotter in Parchasten, where they can get the coke. . . ."

"But we do have a limekiln," Cerdic said eagerly. Then his face fell. "But as for getting them in it—we could only bait one or two at a time, and then they mightn't respond, if the bait was inside the kiln." He glanced hopefully at Antryg. "Unless there were some kind of a summoning spell?"

Antryg sighed. "I'm afraid the abominations wouldn't be the only things such a spell would summon."

"And we wouldn't have time," Joanna put in and nodded toward the horrible movement in the meadow outside. "The things seem to be multiplying pretty fast."

"We may have less time than we think." Antryg shoved his hands in his jeans pockets and cocked his head to one side. "It all depends on whether they're ticks or maggots, you see."

The remark made no sense to Caris, but Joanna went white with horror. Feeling a little as he did when talking to his grandfather, Caris demanded, "What difference does it make?"

The wizard shrugged. "The most attractive thing that can be said for a tick," he responded, "is that it isn't going to turn into anything else that might have wings."

Caris stared at him in shock; the idea that the abominations might metamorphose had never occurred to him. Cerdic whispered numbly, "Mother of God . . ." He swallowed hard. "But if you will not use magic—if poison won't work—"

Caris' eyes went to the wizard's face, reading the struggle obvious there as he tried to figure some way of using his powers without summoning down the Council or the Church dogs, as well. Cerdic was watching him intently, and Caris wondered if he could use this unwillingness to turn the Prince from Antryg's ally to his own.

Then Joanna asked, "What would you need for a spell?"

Antryg shook his head. "Something to draw them. They came like ants after sugar to the body of the dead one. I'd probably send out some kind of an illusion of its smell to draw them to the limekiln. Once they were inside it could be fired."

"We've tried using blood," Cerdic added, clanking forward and awkwardly folding his arms. "Two or three came to it, but the poison didn't stop them. We used plagueroot—the most virulent poison there is— quarts of it. The smell alone should have killed them."

"Try mercury or arsenic," Joanna said. "They're metals. No matter what kind of organisms the things are, a heavy metal should at least slow them down. Whatever they smelled in the dead abomination must be a concentrate of something from the cow's blood, to bring them so fast that they ignored everything else."

Caris shook his head. "One of them attacked me within feet of the carcass."

"Did it?" Antryg inquired suddenly. "As I remember, it attacked your *sword.* Which, of course, was smeared with fluid from the thing's body. It didn't leap after you, once it had the sword. And I'll tell you something else. Whatever they look for in blood, I think they also look for it in earth. At least the stream bank was all chewed with the things tunnelings."

"A trace mineral?" Joanna suggested thoughtfully. She scratched at a fragment of hay in her hair—very different, suddenly, Caris thought, from the painfully shy girl who had accompanied them up from Kymil. She was not, after all, merely a talker to machines, and he wondered suddenly if it was this quality, this knowledge, for which Antryg had kidnapped her. "Blood is mostly water, salt, proteins, and some trace minerals and it carries oxygen. Obviously it isn't water they want or they'd have been in the stream itself. It might be nitrogen. . . ."

"Cerdic." Antryg turned to the Prince, who had stood throughout this with a look of mystification on his round, perspiring face. "Did there used to be a salt lick down by the stream?"

The young man looked blank. "Dashed if I know. Does it matter?"

"A salt lick?" Joanna asked, puzzled.

"Yes—a natural outcropping of salt in the ground. There's a trampled patch on the bank that looks as if it's where the cattle regularly came down. . . ."

At the Prince's signal, the coachman jumped down from the wagon and approached, casting a wary look at Antryg and a disapproving one at Joanna's jeans-clad legs. "Oh, aye," he said, when asked. "That's what the cows were doing in the meadow in the first place, after that good-for-nothing Joe left the field gates open day before yesterday. The cowman drives 'em down there regular, and a job he has keeping 'em out of the hay."

"Well," said Antryg simply, "the lick's gone, now. The whole bank's tunneled in."

"That's probably when they started feeding on the cows," Joanna said. She turned back to the baffled-looking Cerdic. "I think that's your answer," she said, and abruptly, as if she heard and feared the quiet authority in her own voice, her old shyness returned. Diffident but resolute, she continued, "Heavily concentrated salt—as much of it as you can get—with enough water to make it liquid and as much mercury and arsenic as you have. If it doesn't kill them, it should slow them down enough to be shoveled into the limekiln."

Cerdic caught her hand between his two massively mailed ones and said what no knight in gilded armor ever said to any lady of any legend. "My dear girl, you're a genius!"

Joanna blushed furiously and shook her head. "It just took breaking it down into subroutines," she explained self-deprecatingly. "I mean—that's how all programmers think."

The Prince frowned. "Programmer—is that a sort of wizard?"

Antryg, seeing Joanna's confusion overcoming her, put a comforting arm around her shoulders and said, "Yes. And now," he added gravely, "I hope you mean to arrest us, because that would mean we could stop running and have some breakfast."

With equally sober mien, the Prince began to bow, and Caris, the coachman, and Antryg all barely caught him in time, before he overbalanced in the weight of the armor. He substituted a graceful gesture of his arm. "My lord wizard," he said, "please consider yourself under arrest."

"So what happens now?"

Antryg turned from the long rectangle of the window's shadowy luminescence. Far off, a line of smoke marked the first of the limekilns firing up.

"It seems to have worked," he said and smiled a welcome as Joanna gathered up the handfuls of green sprig-muslin skirts and petticoats and rustled her way across the parquet of the drawing room floor. The rooms the Prince had given them at Devilsgate Manor looked east over a short stretch of informal garden to the woods; at this hour, though the greenery outside was still spangled with the last brightness of the evening sun, the rooms themselves were growing dim. "And he was quite right, my dear. It was a stroke of genius, subroutines or no subroutines."

Joanna shook her head again, as self-conscious over the praise as she was over the ribbon-edged flounces and low-cut neckline of her gown. She still wondered who the Prince was in the habit of keeping spare gowns around for. "It comes from breaking everything down for programming," she said. "Talking to a machine, you have to think like one —choose one alternative or the other, decide A on what grounds, decide B on what grounds, if not B, what's C . . . everything in a million little increments." She made a move to sit on the edge of a nearby chair back and gave it up as the unwary move earned her a poke under the ribcage from the boning in the gown's bodice. "It may be slower than talking to a person; but if you do everything right, you always know where you are."

His gray eyes were kind as he heard the years of buried uncertainties in her words, but he only said, "A little like magic, then. To weave a spell, one must know everything about the object of the spell. Thank you," he added softly, "for taking over there. Because you did keep me from having to make a very awkward choice."

Joanna blushed, confused and embarrassed by praise. Fed, washed, and rested, clothed in a gown far more elegant and twice as uncomfortable as her former peasant disguise, she still found herself aching from the hardships of flight. Her wrists still hurt from the kick of the pistol, reminding her of what she had done not forty-eight hours before. That, like the cumulative exhaustion, was something she knew already would take more than a few hours' rest to cure. In a sense it would never be cured—it would always remain something she had done.

Antryg, she was glad to see, looked better, also. He'd acquired a clean ruffled shirt, though he still wore his long-skirted velvet coat and borrowed jeans. The wound on his face was visibly less raw than it had been.

"Any programmer could have figured it out," she protested again. "And you were right—we had no idea of what those things could or might turn into." She hesitated. "And we have no guarantee there won't be others, do we?"

He shook his head—there passed across the back of his eyes some haunted darkness of knowledge, as if he guessed unthinkable possibilities. His voice was very low. "No."

"What happens now?"

Antryg sighed and seemed to brush aside the half-contemplated horrors. "I suppose I could read the cards to find out," he said. "Though the cards are a bit dangerous in themselves."

"Because you can be traced by the Council?"

"No—they're no more magic than dreaming is, really. But the cards have a nasty habit of telling one things one doesn't really wish to know."

Joanna leaned against the opposite jamb of the tall windows and ran her hand down the smooth, gilded molding. "But then you can prepare for catastrophe, if one's coming up."

"Perhaps—unless, like war or jealously, it's the preparation which triggers it. It's easier to let go and deal with things as they arise."

"Maybe," she said, with a rueful smile. "But letting go of things and letting events take their course has always been the hardest thing for me to do." She shook her head, the damp, trailing ends of her hair brushing against her bare shoulders, brown and then white with the changed neckline. "It probably sounds pretty stupid, because I know there's something terrible going on, something evil, but all I really want is out."

He smiled. "It isn't stupid," he said gently. "From time to time, I find myself wishing I were back in the Tower, not because it was comfortable —which it wasn't—but because it was peaceful, and all my things are there, and I was safe."

She remembered her thought on the island, just before she pulled the trigger—*If I didn't have a gun, I wouldn't have to do this.*

"Are we safe?" she asked.

He considered the matter. "I shouldn't think so," he replied judiciously after a moment. "I'm certainly not, and you . . ." There was a long pause, during which, looking up into those mild gray eyes, she noted that they were in truth a very gray blue, flecked with white and hazel-yellow which gave them their silvery cast. There was a triangular pucker of skin, like a small V, among the crisscrossed wrinkles below the left one.

He sighed and said, half to himself, "I wish I knew."

Joanna reflected that she was beginning to feel like the poor *schlemazl* in *North by Northwest,* kidnapped and haled all over the countryside, being shot at by strangers without any idea of what was happening, and on top of it all . . .

There was, she realized, another part to that analogy.

For a long time, their eyes held.

She thought, with a curious sense of shock that was not surprise, *I expected it to be different than this.* For a time it seemed to her that neither of them breathed—that it was impossible that the only point of contact between their two bodies was where her petticoats brushed against his booted ankle in a froth of voile. Part of her mind was saying in its usual cool and practical tones, *This is ridiculous. I don't do things like this*—while another part said, *I want him.*

For a time the sooty-gray shadows of the empty drawing room were like completely still water, fathoms deep and silent but for the distant chatter of the birds outside. The smell of the woods, of grass damp from last night's rain and of the far-off acrid smoke of the burning kilns, came to her through the open windows, mixed with the faint scent of soap from his flesh and hair. He stood so still that one facet of the crystal earring he wore held a gleam of the last light from outside like a tiny mirror, steely and unmoving in the deepening gloom; the only thing that stirred was the white rim of light on the ruffles of his shirt with the rise and fall of his breath.

Everything seemed incredibly clear to her, but without pattern. It had nothing in common with her encounters with Gary and her nervous weighing and reweighing of pro and con. She only knew that she wanted him and knew, looking up into the wide, black pupils of his eyes, that he wanted her.

He turned abruptly, almost angrily, away and walked from the windows into the twilight cavern of the room. "I will not do this," he said softly. She could hear the faint tremor of his deep voice. "You are dependent on me and under my protection in this world. I won't take advantage of that."

His back was to her, the diffuse whiteness of the fading day putting a sheen like pewter on the velvet of his shoulders. She knew well enough that he was conscious of her eyes upon his back. She was aware of her own feelings less clearly, shocked and appalled, not by them, but by their strength. Nothing she had ever experienced with Gary, not even sex, came anywhere near this need—not to have, but to give.

After a moment he turned and walked silently from the room.

"You can't pretend you don't know what he's done!" Caris swung around in his pacing to face the Prince behind his inlaid fruitwood desk. "It is he and not the Church or the Inquisition of your cousin who is the true enemy of the Council!"

Prince Cerdic was silent. His round, smooth, white hands with their old-fashioned rings of gold and rose crystal were folded on the marquetry before him, his painted mouth settled and still. His study, with its old fashioned linenfold paneling and coffered ceiling, looked north; through the tall windows, Caris could see in the distance against the milky twilight sky the first tall outliers of the Devil's Road itself, crowning the bare top of the hill—standing-stones, such as had guarded the way from

Kymil to the Silent Tower long before either city or Tower had been built. Yet the long, silent line of stone sentries led from nowhere to nowhere, traversed only by the wind and by the queer, traveling energies of the earth that only the mages felt.

Caris was coming to see that it was no accident that Prince Cerdic, out of all the manors available to the Imperial Family, had chosen this as his principal seat. Doggedly, he went on, "It is Antryg who kidnapped the Archmage and who gave the Church and the Witchfinders their chance to announce that the mages were plotting against the Empire—gave them their chance to arrest the mageborn without fear of reprisals! Maybe he did it for that reason—maybe for others. He is responsible for the abominations—"

"There's nothing to show that," the Prince protested.

"Then how has he known where they would be? How does he make guesses about what they are or could become?"

The Prince still said nothing, only sat, among his gold and shellwork incense-burners, while the images of the twenty-one Old Gods watched his round, pink satin back. Like many converts, Prince Cerdic was more devout than most Old Believers Caris had met; he was the only one the young man had seen who had statues of the Old Gods, instead of the elaborate calligraphy talismans of their names pasted to the walls with which most Old Believers contented themselves. As he had told the Prince about the abomination in the swamp, about his grandfather's revelations on the fallen stone, and about seeing the old man's glove in Antryg's room as the mad wizard vanished through the Void into that other bizarre and terrible world, he felt the eyes of those small idols upon him —dog-headed Lancres, Tambet with the baby Signius at her breast, Kahieret the God of the Mages with his stork's head rising from the long black robes of a wizard, the horned Dead God wrapped in his burial shroud. . . .

"I need an introduction to the Court," Caris said quietly. "If I bring Antryg to your cousin the Regent openly before witnesses—if I am able to leave freely—the Witchfinders cannot deny either his capture or his confession. They are not interested in truth, but only in what story will best serve their ends; allow them simply to destroy Antryg, and we will never find the Archmage, nor restore the Council's power."

Cerdic rubbed his smooth chin with one lace-gloved hand. "But maybe he is telling you the truth," he said. "The mageborn understand so much more of what is going on than mere mortals like you and me. . . ."

"The fact that they do does not mean he speaks the truth!" Caris almost shouted. "He keeps claiming that the one who has done this evil, who steals the life from the souls of the land, who calls the abominations through the Void, and who kidnapped the Archmage and brought the woman Joanna here is not him, but someone else. But according to the Archmage, there *is* no one else with that understanding of the Void!"

The light of the dozen candles illuminating the opulent study flickered in a rim of fire over the embroidery that laced the Prince's carnation-colored coat. Behind him, on the shelves with the idols of the Old Gods, Caris could see old and crumbling tomes of magic. Some he recognized from his grandfather's study in the Mages' Yard; others he knew only by the sneers of the Council wizards, volumes of piesog and earth-magic and granny-lore, the compendia of every quack and dog wizard for five hundred years. The Prince moved uncomfortably in his velvet chair, his diamond earrings casting a sprinkle of brightness over his shoulders and his pink-and-white cravat.

"In the first place, I'm not sure either my introduction or my patronage would do your cause any good," he said. "My cousin has always been insanely suspicious of everyone. Of late, those suspicious have begun to turn against me as well. It's one reason I'm here and not at Court, doing what I can to help the mageborn. He has me watched in the capital. It's absurd, because technically I am his heir, but I was beginning to fear for my safety.

"But in any case . . ." He frowned and smoothed the lace of his glove. "It is not for us to judge the mageborn. They were our first priests, servants of the Old Gods. They still commune with their ancient powers, beyond the ken of you and me."

Impatiently, Caris began, "That's nonsense! There aren't more than a handful of mages who are Old Believers."

"No matter what they call them," Cerdic said gravely, "the powers they exercise are still the powers of the Old Ones. It is not for any mere mortal to disturb the great webs of destiny, not even for motives which they themselves deem laudable. They say my uncle, the Emperor, had a great deal of respect for Suraklin and went to his prison cell many times to visit him after he was taken; but still, he took it upon himself to destroy a mage, and great evil fell upon him after."

"Twenty years later?"

The Prince's soft mouth pursed, giving his otherwise open countenance a mulish appearance. Caris, though he knew this young man was the second heir to the Realm after the mad Regent, was conscious of an overwhelming desire to knock that pomaded head against the wall.

"He ought never to have meddled in the Dark Mage's affairs. Woe comes to them who hold the mageborn in light regard."

Caris was beginning to understand the viewpoint of those nobles who preferred the Regent Pharos' sadistic madness to this kind of blind obstinacy. Antryg, he realized, knew how to pick his friends.

Slowly, he said, "Woe certainly came to those who held Suraklin in light regard. But that didn't mean that he should not have been stopped. And Antryg is his student, his heir, and privy to all his black arts."

Cerdic leaned across the variegated inlay of the desk surface, to catch Caris' hand. There was that maddening, ethereal kindness in his eyes as he said earnestly, "That is only what you believe, as an outsider looking in."

"I am not . . ." began Caris indignantly, pulling his hand away, but Cerdic's soft, rather high voice rode right over his words.

"It is not ours to judge—not yours, as a sasennan sworn to serve, and not mine, though I am of high rank in the things of this world. Ours is only to serve the mageborn in whatever way we can. I have put a light carriage, a phaeton, at Lord Antryg's disposal, with letters of credit for changing horses from here to Angelshand."

"WHAT?!"

For one instant, behind the gentle and eager convert to the ways of the mages, Caris saw in the Prince's face the stubborn pique of one who has never been crossed in his life.

"Whether he takes you with him is up to him, not you," the Prince said stiffly, and something in his voice reminded Caris suddenly that at Devilsgate, he was entirely in this young man's power. "So I suggest that if you have no respect for your betters in the affairs of air and darkness, you had better cultivate it."

Caris left the study, furious with the Prince's blind stubborn faith and with his own lack of finesse in not sounding out the ground before putting Cerdic on his guard. As he crossed the tall ceilinged hall and ascended the graceful oval of the stair to the higher floor, it occurred to him that he had put himself into a dangerous position indeed. There was nothing to prevent Cerdic from imprisoning him somewhere in the house until after Antryg was long gone—or, for that matter, turning him over to the Witchfinders, though he was unlikely to do that, simply because Caris might then help them to locate Antryg.

The upper part of the house was in darkness. The thought crossed his mind that Cerdic need not have imprisoned him—he need only have delayed him in that stupid interview while Antryg drove the Prince's phaeton off into the night.

Swiftly, he ducked into the room allotted him. His peasant clothes were still there—he had exchanged them for the plain, brown suit of a servant or upper-class tradesman provided for him by the Prince's staff—and his weapons were where he had hidden them in the canopy of the old-fashioned bed, including the sword which he had retrieved from the meadow after the abominations had, as Joanna predicted, been lured away. He checked the pistol—it was still loaded. Though it was forbidden to bear weapons into the presence of a member of the Imperial Family, he had kept a hideout knife in his boot. He checked it, shoved the pistol into the pocket of his short coat and, sheathed sword in hand, strode soundlessly from the room.

He found Antryg sitting in the darkness of the drawing room of the suite allotted to their use. His own mageborn sight picked out the tall, gawky form, sitting in a chair near the window, dealing cards from one of the Prince's tarot decks in silence onto a small ormolu table before him. There was something in the tired angle of those bony shoulders that made Caris think he had been there some time.

Though the sasennan made no sound and there was only darkness in the hall behind him, Antryg said, without turning his head, "Come in, Caris. Are you prepared to leave tonight?"

Caris tipped his head to one side, suspicious. "You're deigning to grant me a place? Or do you just need someone to look after the horses?"

"Well, yes." A stray flick of the last daylight winked from spectacle lenses and what might have been the glint of his half-malicious grin. The long hands moved palely in the dark; the soft pat of cards on marquetry was clearly audible in the still blueness of the room. "And then, I doubt I could persuade Joanna to—er—fly with me unless you were there."

"And her feelings concern you?"

"Oddly enough, yes." The wizard's voice was carefully uninflected. "It's very difficult to carry off a young lady by violence and manage a team of horses, too—at least, I suppose an experienced person could do it, but we should probably attract a good deal of attention. The Regent is on his way here, you know."

Caris frowned and strode forward a step, then paused. "How do you know? He was on his way to Kymil."

"I expect he turned back at the roadhouse, or perhaps the Bishop and the Witchfinders met him halfway." Antryg tapped the spread of the cards. Caris could see over his shoulder the king of pentacles reversed, the eight of wands, the five of swords, the lovers. . . . "And he's going to be married," he added thoughtfully. "Strange sort of thing for Pharos to do, considering, but it does explain a good deal." Puzzled, Caris was about to ask, *Like what?* when, with a flick of his fingers, the mage tossed a seventh card down on the reading—death reversed. "Interesting."

Caris looked down at the cards in silence. As with the vision of wizards in darkness, he saw them without color, shadowless and strange. The Council mages, the academic mages, seldom used the cards, considering them the type of low-class cantrip dealt in by gypsies and dog wizards, but in the darkness he found their arcane shapes disturbing. He asked hesitantly, "Death reversed is . . . life?"

Antryg shook his head, and said softly, "No. It is stagnation."

His long, light fingers gathered the cards and shuffled them restlessly; Caris could see that his eyes were shut. He laid the six cards with the deftness of a faro dealer in their ancient shape and sat for a long time gazing down at them in the darkness. Looking over his shoulder, Caris saw in the center the hermit crossed by the Dead God, whose sign marked the Sigil of Darkness, flanked by emperor and priest, the knight of swords, and the queen of wands. The signs meant nothing to Caris, but he felt the flinch of Antryg's body through the chair back upon which his arm rested; after a moment, he heard the wizard's breath go out in a sigh.

Then the wizard flicked a seventh card from the deck and sat looking at it for some time. From the open windows, Caris heard the voices of the grooms in the stable yard below, calling to one another as they harnessed the horses.

At last Antryg whispered, "So," and got to his feet. Even in the darkness, his face looked strained and more tired than Caris had ever seen him. "It's time we went." Quietly, he left the room.

Caris looked back at the cards, their queer forms as troubling as the voices of things supposed to be dead. The seventh card lay among them —a dead man pierced with ten swords, lying alone in the cold darkness of coming night.

CHAPTER XIII

MOONLIGHT STREAMED BETWEEN THE STANDING-STONES OF THE Devil's Road, bleaching them where it struck or pitting them with inky shadow, like an endless row of broken and rotting teeth. Antryg drew rein beside a fallen one to whose lower extremity earth still clung. The pit where it had until recently been planted was a torn, black hole in the long grass. Looking back along the line of them, Joanna saw how straight they ran, to the top of a distant hill, and down into the unknown night beyond.

The mage said softly, "Hold the horses, would you, Caris." The sasennan, after a moment's hesitation, leaped down from the groom's perch on the back of the phaeton and obeyed.

For all Antryg was still officially Caris' prisoner, Joanna reflected, smiling a little to herself as the mage sprang down from the high-wheeled carriage, at the moment he was the nearest thing to a master the young warrior had.

After a few seconds' hesitation, Joanna gathered up her voluminous skirts and the shawl the Prince had lent her and clambered carefully down after him. Her interview with Antryg in the dimness of the drawing room at Devilsgate had left her shaken, not only by the violence of her own feelings, but by their inappropriateness to everything she had liked to think about herself. She had the sensation of being suddenly in deeper than she had thought, part of her wanting to unfeel what she felt for him and, more, to unknow what it was like to feel. It was that part, perhaps, which in Antryg wanted the safety of the Tower. Down to the taproots of her intellect, she knew that both her friendship and her desire for him were alike utterly stupid—not to mention, she added, that none of this was really any of her business. When she went back to her own world it wouldn't matter. . . .

Except that it did.

He was moving along the double line of the stones, his spectacles and the strings of cheap glass beads around his neck winking palely in the ghostly light.

As when she had killed the two sasenna on the island, she had the feeling of having crossed some line which could not be recrossed. Having seen color, she thought, she would never again be content with black and white.

No wind stirred the long grasses in the shallow dip of ground through which the Road ran; the moon, waxing toward full, outlined not only the stones, but every silken length of grass-blade in sharply contrasting edges of silver and ink. There was a chill on the air, and Joanna hugged her shawl about her; the Prince, a chivalrous young man, had also provided half a dozen dresses for her to wear on the road. Antryg turned at the sound of her step and waited for her, the moonlight picking up a queer, silvery sheen on his outsize black coat. Most of her life, she thought, as she came to his side, she had felt uncertain of her welcome. That, too, had changed.

"What are you looking for?" she asked.

He pointed to the ground. In a week, the resilience of the grass had nearly covered them, but the weight and size of the tracks had left their mark in the soft earth. She frowned, studying them, trying to decide what animal could have made them, and looked at last, puzzled, back at Antryg's beaky face in the moonlight.

He shook his head. "I don't know, either," he said. "But you can see they start here, as if they walked out of a door, then pass close to that fallen stone. The thing must have been massive, whatever it was. Cerdic tells me these high woods are not much frequented, having a bad name in the district. It's very probable its carcass is still rotting up there, while the parasites that lived on it or in it crawled away looking for better fare."

Joanna shivered. A stray touch of wind stirred the thick, fair tangle of her hair; she jumped as if at the brush of a hand. "A week ago," she said after a moment. "That was when . . ." She hesitated. "How far away does the Void weaken when it's open?"

"Generally only a few hundred yards," Antryg replied softly. "But it was open on one of the energy-lines. All things travel along the lines, resonating forward and back; in the old times mages could speak along them or travel down them from node to node, covering hundreds of miles in a day." He turned his head, looking out along the silent Road with its waving, undisturbed grass. The pale light touched the dark blotch of the bruise on his face and glinted in his crystal earrings. "On certain nights of the year, the peasants still drive their herds along them, you know, in commemoration of the Dead God, though they've forgotten why he died. But for the most part they are shunned, as the mages are shunned. No man will summon the voices of the air, if they do not speak personally to him."

He reached out and took her hand with a half-unthinking intimacy; she was conscious of the bigness of the bones beneath the flesh, and the deft lightness of his touch. After a pace or two, she stopped, and he halted and looked at her, his eyes colorless in the moonlight.

"Antryg," she said, "why are you going to Angelshand?"

He hesitated for a long time before replying, his face, which could be so dissimulating, tense with an expression of struggle, as if he debated within himself what he might safely say. Then, bringing out the words with care, he said, "I need to speak to certain members of the Council of Wizards."

Joanna stood for a moment, not certain what to say. It was the first time he had answered her, she thought, without evasion, but it was not what she had expected him to say. "But most—or all—of them are under arrest."

He nodded. "There is that," he agreed, as if she had said, *Most of those telephone calls are toll numbers.*

"About this—this fading? Or what really happened to the Archmage?" After a long moment, she collected enough nerve to add, "About whatever it is you—or someone else—needs or wants me for?"

In the long silence that followed, Joanna could hear one of the carriage team blow softly through its nostrils and heard the faint, bell-like jingle of harness brasses as it tossed its head. The long, odd curves of Antryg's mouth tightened; for a time, she thought he would not answer her or would turn away, as he so often did, with some bit of informational persiflage about ancient cults or botanical lore. But he finally said, "About something which happened twenty-five years ago."

"What?"

"Ah," he whispered, and the old warm, half-demented grin flicked suddenly at the corner of his lips again. "If I knew that, I wouldn't have to ask them."

He started to move back to the carriage, but Joanna tightened her hand around his to hold him still. The bones of his fingers felt large and clumsy entwined with hers and only thinly covered with flesh; through them she was aware of him, blood and sinew and bone.

She said, "I don't understand."

"Don't you?" he asked gently. The ghost of his smile warmed a little. "That's good."

He was not, she sensed, jesting. It came to her again that she was a fool to trust him and an even bigger fool to care for him; for good or ill, she would return to her own world, and it would be as if he were dead and all of this had never happened. Still, when he hesitated to put his arm around her shoulders against the thin chill of the evening, too clearly remembering the interview at Devilsgate, she stepped into the circle of his warmth and slid her own arm around his waist. There was a good deal of comfort in the feel of the ribs beneath the worn velvet and the slight, steady movement of his breathing.

They walked back along the Road to where Caris stood beside the carriage in the brown livery of a groom. Even in the distance, he looked disapproving, his arms folded and tension radiant in his stance.

"Joanna," Antryg said quietly as they neared the spiky shadows of the carriage and the dark horses cropping the long grass in the moonlight. Even pitched low, for her ears alone, his voice was startlingly beautiful, at odd variance with his eccentric appearance. The fractured lens of his spectacles caught the light like a broken star as he looked down at her. "I have no right to ask you to trust me; in fact it would be an insult to your intelligence to do so, but . . . please believe that I won't let you come to harm."

"I've always believed that," she said. They stopped beside the tall conveyance, with Caris still keeping his distance beside the horses' heads. Antryg put his hands to her sides to help her up onto the high step; she shook back the thick masses of her blond hair and looked up into his face again. "Will you return me to my own world?"

His eyes evaded hers. After a long moment, he said, "When I can." He helped her up. She caught the high brass hand railings around the blue leather tuck-and-roll of the seats and stood for a time looking down on him in silence.

Then he said, "I can't tell you the truth, Joanna . . . and God knows I've lied to you enough. All my life I've trusted too easily. I can't risk doing so now."

He climbed up beside her and gathered the reins in his sure, strong grip. Caris, who had watched this tête à tête with deep suspicion, stepped back from the horses' heads and sprang up to his high perch behind as they started forward. For a long time, Joanna sat quietly, hanging onto the sides as the phaeton jarred over the rough ground toward the road. She wondered why she had the impression that Antryg was as appalled by his own reactions to that evening's interview as she was by hers—that, like her, he found himself trusting against his every better judgment. And she wondered, as the carriage rattled into the haythick warmth of the still night, what reason Antryg had to think he ought to fear her.

It took them a day and a night and part of the next day to reach Angelshand, a journey which left Joanna, unused to unsprung, horse-drawn conveyances, cursing the man who hadn't been born yet to invent shock absorbers and almost wishing they had walked. Angelshand was a far larger city than Kymil; from miles away that morning, she had seen the dirty pall of its factory smoke and, when the wind set off its harbor with the cool salt freshness of the sea, had smelled the fetor of its slums. They approached it through a sprawling network of outlying villages and graceful manor houses set in walled parks. Closer in, the phaeton mingled with a rattling press of citybound traffic, passing through dreary streets of crumbling tenements and the ugly brick edifices of the riverside factories. At Joanna's request, Antryg had taught her the rudiments of driving a team of horses on the country roads, but he took the reins back now; as Kymil's had been, the streets of Angelshand were deep in manure and crowded with drays and carts of all description, driven with a disregard for human safety which appalled even Joanna's Los Angelino soul.

They passed over the arches of a crowded bridge to cross the nose of an island that lay like an overcrowded houseboat in the middle of the Glidden River—like the Île de la Cité in Paris, Joanna guessed, the medieval heart of the town. All the buildings of Angelshand were built of the iron-gray local granite, giving an impression of darkness and weight absent in the largely wooden city of Kymil; on Angel's Island, the soot of ages added to the somber hue. The thick, stumpy towers of a fortress glowered above an assortment of crumbling gambrel roofs and gargoyle gutters, like an ogre's frowning brow; elsewhere, beyond, she thought she saw the spires of a church.

"St. Cyr fortress." Caris nodded towards those ancient walls. "The residence of the Bishop of Angelshand—and the prison of the Inquisition." He glanced up ahead of him at Antryg in the driving seat, unconcernedly steering the team around a mender of tin cups who'd set up shop in the middle of the lane and the elegant carriage whose owner had pulled up in the stream of traffic to watch him. In Caris' eye Joanna saw the speculation and wariness with which he'd regarded the mad wizard in the Ponmarish around Kymil and she felt a qualm of unease.

The truce was over. They had reached their goal. From here they would pursue their own purposes once again. At the thought of Caris turning Antryg over to the mad Regent, she shivered, though she knew that, for all his care of them both, Antryg had never proven his innocence of kidnapping both the Archmage and her. He had, beyond denying categorically that he'd had anything to do with any of it, offered no alternative account of his activities, and Joanna was uncomfortably aware that his protestations of complete ignorance were lies.

She glanced up at him now, as he guided the horses through the tight-packed traffic and indescribable clamor of the bridge from the island to the more stylish districts on the far bank. The din on the bridge was hellish, the clatter of iron-shod wheels on granite cobbles striving with the shrieks of ragged beggars, scarf sellers, match hawkers, flower girls and noodle vendors. The sidewalks were crowded with liveried servants and monks in gray, with Old Believers in their black robes and macramé braids, townsmen in coarse browns and blues, fierce-looking sasenna, and whores in bright chintz, painted to within an inch of their lives. The air was rank with the stink of horse droppings and the fetid odor of the murky river below. Beside her Antryg was rubbernecking like a delighted tourist.

He had, she remembered, been a prisoner for seven years.

It took them an hour and more, but eventually he managed to steer them away from the clotted slums and markets of the riverside and toward the more fashionable districts nearer the Imperial Palaces to the north. Knowing she wasn't likely to get an answer that meant anything to her, Joanna refrained from asking their destination. Caris kept silent as well, as much, she suspected, from a desire to remain quiet and have Antryg forget he was there until he was ready to take action as from the fact that, for the moment, there was absolutely no action he could take.

In any case, Antryg seemed to know where he was going; but then, Antryg generally did.

She was still a little surprised when he drew rein in an elegant square; she had been half expecting him to go to some shady acquaintance in the city's underworld for shelter. But this was clearly one of the best neighborhoods of the city. Tall townhouses of graceful, if narrow, proportion looked onto a central square of park, where little girls in miniature gowns and corsets walked under the eye of their governesses. Two other carriages were already drawn up, unmarked and with closed curtains, their coachmen wearing plain livery. Antryg grinned and shook his head as he helped Joanna down from the high step.

"Hasn't changed a bit, I see," he commented, as he led the way up the imposing flight of marble steps. To the footman in flamingo livery who opened the door he said, "Send someone down to hold our horses and tell Magister Magus that the greatest dog wizard in the world is here to see him."

Without batting an eye, the footman murmured, "Yes, sir," and stepped aside to let them in.

"Magister Magus?" Caris sounded scandalized as a second footman escorted them up a curving staircase with graceful iron balustrades and into a drawing room opulently furnished in rose, gold, and black. "That charlatan! That—that toadstone-peddler!"

"What, haven't you been here before?" There was a twinkle of deep mischief in Antryg's eyes. The only other occupant of the drawing room, a handsome if zaftig woman, brutally corsetted into yards of lilac faille, regarded them for a moment and then turned away with a sniff at the sight of Caris' plain livery and Antryg's shabby coat, crystal beads, and bruised face.

Looking around her, Joanna noticed that, for all its rather pseudo-oriental finery, its pink-and-black tufted carpets, and statues in rose agate and alabaster of the Old Gods, everything in the drawing room was of the highest quality and obviously expensive. Peddling toadstones, she surmised, was clearly something that paid extremely well.

"Certainly not!" Caris sounded as if Antryg had asked him that question about a leather bar. "This is . . . ."

The word 'disgusting' was obviously on his lips, but Antryg finished the sentence with ". . . Far handsomer than your grandfather's, isn't it?"

The young man's eyes narrowed. His voice was very quiet as he said, "You should be the last one, wizard, to talk to me about my grandfather." But for just a moment, Joanna had the feeling that a good deal of Caris' annoyance stemmed from just that comparison.

After a few moments, the inner doors of the room opened to the sound of a softly tapped bronze gong. In a vast waft of fragipani incense, another woman emerged from them, also middle-aged and dressed in what Joanna guessed to be several thousand dollars worth of brocade and rose-point lace. She leaned on the arm of a slender, graceful man, whose black velvet robe bore as its sole adornment an emblem, rather like an ankh, of silver literally crusted with diamonds, which hung at his breast. This might have had a religious significance, but Joanna, studying the room, was rather more inclined to believe he'd chosen the combination to match his hair, which was black streaked through with silver, like frosted ebony. His voice, as he spoke to the lady, was low, trained, and extremely beautiful.

"So you see, there is nothing for you to trouble yourself about, Countess," he was saying. "I have seen in your future a young man to whom you were spiritually connected in a former life. Whether it is the young man who now troubles you, or one more fit than he, only time and the gods will reveal. As for your husband, do not worry. Only have faith, and these things will even themselves out, as ripples do upon the lake of time."

Raising one slender, white hand, adorned with a solitaire ruby the size of a man's thumbnail, he made a sign of benediction over the Countess' head. She sank gracefully to one knee, and kissed his hand; then, rising, she drew her veils over her face and at least a foot and a half of high-piled hair and was gone.

Turning to the other lady, Magister Magus said, "My dear Marquise." His eyes, Joanna saw, were the clear green of alexandrite or peridot, deep-set and penetrating under silver-shot black brows. "I can see that your heart is troubled, that you are faced by a situation in which you are caught between two alternatives. But a part of that trouble lies in the fact that today is the Day of Ill-Fortune for you, under the star of Antirbos. It is not a day upon which any advice would bring you good. Go home, then, and to your chamber. Eat only a light supper, drink a single glass of wine, and read and meditate, thinking pure thoughts to combat the leaden influence of the Black Star which weights your heart. If your grief is still with you on the morrow, return to me then."

Joanna privately considered this dismissal rather brusque—after all, there was no telling how long the poor Marquise had been waiting—but, like the Countess, she curtsied reverently and kissed the Magus' hand. "From you," she murmured—somewhat fatuously, Joanna thought— "even silence is good advice. It is all exactly as you say."

Soberly, he conducted her to the door. In a rustle of patchouli and petticoats, she descended the steps, while Magister Magus stood with his arms outspread to touch the sides of the doorway, still as a dark image of ebony and diamond, until the building vibrated softly with the closing of the outer doors.

Then, with a billowing sigh, he pushed the doors to and turned. White teeth flashed beneath his dark mustache. "Antryg, you old faker, where'd you spring from?" He caught the tall wizard in his arms, and the two hugged one another, laughing, like long-parted brothers. "Greatest dog wizard in the world indeed! A fine thing to say in the house of Magister Magus!"

"Well, you're the one who said I had it in me," Antryg retorted with a grin. Then, soberly, he laid one hand on Magister Magus' shoulder, gestured with his quizzing glass, and intoned, "As for your husband, fear not. I see in your future a man, handsome and well-favored, who will treat you with the kindness that a lady of your goodness and exalted destiny deserves. The River of Eternity flows past many shores, and fish of all descriptions glide in its waters. Sometimes its currents are rough, sometimes they are smooth. . . ."

The dog wizard laughed at the imitation with genuine delight. "It pays the bills, my friend—it pays the bills." He frowned suddenly. "But what are you doing here? Don't tell me it's *you* they've been looking for?"

"Well," Antryg admitted, "they *are* looking for me—the Council for getting out of the Tower, and the Regent for insulting him on the road, and the Church . . . Why?"

Magister Magus shook his head. "God only knows—and maybe the Prince Regent. But a week ago Sunday, every Council wizard in the town was dropped on by the Witchfinders, backed up with the Prince's men. They went through the Yard like reapers through corn. I was ready to run; but if I'd been caught running, they'd have asked why." He shuddered, then chuckled ruefully. "Too frightened to run. I'm told even Cerdic cleared out of town." He glanced at Caris, still in his rust-colored groom's livery, and back to Antryg with one brow raised. "A bodyguard? A sasennan?"

"In a manner of speaking." Antryg grinned. "I see trade hasn't been hurt."

"You call only two clients not hurt? Antryg, this place is generally full! They arrive as soon as they wake up—which is about three in the afternoon—and sit here until dark, just waiting to give me money for telling them what they want to hear. I'm almost as popular as a first-class hairdresser! This is the first day anyone's come in a week. The Court's like a bunch of children when someone's told nursie about the games behind the barn."

He sighed, and all the verve seemed to go out of him, leaving him just a thin little man in his elaborate robe and diamond chain, stressed, weary, and very frightened.

Quietly, Antryg asked, "And has your magic faded?"

Magister Magus' head came up with a snap.

"Oh, yes," Antryg said softly. "As I could have been a very good dog wizard, you could have been one of the finer Council mages, if you had had the teaching."

The dog wizard sniffed. "Much good my powers would have done me then," he muttered. "And my teaching was good enough. But for God's sake, Antryg, don't let that about! As I see it, my only defense against the Witchfinders is that they think I'm a complete fake. That's enough to make a cat laugh, isn't it?" he added bitterly. "I advertise powers they don't think I've got to make my living, and you . . ." He frowned again. "But you were always different, weren't you? How do you know . . ." His words caught a little, then he went on, ". . . about . . . about what's been happening to my powers?"

"What?" Antryg's voice was low in the incense-laden hush of the over-decorated room. "Three, four times in the last week and a half and twice or three times before that?"

Magister Magus was staring at him, as his own clients must stare when he revealed some private secret, deduced, as Joanna had seen Antryg deduce them when he was telling fortunes on the road, from the stain on a glove or the nervous shift of the eyes.

"It's happened to all the wizards, Magus—and to all people, hasn't it?"

The dapper little man shook his head disbelievingly, "Last week the Countess said . . . And the quarrels they've been having . . . Senseless, stupid! One woman said she seemed to wake out of a trance, with a knife in her hand, stealing toward her husband's room. Oh, she hates him, yes, but . . . she feared she was going out of her mind. . . ."

"Perhaps she was," Antryg murmured. "Perhaps it was only despair. It is sapping all life, all energy, drawing away both strength and hope for . . . what? I don't know what it is or how it's being done or why. But I know that it is being done. Do you know who's escaped the Church's net?"

"What?" Caught in the frightening vision of the fading of both life and magic, it took Magus an instant to realize his friend had changed the subject again.

"Rosamund? Aunt Min? Old Whitwell Simm? It's an interesting thing," Antryg added, half to himself, "that they're making the distinction not of who has powers, but who can use them effectively—the Council mages, in fact. I wonder whose decision that was?"

The dog wizard shook his head. "God only knows," he repeated. "It must be all of them, mustn't it? Because if any one of the great ones escaped, it would stand to reason he'd rescue the others, wouldn't he?" He led the way through an impressively carved ebony door into a perfectly ordinary dining room and stripped off his velvet robe and pectoral as he went, to reveal beneath them the neat, dark-blue breeches, sober waistcoat, and white shirtsleeves and stockings of a city professional.

"Yes," Antryg agreed mildly, taking the soft velvet weight of the robe to hold for him, "so it would."

On his way to the sideboard for a glass of the wine that stood in the cooler there, the dog wizard paused and regarded Joanna curiously, then came back to her, his dark brows drawn down slightly over his aquiline nose.

"Please excuse me, my dear," he said after a moment's scrutiny. "I'm usually good at guessing someone's trade, if they have one. That so-called groom of yours is obviously a sasennan, for instance." Caris, in the doorway, stiffened a little, indignant. "Your demeanor clearly marks you as possessing a trade, my child, and an income of your own, but I cannot for the life of me determine what it is. Do you mind my asking?"

Confused and slightly embarrassed, Joanna admitted, "Computer systems designer."

"And upon that," Antryg took up, with a smile at Magus' baffled look as he took the wineglass from Magus' hand and gave it to Joanna, "hangs a tale indeed."

"Joanna."

Startled, she sat up in bed, her blond hair hanging in her eyes; the faint scratching noise she had attributed to rats came again from the door. She realized it was the more quiet alternative to knocking and scrambled through the gauzy white curtains which acted as an effective mosquito netting in a world whose wire-drawing technique did not yet extend to window screens. "Who is it?" Somewhere in the humid darkness beyond the tall windows, a clock chimed three; down in the street, a distant, dreary peddler's voice was singing a song about matches.

"Caris."

The moon had set long ago. In Angelshand there was no such thing as the reflected glow of streetlights from outside—there wasn't a streetlight in the whole city—and the only light in the room came from a tiny seed of fire in an amber glass night lamp on the washstand. By its minute glow, she located the nightrobe the Prince had included in her luggage, an amazing confection of gauze and lace, and went to unbrace the chair from the door.

He was standing in the hall outside. The tall, narrow house was silent, save for the soft, sonorous breathing of her host, which could be heard through the open door of his bedchamber next to hers. Caris was dressed, as usual, in the plain livery of a servant, but all of the costume he wore at the moment were the breeches, shirt, and stockings, all creased as if he had slept in them. His blond hair was ruffled from a pillow—she remembered how he had sat silently watching her and the two mages, as Antryg and Magus had exchanged stories and reminiscences until the small hours, and had then followed Antryg silently up to the attics to sleep.

"May I come in?"

She stepped aside. She knew that a month ago she would never have done so, even if he *had* rescued her from an evil wizard's clutches—but a month ago, she hadn't killed two men.

And oddly enough, in the last several days, a little to her own surprise, she had come to like the sasennan. She had formerly been slightly afraid of that silent, beautiful young man, distrustful of the scorn she was sure he felt for her plainness and inexperience. But like Antryg, Caris took people exactly as he found them; if he had not expected her to be able to climb walls and evade armed troops, neither had he assumed she would fail. It was she, she realized, who had held prejudiced expectations of him; but unlike Antryg, he wasn't the sort of man you could apologize to for it.

"Joanna," he said softly, "I need your help."

She said nothing. She knew—or hoped, anyway—that she wouldn't act like one of those whining and putty-willed movie heroines who took pots shots at the hero because of a desperate attachment they had formed for the villain, but she had hoped also that she wouldn't be asked to choose.

That, too, she thought, had been a stupid hope. Whether she wanted to or not, she was in a game for keeps; the riddles locked up behind Antryg's mad gray eyes and lunatic smile affected the fates of both worlds, hers, perhaps, more than Caris'. After a long moment, she found herself asking, "What do you want me to do?"

From his pocket, Caris brought out a creased scrap of paper. In the floating ochre light she saw it was a map. Though one house was marked, there was no number—that was another modern innovation that Angelshand lacked.

"I suspect Antryg is going out soon as it's light," the warrior said softly. "He came to Angelshand for purposes of his own. I can't afford to lose him now. But I must get in contact with Dr. Narwahl Skipfrag. He's the only friend the Council has at Court, the only one to whom the Regent might listen. He's a friend of my grandfather's—a scientist, but one who believes there is something more to magic than hocus-pocus and dog wizardry."

He held out the paper to her. She took it, stiff and heavy-feeling in her cold fingers.

"Tell him what happened and where we are. Tell him that I need an introduction to the Court and that I have Antryg Windrose, if not my prisoner, at least in my sight. Tell him what happened to my grandfather."

She set the paper on the washstand. "I'll tell him your grandfather disappeared," she said slowly, "but to be literally truthful, I don't know what happened to your grandfather—and neither do you."

Caris' mouth tightened a little, and the brown eyes in their wells of shadow seemed to harden to agate.

Slowly, a little gropingly, Joanna went on, "I don't *know* anything, really—only what I've been told, either by you or by Antryg. All I want to do is get the hell out of this mess and go home. . . ." She broke off again, something strange stirring in her heart, because it wasn't, entirely, all she wanted. . . .

"And I tell you this," Caris said quietly. "That Antryg stalked you, and Antryg went to that house where he left his mark upon the wall to find you, and Antryg brought you here, for purposes of his own; and from that I collect that, unless we find my grandfather, unless we free the Council from persecution, you will never return to your home. Do you understand that?"

After a long moment Joanna sighed, and said softly, "Yes."

Caris stood for a time, looking down at his hands where they rested over the hilt of his scabbarded sword, thrust through the sash tied incongruously over his servant livery. Then, not so harshly, as if he, too, were fumbling for the right words, he said, "I am not asking you to do him harm. Whether harm comes to him . . . it could from any number of sources. But I must know what he plans in Angelshand and I must not let him out of my sight. You are the only one I can count on. May I do so?"

Knowing he was right, wretchedly glad that it was no worse, Joanna nodded miserably. With a deep bow, Caris faded into the darkness of the hall. She stood still for a few moments with her hands resting on the satiny wood of the doorframe, wishing she knew, if not what to do, at least what to feel. Though the attic stairs ran close to her room, she did not hear his soundless tread as he ascended.

As Caris had guessed they might be, both he and Antryg were gone from the house by the time Joanna woke. She had breakfast with Magister Magus, during which a solemn manservant in a truly startling livery of rose-hued plush announced that the Marquise of Inglestoke had arrived and awaited audience, and left him robing philosophically for the pursuit of his trade.

Although Antryg's spell of languages allowed her to understand and be understood, Joanna had no idea of the written word. Caris, aware of that, had drawn his map to Narwahl Skipfrag's house on Cheveley Street in careful detail, and she had no difficulty finding the place. It was about two miles from the square where Magister Magus had his lodgings, through crowded streets of shop fronts, offices, and squares of tenement lodgings where coster-mongers yelled their wares from handcarts and beggars whined to the passers-by; but having walked almost eighty miles in the last week, Joanna found the distance no concern.

It was only when she was within half a block of the place that she saw that two sasenna guarded its door.

She halted on the pavement, looking up the short flight of granite steps to the narrow frontage of the house. She shifted her purse on her shoulder, slipped the map from the pocket of her voluminous skirt and checked it, and counted doors from the corner—but in her heart, she knew the guarded door was Narwahl Skipfrag's. He was a friend of the wizards; the black livery of the sasenna was of the soft samurailike cut of the Church sasenna, and she could see the sun emblem of the Sole God like gory flowers upon their shoulders.

For their benefit, she looked up and down the street again, sighed, and shook her head, then walked away down the flagway, still gravely studying her map.

At the corner, she turned and shoved the map into her purse. This was a larger street, bustling with foot and carriage traffic and redolent of horse droppings, garbage, and flies. Across the lane a furniture mender had moved most of his shop out onto the flagway to take advantage of the forenoon sun; a noodle shop run by a couple of braided-haired Old Believers released clouds of steam into the air and Joanna shuddered, thinking what the heat must be like inside. She walked along the pavement until she found the narrow mouth of the alley and, with a slight feeling of trepidation, picked up her skirts and turned into that blue and stinking canyon.

As she had suspected from the layout of Magister Magus' house, the houses of this row all had little yards behind them—by the smell of it, with the privy up against the back fence. Garbage choked the unpaved lane; nameless liquids reduced the dirt underfoot to nauseous slime. Against the faded boards of the fences, the red wax of the Church's seal stood out brilliantly and saved her even the trouble of counting back gates.

She glanced up and down the alley and put her eye to a knothole in the rickety gate. There was no one in the narrow little yard, but, as on the gate, she could see the Church's seal had been affixed to the back door at the top of its little flight of steps. She tested the gate, pulled her Swiss Army knife from her purse, and slipped it under the seal, breaking it from the wood; then she pushed the gate softly open and went in.

The house stood silent. Empty, she thought—but in that case, why post guards?

The only friend the wizards had at Court, she thought. The Regent had turned back, returning to Angelshand, perhaps—going to visit Cerdic, certainly . . . Caris had said he was growing increasingly paranoid. . . .

She was aware of her heart beating achingly as she mounted the steps and leaned over to look through the window beside the door.

She saw a library, shadowy and barely visible giving an impression of comfortable, old-fashioned chairs and a heavy chimney breast with carving over it. No fire—but then in summer there wouldn't be.

Joanna took a deep breath, formulated her cover story about a dying sister who must see Dr. Skipfrag or perish, and thrust her knife under the wax of the seal. It cracked clear; she found her wallet, extracted a credit card, and used the thin, hard plastic to raise the latch.

The house was empty. She knew it, standing in the brown dimness of the hall. Carefully, she untied and removed her low-heeled shoes, cursed her yards of petticoat as she gathered them in hand to keep from knocking over furniture, and moved as soundlessly as she could along the wall toward the stairs.

In the bedroom on the second floor, she found a ruffled bed, the covers flung back but the creased sheets long cold. A drawer was open in the top of the highboy; peering into it, Joanna could see that something had been taken hastily from it scattering cravats and gloves. On the marble top of the highboy a few grains of black powder were scattered, and the experience of the last week had taught Joanna the look and smell of old-fashioned black gunpowder.

Silently, she ascended the next flight of steps.

From uncurtained windows, a whitish light suffused the attic; the trapped heat of days made the room stuffy. The smell of old blood nearly turned her sick. It was splattered everywhere, turned dark brown now against the white paint of the walls and the pale plaster of the ceiling; little droplets of it had dripped back onto the pooled and rivuleted floor. For some reason, the sight of it brought back to her the memory of how hot the sasennan's blood had been, splattering against her face; she shut her teeth tightly against a clench of nausea.

The calm part of her that could analyze program glitches at three in the morning and that told her it was stupid to fall in love with a middle-aged wizard in another universe asked, *What the hell could have caused this?*

Curious, she took a step forward. She drew back her stockinged foot immediately as it touched something sharp. She saw it was a small shard of broken glass. When she bent to pick it up, she saw there were others, sparkling in the wan light on the bloodstained floor and, she noticed, embedded here and there in the walls, as well. She held the shard up to the light. It was edged with old blood.

With a nervous shake of her hand she threw it from her. She didn't know why, but there was something in the touch of it that filled her with loathing and with fear. There wasn't a great deal of glass—not more than one smashed beaker's worth—but it was widely scattered. Picking her way carefully, she crossed the room to the laboratory tables beneath the dormer windows on the other side.

It had been a long time since she'd taken her Fundamentals of Electricity course in college, but she recognized most of what she saw there—primitive cell-batteries with their lined-up dishes of water, a vacuum pump, and crudely insulated copper wire. An iron-and-copper sparking generator sat in the midst of a tangle of leads, and a glass Volta pistol gleamed faintly in the sunlight on a corner of the table. Other objects whose use she did not know lay among the familiar, archaic equipment—convoluted glass tubing and little dishes of colored salts. At the back of the litter sat a seamless glass ball, silvered over with what looked like mercury, gleaming evilly in the diffuse light. Joanna shrank from touching it, repelled without knowing why. Above the table, in the middle of the whitewashed wall, was the fresh scar of a bullet hole; beside her hand, the wooden table's edge was also freshly scarred, as if someone had smashed a glass vessel against it in a rage.

Her first thought was, *Antryg would know what happened.*

Her second, as she heard the soft jostle of an unwary step of booted feet somewhere in the house below her was, *I have no line of retreat.*

They'll have seen the broken-off seals, she thought, even as she scanned the low ceiling for a trap door to the roof. There was none. The windows might have been made to open once upon a time, but they had long since been barred to prevent the ingress of thieves. She thought, *There's a wardrobe in the bedroom—they might pass me by and I could get out behind them* . . . She had to fight with everything in her to walk, silently and carefully, instead of running to the stairs.

It cost her her escape. The two sasenna and the man in the gray garb of a Witchfinder had just reached the second floor as she came silently around the corner of the narrow stair.

CHAPTER XIV

"WHERE ARE YOUR FRIENDS, GIRL?"

Joanna did not look up. The Witchfinder Peelbone's eyes, like his voice, were thin, pale, and very cold and filled her with the panicky sensation that he knew everything about her; she kept her gaze down on her hands, which lay like two detached white things on the grime-impregnated table top before her. She could feel her heart hammering against her ribs beneath the blue striped cotton of her boned bodice and the crawl of panic-sweat down her back, but some small voice in her mind kept repeating, *Don't say anything. He can use anything that you say, but he can't use your silence.*

"We know you have them." She heard, rather than saw him rise from his big, carved chair on the opposite side of the table and heard the rustle of his clothes as he came around toward her. The room was windowless and lit by sconces backed by metal reflectors, one on either side of his chair; his shadow passed in front of one. When he stood beside her in the heat of the room, she could smell his body and the sweat in his clothes. She knew he was going to touch her; but even so, she flinched when he seized her hair and forced her to look up at him. "That's an expensive dress," he said quietly, and she hated the feel of his hand moving in her hair. "And your hair is clean. You spent last night somewhere. Answer me!"

His hand tightened, twisting at her hair unmercifully. She had forgotten from her grade school days how painful it was to have one's hair pulled. She forced herself to look up into that narrow, handsome face, with the eyes of colorless, austere brown under colorless brows, gritting her teeth against the wrenching pain.

If I don't say A, he can't say B, she thought desperately. She had always used silence as a weapon in arguments and had found it an effective one against everyone from her mother to Gary. There was a spy novel, she remembered, wherein someone had sat through hours of interrogation in silence. . . .

She remembered what Caris had told her about the Inquisition's methods and felt sick with fear at the thought.

The grip released suddenly, pushing her away with force enough to rock her on the backless wooden stool where she sat. She caught her balance and looked up at the Witchfinder again, trying desperately not to feel like a sulky, defiant child, trying not to think beyond the moment. The cold eyes stared into hers; she was reminded of a shark's eyes, with no more humanity in them than two round circles of metal.

"Such silence can't spring from innocence, I think," Peelbone said softly. "Very good—we know you are guilty of something. The only question is—what?"

She remembered him saying, *We can't afford these waters muddied.* She would ultimately be guilty, she knew, of whatever was convenient for them, even as they would sooner have killed Caris, back at Kymil, rather than risk him cluttering up their case with truth. When she said nothing, she saw the long, bracketing lines around his mouth move a little, like snakes, with irritation.

He raised one white forefinger. Joanna heard the guard behind her stool step forward and didn't resist when she was pulled to her feet; she was fighting a desperate terror, wondering how much they knew already and whether, if they searched her purse, they'd be able to backtrack to Magister Magus' house from Caris' map. She thanked the guardian god of wizards that she'd put the map in her purse instead of her pocket— there was so much other junk in there that it could easily be passed over.

The guard held her arms behind her, a hateful grip and terrifyingly strong. She expected Peelbone to strike her, as he had struck Caris back in Kymil. All her life she had managed to avoid physical violence of any kind, and the very unfamiliarity of being touched and handled added to her dread. But the Witchfinder studied her in silence for a few moments, then almost casually reached forward and ripped open her bodice, revealing the thin, sweat-soaked muslin of the shift beneath.

"Child," he said quietly, "if I had you stripped naked and thrown into the room where the rapists are kept chained, it would not in any way impair your ability to tell us about your friends an hour later." His disinterested eyes moved to the grinning guard. "Now take her away."

It took everything she had to bite back the desperate impulse to cry *Wait* . . . as the guard pushed her out of the room and into the torchlit hall. Her jaw set, she kept her eyes straight ahead of her, forcing herself not to see the leers of the two other guards out in the hall or hear their comments; she saw only the smokestains on the stone arches of the low ceiling and how the shadows of the torches jerked and quavered in the drafts that came down from the narrow stairways to the guardrooms above. The St. Cyr fortress, at the tip of the island which the city of Angelshand had long since outgrown, was an ancient one, and its very walls stank of the lives that had rotted to their ends there.

The cell to which they took her was a dank and tiny stone closet that smelled like a privy. By the light of the torch that burned smokily in a holder near the low door, Joanna could see that it had only one other human occupant, not counting roaches of a size and arrogance to make the San Serano orthoptera blush with shame—an old woman, wearing the remains of the black robes of a mage or an Old Believer, who sat huddled in the corner as Joanna was pushed inside and the heavy wooden door closed behind her. The woman barely looked up as the heavy bolts were shot outside. Joanna, trembling, stood for a few moments at the top of the short flight of steps down into the room.

I can't cry now, she told herself desperately, her throat suddenly gripped by a surge of betraying pain and her eyes hot. It would weaken her, she knew; unless she kept keyed to this point, she could never face the Witchfinder in silence for the second interview she knew was coming. But neither Antryg nor Caris knew where she was—and even if they did, they would be unable to rescue her. *I never wanted this,* she thought, *I never asked for this! I was hauled here. . . .*

Antryg had said, *You are in this world under my protection. . . .*

Her legs felt weak as she descended the few steps. Raised in the protection of a technological society and under the enormous bulwark of Constitutional Law, flawed though it might be, she had never before found herself in the position of being so utterly without recourse. Her aloneness terrified her. Even if she told them everything they wanted to know and betrayed Antryg, Caris and poor, cowardly, charming Magister Magus to torture and death, she had the horrible certainty that it would not help her. She could not explain how she herself came to this world. She was their accomplice against her will. She had done murder. . . .

You didn't panic then, she told herself grimly, *and it saved you. For God's sake don't panic now.*

A faint snore made her look down. The old woman, thin and fragile-looking, was curled up in the corner, sleeping with the light sleep of the very aged. As she watched, Joanna shuddered to see an enormous roach emerge from a crack in the stone wall and make its unconcerned way down the old woman's shoulder. Her hand cringing from the task, Joanna leaned down and swept the thing away with such violence that it shot across the tiny cell and hit the opposite wall with an audible crack.

The old woman's faded blue eyes opened and blinked up at her under lashes gone white as milk. "She was only walking, after all," she said in a reproving voice. And, when Joanna blinked, confused, the old lady shook her head and gestured with one trembling finger at the other wall, where the enormous insect was just disappearing through a crack. "Not doing harm."

Joanna swallowed queasily.

"They don't eat much," the old lady added, "and nor do I—so it's not that they're taking aught from me." She squinted up at Joanna's sickened face. "Were you raised in privies, likely you'd be loathly, too."

"Sorry," Joanna said and then, knowing what the old lady obviously expected, she turned toward the departed cockroach. "Sorry," she said, more loudly, and the old lady nodded her satisfaction.

For a long moment, those pale, ancient eyes looked up at her in silence; rather gingerly, Joanna gathered up her skirts and sat in the filthy straw beside her. "I'm Joanna Sheraton," she said, and the old woman nodded.

"Minhyrdin the Fair they call me. Are they arresting the dog wizards now, too? For you're none of the Council's."

Joanna shook her head. "No—at least, I don't know. I'm not a mage at all."

The old woman clucked to herself. "Never say so, child; they'll put you in with the street girls or the murderesses, instead of in those cells built to hold the mageborn. They took away my knitting. . . ." She looked fussily around her, as if half expecting to find it hidden under the straw. Joanna shivered and paranoically checked the straw around her skirts, hating the thought that one of the old lady's pet roaches might be crawling in her several layers of petticoat.

You are going to be raped, tortured, and killed, she thought, *and you're worrying about bugs in your skirts?* Tears of wretchedness and fear lay very close to the surface, but she couldn't keep from smiling with wry irony at her own capacity for the trivial.

"How did you come here, then?" the old lady asked, as if they'd met by chance at a Mendelssohn recital.

Joanna folded her arms around her knees, finding a curious easing of her fears in talking. "I was trying to see Dr. Narwahl Skipfrag," she said. "But I—I think he's dead, isn't he? Someone was killed there." She shivered, remembering that gruesome scene. "In the attic—there was blood splattered everywhere, even on the ceiling. That must have been the arteries. It must have happened days ago but the place still stank of it. The Witchfinder's men . . ." She swallowed. The bruises their grip had left were beginning to ache on her arms.

"It was—it was done by magic, wasn't it? There was broken glass scattered on the floor and embedded in the walls. . . ."

"Ah," Minhyrdin the Fair whispered. She folded her little hands and rocked back and forth; the few wisps of her thinning white hair swished against her sunken and withered cheeks. "So," she murmured to herself, "he's at his tricks again."

"Who?" asked Joanna shakily, looking over at her.

"Suraklin." She stopped rocking, but frowned off into the distance, as if trying to remember something. "Suraklin," she said again. "The Dark Mage. He'd call them up, spirits, elementals—hate and rage and destruction—and clothe them in what flesh he chose. He'd cast a handful of pebbles into the whirlwind; and like a whirlwind, they'd grow, till they ripped the flesh from the bone—or fling a handful of water into it, and those drops would multiply, whirling and tearing, till they drownded a man. . . ."

With horrible clarity, Joanna remembered the freshly chipped edge of the wooden table and the nearness to hand of the glass beakers. Easy enough, she thought, appalled, to seize and smash a vessel and fling the shards. . . .

Joanna whispered, "Suraklin is dead."

"Oh, yes." The woman began rocking again, her little hands folded on her knees and her tiny, pointed chin resting on the knotted fingers. "Dead . . . dead . . . for all that poor boy of his drove himself mad swearing he wasn't. But where's he been, eh? Just tell me that."

"Antryg?" asked Joanna, reflecting that Antryg wasn't the only one to be disordered in his wits.

"No!" The old woman looked at her impatiently. "We all know where he's been, meddling and wandering. Suraklin. He's been dead these twenty-five years, but where's he been, if he hasn't, eh?" And she resumed her rocking once more, like a lonely child. When she spoke, her voice had the curious, far-off note of a child's telling a story or a dream. "He wanted to live forever, Suraklin; he hated the thought that he'd die. He ruled all those around him, twisted them all to his will. But he knew he'd die, and it would all fall apart. All fall apart . . ."

Joanna frowned, remembering what Antryg had said in the moonlight of the Devil's road. "Is that what happened twenty-five years ago, then?"

"Twenty-five years ago it was," the old woman murmured, "And the Prince Hieraldus, that was so handsome, and the Archmage, and all the Council of Wizards riding south, with the Witchfinders in arms because they'd been claiming for years it never existed, and the Church lending its hand to us. . . . Ah, those were the days," she sighed. "Terrible days. The Church and the Witchfinders, they gave us help, but they never forgave us, they never forgave."

No, thought Joanna. *How could they, after years of denying your existence and then having to ask your help?* She rested her forehead on her knees, her tired mind trying to fathom the strange whirlpool of darkness into which she had been drawn—kidnap, and flight; the agonizing kick of the pistol against her wrists and the spurt blood on her face; the crawling abominations in the meadow; Antryg's eyes in the wan gray afternoon light . . .

It had been on her lips a dozen times in the last week to ask him, as she had asked that first morning, *Why?*

I can't tell you the truth and I don't wish to lie to you. . . . God knows I've done that enough.

He had stalked her at San Serano—he had come to Gary's, knowing somehow that she was there.

How? She wondered. He had said, *I have always had the misfortune to be a good guesser.*

How had he known about the abominations? What had happened to Caris' grandfather the Archmage, who had vanished into the darkness of the Void with Antryg and who had not emerged from the other side? What did he know about that queer and terrible deadness, that sapping of the life of the world?

She wondered if it would be easier if the mere thought of him didn't shake the bones of her body.

You are in this world under my protection. . . .

As if a blanket of terror had been flung over her head, black darkness fell upon the cell, and the air outside in the corridor was split by a scream of such dreadful agony that Joanna felt as if her liver and lights were trying to leap out her throat.

A second scream followed the first, footfalls thundered, and somewhere a man cried out in terror. The door shook as a running guard blundered into it with a rattle of weaponry; involuntarily, Joanna clutched at the dark bundle of rags beside her, clinging to the frail bones beneath, her heart pounding in her ears so that the hammer of the blood almost sickened her. As if in a nightmare, through a shimmering darkness, she thought she could dimly see the torch, still burning, though its flame was like a wan scrap of white silk, illuminating nothing. Other voices sounded in the corridor, shouts of terror and alarm; under the screaming, Joanna thought the whole St. Cyr fortress was up in arms, blundering in that terrible darkness.

Toward what?

"Joanna!"

Cumulative stress, terror, and weariness broke inside her; she flung herself to her feet with a sob and threw herself to the door. In blind darkness, she groped at the barred judas . . . "Antryg, get me out of here!"

"Get back from the window. I can't touch the door—it's spelled—put your hand up—gently. . . ."

Through the rusted iron of the peephole's crosspiece, she felt the prick of a sword against her fingers. Sliding her hand carefully up the blade, she felt a metal ring with a key on it. Fumblingly, she groped at the side of the door she thought she remembered the keyhole was on. It wasn't. Another scream rent the palpitating air, raising the hair on the back of her neck.

"What is it?" she gasped.

"It's a Screamer, a terror-spell—it's not going to last and neither is the darkness, so hurry!"

A splinter ran into her questing fingers—she disregarded it, guided the key into the lock, and wrenched the heavy mechanism over. Some how that deep, extraordinary voice defused the dread of the dark, reduced the cries of grief and anguish to what they were—noises—and made her expel her breath in a shaky laugh. "I thought you couldn't use magic . . ."

"I can't—this is courtesy of Magister Magus, and he's probably taken to his heels by this time."

She slipped through the half-opened door and felt the familiar strength of a bony arm in the worn velvet sleeve around her waist, dragging her along the corridor in the blackness. Already, shapes were coming faintly clear to her eyes—men running here and there, the torches burning like shreds of fluttering cloth. Another scream rent the air, horrifying with all the despairing pain of torture and grief.

"We can't . . ." she began, trying to stop, remembering old Minhyrdin the Fair.

"Yes we can. Now run!" Inexorably, he dragged her on. She could see him dimly now, the beaky face colorless in its tangled frame of graying brown hair, the spectacles beginning to catch the renewing light of the torches. He held a sword in his free hand, undoubtedly taken from one of the blinded guards. His longer strides made her stumble; he hauled her up a twisting spiral of stone stair and through a guardroom that seemed filled with men blundering about, weapons in their hands, not certain which way to go—shadows against a deeper darkness, their voices a clamor of terror and uncertainty.

"It's a curse!" "It's the mages!" "The Archmage . . ." "Where's it coming from?" "This way, you fools!"

Feeling as if she fled in a dream, Joanna gasped, "The others . . ."

"They'll have to do what they can!" They were in the open court, the darkness mingling into a raw and clammy fog that chilled her to the bone through her ripped dress. Parties of men were running everywhere, pikes and swords and crossbows in their hands; but with belated caution they were already running down toward the court.

The last scream died, and the darkness faded, just as they reached the gate.

Antryg dashed straight to the sentry in the gatehouse, pointed back across the court, and gasped, "In the guardroom . . ."

The man, involuntarily, turned his head to look, and the wizard's knobby fist, weighted with the pommel of his sword, smashed across his temple, even as the two guards who had been beside the gate came running toward him. Antryg caught the first man's descending halberd on the back of his blade, wrenching it up and stepping in under it to kick the man full, hard, and agonizingly in the groin; he was turning toward the second before the first man even hit the pavement. The courtyard behind them echoed with the clatter of boots—city guards, Church sasenna, and, Joanna saw, the Regent's men also, in their gold-braided black uniforms.

As if they'd rehearsed it, the instant the guard in the gatehouse had fallen, Joanna sprang to pull the pistol from his belt. It was double-barreled. She knew, if she tried to hit Antryg's current opponent, she would just as likely hit Antryg, so she swung around and fired at the closest of the black-clothed sasenna rushing toward them out of the fog in the court. Nobody fell, but the lead men flinched and ducked; Antryg was beside her, his blade bloodied to the hilt, shouting, "RUN!"

She gathered up her skirts and ran. She was aware that he was not with her, but couldn't look back—only at the gray arch of fog ahead of her, beyond the stone, shadow, and portcullis ropes. It was as if she ran in a dream, adrenaline scorching her veins and her heart hammering at her that she had to escape—that after this, the consequences of capture would be unthinkable. . . .

She smelled the stagnant little moat that blocked the landward side of St. Cyr from the rest of the old island part of the town; her stockinged feet thumped hollowly on the silly little wooden drawbridge. Ahead of her, buildings bulked in the fog, old-fashioned architecture and slanted roofs mingling with the squarer lines of buildings a century or more old and already fallen into decay. Looking back, she caught the flash of Antryg's descending sword blade in the gatehouse and saw him pelting toward her through the shadows, a last frantic run as the portcullis, its counterweight ropes slashed, rumbled downward. . . .

Joanna felt as if her heart had stopped. Had it been a free drop, he could never have made it, but the geared wheels, even rolling loose, slowed the fall of those tons of iron just enough. He flung himself down and rolled, the weighted iron teeth of the grillwork gate grinding into their slots inches behind his body. Then he was on his feet and running toward her again, the ridiculous skirts of his too-big coat billowing behind him like a cloak. His face, she noticed in the fog, was as white as his shirt ruffle.

Men were crowding up against the portcullis, trying vainly to lift it without the counterweights. Pistols were thrust through the lowered grille; there was a deafening roar and a stench of black powder as Antryg reached her and caught her arm. Together they made a dash across the small, cobbled square. The rough paving-stones gouged her feet and the puddles soaked and chilled them through her thin stockings, but she scarely noticed. Three men started to run down the steps of a tavern toward them, waving sticks. From the portcullis behind them, Joanna heard the *whap* of a crossbow firing and from the corner of her eye saw the bolt of it bury itself with hideous force in the tavern's wall. The three men flung themselves flat, and Antryg dragged her into the noisome mouth of the nearest alley.

Voices were echoing behind them in the square, dimmed and muffled by the fog, which was growing thicker, drifting clammily between the somber buildings and limiting their visibility to a few feet. Holding up her skirts with one hand and thanking all the Fates that watch over heroines that she'd had, by this time, plenty of practice fleeing in pet-ticoats, Joanna stumbled along after Antryg as he walked rapidly down the slimy mud of the lane. The first jet of strength that had carried her over the drawbridge was fading. She felt weak and suddenly cold.

He ducked through a back gate into a narrow yard which, by the smell of it, was used promiscuously as a toilet facility by the entire over-crowded tenement it served, led her across it, through a dark doorway into what had once been the lower hall of some great house and was now the black and gloomy bottom floor of tenement lodgings, and out again through the front door onto the street. The fog seemed, if anything, thicker there. Holding her arm, he led her across a narrow, cobbled street, dodging aside as the shape of a horse-drawn vehicle of some kind loomed suddenly out of the gray mists, and then into another alley beyond. She heard voices shouting from somewhere and the clash of weapons, and all she could think was, *We can't get caught. We can't get caught. . . .*

"Here." Antryg stopped. It seemed they were alone in a tiny bubble of solitude and the stink of rotting fish which permeated the mud underfoot. He seemed to see for the first time her torn bodice and disheveled hair, and a small, upright line that could have been pain or anger appeared between his brows. "Did they hurt you?"

Joanna shook her head. "Just threatened real good."

A corner of his mouth quirked at that, but his eyes remained grave, as if he guessed that, had she been hurt, she would have been too ashamed to admit it. "You're sure?"

Why this concern for her true feelings should make her throat hurt with the urge to cry again, she didn't know—possibly because he was the first not to take her brusque, "I'm fine," at face value, possibly simply because she was cold, frightened, and overwrought. She nodded, and he seemed to accept that. He pulled a tattered silk handkerchief from his pocket and wiped his swordblade with it, then sheathed it in the scabbard that was thrust, as Caris bore his when battle was at hand, through a sash at his waist. It made a sharp angle under the voluminous skirts of his coat. He took the pistol gently from her hand, checked it, and handed it back; then he stood for a moment looking down at her.

She thought he had been going to say something else, but he did not. It was coming to her that she was still alive and, at least for this second and possibly the next two, safe. It was against considerable odds that they both weren't lying dead in the shadows of the St. Cyr gatehouse. He put his hand up to touch her hair; then, as if half-doubtful of the wisdom of his action, bent and kissed her lips.

And he was right, she thought, to doubt. The kiss was probably intended to last much less time than it did. On the road their bantering had occasionally edged on flirtation, but he had been careful never to be alone with her, and for this she was, in a way, grateful. But now she was only aware of her own desperate need to hold him, all the terrors and dread of the last six hours swelling to bursting point within her, tightening her grip around his ribcage, the lock of the pistol she still held pressing awkwardly against his back, until she could feel every edge of shirt-ruffle and every button through her sweat-soaked shift and into her icy flesh. She was aware of his body against hers, holding her up as her knees shook, of the softness of the worn velvet under her hands, of the warmth of his breath on her cheek, and of her passionate desire to press her face to his shoulder and weep.

She tore her mouth free of his. She found she was breathing hard, trembling even as he was. She thought, *This is crazy!* But their eyes lingered, with a desperate knowledge that both of them were well aware verged on madness. Then he caught her hand and led her swiftly in the murk.

"Nothing quite so useful as a good fog," he said after a few moments. "They said that the Archmage Elsheiyin used to summon fog by combing her hair, but most people need water of some kind. Suraklin could do it with water dipped up in his hand. Mind you, it isn't easy to summon one this early in the year."

"Did Magister Magus do this?"

He shook his head. "No, this is mine. Tinkering with the weather is relatively safe because it's so difficult to detect. Magus is probably home under his bed by this time. No mage likes to get too close to St. Cyr, and he had to be almost up under the gatehouse to cast the darkness and the screams. To do him credit, he stayed much longer than I'd have thought."

"What would you have done, if he hadn't agreed to help you?" Joanna asked, as they dodged across what appeared, in the clammy mists, to be a small courtyard, where the ghostly forms of men and women crowded in house doorways around mephitic braziers of coals amid a strong stench of smoke and gin.

"Given him a case of itches that would have worn out his fingernails for scratching," Antryg replied promptly, and Joanna, in spite of herself, the danger, and the fact that a moment ago she'd been perilously close to exhausted tears, was shaken with the giggles.

"We've got to get off the island," he added. "It's small enough that the Church's soldiers and the Regent's can quarter it between them. I was surprised to see the Regent's men; he must have returned to Angelshand. They'll know these alleys better than the Church sasenna will." He stopped, turning his head to listen in the fog, his hand tightening on Joanna's arm. She sensed shapes moving against the darker bulk of an almost unseen building and felt a sudden qualm of terror of being caught in the open, fog-cloaked though it might be. It was late afternoon, and the vapors were suffused with a thin gray light; shapes within them shifted, dark and indistinct. . . .

Silently, Antryg melted back into a doorway to let them pass. Like the faint drip of water, their footsteps tapped away into the distance. Above the stench of greasy cooking and stale urine in the doorway around them, Joanna could smell the murky river somewhere close by. She shivered, the pistol feeling suddenly heavy in her grip. The wizard's hand was very warm where he patted her back through the thin, sweat-damp muslin of her gown. Like a pair of ghosts, they stepped from the doorway again and drifted through the vaporous dimness toward the chuckle of the water. It occurred to Joanna that, whatever the reason Antryg had kidnapped her—if he had kidnapped her—she seemed to have thrown in her lot entirely with him now. There was no longer whatever alternative course Caris could offer. If she—

In the darkness of an alley to their right, a sword clanked on stone. Antryg whirled, his hand going to his sword hilt. At the same instant, Joanna saw in the black, eyeless socket of a doorway to their right the shadows solidify into the shapes of men with swords. She hadn't even the span of an intaken breath to cry a warning. Antryg, alerted by some sixth sense that he'd walked into crossfire, was already turning back as the weighted pommel of a sword cracked down on the back of his head.

In a telescoping instant of time, Joanna was perfectly well aware that she was unable to carry him as he crumpled down against her; she was also aware that she had only one shot in her pistol and that, if she fired it now into the thick of the half-dozen sasenna closing in on them from the mouth of the alley opposite, she might buy herself the time to flee. Instead, she swung around on the man in the doorway as he pointed his crossbow down at the wizard's crumpled body on the wet cobblestones and cried, "Don't!"

Iron hands seized her from behind, dragging her back against an iron body as hard fingers wrenched the pistol from her grip. She knew it was useless to struggle, so she didn't. Looking up, she saw the red-haired sasennan who'd caught her at the posthouse on the Kymil road, the captain of the Regent's guards.

CHAPTER XV

"It's them, my lord." The captain of the Prince's sasenna spoke softly in the black arch of the stone doorway. "We brought them here as you said, instead of back to St. Cyr."

"Very good, Joris," the Regent's shrill, edgy voice replied. "Keep the men within call." A ripple of gold flashed in those inky shadows. Then the Prince stepped into the room, into the dim circle of the charcoal brazier's softly pulsing glow. "And I warn you, wizard," he added, his words brittle as chipped glass, "at the first sign of trouble from you, Kanner has orders to kill the girl."

Thanks, Joanna thought tiredly, fighting tears of sheer exhaustion and fear. The guard who stood beside the chair of ebony and ormolu where she had been tied didn't even move his head at the sound of his own name; his dark eyes wavered from her no more than did the barrel of his pistol. His uniform was crimson, though he moved with the quick-footed grace of the inevitably black-clothed sasenna. His face was a mass of scars and old angers. Joanna looked away from him, shivering. She could not seem to stop shaking with cold, wretchedness, and fear. She felt, as Antryg had once said, a weak longing for the relative safety of the roach-infested cell in the St. Cyr fortress. At least, the Witchfinders were bounded by a sort of law—if nothing else, their self-deceptive righteousness might keep them from the baser forms of cruelty. Looking into the Prince's mad eyes, she knew that what he would do would be done without compunction, for his own pleasure.

Here—wherever this small stone chamber was, at the foot of its twisting stair—they were entirely in his power.

She had thought Antryg was still unconscious, chained by his wrists between the two pillars which supported the central groinings of the ceiling. But he raised his head groggily at the Prince's words, sweat shining along jaw muscles tense with pain. "The girl has nothing to do with this, Pharos," he said. "She's only my servant. She knows nothing of any of this. I forced her to accompany me."

"And took two cuts with my whip out of indifference to her fate?" The Prince walked slowly over to Joanna and caught her chin with one small, black-gloved hand as she tried to shrink away. His pale-blue gaze traveled over her throat and half-bared bosom; his mouth widened a little, but what was in his eyes could never have been called a smile. Terrified and loathing him, Joanna felt, as she had with the Witchfinder, that her best defense lay in silence. She met his eyes; it was the Prince who looked quickly away.

He turned back to Antryg. The wizard had gotten his feet under him, taking some of the strain of his unsupported weight from his stretched-out arms. His face was chalky with exhaustion and running with sweat in the hot closeness of the little room; Joanna could see the shift of his knuckles where he held the manacle chains, trying to ease the cut of the bracelets in his wrists. The chains were twisted through with thin red silk ribbon, incongruously gay—spell-cord, she recognized from Magister Magus' description. More of it was twined around the ropes that held her own wrists to the arms of the chair.

Though he was weaving a little on his feet, Antryg's gray eyes were calm. Through his open shirt, Joanna could see the steady rhythm of his breath. If he was even half as afraid as she was, he hid it well.

The Prince asked softly, "Who are you?"

Antryg sighed, and some of the tension seemed to drain from his body. "Antryg Windrose," he said.

The chill, pale-blue eyes narrowed. "So." For a long moment the Prince remained still, studying the form chained between the pillars in the ruddy, reflected glare of the brazier. Joanna could see the lines of sleeplessness on his face beneath a thick coating of rice powder and rouge; the dark rings of bister and fatigue made the queer eyes even paler. The Prince wet his lips, as if he feared the wizard, even chained and helpless, and had to nerve himself to approach. Then he stepped forward and, as he had before, reached up one gloved hand and carefully removed Antryg's spectacles from his face. Antryg flinched a little as the metal temple piece nicked the bruises, but his eyes never left Pharos' face.

The Prince folded up the spectacles and set them on the narrow ledge of the pillar's capital beside him. The firelight slid along the soft black leather of the gloves as he put out his hands to frame the wizard's face between them, shoving back the loose lion's mane of graying hair to outline the delicate bones and wide, lunatic eyes.

"So," he said again. He stepped back. "Is what the Bishop of Kymil said about you true?"

Antryg tipped his head a little to one side. Without the cracked mask of the spectacles, his gray eyes looked even wider and strangely luminous in the dark smudges of fatigue. "Oh, probably not," he said mildly. "How much of what is said about you is true?"

The white gleam of teeth showed, very briefly, with the parting of the painted lips. "Everything," the Prince whispered. "I could flog you to death, you know, just to see how long it would take a wizard to die under it. No one would know. My palace—" He gestured to the dark room around them and the shadowy, convoluted vaults overhead "—stands in its own grounds, away from the main Palace and away from that stinking rabble of wizards my father used to surround himself with. Away from prying eyes, away from people spying on me, trying to kill me—yes, even my saintly cousin Cerdic!—whispering among themselves that I'm mad. Of course I'm mad! My father is, isn't he? And I am his true son . . ." His voice sank even lower, so that Joanna, watching that slender black figure, barely heard. "Aren't I?"

Antryg said, his tone quiet and conversational, "You would know more of that than I, Pharos. But being quite mad myself, I wouldn't hold madness against you; one sometimes does it in mere self-defense, you know."

The Prince's glance cut sharply up to Antryg's eyes for the first time. "What?"

"Goes mad."

The beauty of that deep voice seemed to calm the Prince; for some moments the blue eyes held the gray.

"Yes," Pharos said slowly. "Sometimes one must—go mad—or die. They said that you were mad." His glance shifted away again, as if he could not bear to show even that part of himself to another human being for more than a second or so.

Antryg nodded. Still low, still soothing, he said, "It was—the only thing that I could do at the time."

"Is it true that you've been a prisoner of the Church for seven years? That you were condemned to death?"

The harsh, metallic voice was uninflected, impossible to second-guess. Antryg said, "Yes," and the Prince looked back at him again, suspicious, waiting for something. The wizard went on, "The rebels were my friends.

The Emperor's dragoons had no right to do what they did. Not to the children. I thought that the Emperor . . ." He paused, for a long moment, then shook his head, weary, defeated by the old memories. "Yes, I was imprisoned under a commuted sentence of death."

"And the Archmage helped you escape?"

"No." Joanna saw Antryg's hands tighten again on the chains, holding himself upright against fatigue, shock, and the sick aftereffects of a really appalling crack on the head. In the dead-still, heated air, she could smell the musky stink of the Regent's perfume and the faint sourness of sweat from the guard Kanner, who stood beside her, silent as a statue, so close she could see the runes of na-aar written on the pistol barrel. Antryg moved his head a little, shaking aside the sweat-dampened ends of his long hair, where they clung in little circles to his temples and cheeks. "I escaped when the Archmage disappeared, but I had nothing to do with his disappearance, nor he with my escape. He had neither the intent nor the desire to set me free."

"No," the Prince murmured. "He knew our fat Bishop well—he knew the Witchfinders—he knew me. If he had helped you escape, it would have been far better done, wouldn't it? Not leaving you wandering the roads like a vagabond, nor leaving the other members of the Council to take the Church's wrath unaided. And you—you would have risked your life to rescue more than a chit of a girl. You can tell me nothing of them, can you?"

Antryg shook his head exhaustedly, the fatigue telling on him, sapping his strength. His voice remained calm, low and weary with memory and hopelessness. "I haven't seen any of them in seven years."

"Then why did you come to Angelshand?" the Prince asked, his voice soft now, evil as the Witchfinder's and infinitely more deadly. "Surely, if you are a fugitive from the Council as you say, you would have run in the opposite direction?"

Antryg turned his face away. The gold light of the brazier shining through the damp, thin fabric of his shirt outlined his body as he drew a deep breath, then let it out, struggling, as Joanna had seen him on the road, between trust and silence. Then he looked back at the Prince, his deep voice still level but desperation in his eyes. "I have to reinstate myself somehow," he said quietly. "I can't go on like this. Not for the rest of my life. I'm a wizard, Pharos, and I haven't been able to touch that reservoir of power within myself for seven years. Even now I can't use it, for they would find me through it—the Witchfinders, the Church mages. I need to speak to them. . . ." He broke off, gazing into the

Prince's face, the dark lines of strain suddenly cut deep in the discolored flesh around his eyes, hardening and aging them.

The Prince said nothing for a time, but stood with his gloved hands clasped together, an oily gleam of moisture glazing his maquillage and a sprinkle of reflected flame dancing over the bullion lace at his wrists as he shivered, as if with sudden chill. At last he whispered, "Is it real? This—this magic. This mumbo-jumbo—old women calling the weather among the fallen stones on the hills, things that mumble in the crypts, men who can summon storms by looking into a bowl of water—is it real? Not just stories with which to frighten us into obedience as children? Not just charlatans like those fakers my cousin fills his house with? Not just hags deluding themselves from their own helplessness?"

"No," Antryg murmured. "No, it's real."

The Prince stepped close to him, his voice hoarse with fear to believe. "Show me."

Antryg's fingers moved, brushing the spell-ribbon that knotted through his chains. "You've taken care to see that I couldn't," he said softly. "Surprising care, for a man who believes it's all mumbo-jumbo and granny-rhymes. And, as I've said, I would not, even if you released me. They are seeking me—they would find me through it; and believe me, Pharos, I fear them more than I fear you."

"The Church dogs?" Pharos sniffed with scorn touched by the bravado of one half-afraid himself. "I gave the Church their mandate to act, when they said there was a plot by the Archmage and the Council. I can take it away again. I could protect you."

"Not from the Council." Antryg looked down at the Prince, the top of whose golden curls came barely to his lips. "I don't know how many of them managed to escape from St. Cyr this afternoon, but you never had them all, did you?"

Suspicion flared again in the Prince's mad eyes. "What do you know of it?"

The chains clinked faintly as Antryg shrugged. "If you had," he said simply, "you wouldn't still be afraid. And you are afraid."

The Regent stood for a moment, his face averted. In the absolute stillness, Joanna could hear how shaky was the draw of his breath. There was a cracked note to his shrill voice as he called out suddenly, "Joris!"

The captain of his sasenna, the tall, heavy-boned, red-haired woman who had captured them, emerged from the utter darkness of the hall.

"You haven't touched magic for seven years," the Prince said softly. "You couldn't have, not from the Tower, not as their prisoner." He signaled to the woman Joris.

Taking a key from the nail beside the door, she crossed into the dim circle of the firelight and unlocked the shackles from Antryg's wrists. For a moment, Joanna thought the wizard would collapse without the chains to hold him up, but he only leaned against one of the pillars, rubbing the flesh of his bony wrists where the metal had scraped the skin off it. At a nod from the Regent, Kanner stepped aside, though he did not put down his pistol. Joris came over to Joanna's chair and untied the ropes that held her. When the sasennan left, the big guard remained, his pistol still at the ready, silent as a sword.

During all this, Pharos stood with his hands folded in front of his breast, palms and fingers locked and pressed together so tightly that Joanna could see the knuckles bulge and work through the soft kid of the gloves. His eyes, when in their restless flickering Joanna could glimpse them, had lost their malice and were haunted and anxious; he caught Joris by the arm as she moved toward the door. "Be ready," he said softly, and the woman nodded briefly. She stepped back through the door into darkness, but in that darkness a shadow moved, and Joanna caught the gleam of pistol barrels, leveled at Antryg's heart.

After a long moment, the Prince began, "I need . . ." He stopped, standing close to Antryg, closer than Joanna would have found comfortable, the closeness of intimacy; but still he did not look at the wizard. It had undoubtedly been a long time, Joanna thought suddenly, since this dainty, evil little man had said, *I need* to anyone.

He swallowed hard and tried again. "Narwahl," he said quietly. His voice was very different now from the arrogant and perverted Prince who had held them at his mercy. Caris had said Skipfrag was the Regent's friend. There was a terrible tension in the Prince's words as he tried to speak calmly of that friend's death. "The neighbors heard a shot and then a shrieking like all the souls of the damned. They found . . ." He paused, unable to go on.

"I know what they found," Joanna said. "Broken and shattered glass. And blood all over everything—the floor, the walls, everywhere."

The Regent glanced to where she still sat in the carved ebony chair to which she had been tied. The corners of his mouth twitched. "Ah, yes. You were there, weren't you? At least, that's what Joris tells me the Church sasenna said." He took from one pocket a handkerchief—black, she noted. All his linen was black, an affectation that reminded her irresistibly of a Hollywood pimp. With the care of one long used to working around makeup, he wiped his face, and she saw that his hand shook.

"I never knew he was associated with mages," he began again in a strained voice. "The Witchfinders said they found evil things and evidence of some horrible, angry spirit in his workroom. They asked me to order the house put under seal. I think they wanted to see who would come for them."

Joanna sniffed. "They would. All he was doing was experimenting with electricity. Peelbone would burn the inventor of the clock for daring to interfere with the Sole God's prerogative of determining time."

"Perhaps," Antryg said quietly. He took his spectacles from their ledge and seated himself carefully at the base of one of the pillars, wincing a little as he folded his long arms around his drawn-up knees. "But the fact remains that someone broke into his workroom. And I suspect, from what you two say, that it was someone who could summon and control elementals, give them body and form." He cocked his head up at the Regent. "Is that why you fear the Council?"

The Prince stood looking down at him for a moment, holding back that last surrender, that last admission. He drew a short, sharp breath that hissed through his nostrils and looked away. Joanna could see his mouth work for a moment. Then, as if he were aware of it, he pressed his hand to his lips, forcing it still. When he took his hand away, his fingers were shaking. "I don't know," he whispered wretchedly. "They are the ones who—who are supposed to have power. When the Bishop of Kymil said there was a plot and asked for my sanction to investigate it, I thought . . ." He took a deep breath, like a man fighting to steady himself against some terrible strain. "I do not know who it is I have to fear," he said at last. "I only know that, if you have been a prisoner these seven years, Antryg Windrose, it cannot be you."

Antryg said nothing, waiting in silence while the Prince considered what he could say. After a moment, Pharos went on, still in that hoarse, frightened whisper, "And you are a mage. It is why I ordered my men to bring you here when they caught you, instead of turning you back to the Witchfinders. Since Herthe told me you had been a prisoner in the Tower, unable to work magic, I knew that I had to find you. You are the only one I can speak to, the only one it is safe to speak to—if it *is* safe—of certain things."

The wizard's deep, beautiful voice was gentle and unalarming in the buried stillness of the firelit stone room. "What things?"

The Prince drew another deep breath and was quiet a moment, sorting his thoughts; even his restlessly twisting little hands grew still, clasped before him. "It was—balderdash," he said at last. "I was always told that. Magic. My father . . ." He swallowed. "He—he favored the wizards, but he kept them all at arm's distance. My tutor never approved. I thought his favor was excessive; certainly I never thought their powers were any more real than those cheapjack toadstone-peddlers or the granny-wives who claim they can put a bad word on someone's cow. They spoke of powers, but they never did anything at all. Even now, I don't know if I'm mad or sane, whether this is part of the old madness or some new twist."

Gently leading him, Antryg looked up at him and asked, "What?"

The Prince paced a few steps, then turned back again, some of the tension easing out of his body with a kind of hopeless inner surrender. When he spoke again, his voice was deliberately matter-of-fact. "About three months ago, I fell in love with a boy in the household of the Duke of Albrete—an enchanting youth, amber and alabaster, with skin so clear you could trace the path of a swallow of wine down his throat. Elfwith was his name—not that it matters, and I certainly didn't expect to remember it three months afterwards. I probably wouldn't, except for what happened to him." He stilled in his pacing and swallowed again, looking down at Antryg, who sat unmoving at the base of the pillar, the tawny light playing restlessly across his absurd, bespectacled face.

"He—died. I'd asked him to go up to my rooms and given orders for the guards in the secret staircase to let him pass—even the secret stair into the room is guarded. I was delayed by a matter of state—those wretched ambassadors from Senterwing about that brainless bitch I'm to marry. All very secret."

Antryg nodded. Joanna remembered, sometime on the carriage journey, Caris saying the wizard had read that marriage in a spread of cards. She felt very little surprise, even in the face of what she knew about the Prince's preferences, in hearing that it was true.

"Well, Elfwith came hurrying down to the guard on the secret stair, saying he thought there was someone in my rooms. They turned out and searched, they said—I heard all this later—but there was no sign of anyone having been there. So Elfwith went in to wait. And I found him, an hour and a half later, dying—dying horribly in my bed, his limbs covered with sores, eaten with them. If it was a sickness, it was nothing Narwahl had ever seen, but he claimed there was no poison that could do it, either. I swore him on his life to secrecy, because there was the boy's family to consider as well. Of course the bedding was all burned, but there was no other case of such a sickness ever reported anywhere, before or since. I know that, for Narwahl looked in every book and journal he possessed.

"Then—it might have been two weeks later—I was sleeping . . ."

"Alone?" Antryg inquired, and Pharos managed an ironic smirk.

"You don't think I ever let myself fall asleep in the presence of those stupid little creatures, do you? I send them away. Lately I've kept Kanner in my room when I sleep, though I didn't do so then. He's very loyal to me. He was sasennan until he lost his hearing through a fever. I know that, when sasenna become flawed, they're supposed to kill themselves, I suppose he's added the flaw of cowardice to that of deafness, but I've made it worth his while. I find having a deaf servant supremely useful. In any case, I woke up—I don't know why—it might have been a dream. I dream . . ."

He paused again, then visibly shied from the subject, like a nervous horse, and resumed his pacing. His gestures, repeated in vast, amorphous shadows on the wall at his back, moved as if they would shape the scene from air. "The bed curtains were open a little, and I could see part of the paneling of the wall by the light of the night lamp. There was a shadow on it, clearly thrown, but huge, distorted—the long robe of a mage. I saw him move his hand, doing something at the lamp table I thought. I cried out for the guards; but when they came in—nothing. There was no one there, nor was there a way he could have left; the corner he was in is near the outside wall, and there was no possibility of a secret passage, even if I had not had the room sounded a dozen times. I had the water in the pitcher that stood on that table given to one of the palace dogs. It seemed all right at the time, but the dog died four, five days later. Too long for poison, much too long. And yet . . ."

He pressed his hand to his mouth again, a nervous gesture, to still or to hide the unsteadiness of those too-full, painted lips. "I couldn't tell anyone after that, you see," he went on, a little thinly. "There was no proof. They would have mocked me if I'd said I thought it was magic, as they mocked me when . . ."

He caught himself up again, over some old memory, and went hastily on, "They would have said I was mad, as they did before. And I am mad. But not—not mad in that way. Not until now. Twice I've waked in the night and heard knocking somewhere in the room—it's vanished when I called the guards; and after the second time, I had Kanner in the room with me and at least one other guard. I don't even know whether I really heard it the second time or not—I was dreaming—I don't know."

He ran his hands through his barley-gold hair, twisting the careful curls awry; in the firelight, the muscles of his long, narrow jaw quivered with the violence of their compression.

"I fought against it for a long time," he said at length. "I did not believe in magic, but—I think someone is trying to kill me through its use. Is this possible?"

He turned back to look at Antryg, hungry desperation in his eyes.

After a long moment, the mage nodded. With a movement oddly graceful for one so gawky, he got to his feet, still steadying himself against the pillar, and put a gentling hand on the Prince's shoulder. "How long since the last attempt?"

"If it was an attempt," Pharos whispered. "It was only knocking. . . ."

"It was an attempt," Antryg said, and there was no doubt in his voice. "How long?"

"Two—three weeks. Shortly before—shortly before the Bishop of Kymil sent word that she had uncovered a plot of the Council of Mages against the Church and against the Realm. I issued jurisdiction for their arrest. Then, two days later, Narwahl . . ."

As if quieting the hysterics of a child, Antryg closed his hands around the Prince's trembling fingers. It occurred to Joanna to wonder whether Pharos had seen that attic room, sprayed with fresh blood and glass.

"And you went to Kymil?" Antryg asked, and the Prince nodded. "To find out what Herthe knew?"

"Yes." The Prince nodded again, his voice a little stronger, a little steadier. "Herthe and her guards came and met me at the posthouse. She told me who you were. I knew then I had to find you, get to you before the Witchfinders did. I knew you were the only one who couldn't have done it, who couldn't possibly be in on it. She spoke of abominations in the land and said that it seemed likely you were coming to Angelshand. I made some excuse, turned back, and ordered my men to search for you, find you before the Church could have you killed. I thought you might have gone to Devilsgate, to take refuge with that stupid, saintly hypocrite Cerdic. . . ." A flash of vicious bitterness surfaced in his voice, like the glint of paranoia that suddenly gleamed in his narrowed eyes at the mention of his cousin's name. Antryg said nothing, and Joanna, who had been thoroughly charmed with the Regent's cousin, likewise refrained from adding her two cents to the conversation at this point.

After a moment, the madness faded from Pharos' eyes, and with it, his hard-held calm. He swallowed; his voice came out small and cracked with strain. "I came back here today. But it was as if—as if from the time I spoke to Herthe, the morning after I met you in the posthouse, I knew it was hopeless. It seemed to me then that I could see my whole future, and it was empty—that I was mad, like my father." He faltered, then went on, "And in time I would become an imbecile like him. Even though these things I feared had no existence, they would destroy me, and there was nothing to do, nowhere to come, except back here to my death. I tried having the Council mages imprisoned, but the Church has its mages, too. And there's still tonight to sleep through—"

His voice broke suddenly, as if weight had been put on a flawed beam; his breath hissed, and he stood for a moment, shivering in silence and, Joanna realized, shame at his fears.

Very gently, his hands still in the Prince's convulsive grip, Antryg said, "Here?"

When Pharos glanced sharply at him, Antryg went on, "I take it this is the dungeon under the original part of the old Summer Palace."

The Prince's lips moved in a quirk that might have been a smile; he glanced down at the big hands he still held and released them. As if aware of the wreck he'd made of his coiffure, he put up one gloved hand to straighten a snail-shell curl. "Yes. I've taken it over for my own. It's sufficiently isolated in the grounds to keep gossip mongers away when I want a little private sport."

"Is there anywhere else you could sleep?"

"Would it make a difference?"

"It might," Antryg said mildly. "If you were more superstitious, you'd probably have thought yourself of the possibility that there's a wizard's mark in your rooms."

There were seven of them.

Wearing a ruffled shirt and breeches fetched by Joris from the wardrobes of the Prince's pages ("I'm tired of walking around looking like I've just escaped from the cover of a historical romance!") Joanna followed Antryg and the Prince up several flights of stairs, passing from the ancient stonework of the dungeons to the renovated rococo grace of the Prince's palace above. It was now quite dark outside, but the Prince's private apartments blazed with the light of a thousand candles and lamps; as they moved from room to brilliantly lit room, followed by Joris, Kanner, and two other guards, it occurred to Joanna that the Regent was probably terrified of the dark.

The warm brilliance of the candles, so different from the hard and prosaic electricity Joanna had grown up with, lent a curiously dreamlike air to those rooms, with their shell-shaped curlicues of gold and scarlet, their delicate furniture, and their sinuous marbles. In his shabby black coat, spectacles, and quizzing glass, Antryg moved through them like some daft Victorian ghost hunter, tapping at the chinoiserie of the panels and calling the marks, one by one, to faint and glowing life.

One mark, on the ancient stonework behind the paneling itself, was extremely old, readable only when Antryg pressed his hands to the painted wood. Another made him smile. "I wonder what the mage Nyellin was doing here? It's six hundred years old—nothing to do with you, Pharos—but she did have rather a reputation as a meddler herself."

His hand brushed the scarlet-lacquered wood between the bedroom windows. Under his fingers, another mark appeared, only to be seen from the corner of the eye—a chance glimmer of candlelight, floating, it seemed, above or below the actual surface of the panel, as if someone had scribbled with a finger on the air in light.

Joanna remembered, with an uneasy chill, the sign on the wall of the main computer room at San Serano, seen past the dark shadow of the strangler's shoulder; she remembered also the darkness of Gary's upstairs room and the red reflection of computer lights off Antryg's spectacles as he'd brushed his hand, just so, along the wall by the door.

I can't tell you the truth and I don't wish to lie to you. . . .

You are in this world under my protection. . . .

"A wizard's mark will call him to it," Antryg explained over his shoulder to the Prince, who followed, cautious as if the marks themselves could kill. "He can find it, wherever he is, and go to it. If the mark is strong enough, he can use it to influence things near it, even when he is not present, sometimes even work certain spells through it without being there."

He stood for a long time, staring at the paneling between the windows, where the mark had glimmered so briefly to life. Then he sighed and shut his eyes.

The Prince glanced nervously over his shoulder. "What is it?"

Antryg turned away and touched briefly the elaborate marquetry dressing table that stood beneath the mark. A branch of candles in the twining shapes of naked goddesses stood on it and beside them a pitcher of creamy, rose-colored porcelain, half-filled with water. "The mark is less than two months old," he said quietly. He looked suddenly very tired, his mouth taut and a little white, as if he had drunk some bitter and poisoned brew. "This one—" He crossed to the door of a dressing room and brushed a faint, brief shimmer of sign from its topmost panel, "—about ten years. Both by the same wizard."

"Who?" demanded the Prince, and Antryg shook his head.

"The second mark would reinforce the influence of the first," he went on, staring up at the place where the mark on the door had been. "But ten years ago . . ." He paused, his eyebrows drawn together over the absurd beak of his nose. "Ten years . . ."

"What is it?"

Antryg looked back at the Prince and shook his head. "I don't know," he said. "These have always been your rooms?"

"Yes. Since first I was given my own establishment when I was eighteen. I am thirty-five now and I assure you, my lord wizard, that no mage has been in here to make that first mark since they have been mine."

"Knowing how you've kept yourself guarded, I'd say I believed you," Antryg said, "except, of course, that one obviously was."

"They were always about the Court, of course," Pharos said. "My father . . ."

He hesitated.

"Exactly," Antryg said quietly. "Your father. And Cerdic later. I know your father had a good deal to do with Salteris, as Head of the Council." Listening, Joanna wondered if she detected the faintest of flaws in Antryg's voice when he spoke the Archmage's name. "Do you know who else?"

The little man shook his head. "I didn't want to know. I considered it—" He licked his lips, shying again from the subject, and then simply concluded, "I didn't want to know."

Antryg was silent for a long time, his arms folded, his head down, and his strange, wide, light-gray eyes distant with thought. From somewhere, Joanna heard a clock speak eleven silvery chimes and felt all the deathly weariness of the day closing in on her—flight, fear, and sudden, starving hunger.

Then the wizard sighed and pushed up his spectacles to rub his eyes. "It's very late now," he said, "and Joanna and I both are very tired. At least I am and, if she isn't, I suggest you hire her as your bodyguard. Unless you're going to lock us away for good, Pharos, there are two things that I'd like to ask of you in the morning. Three things, actually, counting breakfast. Can your cook make muffins?"

It was the first time Joanna had seen Prince Pharos laugh, the pale, pretty face and sinful eyes screwing up in genuine amusement. "My dearest Antryg," he said, laying what Joanna privately suspected of being an overly friendly hand on the wizard's arm, "if the muffins are not to your satisfaction, I give you full permission to flog the cook. He won't quit, I assure you; he'd never relinquish his position as *my* cook. It's far more than his reputation would be worth."

"Excellent." Antryg smiled and pushed his spectacles up on the bridge of his nose with one bony forefinger. "The second is that I'd like you to send for the contents of Narwahl Skipfrag's laboratory, and the third . . . I'd like to look at your father's rooms."

* * *

"By the way," said Joanna quietly, "I never had a chance to say thank you."

Antryg, sitting in the dark window embrasure of the room the Prince had given him, up under the eaves of the Summer Palace's mansard roof, looked around at her and smiled. A flicker of bluish light appeared in the air of the room between him and the door where she stood; it floated, like a negligent firefly, over to the exquisite ormolu table in the room's center and came to rest on the wick of one of the unlit candles there. His voice was deep in the gloom. "I ought to say it was my pleasure, but diving under that portcullis—I can only think of two times I've been that frightened in my life. It is my pleasure," he added, "that we're both alive."

"I wouldn't say pleasure so much as stunned surprise." She crossed the room to him, and he drew up his feet on the window seat to make room for her. Through the open casement, she could smell the smoke from the lamps and torches of the guards in the courtyard three storeys below and, when the wind shifted, the thick green smells of the palace park. "Decent of the Prince to send us up supper."

"Considering what it took to get lobster patties at this hour," Antryg agreed. "No matter what the muffins are like for breakfast, I shall have to lie and say I like them. Such a cook ought never to be flogged more often than is necessary, as the Prince says, to keep him smart."

Joanna chuckled. "Not to mention the clothes," she added, touching the high, pleated collar of the pageboy's shirt she wore. "He sent me up a gown for tomorrow. I'm wondering where the hell he got it."

"Possibly one of his boyfriends . . ."

She poked him reprovingly in the knee with her foot and laughed. "*Is* one of the mages trying to kill him?"

"Oh, yes."

"To put Cerdic on the throne?"

"If I were the sort of mage who routinely meddled in human affairs," the wizard said gravely, "it's what I'd do."

She remembered Cerdic's enthusiastic and unquestioning welcome of Antryg because he was a mage and the blind acceptance of the inherent rightness of wizards, started to speak, then was silent. For a moment, she contemplated that long, peculiar profile in the bluish glow of the witchlight, noticing how the reflections of the fires in the courtyard below touched hard little glimmers in the steel of his spectacle frames and the dreamy grayness of his eyes. He looked a little better than he had, less strained and gray, but the nervous energy that had gotten him through the last several hours was fading, even as it was for her. He looked tired and very vulnerable, sitting with his knees drawn up in the window seat, and she had to resist an overwhelming impulse to put out her hand and touch his arm.

Slowly, she said, "Are we dealing with several problems here or just one? The fading and the abominations—but you said you were coming to talk to some member of the Council? and there's the Archmage. . . . And poor Caris—whatever's happened to him?"

A smile tugged briefly at Antryg's lips in the wan lucence of the witch-light. "I imagine poor Caris is still waiting for me outside a vacant building on the south side of the river. He's very patient when he's on a trail."

"One of these days," Joanna said severely, "Caris is going to murder you—and not because of his grandfather, either."

"Of course," Antryg said. "That's been the—" He stopped himself as Joanna's eyebrows came together, then went on quickly, "He's come very close to it twice. As for what we're dealing with here . . ." He shook his head. "There seem to be a lot of events unrelated to one another, except by juxtaposition in time—Narwahl's death, your kidnapping, the Prince's marriage . . ."

"Or things that happened twenty-five years ago," she said, remembering the old woman in the prison. *At his tricks again,* that one had said, rocking back and forth, and for the dozenth time Joanna found herself reminded that what Suraklin had known, Antryg undoubtedly knew. There was no way he could have murdered Narwahl—on the night of the physician's death, as far as Joanna could calculate, they had all been sleeping in the hayloft of some posting inn on the Kymil road. . . . Or could he?

She wondered suddenly whether an examination would reveal wizards' marks in that stuffy, blood-smelling room.

She was aware that Antryg had fallen silent and was looking at her with wary uncertainty in his eyes.

"How did you know I was there, by the way? Thinking about it, I was desperately glad to see you, but I don't think I was surprised; and now I realize I should have been."

"Not really." His earring winked in the tangled mane of his hair as he turned his head. "I was looking for mages, remember. Considering the current situation, the logical place to look was St. Cyr. I was loitering around inconspicuously outside when they brought you in. I assume Caris sent you to Narwahl's."

"How did . . . ?" she began, and then remembered saying to the Prince that she knew what the neighbors had found in that hideous upper room.

"Will that screw you up?" she asked after a moment. "All the mages getting away from St. Cyr—or did they all get away?"

He shook his head. "I imagine most of them did. I've spoken to Pharos about releasing the others. There will be time enough to find them and to speak to them, after I've seen the Emperor's rooms."

"Will having them loose increase your danger?" she asked, and he shook his head absently. "Then you know which one to be afraid of?"

He looked quickly at her, his eyes suddenly wide in the dim gleam from the court below, as if he had suddenly seen that he'd walked into a trap. But it wasn't a trap, she thought, baffled; she had sensed him holding her at arm's length, picking his way carefully over conversationally shifty ground. He was braced for something, she knew, but she only asked, "Why are you afraid of me?"

He started to say something, then checked himself; for some moments, the little room under the eaves was quiet, save for the noises that drifted up from the court below through the opened casements and the faroff creak of some servant's foot elsewhere in the palace. Then he changed his mind and said, "Like the Prince, I'm afraid of a good many things. I've spent most of my life terrified of a man who's been dead for years."

He got to his feet and helped her to hers. The vagrant foxfire drifted after them as he led her to the door. She paused in its darkness, looking up at him, knowing he was evading her and coming up with an uncomfortable number of reasons why. But none of them accounted for the care he'd taken of her, none of them accounted for risking his life that afternoon to save her from the Inquisition.

She said, "I get the feeling that there's a pattern here somewhere—as you said, some connection between the fading and the abominations and between Narwahl's death and the Archmage disappearing and my being kidnapped. It's all subroutines of a program I can't see. I understand the kind of thing you hope to learn from seeing Narwahl's experiments—though they looked to me like perfectly straightforward let's-make-electricity stuff—but what do you hope to learn from seeing the Emperor's rooms?"

He shook his head. "Confirmation, perhaps, of a theory I have." He leaned against the doorframe, the will-o'-the-wisp light edging hair and spectacles and the curlicue line of shirt-ruffles with their snagged tangle of quizzing glass and beads. "And maybe the answer to something that's puzzling me very much."

She didn't really expect an answer, but asked, "What?"

After a long moment's hesitation, Antryg seemed to come to some decision within himself. "Why they would send him mad, instead of killing him."

At two in the morning the terrible, draining deadness began again and tortured Joanna's exhausted dreams with visions of old Minhyrdin until dawn.

CHAPTER XVI

"THEY SAID IT WAS A JUDGMENT, YOU KNOW." THE PRINCE REgent's pale, shifty eyes flicked from the parklike vistas of topiaried garden visible to both sides of the open coach back to the man and woman opposite him on the white velvet carriage seat. The deadness that had lasted until almost dawn had left its marks on him, adding to the keyed-up, exhausted nervousness of the previous night. His full-lipped red mouth twitched as he explained, "for his sympathy to the mages."

"I wouldn't say sympathy was your father's outstanding characteristic at my trial," Antryg mused. "Hanged, drawn, sliced, and broken—it was *years* before I could contemplate chicken marinara, not that I was given the chance to, mind you. But then, he never did like me. How did it happen?"

Pharos shook his head. "Would to God we knew," he said, quite simply. "He woke that way one morning four years ago. He . . ." He swallowed, wiped his moist hands on a black silk handkerchief, and tucked it back up among the sable festoons of his sleeve lace. "We didn't know whether it would go as suddenly as it had come—we still don't, but back then we hoped more than we do now. He used to try and talk then, or at least it looked like talking. In the first day or so, I sometimes thought he knew me. Now . . ." He looked away again, over the sun-splashed morning beauty of those manicured lawns and carefully pruned groves. Then his glance, half-embarrassed and half-warning, returned unwillingly to Joanna. "When you see him," he said carefully, "you must remember that he is a very sick man."

Joanna guessed what he meant and suppressed a qualm of apprehensive disgust. It interested her that he would feel enough concern for his father—who couldn't possibly have cared one way or the other—to warn her against showing repugnance. And afraid as she had once been of him, she now felt oddly sorry for this bejeweled little pervert.

Antryg asked, "Who were the mages who were habitually admitted to his rooms? Who would have had access to his bedroom, for instance?"

"No one," Pharos said promptly. "Well, they might have entered there from the rest of the suite. Rosamund Kentacre—her father dragged her there for him to convince her not to take the Council vows. Thirle, I believe . . ."

"Minhyrdin?"

Pharos sniffed. "That senile crone? My father's interests were in magic, not particularly in those who worked it or who were at one time able to work it. The members of the Council were admitted—Salteris, of course, Lady Rosamund, Nandiharrow, Idrix of Thray, and Whitwell Simm, and you."

"Not me," Antryg said. "Well, once, after I'd been elected to the Council, I had to be presented formally to him. But as I said, he never liked me." He frowned a little. "During the Mellidane Revolts, I had the impression I was not precisely entrapped, but certainly maneuvered. He *can't* have been that ignorant of what was going on. But I never understood why. From my little acquaintance with him, he was perfectly capable of it, of course. . . ."

"Did you know him before . . . ?" began Pharos, then stopped himself. "No, you couldn't. You were Suraklin's student. Perhaps that was the reason." The dappling sunlight passed like a school of shining fish over his bright hair as the carriage moved through a grove of maples whose leaves were already edging with blood-red autumn flame. It was difficult to believe that beyond the park walls in three directions stretched the sprawling gray city, the dingy factories, and the crowded wharves of Angelshand.

The strain and tiredness were apparent in the Prince's voice as well as his face. Joanna heard the harsh, shaky shrillness of last night still there, held rigidly in check, as it had been, she thought, for weeks—perhaps for years. After a moment, he went on, "He never would have handed down a judgment like that before—before he rode with the Archmage to Kymil, you know. He—changed afterwards."

"If he saw anything of Suraklin's Citadel," Antryg murmured, "it would be surprising if he hadn't."

"No." The Prince's voice sank. "Sometimes he spoke of it—of the things Suraklin kept in darkness, things that he bred or called up, things that he fed on the blood from his own veins. . . ."

Beside her, Joanna felt Antryg flinch at some memory, but he said nothing. Back in Kymil, she'd noticed the old, tiny scars that marked the veins of his arms like a junkie's tracks.

"But I hated him for it," Pharos continued, "as much as I had loved him before. And I did love him. It's strange to say, but since he has—since he has become an imbecile, oddly enough, I love him now." He swallowed and passed his hand over his mouth, a nervous gesture. He spoke from behind the white, delicate fingers with their bitten nails, as if from behind a barrier. "They said of Suraklin that he had a terrible, almost unbelievable influence over the minds of all who had to do with him. They said he could break anyone's mind to his bidding, if given his chance. . . . But looking back, I realize it was only the things that he'd seen . . ."

His voice faltered. Feeling Antryg's eyes on her, Joanna turned her head and caught again the wariness and fear that lurked in the water-gray depths. After a moment, Pharos went on, his words coming rapidly to cover old guilts. "But I was only a child and a fanciful one—I understand that now. It must have been only that I was ten . . ."

"You were ten?" Joanna had been watching Pharos, but the note in Antryg's voice drew her eyes, as if he had shouted the words instead of whispering them almost inaudibly. There was shock on his face, as if he had been physically struck—shock and a terrible intentness that Joanna was at a loss to understand.

Pharos nodded, too sunk in private nightmares to notice the wizard's reaction to his words, the presence of the coachman on the box, Kanner on the footman's stand, the scrunch of the horses' hooves and the carriage wheels on the gravel path, or Joanna. Hands pressed to his mouth, he stared out ahead of him with the glittering gaze of madness.

"What happened?" Antryg whispered, leaning gently forward to take the Prince's hands. He drew them down, denying Pharos that hiding place, and asked again, "What was it that happened twenty-five years ago when you were ten?"

"Nothing." The Prince shut his eyes, squeezing the painted lids together like a child hoping desperately to deny the reality of what he was helpless to fight. "That's it—nothing happened."

"Except that you went mad."

"I was a child." The words came out as if strained by main force from a throat so constricted it barely passed the air of life to his lungs. "There was nothing I could do, no one even that I could tell. I used to dream about him, after he came back, and in my dreams . . ." He broke off again, his hands trembling violently in Antryg's sure, light grip. The mage said nothing, but his wide eyes were filled with horror, grief, and enlightenment—not for the Prince's sake, but as if, looking into the younger man's madness, he had seen the terrifying reflection of his own.

Blurtingly, the Prince sobbed, "In my dreams he was not my father!" Tears tracked down through the heavy paste of makeup; he wrenched his hands from Antryg's and fumbled for his handkerchief again, his body racked by tremors of grief and horror he could not stop. "I was only ten," he repeated, "and there was no one I could tell; they wouldn't believe me. But for years, I believed that the wizards had somehow stolen my father and put someone else in his place. And afterwards, when I realized it couldn't possibly be true—when I realized it was all charlatanry and faking—I hated them for that! God, how I hated them!"

Bitterness scorched his voice. As if something had broken in him, and he could not stop, he continued to sob, thrusting Joanna's comforting hand roughly away and huddling in his corner of the carriage, fighting alone for control over himself, as he had always fought alone. Antryg, perhaps understanding that the Prince would take comfort from a man that could not be taken from a woman, moved over beside the Regent and put his hands on those quivering black satin shoulders; though the touch seemed to calm the Prince, the tears would not stop flowing—a reservoir of them, dammed for years.

As for Antryg, his face was that of a man who has spoken a spell-word in jest and seen hell open before his eyes.

"He changed," the Prince whispered wretchedly. "How could I ever trust? There were other things to it. . . ."

"I'm sure there were," Antryg murmured, as if he spoke to himself of some hideous vision that only he could see.

"But that was the source of it. I'd loved my father, and they took that from me forever. In dreams . . ." With a final sob, the Regent sat up and made a clumsy effort to mop his face. "Curse it, there's the Palace."

With some startlement, Joanna saw that they had almost reached the gilt-tipped gates of the Imperial Palace's marble forecourt. His hands shaking, Pharos wiped with his black silk handerkerchief at his smeared cheeks. "I must look like some sniveling girl."

Antryg managed to grin, the enlightenment and the horror alike gone from his eyes, except for their shadow lurking somewhere far down in the water-gray depths. "I'm sure your father won't care."

From the short flight of marble steps, guards in white and gold were descending to meet the carriage as the shadows of the Palace's vast wings enfolded them. Rows of eastward-facing windows blazed with the reflected sun, and the gilded spines of the roofs sparkled like a frieze of fire.

The bitter rictus of a smile pulled the Prince's mouth, "No—not that he cares about anything. But . . ." The expression softened. Joanna saw that the Regent had spoken the truth; whatever hatred and fear he had borne his father through his adolescence and early manhood, the love of his childhood had been able to reassert itself since their roles had been reversed, since he had now become the stronger, and since his father was dependent upon him for care.

"And if any of the servants comments," Antryg added cheerily, as the footmen stepped forward in matched unison to let down the carriage step, "you can have him flogged."

The Prince shot him a devil's grin as they descended. "Ah, you know how to gladden a man's heart," he retorted. Joanna followed them, wizard and prince, up the palace steps.

From what he had said last night, Joanna had expected Antryg to make a careful investigation of the Emperor's rooms; but either he had misled her or something had caused him to change his mind. The Emperor Hieraldus occupied a suit of rooms on the third floor of the north wing, reached by a small stairway from the State Rooms on the second. "One of my less creditable ancestors furnished them to house his mistress," the Regent explained sotto voce as he opened a painted panel in the gilded oak wainscoting by the fireplace of what was referred to as the Emperor's withdrawing room—a chamber the size of some barns Joanna had slept in during the course of the last two weeks. "He had the stair built—it's overlooked by the guard outside the door there. Father and Grandfather both used the rooms as their private living quarters, since they're more comfortable than the State Rooms."

Antryg looked around the huge withdrawing room, with its stately dark furniture and elaborate tapestries. "In the wintertime, I should imagine it would be difficult to find anything *less* comfortable. Your father always lived upstairs, then?"

The Prince nodded. Since his breakdown in the carriage, much of his suave deadliness had deserted him; Joanna, though she knew he was perverted, mad, and cruel—though the bruises of his whip had not yet faded from Antryg's face—found herself almost liking as well as pitying him. As she followed mage and Regent up the narrow stair, holding up the inevitable voluminous ecru petticoats, she shook her head at herself. *First you fall in love with Antryg,* she thought, *and now you like the Regent. I see you're batting a thousand on this trip.*

"He is looked after constantly," she heard Pharos say as he turned the gold knob of the door at the top of the flight. It was typical of the Palace, Joanna thought, that even the doorknob was a minor work of art, with gilded scrollwork and a tiny cloisonné painting of mythical gods disporting themselves among giggling nymphs. "None of his attendants have reported anything amiss."

"No," Antryg said, almost absently. "No, they wouldn't."

His examination of the rooms was almost cursory. Chamber after delicate chamber was crammed with all the beautiful things a man with unlimited wealth and good taste could accumulate, from delicate clocks to exquisite paintings, oppressive with the trapped, unventilated heat of early autumn, and pervaded with the sick, musty odor of a body that had ceased to look after itself.

The Emperor himself, led out by a careful and cheery attendant, did not shock Joanna nearly so much as she had been afraid he would. He was only a man of about her father's age, his scanty white hair clean and combed, his tidy clothes, apart from fresh food smears down his plain, dark waistcoat, speaking worlds of diligent and neverending care on the part of his guardians. His mouth hung slightly open, and he stared straight ahead of him with blank eyes that barely tracked movement, but Joanna, who usually felt unease bordering on revulsion in the presence of the crippled or retarded, was a little surprised to find in herself nothing but an overwhelming sense of pity.

"Were the rooms marked?" she asked as they descended the steps once more, with courtiers bowing to them when they passed through the State Rooms and headed once more toward the courtyard where the carriage waited.

Antryg glanced at her, as if startled from a reverie of his own. "Oh, yes."

"Did it confirm your hunch?"

He hesitated, and she sensed he was trying to decide whether to tell the truth or to formulate some other evasion, and suppressed a strong desire to shake him. At length he said, rather carefully, "No, it didn't. I'd thought that the rooms would have been marked to—to do that to him by means of a spell. I don't think that was the case."

"Then what did happen?"

With his usual care, he helped her up into the carriage again and swung up to settle himself beside her; the Prince looking rather pensive, was handed in by his footmen, and the carriage started off again. "I'm not sure," Antryg replied, a trifle too airily.

"Look," Joanna began, exasperated, but Pharos cut her off.

"Is he in danger?"

"I don't think so," Antryg said. "Not as long as you're alive, at any rate. Whoever wants you out of the way doesn't want to contest the issue of the succession yet. The Regency will do."

"Of course," Pharos said thinly. "There would be civil war before the nobles would assent to dear Cousin Cerdic being crowned, unless he had a nice, long Regency to get them used to the idea. I take it that is the plot?"

"Something of the kind, yes." Antryg's long fingers steepled over his chest. He had, she noticed, acquired a chain of sapphires and gold, a gift from the Prince that stood out like Fabergé work against dime store finery among his other tawdry necklaces. His voice was light, but his eyes, Joanna saw, were still deeply troubled, as if the information the Prince had supplied him, which had meant so little to her, had given him an answer to questions he did not want to understand. Typically, he pursued another subject. "Who knew of your marriage?"

Pharos sniffed. "Few enough."

"Did Narwahl?"

"He was my physician." The blue eyes narrowed within their discolored sockets. "Of course he knew. You're not saying it was because of that knowledge that—that he was killed?"

Antryg was silent for a moment, studying the Prince's face, as if calculating what would be best to say. Then he said gently, "I doubt it. I think he was killed because of what he was doing in his experiments. The intruder was standing beside his worktable when Narwahl surprised him. . . ."

Pharos, who had been looking out across the park toward a miniature pavilion beside a toy lake, whirled with the suddenness of a mad dog, suspicion and rage blazing in his eyes. Before he could speak, Joanna, familiar by now with Antryg's Holmesian reasoning, said hastily, "He'd have to have been. The pistol ball was lodged in the wall just above the worktable."

"Of course," Antryg said, a little surprised the point would need further elucidation and blithely oblivious to how close he'd come to a quick trip back to St. Cyr. "At fifteen feet in the dark, Narwahl's shot could have gone wide, even if he wasn't shooting at a mage—and even in broad daylight at half the distance, the mageborn are notoriously hard to hit."

"So he could have told any one of the mages about the marriage," Pharos said, after a moment, his mouth suddenly wry with distaste. A mad flicker of suspicion danced like flame in the back of his eyes for a moment, and he added, "He could have been in a string with them too, couldn't he? All of them—Cerdic, the Council. . . ."

"In that case, it's hardly likely they'd have killed him."

The carriage drew to a stop before the old Summer Palace, on the far side of the grounds from the vast Imperial edifice. In the daylight, Joanna could see no sign of its greater age, except perhaps in the somewhat irregular lines of its facade. Like the greater Imperial Palace, this smaller building was faced with mellow, red-gold stone and trimmed with white marble. The statues of its niches were made of several particolored stones which reflected the Regent's more outré tastes.

Only inside, as they left the classical symmetry of the entrance rooms, did the building's age become evident. Though no architect, Joanna sensed that the lower ceilings and rambling, irregular layout of the inner rooms bespoke tastes less self-consciously elegant than those which had renovated the older palace in the classical style. As they moved down a long, narrow gallery, her eye was arrested by an occasional pointed arch or deeply coffered ceiling.

They ascended two or three steps to another hall and from there climbed an old-fashioned, enclosed staircase to the attics in the original wing of the building. "My men brought Narwahl's equipment here, just as it was," the Prince said as they paused before a thick nine-panel door into one of the attic rooms. "I also obtained your reticule, my dear Joanna—though the Witchfinder wasn't pleased to give it up. It contained devilish things, he said."

"Floppy disks?" Joanna asked, puzzled at this construction of the diabolical.

"To the pure, all things are pure," Antryg remarked, in Magister Magus' best soothsayer voice, "and to the unimaginative, all things are devilish."

The Regent sniffed. "Evidently most of the wizards in Peelbone's custody escaped in the confusion you caused. He suspects deep plots."

Antryg's hand moved for the door handle, and the Prince's small, white fingers touched his frayed sleeve ruffle. The blue eyes gleamed strangely in the gray-white light of the outer attic's small, round windows.

"And so help me, if by some chance he is right," Pharos added softly, "you will long for the death my father ordered for you as a man in the desert longs for water. Do you understand?"

Antryg was silent for a moment, like a man standing with one foot in a trap not yet sprung. Afraid of the Prince's suspicions? wondered Joanna, prey to the now-familiar sensation of being torn between her affection for him and her better judgment. Or of something else?

In the end he said nothing, but silently turned, opened the door, and ducked under its low lintel to enter the attic beyond.

Dust sparkled faintly in the still air of that long, low-ceilinged room. The place reminded Joanna uncomfortably of the other attic from which they had taken these things, with ceiling and walls splattered with their creator's blood. This room was over twice as long, its far end heaped up with a vast tangle of heavy furniture in dark wood, with closed chests and occasional bolts of thick cloth whose nap and weave were unsuited to the stiff lines of current fashion. The inner walls and ceiling were plastered coarsely; the outer one, in which the three square, high windows were set, was the raw stone of the old Summer Palace. Against this wall stood a table, jammed with the gleaming, Frankensteinian coils of Narwahl's experiments, the archaic workmanship of the components making wonderful the prosaic collection of resistors and connectors. On one corner, her purse lay like a dead and lumpy dog.

Walking over to the table, Joanna began to check the equipment over. It was, as far as she could tell, as it had been in Narwahl's laboratory. She traced the leads and grounding wires, set up the tall sparking rods and the hand-crank generator. Amid the chaos, the queer, shining sphere that had caught her attention before seemed to gleam with a baleful half-luminescence that made her uneasy.

Beside her, she was aware of Antryg's silence. She glanced back and saw that his eyes had been drawn to the sphere; there was recognition in them and an uncomfortable enlightenment, but no surprise.

"What is it?" She pushed aside her pink silk sleeve flounce, whose laces had become entangled in a switch. "All the rest of this I recognize. . . ."

"Do you?"

She nodded. "My whole world runs on electricity." Her fingers traced the sinuous glass curve of a Volta pistol and brushed the awkward brass vacuum pump, but she found herself shying from the evil refulgence of that quicksilver sphere. "Hardware was never my field, but I know enough about it not to electrocute myself changing the chips on a breadboard—and Gary *is* a hardware man. So I know what Narwahl was doing. But that—that thing . . ."

As with her bizarre depressions, before she had realized they were something thrust upon her by an outside force, she found herself unwilling to speak of the loathing she felt for it. *What has no name isn't real,* she thought. She looked for confirmation of her repulsion in the wizard's eyes.

"Yes," Antryg said softly. He pushed up his spectacles and came forward to where she stood beside the table. "Yes, it is evil. An implement of forbidden magic. Making such spheres is forbidden; passing on to others the knowledge of their making is punishable by the Council by death."

"Why?" Even as she asked, she wondered why she wasn't startled to hear it.

"It is called a teles." Antryg's long, light fingers brushed the gleaming surface of the ball. "They have many uses. Suraklin used them. . . ." He hesitated on his ancient master's name, and an expression flickered through his eyes of some old horror, as if he had unexpectedly touched an unhealed wound in his mind. He recovered quickly and went on, "Suraklin linked them into the energy-lines and used them to extend his power over territory beyond his line of sight. He could control . . ." He hesitated again, frowning, and then glanced at the prince who stood in silence, framed in the attic doorway. Kanner, as always, loomed like a crimson shadow in the half-light of the hall beyond. "By the way, Pharos, what is the longitudinal coordinate of the palace?"

"What?" The Prince stared at him as if he had taken leave of his senses —which, of course, Joanna thought with irrelevant frivolity, he had, but that had been a long time ago.

"The longitudinal coordinate of the palace. Because, if I recall correctly, the energy-line marked by the Devil's Road runs through Angelshand, with a crossing-node of the Kymil line at the old stone circle on Tilrattin Island up the river. Suraklin . . ." He fell silent again, his hand resting on the side of the silvery teles ball. The high, sharp sunlight glinted on the fractured lens of his spectacles and touched Joanna's fingers on the table without warmth.

"Suraklin," Pharos echoed. "Always, we return to the Dark Mage."

Antryg's eyes flicked back to the prince. In them she saw again that braced look, as if he knew he walked among his foes. With a forced lightness he said, "Well, Suraklin wasn't the only one who knew how to make them, of course."

"Presumably," Pharos said softly, "he taught you."

"Oh, yes," Antryg agreed equably. "But it's a tedious and exhausting process. One's laid up for weeks afterward. Suraklin mostly used old ones that others had made centuries before. This one's very old." Joanna shivered as he picked it up, handling it with the tips of his fingers. "Suraklin had some that were thousands of years old and that had been absorbing power from the mages who touched them until they almost had voices of their own. No one really understands them well. Suraklin certainly didn't. But then, he used a lot of things he didn't understand properly. It was," he added, with a sudden hardness in his voice, "one of the things which made him so dangerous."

Pharos' voice was suspicious. "But how did Narwahl come to have one? My father . . ." He stammered on the words lightly. "They should have been destroyed when Suraklin's power was broken."

"Indubitably." In a billow of coat skirts Antryg turned with swift, sudden lightness and hurled the teles at the stone wall like a volleyball center spiking down over the net. Joanna flinched with the involuntary reaction as one flinches in the quarter-second between the dropping of a light bulb and its explosion on a concrete floor, but the teles did not break. It hit the stone with a queer, terrible ringing noise and bounced sharply back into Antryg's hands. The ringing seemed to vibrate horribly on in Joanna's skull. "If you can figure out a way to destroy a teles, the Council will be delighted to hear about it. And in any case, this one may not have been one of Suraklin's. My guess is that Narwahl got it from Salteris. According to Caris, they were friends. Obviously, if Narwahl told Salteris enough for him to use electricity against the abomination at Kymil, Narwahl was using Salteris' help and advice for—what?"

"Experiments with the effects of electricity on magic?" Joanna guessed. She touched the concave metal bed in which the teles had rested. Copper wires led out of it, their ends twisted, showing they had been joined to other leads. *"Does* electricity have an effect on magic?"

"I haven't the faintest idea." Antryg set the teles back in its bed and looked over the tangle of wires and resistors with interested eyes. "I shouldn't think so. I've worked magic during lightning storms; and, according to the scientific journals I've read, not only is lightning electricity, but the air is charged with it at such times." He tracked a pair of wires to the generator and experimentally turned the crank.

"Hold on," Joanna said. "That's not connected to anything yet." She found the leads to the sparking rods and twisted the wires in pairs. Pharos, who had remained warily in the doorway, stepped forward, but drew back again as Antryg started turning the small generator crank. She saw the fear and suspicion on the Regent's face, as thin trails of purplish lightning began to crawl up the rods, and said, "It isn't magic, your Grace. If I turned the crank, or if you did, it would act the same. Here." She pushed up her sleeve flounces and took over in mid-turn from Antryg, feeling the stiffness of the crank as more and more power built up. Ghostly in the diffuse sunlight of the attic, the lightning continued to spark. "Don't touch it," she added quickly, as Antryg advanced a cautious finger towards the rods. "You'll get a hell of a shock."

She let the crank go. The iron-wrapped wheel whirled itself to a halt.

"So what was he trying to do?" Pharos advanced warily into the room once more. "Use electricity in some way to contain magic or protect against it? Make a shield of this tame lightning through which magic could not pass?"

Antryg, his hands in his jeans pockets, shook his head. "Salteris would have been the first one to tell him it wouldn't work as a protection," he said. "In fact, if you stood in a field like that and I was a mage who wished you dead, Pharos, it would be the simplest thing in the world to turn that tame lightning inward on you. Joanna . . ."

She paused in the act of tracking the compression on the vacuum-pump.

"What does it look as if he was doing?"

She shook her head, puzzled. "I don't know, but it sure as hell appears that he was running electricity either into or out of the teles. Look." She held up the wires from the teles' dish. "That means the teles is either conductive or is itself the source of electricity. Is it?"

"Not that I've ever heard," Antryg said, studying the wires emerging from the generator, then looking thoughtfully back at the teles.

Her fingers shrinking a little from touching the thing, Joanna lifted the teles from its metal bed. Aside from feeling slick and queerly cold, there was nothing untoward about it. She set it aside and examined the connections. "That's funny. The ground wire here's a closed loop—as if it was grounding into itself." Frowning, she replaced the ball, then untwisted the generator wires from the sparking rods and connected the teles to the rods.

Not much to her surprise, nothing happened.

"Closed system," she said simply. "Read only. Nothing going in, so nothing's coming out. Electricity isn't created out of nothing—all power has to come from somewhere."

"A sound metaphysical and magical surmise as well," Antryg agreed quietly. "But on the other hand . . ." He reached forward and brushed his fingers along the oily-looking, slightly phosphorescent surface of the ball.

Joanna felt it as clearly as a sudden drop in temperature—like the heroine of *The Wizard of Oz,* as if she had wakened after the magic and color into a gray world of black-and-white. She felt sick and utterly weary, uncaring about what they were doing, hating Antryg for his lies to her, for his evasions, and for what he had done to her. He had brought her here and taken advantage of her dependence on him. He would keep her there, stranded in this filthy, dreary world in which she had no place. . . .

The rods began to spark. Lightning crawled up them, faster and stronger than before, bright enough to illuminate Antryg's strange, angular face as he stood looking down on them, his earrings flashing like diamonds in the suddenly sickened light of the gray sun.

"Stop it!" Joanna said, suddenly furious at him for doing this to her to satisfy some stupid academic curiosity of his own. "Turn it off. . . ." Some part of her was screaming, *This is important! This is the key to it all!* But smothered in the effects of the experiment, she scarcely cared.

Pharos pressed his hands to his eyes. "So this was it!" His voice shook. "In these past weeks—the morning I spoke to Herthe at the posthouse— and last night—I thought it was only me! Only some new phase of my madness!"

"No." Antryg jerked free the ground wire, which ran so oddly from the teles back into itself. The lightning died on the rods; and like a cloud from the face of the sun, the cold grief lifted from the room. "The life-energy was being drained from you, Pharos—as it was being drained from everyone. Not enough to kill, but only enough to maim in a way for which there is no word."

Eerily, phosphorescent light continued to gleam for a time from the teles itself, shining wanly up through Antryg's fingers where he rested them on the silvery ball. His eyes were focused on some endless distance. Though Joanna could not understand what it was that he saw, she shivered at the reflection of dread, grief, and a knowledge that he did not want that she saw in his eyes.

"It was the whole course of Narwahl's experiments, I think," he went on after a moment, speaking as if to himself, his voice nearly unheard in the stillness of that sunwashed, enormous room. "It was for this that he was killed—not because he'd discovered how electricity might affect magic, but because he had discovered how to use magic to draw off the life-energy which fills all the earth and use it to create electricity."

CHAPTER XVII

"BUT WHY?" JOANNA TUCKED HER FEET UP UNDER THE VOLUMINOUS masses of her rose and cream petticoats to sit cross-legged on the throne-like oak chair Antryg had fetched for her out of the tangle at the far end of the attic. "Why electricity?" Her eyes went from the enigmatic snarl of glass, copper, and iron on the table to the ridiculous and equally enigmatic face of the man perched on the corner of the worktable beside her.

The Prince had gone, though his guards remained inevitably within call outside the door. A footman in the Prince's ruby livery had brought them lunch, which lay in a picked-at ruin on the tray on the floor at Joanna's side. Antryg had barely touched it or spoken.

Twice while she was eating the honeyed ham and comfits, Joanna had been aware of him watching her, as he had watched her in the silvery moonlight of the Devil's Road and again that morning in the Prince's carriage. Evasive he had always been, but the closer they had come to Angelshand the closer they had drawn to the dark heart of the tangle of riddles surrounding them, the more pronounced that wariness, that fear, had become.

Studying his preposterous profile against the flat brightness of the windows, she wondered for the thousandth time why.

Was it because he knew her expertise lay in matters technological and he knew she would eventually scent through his lies and evasions to the mystery's real heart? But though she had a sense of pattern, a feeling that events connected, she had no idea what the heart of it all was.

The Prince's upcoming marriage, the attempts on his life, and Cerdic's stubborn attachment to the mages seemed to form one subset; the abomi-

nations, the original murder of the mage Thirle, and the fact that someone was going back and forth across the Void formed another. Her own
kidnapping and that of the Archmage seemed linked in time, but not in
any other way. The recurrent theme of madness—the prince's, Antryg's,
the Emperor's—seemed broken by a hiatus of over twenty years. Like
Ariadne's thread, the glittering trail of wizards' marks ran through the
dark labyrinth, but it seemed to lead nowhere. As a programmer, used to
breaking all situations down into manageable subsets, she found that this
computerlike logic failed her when it came to working in the other direction.

Or was Antryg's fear of her, she wondered, simply because he feared to
trust? He had trusted, he said, once too readily and once too often. Did
he fear to care for her, as she feared her caring for him, because of the
power such caring gives?

Maybe, she thought, if she were better with people than she was with
programs and machines, she'd be able to tell whether he was lying or
telling the truth. But in a sense, she felt that he had always done both.

Still he did not answer her, and she said quietly, "It would help if
you'd trust me."

She saw the quick shiver that went through him, succeeded immediately by the wry flicker of his grin. "Believe me, Joanna, it would help if I
could trust anyone. But I'm like Pharos—afraid the person I hire to
protect me is the one who's been trying to kill me all along."

She frowned, hearing some note in his voice. "*Is* someone trying to kill
you?"

He regarded her with surprised gray eyes. "Of course, my dear. Caris,
for one . . ."

"He isn't the one you're thinking of, however," she said. Though he
did not reply, he seemed to withdraw a little into himself again, not
willing to give anything away. "You said you wanted to find out from the
Council of Wizards what happened twenty-five years ago. Was whatever
it was connected with why the Prince went mad? It happened at the same
time. But if it was hereditary, from his father . . ."

He shook his head. "The Prince went mad because he could not accept
the fact that two and two equal four," he said gently. "Even as I did. As
for his father . . ." He looked away from her, his eyes suddenly shadowed again with horror and grief. "That is another matter."

"But it connects somewhere, doesn't it?" The pearl rosettes of her
sleeve bows glimmered softly as she folded her arms. "And it connects
with the fact that someone's been moving back and forth across the Void
to get something from my world, something that needs electricity to

operate. They heard about Narwahl's experiments with the teles . . ." She paused, frowning, and pushed at the corner of the tray at her feet with one slippered toe. "But why didn't they steal the teles when they killed him?"

"Obviously, because they had one of their own." He unfolded his thin legs and hopped lightly to the floor, pacing with his hands thrust deep in the pockets of his trailing black coat. "More than one, since the power seems to be drawn from such an enormous area. Suraklin used to link them in series to increase their power, and presumably that's what's being done here. What runs on electricity in your world?"

Joanna half-laughed, reminded absurdly of her mother's request that she "explain this computer stuff to me."

"God—What doesn't? Television . . ."

"It needs a transmitter as well as a receiver," the wizard objected. Joanna had explained to him some time ago the intricacies of television, though the ramifications of game shows and televised pro football had eluded him. "And no wizard with a good scrying-crystal would need one."

"Not unless he'd become secretly addicted to *Gilligan's Island* reruns," Joanna agreed. She started to lean back in the chair, then sat hastily up as the bodice boning poked her under the arm. "Same argument puts the kibosh on telephones. A factory, maybe? It would have a hell of an economic advantage over waterpower."

"With a supply of raw materials coming in, it would be a bit tricky to hide." Antryg paused in his pacing, toying thoughtfully with his gim-crack necklaces.

"Could they use magic to hide it?" Joanna suggested. "No," she answered herself almost at once, "because such generation of the electricity kills magic, doesn't it? Or could that be what they're trying to do? Cripple everyone's magic permanently? So whatever they're doing, they won't be found out?"

"It's a possibility." Antryg frowned. "And very like him, now that I think of it."

"Like who?"

He hesitated. "Whoever's doing this—whoever it is. He—or she—is very clever . . ." His frown suddenly deepened, and Joanna would have given much to know whether what he next said was his true thought or something to turn her from the subject. "Cripple everyone's power? Or drain it—and use it?"

She was silent for a moment, struck by the monstrousness of the impli-cation. *"Could* they?" She remembered suddenly Caris' bitterness over losing his powers and Magister Magus' fears. It crossed her mind to wonder where Caris was now and what he'd been doing since . . . was it really only the night before last?

"I don't know." Antryg came over beside her and rested his long hands on the elaborate poppy-head finials of the tall chair back. "But power does move along the energy-lines. If it can be channeled into a central point . . ." Then he shook his head. "But I don't see why electricity."

"No?" Joanna turned in the chair to look up at him, and the boning of her bodice stabbed her sharply again. "Ever since we talked at Devilsgate and you said spells were similar to programming, I've been wondering. Would it be possible to program a computer to do magic? A big one, like a Cray, that reproduces all the functions of the human brain?"

"Reproduces the functions of the human brain," the mage echoed softly. He was silent for a long time then, his gray eyes staring off into some inner distance. What he saw there Joanna could not guess, but his eyes slowly widened, as if they looked upon some unimaginable nightmare. So he had looked, she realized, that morning in the Prince's coach, when he had learned or guessed what it was that had happened twenty-five years ago that had driven both himself and the Prince into the comforting refuge of madness. "Dear God . . ."

"What is it?" She half rose; her hand on his velvet sleeve seemed to pull him from some private hell-vision of that final revelation. His eyes returned to hers, like the eyes of a man newly come from some other world to find all things in this one not as he had left them. *"Tell me!"*

Their gazes locked; in his she saw the struggle of fear and trust, unwilling love, and the knowledge that he should not, must not, give to her more than he had. Then he looked away. "I—I don't know," he lied. "You've spoken of programs which can write, draw, and project events—which can lie, even, about their own existence!"

"That's not what I meant!" When he tried to turn away, she caught a handful of frayed lapel, the velvet soft as moleskin in her fist. "You've known something all along, something you've been lying about . . ."

"It's nothing," he said, his voice a little breathless. "It may not even be true—much of what I fear isn't, or so they keep telling me. What functions of thought can a computer reproduce?"

"Not a computer." Joanna released her hold on him and rose from the chair herself, standing separated from him by the width of its thickly carved, black oak back. "A program. A series of subroutines, done infinitely fast. A computer can't perceive patterns, but it can recognize them, if it breaks them down line by line. It's why programmers think the way they do. You say magic is predicated on visualization and hope. With a computer, that's graphics and statistical projection, since a computer doesn't care what should or shouldn't exist. But to write a series of programs that complex, you'd need a programmer who was also a wizard —or a programmer and a mage working together. Which you aren't likely to find in either of our worlds."

She stopped. They stood for a moment, looking at one another. In a hard-hearted and detached corner of her mind, she suddenly knew how Antryg had felt when he had seen whatever hideous realization had been reflected in the Prince's madness. Her own enlightenment beat upon her mind, as if she had walked from darkness into the agonizing glare of a magnesium flare.

Looking up into his face, she saw that he knew she'd guessed.

"You aren't likely to find it in either of our worlds," she repeated softly, "unless a mage came across the Void and kidnapped a programmer."

"Joanna . . ." There was neither surprise nor innocence in his face.

"And got her to trust him," she went on, and her voice suddenly shook. He had said, *I will not take advantage of you.* . . . She saw now that he had been like a cardsharp who passed the deal, using that, too, to gain her trust. Anger hit her—at him and at herself for falling for him, for caring. He had used her, played upon her sympathy for him and her dependence on him, as Gary had done years ago. He had seen her with Gary at the party. He must have known exactly what to do to gain first her trust and then her love. Her hand closed around the chair's carved finial until the edges of the wooden leaves dug painfully into her fingers. Her voice in her own ears sounded cold and distant, like someone else's.

"Or was there some other reason you brought me here?"

He said nothing, but there was despair in his eyes, the wreckage of all his hopes.

She turned and left the attic, each step that carried her through the old door and past the guard in the corridor seeming like a separate action, unconnected with any before or after. He neither called nor tried to follow as she walked down the stuffy enclosure of the stair and away through the quiet vistas of the palace rooms, her mind blank of thought and bitter confusion in her heart.

"Joanna!"

In contrast to the strength of the butter-colored sunlight on the lawn, the shade of the grotto where Joanna sat was like dark indigo. She wasn't sure how long she'd been sitting—not long, she thought. The shadows of the marble statues lining the lawn—heroes in archaic armor overwritten, as Cerdic's had been, with protective runes or the old, strange, animal-headed gods—hadn't lengthened much. She looked around at the whisper; but in the shade of the artificial bower's pink marble columns and twining roses, she saw nothing until Caris moved.

"Caris!" She untucked her feet from beneath her petticoats and sprang up. The sasennan had gone back to the matte, dark, flowing coat and trousers of his vocation, his long sword held ready in its scabbard in his left hand. Confused and shaken by her realization of what Antryg wanted of her and by the violence of her own feelings, she found herself suddenly weak with relief at knowing she was not, after all, utterly without options.

In the time she had been sitting here, it had dawned on her how absolutely in the wizard's power she was. She had always known she depended on him, but now it had come to her that she *could not* leave him, even if she were willing to risk being stranded forever in a world that was at best miserably filthy and inconvenient and at worst perilous even to those who knew what they were doing in it. There was nowhere in this world for her to go and certainly nowhere that Antryg couldn't talk the Prince into sending men to find her.

She felt ridiculously like bursting into tears, but Caris, she knew, wasn't the sort of young man who could cope with lachrymose females. Instead she took a deep breath and said, "You're all right."

He nodded. The smoke-colored shadows didn't hide the marks of strain and sleeplessness on his face. Some irreverent part of her came within an ace of asking him, *How long did you wait outside that vacant building?* but she pushed that thought away.

"We've been seeking you in a scrying-crystal," he said. "It wouldn't work while you were with Antryg, but when you were at a distance from him . . ."

"We?" she demanded. "The mages who escaped from St. Cyr . . ."

"The rest of them were released this morning," the sasennan said. "But I . . ."

"That was Antryg's doing," she said and frowned, puzzled. "Though I don't see why."

"He is closing in on his goal," a quiet voice said from the rose-hung shadows of the pillars. "And perhaps he fears what some of them might say of him, should his name arise."

In the fawn-spotted, green gloom a shadow emerged from the deeper shadows, a slender old man of medium height, his tall forehead laddered with wrinkles and his long white hair hanging to square, narrow shoulders clothed in the black of a wizard's robe. His eyes were the same dark coffee-brown as Caris', with the same slight tilt to the corners. Joanna knew at once who he had to be.

She stammered, "Your—I'm sorry, but I'm a stranger here, and this sounds really stupid, but I don't know whether I'm supposed to genuflect or kiss your ring, and I've *never* figured out how to curtsy in these damn skirts." She kicked aside the intrusive petticoats and stepped forward to take his strong, slender hand and to be greeted by the winter sunlight of his smile.

"Then we'll take your greeting as read," he said. "Caris told me of you. I must say I am both astounded and relieved beyond expression to see you alive, free, and—in possession of your own mind."

She stared at the Archmage in shock. *"What?"*

Dourly, Caris remarked, "I gather Antryg lost no time in getting on the good side of the Regent."

"The Regent needed his advice," Joanna said. "He needed a wizard who couldn't possibly have done magic in the last seven years."

"A convenient, if specious, argument," Salteris said drily. "Antryg has been coming and going from the Silent Tower as he pleases for some months now."

"I—wondered about that." She stepped back and gestured the old man to the marble seat she had been occupying, a carved bench the size—and function, she suspected—of a love seat, embellished at both ends with cupids and wreaths of carved roses the size of cabbages. Neither it, nor the marble statues in the gardens, she had noticed, bore the usual festoons of bird droppings; the Prince's predilection for flogging his servants evidently had certain valuable side effects beyond his ability to get lobster patties for his guests in the middle of the night. "That is—Antryg always seems to know more than he should and he can't be *that* good a guesser."

"No." The old man gently shook off Caris' efforts to help him down and seated himself at Joanna's side. "He is in precisely the position of a doctor who doses a man's coffee with poison and then claims a miracle cure for producing the antidote—a favorite dog wizard trick. And Pharos, I fear, has placed his trust in him, to the exclusion of every mage who has been abroad in the world. In many ways, Pharos is as credulous as his cousin, though far more dangerous. I am only pleased, my child, to see you safe."

"Believe me, the feeling's more than mutual." She glanced up at Caris, who stood quietly at his grandfather's back. "I'm glad he found you safe."

"I did not find him," the sasennan corrected her. "He found me. No one finds the Archmage unless he wills it."

"But where *were* you?" She looked back at the old man. "Did . . ." But she found herself almost unable to speak Antryg's name.

He must have sensed it, for the dark, severe eyes softened with pity and understanding. "Lost," he said. "I don't know—the spell was one of confusion. I wandered for days, it felt like, but I had no way of telling how many, for there was neither day nor night where I was. Only darkness . . ." He shook his head. "I don't know. I escaped, but it has left me exhausted."

Quietly, Caris asked, "Could he have pushed you into the Void itself? To wander between worlds?"

Salteris passed a hand over his brow and shook his head. "I don't know. Suraklin had a black crystal with a labyrinth inside. He could trap a soul within it, to wander forever in the lattices of a gem small enough to pick up in his hand."

"And Antryg was Suraklin's student," Joanna murmured, remembering the teles, the elementals that had slain Narwahl Skipfrag, and the abominations. . . .

The Archmage's dark eyes rested on her for a moment. Then he sighed. "No," he said softly. "No—it is worse than that. Antryg . . ." He hesitated, folding his hands with his forefingers extended against his lips, his deepset eyes gazing out into the sunlit vistas of the garden beyond the shadows. "My child, I fear that Antryg Windrose has not existed for a long time."

She didn't know why her eyes burned or her throat seemed to constrict with grief; it was grief, she understood, for someone she had never known. In the silence, she could hear the twitter of sparrows marking out their territories among the trees and the far-off clatter of carts beyond the walls of the palace parkland in Angelshand, a quarter-mile away. Words drifted through her mind:

> *He could break anyone's mind to his bidding . . .*
> *. . . He wanted to live forever . . .*
> *. . . Where's he been, if he hasn't?*
> *. . . I felt him in dreams . . .*

Even before the Archmage spoke again, she knew what he was going to say.

"Suraklin had worked for a long time on the notion of taking over the minds of others," the old man said. "With his slaves, of course, he controlled their minds with his own; those under his influence did as he bade them and were his eyes and ears, without thinking to ask why, and his influence was incredibly strong. That is why I said I am glad to see you still capable of leaving Antryg's side. But he wanted more than that." The old man sighed, his thin mouth taut and rather white, as if sickened by some unshared knowledge whose bare bones only he would reveal, not out of secretiveness, but out of mercy. "He took the boy Antryg, the most powerful child adept he could find. He taught him everything he himself knew, like a man furnishing a house with his own things. . . ."

"No!" Joanna pulled her mind from the hideous picture that swam there unbidden of a gawky, thin-faced, frightened boy staring with hypnotized gray eyes into the terrible yellow gaze of the old man. Intellectually she knew that she had never truly known Antryg. Why did it cross her mind that the nervous, gentle man, the man who had whispered, "I will not do this . . ." and turned away, rather than take her in his arms when she could not have afforded to say no, even had she not consented, had been in fact that boy and not the mage who had raped him of mind and body so that he could go on living in his stead. "Oh, Christ, no."

"I'm sorry," the wizard said softly.

She pressed her hands to her mouth, suddenly trembling, remembering the soft force of Antryg's lips on hers. It was Suraklin who had kissed her, an ancient intelligence in stolen flesh. She thought how close she'd come to lying with him on the road from Kymil to Angelshand and felt almost ill.

Slim and strong, the hand of the Archmage rested upon her arm. "When Caris told me you were with him, I was afraid. I know how strong a hold Suraklin could take, even over those he did not fully possess." He glanced back toward the irregular roof line of the Summer Palace, visible over the sun-spangled trees. "I fear he has the Prince's trust already; he will consolidate that hold in whatever way he can."

Sick with disgust, she recalled the mage's mock flirtation with Pharos; a game, she could have sworn at the time. But then, she could have sworn that Antryg's care for her was genuine and not simply the means to some other end.

"Antryg said . . ." She hesitated. It was not, she knew now, Antryg who had spoken. "He said he had loved Suraklin. Was that true?"

"That Antryg loved him?" Salteris nodded. "Yes, very probably. Suraklin had that talent of winning the hearts of those who came in contact with him. Their loyalty to him was unquestioning, almost fanatical, even in the face of evidence that he was not what he said he was."

Joanna blushed, not, she knew, because she had trusted Antryg, but because there was some large portion of her which cared for him still—or, she thought, confused, cared for the man who'd sat by her in the roadside inns and who'd talked with her on those long, weary afternoons on the road about television and computers and friends he'd met during the Mellidane Revolts, the man who'd stood so close to her in the dimness of the drawing room at Devilsgate. Why did she feel it was so absolutely impossible that that man was the Dark Mage?

His voice quiet in the gloom of the arbor, Salteris went on. "That was the thing I never understood, after I found Antryg in the monastery, years after the destruction of Suraklin's citadel—his story that he had fled shortly before the Imperial armies gathered. But I thought . . ." He sighed again and shook his head.

"Twenty-five years ago," Joanna said suddenly.

"What?" The Archmage raised his head sharply, an amber glint flickering in the onyx depths of his eyes.

"Antryg said he—he had to ask some member of the Council about something that happened twenty-five years ago."

"So." The old man nodded. "He feared someone else might have seen or known or guessed. And if he found them, if he learned that anyone had seen Antryg make a final visit to Suraklin before the execution . . ." The dark eyes narrowed. "And did he?"

Joanna shook her head. "He never found another member of the Council—or at least, not that I knew of. Pharos told him that his father had seen something or knew something after the taking of Kymil which changed him; and that seemed to horrify Antryg. But later . . ." She shook her head. "I don't understand."

"If I were trying to bring the mad Prince under my influence," Caris sniffed, "and learned his father knew anything, had any suspicion which he might have passed along, I'd be horrified, too."

"Maybe," Joanna said slowly. "He did say the Emperor never liked him. Somebody—I forget who—told me the Emperor visited Suraklin several times during his trial. Do you think he could have recognized him in Antryg? Or suspected, at least? Because he did sentence him to death seven years ago."

The old man sighed bitterly. "And I, to my sorrow, had the sentence commuted. But as Archmage of the Council, I could not permit the Emperor, the Church, or anyone else to hold the power of life and death over any Council mage, be he never so forsworn of his vows. At the time, I believed that that was all there was." He frowned into the distance again, all the parallel lines of that high forehead seeming to echo and re-echo his speculations and his grief. "Hieraldus was a brilliant man and a perceptive one. He would have felt the similarity. So did I, once or twice, at first. But I put it down to the fact that for many years the boy Antryg had been virtually Suraklin's slave. After that . . ." He shook his head, and a stray fragment of sunlight turned the edge of his long hair to blazing silver against the black of his robe. "Perhaps elements of Antryg's original personality survived—enough to keep those who knew him from suspecting the change. No one but Suraklin had really known him well—and then, of course, he was always known to be mad."

"Useful," Caris sneered.

Joanna remembered the shadows of the roadhouse hearth and Antryg's lazy smile over the tankard of beer. *I never knew him,* she thought. *I only knew the lie. Why do I grieve for the lie?*

"Was he?" she asked. "Mad, I mean."

"The original Antryg?" Salteris shrugged. "Who knows? He may have become unbalanced by the struggle against Suraklin's will. Afterward, the reputation was Suraklin's shield and cloak, an armor fashioned to resemble vulnerability. I pitied him, but never suspected—until he struck." The old man's mouth tightened again, all the delicate muscle of cheek and jaw springing into prominence under the silky cloak of white hair. She understood then that hers had not been the only trust, the only love, betrayed.

"Where is he?" Caris' eyes sought the clustering turrets of the Summer Palace.

"I left him in the attics of the old wing." She looked down at her hands, folded among the silly profusion of ruffle and lace in her lap. "He —He and I looked over Narwahl Skipfrag's equipment. I don't suppose I told him anything he didn't already know. He's going to program a computer to do magic. With a big enough computer, the scope of the subroutines would be infinite. I think . . ."

She hesitated, then went on, ashamed at how nearly she'd fallen for something that now seemed so obvious. "I think the scenario he planned to use was that some other evil wizard—the one he said had kidnapped you and me and tried to murder the Regent and all the rest of it—was doing it, so why didn't I help him steal equipment and work out programs as a countermeasure. At least that would be the logical course of action. He was working up to it very gradually, winning my trust. . . ." She swallowed, her throat hurting again at the loss of that gentle consideration with which he had, she now knew, baited his trap. "If I hadn't guessed, I probably would have done it."

Cool and very strong, Salteris' thin hands closed over hers. "It is perilously easy to come to care for one upon whom one is utterly dependent," he said. "Particularly if he has gotten you out of danger—which he did, didn't he?"

She remembered the vicious whine of Pharos' riding whip in the darkness of the inn and the heartbreaking exhaustion of that last desperate run through the muddy lanes around St. Cyr—remembered, too, Antryg's arms, surprisingly strong around her, and the desperate hunger of his mouth on hers in the fog-bound isolation of the alley. She felt hot all over with shame.

The old man's voice was like a gentle astringent. "He miscalculated your strength, child, and your wits—but it is as well you left him when you did. Because he would not have stopped with simply winning your . . ."

He paused, and Joanna finished for him cynically, "Heart?"

"Confidence, I was going to say. He could have gone into your mind—you would have let him—and used your knowledge of—computers?" He pronounced the alien word hesitantly.

Joanna nodded. "Not only computers—systems and program design. That's my job. It's what I do."

"He could have used your brain, your knowledge, like a tool, even as he could have used your body."

She glanced up quickly at that, sensing different meanings behind the phrase, but Salteris' dark gaze was already fixed again on the distant vista of parterre and statues and on the far-off glint of the roofs of the Imperial Palace, which rose like a mellow sandstone cliff beyond the trees.

"As he used me," he murmured. "I was the one who originally told him of Narwahl's experiments with the teles, little suspecting that the dozen or so teles never found of Suraklin's hoard had been hidden away by him." He shut his eyes for a moment, bitter grief deepening the lines already graven in the soft flesh of the lids. "Narwahl was my friend," he added in a voice barely to be heard. "It seems that in striving after justice, I have done naught but ill." The narrow, sensitive mouth quirked, and he glanced beside him at Joanna again, the bitterness of wormwood in those deep eyes. "Like you, I have been victim to that accursed charm."

She put her hand over his, feeling the warm flesh, thin as silk over the knobby shapes of knuckles and tendon. Archmage though he was, she felt in him suddenly only an old man who knew himself responsible for his dear friend's murder. She hoped he knew nothing of the blood-splattered attic with its tiny shards of glass; but she also knew that the hope was impossible, since he was the Archmage.

"I'm sorry," she said, and some of the bleak horror faded from the old man's eyes.

"We have both been his dupes," he said gently.

Joanna shook her head. "All I've lost is some illusions," she replied. "Not—not anyone I know." *Only someone I hoped to know. And the hope,* she reflected wryly, *was my problem.*

His fingers tightened over hers, remarkably strong for so old a man's. "Come," he said and rose to his feet, the long, dark robe falling straight about him. "It's best we find him, before he learns that I've escaped and am here."

The Summer Palace was curiously quiet as they approached it; the Regent's high, harsh voice was audible from the terrace, but his words were indistinct with distance. Like three ghosts, they moved through the shrubbery, which, in accordance with the Prince's Gothic tastes and desire for privacy, grew closer around the walls than the formal vistas of topiary which surrounded the new Palace. Away from the graceful symmetry of its remodeled facade, all pretense of the building's modernity faded. The stable and kitchen courts were even to Joanna's untrained eye a jumble of styles and periods, mansard roofs crowding comfortably shoulder to shoulder with the oddly angled gambrels and projecting upper storeys of the Palace's earlier incarnations. "Won't someone ask us what we're doing here?" she inquired, glancing uncertainly at Caris' dark uniform and sword and at the old man's flowing dark robes.

They paused in the gloom of a grove of cypresses opposite the round, gray turret of the stable tower. Through the tower's broad gate the stable court was visible; grooms in the Prince's flame-colored livery were working with neat efficiency to harness a pair of coal-black horses to a light carriage of some kind. At Joanna's side, Salteris murmured, "I scarcely think so," and made a small gesture with one hand.

The nearer of the two horses, which had been standing quietly up until that instant; flung up its head in panic. A stableboy caught too late at the bridle, and the beast reared, frightening its harness-mate. Men began to run from all directions under the shouted orders of the gray-haired coachman in his gold-and-crimson braid. "Stay close to me," the wizard admonished. With Caris glancing watchfully in all directions and Joanna holding up the voluminous handfuls of her beruffled skirts, they calmly crossed the drive and passed unseen by the shouting confusion around the carriage.

"It's always easier to enter a house through the servants' quarters," the old man said softly, "provided you know what you're doing." The oppressive heat of steam and the damp smells of soap and linen enveloped them as they passed into the shadows of the brick laundries on the far side of the court. Salteris turned unerringly along a brick-paved corridor with a low, groined wooden ceiling, under which the day's heat collected with the mingled smells of smoke, cooking meat, and spices from the kitchens beyond. A man started to emerge from an archway of reflected daylight to their right. Joanna, startled, paused in her stride, but the old man beside her only flicked a finger; from the room beyond came a crashing noise that made the servant turn hastily back, yelling "Not that way, you stupid jolterhead!"

Something stirred in Joanna's consciousness. A dark, cold feeling of half-familiar strangeness, like an unheard sound, seemed to go through her, and she was aware of the sudden hiss of Caris' breath beside her. Salteris checked his steps in the narrow seam of the kitchen passage, his dark eyes narrowing and a flame seeming to spark suddenly in their depths. . . .

Joanna identified where she'd first felt that queer, haunted sense of terror a split-instant before Caris and his grandfather's glances met.

Then they all began to run.

There was a backstairs at the end of the corridor, leading to apartments in the old wing. Salteris, dark robe billowing about his thin limbs, led them unerringly to it, across an unused state chamber with its ancient linenfold and gilded coffer and up the stairs to the attic; Joanna followed in a sursurrus of silk taffeta. The memory of the blood-splattered attic in Narwahl's house and of Minhyrdin the Fair mumbling, *He'd call them up, spirits, elementals* leaped to her mind. Panic chilled her heart as she realized that Antryg had electrical equipment at his disposal.

But when they burst past the startled guard into that vast room, nothing met their eyes—nothing, hanging dark and shimmering where the sunlight had been, as if a hole had been opened in the fabric of the world and the night, momentarily, allowed to breathe through. It grew smaller and smaller, like a shrinking bubble of darkness, even as they watched, seeming to retreat without ever reaching the far wall. Along it, Joanna thought she could see something moving.

Salteris strode forward and Joanna reached involuntarily to catch the black fabric of his sleeve. The smells of woodsmoke and herbs came to her from it as he turned, as they had come from Antryg's—the smells of wizardry that had smothered her at San Serano, with the strangler's grip around her throat. She gasped, "Don't . . . !"

At the same moment, Caris shoved her roughly aside, his sword whining from its sheath. "We'll lose him!" The wind of the Void lifted his blond hair back from his forehead, and anger blazed in his eyes. For a terrifying instant, Joanna saw that her choice was either to fling herself willy-nilly after them into whatever second gap in the Void Salteris should open or to be trapped in this world, with neither good mages nor evil to help her, forever. . . .

She gritted her teeth and tightened her grip on her gathered-up petticoats, ready to run. But Salteris did not move. He only stood watching as the hideous black shimmer of the Void faded and vanished.

"No," he said. His voice echoed queerly in that enormous room, with its jumble of antique furniture and the sun glinting harshly on the glass tubes and copper wires coiled beneath the window. He turned back to consider them—Joanna in her ruffled and borrowed gown, and Caris with his sword half-drawn, his eyes the eyes of a hawk stooping to its prey. "No. I know where he has gone, my children. I read the marks of Suraklin that guide him like candles through the darkness." As if he guessed her fears from her grim eyes and braced chin, he smiled and, reaching out, gently touched Joanna's cheek. "I will not leave you alone here, child. Indeed," he added quietly, "when I cross the Void to trap him, I shall need you both."

CHAPTER XVIII

WHEN THEY REACHED GARY'S HOUSE IN AGOURA, THEY FOUND IT empty and silent. Just as well, thought Joanna, watching Caris make a rapid, wary circuit of the den, kitchen, and party room, naked sword blade in hand. The last thing she wanted at the moment was even to see Gary, let alone explain to him where she'd been for the last two weeks and who Caris and the Archmage were.

Letting herself in with the hideaway key, she had a strange sense of *déjà vu,* like the dreams she occasionally had of being in grade school again with her adult knowledge and experience. Some of it was simply aesthetic—her eye, used for weeks to rococo curves and molded plaster ceilings, found the high tech starkness of the place alien and strange, and her lungs gagged on the quality of the September air. But it was emotional as well—a sense of reality-poisoning that was increased by the impersonality of the house, the party room with its ugly, comfortless couches and prominent television set. Everything around her seemed almost audibly to speak Gary's name.

For no reason, she remembered the ragged little mill girls in Kymil, hastening through the silent glory of late summer dawn, and the bitter, weary pity on Antryg's face as he'd asked, "Is it worth it?"

"It's all dead," Caris said softly. He came back from the big glass-and-chrome kitchen, sword still in hand, cautiously touching television, bar, and couches in passing. "I mean—it never was alive." He paused, his dark, beautifully shaped brows drawn down over his eyes with puzzlement as he looked at Joanna. "What is it all made of?"

"Plastic, mostly." She shoved her hands into her jeans pockets and looked around her at the house, realizing at last what it was that had chiefly bothered her about Gary. "It's cheap, and it'll do."

"But it isn't—it isn't *right,*" the sasennan insisted.

Salteris, who had been standing by the patio doors, gazing thoughtfully out at the smog, let fall the drapes and turned back. "I doubt one person in ten notices, anymore," he remarked, almost casually. "People get used to things. In time, they cease to remember and don't miss what they've forgotten they had." He came back to where Joanna stood, once again in the well-worn comfort of jeans and t-shirt, and said, "The mark is upstairs, isn't it?"

The mark was at Salteris' own eye level. He brushed his hand along the wood, as Antryg had done on the white, curlicued paneling of the Emperor's suite. Like a glowing pixel, the scribble of light seemed to float up out of the depths of the grain. The wizard stood for a long time gazing at it; even when it faded again, as it did almost at once, he did not move, but remained, as if he could read it still.

"Was that the mark," he asked her at last, "that you saw in San Serano? In the great computer room there?"

"I think so," she said hesitantly. She pushed back her unruly blond hair from her face, trying to remember something beyond the terror, the queer, smoky smell of the robes, and the scorch of a man's breath on her temple.

"His influence can be incredibly strong upon the minds of those who know him," the old man murmured. Sharply through the curtains, a scissor edge of late sunlight rimmed his angular profile, so like Caris', and haloed the free-floating strands of his silver hair. "And even those who do not know him yet—the mark influences their minds, as if he spoke to them when their thoughts were elsewhere. The mark prepares the way. I see his influence in your eyes still."

She looked away, feeling her face go blotchy red with shame that he should guess.

"You do not want to believe entirely ill of him," Salteris continued gently. "You search for the reasons he did what he did, motives to make his use of you other than what it was. It says better of you than it does of him."

Her throat tight and aching as if she had screamed her heart out, she stood staring at the silent red eyes of the IBM in its bank of 20-megabyte disk drives.

"I know, Joanna." The slender, powerful hands rested on her shoulders. "Even now, even knowing what I know through the memory of the grip of his mind upon mine, even knowing I must meet him again, it is my instinct to trust him. That is the terror—and the strength—of his spell."

Caris turned sharply from examining the neat shelves of additional ROM and backup floppies, the sunlight slicing through the single chink of curtain bursting against the brass of dagger hilt and buckle. "Must you meet him?"

"He has not yet been here." The old man folded his hands in the sleeves of his robe. "He will come to this, his mark."

"Why?"

The dark gaze rested gently on her for a moment before the Archmage replied.

"Perhaps there is something here he wants," he said. "Perhaps—for very little, if any, magic operates here, and it is hard to say—perhaps because he will sense you near it. But he will come—he must. And I must meet him."

Caris asked softly, "Alone?" In the inflection of his voice, Joanna could hear that he already knew his grandfather's reply.

Salteris sighed and folded his hands before him, forefingers pressed to his lips. At length he said, "Caris, I am sure of myself. To introduce a second factor, even one that I trust implicitly, as I trust you, would be to increase the danger."

"But your magic doesn't operate here," Caris began protestingly.

"Neither does his."

"But he is twenty years younger than you and a half a foot taller! He can . . ."

"My son," the old man said, with a smile, "do you think me that defenseless?"

Caris said nothing.

"And then, someone must stay with Joanna." The dark gaze moved thoughtfully to her in the close, hot gloom of the computer room. "I do not think he will pass me unseen, but he might. If he does, he *must not* be allowed to speak to her."

Neither Caris nor Joanna spoke; but judging by the sasennan's face, he wasn't any more thrilled with the idea than she was.

More gently, Salteris went on, "You stand in grave danger still, Joanna. Even knowing what you know, you want to trust."

She looked away again. Hating herself, she nodded. Dark and compelling, the old man's glance went to his grandson. "If you cannot prevent him from speaking to her in any other way, kill him." He turned and walked to the window, flinging back the curtain to admit a drench of harsh and smog-stained afternoon light. Beyond the window, the hills that hid San Serano bulked in the haze, and between them, like a gun sight, stood the dusty little shed in which they had stepped from the dark of the Void.

"I will wait for him there," he said. "He is sly. . . ." He lifted his thin, white fingers at the intake of Caris' protesting breath. "He will not speak with me, if you are near. He has reason to fear you, my son. Trust me." He looked back at them, the hot sunlight outlining the worn contours of his face, suddenly very fragile-looking in his faded black robe. "I know what it is that I do."

The light had shifted again to the sharp-edged champagne brilliance of the long Southern California afternoon when Antryg came walking over the hills.

Caris and Joanna were in the computer room, where they had been since Salteris left them, alternately speaking of what had passed since they'd parted at Magister Magus' and watching for movement in the parched ochre vastness of grass and dust.

Caris had turned from the window to regard Gary's monstrous new IBM among its red-eyed banks of monitors and surge suppressors, as he had done at intervals, all afternoon. After some moments, he said, "This is the thing that is your life and the life of all your world? The machine that thinks like a man?"

"Not like a man." Joanna folded up her legs to sit cross-legged on the corner of the computer table, the weary portion of her mind that was not trying desperately to avoid thinking of Antryg taking considerable comfort in the freedom of jeans. *He is walking into a trap,* part of her said, and she pushed the treacherous impulse to care aside. "Computers can arrive at the same conclusions a person can, with the same kind of logic people are capable of, when they aren't hoping that two and two won't equal four. . . ." She paused, then went on. "But not like a man." She reached for the switch on the main terminal. "Would you care to try?"

He stepped back hastily and shook his head. Then, seeing her startled expression, he flushed a little and explained, "It is not the Way of the Sasennan. We are trained to be what we are, and to do what we do. All this—" He gestured around him at the high tech fixtures of the house, the soft hum of the air conditioner, and the alien richness of the world, "It is not supposed to matter to the sasennan. We are weapons, honed to a single end. That is all."

She remembered Kanner—remembered, also, Caris' uneasiness at operating without a master, or with only the dottily masterful Antryg to give him orders. In his own way, she realized, Caris was as bad with people as she.

Curious, she said, "But you were mageborn. You were going to be a wizard. Isn't that just the opposite?"

He hesitated, as if it were something he had never quite articulated to himself, let alone anyone else. As he always did when he was trying to say what he really meant, he spoke slowly. "It is, and it isn't. As a mage, one can't give oneself to any of it, either. They say neither the mage nor the sasennan drinks the world's wine, as street-warriors and dog wizards do. So it isn't—" He shook his head. "It isn't safe to sniff at the fumes. At least," he added more hesitantly, "it isn't safe for *me*. To be what we are, and only what we are, to put everything into that, is what hones us to a killing edge. Anything else is a softening."

"The more you do, the more you do." Joanna sighed. He had a point. It was a definite changing of mental gears to go from dealing with computers to dealing with people, particularly after she'd been programming for hours or days at a time. And indeed, most of the time she did feel more at ease dealing with her IBM than she did dealing with Gary or with any other human being . . . at least, until recently.

Antryg . . .

Not Antryg, she told herself wretchedly. *Suraklin. Suraklin.*

Caris turned suddenly. Though he did not speak, Joanna was on her feet and at his side, looking out toward the tiny, ragged outline of the shed.

In the fulvous sunlight, Salteris stood in front of the shed, unmoving save for the wind stirring his black robes and silky hair. After what seemed like a long moment, Antryg came into view above the tawny crest of the hill.

He had changed back into the jeans and scruffy t-shirt in which she had first seen him, here in this house. The slanted afternoon light caught the silver-foil HAVOC across his chest; though she knew it was only the name of a rock group, the word had a grim significance to her, knowing what she now knew. His cracked spectacles glinted as he held out his hand to the unmoving Archmage and took a step closer to him. Joanna thought he spoke; but at this distance, it was impossible to tell.

She could not see whether the old man replied. In her heart she knew her fears should be for Salteris' safety rather than Antryg's.

After a moment, the younger wizard stepped forward and bending his tall form, embraced the old man. After brief hesitation, Salteris' arms came up to return the embrace. Antryg led him gently into the shed.

Beside her, Joanna heard Caris whisper, "No . . ."

She caught him by the arm as he turned away. "He said he had to meet him alone." She was aware her hand shook.

"He also said that the one thing he feared was Antryg's charm." He stepped back from Joanna, the first true kinship she had ever seen for her in his face. "I know. I—when I first met him, I trusted him. And I've had to fight all this time to keep from trusting him again. I know." He nodded towards the silent shed in the puma-gold emptiness of the hills. "Are you coming?"

The air in the patio was hot, in spite of the cooling proximity of the pool. From the iron gate that looked out into the hills, they saw Antryg emerge from the shed and stand for a time, his back leaned against the splintery wood, his head bowed in exhaustion. Caris glanced quickly at Joanna, fear in his eyes; when they looked again, the mad wizard was gone.

Caris, at a dead run, reached the hill long before Joanna did.

Parching and oppressive, the heat of the afternoon seemed to have imbued itself into the coarse wood of the shed, along with the stinks of dirt and old oil slowly baking in the summer silence. Pierced by splinters of blinding light from the chinks in the walls, the shed's darkness defeated Joanna's eyes as she stepped through the open door, but it seemed to her that she already knew what she would find inside.

The Archmage Salteris lay in a corner, behind a crazy pile of splintered plywood and the dismembered parts of a car. He had been laid out carefully, a small, frail form under his black robes. There was dust in his white hair. His eyes had been closed, and his mouth, also, though his face was still a hideous mottled gray-blue with strangulation. Even with the merciful masking of the shadows, Joanna could not deceive herself that he might be somehow revived. She had killed two men. She knew what death looked like now.

The unbearable brilliance of a crack of sunlight outlined Caris' face in gold as he knelt beside the corpse. He stared out straight ahead of him, his face blank with a kind of shock. He had relied on the old man, Joanna realized, as much as he had loved him. His rage at Antryg had come as much from fear of losing Salteris' support as it had been from his fanatical loyalty. He had been able to believe in his grandfather's disappearance, she remembered, but not in his death. He had made himself a weapon for those slender, blue-veined hands. It had always been inconceivable to him that they would one day fall slack.

His face inhumanly calm and still, Caris lifted one of those hands, limp now as a bundle of jointed sticks. he turned it over to look at the white fingers and palms, then laid it as it had been, back upon the breast.

Tenderly, still with that odd, almost wondering numbness, he brushed aside the white silk of the hair and looked for a time at the bruises on the colorless, crepey flesh of the throat.

Joanna thought it was only some final seeking for contact with the old man he had loved, until she heard him whisper, "Why? Was your trust in him so great that you didn't even struggle when you felt his hands around your throat? Could he do even that to you?"

Then suddenly he doubled over, as if some poison, drunk unnoticed, had finally taken grip. The big, well-shaped hands pressed his face, and shudder after silent shudder of grief racked through his body. He twisted aside from the hand Joanna tried to lay on his back and knelt in the stifling dust, hands pressed to his face as if he could squeeze all tears, all sound, all feeling back inside of him, as it was the Way of the Sasennan to do. Barred with sunlight, Salteris' distorted face seemed strangely calm, as if he knew that none of this, nor any further machinations of the Dark Mage, concerned him any longer.

After a long time, Joanna asked, "What can we do?"

Joanna heard Antryg's light footfall in the party room an hour and a half later. Outside the kitchen windows, the afternoon light had slanted further, then taken on the curious crystal quality of evening, as the wind moved the smog further east. She had been sitting and staring out at the changes of the light since returning to the house. She felt empty and cold inside, as if some final illusion had collapsed; her thoughts seemed to have slipped into read-only mode, going round and round until they were exhausted, without producing anything except that, like Caris, she must do what she must do.

But when she heard the footfalls that she knew for Antryg's, it felt as if everything within her were passed suddenly through a wringer.

She heard him pause in the party room. Forcing a calm upon herself she had never known she possessed, she got to her feet, walked to the stove, and poured the water she had heated in the teakettle over the combination of instant coffee and crushed sleeping pills in the cup on the counter. She took a deep breath and conjured again for herself the vision of Salteris' dead, swollen face in the brown gloom of the shed. Then she picked up the cup and went into the party room.

He was standing near the curtained glass of the doors, looking sick unto death.

The naturalness of her own voice astounded her. "Did Salteris find you?"

He looked up at the sound of her voice, and some expression—shock, dismay, despair of a situation that was hopeless—superseded the misery and exhaustion on his face. He shut his eyes for a moment, fighting some terrible inner weight which seemed to have descended on his wide, bony shoulders, and whispered hopelessly, "You came with him?" Then, realizing that he should not even know of Salteris' presence in this world, he looked at her again and added, "Salteris?"

"He brought me back here," Joanna said. "He came to me in the garden—he said he had to speak to you. He didn't say why. We went up to the attic but you had gone. So I asked him to bring me back, and he did."

He closed his eyes momentarily. The lines around them looked as if they'd been put in with a chisel in the discolored flesh. He said, "I wouldn't have left you."

"I didn't know that."

He looked so shaken, so drained of all his usual ebullience, that it was absolutely natural that she should hand him the coffee. She had to force her hand to it, force herself to look into his face as she did it, telling herself he was Suraklin. Suraklin! He drank it without a word, grateful for the warmth of it. After a moment he said, "Thank you." Going to the couch, he sat down as if he had only just recalled that it was possible to do so.

He ran his fingers through his graying hair and seemed to pull himself together. "I'm sorry," he said. "I didn't mean to leave you long—not even this long. I should have returned earlier than this." He swallowed, and she saw the muscles of his jaw harden for a moment. "And Pharos would have looked after you, kept you safe. But there was something here I had to find."

She remained standing in front of him, her arms folded and her heart hammering, but her whole body feeling strangely numb. "And did you?"

He shook his head, a small gesture, defeated. "No." He looked down, turning the remains of the drugged coffee in his big hands, staring down into the dregs as he had once studied tea-leaves in the posthouses to buy them supper. He asked carefully, "Did Salteris say where he had been?"

"No," Joanna said. "And frankly, I didn't care."

He looked up at her quickly, that look she had seen before, with the ruin of all that he had ever sought or hoped in his eyes.

"I don't want anything further to do with this," she said, fighting to keep the tremor out of her voice. "I only wanted to come home, to get out of whatever is going on. You said once . . ." Her voice faltered. "You said once you'd see I came to no harm. If you meant that, just leave me alone. All right?"

He said nothing for a time, but their eyes held, and for a long moment she had the impression that he wavered on the brink of telling her the truth, of stepping beyond that self-imposed wall and trusting her, as it was still her instinct, fight it though she might, to trust him. Then he sighed, and in an almost soundless voice, agreed. "All right."

She couldn't help herself. "Will you be all right?" *What a stupid question,* she told herself an instant later.

He managed the ghost of his old warm, half-demented smile. "Oh, yes." He set the cup down at his side. "As long as I stay a step ahead of the Council. As long as I can . . ." He paused and shook his head, as if trying to clear it. "I'm sorry, Joanna. But the mark on the wall . . . the mark on the wall . . ."

Then he slumped sideways and was asleep.

CHAPTER XIX

IT WAS LONG AFTER DARK WHEN HE AWOKE. JOANNA WAS STILL SIT-ting on the curiously comfortless gray chair beside the couch, her mind blank, her body and bones cold with exhaustion. She almost literally could not believe that she had awakened that morning in the old Summer Palace at Angelshand or that it was only fourteen or fifteen hours ago that she had sat in the Regent's carriage, while he had wept as he'd spoken of his father. It was as if it had happened to someone else.

And in a way, she thought, it had.

The heat of the day had passed off. The party room was dim, illumi-nated only by the reflected yellow glare of the kitchen's lights. Through the open glass doors of the patio, the smell of chlorine came in off the pool with the warmth of the tepid night.

She saw Antryg stir, fighting his way to the surface of the dark well of his dreams, saw him try to move, and saw how his breath stopped, then quickened when he realized that he could not.

His eyes opened, and he looked up into her face.

"I'm sorry, Antryg." Oddly enough, she meant it.

He made a quick motion and ceased at once. His wrists and ankles were knotted tight with the plastic-wrapped wire Joanna had carried in her purse and which she'd gotten, weeks ago, from the telephone man at San Serano. With weary irony, she remembered thinking at the time that it would come in handy. More than that, Joanna realized, recalling her own first experience with barbiturates, he must be prey to the grand-mother of all headaches. The eyes that stared up into hers were dark with despair and terror, but showed no surprise.

"Caris is summoning the Council," she said quietly. "Salteris had something called a *lipa* in his robes."

His head dropped back onto the cushions of the couch. She saw the shudder that went through him; but curiously, as he closed his eyes, what was in his face was a kind of relief.

"Why?" she asked. "Who were you expecting?"

The bruised eyelids moved a little, but did not open. He whispered, "Salteris."

Bitter heat went through her as she remembered how the old man had embraced him, just before he'd led Salteris into the shed. Her voice shook. "You know as well as I do that Salteris is dead."

His eyes opened again and looked up into hers. "You saw?"

"I didn't actually see you strangle him, no—but we saw enough."

The breath went out of him in a sigh. Two and two, Joanna thought numbly, once again and inevitably equal four. She went on, "But he told us."

His head turned so sharply that he flinched, and the color drained from his face. In the sidelong light that came from the kitchen, she could see the sweat gleam clammily on his cheeks and the bridge of that absurd nose. "Told you what?"

"Who you are."

"Who I . . . ?" His eyes widened, as he understood. "No," he said softly. "Joanna, no."

"He had no reason to lie."

"He had every reason! Joanna, don't you understand? When Suraklin escaped for the last time from the body he was born in—the body that the Archmage and the Council slew and burned in Kymil twenty-five years ago—it was not my being, not my body, that he stole for his escape."

"Then why did he teach you everything he knew?"

"I was his chosen victim, yes," Antryg said quietly, and she could hear the desperation buried under the forced calm of his voice. "Although I didn't know what was intended for me, I suspected—I don't know what. It all became tangled with dreams and madness in the years I lived in hiding, knowing he was dead and feeling his mind seeking mine in my dreams. It's why I had to find a member of the Council in Angelshand to confirm what I feared, though I already knew it to be true—to find where he'd been, *who* he'd been, all those years. For I knew he was alive. In nightmares, I'd see someone I knew looking at me with Suraklin's eyes. . . . And then, in the Silent Tower, he came to me, and I knew him."

"Who?" Joanna demanded, closing her mind furiously against what she knew to be a trap.

"Suraklin," Antryg said softly. "Salteris."

"You expect me to believe that?" Panic made her hands tremble, and she closed them tightly on one another against the arm of the couch. "You expect me to trust your word, after you've lied and evaded me—"

"I had to!" Antryg cried desperately. He twisted against his bonds, then shuddered and went white again, to lie still, teeth clenched, until the nausea passed. "He had an accomplice in this world, Joanna. I knew that much from the marks on the walls here and at San Serano. None knows better than I the terrible strength of the hold he has on the minds of others. And I—I was afraid it was you."

She looked away from him, understanding suddenly why he had feared her; why he had feared even more the attraction that she knew he had felt toward her. Suraklin's gift was to win the trust of others, she thought. No wonder Antryg would mistrust even his love for her—if he was telling the truth.

"I wanted to trust you," he went on. "I couldn't. I didn't dare. If he even suspected I'd guessed he was still alive, he would have hidden, gone underground in some other body, as he did before. I'm only a man, Joanna—one of the very few left who knew him, who might be able to recognize him. And in this vampire state, going from body to body, he is deathless. He had to be stopped. . . ."

"And you're saying that's why you killed Salteris." She shifted her feet beneath her in the chair. Somewhere outside in the night, a warm stir of wind brought her the far-off sounds of the Ventura Freeway and the distant boom of a plane heading into Burbank. "Because Suraklin had taken over his body."

"No." The crumpled, weary lines around his eyes darkened with something deeper than horror or grief. "I killed Salteris because Suraklin had departed from his body. Don't you see? The body he first stole, the one in which he escaped from Kymil, was the Emperor's. As Emperor, he ruled Ferryth for twenty-one years. Only Pharos guessed, and Pharos was a child and could do nothing—could not even dare believe what his heart told him was true, that his father had ceased to be his father. As the Emperor, he tried to have me executed after the Mellidane Revolts—and maybe it was he who pushed me into aiding the rebels in the first place. I don't know. But four years ago, he left the Emperor, left him mindless as he is now, to take over Salteris' mind and body, to become Salteris—and he left Salteris today, to go on to someone else. I killed Salteris . . ." He forced his voice steady, against the sudden stress of fatigue and grief. "I killed him because I had loved him, because he had been my master, and my friend. I could not bear to leave him as the Emperor is, a mindless, imbecile shell, cared for by others. And except for leaving Suraklin to begin with, it was the hardest thing I have ever done."

Like a litany, she whispered, "I don't believe you. They told me . . ."

"*Suraklin* told you," Antryg insisted desperately. "He had to discredit and kill me. He left one of his gloves in my room, the first time he visited me, and by sleight of hand got Caris to believe he had them both with him. He never came into my rooms the second time, never entered the Tower at all. He couldn't have touched the Void from within its walls; no one could, unless it was opened just outside. But he made Caris think he had by a spell of illusion, and if the Void had not weakened enough for me to escape then, Caris or the Bishop or the Witchfinders would have killed me that night, as he'd intended they should. He cannot afford to leave me alive. You must believe me, Joanna. Please believe me. . . ."

"Shut up!" She turned her face away, panic struggling to the surface of her heart. *If you cannot prevent him from speaking to her, kill him,* Salteris had said. Because she would hear the truth, she wondered, or because she would want to believe the lie?

She heard the rustle of his body as he tried to move again; then it stilled. His voice, when he spoke, was rapid, as if he knew his time were running out.

"He wanted to live forever. From a goal, it became an obsession with him. He had the magic by which he dominated the minds of others; he used spells to break down his own mind, his personality, into thousands of small cells—subroutines, you call them—as if he visualized and formed by magic a duplicate of his personality, which he put into the mind and body of another. I had to learn who it was he'd taken to flee Kymil the first time after his defeat. Until this morning, I didn't know who. And until this afternoon, when you said computers can reproduce the human brain, I didn't know what his ultimate intentions were."

"A computer," Joanna said quietly. She turned back and looked at the tall, gawky form in faded jeans and black-and-silver t-shirt, lying on the couch with his tawdry beads glinting in the reflected light. "Not program a computer to do magic—program a computer to be a mage. And use the teles to feed it electricity."

"At the cost of the life of your world and mine. At the cost of that dreadful pall of colorless grief, of unliving and uncaring, that will cover both our worlds when the computer is ready to run. And no one will understand quite what they are paying, or why. In a generation or two, they will not even remember what it was like before."

Something Salteris had said in this room caught at Joanna's mind. Past the open patio doors, she could see the dark shed against the black of the evening sky where Caris sat alone with the *lipa*, the summoning-spell, and with the Archmage's cold body. She felt a queer stirring along her nerves, the half-sensation of fear and cold, and knew that somewhere close the Void was being opened.

"Just because you're telling me this now," she said softly, "doesn't mean you're not Suraklin."

The muscles of his bare arms moved again as he twisted against the wires. "Joanna, I swear it," he said softly. "What can I say to make you believe me?"

"Nothing," she said. "Because if you are Suraklin, you would say anything. Even . . ." She shut her mouth on the words, *Even that you love me.* After a moment she went on, "Salteris said Suraklin had the gift of making others trust him."

"I see he was right," Antryg said bitterly.

Joanna felt herself grow red. "He didn't give me lies and half-truths and evasions."

"He told you a lie that was consistent from beginning to end," the mage retorted. His breath was fast and uneven. Like her, he could sense the movement in the darkness outside. "Joanna, I followed Suraklin's mark to this place, to the room where I first met you, upstairs here. Later, when I felt the Void opening again, I followed him back and found you in whatever hideout in the hills of Kymil he'd brought you to after his accomplice had kidnapped you from here. I didn't know what he'd done with you before, if anything. For all I knew, *you* could be his slave as well. And then," he said, "at Devilsgate . . ."

She thrust aside the memory of the cobalt dimness of the drawing room, her overwhelming need for him, and the softness of that velvet voice in the gloom. "I don't want to talk about Devilsgate," she said stonily. "I was a fool. . . ."

"As was I," he murmured. "I saw in the cards there that you would betray me. The sixteenth card, the Dead God—the sign they put on wizards to cripple their power when they lead them out to execution. In spite of that I wanted to trust you and found myself doing so, although I knew it was insane. I have always trusted too easily. I could not risk it."

"And I," Joanna said quietly in the darkness, "I can't risk this."

He lay silent then, the kitchen light shining on the sweat on his face and on the lenses of his specs. He stared at the ceiling. Gary, Joanna found herself thinking, would have been gazing accusingly at her; she pushed the comparison from her mind. The fact that Antryg had never shown her anything but caring, kindness, and, she suspected, love, the fact that he had risked his life to save her from the Regent and the Inquisition, and the fact that she loved him did not alter the fact that he was Suraklin, the Dark Mage. Or—was he?

It was not a case of two and two equaling four, but rather a hellish quadratic equation, in which there were two equally correct answers and no way to choose between them. Either everything Salteris had said was a lie or everything Antryg had said was. There must be some logical way to learn the truth, she thought, but she could not arrive at one. She wished desperately that she were better at understanding people or that she had more data.

In the darkness outside, she was aware of movement, and dread chilled her like the onset of fever.

"Joanna," Antryg said quietly, and under the forced calm of his deep voice she heard the tremor of his panic. "I can't prove any of this to you. I know I can't. And it is unfair to ask anyone to make a choice based only on the heart. But you are in danger, too." He shook aside the dampened ends of his hair, where they clung to his bony temples and the last bruised remnants of the Regent's whip marks.

"Suraklin left Salteris' body. He can only have taken over someone else's—at a guess, the accomplice in this world who's been doing his programming for him. The accomplice would have met him at the shed —the shed's marked with his sign as well, you know—when Suraklin guessed Salteris would be more good to him dead than alive, if I'd get the blame for his imbecility as well as the Emperor's. But Suraklin wanted you for something. He stalked you in San Serano—he had his accomplice kidnap you from here and came here to get you, to bring you to that hideout of his, wherever it was. And it's my guess he still wants you."

"Of course," Joanna said, fighting the fear his words brought and her anger at the thought of how easily her fears were manipulated. "He might want me enough to save me from the Regent, or break me out of the Inquisition's prison . . ."

His eyes met hers in the darkness. "You know perfectly well why I saved you."

She turned away. Her voice shook again. "I don't," she said. "That's the whole point. I don't know."

In the hot, gluey darkness outside, the patio gate creaked. Antryg's head came around quickly, and she saw the track of sweat along the high cheekbone. Low and very rapidly he said, "Let me go, Joanna. Please. When they're gone, he'll come back for you, whoever he is now. . . ."

"You're trying to scare me into releasing you. . . ."

"I'm trying to save you, dammit!" He wrenched his arms furiously against the binding wires. In the patio, Joanna could see nothing in the dark, but thought she heard the slur of homespun robes against the stiff leaves in the planters and the pat of quiet feet on cement. Desperately, he said, "Joanna, they'll kill me. . . ."

His eyes changed, looking past her to the doors. Joanna turned her head. Caris stood framed by the night, his face, for all its dust-covered exhaustion, set and queerly serene, but much older, a man's face, not a youth's. His naked sword blade flashed coldly in his hand. Behind him, nearly invisible in their dark robes against the darkness, she sensed others. From that shadowy assemblage, a woman stepped, tall and beautiful in her sable garments, the silver embroidery of the hyacinth stole she wore a pin-prick of reflected light beneath the loose curls of her dark hair.

"Joanna," she said softly. "I am Lady Rosamund Kentacre. In the name of the Council of Wizards, I thank you for what you have done."

Beside her, Joanna was aware of Antryg looking at the Council with the face of a man who knows that nothing he can say will save him.

"Caris told us what happened," the mage said, still in that low, sweet voice that, underneath its beauty, was colder than an assassin's knife. "On behalf of the Council, I can only ask your pardon for the fact that you were drawn into the affairs of wizards. I promise you, for whatever it is worth, that this man will be punished, not only for what he has done to you, but for what he has tried to do to both our worlds."

Caris stepped forward, his dark eyes remote, stern, and curiously peaceful for all their weariness. He was once more a weapon of the Council; he had fulfilled his mission and encompassed his revenge. He had returned to being what he was, something Joanna knew already that she would never do. Three other mages stepped forth from the darkness behind him—all young men, strong, and grim-looking. Two of them wore the blood-colored robes of the Church wizards, and Joanna guessed that peace had been made with the Bishop and the Witchfinders.

Her stomach felt cold at the thought that it would be Peelbone who presided over Antryg's questioning. With the Council and with Caris' account of Salteris' murder, the Regent would not protect him. She remembered the sudden iciness of those evil blue eyes and the shrill voice saying in the dimness of the attic, *You will long for the death my father ordered for you. . . .*

In a kind of daze, she stepped aside, and the mages untwisted the wire bonds from Antryg's booted ankles and pulled him to his feet. He looked deathly white. He knew as well as Joanna did what waited for him on the other side of the Void. *I want to be done with this,* Joanna desperately thought, sick and wretched, knowing that whatever the necessity for destroying Suraklin, this would always remain something she had done. *I want this to be over. . . .*

Lady Rosamund had turned back to the patio doors. Beyond them, Joanna could see forms moving, the stray glint of light on the pool, pale hands uplifting and with laborious concentration making the signs necessary to open one last time the gate in the darkness which separated world from world, time from time. Wind moved the gray draperies and lifted back the dark sleeves from Rosamund's arms. It touched Joanna's cheek and stirred in the graying mane of Antryg's hair. Queer and cold, the smell of the Void filled the room with the terror of the haunted abyss. She thought, but wasn't sure, she heard Antryg whisper despairingly, "No . . ."

Beyond the doors lay nothing, an empty gulf of blackness, as if, beyond the frame of curtain and glass, all the universe fell away.

Caris turned his head. For a moment his eyes met Joanna's. Through the wall of his grief, which was already transmuting into a desperate perfectionism of his warrior's vocation, she saw the last glimmer of his regret—regret at leaving her, perhaps his only nonsasennan friend, and at leaving the possibilities of the strange affairs of the world beyond the perfections of the killing arts. Joanna realized she would never see Caris again. When the Void closed up this final time, it would all be gone—the beauty of dawn on the marshes of Kymil, the twisting, cobbled streets of Angelshand, Magister Magus, and the poor, mad Regent. . . .

With a violent wrench, Antryg twisted free of his guards and made a last, desperate run for the room's other windows. He didn't make two strides. Caris and the mages fell upon him like dogs, bringing him to the floor. Caris' sword flashed as he raised it and brought the weighted pommel down on Antryg's skull with a crack Joanna felt in the roots of her teeth. Then they dragged him to his feet again, still struggling, though he couldn't have been more than half-conscious.

In a chill voice Lady Rosamund said, "Bring him." Caris and the Church mages half dragged, half carried him through that terrible door and out into the eternal darkness that lay beyond.

From where she stood in the doorway, it seemed to Joanna that she could see them for a long time, vanishing down the endless corridor to nothing. She saw a last glint of light on Antryg's spectacles—or perhaps it was only the glimmer of the water in the swimming pool. The air around her was warm again. The wound in the night was healed.

Only what they had been and what they had done remained, tracked indelibly like footprints across her soul.

She realized it was Wednesday. She'd have to go to work in the morning and unravel the hideous mess left by her disappearance.

It was only then that she shed tears.

She knew she could have lain there on the couch where Antryg had been bound and wept all night from weariness, self-hatred, and the stress of shock after shock. But the detached part of her mind told her it was God knew how late already, and Gary would be coming. Of all the people in the world, the last one she wanted to see, to deal with now, was Gary. The thought of listening to that whining self-pity nearly nauseated her.

If only she'd had some proof, she thought, weary at last to numbness. One clue, one way or the other . . .

Antryg could have figured it out. She recalled the blithe, Holmesian quickness of his deductions. *It has been my misfortune to be a good guesser.* . . . Except, of course, if Antryg were really Suraklin, he'd lie.

But the memory of Holmes' name triggered another thought.

She shook her head, telling herself that, for better or worse, it was over. What she wanted to do was useless. But in spite of that conviction, she felt the sudden lurch of her heart as she realized that there had, in fact, been a way to tell.

As she had felt on the island, with the pistol heavy in her hand, she had the sensation of not wanting to know, of wanting to be powerless because then nothing would be expected of her. After a long time, she mounted the stairs to the computer room again.

Only the small orange lights of the surge suppressors and backup batteries illuminated the darkness, with the ruby gleam of power lights and the green luminosity of the clock. She stood for a long time, looking at the doorframe where Suraklin's mark was. When she had first seen Antryg at the party, she remembered, he had brushed his fingers along the wall, not making the mark, but calling it forth, as Salteris had done only a few hours ago. She'd seen Antryg do the same in the hot, smelly closeness of the rooms upstairs in the Imperial Palace—God, had that been only this morning?—and the Prince's rooms last night. The memory was very clear. All her memories of him were. Antryg in his long, black coat and shabby ruffles, passing his hands in wide sweeps over the lacquered paneling, until his fingers paused on one spot or another . . .

Except for one deliberately placed high up, the marks had all been at only slightly different heights. Hadn't Conan Doyle written in *A Study in Scarlet* that a man will mark a wall at his own eye level?

With terrible vividness, she saw Salteris in this room again, calling forth Suraklin's mark—at the level of his own eyes, six inches below the level of Antryg's.

It proves nothing, she thought desperately. *If he'd thought about it, Suraklin could have made his mark at the level of his chin. . . .*

But other memories crowded back of hands strong around her throat and the hot stir of breath against her temple at San Serano—and then of how, in the alleys near the St. Cyr fortress, panting and exhausted in the silence of the enclosing fog, she'd had to reach up even to put her arm around Antryg's neck so that their mouths could meet.

The man who'd attacked her at San Serano was a shorter man.

Through the open window, she heard the scrunch of tires on gravel. Headlights tracked across the drive, and the barred shadows of the iron fence chased each other over the flickering surface of the pool.

Gary, she thought, sickened with a bitter distaste. She could hear his voice now: *Hey, babe, you can stay here if you want, you know. . . .*

All she wanted was to be alone and to cry for hours, not knowing what it was that she'd done.

The Void was closed.

She would never know for sure if Antryg had told the truth or lied.

No, she thought. If Antryg told the truth—if he was not Suraklin— that uncaring deadness would return, to drain the life and hope from the world. And by that time, Antryg would be dead. She pushed aside the hideous details Caris had once given her. On the other hand, it might be that Antryg's—or Suraklin's—death would prevent that from ever happening.

She was back to the quadratic equation again, with positive and negative solutions, and no way of telling which was which.

He would have come back to this world, she thought, to find Suraklin's computer, and the teles relays which powered it.

Or, she thought, to find another dupe.

She hated to leave the darkened sanctum of the computer room. She felt safe in the fortress of those tiny, steady lights, as she always had. They were idiots savants, but in their inhuman way far more reliable than anyone she'd ever met . . .

. . . If it was inhuman reliability she wanted, that is. If all she wanted to get out was what she herself had put in.

She heard Gary moving around downstairs and knew she had to go.

Done is done, she thought. If Antryg was Suraklin, she had just saved the world.

If he wasn't . . .

There was nothing, literally nothing, that she could do.

Quietly, she descended the stairs.

Gary was sitting at the kitchen table, a glass of red wine before him, the glare of the electric light shining harsh and yellow on his soft brown hair and catching like blood in the highlights of the wine. His elbows were propped on the table, his hands folded before his chin, and his forefingers extended against his lips.

Joanna stopped in the doorway, her first thought only that Gary hated wine.

She wondered where she had seen that forefingers—extended gesture before. Then he looked up at her with an ironic half-smile.

"Joanna, my dear," he said. "I see you've returned. You should probably telephone your friend Ruth. She's been pestering the police of three states to distraction."

She thought, *Oh, God.*

And for a moment it was just that.

The only answer to two and two seemed to be four, and she understood then why the Prince Regent had gone mad at the age of ten.

Praying she was wrong, knowing she was right, she was perfectly sure where she'd heard that alien, unGarylike speech pattern and seen that gesture. She knew then why she had been stalked and kidnapped, why Gary had insisted she come to his party, where Suraklin was getting his computer, who his accomplice had been, and what had happened to that accomplice when Suraklin had gained what he needed.

She said something—she didn't know what. She felt numb and half-drowned in implications that were pouring into her mind like the sea pouring over a cracked wall; her mind revolved back on itself in a single phrase: *Oh, God—oh God ohgod . . .*

And she knew that Antryg, beyond any ability of hers to find or save, had been right.

The same personality she had known as Salteris—the one who was, she understood now, the Dark Mage Suraklin—was looking at her out of Gary Fairchild's eyes.

EPILOGUE

A CAR SWEPT BY ON VICTORY BOULEVARD, WITH A RISING ROAR, then a soft swish of retreating tires. One of the pile of cats on Joanna's mangy fake-fur bedspread stretched a hind leg, shook its head, and settled back to sleep. Bright in the darkness of the room, the glowing green list on the monitor screen reached its end: ZYMOGEN ZYMOLOGY ZYMOSIS ZYMOTIC ZYMURGY OK>.

Joanna sipped her tea, and stared at the screen for some moments in silence.

She thought, *Scratch one.*

With the calm persistence of one who works with computers, Joanna hit the reset key and began again, opening the modem, dialing up the communications directory, hitting the S on the menu to call up the San Serano mainframe. When the carrier tone whined, she punched in, not her own user number, but Gary's, tracked down out of the membership directory.

PASSWORD? swam into the screen.

She hit the break key, and typed BABY.

It was a long shot, one of several breaker programs she'd devised to keep herself amused while waiting for the engineering department to bring in test results when she was working overtime at San Serano. In spite of the fact that the computer at San Serano contained classified information and was allegedly protected, breaking into it was relatively simple. Once into the computer itself, she had only to get into whatever files Gary was using to program Suraklin's mind, memories, and magic, preparing them for later transfer to whatever computer it was he'd stolen, piece by piece, by breaking shipping codes—the computer that would be fed by the teles relays.

She took a sip of her tea, scarcely noticing that the liquid, dark and strong as coffee, had long gone cold. The green glow of the clock proclaimed it to be 3:48 A.M. She'd have to be up at seven, if she were going into San Serano to report.

Gary said he'd covered for her with management, creating a tale of family emergency. His questions to her regarding her actual whereabouts and activities for the last two weeks hadn't been particularly convincing, but it had confirmed in her mind that he didn't suspect she knew. They were the questions she'd have expected him to ask, the questions she'd have wondered if he didn't. He'd even pestered her to stay with him—for the sake of appearances, she hoped, though it had taken all her self-control to conceal the loathing and terror she felt, looking into those ironic dark eyes.

I doubt one person in ten notices . . . Salteris—Suraklin—had said. *In time, they cease to remember and don't miss what they've forgotten they had.* . . .

She wondered why she hadn't realized then that there was something wrong or guessed it when Salteris had gotten them into the Summer Palace by terrifying the Prince's horses, injuring them and undoubtedly earning a flogging for the innocent grooms. Antryg would never have been that careless of the safety of others.

Around her, the bedroom of her little apartment was silent. The cats slept again across the foot of the bed like a carelessly dropped fur coat; the dark leaves of the plants glistened with the yellow reflections of the street lamps outside. No breeze fingered the curtain of the open windows. In the dimness, the flashing of the green cursor on the CRT seemed very bright.

Program Baby didn't take long to run. When it finished, the words PASSWORD INADMISSIBLE were still shining on the screen, the cursor flashing expectantly.

Joanna sipped her tea again and stared at the screen. She was beginning to have a bad feeling about this. Getting another user's number was easy enough—it was getting the password that went with the number that was the hard part. The files had to be there—there was no other computer large enough to which Gary would have access and on which he could devise programs for something as complicated as all of a wizard's mind, all of his knowledge, all of his personality, and his magic. It would also be child's play for Gary to write these programs so that they would lie about their own existence, assign larger numbers of bytes to other programs on the directory so that the discrepancy of available space would pass unnoticed. Joanna had similar files of her own in the mainframe. To get into them required a password of up to eight characters, and therein lay the hacker's problem.

Joanna's first hacker program consisted of all words in a standard directory of up to eight letters. In spite of the vast number of random combinations of 26 letters plus 10 digits available, most users selected some easily remembered English word as their password, and the program was written to try them all in succession, with the sublime, uncaring patience of a machine. In her spare hours at San Serano, it had gotten her into any number of classified defense files which the United States government and San Serano's management fondly believed to be secure.

That in itself took several hours. Her second program was the contents of a "What to Name the Baby" book, since most users had a tendency to select names as passwords—that of a wife, lover, child, or dog. She had a third, with those random proper nouns culled from popular culture: Tardis, Gandalf, dilithium, Yoda, Mycroft.

If not A, go to B.

She rubbed her eyes, dialed into San Serano, and punched through Gary's number. The green letters inquired, PASSWORD? and she hit the break key and ran in that third hacker program. As the pixels shimmered across the screen, she massaged the stiffened muscles of the back of her neck, praying this one would work. She'd calculated that trying all combinations of 36 to the eighth power, at the some ten tries per second of which her small desk computer was capable, could take, 3,265,173.5040 days, or roughly eight thousand years. Usually she'd hit pay dirt before that time, but even if it was weeks, she had no way of telling how many days Antryg had left to live.

When she thought about what she knew she had to do, she was perfectly well aware that she was terrified. Throughout the dark hours of the night, since her return from Gary's, intermittent rushes of adrenaline had coursed through her, making her shiver as only social encounters and conversations with her mother or Gary had done, up until two weeks ago.

Caris had told her once that for all his training in the killing arts, he had never, up until a few weeks before, used his skills to protect his own life. Joanna knew nothing about heroism or rescues, but she did know about the patient phlegmatism of computers. As with the problem of the abominations in the meadow, her mind was breaking her task into manageable subroutines.

First, she thought, get the contents of Suraklin's files.

Then stick close enough to Gary to follow him through the Void. Magic wouldn't work on this side of it. He had to go back through. She remembered Antryg's words about Gary's still needing her and shivered. Getting through the Void might be easier than she was prepared to think about at the moment.

Then—Caris? Scarcely likely. The Prince? She shuddered again, recalling the evil glint of those pale eyes. For all his paranoia, he had put his trust once, hesitantly, in Antryg. He would never forgive the violation of that trust.

She pushed the panic urge to hurry to the back of her mind. First things first. You can't get to C until you've gotten A and B out of the way. Part of her wailed, *But they'll torture him,* and the cool, semicomputerized portion of her brain retorted that there was nothing to do but what she was doing. Hurrying would only make it last at least fifty percent longer.

She hit the reset button, opened the modem, dialed, and selected the S for San Serano from the menu. When the carrier tone whined, she punched in Gary's user number and stared at PASSWORD? flicking into life at the center of the screen. Her finger touched the break key, to interrupt function so she could run the main hacker program through.

I can't do anything else, she told the sudden, anxious misery in the pit of her stomach. It could take days—breaking into the files of an employee at San Serano whom she'd idly suspected—correctly—of being a CIA employee had taken weeks.

Antryg was in the hands of the Witchfinders. He didn't have weeks.

Whether Antryg had killed Salteris or left him alive, imbecilic as the Emperor was, he'd been extremely lucky that Caris hadn't cut his throat on the spot. Perhaps that's what Suraklin had been angling for.

There's nothing else I can do, Joanna told herself again. It will take the time it takes. There are other preparations I have to make in the meantime. If I'm too late . . .

With sinking heart, she knew she almost certainly would be. There were 2,821,109,907,456 possible combinations of eight letters and digits. Even subtracting the some 60,000 entries from the dictionary breaker program and the baby-name program combined, the number remained astronomical . . . and that was only the eight-letter combinations. It could conceivably be smaller. Eight was only the outside limit.

Then she thought, *Suraklin* has eight letters.

So does *Salteris.*

She hit the escape key, and typed, SURAKLIN.

PASSWORD INADMISSIBLE.

She muttered a word she'd picked up from Caris and tried again.

SALTERIS.

PASSWORD INADMISSIBLE.

It had been, she thought, too easy. But the ebb of the rush of hope was hurtful, more so than if she had simply put through the hacker program and gone to bed. Her throat aching, she thought, *I can't be too late to save him. I can't. . . .*

The cursor blinked at her in the gloom. Across the room, the window was no longer black, but a sickish gray, surrounded by a frame of inky shadow. The tepid air felt clammy and close. She was sorry she had hoped. She had been a fool—as Antryg was a fool. Magic was predicated upon hope, he had once said. And it was upon hope, upon life, that the Dark Mage's computer would feed, draining the life of the world.

Joanna frowned to herself, something snagging in the back of her mind. She looked back at the screen. She had one more try at manually breaking into the password, before turning it over to the hacker program, and it occurred to her there was one other eight-letter combination some-one connected with Suraklin might use.

She typed in, DARKMAGE.

The screen went blank, the green shadows of the letters fading sharply out. Then in the middle of the darkness blossomed the words:

WELCOME TO THE SAN SERANO COMPUTER

Her breath went out in a shaky sigh. Her hand a little unsteady with tiredness, she hit the printer switch. The machine hummed to life with a faint, preliminary whirr.

She glanced at the clock again. It was nearly six—time enough to start that long line of subroutines toward a goal too frightening to think about whole.

She typed, PRINT FILES, drained the remains of her cold tea, stood up achingly, and headed for the shower. Behind her, the printer chattered to itself in the darkness.

THE SILICON MAGE

FOR BILL THE TIME LORD
AND THE BIONIC GIMP,
TWO TRUSTED FRIENDS.

My special thanks to Sam Pahalnuk, Diana Paxson, Carrie Dougherty, Adrian Butterfield, and Brynne Stevens for technical advice on a variety of subjects about which I knew nothing. This story could not have achieved its present shape without the wisdom and skill which they so generously shared.

CHAPTER I

THE WORST THING ABOUT KNOWING THAT GARY FAIRCHILD HAD been dead for a month was seeing him every day at work.

"So whatcha doing after we get outta here tonight, babe?"

Joanna Sheraton tried not to stiffen, tried to recapture the half-tolerant, half-evasive tone characteristic of her conversations with him before . . . before. "I don't know, Gary. Ruth and I had talked about going to the movies." It sounded tinnily unconvincing even to her own ears.

Gary's face, as he leaned around the avocado burlap-padded partition into her cluttered programming cubicle, fell into its familiar pout. But there was a rehearsed quality to it, as there was to the slouching stance of that compactly muscled body in its assortment of Sears' best polyesters. It was something he knew Gary used to do, but now and then he forgot and stood straight and poised. There was an amber glint far back in the brown eyes, worlds distant from Gary's doglike eagerness.

Joanna felt her heart pounding fast and turned back to comparing the green lines of information on her terminal with the bug-riddled runout of the Tiger missile test analysis program, so he wouldn't see the nervous tremor of her mouth.

"Babe, what's the matter? You mad at me?" He had the whine down perfect that time.

She swung around a tad too quickly. "No. That is . . ." It was astonishingly difficult to remember patterns of voice and behavior several months old, particularly when she thought about them consciously—particularly with those brown eyes, watchful now, studying her face. She swallowed hard and pushed back the feathery tangle of untidy blond curls from her face.

"Babe, listen." He came around the partition, removed a stack of printouts from the cubicle's other chair, and sat down with that new, lithe grace, reaching out to take her hands. The nails were growing back —Gary had habitually bitten them to the quick. It was the closest that she'd let him get to her since she'd guessed what had happened to Gary —to the real Gary.

She made herself calm, made her eyes meet his.

He went on, "I don't know where you went when you disappeared at the end of August, or what happened to you . . ." That was a lie. He knew, all right; the only thing he didn't know was how much she had realized on the night of her return. "But I know something's been bothering you ever since you came back. You've been avoiding me."

"No!" Again it was too quick. The management of San Serano habitually turned off the air conditioning in Building Six around three in the afternoon; the close swelter of the October heat was, she hoped, enough to account for the crawl of sweat down her face and neck. Stammering, she tried to recoup. "I've been sort of avoiding everybody, Gary. Really, I just—I just don't want to see anyone now."

He smiled a little. "That's why you're going to the movies with Ruth?" His fingers tightened over hers. She hoped to hell they didn't feel as cold to him as they did to her. His eyes warmed with all Gary's old shallow charm. "You've got to deal with it sometime, babe. Get it out in the open." Past the cubicle door, voices sounded, and the scuff of feet echoed oddly in the high ceilings of the plant's testing bays just beyond the computer section where they sat. It was five o'clock. People were going home.

Hastily she pulled her hands away from him. Over her shoulder, as she began to stumble through backup procedures, he went on. "Why don't you come out to dinner with me, we go back to my place, and we talk. Okay?"

Two and a half months ago the invitation would have meant merely that he was going to try and talk her into bed with him. Now she knew, with a cold that seemed to spread from her hands and feet to the very pit of her stomach, that what he wanted was to get her alone.

"Another time, Gary." Her hands fumbled the typed commands; she hit the ESCAPE button and tried again, hoping he wouldn't read her fear and begin to ask himself why.

"Babe . . ." He came around behind her and put his hands on her shoulders, bare in the sleeveless top that was the only answer to the heat of an unspeakable California autumn. She had to clench her teeth and fight not to strike his hands away with loathing and terror. "Next week?"

"Maybe . . ." For a horrifying instant she blocked on the proper command to get out of the mainframe, her distracted mind praying he wouldn't notice.

"Tuesday?"

She was about to say "Maybe" again, then realized that every moment the discussion lasted, people were leaving the plant. In a very few minutes Building Six would be virtually empty, and he wouldn't have to maneuver to get her alone . . .

She turned in her swivel chair, looked up into his eyes, and conjured up a sigh. "All right."

He smiled, but there was a gleam of a different triumph in his eyes.

She was shaking all over as she walked out to the parking lot.

He had been trying for weeks to get her alone, sometimes subtly, sometimes blatantly; like her, he was working delicately around things that he wasn't supposed to know, pretending he didn't know exactly what had happened to her in those weeks at the end of summer when she'd been gone, pretending he hadn't met her on the other side of the dark Void that separated universe from universe.

He hadn't been Gary then, of course.

Joanna shivered as she started up the car, a decrepit blue bomber of a '75 Mustang, remembering the frail, delicate old Archmage, the head of the Council of Wizards, Salteris Solaris. He'd fooled them all: his grandson the young warrior Stonne Caris; Gary—the real Gary, in those days —whom he'd duped into acting for him on this side of the Void; and all the Wizards of the Council . . . herself . . . He'd fooled them, and had left poor Salteris' stripped-out husk of body and mind to migrate on and devour Gary's self in his turn, as he'd left others.

He was Suraklin the Dark Mage, now after her.

The damnable thing was that there was no proof.

It was no wonder, she thought, that Antryg Windrose went insane.

She guided the car down the long stretch of Lost Canyon Road to where the Ventura Freeway lay, a glittering snake of constipated steel wavering with heat-dance, and wondered bleakly if Antryg were still alive.

He has to be, she thought, a threadbare litany with which she had tried to sustain herself for the last four weeks. *Please, God, don't let him be dead.*

She had no proof of that, either.

Tears of remorse, anger, and shame burned her eyes.

Likewise, she had no proof that those blank periods of gray and cause-less depression that had more and more often troubled her and everyone she knew were anything other than her own unsettled mind. Yes, at such times no one at San Serano seemed to be able to do any work or to perform such tasks as they attempted correctly; yes, such spells coincided with an increase in newspaper accounts of both suicides and senseless gang violence, not only in Los Angeles, but in San Francisco, New York, Tokyo, London, or anywhere else she could read about. One or two newspapers had come up with facile sociological theories about economic anxiety and shifts in demographics. They might even have been right. But going downstairs to visit her friend Ruth after one such spell, Joanna had seen the painting on which Ruth had spent weeks, gessoed over with great, impatient smears of hardening white.

That was still not proof that the life-energy of the world was being intermittently drained and bled—not fatally, or at least not intrinsically fatally—across the Void, to create electricity to power a computer in a world which had neither.

In the last four weeks, Joanna had read a great deal about that com-puter in Suraklin's files.

She nosed the Mustang up the freeway on ramp, one tedious car length at a time, and into the sluggish flow of traffic. Whatever air-conditioning system the car had once possessed had bitten the big one years ago; she relied on what Ruth called four-eighty air conditioning; one opened all four windows and drove at eighty. It worked when one wasn't trying to get down the 101 at five-fifteen on a Friday afternoon with everybody else in the southern half of the state of California. At least she was inbound, toward L.A. instead of away from it; the traffic *was* moving—at about two yards per hour, but moving. The outbound lanes were stopped in both directions as far as the eye could see.

The slowness gave her time to think about tonight, and with thought came fear.

She'd been living with fear for over a month now and she hadn't gotten used to it yet. The abnormally heavy traffic reminded her again that it was Friday, making her heart triphammer with dread. There was a good chance that it would be tonight. . . .

She and Antryg Windrose had guessed that Suraklin had a computer whose electrical/magical power relays fed on life, hidden in some for-tress, some cavern, or some other hideaway in the Empire of Ferryth, the world on the other side of the Void, before she'd ever tapped into Surak-lin's files. For months Gary had been programming them into the big Cray mainframe at San Serano, while he'd worked at stealing by modem-powered computer-scam an experimental mainframe of artificial-intelligence proportions to set up on the other side of the Void. It was ultimately ironic, she thought wryly, that, having stolen via computer, Gary's personality, his self, should now be nothing more than a series of programs logged in a computer's electronic guts.

She'd seen that program. Everything about Gary—his likes and dislikes, his intricate network of computer-tapped bank accounts, the affairs he'd carried on with other women while he'd sworn his undying love to her, and the details of the particularly nasty variety of pornography he'd favored—had all been neatly digitalized. In other files, she'd found the details of the old Archmage Salteris' personality and what had been that of the poor imbecilic Emperor of Ferryth, whose shell still stumbled drooling through the palace at Angelshand while his mad son ruled the Empire.

And with them was the personality, the memories, and the knowledge of the man who had stolen and inhabited the bodies and minds of the Emperor, of Salteris, and of Gary in turn—the evil old man whose speech patterns and gestures Gary occasionally used and whose amber cat-glint eyes had watched her so intently today, the wizard Suraklin, whom all had once called the Dark Mage.

The computer was his ticket to eternity. Joanna knew it existed and knew he was programming his personality, petrifying it in everlasting silicon, so that he would at last live forever. The drain on the life-energies of her own world and of the world in which the computer itself was situated—the world across the Void—wasn't strong enough to kill. It would only maim, in a way for which there was no word, forever.

She knew it existed, but she had no proof.

She was fighting him absolutely alone.

She edged the car out of traffic, off the freeway and into a supermarket parking lot in Encino, still halfway across the San Fernando Valley from her home. From the front seat, she fished her purse, a monstrous affair of macramé and bunny skins the size and weight of a dead Labrador dog; from the trash pit of the trunk she dug a blue nylon backpack of the kind schoolkids carry books in, crammed to bursting and heavy as if it contained lead. Slinging these over her shoulder, she locked up the car and crossed the parking lot on foot, a small, sturdy girl, her untidy blond curls now damp and matted with sweat, like a schoolkid herself in her worn blue jeans and sleeveless top. Within fifteen minutes she was on a bus headed back toward San Serano.

Definitely, she thought, *a candidate for the Academy for the Bewildered.* Her behavior in the last month—breaking into computer files, hiding her car and sneaking back to the darkened plant after everyone was gone, avoiding the man she'd been sleeping with for the last two years—was bizarre enough to qualify her as a paranoid in anybody's book. Her dreams were something she wouldn't wish on her worst enemy.

"I've spent most of my life terrified of a man who's been dead for years," Antryg Windrose had told her once. And she understood now how the Prince Regent had become a hopeless paranoid at the age of ten, positive that his father the Emperor had ceased to be his father and unable to prove it to a soul.

She leaned her head against the vibrating metal of the window frame of the bus, closed her eyes, and tried not to smell the fattish man in a brown leisure suit who'd come to sit next to her on the crowded conveyance.

The whole situation—the events of her disappearance, the terrible thing she had learned, the tall, gentle madman who had kept her safe both from the Inquisition and from the random abominations traveling now through the Void between universes—had the aspect of some hideous quadratic equation, with two solutions and no means of determining which was correct.

The daylight side of the equation was simply that she had been temporarily insane. That was easy. At Gary's house party last August, she'd imbibed some chemically enhanced punch, of which there'd been a fair amount, and had undergone a long period of illness and violent hallucinations, peopled by wizards, warriors, evil princes, and the kind of man whose love she had always craved. And, like Judy Garland in *The Wizard of Oz*, she had waked again to a black-and-white world of people she had known all her life saying soothingly to her, "It was only a dream, dear; only a dream."

The night side of the equation was also a dream.

That dream had come to her a few nights after her return to this world from wherever she had been. It had recurred—cloudy, haunting, terrible —five or six times since.

In the dream she was in a stone-walled room, like the dungeon of the Inquisition from which Antryg had rescued her; by its heavy proportions, it was somewhere underground. Clammy cold radiated from the damp wall behind her, but she was sweating from the heat that blazed from the condensed cherry flames on the room's small hearth. A man was working at the fire, bent over it with his troll shadow flung vast and fidgeting on the curved stone of wall and roof groin, stripped to loincloth and shoes in the heat, with his skull shaved bald. In the corner where she stood, Joanna could smell the acrid reek of his sweat. The faint, brisk tapping of his little hammer on iron sounded loud in the silence, punctuating the crackle of the coals and the asthmatic hiss of the bellows being worked for him by a girl apprentice whose sleeveless shift showed biceps like a man's. She, too, was shaved bald, as was the big, clumsy-looking woman in gray velvet robes who stood before the hearth, perspiration trickling down the fatty rolls of her neck. The smell of unwashed wool, wet earth, and smoke lay heavy on the air.

That fat woman was looking, not at what the smith was doing by the fire, but at the doorway opposite, a low black arch of shadows, sinister as the maw of some Boschian beast.

In time, there was movement in that dark, and the fat woman in gray folded her hands over her stomach and smiled.

The man they brought in was taller than all but two of the guards who held him. When Joanna had stood in the circle of his arms, her head had not come as high as those broad, bony shoulders. Framed in a tangled explosion of graying brown hair, his face was chalky with exhaustion, the wide gray eyes in their bistered hollows dilated with drugs.

The big woman stepped forward, her eyes like pieces of chipped blue glass in the pouchy flesh. "Antryg Windrose," she said, and the prisoner raised his head.

Without his spectacles, Joanna knew he was half-blind. She saw the swooping network of lines—raying back from eyelids to temples and down over his cheeks—tighten as he tried to get her into focus.

"Antryg Windrose, do you confess to the crimes of which you have been accused?"

He drew in breath to speak, then paused. Sweat shone in the torchlight on his upper lip, the preposterous arch of his nose, and the pit of his throat, visible through the tattered collar of the coarse robe he wore. Asleep, dead—fifty years from now, Joanna knew she would recognize his voice in her dreams.

"Herthe, I don't care what you do to me, but please believe that killing me will not remove the danger you're all in. Suraklin . . ."

A guard behind him did something to one of his pinioned arms; he cried out and the other guard caught him as his knees buckled. In the crazily leaping shadows, Joanna could see that the first guard was Stonne Caris, the Archmage's grandson.

The woman Herthe stepped forward as the guards dragged Antryg upright again. "Do not name your master to us," she said softly. "And do not think to frighten us into letting you live. You have already signed the confession of your crimes." Her voice sank lower, cold as poisoned ice. "Is it necessary that, as Bishop in charge of this Inquisition, I require you to do so again?"

He looked away from that flat stare, and a shudder went through his body. His voice was almost inaudible. "No."

"Do you confess to violating the first law of the Council of Wizards, to breaking your vows to the Council never to use your powers, either for ill or for what seems good, in the affairs of humankind?"

He nodded, still not meeting her eyes. "Yes."

"Do you confess to attempting to murder the Prince Regent Pharos by means of magic?"

"Yes."

"Do you confess to the murder of Salteris Solaris, Archmage of the Council?"

He closed his eyes, fighting within himself against grief, guilt, and despair. It was a long time before he could speak; and then, it was only the soundless movement of his lips. "Yes."

The Bishop signed to the blacksmith beside the hearth. He straightened up, holding in his hands the thing he had been forging. Those of Antryg's guards whom Joanna recognized by their black robes as wizards fell hastily back. Caris, too, a wizard born, flinched and averted his face from it, though he did not release his grip on Antryg's arm.

Panic and despair flooded the mad wizard's gray eyes. "No," he whispered desperately, and tried to back away; Caris twisted his arm again, brutally forcing him forward. "Herthe, that isn't necessary. The Sigil of Darkness is on the Tower door; that is enough. I can't touch it, can't pass it, no wizard can . . ."

"Yet you escaped from this Silent Tower before," the Bishop said impassively. A spurt of yellow firelight winked balefully on the iron collar in the smith's hands, flaring across the crooked symbol of lead and jewels worked into its center. "The Sigil of Darkness is the Seal of the Dead God, the death of power. It should keep you from escaping again until the time of your execution."

"I won't," Antryg said, his voice low and desperate, staring at the thing in the smith's hands as if hypnotized. "I swear to you I won't try to escape, only don't . . . You don't understand, you're not a wizard, please . . ."

The smith stepped forward, the iron collar in his hands. It took four guards to force Antryg to his knees, to strip back his faded robes, and to hold him immobile by the hair, the arms, the shoulders, while the smith fixed the collar around his neck and soldered shut its lock. Caris was one of them; but, mageborn as he was, even the proximity of the Sigil left him sweating and gray-lipped. Though his grip never slacked, not once throughout did he look at the thing they were fastening against Antryg's flesh. Only when they were done and the other guards released him did Caris thrust the renegade wizard from him, sending him sprawling to the filth of the stone floor.

Every time she had dreamed this, Joanna fought to leave the shadowy corner where she stood to go to his side. It was like trying to move, not under water, but smothered like a fly in the treacly amber of the firelight. Even her cries were stillborn in her aching throat. For a long minute, there was no sound in that dreadful room, save the cracking of the fire, and Antryg's hoarse, sobbing breath.

Then Caris asked quietly, "Why this?"

The Bishop fixed upon him her clammy blue gaze.

In a face still white from the mere closeness to the Sigil of Darkness, the young man's brown eyes smoldered with hate. "He has confessed and been condemned by the Emperor, by the Witchfinders, and by the Council of Wizards. Why take the trouble of binding his powers, instead of killing him now? Has someone on the Council gotten jealous of the Council's rights to judge its own?"

"You are a sasennan of the Council, Caris, their living weapon." The words came out as flat and cold as her fishbelly eyes. "It is not for the sword to question the hand that wields it."

Passion shook his low voice. "Salteris was my grandfather, damn you!"

"Caris." Ghostlike, the form of the wizard Lady Rosamund materialized in the darkness of the low doorway, the mage who had led in Antryg's arrest. Behind the glitter of her bullion-stitched stole of office, she seemed little more than shadow within shadow, and those gathered behind her even less than that. "You put that away," she reminded him, "when you took your vows as sasennan. From that moment, you had no grandfather. It is nothing to you which member of the Council has spoken for this man's life, or why. Until that vote changes, he remains as he is."

Huddled in the shadows, Antryg had turned his face from the other wizards and covered it with his hands, as if by so doing he could hide from them. Twice Joanna had seen his fingers move toward the iron collar, but he could not bring himself to touch it. His whole body shivered. She thought he wept.

The hearth fire had sunk to a bed of rubies on powdery ash. The smith and his apprentice had already departed. In the blood-colored glare, the Bishop gave that crumpled form one last scornful glance and followed, with her black-clothed guards about her; the wizards faded back into the shadows from whence they had come. For a time Caris alone remained, looking after them, his face like carved bone dyed by the sinking embers, motionless but for the somber glint of his eyes.

Then he turned and walked to where Antryg lay.

The wizard was silent. Only by the shaky draw and release of his breath could Joanna tell that he was alive at all or conscious. The rags of his robe had been pulled down off his shoulders; in the dull carmine light, she could make out the angles of scapula and vertebrae under taut, fine-textured white skin.

Caris knelt beside him and drew his dagger. At the noise, Antryg raised his head, struggling up against some great weight of despair. Seizing him by the shoulder, the young man thrust him back against the stones of the wall. Coppery reflections of the fire glinted on the long blade, on the sweat that ran down Antryg's face and chest, and on the evil jewels in the iron and lead of the collar.

For a time Antryg looked, not at the blade that hung inches from his naked throat, but at the sasennan's eyes. Then very slowly he brought up his hands, and Joanna saw that his fingers were all splinted and bandaged, swollen as if every joint had been dislocated. Gritting his teeth slightly against the pain, with the edge of one wrist he pushed back the sleeve of his robe to expose ropy muscle and veins tracked to the elbows with whitened scars.

"Please," he said softly. "I'd take it as a great favor."

In one savage move Caris hurled him aside and jerked upright to stand over him. For that instant, no matter how many times Joanna had dreamed this scene, she thought that he would kick Antryg with fury and frustration and hate. But he turned on one booted heel and snapped the dagger back into its sheathe. The firelight blinked on its hilt as he strode into the darkness of the doorway, leaving Antryg lying alone, like a broken scarecrow in the gathering dark.

After a long time, the wizard crawled to his feet. Holding himself upright against the walls with his bandaged hands, he stumbled toward the door and beyond its darkness to the stair that led to his prison in the Silent Tower above.

The bus lurched to a stop at the gates of San Serano, and Joanna got out. The shuddering heat of the day radiated through the soles of her battered hightop sneakers from the asphalt as she crossed the parking lot to Building Six; the empty hills that surrounded the plant loomed like brownish cardboard cutouts in the smog.

You mustn't think about Antryg, she told herself wearily. Not of the lightness of those big hands as he'd taught her to drive Prince Cerdic's carriage nor those evenings they'd spent at the posthouses along the road from Kymil to Angelshand, drinking ale and talking. Not the tones of that remarkable voice, deep and beautiful like some lunatic Shakespearean actor's nor the desperate heat of his lips against hers. That was one thing nobody ever mentioned, she thought wryly—that the obverse side of learning to care for someone was that you couldn't stop caring when it hurt.

The straps of the heavy backpack cut into her shoulder. It contained a variety of things, mostly bought out of money pilfered by computer from Gary's various illegal bank accounts—bank accounts he had filled by computer theft from financial institutions across the United States. She'd found everything about them—account numbers, amounts, even the break-in program he'd modemed into all those banking computers after hours—in the programs of his personality in the DARKMAGE files. It hadn't taken much tinkering to help herself. Gary and Suraklin between them—*between him?* she couldn't help wondering—had done a good deal of evil. She considered it only right that they should finance her expedition to free Antryg—And he *is* alive! she insisted desperately to herself. He *is!*—and defeat Suraklin's plan.

She couldn't go on fighting him alone.

So she'd bought cultured pearls and synthetic sapphires and rubies, beef jerky and Granola bars, a lightweight water bottle and a six-inch sheathe knife to go with the Swiss Army knife she already had, duct tape, nylon cord, a bundle of plastic-coated copper wire, carbide hacksaw blades, and various other supplies. From a pair of costumers she knew who catered to the Renaissance Faire crowd, she'd ordered a gown made to the best of her recollections that would pack small, but, once unpacked, would allow her to pass inconspicuously in a society that frowned upon women wearing trousers. The thought of passing herself off as a boy, as so many romantic heroines seemed able to do, had crossed her mind, but one glance in the mirror put the kibosh on that one.

She'd bought a .38 Colt Diamondback and a cleaning kit and had practiced until the blasting roar and the kick no longer twitched at her aim. She had toyed with the notion of going to one of the jock hackers she knew for some kind of portable induction coil simply to degauss the stolen computer's circuits; but from what she had read of its specs, she knew its shielding was up to anything a battery was likely to generate, and there was no guarantee she'd be able to tap into the computer's magical electrical source herself. The idea of high explosive she'd simply discarded; aside from the legal restrictions entailed in acquiring it, she

knew herself to be far too inexperienced to use or transport it with anything resembling safety.

But input is input. If Gary—Suraklin—could transfer programs from
the San Serano mainframe to his new computer, so could she. So in a
special pocket of her backpack, reinforced with metal and wrapped in
layer after layer of plastic, was her best and most illegal wipe-the-disk
worm program.

For the rest, her backpack was jammed with hardcopy. Some of it
photoreduced and Xeroxed almost to illegibility, some merely shoved in
at random as it came off the modem-lines that she hadn't even had time
to look at. She'd been hacking into the DARKMAGE files for a month;
but owing to the sheer volume of them, there had been so little time. So
little time, she thought—but more than enough for Antryg to be . . .

Stop that! she ordered herself. *Antryg is alive. He has to be. He has
to . . .*

And if he wasn't, she knew, with cold and sinking dread, she'd have to
stop Suraklin herself.

They'd already shut down most of the lights in Building Six. Very
quietly, Joanna moved down the blue-carpeted corridors of the empty
typing pools, between programmers' deserted cubicles. She had stolen
back into San Serano this way at least twice a week for the last month,
and it always brought up in her a variety of emotions; but paramount,
horrifying, in her mind was the knowledge that Suraklin still needed her.
He had kidnapped her once before when he was planning to take over
Gary's body, and knew he'd need a programmer in his universe under his
influence to take Gary's place. Rather, he had gotten Gary to kidnap her
and had himself taken her across the Void. Had Antryg not been following him, she would even now be the Dark Mage's helpless puppet and
slave.

Almost the last thing Antryg had said to her when they'd finally taken
him was to warn her. And of course she hadn't listened.

Nearly ill with the violence of her hammering heart, she walked swiftly
along those darkened halls. If he met her now, he'd have her, and every
step she took closer to the Main Computer Room made her danger
worse.

Relax, she commanded shakily. *You've done this a dozen times.*

She was still shaking all over by the time she slipped into one of the
programming cubicles across the hall from the mainframe.

You've done this a dozen times . . .

*Left work with everyone else, to stash your car in a parking lot, en route,
but never the same parking lot, and sneaked back here by bus to take a*

roundabout way back into the plant to wait . . . Spent your time raiding computer files and toting around twenty pounds of backpack . . .

Altogether, she thought wryly, to quiet the shakiness in her chest, *this had damn well better not be a hallucination after all.*

She felt a little like a white-robed cultist who, having sold everything he owns, stands expectantly on his mountaintop, awaiting the end of the world. *And I'm going to feel just as silly,* she added, *trudging down home again . . .*

Feet swished softly on the carpet outside. Joanna flattened her body against the wall behind the cubicle's half-open door and angled her head sideways to look through its crack. For one flashing instant she identified Gary as he passed.

The Gary who was no longer Gary now, in the absence of anyone who had known Gary, didn't bother to keep up the pretense. In spite of years of conscientious weight-lifting, Gary—of medium height and slender build, despite a recent tendency toward paunchiness—had never looked particularly comfortable with his body. He walked now with an animal grace subtly at odds with the sensible gray polyester trousers and the pale quiana shirt.

Joanna saw he was carrying a briefcase, and her heart turned perfectly cold within her.

It was, after all, going to be tonight.

She'd guessed it when she'd tapped into the DARKMAGE files early this morning and found large sections of them gone. No modem-lines stretched across the Void. He was doing his programming on the San Serano mainframe, but he had to transfer his files across the Void by hand.

She felt the terrified urge to cry. *Don't think about it,* she told herself severely and tiptoed soundlessly across the darkened cubicle to the phone. To her infinite relief, she got Ruth's answering machine. It had been a good bet she would—Ruth was rarely home—but the last thing she wanted right now was questions.

She said, simply, "Ruth, this is Joanna. Use your key to my place. There's a manila envelope on the table, with some instructions. *Please* carry them out. I'll explain when I see you, but that might not be for a few weeks. I'm not in any trouble. 'Bye."

Paranoid, schizo, obsessive, insane.

Why does it have to be me?

Antryg, she thought, must have felt the same.

Then something changed in the air. It was a sensation she would have been totally unable to describe—an unreasoning terror, a strange tingling of the nerves, a sense of standing on a beach whose shoreline is not water but the black drop-off into eternity. But once felt, it could not be mistaken for anything else. Dark winds seemed to whisper across her bones; she felt she could hear the murmuring echoes of unknown forces, moving in blackness.

The Void between the universes was being bridged. Suraklin was going across.

She was keyed to the shaking point as she slid out the cubicle door. *I can't let Suraklin see me,* she thought desperately. *As of now I've disappeared and left a plausible story for why I won't be seen for a couple of weeks. No one will look for me.*

But of course, if Suraklin took her now, it wouldn't matter if the search started tomorrow. No one would find her until she returned, her mind not her own.

Cold white light poured through the computer room door into the darkened corridor. The backpack with the purse strapped to it now dragged her shoulders, but she scarcely noticed. She thought, quite reasonably, *There's a nine o'clock bus back to Encino . . .* and put her head around the door.

And the good news is, she thought half-hysterically, *it wasn't all a hallucination.*

That is, unless I'm having a hallucination now.

There was darkness in the computer room.

Darkness, hideously, surrounded by the fluorescent blaze of the lights; like a cloud of gas, but definitely not a vapor, not a substance at all. A darkness that seemed to stretch away, never reaching the rear wall with its banks of green-eyed monitor lights, but seeming to extend far past it, a ghostly corridor that stretched to the abysses of infinity. Far off, along that great gulf of nothing, she sensed movement.

There was no one now in the computer room. At its edges, the darkness was already beginning to disperse.

And the bad news is . . .

. . . It wasn't all a hallucination.

And you're going to have to walk into it.

A small voice within her suggested timidly, *Can't I just go home and forget the whole thing?*

Not allowing herself to think any further about that very real option, Joanna strode forward into that darkness.

CHAPTER II

IT WAS BEYOND A DOUBT THE MOST FRIGHTENING THING SHE HAD ever done. She hadn't gone two steps when she wanted to turn around and go back, but she knew already she dare not even look over her shoulder to see if it were possible. Far in the lightless Void ahead of her Gary's—Suraklin's—yellow polyester shirt was a flitting blur. If she lost sight of that, she would be lost indeed.

Vertigo swamped her, the sensation of falling, the terror of feeling nothing beneath her feet. She struggled forward, half-running, half-swimming, tractionless and desperate to keep that pale will-o'-the-wisp in sight, smothering in darkness such as she had never known. Tears burned her eyes, tears of terror and resentment. When she had gone through to that other world the first time she had been unconscious; coming back, Salteris'—Suraklin's—thin, strong hand had been her guide.

Don't think, she told herself. *Caris could follow a man through the Void unguided; you can, too.* Cold that was not really cold was leeching the strength from her veins. She ran/swam/flew through the darkness, fighting frantically not to lose sight of the man who would destroy her if he found her now.

The darkness was alive. She knew it, felt it, sensed the vast amorphous things that floated in that frozen emptiness; she heard the dry, glittery whisper of something close behind. Panting, wheezing breath, she wondered, or her own desperate gasping as she struggled to keep Suraklin in sight? Her sweat, dripping from her hair in icy droplets, cold on the bare flesh of her arms, or . . . ?

She ran harder, sobbing, not daring to look behind her. Only the fact that she could not stop to get her breath prevented her from screaming Suraklin's name, pleading with him to come back and fetch her. If he needed her services as Antryg had said, he couldn't let her be lost in the Void.

He was gone.

Darkness was around her, wind—or something else—clawing the ends of her flying hair. There was no blur ahead of her, only plunging darkness, livid with the sense of writhing things. Far off to her right, something bright caught her eye, fragile, milky light, and she sensed the smell of rain. Though it was nowhere near the direction she had last seen Suraklin, she veered toward it, running as she had never run before, running in heartbursting panic, with the pack dragging her shoulders, like the weighted flight of nightmare. Something swooped at her, some winged and flabby thing whirling out of the aphotic pits of this nonbeing; she felt it cut her arm, felt blood hot on the cold flesh. She didn't look, only ran harder. Time had stopped; she felt as if she had been running for hours, aimless and in terror. What if she had been? she wondered frantically. What if the light before her vanished as Suraklin had? What if it was only a lure? What if she never got out, if this would go on until she died? What if she didn't die? Her hair tangled in her eyes, the pack was dragging on her, pulling her back, and the light was drifting away, fainter and fainter . . .

Then it was clear before her, a white moon burning full and clear in a wide-flung double ring of ice mists above a broken line of standing-stones. Sodden grasses whipped Joanna's calves as she ran; cold sliced her arms, damp and raw. Behind her she heard the chitter and hiss that had filled her ears in the Void. Risking a glance over her shoulder, she saw it, as much of it as there was to see—something dark and floating, a chitinous tangle of long, knobby legs, with moonlight edging an aureole of floating tendrils like a woman's long hair in water. The tendrils reached out toward her, and, in the knot of darkness at the creature's center, things like specks of faceted glass caught the moonlight.

Her mind blurred with terror she ran, stumbling on the rough rise of the ground, racing until she felt her heart must burst toward the staring silver eye of the moon. She had the confused impression that, if she could get her back to one of the bigger standing-stones, she might at least have some chance. Where she had come through the Void, they were only low stumps, like broken fenceposts along the ancient path, if anything remained of them at all. Even as she ran, she cursed herself. Her knife was in her pack; she'd never get it out in time. *Caris would never let himself get caught like this . . .*

She flung herself against the nearest of the large stones, the pitted surface tearing at her hands. Blind with horror, she scrabbled at her pack and ripped free the velcro pocket. The blood was hot on her arm where the creature had cut her. In another second all those dangling claws would be on her. She dropped the pack and jerked the knife free of its sheathe, the blade jamming in its newness. Any second . . . Any second . . .

Barely able to breathe, she flattened back against the stone and faced her adversary.

It was gone.

It was out there in the darkness; she knew it, felt it, and could almost hear its faint, crackling whisper. But there was another sound, a muffled, rumbling thud in the earth, a groan.

She spun around, looking down the track into the moonwashed slot between the stones.

A rustling, moving shadow spread over the ground like water. Even with the thin lucency of the moon, it was hard to distinguish shapes, but after a moment she heard the groan again, deep and plaintive, and realized it was the lowing of a cow. Sheep bleated. Straining her eyes, Joanna could make them out now in the shadow: cloudy blobs of whitish wool; the blunted spark of brass horn-tips; and a vertical shape that could only be a walking man. Sweet, cold, and unbearably lonely, music curled like a black ribbon into the night, a haunted piping that threaded its way like wind between the stones. Like a counterpoint against the thudding of her heart, she heard the hollow pat of a drum.

Somewhere beyond the line of stones, out in the huge gulf of blackness that lay like a single velvet entity up to the glowing violet hem of the hill-crowded sky, the abomination waited.

Joanna remembered Antryg saying that whenever the Void was breached the whole fabric of the universe weakened; holes appeared not only in the vicinity of the Gate, but elsewhere in other universes, and through these holes abominations would drift. In veering from Suraklin's route, she might have stumbled through a hole opened along one of the energy-tracks that crossed the Empire of Ferryth. Or, she thought with a shiver, she might have fallen through to some other universe altogether, neither her own nor the one she sought.

Fine, she thought, with half-hysterical irony. *I've managed to screw up before I even got through the Void.*

She stepped cautiously back out of the main track between the stones, keeping her body still pressed to the icy, uneven surface of the menhir, the cold making her hands ache around the unaccustomed handle of the knife. The bobbing darkness down the track was coming nearer, resolving itself into a blur of dark shapes and green eyes flashing queerly in the moonlight. She smelled dung and dust in the sweetness of the trampled grass; fragile and terrible, the aching, single voice of the pipe tugged at her heart.

A sheep passed her, then a cow with a yearling calf. More cows followed, jostling one another, one of them so close she could feel the warmth of its body, then sheep in a dusty choke of wool-smell and hay. Dogs trotted between them, silent; then goats, a couple of pigs, a plowhorse the size of a Panzer tank, with a small boy walking nearly hidden in its shadow along that dark and silent track toward the moon. Other men and women walked among the animals, silent as they in the false, quicksilver light; dogs trotted at their master's heels, and half-grown girls carried cats in their arms.

In the trampled wake of the beasts walked a line of men, heads dark and disfigured by the horned beast masks they wore. There was something indescribably lonely and terrible about the dirge they played, like no music Joanna had ever heard, mourning for something no one understood anymore. The black horns bobbed and swayed in the ashy moonlight. Under the jutting muzzles gleamed the silvery reflection of masked eyes. If they saw her as they passed her, standing shivering in the black pool of moonshadow, they gave no sign.

Last of all she saw what she thought was a catafalque made up from a farm wagon, drawn by cows and sheep, though it was almost impossible to tell in the darkness. She thought that on it lay the body of a man, eyes shut, face and hands blackened, clothed in rags, with a deer's antlers fixed to his dark forehead. She seemed to hear Antryg's deep voice: "All things travel along the lines, resonating forward and back . . . On certain nights of the year the peasants still drive their herds along them, in commemoration of the Dead God, though they've forgotten why he died . . ."

Well, at least, Joanna thought wryly, *I've come to the right world. Fine. Now you have to worry about Suraklin.*

Her first impulse was to follow them, knowing they would lead her eventually back to their village, to shelter and warmth for the night. It was bitterly cold—belatedly, Joanna remembered that, for all its damp and smothering heat in midsummer, the Empire of Ferryth lay well to the north of the latitudes of California. The thin windbreaker wadded in her backpack would be about as much use to her as a pair of lace ankle sox. *Swell. You not only screwed up while you got through the Void, but you didn't do so good before you entered it, either.*

But even as she moved to pick up her backpack and follow, Joanna glanced out into the darkness, and saw something moving, like a floating spider, far out in the darkness, paralleling the course of the stones. Moonlight tipped the end of a floating spun-glass tendril. The abomination, too, was following the funeral of the Dead God.

Was it the music that drew it? she wondered. Or the smell and the heat of blood? She huddled down again, her back to the blue-black shadow of the eroded stone, trembling as she pulled the useless windbreaker from her pack and prepared to wait out the night. Far off, like the voices of the dead, the pipes cried alone in the darkness.

Had it not been for the abomination, Joanna might have backtrailed the swathe of trampled grass and animal dung back to the village from which the macabre procession had set out. She felt cold and hungry and, once the first rush of adrenaline seeped from her veins, exhausted; even if the villagers had left watchdogs prowling around their homes, even if they weren't likely to welcome a stranger snooping about the place in their absence, surely she could take refuge in some friendly haybarn until dawn. But the thought of being in any enclosed place in this black gloom —the thought of being without a clear line of sight in all directions and something absolutely solid at her back—gave her a shrinking feeling in the pit of her stomach; she huddled all the tighter into her thin jacket and stayed where she was. The long trough of the energy-track, marked only here and there with an occasional small menhir in the direction of the village, but as visible in the wan moonlight as a paved highway, stretched away into the shadowy hills. It was a long walk, not knowing what might drift above or behind her in the dark.

The depression, when it came, turning the fragile beauty of the moonlight to flint, even as it sucked the hope from Joanna's soul, made everything a thousand times worse.

Joanna knew what it was and had been expecting it. After all, Suraklin had crossed the Void to use his computer on this side of it, and the computer fed on electricity converted by relays of teles-balls from the energy, the hope, and the life-force of every human being in her own world, this one, and who knew how many besides.

She, at least, was aware now that the numbness in her soul was externally caused, not the result of some fading within herself, and that put her ahead of literally every other victim of the computer's far-reaching field. It didn't help, of course. She was still tormented by the knowledge that she would fail and that what she did was pointless and would result, at best, in her permanent exile to this inconvenient, smelly world and, at worst, in her death or enslavement. She felt a growing conviction that Antryg was, in fact, long dead. It had been a month and more since the wizards had taken him. Even worse was the part of her that shrugged and said, "So what?" That part of her was seized with an impatience to get up and set out through the darkness for the village, half forgetting, as an alcoholic forgets his last bender when the liquor-fumes rise to his nose, that the abomination was somewhere out there. *It's following them —it won't get me,* she thought, resentment at her chapped hands and cramped knees flooding her, and only a mechanical resolution to do everything completely by the numbers made her stay where she was.

When a steel-colored dawn finally gave her a clear enough view of the surrounding countryside to make sure she was absolutely unthreatened and unobserved from any direction in the crowding shoulders of the hills, she got stiffly to her feet and changed into her dress—not particularly easy to do while keeping an eye on the landscape. The depression that choked her soul like sifted ash had not abated. Since this was Saturday, she didn't particularly expect it to. Gary—Suraklin—would undoubtedly continue his programming all morning and into the afternoon, and there would most likely be another such spell tomorrow.

At least, she thought, viewing the bony landscape of granite hills beneath its thin garment of rusty autumn grass, *I seem to have come to the right place.* But Antryg had said that the Sykerst, the rolling, barren lands of steppe and moor and waving lakes of grass through which they had walked from Kymil to Angelshand that summer, stretched two thousand miles to the east of the more populous areas of the Empire. If she were somewhere in the Sykerst—and these hills looked exactly similar to those she remembered—she could easily be anywhere in them.

Please don't let me be fifteen hundred miles from the nearest civilization, she prayed drearily, hoisting her backpack to her shoulder and cursing herself for filling it with paper. *Gimme a break, for Chrissake. This is going to be tough enough.*

As she trudged down the trampled path of the Dead God and his followers, the hem of her petticoat swirling around the hightop sneakers she had decided would be better for walking in, the other half of her mind retorted, *Don't bitch, baby, you made it to the right universe, didn't you?*

Did I?

I should have taken that nine o'clock bus back to Encino. Oddly enough, a glance at her watch sometime in the course of the night had showed her that, though it had felt as if she had run through the Void for at least half an hour, the time had not registered on her watch at all. As near as she could calculate, she had emerged a few minutes before nine o'clock—precisely the same time that she had stepped in.

It was now full daylight, the morning hard and clear and hot in the sky, when she saw the village, tucked into a little pocket of semifertile land among the looming gray hills. A few workers toiled desultorily among the tawny grain in the fields; harvesting, guessed Joanna, by the half-shaved stubble, but not going about it with any great enthusiasm. The sun seemed stiflingly hot on her unprotected head. *I should have remembered to bring a hat,* she told herself irritably, *and a groundcloth to sit on last night would have helped, too.* But here on the tall slope of a granite hill, she could feel the bite in the wind. She remembered how, all through the tail end of summer, the bleak weariness of these times had kept the haymakers from the fields—a physical exhaustion as much as an emotional one, for the drawing of energy down the paths to Suraklin's computer affected the body as well as the soul. Part of her recognized that the ruin of the harvest would mean hunger throughout the land. Another part simply did not care.

All she wanted now was a meal and a bed to sleep in. If possible, she wanted to sleep through tomorrow—to deal with all this later.

The wind turned; the smell of blood hit her nostrils as if she'd inhaled a dose of ammonia.

She knew the smell of blood. At the summer's end, on an island in the sluggish green Shan, she'd shot a Witchfinder at a range of under two feet. The blood had sprayed her as if from a hose. Antryg had dragged her into the water, washed the sticky horror from her clothes and hair almost before what she had done sank into her. But she'd never forget that cloying, sweetish reek.

Turning her head, she saw the distant clump of gorse on the hillside and how the iridescent cloud of flies glittered around it in the early sun. Not wanting to, but knowing that she'd have to know, Joanna gathered up handfuls of petticoat and skirts in a gesture that was to become second nature to her, and picked her way over the sloping ground.

It had been a pig. It lay in a little hollow, behind the stiff, gray-green clump of the gorse. Flies swarmed over it, industrial-strength rural flies, some of them two inches long, buzzing like B-52s in the stillness of the sheltered hillslope. The pig's flesh had fallen in over its bones, like a punctured balloon, as if all the fluids of its body had been sucked forth at once, though Joanna could tell that the kill was fresh, last night. It had not yet begun to stink. Its hide, what she could see of it, was beaded all over with dots of blood, as if it had been pricked with a thousand needles simultaneously. She remembered the floating, angel-hair tendrils of the abomination, reaching out in the shimmer of the moon.

Stumbling jerkily on the uneven ground, Joanna turned and walked swiftly away from it. She made her way downhill, not toward the village, where people might delay her with questions, but toward the narrow wagon track of ash-colored dust that wound away from it to the south. In spite of the exhaustion that dragged upon her and the dreadful sick weariness that filled her body like a bloating disease, she wanted to get away from this accursed country as far and as fast as she could.

A wagon was coming from the village, driven brutally fast, with an angry disregard of the horse or the road. Joanna thought, *To hell with him, I don't need that kind of driving, I'll wait for the next one,* and then realized that, as small as this village was, in the midst of the harvest season, this was probably the only outgoing vehicle she was going to catch all week. The fear of the abomination alive in her mind, if not in her numb heart, she ran to reach the edge of the road before the wagon passed.

"Stop!" she pleaded in English, hoping to goodness the spell of tongues Antryg had once laid on her would hold. "Help me!"

The driver stopped the horse with a savage yank of the reins; she saw the flecks of foam spray from the beast's wrenched mouth. The driver was a youngish man who had once been stout, but now had the slightly wrinkled, fallen-in appearance of a fast and unhealthy weight loss; his face was gray and pinched with anger. "What the hell do you be wanting, girl?" he yelled at her.

Thank God the spell works. "I'm trying to get to Angelshand. We were set on by highwaymen—they killed my brother." She wished as she said it that she could work up a more convincing delivery, but with the hot buzzing weariness in her head it was the best she could do. "Can you take me to the nearest town where I can get a stage? I have money . . ."

"What, that the highwaymen left you?" the driver jeered. "Money you stole from those you worked for, more like, when they turned you off!" He lashed his horse. The wheels flung dust on her as the wagon pulled away.

Joanna stood for a moment, her throat hurting with tears of resentment and rage. Blindingly, crazily, she wanted to fling rocks after the departing wagon and scream curses at its driver, the horse, and their whole smelly little village. Suddenly, overwhelmingly, she wanted to pull the gun from her pack and . . .

LIQUOR-STORE ROBBERS SHOOT THREE, the headlines had said last

week. GANG SHOOTING SPREE KILLS FIVE. WOMAN SHOOTS TEENAGE
DAUGHTER . . .

Among other things, that deadness, that uncaring in the soul, made it
very easy to pull a trigger if you happened to have one in your hand.

Joanna sighed. Beyond a doubt the yokel in the wagon had spoken out
of the same bled, gray ache that filled her own heart. After this spell of
draining ended, she supposed she'd feel sympathy for him. Right now the
rage in her, like the pus of an unburst boil, began its nauseating reabsorp-
tion into her body. She scrambled over the weed-grown ditch and bank,
brambles snagging her petticoat and the backpack straps cutting into her
shoulders, and began walking away from the village, but not really caring
where she went or why.

She was almost on top of the wagon before she realized it had stopped
and was waiting for her.

"I'm sorry, lass," the driver said in a weary, beaten voice. He pushed
back his sweat-stained felt hat and wiped his brow with an arm that
Joanna could have done chin-ups on, had not such exercises always been
beyond her. "I didn't mean to shout at you as I did." He extended a hand
the size of a small typewriter to help her over the high front wheels to the
straw-strewn board of the seat. Puzzlement and exhaustion struggled for
a moment behind his clear green eyes, and with them a hidden fear. "It's
just . . . I don't know what it is that's come over me of late."

Joanna could have told him, but it was no more believable in this
world than it was in her own.

It took her nine days to reach Angelshand; nine exhausting days of
being jolted, first in wagons, then in the public stagecoach, elbow-to-
elbow with coarse country squires, broadcloth-suited businessmen, talk-
ative matrons, and bald-shaved prelates, over roads deep in autumnal
mud. The gap in the Void through which she had come had opened deep
in the Sykerst, hundreds of miles from either Kymil, where she was
almost certain Antryg was being held, or Angelshand, where she hoped
to find help in rescuing him. Once the weary spell of deadness lifted, as it
did late that first afternoon, she realized she was extremely lucky she
hadn't come through on the other side of the world.

Still, it meant eight nights in some of the worst accommodations she
had ever encountered, sharing straw mattresses crawling with bedbugs
with whatever other female passengers happened to be on the stage that
day—and their babies, if they had them—lying awake, half-choked with
the foetor of unwashed clothes and bodies, scratching furiously at flea
bites, staring at the dark rafters overhead, and listening to the steady beat

of the rain on the shingles. *This doesn't even qualify as one-star,* she thought tiredly. *I'll give this two black holes. Why couldn't I be like those heroines who come through the time-warp or the dimensional vortex at most a day's walk from where they're trying to get to?*

The farmer who had given her a ride had introduced her to a friend of his in the next village, with instructions to take her on to a mutual acquaintance, a trusted Old Believer merchant in Sug's Beck, the nearest large town. Neither would even listen to her offers of payment, but she had left a sapphire with the merchant, who, like most of his faith, turned a few crowns in whatever he could, telling him to give them both whatever credit the jewel would buy. The merchant, an elderly man in the long black robes and elaborately braided hair of his people, had bought other jewels from her to give her money for the journey and had thrown in gratis a hot meal—care of his wife—a cloak, since by then the rains had begun, and a new dress, "Because a nice girl like you needs more than one dress."

The journey itself was exhausting and uncomfortable beyond belief. Joanna spent the first three days in a stupor of exhaustion and afterward alternated between almost unbearable anxiety over how long it was taking, the gnawing awareness that if Antryg were dead or if she couldn't manage his escape there was no way out of this world for her, and the unspeakable tedium of her fellow-passengers' conversation. The Council could change their vote and execute Antryg at any time, if they hadn't done so weeks ago while she was still raiding the DARKMAGE files from the San Serano computer.

Altogether, Joanna was heartily glad when the huge, unwiedly coach pulled into the yard of the Horn of the Hunter on the southern outskirts of Angleshand, and she stumbled—cramped, weary, and, she suspected, lousy—out of it for the last time into the raw, misty gloom of the early afternoon.

"Call you a hack, ma'am?" one of the porters inquired, and Joanna nodded, though the thought of getting into another horse-drawn conveyance affected her with an almost physical nausea. As the cab rattled north through first the suburbs, then the outlying slums and factory districts of the capital of the Empire of Ferryth, Joanna felt again the quickening of her heart and the hard twist of anxiety in her belly as she recognized landmark after landmark in that dark granite city. Buildings the color of iron loomed above the sheet-steel of the river against a sky dark with autumn and factory soot. Above the jammed higgledy-piggledy of rotting half-timbered gambrels on Angel's Island she caught a glimpse of the towers of the St. Cyr fortress, where the Bishop of Angelshand presided over the Inquisition and its Witchfinders. Even in this raw weather the streets teemed with beggars in rags, servants in a rainbow of livery, and swaggering sasenna in their black uniforms and razor-bright swords. Scarf-sellers, whores, and match and noodle vendors rubbed elbows with bourgeois ladies out for walks with their companions, clerks hurrying to their countinghouses, crossing-sweepers busily clearing horse dung out of the way for a copper, chimney sweeps, pickpockets, constables in red and blue uniforms, and butchers' boys driving their quick-footed ponies and trailed by gangs of yapping pariah dogs. From the packed bridge that joined Angel's Island with the wealthier precincts north of the river, Joanna glanced downstream to the harbor, where masts rose like a fire-stripped forest and the faint cries of the stevedores unloading all the wealth of the Empire mingled with the melancholy mewing of the gulls. Swirling below against the arches of the bridge, the river stank like the sewer it was.

The cabman had known the house she'd asked for—a fortunate circumstance, since Joanna couldn't remember the name of the square. By the time she climbed down and paid off the jarvey, the tightness in her chest had become almost unbearable; the fear that had slept in her all these last nine dreary days swelled again to smother her, the fear of being done with one stage and having to start on the next.

It was Joanna's nature to think in subroutines. It was, she supposed, the only thing which had permitted her to undertake her current impossible task. She had obtained as much of Suraklin's files, Suraklin's knowledge and personality, as she would be able to; she had prepared herself for the expedition—with the omission of a warm jacket, a hat, and a groundcloth, she reminded herself; she had made it this far. Over the course of the last nine interminable days she had tortured herself, like the victim of a Sunday-afternoon toothache, prodding at the pain and waiting for the dentist's office to open on Monday, by wondering, *What if he's gone? What if he was arrested? What if he won't help me . . . ?* until she was almost ill with apprehension.

But the narrow, disdainful townhouse in its fashionable setting was unchanged as she crossed the broad rectangle of autumn-brown grass in the center of Governor's Square. Five or six carriages, their teams thickly blanketed and puffing steam from their nostrils like dragons in idle, stood near the curb. The coachmen, both male and female, had gotten up a coal fire in a brazier on one corner and were huddled around it, warming their hands and talking shop. Her heart pounding, Joanna hitched her over-stuffed backpack up over one shoulder and climbed the marble steps of the one house in this world in which she hoped for refuge while she made her plans.

An extremely gorgeous young footman in fuchsia livery answered her knock, and looked down his beautiful nose at her when she admitted, blushing, that she didn't have a card to lay upon his little silver tray. *Add calling cards,* she thought irrelevantly, *to the list for next time.* "I'm afraid I haven't any with me," she said meekly, wishing she had had access to a hot bath and a dress that hadn't been worn for six or seven consecutive days in a crowded coach. The young footman's expression of disbelief deepened; Joanna found herself picturing what the Prince Regent would say about him, and immediately felt better. "If you'll tell Magister Magus that Joanna Sheraton is here, I think he'll want to see me."

The young man looked as if he did not see how this could be possible, but only said, "Very well, Miss. Walk this way," an unconscious Marx Brothers straight line which made Joanna want to giggle. It was odd, she thought, following him up the oval curve of the open stairway, how fleeing for her life from the abomination in the darkness had seemed less anxiety-producing than facing another person and asking for help.

And he has to help me, she thought blindly. *I have to start somewhere . . .*

Magister Magus' drawing room was, as usual, crowded with over-dressed ladies with high-piled hair, an ocean of jacquard petticoats, lace sleeve flounces, and jewelry that reduced Joanna's paltry hoard to bargain-basement gleanings. Most of their maids were better dressed than Joanna, and all of them looked down their rice-powdered noses at her travel-stained blue dress and the limp cloak that the footman took away. One elegant young matron who couldn't have been more than eighteen nudged her neighbor and nodded toward Joanna with a remark concealed behind a painted chicken-skin fan. The others, after a cursory glance, simply ignored her.

After nine days of stagecoach gossip and the endless accounts of her fellow passengers' illnesses and childbirths, Joanna was just as glad.

She was human enough to be thoroughly gratified, however, when a second footman opened the inner ebony doors of the drawing room, to usher out a solemn-looking lady in her sixties, and said, "Miss Sheraton?"

Demurely, Joanna got to her feet. As the doors shut behind her she heard a muffled, "Well, *really!*" The footman lifted a curtain from an arch, and Joanna found herself in a small consulting chamber even more opulently furnished than the lush pink-and-black room outside. Incense burned before a hematite statue of Kahieret, God of the Mages, with-drawn and dark as the velvet that draped its niche, and Magister Magus himself was just rising from his chair of inlaid ebony.

"My dear child!" He strode to her across the tufted silk of the carpet and caught her hands. "Antryg's friend the systems designer—your hands are freezing! I can spare but a moment now, my dear, but I've ordered tea for you in the dining room . . ."

She grinned shakily, relief at being recognized, let alone welcomed, making her throat feel suddenly hot and close. "It's all right. I can't have your customers getting in a snit."

"Are you hungry?" His eyes were anxious—light, almost white-green, within startling dark rings around the irises; he must have been months tracking down the peridots of just that color set among the diamonds of his pectoral cross. In spite of the black velvet robe and all the trappings of a fashionable society charlatan, there was a genuine warmth to him, a caring wholly apart from his professional charm. "My dear child, I'd heard . . ." He hesitated, seeing the sudden tightness of her expression, and veered from mentioning what she already must know. "Well, I was afraid you'd been hurt as well."

She shook her head, furiously fighting the urge to lean on that slender velvet shoulder and cry. It was unexpectedly, achingly good to be with someone who believed her and who would understand.

She was looking away from the Magus, and in any case her sight was suddenly blurred, but she felt the gentle touch of his hand on her shoul-der. "Now, my dear," that fluent, beautiful voice said. "We'll talk about it after you've rested a little and eaten. Are you . . . ?" He hesitated again. Looking up, Joanna saw tact and concern for her struggling in his face with worry for himself and almost laughed in spite of her tears.

"No, I'm not on the run. Nobody's after me." *At least,* she amended, *not the authorities.* She decided not to mention Suraklin until Magus was sitting down.

He made a deprecating noise, as if such considerations were the fur-thest thing from his mind, but looked relieved.

Then silence hung between them, silence balanced on the edge of an indrawn breath, like the silence in a lovers' quarrel in which neither dares speak for fear of the chain of events the next, inevitable utterance must unleash. The swollen hurt of the dread she had carried in her for nearly six weeks was nearly unbearable, but now that she faced the first person whom she could ask, the first person who could tell her, she found the words stuck in her throat.

And the Magus, looking down into her eyes, wore an expression of such pity and such unhappiness that he must be the one to answer the question which he knew she would ask that she felt her heart and bowels turn to sodden and ruinous ash. He knew what she was going to ask him, she thought, and he knew he'd have to be the one to tell her she had failed before she had begun.

Her voice was very small. "He's dead, isn't he?"

Magus sighed, not pretending he did not understand of whom they spoke. "I wish it wasn't me who has to tell you this," he said gently and took her hand in his, as if the touch of his fingers could somehow lessen what was to come. "No, he isn't dead, but—his mind is gone. The Inquisition tortured him, you know. I'm not sure what all they did, but when they were done, there wasn't much left. My child, I'm sorry."

CHAPTER III

I'M GOING TO HAVE TO DO THIS ALL BY MYSELF. JOANNA STARED blankly out into the misty charcoal gloom visible beyond the dining room windows, feeling the weight of terror constricting her chest like an iron band.

And then, *Oh, Antryg, I'm sorry.*

Joanna had never been a believer in *sorry.* Up until the last moment, when the wizards walked through the patio doors of Gary's house in Agoura, she could have cut Antryg's bonds and let him flee into the night.

She wondered why she had believed that a love as intense as the one she felt for him had to be suspect, that anything she wanted that badly couldn't be right.

Weak tears gathered in the inner corners of her eyes and she gritted her teeth against them, thankful for the warmth of the cup of steaming tea cradled in her cold hands.

"I doubt that either of us would even recognize him anymore," Magister Magus was saying gently. "They say for days all he did was huddle in a corner and weep, or scream and pound on the walls with his hands." Joanna shut her eyes, remembering the splints on those twisted fingers. "I've heard that these days he has visions and holds long conversations with obscure saints."

I betrayed him to that, Joanna thought, her mind numb with fear and grief. *I betrayed him and now I have to face Suraklin alone.* She didn't know which was worse.

It was six in the evening and already quite dark. The Magus' ladies had all departed to have their hair done up for the evening's balls and opera visits, and the narrow townhouse was quiet, save for the distant clink of metal and porcelain in the kitchen where dinner was being prepared. A steady drizzle pattered against the window beyond its claret-red velvet drapes, and Joanna felt cold to the bottommost reaches of her soul.

She realized she had let her silence last too long. Looking around, she saw the Magus regarding her anxiously, kindly concern in his fashionably painted eyes. She swallowed and set her teacup down unsipped, forcing her voice steady. "Who told you that?"

He shook his head, as if to dispel her forlorn hope it was all rumor. "It's common knowledge, child. I've spoken to Church sasenna and hasu who've guarded him. The guard on the Tower has been trebled; since he's taken to having visions, the Bishop changes them nearly every week. Most of the Church sasenna have taken monks' vows as well; the visions inspired a certain amount of sympathy and awe, since he describes quite accurately saints of whom he's obviously never heard."

He folded his slender hands, clearly concerned both for his friend and for her. Out of his impressive black velvet robes, he looked like any well-to-do professional of the city in his white shirtsleeves, stockings, dark breeches, and vest. The Prince Regent, Joanna reflected with tired irony, in his sable linen and black-jeweled rings, looked far more like a necromancer than this dapper little faker.

"Would the Sigil of Darkness do that to him?"

The Magus thought about it a moment, frowning. "I don't see how it would," he said finally. "After all, he was imprisoned under its influence for seven years and it did him no harm."

"But then it was just on the doors of the Tower, wasn't it, and not around his neck?"

"Around his neck?" The revulsion on his face was almost nausea.

"On an iron collar," Joanna said. "They soldered it there, after he had signed his confession, I think because someone on the Council was holding out against voting for his execution."

The dog wizard looked away, utterly sickened.

Hesitantly, she added, "I saw it in a dream . . ."

"I don't wonder that you did. The screaming of his soul at the touch of that thing . . ." He swung back to look at her. "Do you know what the Sigil of Darkness is, child? What it does?" And, when she only looked blankly at him, he went on, "It is an utterly abominable thing to wizards, utterly abominable. It does more than cripple our power. It is the antithesis of power; it is anti-power, and the greater one's strength, the greater the—I suppose pain is the closest word, but it isn't that. It eats power, eats at us through our power. Torturing him these last six weeks would have been more merciful. God help him, no wonder he went mad." He flinched, pressing his long fingers against his mouth in the frame of its silky little Van Dyke beard, as if he could feel the cold stain of that poison through the secret magic that underlay his flamboyant charlatanry.

Frostbitten fingers hurt when they were warmed—Joanna recognized the stabbing ache somewhere in her chest as being of the same order, the pain of hope flaring in the ash. "Then if the Sigil were removed . . ."

Pity in his thin face, the Magus took her hands. "Child, it's hopeless. You would only destroy yourself. Antryg is my friend. Since I wasn't blind when you were here with him, I know you love him . . ."

"It isn't that," Joanna said stubbornly. "My—love for him—has nothing to do with this, nor the fact that I put him where he is now, that I was the one who drugged him and gave him to the Council . . ."

Magus made a shocked noise.

"It's that I have a job to do and I can't do it without a wizard's help. I can't do it without Antryg's help. He's the only one besides myself who even believes there *is* a threat, a worldwide threat, in these—these periods of deadness, of draining, of the death of magic and hope. And from everything I've heard, he's for damn sure the only mage who's capable of taking on Suraklin."

She hadn't meant to speak that name to him so soon. The silence that followed it was curiously like that which follows thunder in the night, a hush through which the tiny sounds of the servants in the kitchen, the faint patter of the rain, and the tinkly rattle of a carriage over the wet cobblestones outside seemed clear as music. Magus' black eyebrows seemed to stand out like smudges of ink against a face gone suddenly very white.

He said softly, "That's impossible. Suraklin is dead."

"Suraklin's original body is dead." Joanna's grip tightened slightly over the Magus' fingers as they flinched, as if to keep him from flight at the mere mention of the Dark Mage. "Suraklin's mind, his knowledge, and his personality have been living in the minds of others, like a self-perpetuating worm-program on a computer disk that lies about its own existence and eventually eats up all the other programs. And now he's getting ready to download into a computer for real, a computer powered by electricity that will be generated by the life-energies of everyone in the world. The deadness is going to become permanent, Magus. Everyone's magic will fade, as yours has faded. Suraklin will have it all."

She looked across the table at the Magus and saw in his horror-stricken green eyes that, deny it though he might to her, to others, or to himself, he knew she spoke the truth. He whispered, "Then when Antryg was here with you in the fall . . ."

"He was looking for Suraklin."

The Magus pulled his hands away from her and stared out into the rainy darkness. "Dear God."

"And he couldn't confide in you or me or anyone, because he knew that anyone at all might be under Suraklin's influence." *As Magus might be,* Joanna thought, with sudden disgust at herself. *Oh, well, too late now. No wonder Antryg came across as a hopeless paranoid.* "Magus, I need help."

"Not against Suraklin."

"He doesn't know I'm here."

"He will. By the saints, girl, don't you listen to anything?" He swung back to face her, anger struggling with fear in his absinthe-colored eyes. "I never lived in Kymil—the Church has always been too strong in that town for a dog wizard to be comfortable—but I passed through it when Suraklin was alive. I tell you there was nothing that went on there that he didn't know, no one whose life he could not tamper with if they did not obey his . . . He called them 'requests.'

"The first time I saw him was in the marketplace, a thin, biscuit-colored man with his long hair tied in a tail down his back and his yellow eyes like a cat's, watching the stall holders' children playing in the gutters. He walked over to a little girl of about four and took her—just took her by the hand and led her away through the market, in front of the whole population of Kymil, *and nobody did a thing!* I was so shocked I wondered for a moment whether he mightn't have been using some kind of cloaking-spell—which, as mageborn myself, I could see through when others couldn't. But one of the little boys ran to the girl's mother, pointing after them and telling her. And she shushed him. I'll never forget the tears running down her face as she watched them leave the market nor that damned, smug look of satisfaction on Suraklin's. My child, I'll have nothing to do with Suraklin."

Had Suraklin done that with Antryg? Joanna wondered—just walked up to that overgrown, skinny boy of nine in some outback Sykerst town and taken him by the hand, smelling out the powers in his mind and wanting them for his own? Or because of the boy's powers, had he seduced Antryg through dreams, as he had seduced Gary, long before they met, to win *his* trust?

"Then help me save Antryg," she said quietly. When he averted his gaze from her again, she reached across the table and caught at the pleated ruffle of his wrist. "Magus, please! I have to start somewhere . . ."

"Even if you could somehow get into the Tower itself, getting the Sigil off him might not help, after this long."

Her voice breaking with despair, she cried, "I have to try! Magus, I can't do this all by myself! Suraklin has to be defeated . . ."

With the gentle swiftness of one long used to dealing with female hysterics, Magister Magus was on his feet, around the table, and holding her comfortingly in his arms. And, in spite of her fury at him and her frustrated rage at his cowardice, Joanna found a great deal of comfort in the firm strength of his hold, the warmth of his hands on hers, and the mingled smell of perfume, candlewax, and incense that clung to his clothes. "My child, I'm telling you he can't be," the Magus said softly. "I know you consider me a coward and a villain . . ."

She raised her head from that strong, slender shoulder and looked into the green eyes beneath the silver-shot black brows, seeing in them the man's genuine quixotic chivalry struggling with his fear of pain and death.

He went on, with a kind of apologetic dignity, "My position was bad enough before, with the Witchfinders always sniffing at my heels and the Regent staring daggers at me every time our paths crossed at the Palace, in spite of my being under the protection of his cousin and heir. Now with the abominations multiplying in the countryside, with the harvest on the verge of failing, the Saarieque trade-fleet not yet in and every fortune in the Empire in a tizzy, with rumors of plots by wizards flying thick as grasshoppers in a dry summer . . . My child, it would take so little for me to end up before the Inquisition myself. It would be safer for me not to let you stay here at all . . ."

Panic clutched her; he touched her hair reassuringly, the dozen candles in their holder on the table throwing faint, multiple shadows across the tired lines of hopelessness on his face. "I can only beg you to remember my position here and not bring down the Witchfinders, the Council of Wizards, or the abominable Prince Regent's notice on me while you're under my roof. Further than that I cannot go. I have met Suraklin, my child; I've seen his power. Believe me, the consequences of going against him are one of the few things I can think of worse than death."

Joanna sighed, feeling very weak and wishing there were someone else to do all this for her. "Unfortunately," she said, "so are the consequences of not going against him. So I really have no choice."

*　*　*

The noodle vendor whose little cart leaked steam into the damp air looked askance at Joanna, but pointed out to her the direction she had asked. This part of Angelshand was a far cry from Governor's Square. Crumbling brick tenements and soot-rotted half-timbered edifices leaned against one another in the fog like homeward-bound drunks. Down alleyways which Joanna could have spanned with her arms, mazes of laundry fluttered above reeking streams of half-frozen sewage through which beggar-children splashed, shrieking, their feet wrapped in rags. The shops that gazed like the gloomy eyesockets of skulls into the narrow lanes seemed to be of only three types—secondhand clothes, pawnshops, or gin palaces from whose doors, even at this hour of the afternoon, trickled snatches of drunken singing. The men and women whose feet churned at the icy slime that smeared the flagways increasingly wore the dark gabardine and looped-up braids of the Old Believers, and once Joanna glimpsed across the street a red-haired girl in the billowing black robes of a mage.

Nervously, Joanna patted under her cloak the awkward bulge of the .38 that distended the pocket of her dress. She wasn't sure what Caris' reaction to her return would be, but she didn't believe in taking chances. Knowing what he knew, Caris would guess at once that there could be only one reason for her to come back.

The Mages' Yard was a narrow court of eight or nine shabby houses, brooding in the raw brown mists over scummed and uneven cobblestones. As she passed it, Joanna saw few people about, save for an Old Believer woman sweeping her doorstep and a boy in rags peddling kindling from house to house. Autumn in Angelshand was a dreary time. The long winds from the southwest, the ship-winds, slacked as the trade season drew to its close, and the fogs and rains settled in. Iron cold was locking down on the land. The Sykerst would already be under snow.

The harvest had failed; from the number of beggars Joanna had seen she guessed the cost of bread was up. According to Magister Magus, poverty was always worst in the city in early autumn, just before the great silk and tea fleets came in from Saarieque to provide their annual stimulus to the economy. He had spoken of this philosophically. Joanna, raised with the comfort of a public welfare system that never *really* let anybody starve, found those hollowed eyes and emaciated faces horribly disquieting.

As she lingered at the head of the Mages' Yard, one of the house doors opened, and a small group of wizards and sasenna emerged. In their center she recognized the Lady Rosamund, coldly beautiful and seemingly oblivious to the bitter chill of the afternoon, laying down the law about something to a silver-haired androgyne who flitted along at her side like a dandelion seed. Her breath steamed cloudy in the grimy air, and her voice struck fragments of words, like glass chimes, from the hard walls of the court. Mindful not to call attention to herself by hurrying, Joanna idled away down the street, glad for the concealing hood of her cloak.

Of all the mages, she feared most to meet the Lady Rosamund.

In a tavern down the block, she gave the innkeeper's boy a copper bit to take a message to Stonne Caris in the Mages' Yard. Sitting in the half-empty ordinary room, she wondered what she would say to the Archmage's grandson, the young man who had risked his life to pursue and capture Antryg and bring him to the Council's justice. The last time she had seen him came back to her, when he and the Church wizards had beaten Antryg to his knees at his last, desperate attempt at flight, and had dragged him back through the dark Gate in the Void. Caris had worn a look of calm, the serenity of a man once more back in the world he knew. She recalled, too, the dark scenes of her dream.

But Caris had traveled with Antryg and her from Kymil to Angelshand. With his rudimentary powers, he had felt the draining-off of the world's life to fuel Suraklin's computer; he had dealt with the abominations which came through the Void at its opening; and he had heard Antryg speak of the danger that lay in those gray times of grief. He was, Joanna realized, one of the very few people who might conceivably believe what was going on. And, though she wasn't sure how much bearing it would have on Caris' attitude, Antryg had saved his life.

The door opened. Murky whitish light filtered dimly into the brown gloom. Looking up, Joanna saw Caris silhouetted against the gray cold of the street—a young Greek god, foster-raised in Valhalla, with the loose black clothing of a sasennan and a thickly quilted jacket not quite blurring the gymnast poise of the body and his short quiff of cornsilk-yellow hair falling over his forehead. The sword and daggers of the ancient order of sworn warriors glinted among a brass-buckled strapwork of weapons belts and a dark silk sword sash. Coffee-brown, tip-tilted eyes touched her, went on to scan the room for potential dangers, and returned to her.

His face expressionless, he turned on his heel and strode out again.

Startled and hurt, Joanna lunged to her feet, tripped on her petticoats, and cursed. The cold outside was like a slap in the face; in the bleak, narrow street, Caris was nowhere to be seen. A glance at the black mud underfoot showed her the marks of his soft-soled boots; holding up her skirts, she followed around the corner into an alley . . .

Hard hands grabbed her elbows from behind. Joanna cried out with shock as she was shoved face-forward against the sooty brick of a wall; a hand blocked her jabbing elbow as another clawed through the layers of her cloak at the pocket of her skirt.

It was all over in less than a second, and Caris turned her around, holding her hard against the wall with one hand while he shoved the .38 into his sword sash with the other. His brown eyes were flat and cold, as if they had never met.

"Come with me," he said.

She braced her feet against the jerk of his hand. His beauty had always intimidated her, but she had never had cause to feel his strength before. It was terrifying. Of course, she thought, he's been working out eight hours a day since he was fourteen. "Caris, no . . ."

He paused. His face was as she had seen it in her dream, expressionless, but with emotion raging far back in the depths of his eyes. "You shouldn't have come back, Joanna. You understand that now the Archmage won't be able to let you go." Like his face, there was nothing in his voice.

It was something Joanna hadn't counted on and it hit her like a blow to the stomach. She had known that if she met Lady Rosamund she would be recognized and identified as what she was now, Antryg's willing accomplice instead of his victim. The thought that she, too, might be imprisoned by the wizards hadn't even occurred to her. With it came the sinking realization that, while she had given plausible reasons for her disappearance in her own world which would prevent people from looking for her, in this world, legally, she did not exist at all. If she vanished, no one would know, except Magister Magus, who would undoubtedly be too terrified to inquire.

Her first impulse was to plead. But something in Caris' inhuman blankness sparked anger in her instead, and she set her feet and twisted her arm defiantly against the steel grip. "Look, would you pretend you have a will of your own for about five minutes?"

She saw the flare of his nostrils with his responding anger; but, as is the Way of the Sasenna, he mastered it and only said levelly, "Having a will of my own kept me from killing Antryg Windrose the moment I caught him. Had I been obedient to the dictates of the council, my grandfather would be alive today."

Joanna used a phrase she'd picked up from the stagecoach drivers on the way to Angelshand and added, "You were obedient to the dictates of the Council when you let your grandfather go to meet him alone, both times, first at the Silent Tower, then at Gary's. Even if he wasn't duping you, do you think your unthinking obedience helped him any?"

The breath steamed from his lips—one, two breaths. His grip didn't change. "When I took my vows as sasennan, I turned my will over to the Council of Wizards," he said. "Whether your arguments are right or wrong doesn't concern me."

"Does it concern you that even having Antryg under lock and key, sealed in the Silent Tower under the Sigil of Darkness and driven out of his mind by what they've done to him, the fading of magic, the draining of life, *is still going on?* If the abominations were Antryg's doing, why are they still appearing?"

"Because he still lives." He thrust her toward the mouth of the alley; Joanna pulled vainly against that frightening strength. Terrified at the thought of facing the Council, she forced her mind to focus, not on her fear, but on her rage.

"Dammit, would you act like a man instead of a goddam computer!"

That offended him out of his stony calm. "It is a man who is loyal . . ."

She finally succeeded in wrenching her arm free of his grip and stood, angrily rubbing it through her cloak. "I've talked to a lot of computers in my time and, believe me, I've gotten more discrimination and judgment out of a six-K ops program than I'm getting out of you!"

They stood close together in the murky shades of the alley, like a fair-haired brother and sister at the tail end of a shouting match. Caris was breathing hard now with fury, his hand half drawn back, as if he would strike her. *If he does,* she thought, too angry now to let herself fear, *so help me I'll rip his ears off.*

But slowly, the iron expression on Caris' face faded. Fleetingly, it looked young and troubled—she remembered he was only nineteen—as it had before his grandfather's murder had hardened his soul into the perfection of his vows. Quietly, he said, "It isn't up to me to discriminate or to judge—or even to listen. I know you to be an enemy of the will of the Council. You're here to rescue Antryg, aren't you?"

"You flatter him," Joanna said slowly. "And you insult me, by the way. I'm here because I know, and you know, that Antryg's old master Suraklin didn't die twenty-five years ago when he was supposed to have been killed. Only two people knew that—Antryg and Suraklin himself. Caris, for the last four years Suraklin was occupying the brain and body of your grandfather Salteris."

"No." The flat harshness returned to his voice, the rage to his eyes.

"He told you that, didn't he? To save his own skin. Had I known he had calumnated Salteris so, I would have . . ."

"Slit his wrists back at the Tower when he begged you to?" That threw him off balance. She pressed on. "There was a man I knew back in my own world, the owner of the house where we were, the house where all Suraklin's marks were found. After your grandfather died—after Suraklin left his body, imbecile as he left the Emperor's—this man had all the mannerisms and the patterns of speech that I knew in your grandfather. According to your grandfather himself, who else could download his personality from body to body, from brain to brain, except Suraklin? Caris, we got the wrong man. We were both duped. And now we have to stop Suraklin, and Antryg—*if* we can get him out of the Silent Tower, *if* we can get the Sigil of Darkness off him—is the only one who might be able to help us."

"That's a lie," the sasennan said, his voice like the iron earth of winter. "Antryg murdered my grandfather. He betrayed his trust—*he* was Suraklin . . ."

"Caris," Joanna said quietly, "wasn't there ever a time when your grandfather—changed?"

He looked away. "No. . . . It was because of my grandmother's death. He loved her." His jaw tightened. For a moment, the grief and anger in him seemed to seethe up beneath the stiff rock barriers erected by the Way of the Sasenna. When he looked back at her, there was something close to hatred in his brown eyes.

"Don't you understand that what I think about it doesn't matter?" The words came jerkily, as if the very framing of them were difficult. "Your telling me this . . . I am sworn to be the weapon of the Council and only that. I'm not—qualified—to judge these matters. It is not the Way of the Sasenna to be."

Looking up into his face, Joanna suddenly felt very sorry for this gorgeous, muscular young man, this honed and glistening blade. After all, she thought, he had traded in the pain of making decisions for the steady comfort of knowing that in following orders, no matter what they were, he would always be in the right. Pain like that could be turned away from, but it was always there waiting, and now he had no experience in dealing with it.

Her anger at him faded. "I'm sorry," she said. Turning, she walked away down the alley toward the muddy pavement of the street. Grief and defeat filled her, as exhausting as if she had indeed fought him hand to hand. Caris remained standing where he was, looking after that small, cloaked figure, like a statue, save for the mist of his breath. Only when she was halfway back to Magister Magus' did Joanna realize that he hadn't, after all, followed his duty and caught her again and only much later that evening did she remember that he had kept her gun.

CHAPTER IV

THIS IS MY LAST CHANCE. A FOOTMAN IN THE EMERALD GREEN VELVET livery of the Prince Cerdic's household opened the door of Magister Magus' anonymous dark carriage, and helped Joanna down—a gesture she had always considered a quaint formality until she'd actually tried getting out of a high-slung vehicle in half a dozen layers of petticoats and skirts. *This had better work.*

If it didn't, she had no idea where to go next.

She tipped the man the amount prescribed by Magister Magus, that expert in the nuances of Court conduct, and walked up the pink marble steps of the Dower House, one of the smallest of the several palaces which dotted the vast, fairy-tale parklands comprising the Imperial Seat. She found that, on the whole, she felt worse than she had when she'd knocked on Magister Magus' door for the first time. On that occasion at least, she reflected, she'd had the comfort of several courses of action open to her—if not Magister Magus, then Caris; if not Caris, then Cerdic the Prince, first cousin of the Regent and Heir, after him, to the Empire.

She was now down to one, with nothing open to her beyond that, and no way of getting home.

Literally no way of getting home, she added to herself with a rueful grin, watching the coachman turn the small, single-horse brougham in the drive and move briskly away down the rain-puddled road up which they had come, until it vanished beyond a copse of wet trees. Magister Magus had been horrified by her request to be taken to Court. "Are you mad, girl? With things as they are? The abomination that killed those children in the factory district last night; the rumors in the Sykerst that the religion of the old gods is coming back; the Witchfinders up in arms; pogroms in Mellidane; the Stock Exchange shaky—it always is, in autumn—mutinies on the trade-ships coming back from Saarieque and the Spice Lands; the worst harvest in thirty years . . . My life wouldn't be worth two coppers if I went anywhere *near* the Imperial Palaces!"

"But I have to see Prince Cerdic," Joanna had insisted quietly from the depths of one of the dog wizard's gilded ebony armchairs. "I may not know a lot about Courts and Princes and things, but I do know you can't just walk in off the street and ask to see the dude who's second-in-line for the throne. But he's a friend of yours and he favors the wizards. If anyone could help me get Antryg out, he could."

"*If* anyone," the dog wizard repeated softly. That had been last night, after Joanna had returned from her abortive interview with Caris; they had shared a glass of port in the library while the Magus had read over the various newspapers, broadsides, and scandal sheets from which he gleaned the raw material for his seemingly magical deductions about his clients' lives. "The problem is, child, I'm not sure anyone can help Antryg now. And in any case, I'd hesitate to ask. Part of the secret of dealing with Courts is knowing when to disappear. Now that the Prince Regent is married, he keeps an even closer eye on Cerdic . . ."

"Married?"

"Last month—my dear child, the town rang with it."

The Regent's high, harsh voice came back to her . . . *that brainless bitch I'm to marry* . . . and Antryg's, in the firelight of the posthouse, *Come, Pharos, you know you haven't any use for a woman* . . .

"Pellicida, niece of the King of Senterwing," the Magus went on. "They say at court his Grace calls her the Black Mare. But until he gets her with child—if he ever manages to—Cerdic is still his heir; and at the moment, both Cerdic and I know it is not the time for Cerdic to be seen associating with the mageborn."

By dint of coaxing, Joanna had managed to secure the loan of his carriage and a letter of introduction. "Anything else?" the Magus had inquired, with some acerbity. "A team of running-footmen to announce you? A brass band? Fireworks, maybe?" But he had flung himself gracefully into a chair before his desk, waved absentmindedly in the direction of the two branches of candles flanking its inlaid writing surface and caused all twelve wicks to burst into a simultaneous flutter of light, then began to write.

His sole condition had been that his coachman wait for her at the gates of the Imperial Park, not at the Dower House where Cerdic stayed when he was in Angelshand. Knowing that the Regent would probably have spies in the stables, Joanna had agreed. Last night, with the rain drumming softly on the roof, this had not seemed like such a good idea, but this morning the soft autumn ship winds had blown again from the southwest, dispersing the clinging mists. The first of the Saarieque trade fleet had finally been sighted, a day or two off the out-islands. Magister Magus, like everybody else in the city, had money invested in their cargoes and had cheered up considerably and given Joanna innumerable small pointers about the proper conduct at Court.

It appeared that Magister Magus wasn't the only person in Angelshand familiar with the secret of knowing when to disappear. Pharos' paranoia about Cerdic was evidently only too well-known. After a condescending scrutiny which made Joanna glad she'd invested the remainder of her dwindling funds in a new gown, an elderly majordomo conducted her to what was apparently the reception room for the better class of petitioners, a sort of long drawing room in oak and red velvet, whose French windows looked out on a vista of wet, brown garden, shivering in the wind-blown restlessness of the sunlight. The room boasted several life-sized bronze statues in velvet-draped wall niches, a marble fireplace in which a fire had been newly made up, and not another living soul.

"His Grace is rather occupied this morning," the majordomo said, with a chilly bow, a statement which Joanna interpreted as a warning that she was in for a long wait. "I will inform him of your presence." And he departed, bearing her letter of introduction and the sizable tip the Magus had advised would insure its prompt delivery.

At least, Joanna thought, there was a fire in the fireplace, not at all a usual consideration, according to Magister Magus, in the rooms where the humble waited to present their petitions to the great. Thinking back on it later, she knew that it should have alerted her that someone else was expected and, in fact, someone fairly important—but it didn't.

Thus the first warning she had was the sound of voices approaching in the garden beyond the French doors. She looked up, startled, in time to see through the glass Prince Cerdic himself coming up the steps of the small terrace just outside, looking back over his shoulder to talk to a man behind him.

The second man was Gary.

Joanna was so shocked, so disoriented at seeing Gary—possessed by Suraklin or not, her first impression was that it was Gary—in the context of this world that Prince Cerdic was actually starting to open the door before she moved. Her mind was staggering under the realization of what Suraklin's presence here implied, the collapsing hurt of her last hope vanishing; only a half-second later did she realize her own appalling peril, and then it was far too late to make it across the room to the inner door. Her only refuge was in the velvet-draped niche beside the fireplace which housed a heroic bronze of some ancient warrior who bore a startling resemblance to Tom Selleck, close enough to have reached out and touched either of the two men as they came to warm their hands at the fire.

"My dear Gaire, of course he's mad, but why should the nobles care about that?" Cerdic was asking. "As long as he doesn't offend the Church, retains a favorable trade balance with Saarieque, and keeps the peasants in line, they wouldn't care if he slept with sheep and pigs, never mind boys." The young Prince had put on a little weight since Joanna had last seen him, his round cheeks somewhat rounder against the artful clusters of dark brown curls. But he still had the same pleasant expression in his painted hazel eyes and the same open brow and air of clean, healthy good looks. Against Cerdic's resplendent mauve satin and clouds of rose-point lace, Suraklin's dust-colored velvet seemed almost severe.

"So far." The Dark Mage had discarded all of Gary's old mannerisms. Even the voice sounded different, though its pitch and timbre were the same. "Nobles favor any man under whose rule they prosper. When they feel the pinch of lost revenues and when they come to you for money, you'll find yourself a good deal more popular."

Cerdic nodded in eager agreement. "Of course your investment advice is superb, as all advice from one in touch with the Ancient Powers of Magic must be." Suraklin nodded in deprecating agreement. Joanna, in her hiding place and half-suffocated by the heat trapped between the fireplace wall and the crimson velvet draperies, remembered the young Prince's slavish adherence to anything Antryg had said, too, and wondered how she could possibly have considered that kind of unthinking championship anything but moronic.

"But all support doesn't come from money alone. Popular feeling plays a great part in it, especially now . . ."

"And so it shall," the wizard responded kindly. "It's why I asked you to extend your invitation to both your cousin and his bride today. The Lady Pellicida is surprisingly popular . . ."

Cerdic's plucked eyebrows lifted. "Pella? That overdressed, homely gawk of a girl?"

"They see in her one more victim of your cousin's evil." He shrugged. "As indeed she is. When you have your conference with the Regent, then I shall speak to Pella, to offer her your support and help."

"But . . ." The Prince frowned, genuinely concerned. "I can't allow you to endanger yourself by remaining. Indeed, the Regent might have with him one of those disgraceful catamites he keeps about him. He often brings them with him. That poor girl! If you're seen here—if word gets to my cousin that you're one of the mageborn . . . Your person is too precious to go into such peril alone!"

Suraklin smiled, like a saint making light of an impending martyrdom, but there was an amused glint in his eye, as if he snickered up his sleeve ruffles at his patron. Had he done so, she wondered, suddenly angry, at her belief in him and at Caris' love? "Do you think I cannot deal with such matters?" he asked mildly. "You'll see; there will be no danger or certainly not much. And in any case, it's your cause I'm thinking about, my Prince, not mine."

And if you were Pinocchio, Joanna thought sourly, *the Prince would have just gotten impaled on about seven feet of nose.*

The two men strolled back to the French window together, talking quietly of a masked ball to be given by the merchant noble Calve Dirham the following night; against the misty brightness of the glass, Joanna saw with some surprise that Suraklin and Cerdic were the same height. She had gained the impression that Gary's very body had altered and that he was taller, thinner, older—so much older. She knew Gary was thirty-four, ten or twelve years older than Cerdic at the most. But those brown eyes, with their disquieting yellow glint, were the eyes of fathomless age.

The hold of Suraklin over the minds of those he sought to control was almost unbreakable. She had been warned of it, over and over again; she had seen it only yesterday, in Caris's stubborn adherence to his love for the old man. She was far too familiar with it to believe that the credulous Cerdic could be convinced to help her, or indeed to do anything but turn her over to Suraklin.

The thought made the sweat trickle down her sides under the forest-green satin of her gown. *Jesus Christ,* she thought suddenly, *if he's here at Court, he'll be maneuvering to get Antryg's death expedited.* The fact that to do so he would probably have to go through the Regent, suspicious of all mages, didn't matter. She'd had devastating experience with the Dark Mage's abilities as a manipulator. *I have to get Antryg out of there!*

But without support of any kind, she could see no way that she could.

There's nothing further I can do in Angelshand, she began, falling subconsciously back into programmer mode and groping for a next step to get her beyond the panic that began to hammer in her chest. *First, I have to touch Magister Magus for a monster loan. Second, I have to get to Kymil . . .*

"My lord," the majordomo's voice said from the inner door. "His Grace the Prince Regent is here."

Cerdic laid a hand on Suraklin's sleeve and said softly, "Do be careful, lord wizard." Turning, he hastened across the room and out into the main hall beyond. With an ironic smile, Suraklin slipped through the French doors onto the terrace.

Oh, swell, Joanna thought, weak with fear. *So now I have a choice of splitting and walking smack into him outside or staying where I am and getting rousted out by Pharos' sasenna, if they decide to search the room . . . Holy Christ, Pharos will recognize me, too!* She leaned her head back against the paneling behind the drapes, caught between panic and an ironic understanding of the impulse to pound one's head against a wall.

But stronger than either of those was a violent and personal loathing for the wizard Suraklin. Seeing him at San Serano, in Gary's body, was one thing; while he was imitating Gary's mannerisms it had seemed, at times, that it was in fact only a segment of Gary. She had known that Gary was dead. But not until now, not until she had seen Suraklin *as Suraklin,* gesturing casually with Gary's hands and smiling his lies through Gary's mouth, did it come home to her that Suraklin had killed Gary for his body and the contents of his brain as surely and as offhandedly as he'd have killed a rabbit to make slippers out of its skin. In the last year she hadn't liked Gary much and, reading his programs and the motivations and thoughts that had watchspringed his actions, she liked him less. But her dislike of him in no way altered the callous brutality of his murder.

The door opened. The elderly majordomo ushered in the Prince Regent Pharos Destramor, Heir to the Empire and its de facto ruler, small and dainty as ever in his gold-laced black velvet and leaning on the arm of the prettiest teenaged boy Joanna had ever seen. Only a year or so younger than Caris, the boy was darkly handsome in blueberry silk; but unlike Caris, he appeared highly conscious of his own good looks and preened himself at the Prince's every admiring glance. Behind them walked a girl of about the same age, fully as tall as the Prince's companion and nearly a head taller than the Prince himself, her coarse black hair curled unbecomingly around a dark, strong-featured face, wearing far too much makeup and an overdecorated pink satin gown. A pampered-looking lapdog trotted at her heels, like a miniaturized Borzoi with a diamond collar on its neck.

The Black Mare, Joanna thought, looking at that broad-shouldered, big-boned figure. It was a cruel nickname and regrettably apt. Only at second glance did Joanna see how young she was.

The Regent and his eromenos had come to stand near the fire. The perfume they wore was rank and sweet in Joanna's nostrils. The girl

Pellicida lingered awkwardly in the background, and Joanna saw a private smirk of triumph at having shut her out slip between the Prince's pale-blue, paint-crusted eyes and his boyfriend's violet ones. The boy whispered something and glanced; the man giggled.

At that point the lapdog, sniffing exploringly around the room, reached the wall niche in which Joanna had taken refuge. It cocked its feathered ears toward her. Joanna had one instant's total fright; then the Prince said, loudly enough for his miserable bride to hear, "Useless bitches, all of them." He knelt and snapped his fingers peremptorily. "Kysshenka—Kyssha . . ."

The little dog, her attention diverted from Joanna, trotted obediently over; the Prince's soft hand stroked the tiny head. "Mangey little ragmops—this one and those two fat pugs. I've always wanted to shave the lot of them . . ."

"Stop it," Pellicida said from the other end of the room. Hearing her voice, the little dog made an effort to get away, but the Prince, with that surprising quickness of hand Joanna had noticed in him before, caught the scruff of the slender neck.

" 'Stop it,' " Pharos mimicked in a nasal whine and added to the dog, "Bite me, would you?" as the little creature, panicking, made a hesitant nip or two at his sleeve ruffles, though it was obvious she knew full well she was forbidden to bite humans. There was a look of terror and horrible dilemma in her enormous brown eyes.

Pellicida strode down the length of the salon, her vast carnation petticoats bringing down a small table unnoticed in her wake. "Let her go."

"Why should I, my little Princess? She's my dog, after all—as all your property is mine to do with as I choose. If I decided to set that fluffy little tail on fire . . ." He caught the dog Kyssha's feathery tail in his other hand and pulled her by it toward the blazing hearth.

Whether he would actually have thrust the terrified lapdog's tail into the fire or not Joanna never found out, though she had her suspicions. This was because Pellicida, reaching him, grabbed him by the shoulder of his coat and hauled him to his feet, making him release the dog in sheer surprise. With the other hand she delivered an open-hand slap across his face that staggered him back against the marble mantel.

For an instant Joanna thought he would strike at her; from where she hid in the thick folds of the niche curtains, she could see him pressed against the pink and white carvings like a snake coiling, an ugly red bruise mottling his pasty skin. Pellicida faced him, tears of anger blazing in her hazel eyes. Kyssha, flattened against her mistress' skirts, seemed to sense the violence of his rage and bared her tiny fangs in a soprano growl.

Quietly, Pharos said, "You'll regret that." He walked unhurriedly past her and out the hall door, his boyfriend hurrying solicitously in his wake. The Princess looked after him until the door shut. Then she crumpled down onto one of the settees near the fire, gathered up the dog who had jumped immediately into her arms, and began to cry.

As in her dream of the Silent Tower, for an instant Joanna felt trapped where she was, held from comforting this big, dark, homely child by her fear of discovery should Pharos come suddenly back. *To hell with that,* she thought, stepping out of the dusty tangle of crimson curtains. *Anybody who has to put up with that kind of public humiliation every day needs all the help she can get.* She was halfway to the settee when a shadow crossed the garden windows and the dog Kyssha raised her head with a quick, high-pitched growl. Looking across at the tall, narrow bands of window light, Joanna recognized Suraklin's returning shape.

The Princess had seen him, too. Still holding Kyssha in her arms she got quickly to her feet, stumbling when she trod on the hem of one of her flowerlike layers of skirts, and headed for the curtained niche by the fireplace, blundering straight into Joanna.

For an instant the two women stared at each other, startled and disoriented; then Joanna turned back and made a dash for the niche, the tall Princess at her heels.

"I can't let him see me!" Joanna gasped, and Pellicida shook her head in agreement and felt quickly behind the deeply carved molding of the wall panels at the back of the niche. A narrow door opened.

"Through here," whispered the Princess. "I can't let him see me, either."

The panel slid back into place behind them, the sigh of air settling from beneath the heavy drape as Suraklin the Dark Mage was left to enter an empty hall.

"Why not?" asked Joanna quietly. "Gaire, I mean." She used the name Cerdic had called him.

Pellicida glanced quickly down at her, then away. After a moment she let out her breath in a sigh. "It isn't important." Her mouth trembled on the words, but she pursed it closed.

The sliding panel had admitted them into another room along the garden side of the house, this one a sort of private bookroom-cum-study filled with Cerdic's usual collection of statues of the Old Gods, tomes of cantrip and quackery, star-mandallas, and armillary spheres. From it the two girls had stepped through another French window into the gardens, crossing to the nearest copse of trees and taking one of the winding paths that would lead, eventually, to the other palaces of the grounds and to the outer gates where Magister Magus' coach awaited Joanna. In spite of the sharp-edged sunlight, the afternoon was quite cold, but by tacit consent neither suggested returning to search for their cloaks.

The Princess sniffled, and Joanna dug into the deep pocket of her dress for a clean handkerchief to offer her. Pella was not the delicate type of girl who could cry without rendering herself hideous; her nose was swollen, and her face, under a layer of half-wiped-off cosmetics, reddened in fading blotches. Kyssha, trotting at the hem of her swagged petticoats, looked up at her and whined in concern, and Pella reached down and took the little dog into the crook of her arm.

Joanna sighed. "I realize this is a stupid question under the circumstances, but can I do anything? Short of murdering Pharos, that is— though honestly I don't think Cerdic would be an improvement as a ruler."

Pella glanced quickly at her again, as if to reassure herself of the jesting tone in her voice. In spite of the japes about it, her height wasn't excessive, though at five-nine or so she was a head taller than Joanna and the diminutive Prince. It was her air of hesitancy which made her seem clumsy and outsize, something not helped by the bouffant extravagance of her gown. "It's all right," she said wearily. "I suppose I'd agree with Gaire about—it—if I didn't know what kind of ruler Cerdic would make." She gave her eyes a final wipe, completing the ruin of her makeup, and stroked Kyssha's head protectively. The little dog licked at her hands and whined again, shivering in the sharpness of the wind. Pella's mouth twitched in a bitter expression far older than her years. "Do you know Gaire well?"

"I did," said Joanna softly. "Once."

"I didn't know he'd come back." They emerged from the trees into a long, formal parterre which must have been like close-napped green velvet in the summer, brown now and edged with naked trees gray as pewter in the changeable brightness of the day. "Tell me about him."

Joanna shook her head. "I don't know if I can. It's—it's hard to explain."

"I have to know."

The urgency in her voice and the intentness of those hazel-green eyes stopped Joanna. She stood looking up at the girl, sensing the echo of that hateful sensation of knowing but of having no proof. Suraklin must have tried to put the influence of his mind over hers; she had fled him, not knowing why.

Then, rather quickly, Pella looked away. "He comes and goes. Nobody knows anything about him. Except what signifies—that he's Cerdic's latest fad, his 'Spiritual Advisor,' which is what he calls himself so no one can point to him and say 'wizard.' But he is a wizard, isn't he?"

"Yes," Joanna said softly.

Pellicida let out her breath in another short little sigh and stood for a time, cradling her little dog in her arms, staring out across the two acres of flawlessly smooth brown lawn toward the gilded roof trees of the Imperial Palace, visible beyond the cindery lace of the trees. "He made me . . ." she began, and broke off. Then she said, "I didn't even *like* him —I didn't understand what happened. I haven't—haven't ever been in love, but I didn't think it could be like that. It was a spell, wasn't it?"

"Yes," Joanna said, guessing what had happened and why Pellicida had run from him rather than face him again. After a moment she added, "I think legally that counts as rape—or it should, anyway."

Pellicida's glance was wry, to hide a hurt that had clearly been one of many in the last wretched month. She started walking again, a solitary figure, like a huge pink peony dropped on the sepia ground. The wind pulled loose strands of her black hair from their ridiculous masses of curls and tangled them with the dog's silky fur. "Did he do that to you?"

"He tried."

"Because you could be useful to him?"

Joanna nodded. She wondered morbidly whether, if she had agreed, he would have imitated Gary's rather unsatisfying sexual technique.

"Why did he do it?" Pella asked, as if asking about something that had been done to someone other than herself. "To get me to—to connive at his killing Pharos?"

She was a stranger in a strange land, a world alien to her own customs and wants, eighteen years old and married to a man who scorned and humiliated her. She held herself straight as any of the marble statues of heroes that lined the parterre, her profile cut like stone against the dark chaos of her hair.

Joanna said, "Probably."

"Tell me about him," Pella said again. "There's something about him, something evil . . . I don't know. Tell me who he is, and what he wants; tell me what's going on."

During winters in Angelshand, dawn came late; in the pre-solstice depths, a heatless daylight lasted five or six hours. Now, with autumn fully come, workers sought the grim riverside factories in darkness. The bells of the city's many churches were tolling matins. In summer the sky would have already been pale. Unnaturally clear and cold for this season of the year, the stars blazed queerly above the black angles of jutting roofs.

Stonne Caris, grandson of the dead Archmage Salteris Solaris, thrust his hands into the sleeves of his padded jacket and shivered as he strode the silent alleyways. In spite of the unseasonal clearness of the predawn darkness, it was bitterly cold. Usually at this hour of the morning from where he stood at the top of Threadneedle Street, where its cobbled slope turned down toward the river, nothing could be seen but a sea of white mist rising from that oily brown expanse, but now even the winking nets of riding lights on the ships in the harbor seemed to dance in the dark. It made him uneasy, with a strange sense of things not being as they should be. But his mageborn eyes showed him nothing to fear in the darkness of the alleys around him, and his hearing, trained through grueling blind-fold obstacle courses, spoke of no danger. Still, he hesitated for a moment at the top of the street, as if his nose could tell him what was wrong.

But all he smelled was the usual fishy reek of the bare mudflats below the granite embankments and, more strongly than usual, the nauseating whiff of spoiling meat and cheese from the garbage dump near the Grand Market.

Cautiously, he felt the pistol he had taken from Joanna, thrust through his sword sash, hard against his stomach through the padding of coat, jacket, and shirt. He slid his sword, still in its sheathe, from his sash; carrying the sheathe loosely in his left hand, he descended to the flats, his footfalls a moist whisper in the iron dawn.

He was pleased to find the mudflats empty. At this hour, they often weren't—during the summer they were a favorite dueling ground for young blades with scores to settle. Generally the coming of the autumn mists put a stop to such proceedings. This morning, however, was exceptionally clear. His breath escaped him in a cold thread of white; somewhere a dog barked, but he missed the crying of the gulls usually to be found arguing over the river garbage left by the turn of the tide.

He stopped, puzzling for a moment over that.

Upriver and down, dull orange lights glowed in kitchen windows of the dark houses that overhung the embankments. Across the rippling sheet of the water, the lights of the massive St. Cyr fortress gleamed unnaturally bright. An icy skiff of wind tugged at his cropped blond hair. He slipped the sword sheathe back into his sash and took out the gun.

When he had taken it from Joanna, he had assumed it was a gun like any other; only when he had examined it later, after he had come off-shift in his duties as guard at the Mages' Yard, did he realize that, in their weaponry as well as their strange machines, Joanna's people were vastly

different from his own. The weapon itself was alien to those with which
he was familiar, but the principles were the same. Instead of a ball, it
fired pointed projectiles, encapsuled in what he guessed were cartridges
already filled with premeasured loads, apparently loaded from the breech
instead of the muzzle. In addition, this weapon had a revolving chamber,
holding six bullets.

Lost in admiration of the efficiency of it, he had at first not realized
what it could mean—that a weapon existed which fired several times in
rapid succession.

When he realized it, it had shaken him to the roots.

The air down here was still, though he could now hear the rising whine
of wind across the roofs of the houses above him. The cold damped much
of the smell of the mudflats. It was not an ideal place for his experiment
—it was more open here than it had been in the Mages' Yard on the night
of Thirle's murder, and there was some movement of air—but it would
do.

He pointed the gun downriver, aiming high in the air, braced both his
hands on the butt in case it kicked more strongly than an ordinary pistol,
and squeezed the trigger. Instantly the flat crack of it echoed out across
the water; there was no delay between the fall of the hammer and the
ignition of the powder, and it hardly kicked at all. He fired a second shot
immediately, the cylinder revolving with deadly, beautiful smoothness
into place. There was a little flash. That was all.

There was very little smell of powder and no smoke whatsoever.

Caris felt his stomach sink.

This is none of my business, he thought despairingly. *I shouldn't even
be here. I am sasennan of the Council—it isn't up to me to decide right
and wrong. Antryg confessed to the murder of Thirle and other things
besides . . .*

But the murder was done with a gun like this one.

Where had he gotten it?

The thought intruded itself into his mind that Joanna could have been
right.

And if that is the case . . .

The wind was rising as Caris strode up the steep angle of Threadneedle
Street again. Black clouds had moved in to blot the stars. The ships at
rest in the harbor began to rock uneasily, like horses tied in a barn,
nervous at a sudden whiff of smoke.

As he made his way back through the alleys to the Ghetto, Caris
remembered the scene. It was his dreams that had wakened him then,
troubled, inchoate dreams of loss—his dreams and the fading of his

magic. His powers had never been much, but once before he had sensed their waning; that second time, waking in the muggy, stinking heat of the summer night, it had been like death. He had, he remembered, some notion of crossing the Yard from the house where the sasenna slept to see if his grandfather was back; but with the desolation that had come over him, it had suddenly seemed pointless. It was as if, with his magic, all hope had been bled from the world.

Then he had heard Thirle scream.

Thirle had been standing in the mouth of the alley known as Stinking Lane, the alley where that dreadful Gate of darkness had opened through the Void. He had been shot from the shadows of the houses on the opposite side of the square, and from those shadows a man had come running. A second shot had been fired at Caris, but he did not know, now that he thought of it, whether the fleeing man had fired it, or it had come from the shadows of the houses, like the first.

The killer had not been the man he had seen—the man who had run back through the Void—at all, but rather someone who had remained in the Court, who had fired the shots to cover the fugitive's tracks and to get Thirle out of the way.

Although Caris' memories of that time were surprisingly blurred—due, he supposed, to the draining hopelessness which had been on him then—it came to him now that the aim had been startlingly good for a running man's.

The first spits of rain were beginning to fall by the time he reached the Mages' Yard.

It made it easier for him. Though no sasennan would take shelter to the neglect of his duties, the noise of the wind howling through the narrow alleyways around the Yard would cover any sounds he might make better than the foggy stillness typical of autumn. After his grandfather's death, there had been talk of the narrow little house being taken over by the Lady Rosamund, but nothing had been done about it yet. The place had been locked and fear-spells put on the doors and windows; Caris could see them, glowing faintly through the slashing rain. He had not the power to override them, but simply his awareness of them—his knowledge that they were merely spells—let him force the catches on the rear window and scramble through with hammering heart, where an ordinary housebreaker would have thought better of the entire project.

The whole house spoke to him of his grandfather, with a terrible immediacy which brought back all his grief and rage at the old man's death.

If Joanna had been right . . .

Had there been a time when he had changed?

Standing in the close, crowded darkness of the narrow room that had been Salteris' study, while the rain slammed dementedly against the window glass as if hurled from buckets, Caris let his mind rove back.

He had not seen his grandfather from the time he was thirteen until he was eighteen, nearly two years ago now; he was aware that there was no greater gap in perceptions than that which existed between those two ages. His memories of his grandfather before that were a child's memories—running behind the old man through the sweetmarshes of the river Strebwell, hunting polliwogs while the Archmage gathered mallows or observed the comings and goings of birds. One summer there had been an epidemic of little pox in the village, and Caris had been drafted as assistant, to brew tisanes and hunt herbs; later his grandfather, still young, with the wiry strength of wizards, had stripped to a breechclout, braided back his long dark hair, and had helped Caris and the few villagers who were still on their feet get the hay in. Caris remembered as if it were yesterday the shine of drying sweat on the muscles of Salteris' arms and back as he'd sat with the other villagers under shelter, drinking beer as the rains swept in over the stubble fields; he remembered the thick, green smell of the air, heady as brandy, and Salteris' joyful laughter.

Since Caris had come to serve the Council of Mages as sasennan, since he had sworn his unthinking allegiance to his grandfather as head of that Council, he had not heard his grandfather laugh. He thought the glint of ironic mockery in the old man's eyes was new, but couldn't be sure; he did not remember in any of his childhood the haughty touchiness of temper which had characterized the wizard lately, nor that suave note in the voice which seemed to speak of some private joke with himself at his listener's expense. It might, Caris had thought, have had something to do with his grandmother's death, which had happened after he had gone to Innkitar to begin his training as sasennan; it might simply have been that, as a child, he had not seen that side of his grandfather.

Or it might be as Joanna had said.

It if was, he thought, sudden heat firing through his veins, it was Suraklin who killed him—Suraklin who ended that laughter, who stripped away that joyful life. Suraklin the Dark Mage . . .

I will kill him, he thought. *Dear God, I will kill him . . .*

Antryg, too, he realized, had loved Salteris. If what Joanna said was true—if Suraklin had left his grandfather alive and imbecile, to go on to this other man, this man of her world who understood computers—what must it have cost Antryg to kill in mercy the part that was left?

Stop it, he told himself. *Stop it until you have proof.*

He knew in his heart that the Way of the Sasenna is not to ask for proof. The Council had decided; it was no longer his affair. Nevertheless, he began to search the darkened study.

As it had been in Salteris' lifetime, the room was crowded with books, tablets, charts, astrolabes, and armillaries, but scrupulously neat. The old man's desk towered above it all in its little niche near the fire, like some massive black castle, turreted and crenellated with scroll-edged pigeon-holes and a treasure house of secret compartments. A couple of candleholders arched out over the slanted writing surface, but the waxen shafts they bore were unburned and covered with dust. Salteris had seldom bothered to light them when he worked, seeing, as all mageborn could, in the dark.

Caris' own sight in darkness was not as good as most mages', but it would have to suffice. The wind, which had risen to a screaming frenzy over the rooftops, would cover any noises he might make, but he could not hide light.

Methodically, he searched.

His grandmother, Salteris' wife in all but name for forty years, had told him of this desk, fascinating him with its marvels while he, a fair-haired child with dirt on his hands, sat on her knee. His fingers, light and sure as a craftsman's, probed delicately for hidden springs and secret doors, compartments tucked into what appeared to be mere partitions. Outside, the wind howled down from the north, driving sleet and rain before it; in the darkness around him, the old house rocked uneasily on its timbers. In one compartment he found his grandfather's porcelain flute—a flute that he remembered the old man playing for his grandmother, but had not heard Salteris play since.

In another, he found a handful of bullets. There was no mistaking them—point-nosed, gleaming, wrapped in their brass cartridges. He drew the gun from his sash, and broke open the cylinder; they were too large to fit, but clearly of the same manufacture. A little more search of the desk yielded the gun itself. Two of its chambers were empty.

Caris set the gun down on the desk. He was so angry his hands shook, cold, furious rage that felt queerly impersonal in its intensity. Suraklin had murdered his grandfather, years ago, calmly, greedily, tricking him with a play of friendship and understanding in his former guise as the Emperor Hieraldus until he was ready to strike. He had murdered poor Thirle, stout and affable and trusting, simply because he was in the way. Who knew how many others besides? He had used Caris' love, twisted and tricked him and tried to manipulate him into killing the one man who might have been able to offer effective opposition.

Caris' fisted hands tightened until the bones hurt.

And Suraklin had gotten away with it. He was still at large. Bound by his vows to the Council, there was nothing Caris could do.

Though the storm-darkness still blotted the windows, Caris knew it would soon be time for morning training with the other sasenna. Quietly, he wrapped both guns in the oiled cloth, along with the bullets. Then he rose and slipped the catch from a window nearby, to account for the rainwater that had dripped from his clothes. Retracing his steps to the window at the back of the house, he scrambled out again into the storm, taking guns and bullets with him.

CHAPTER V

THE STORM, THE WORST IN HUMAN MEMORY, LASTED UNTIL EARLY the following afternoon. Joanna watched its fury from the secrecy of a small boudoir attached to Princess Pellicida's rooms in the north wing of the Imperial Palace, a hidden love nest furnished for some forgotten princely mistress of the last generation and enterable only through a hinged wall panel near the head of Pella's bed. The previous night she and the Regent's wife had arranged to meet at a masked ball at the merchant prince Calve Dirham's extensive townhouse near the palace park. They had talked until nearly four in the morning, watching Prince Cerdic, who probably believed himself incognito behind a mask of seashells and pearls, winning thousands of Imperial Eagle coins in the gambling rooms while Suraklin had looked on, his suit of old-fashioned blue velvet and lace transformed into a macabre incongruity by the grinning mask of a skull.

The Prince's streak of uncanny luck at cards, at dice, and at roulette—Dirham's gaming room had boasted a roulette wheel, which for some reason reminded Joanna of the arcade-size videogame which Gary Fairchild had made available to his guests—had lasted for four hours, causing Joanna to remark, "I bet that's the *real* reason they outlawed wizards meddling in human affairs." She'd seen Cerdic's old suit of magic-proof armor, and wondered facetiously if there existed, in the attics of the nobility, na-aar roulette wheels, dice, and card decks.

It was not until this morning that she understood the true reason.

By the time she and Pella had discussed plans for freeing Antryg, the wind had begun—violent, unseasonable, arctic. Rather than have Joanna go seeking a cab in the pouring rain or scandalize the entire servant population into an orgy of gossip by instructing Pellicida's coachman to drive to Magister Magus' house, Pella had offered her the hospitality of the little hideaway in her suite. "You don't have to worry about Pharos," the Princess said, as the carriage had pulled away from Dirham's in the pitch-black, screaming darkness. "He stays in his own palace. I'm told he's even given his paramour Leynart rooms there."

Joanna had laughed. "I don't imagine Pharos even knows where your rooms are."

Beneath the trailing black-and-white feathers of the mask she still wore, Pella's mouth had tightened. She looked away. Her voice sounded very small. "He does."

Joanna blushed hotly in the darkness of the coach. Whatever brief honeymoon this girl had known with the Regent, Joanna thought, as a first experience Pharos would undoubtedly tie for last with Jack the Ripper. No wonder Suraklin had found her easy prey. As they drove slowly through the palace park, blind with the rain and stopping continually as huge branches and even young trees were literally ripped from their roots to come careening like drunken witches through the howling air, Joanna could see the dim lights of the Regent's palace, glimmering through the thick trees that hemmed it in. She wondered if he were in his study reading a good book—the Marquis de Sade, for preference—or merely spending a quiet evening in the basement, whipping his servants.

"I wish it didn't matter to me," that sweet, curiously husky voice went on after a long time of silence. "I wish I could just—I don't know. Shut my eyes and not care whether someone murdered him or not. Then I could be rid of him, and not—not have to put up with . . . with all this." She sighed, and looked back at Joanna, her white wig, mingled with the long black feathers of the concealing mask she wore, starkly pale against the dusky oval of her face in the reflected glow of the carriage lamps. "The thing is, I know he's a good ruler. I've seen good rule at home. Senterwing isn't a very large country, but Uncle Tye makes the most of what he has. He's always spoken well of Pharos' policies. Pharos understands trade and industry and all the things landholders aren't supposed to concern themselves with. That's why he married me, because Senterwing is a country of factories and banks. It's just that—I suppose being a good ruler is different from being a good man."

"I know," Joanna said. "And as a matter of fact, it's because he's a good ruler—or a strong ruler, anyway—that Suraklin wants to get rid of him and put Cerdic on the throne. Cerdic would sure as hell let him run the country."

Pellicida sighed. "It sounds—I don't know, pompous I suppose—to say so, but it's one reason I want to help you. It isn't fashionable here to be concerned about it, but I was brought up to believe in good rulership. So much depends on it." She toyed with her fan, her big, awkward hands dwarfing the delicate confection of ivory and silk, keeping her eyes on it rather than meeting Joanna's. Silhouetted against the sodden gloom, her strong-featured face seemed older than its eighteen years, momentarily the face of a woman and a queen. Then she ducked her head—Joanna sensed rather than saw her blotchy, unbecoming blush. "And then these times of deadness, these drained patches, that you say are caused by this machine of Suraklin's . . . One of them took place not too long after I let him seduce me. I came very close to killing myself then. Not out of guilt—not really. Just a kind of hopelessness. It seemed to me that from then on there would be nothing else for me but that, going from lover to lover because there was nothing else to do here. It all seemed so stale and dirty. And I wonder how many other people have felt like that during those times, and how many went through with it?"

The Princess was out when Joanna woke. It was eleven o'clock by the digital watch stashed in the pockets of her petticoats and by the delicate ormolu clock on the mantelpiece, but there was a covered breakfast tray in the empty sitting room. A fire burned in the small marble grate, warming the little suite; indoor plants clustered near it like fragile children shunning the rough world outside. The place was cluttered and cozy, filled with knickknacks and pets: a cageful of ornamental finches whose aimless twittering gave Joanna a whole new insight into the term "bird-brained"; Pella's two fat pugs about whom Joanna, a cat person, privately agreed with the Regent; and, to Joanna's great delight, a five-foot boa constrictor dozing in wintry torpor in a big glass cabinet built into the side of the chimney. "Mellachior spends most of his winters asleep," Pella had remarked, tapping the glass gently; the shinning earth-colored coils within did not shift. "They laugh at me around here, but I was brought up with animals. As things worked out, I'm glad I brought them along."

Wind still ravenned at the windows, though, by the sound of it, the storm was lessening. Pella's two fat pugs, clearly unhappy at the tumult, crouched beside Joanna on the windowseat as she looked out across the devastated park. The naked shrubs had been stripped of most of their branches and whole trees snapped off short, to lie tangled and dead in the slate-colored lakes of the flooded paths.

Joanna pulled more closely about her the overlong plush robe she'd borrowed from her hostess and shivered. Through what little had remained of the dark hours, she'd listened to the rain slashing against the secret room's small, round window. It had come to her then why the interference of wizards in human affairs was—and should be—punishable by death.

The door opened. She glanced up as Pella entered, Kyssha pattering restlessly at her heels. The little dog dashed over to greet Joanna, then to engage in an orgy of sniffing and licking with the two lapdogs. Pella only stood like an outsize bird of paradise in her primrose and green riding dress, her face somber and her eyes filled with sorrow and concern.

Pella was the daughter of merchant kings. Joanna guessed that she, too, had understood what the storm had done.

"It destroyed the trade-fleet," she asked quietly, "didn't it?"

Pella nodded. She seemed stunned, shedding her enormous greatcoat and shaking the last flecks of the fitful, windblown drizzle from her coarse black hair. "All the first-comers, the ones that would have put in today to get the cream of the market. God knows how many others out among the islands." She dropped her gloves and her coat, moving as if the loss, the tragedy, were hers and not others'. "Autumn's a quiet season," she went on. "Fogs and rain, yes, but never winds like that. The whole harbor is one lake of fouled masts; they've pulled hundreds of bodies out so far. They say Calve Dirham hanged himself this morning, rather than face his investors."

Joanna remembered him vaguely from last night, a jovial little man, vulgar but anxious for everyone to have a good time. Wrath stirred in her, the hot wrath she had felt yesterday while watching Suraklin smiling through poor Gary's mouth. She felt the cold of the window glass breathe against her back as she leaned against it. Her voice came out surprisingly level. "Were any of the ships Cerdic invested in wrecked?"

The Princess shook her head wearily. "I don't know, Joanna. There were so many . . ." Then she stopped, realizing what Joanna had asked. She stared at her in silence, her hazel eyes wide with first shock, then dawning horror. "That's impossible."

"Think about it." In her mind Joanna saw Suraklin again as she had seen him last night—the skull smiling above blue velvet and lace.

"He *couldn't,*" Pella whispered. "I know Cerdic's ships were supposed to be far in the rear, but . . . Most of the fleet was wrecked, Joanna! Hundreds were killed . . ."

"It wiped out fortunes, didn't it?" Joanna folded her arms across her drawn-up knees, regarding the gawky young Princess in her coat of daffodil velvet, still standing beside the hearth and the gilded snake cage.

"And people who lost their year's income will be turning to a man who has money. You saw how much he won last night, and I'd be willing to bet none of the ships he invested in were in the harbor last night. I don't think Cerdic's going to let himself believe Suraklin did this to buy him power, and Suraklin's probably going to come up with some plausible explanation so Cerdic doesn't have to believe it. But I think that's what happened.

"I didn't really understand before," she went on, standing up, the folds of the robe falling thickly around her feet, "why the Council would make it punishable by death for the mageborn to interfere in human affairs." She kicked the dragging weight of the lavender velvet out of the way and crossed to where Pella stood. "Even watching Suraklin making the cards fall right for Cerdic, or spinning the roulette wheel his way . . . Maybe there are people who'd even forgive a love-spell or two, like the one he put on you. So what? they'd say. But I know now the kind of thing that they meant, five hundred years ago, when they fought the Battle of Stellith over it; I know the potential for destruction of someone really powerful who doesn't give a damn, so long as he gets what he wants. And do you know what else I know?"

The Princess looked at her apprehensively, this small, outlander woman with her tangled blond curls hanging over the robe's gray fur collar, her arms folded over her breasts.

"They're going to find some way to blame it on Antryg."

"The Prince won't ask questions if I say I'm going to one of the royal residences near Kymil." Pella deftly steered her chestnut team around the ruins of a chimney which had literally been blown into the street, the long wreckage of brick stretching like a snake across the flooded cobblestones and on into the tangle of glass, broken shutters, and ruined goods in a shop window. "Everyone makes jokes about Senterwing being a swamp, but it's warmer than Angelshand. I can probably get away with saying I can't stand the cold."

With her black hair braided up under a close-fitting cap and her tall form muffled in a many-caped cloak such as coachmen wore, the Princess was sufficiently anonymous at the reins of her unmarked phaeton. The masculine style suited her far better than her frilled court dresses did; by no longer trying to apologize for her square jaw and wide mouth, she gave them dignity and a kind of severe beauty. Joanna, huddled beside her on the high seat with a cloak covering the elaborately silly gown she'd worn to the ball last night, had leisure to look around at the swamped streets of the town.

Most of them were flooded right across, and the phaeton's wheels threw up little wings of water as it passed servants and laborers working ankle-deep at clearing away the wreckage of broken trees, fallen chimneys, and scattered roof tiles. In the poorer districts of the town south of the river, Joanna thought, the damage would be worse. She remembered the rickety tenements that leaned so perilously against one another and the vendors' stands in the streets. Even in the relatively affluent neighborhoods near Governor's Square, there was a silence, an air of calamity, and a ghastly realization that money borrowed or spent against the expectation of those investments was truly gone.

But in the poor quarters it would not be a question of money, but of husbands, brothers, fathers, and sons, dragged dead out of the broken tangle of fouled spars and lines that stretched for miles along the smoke-colored waters of the harbor. It was a question of marginal poverty turning into starving destitution and of cold beds and children who would never see their fathers—or days without hunger—again.

Joanna shivered, oppressed as she had been her first morning in Kymil, by the sense of being brought face-to-face with intolerable situations which she had no power to rectify—except, she thought, by doing what she was doing, by attending to the matter at hand. "Can you get a copy of Pharos' seal?" she asked and Pellicida nodded. For all her youth she had a bluntly matter-of-fact grasp of the essentials.

"He keeps the seal itself guarded, I don't know where. But I have two or three letters from him with it on the bottom."

"Magister Magus will know how to remove them," Joanna said. *And he'll do it,* she added grimly to herself, *or I'll know the reason why.* He'd be horrified, of course, as he'd been horrified yesterday when Joanna had told him she'd found an ally in the Regent's wife, but it couldn't be helped. If they were to free Antryg, they'd need forged signatures and faked seals to get into the Tower, and she had a shrewd idea the Magus knew who in Angelshand could provide such things at short notice.

And the notice, she thought, looking around her at the sheets of leaden water and at the desperate, angry faces, would be very short indeed. They were people mortally injured, seeking someone to blame. It wouldn't take much of a manipulator to turn that anger against anyone who might stand in his way.

She stroked Kyssha's fluffy head; the dog lay like a little muff across her lap, Pella needing all her freedom of action to control the team in the flooded debris through which they passed. Clumsy and gawky as the tall Princess seemed on foot in her tasseled and overjeweled gowns, she was a steady and light-handed driver. She was careful of her team, too, getting out and testing the deeply flooded patches of street for submerged wreckage; and restive as they were, the horses stood obediently with Joanna's hand on the rein until Pella had scrambled up to the high seat again.

"I helped train them," she said, when Joanna spoke of it. "We had a marvel of a trainer at home. He taught me everything he could when Mother wasn't looking. I was always more at home in the stables than I was at dancing lessons. At least no one laughed when I tripped over my own feet." She sighed, looking out across the team's sharp-pricked ears as she guided them around the broken corpse of a tree that blocked half the lane. "I never really cared for being a Princess."

Down at the far end of the street, voices shouted, a rumble of angry sound punctuated suddenly by a yell. "Lynch him! String him up! Storm caller—he did this!" Other voices joined in like a hellish chorus baying, "Hang him! Hang the wizard!"

"Oh God," Joanna whispered, knowing what it had to be. Pella exchanged a quick, scared glance with her, then clucked encouragement to her team, who trotted nervously forward with a hissing swish of muddy water.

There must have been thirty or forty people in Governor's Square, men and women both, mostly laborers and servants. They were rudely armed with makeshift clubs, bread knives, and bits of timber from broken shutters. A knot of black-clothed sasenna clustered around the steps of Magister Magus' house, keeping them back.

". . . behind it all summer!" a man in the long caped cloak and muffler of a cab driver was yelling. "It's him that called up them abominations, those things setting fire to the houses in the Haymarket! Ruined the harvest, belike, too! And now this . . . !"

The doors opened. Four sasenna and two men in the narrow gray garments of Witchfinders emerged, leading Magister Magus between them. Around the steps, the crowd set up a yammering like the hounds of hell. Clods of dirt and horse dung splattered against the wall on all sides of the door, and Magus flinched, trying to hide his face against his shoulder as best he could in wretchedness and shame. His hands were bound behind him; even at this distance, Joanna saw the blood-bright ribbon of spell-cord twisted through the bonds. She only realized she had half risen in the phaeton seat when Pella pulled her back down.

"There's nothing we can do."

The mob was pushing in. The sasenna descended the steps, thrusting them back. Two remained by the door with their prisoner, their crossbows leveled on him, as if they expected him to attempt to fell them with a Bruce Lee wheel kick, leap over the heads of the crowd, and make good his escape. The dog wizard's thin face was white against his disheveled black hair; a bruise was already blackening on his temple.

Joanna looked across at Pella, fear kicking hard at her chest. "It isn't that. My backpack's in the house. It's got the program disk in it, the only thing that can take out the programming in Suraklin's computer."

Pella's full, square lips pressed taut; her eyes narrowed as she scanned the square and the little group before the house. "They'll need their whole force to keep the crowd off him. One of us could get in the back now before they search the house."

Joanna's stomach curled up in terror at the possibility of capture by the Witchfinders and the thought of facing the Witchfinder Peelbone again. But she knew the Princess was right. She took a deep breath, "Okay. If I'm not back in . . ."

Pella handed her the reins. "I'll go. Can you hold them?" And when Joanna moved to make a totally half-hearted protest, she asked, "What can they do to me if they catch me? I'm the wife of the Heir. What does this backpack thing look like?"

Joanna told her and held Kyssha back from joining her as the tall girl sprang down from the seat and pushed her way off through the crowd.

A small black carriage had been brought up to the house doors, enclosed and heavily curtained. Joanna remembered it well. She had ridden in a similar one from the house of the murdered Dr. Skipfrag to the St. Cyr fortress after her own arrest.

The guards formed a flying wedge around Magus, breasting like swimmers through the crowd to get him there; angry fists were shaken at them, and now and then a stick flailed out of the mob to strike one or another on their shoulders. The Magus cowered in the midst of his guards, with the look on his face of a rabbit in a trap. Remembering his kindness to her and the fact that it was he who had helped Antryg rescue her from Peelbone and his Witchfinders, Joanna felt like a traitor.

A voice said close to her knee, "You know he'll be safer with them than he would if he stayed in his house."

Startled, she looked down. Caris stood beside the phaeton.

"What will be done to him?" she asked quietly.

"Magus?" Caris shrugged, watching the progress of the mêlée by the steps with a professional eye. "If Cerdic speaks up for him, probably only a public flogging and banishment. But rumor has it that Cerdic's found himself a new Spiritual Advisor these days."

Voices rose, and dung and pieces of broken brick rained down on the closed black carriage as it began to move away. A stray chunk of dirt struck one of Pella's phaeton team and the horse flung up its head ner-

vously. Caris caught the rein and drew the beast back down, talking
gently and stroking the soft nose. A moment later Pella reappeared, the
bulk of her tweed cloak appearing even bulkier with the backpack hidden
beneath it. She saw Caris and stopped, her brisk competence fading to
awkwardness at once.

"It's all right," Joanna said. "At least—I think it's all right. But we'd
probably better get out of here." The crowd around the Magus' house
was dispersing as three sasenna went back up the steps. One of them
removed from the pouch at his belt a bar of red wax and a seal; Joanna
suspected reinforcements would be on the way.

"It's all right," Caris assured her. His voice even and impersonal, he
went on, "I've just heard that Cerdic's two ships have been sighted coming in past the Chittern Islands. It seems one of them sprang a plank or
something and had to put in at Felwip a few days ago. I don't know what
happened with the other, but something similar, some accident that kept
them in port in the islands."

"Dear God," Pella said softly. Her green-gold eyes filled with pain,
either at the destruction itself or at this final proof of cold-blooded per-
fidy; half-subconsciously she put out her hand to touch the flank of her
near horse, as if seeking in the animal contact some grounding to the
gentler life she had left behind. After a silent moment, she handed the
backpack up to Joanna, swung herself up onto the high driver's seat
again, and collected the reins.

Without a word, Caris sprang up to the groom's perch behind them.
Still in that same automatic fashion, as if she were handling a car instead
of two nervous animals, Pella backed her team neatly, turned them, and
guided them across the flooded cobbles of the square. She looked
stunned; Joanna found herself remembering that most people in this
world only half believed in magic, if they believed in it at all. It was one
thing, she supposed, to have a love-spell put on you. It was another to see
spells used on that scale with that kind of cold-blooded selfishness.

To Caris, Joanna only said, "Suraklin's staying with Cerdic. He's been
helping him win money in the gambling halls; Cerdic will have a fortune
now to buy friends with. We don't know, but we think Suraklin means to
murder Pharos and get control of the Empire."

"That would make sense," Caris said quietly. "He will be trying to
protect himself, if it is in fact his aim to become one of these computer
machines." Then for a long time he said nothing, only held onto the brass
railing of the groom's perch, staring out in front of him as Pella drove
through the flooded, half-empty streets of the town. Kyssha put her paws
on the seatback and nosed at his hand; Caris stroked her head absently,

as if not truly aware of her presence. Then he sighed. "I found this in Grandfather's house." He took a revolver from his belt. Glimpsing it there earlier, Joanna had assumed that it was the one he'd taken from her, but she saw now it was a .45, not a .38. She glanced quickly up at his face, and saw it strained and bitter, as if he had taken some scouring drug.

He had wept, she remembered, over the dead Archmage's body, sobs that had seemed to tear him apart. "I'm sorry."

He shook his head, as if he would say something; but after a false start, he was silent.

Hesitantly, Joanna said, "Maybe if you showed it to the new Archmage . . ."

"It wouldn't do me any good," Caris said, his voice quiet but hard as stone. "For one thing, it is not for me, as sasennan, even to have investigated; the Lady Rosamund has already told me that the matter is closed. Then, too, most of the mages have left the Yard. They know the storm was caused by magic. They tried to trace it, but weather tampering is very hard to track. They knew they'd be blamed. After their arrest last summer, even the few who stayed in town have kept getaway bags packed. The last of them left before noon." He sounded remote, as if it barely concerned him; had she trained with him as sasennan, Joanna would have recognized the tone he used when he was injured and trying to speak around gut-tearing pain. Pella glanced back at him, comprehension and worry in her eyes. "Some of them took sasenna with them, but I was one of the ones ordered to stay as a guard against looters."

There was a moment's silence, broken by the milky swish of the wheels in the flooded street and the splashing of the horses' hooves. Joanna knew it was an unfair question, but asked it anyway. "And will you?"

He didn't look at her. "Joanna, you don't understand."

She half turned in her seat, looking up at that tense, beautiful face in the sunless light. "I do understand, a little—at least as much as anyone can understand who hasn't been brought up with that strong a concept of honor. And after seeing the destruction Suraklin has wrought, I think I understand the vows of the sasenna as analogous to those of the mages; that one who is trained to kill *can not* be permitted to choose his own places and times for it, any more than one who has been trained to alter the physical world by an act of his own will. But that doesn't change what Suraklin is doing. It doesn't change the fact that he's got to be stopped at whatever the cost."

Keeping clear of the poorer districts near the river, Pella guided her horses through a broad square past a neoclassical domed building that was obviously a bank. Its granite steps churned with businessmen in dark broadcloth like a hosed-out anthill. One young man came quickly down the steps and climbed into a closed carriage as Pella drove past. Through the windows, Joanna could see him, once he thought himself out of sight of his colleagues, bury his face in his hands like a man who has heard the sentence of his own death.

Behind her, Caris' voice was desperate. "Don't do this to me, Joanna."

Antryg had said that, she remembered, lying with bound hands, waiting for the wizards to come for him.

She did not look back at him, only pleated at the knots of green silk ribbon that bordered the sleeves of last night's ballgown. "Why did you come looking for me, then?"

Caris sighed, bitter and weary, as if he had not even been sure he meant to speak to her until now. "To tell you that the rumor in the Mages' Yard is that Peelbone the Witchfinder left Angelshand this morning, as soon as the wind eased enough to let him travel. He's heading south, for Kymil."

"Are you angry with Caris?" Pella asked later, pausing in her search for a spill of kindling to light the candles in the rapidly encroaching gloom of her apartments. "Because you shouldn't be."

"Not really." Joanna's small hands continued to move as she talked, folding the mountains of petticoats, nightdresses, and chemises whose packing she had taken over after Pella had, for the fifth time, gone wandering around the chaos of the room looking for a mislaid glove. "I know he takes his vows as a sasennan very seriously; I suppose it's like a devoutly religious person being asked to deny God in order to save the life of someone he loves."

Pella nodded. "Only of course all sasenna are automatically excommunicate—except the Church's, that is. They don't deny God, but they certainly must choose their master's wishes over the Church's without an instant's thought. It's the same reason they don't make legal marriages." Around her feet, Kyssha and the two lapdogs played hide-and-seek among the lace ruffles of half a dozen petticoats tossed carelessly on the floor. "You know it is in the Council's power to have him killed for disobedience?"

"I know if a sasennan becomes—flawed, or crippled, he's supposed to kill himself," Joanna said slowly, thinking of the Regent's deaf servant Kanner. "But I don't think that fear was a factor in Caris' decision to stay here."

"No," Pella agreed quietly. Forgetting her quest for illumination, she returned to the dense shadows of the bed and helped Joanna dump the latest heap of lace-edged lawn into the trunk at her side. "Do we *have* to pack all this?"

"We do if it's going to look as if you're heading south for a leisurely change of climate," Joanna declared. In straightforward matters of animals or physical courage or, Joanna suspected, policy, the Princess had a powerful and instinctive grace, like an animal herself; but faced with the nuanced complexities of clothing or behavior, she lapsed into gaucherie. Joanna, morbidly sensitive to all the things she herself had been urged to do, felt an overwhelming sympathy. She fished her backpack from the floor and dug from it a notebook, from which she ripped half a page. She twisted the paper into a makeshift spill and handed it to Pella, who remembered what she was about and hurried to the fireplace to touch one end to the small blaze there. "The minute it's light enough and we're away from Angelshand, we're going to leave it behind with the baggage wagons and go on in your phaeton, remember."

The Princess froze in the act of touching the lighted end to a candle wick. "The letters of credit for changing horses . . ."

"I have them here." Joanna nudged her backpack with one toe. After watching Pellicida's absentminded packing all afternoon, she had taken the precaution of stowing everything they would truly need in various pockets of the bulging sack—the aforesaid provision for changing horses en route, a great deal of money, and a sheaf of letters and orders from Pharos, several of which bore his seal which Joanna hoped she'd be able to remove with a hot knife, once she'd forged permits to get in to the Tower itself.

Returning to the former topic, she went on, "I think it would be easier for one of us to get in to see Antryg if we had a sasennan along to make it look more official . . ."

"At a pinch, I could pass myself off as a sasennan," Pella said thoughtfully. "That is, I've had some training. We all did—my cousins and I, back home, though of course, since we would never be allowed to take vows, we were never trained at the higher levels. But I've got a uniform and a sword, as well as a clerk's robe for you."

"*Are* there female clerks?"

Pella looked startled that Joanna would ask. "Of course. A man doesn't write with his—er—whiskers." The spill burned down to her fingers; looking startled, she hastily lit the candle with it and tossed the flaming paper into the hearth. Then she proceeded to rove restlessly around the little bedchamber, lighting the candles that stood in holders of crystal, gilt bronze, and creamy porcelain. "Speaking of writing, I can fill out the text of the passes to get us into the Tower—any clerk would do that—but Pharos' signature is another matter. I was never any good at drawing. Besides, he's left-handed."

"I think I can manage that," Joanna said. "At least, I could always forge my mother's, and *she's* left-handed, not to mention signing her name like a Rorschach test. You know, in a way I feel rather sorry for Caris."

"Sorry?" Pella bristled.

"He's in an almost impossible situation," she explained quietly. Elsewhere in the palace, on the floor below, voices were momentarily raised and a hurrying of feet was heard; Pella swung around, her greenish eyes darkening, and she stood frozen like a deer in stillness until the sounds passed away. "What is it?"

"Nothing," the girl said and blushed again. "That is—whenever my mother went traveling, which wasn't often, my father used to come up to her rooms and bid her goodbye. It isn't that I expect Pharos to, but . . ." She stammered to a conclusion, as if realizing how ludicrous the comparison was.

Her parents must have loved one another a great deal, Joanna thought, torn between cynicism and envy, to have given her such ineradicable hopes about marriage.

She, too, had been listening for Pharos' chance coming, though for different reasons. When she went back to her packing, the leftover adrenaline flash made her fingers shake.

All it would need, she thought, was the smallest suspicion on his part. All it would need was one servant's rumor, one bit of gossip about his wife's new friend. For he would recognize her, of course. He might or might not take out his vicious sense of betrayal by Antryg on her, but whatever happened, at a screamingly optimistic least it would mean delay.

There could be no delay. Not now.

On their return to the north wing of the Imperial Palace Pellicida had been all for ordering a fresh change of horses for her phaeton and setting forth then and there, in the hopes of overtaking the Witchfinder's equipage and holding the lead all the way to Kymil. It had taken considerable persuasion on Joanna's part to convince her to wait for tomorrow morning, as even the most precipitate journey would under normal circumstances. Hence the long and tedious business of packing, of ordering the great traveling coach and a smaller vehicle for the servants and extra luggage, and of sending postriders ahead with orders to prepare Larkmoor, the small royal manor near Kymil.

Much as it drove Joanna insane to watch the failing of the afternoon light—it was only three-thirty—and to know that they couldn't leave for another fifteen hours or so, she knew that it was necessary to avert suspicion. She had no idea whether Suraklin was still with Cerdic at the Dower House and no idea if or how intently he kept track of Pella's movements. Throughout Pella's packing—or rather Joanna's packing of Pella's things while the Princess roved abstractedly around the apartment, looking for items Joanna had already packed—Joanna had been burningly conscious of the slow-moving gilt hands of the mantelpiece clock, half-buried under an orgy of enamel-and-gold nymphs, and of the gathering darkness outside. Peelbone the Witchfinder was on his way south, undoubtedly with the final warrant for Antryg's death in his pocket. At this point, the Council of Wizards was in no shape to prevent it, as Suraklin had clearly intended. And she knew she was doomed to sit in these rooms until enough time had passed for someone to sleep and wake up before she could do anything about it.

Screaming with frustration will not help, she told herself firmly, with wry and involuntary humor, *and will only cause talk among the servants.* With the hideous sensation of having her plans ravel once again from her hands, she went back to her packing, wondering how she would pass the night until morning.

It was seven A.M., black as the pits of hell and bitterly cold, when the Princess' huge traveling carriage finally lumbered away. To the last, Pellicida had been listening, waiting for some sign of her husband's coming, some acknowledgment from him that her movements mattered to him, and Joanna had fretted herself nearly ill with apprehension. He had not come, of course. Perhaps the girl did not consciously expect that he would, but Joanna could sense her disappointment and her hurt, ridiculous though it was, and was fond enough of the big, gawky girl to feel sorry for her. She herself had been more fearful that Suraklin would choose that inopportune moment to renew his attempt to seduce the Prince's wife. Then the game would have been up indeed.

River fog had risen to blanket the palace grounds and the city that lay beyond the walls; through it Joanna could see nothing, but now and then she heard the slop and drip of the horses' hooves in puddles and knew that the landscape would be one of absolute desolation. It was wretchedly cold in the coach, in spite of heated bricks wrapped up in the fur robes at their feet, and Joanna watched the soft steam of her breath float in the reflected glow of the carriage lamps. The coach was badly sprung; though the Princess' phaeton, which followed behind, ostensibly for Pella's use once they reached Larkmoor, was slightly better, she was miserably anticipating several days of jolting discomfort. She tried to keep herself from thinking about Antryg, about what would happen to her if she failed to rescue him, or if, having gotten the accursed Sigil off his throat, she found him permanently mind-broken as Magister Magus had feared. She tried not to think of the Magus, either.

He would be in the St. Cyr fortress now, in one of the vermin-ridden cells whose walls, like those of the Silent Tower, were spelled against the working of magic, perhaps the same cell in which she and the tiny, decrepit old crone Minhyrdin the Fair had been locked. It had been his spell, she remembered unhappily, that had allowed Antryg to break her out.

She leaned her head back against the soft plush of the seat squabs and shut her eyes, her head aching. She could think of no way in which she had betrayed him; it was sheer luck that she herself had spent last night at the palace instead of going home to be arrested with him. She could not help him. In fact, tarrying here would put her in danger of arrest herself when the Witchfinders began questioning him, even had Antryg not been facing immediate death. But she still felt guilty at abandoning the poor little quack to his fate.

The jolt of the carriage as it lurched to a stop made her open her eyes. At the same time she heard Pella gasp, and the Princess' big, clumsy hand sought hers under the velvet softness of the furs. Her heart seeming to shrink in her breast to something the size of a filbert, Joanna sat up and followed the younger girl's gaze through the carriage window, out into the blackness of the iron dawn.

Dark against the fog, a black shape stood on the verge of the road; a black cloak fell back from a raised arm. The horses drew up, their breath smoking like dragons' in the cold. Wet gravel crunched under soft boots. The lamps caught the glint of blond hair.

After an instant's frozen shock, Pella opened the carriage door. Caris climbed in without a word, the soft leather of his dagger belts creaking as he slumped back into the seat opposite the two girls. He did not look at them, nor did he speak; he just stared furiously out into the charcoal blackness of the mist as the coachman whipped up the horses, and, with a rattle of brasses and leather, they started forward again.

CHAPTER VI

AT THE SUMMER'S END, CARIS REMEMBERED, IT HAD TAKEN HIM and the Archmage Salteris Solaris a week to walk from Angelshand to Kymil, ostensibly to seek the answer to the riddle of the mage Thirle's murder from Antryg Windrose, imprisoned in the Silent Tower. He had made the journey many times before, though that had been the first time he and Salteris had taken that road together. Always, as befitted the weapon of the Council of Wizards, it had been on foot.

Thus his memories of that journey had a slowness to them, in contrast to the hurried beat of the carriage team's hooves and the sting of wind on his face; then there had been the rhythm of a foot pace, the long flux of the amber and cobalt wings of summer days and nights, and the taste of dust and dew. The weather was well and truly winter now, the winds like flint and the roads either foul slime troughs or slicked with ice. Joanna and Pellicida were wrapped in rugs and mittens in the Princess' open traveling carriage, but Caris himself, high on the footman's perch behind them, barely felt the cold.

At times, the rage in him felt so hot that he thought he must smother; at others, his whole soul seemed to be nothing, down to its bottommost depths, but a pit filled with broken black ice. He hardly spoke, although, when Pella drew the team to a stop and jumped down to check their hooves for ice balled in their frogs, Caris sprang from his high perch to hold their heads.

Only that night, when Joanna had clustered all the lamps available on the table of the smoky, stinking, private parlor they had rented at the posting inn of the Plucky Duck to practice forging the Regent's signature, did he say, "Do you really think that's going to do us any good?"

He was weary, and the weariness came out as scorn; Joanna's head came up, her dark eyes hurt and a little puffy with sleepiness. But there was a spark in them, that spark of anger he had first seen in the alley behind the Standing Stallion in Angelshand, when she had cursed at him to act like a man. "If you've got a better plan for getting Antryg out of the Tower, I'd like to hear it."

Her fingers were chapped and red—it was very cold in the room, in spite of the grimy fire in the grate—and the imitation of Pharos' writing wouldn't have deceived a child.

He didn't, but Joanna's high-handed assumption of command chaffed him like a too-tight sleeve. "You haven't seen Antryg," he told her bitterly. "I have."

"It's the Sigil of Darkness . . ."

"Pox! It may have been the Sigil of Darkness that pushed him over the edge of madness, but taking it off him isn't going to restore what few wits he may once have possessed! *If* you can get it off him at all, which I'm waiting to see, in a Tower full of guards. And he's physically deteriorating as well . . ."

"Whose fault is that?" Joanna lashed at him.

"You're the one who put him there."

He could see her whole body tense, like the shutting of a fist. In the greasy orange glare of the two or three lamps before her, the thin face seemed to tighten in on itself, cold anger holding itself in. Stiltedly, as if counting out every word, she said, "I know I'm the one who put him there. But there's nothing that I or anyone can do to change things that have already happened. I can't know what to do about getting him out until I've seen him. For that, I need to get into the Tower . . ."

"And you think they're going to take the Sigil of Darkness off the outer doors to let *me* pass inside with you? Or that they're not going to ask about you having a mageborn sasennan with you?"

Her mouth stayed clamped shut, but he could see the tears of helpless anger gather in her eyes, and her small hands, that could not even wield a quill properly, shake.

"If that's how you feel about our chances of success, why did you come?"

"Because when you try to break Antryg out of the Tower," said Caris, quiet but suddenly harsh as broken stone, "Suraklin's going to hear about it. Suraklin will come . . ." He got to his feet, almost throwing the crude, heavy chair from him. "And then I will kill him for what he's done to me."

She answered him in a voice thinned with spite, "What makes you think you can?"

He took a step forward, wanting to slap her and hating that new spitfire glint in her eyes "If I can't," he said slowly, "then at least I can die as a sasennan should."

Joanna drew breath to speak, then stopped. Her brown eyes, in this uncertain light as black as the coffee cooling in its cup between the lamps, met his, narrow and gleaming; around her sharp face, her hair hung like a sulfury cloud. She said nothing. After a moment Caris turned on his heel and strode from the room.

If she had thrown it in his face that he was sasennan no longer, that he had broken his vows, and deserted the Way to which he had sworn his life, he thought he would have struck her. Sitting alone in the darkness of the inn stables, listening to the groan of the wind in the rafters and filling his nostrils with the clean, warm scents of horses and hay, he felt his rage rise at her, at Suraklin, at the mages who had disappeared from the Yard, at the stolid, silent, unimaginative Princess, and at the fool of an inn-keeper who was little better than a robber for charging them a silver bit for a ladleful of stew and a hunk of bread the size of his fist. It was not the Way of the Sasenna to show rage, but he collected his rage, like steaming black liquid in a cup; a bitter drink that was all now that gave him strength.

It will sustain me, he thought, *until we reach Kymil.* After that it would not matter.

"Caris?"

The deep, husky voice made him realize with a start that he had no idea how long he'd been sitting out here. The sounds from the inn had fallen into muffled silence; the wind had risen, and when the door opened a crack, in the swimming well of shadows below the loft where he sat, he could smell the blowing snow. Mageborn, he could see in the dark when the tousled black head poked up through the ladder hole. He saw her looking around for him, peering in the blackness; he had automatically sought the deepest shadows, as it is the Way of the Sasenna to do, with the best field of fire to cover the entrance to the loft in case of attack.

He said, "Here," and the girl turned, tracking his voice without error. He heard the crunch and slither of her boots on the straw and the faint, light patter as she set Kyssha down beside her. He knew very little of this girl, save that she was a good driver, hopelessly disorganized, and that Joanna had somehow convinced her of her story. As the wife of the

Regent she was, he realized, the first lady of the Empire, but it was difficult to remember that. For all her height, in her plain traveling dress she was curiously unobtrusive, speaking very little to the tense and preoccupied Joanna and not at all to him.

Not, he reflected dourly, that he would have made much of a reply if she had.

"Do you really think Antryg won't be able to help us?" She settled in the hay near him, drawing her thick tweed cloak about her. A moment later, Kyssha's small, cold nose came questing at his hand.

With a rueful smile, he gathered the little dog into his lap, like a folded marionette. Softly, he said, "You know, I think the hardest thing to give up when I went into training was my dog? Her name was Ratbane." He sighed, not adding that the closest he had come to crying during the time of his training had been when he'd received news of her death. Of course he had not cried. He had been sixteen by then, and it was in any case not the Way of the Sasenna to mourn even the passing of one's parents, let alone a shaggy-coated shepherd bitch with one blue eye.

After a moment he went on, "I don't know. Joanna isn't sasennan, and she isn't mageborn. She doesn't understand . . ." His mind shied from the thought of the Seal of the Dead God. It had taken every ounce of strength, every knotted fragment of the hate within him, not to shrink away when they'd fixed the iron collar around Antryg's throat. The thought of touching the thing made him want to vomit. "The Sigil's strength is in proportion to the strength of the mage. It broke Antryg. He seemed to come through the torture as well as anyone does."

Her voice was quiet in the gloom. "So you think it's hopeless?"

Bitterly, he said, "Don't you?"

She made no reply, a curiously comforting silence, as if she knew he had more to say and didn't want to divert the course of it with words of her own. Outside, a gust of wind struck the stable, like the flat-on blow of a monster hand, and below them the horses stirred in their stalls. The air was heavy with their smell, clean and curiously sweet, and the sweetgrass scent of Pella's hair. Caris knew he should rest, for they would be on the road as soon as it grew light enough for the horses to see, but his whole body felt charged with restless elation, as if he had drunk the *zam* that professional boxers quaffed before their matches.

"I want one thing, Pella, and one thing only. I want to kill Suraklin. I . . ." He hesitated, all the rage that had seethed in him since he had first stood in his grandfather's study with a handful of alien bullets in his hand taking shape, for the first time, into words. Slowly, stiffly, he said, "I loved my grandfather. A sasennan isn't supposed to love, but I loved him more than anyone else in the world, maybe—certainly more than my parents, though they were as good to me as they knew how to be. It's just that they were farmers, and he was . . . he understood what it's like to be born with fire inside." He swallowed, struggling with the memory of those old hurts, wondering how after all the buried years they still seemed so fresh.

He went on, "I swore my vows to the Council because I loved him. He knew I loved him, maybe the only person I've ever told that I did. When Suraklin took over his mind, Suraklin knew that, too. And Suraklin used that, did all the things my grandfather did, things that I loved him for, played at being my grandfather, and used my love. He murdered him, killed him like a—a robber who wanted his cloak, only I was part of the cloak. He used me like a pimp."

It was the insult and the hurt, as well as the taking-away of the one person he had loved, Caris realized then, staring into the warm blackness, his blunt, powerful fingers toying with the soft fluff of Kyssha's ears. In his rage at the murder there was also rage at betrayal, as a man might feel who learns that the woman who came to his bed in darkness was not his wife, but a grinning succubus, counterfeiting the sound of her voice and the touch of her hands, in order to steal his seed. "There is no way back for me now," he finished softly. "I have betrayed my own vows. I'll have his life for what he has done and die."

They were under way again before dawn, the ice cracking sharply beneath the hooves of the newest relay of horses. Joanna dozed, exhausted from staying up half the night trying to master the techniques of forgery in an unfamiliar alphabet with writing implements she barely understood; when awake, she seemed anxious and preoccupied, as if calculating how long a start the Witchfinder had on them and whether he was able to make better progress than they. At every postinghouse, she asked news of them, and the news was depressingly the same. Peelbone was moving south fast, not lingering more than was absolutely necessary to sleep or to eat.

"Can we pick up time by driving through the night?" she asked worriedly as Caris helped her up into the phaeton again after the barest stop for lunch while the horses were changed. "Or part of it, anyway, since we're going to need some time to work on those orders."

Pella and Joanna had both ended up practicing Pharos' signature. In spite of Joanna's inexperience with the Ferr style of writing, her efforts, though less than convincing, were still far and away the best. Pella was simply too clumsy-handed to be an artist. An attempt to transfer the

Imperial Seal from one document to another had already resulted in cracking one of the three available; the other two were secreted in one of the few corners of Joanna's backpack not jammed tight with computer programs.

The backpack never left her these days, its straps wearing grooves in the thickly quilted crimson coat of one of the Regent's pages which she wore over her gray traveling dress. The scare she'd had when it had been in Magister Magus' house at the time of his arrest had been enough. Whatever the disk she carried would do to destroy Suraklin's plans—and Caris, in spite of her explanations, wasn't certain he understood it—she was determined never again to let it out of her sight.

Oddly, as he handed the backpack up to her, Caris found in himself no trace of last night's impatience and scorn. Though Pella had said very little in the stable loft, it was as if her mere presence had allowed him to vent some of the leading edge of his fury and, by speaking of it, to understand himself the hurt and the fear that underlay his wrath.

Standing by the horses' heads, Pella looked doubtful. "Even without the clouds we haven't had much of a moon lately . . ."

"If we get anything like a decent team, I can drive them in darkness," Caris said unexpectedly. "My sight in the dark isn't as sharp as a true wizard's, but I can see to drive." And, seeing the surprise in Joanna's glance, he added gruffly, "I'm not saying it will do us any good, but I'd be pleased to find out you're right about Antryg."

The words came harder than he'd thought—or would have liked to think—they would.

What they would do with the mad wizard or what was left of him if the deterioration brought on by the Sigil proved to be irreversible, Caris refrained from asking. Clinging hour after hour to the high footman's perch, or trading off the reins with Pella—Joanna not being a good enough whip to manage on the fouled roads—Caris watched the blond woman's sharp, worried face and wondered whether she was aware of the only possible option in that case. If Antryg could not be a help to them, with as powerful a mage as Suraklin alerted to his danger by the rescue, there was no way they could afford him as a hindrance. Caris knew Joanna to be not only learned in the ways of these mysterious computers, but intelligent as well. Her love of Antryg had not blinded her to the priorities of the situation. At least, he thought, it didn't seem to have blinded her mind.

And in any case, shooting the wizard like a lamed horse would be a far more merciful death than whatever was commanded by the Witchfinder Peelbone's warrant. Of that Caris was positive.

That night Caris got three or four hours' sleep in the hired parlor of the inn, while Pella and Joanna worked at what Joanna called their penmanship exercises and tried to figure out the tricky business of removing a seal from parchment without cracking it. They set out shortly before midnight in the teeth of a driving wind. Pella had to pay thrice the usual fee to take the horses out; but even driving with great care in the howling darkness, they managed to pick up six or seven hours on the Witchfinder's equipage. They had left the calmer weather of the Glidden Valley for the fringes of the Sykerst, and by dawn Caris could make out the barren gray hills rising beyond the ghostly clumps of birches beside the road.

"He's ten or twelve hours ahead of us," Pella reported, coming out of the stables of the next posting inn to where Caris and Joanna waited by the phaeton. Unlike those in the Glidden Valley, this inn was not attached to a village; it was a small affair and rather shabby, subsisting entirely on the traffic of the Kymil road. Indeed, there were no more villages between here and Kymil, only the bare gray hills of the Sykerst, stripped now even of their summer crop of wandering sheep.

It was also the inn at which, in Antryg's company, Caris and Joanna had once encountered the Regent and had been forced to leave the main road to flee his pursuit. Sitting at Joanna's side, the hood of his brown servant's cloak pulled well over his face, Caris felt just as glad they weren't staying. The events of that night had been far too spectacular for anyone not to recognize Joanna as the woman who had triggered them.

"Then if we drive all night, we can overtake him in the morning." Joanna looked exhausted. Unlike Caris, she had had no sleep last night, and she lacked Pella's ability to sleep in a moving carriage. Indeed, it took a special constitution to sleep in a small racing vehicle which could seat only two and was scarcely designed for even the small amount of luggage they carried.

"Did you come up with orders that will pass muster at the Tower?" Caris demanded.

She passed her hand over her eyes, pushing back the tangle of her fair hair. In the shadows of her dark green hood, her face looked white beneath the remains of its curious, unseasonable tan. "If we don't overtake him tonight, he's going to reach the Tower before we do anyway. I think what we have will do." Her jaw tightened. In a very small voice she added, "It will have to."

Pella swung up to the footman's stand, in spite of Caris' shocked admonition. Though no sasennan save those who had specifically sworn it owed allegiance to the Imperial Family, it still horrified his peasant heritage to see the wife of the Regent hanging on the footboard like a common groom. Caris steered the team out of the inn yard and once more onto the road.

It was a bitter day, the sky above the hills dark as a roil of ink. Periodic flurries of sleet soaked the road, the horses, and the passengers of the open phaeton, and made driving treacherous; the hard cold froze the road into a sheet of oiled glass. Caris and Pella traded places frequently, for driving under such conditions exhausted them both, and neither would even think of giving the reins to the inexperienced Joanna. Nor would either seek warmth from the bottle of plum brandy Joanna wordlessly produced from her bottomless backpack.

"I'm a cheap drunk," Pella admitted with a shy grin. "One glass of May wine and I start to sing."

Caris, holding the near horse's head while Pella picked the balled ice from its hoof, found himself thinking he would one day like to hear her sing. Her speaking voice was deep and husky, but had a sweetness to it, like an alto flute. At the moment there was nothing else sweet about her. Like him, she was splotched from head to foot with mud, her travel-dirty black braids twisted tight beneath her flat coachman's cap and her heavy mouth and chin pinched with exhaustion.

"I can't afford to take any of the edge off my concentration," Caris added. He and Pella scrambled back to their respective perches, and he took up the reins once more. "By the look of the sky, it's going to get worse tonight. But thank you."

It was four o'clock and graying toward sunset somewhere above the bruised darkness of the clouds, when the gray deadness, the numbness of body and soul, descended like a plague on the land. Joanna cursed, her small fists closing tight; she looked over at Caris, who had let the horses drop to a walk, feeling suddenly overwhelmed with a terrible sense of the futility of it all. "Do you feel it?" she asked, as if she hoped against hope that it was only her own weariness and not the draining of the world's life.

He nodded. Suddenly weary, furious with the exhaustion of the journey, he said, "It won't stop us. We can go on . . ." He picked up the whip, and Joanna reached out and caught his wrist.

"No. I *think* this is only a—a testing-out of one of the programs, rather than a major download. He only does that on weekends. It shouldn't last more than a few hours."

"And if it does?" Caris asked brutally, "Are you willing to risk that?"

"I think we have to." Pella leaned forward from her rear perch. "The roads are bad, Caris. It would be too easy to make a mistake and lurch us all."

"I've never lurched *anything* I drive . . . !" he yelled, suddenly furious. Another time it would have cut him to the heart to see her cringe. Now it gave him a kind of savage satisfaction.

Wearily, Joanna said, "We'll stop at the next inn and wait till it passes. We can't risk losing the time an accident might cost us."

Furious, frustrated, Caris made a move to lash the horses back into a canter. It was only when Joanna stopped him again that he realized the stupidity of the action in the dark and on such roads. Even so, he drove on, slowly, with blackness in his heart.

The spell lasted for just over four hours. It was less than half the long night, but sitting in the overpowering warmth of the posting inn's common room—for the place boasted no private parlors—it seemed to last forever. Pella came over to the inglenook where Caris sat, scruffy as a stagecoach driver in her travel-stained brown dress, with Kyssha huddled shivering in her arms. In spite of the poisoned weariness in his veins, Caris felt the stir of pity for them both, wordlessly facing a pain they could not understand; he moved to put his arm around those firm, square shoulders, then stopped himself, confused. It was not the Way of the Sasenna to give comfort—and certainly not to need it as he did. But even so, he found there was a certain amount to be derived simply from sitting in silence side by side and knowing he was not alone.

It had passed, and Pella had just paid the usual exorbitant fee to have the horses put to, when the Witchfinder Peelbone walked into the inn.

Caris heard his voice over the sound of the wind outside in the inn yard. For an instant, he did not recognize it. He was talking to Pella and Joanna by the fire in the nearly deserted common room, his mind on the drive ahead and on the nearly hopeless task of overtaking Peelbone before the Witchfinder could reach Kymil and deliver his warrant. He was aware of figures in the doorway and subliminally aware that he had heard no horses in the yard. Then the voice, thin and cold, said, "It was you who had the charge of such things, Tarolus. Such carelessness speaks ill for your devotion to our cause."

Caris' heart turned to ice in his body.

"My lord, I told you . . . I don't know what came over you . . ."

"Nothing came over me save the knowledge that each day Windrose lives, the chances increase of his rescue."

Joanna's head snapped around, her brown eyes wide with alarm. She made a move to leave, and Caris stayed her, knowing it was too late to do so without calling attention to them. Unobtrusively he turned his back to the room, and Joanna turned with him, holding her hands out to the fire. Caris found himself remembering that Peelbone knew them both.

"Rescue? My lord, surely no one . . ."

Behind him, the sasennan heard the Witchfinder's long tread. In the grimy mirror over the mantelpiece, Caris saw him, thin and middle-sized, a gray man—gray clothing, wispy gray hair. Even his eyes, though brown, seemed flat and colorless beneath the wide brim of his gray hat. He moved like a spider, slightly awkward, but with frightening speed; in his expression there was nothing, save a cold knowledge that whatever he chose to do was correct, and none would gainsay it.

"You are naive, Tarolus." The Witchfinder turned to his companion, older and shorter, like him clothed in the close-fitting, colorless suit of that self-righteous order. "There are many who would free him, either from desire to use his power or from mere perverse adherence to the heresy of witchcraft. Now that it is in our power to forestall such an attempt, we should lose no time."

"But driving at night . . . !"

"I see perfectly well in the dark!" The cold facade cracked; for the first time, Caris saw the vanity of the man behind it.

Beside him, Pella whispered, her voice barely able to contain her glee, "He lurched them! He put them in the ditch somewhere up ahead. They must have been walking for hours . . ."

The soaked clothing and muddied boots of Peelbone and Tarolus bore ample witness to this hypothesis. In the mirror Caris saw them making for the fire. His heart thumping heavily against his ribs, he moved away with what he thought was naturalness, still keeping his face averted. Peelbone had once gotten a good look at it, by the red glare of the burning books in the library at the House of the Mages. *Kill him,* he had said, as casually as if ordering the destruction of a stray dog. *We can't afford these waters muddied.* Even clothed as Caris now was in the rather grubby brown corduroy breeches and coat of a rich lady's groom, he knew the Witchfinder as a man who would not forget a face.

The innkeeper had come over to speak to the newcomers. Caris heard that chill, hated voice again. ". . . accident to our chaise . . . ten miles up the road . . . broken axle . . ."

"He must have tried to drive on after dark, during the dead time," said Pella softly. Caris remembered his own violent impatience and felt an odd twinge of shame at himself. He would, he knew, have tried to do the same. "It will give us at least six hours . . ." She turned toward Joanna, but Joanna was gone.

Caris muttered a curse. They still had several minutes until the phaeton was brought around, owing to the fact that the dead time had triggered in one of the ostlers a great desire to drink most of the contents of the inn's wine cellar. By remaining in the common room Joanna might have run the risk of being recognized by the preoccupied Peelbone, but disappearing and forcing himself or Pella to go search for her was not usual behavior in travelers, and would rouse more suspicion still.

Tarolus was arguing, ". . . a broken man. All he does is weep, and speak to the saints. He could help no one . . ."

"He could help anyone who took the time to force from him the secrets of his former power," Peelbone retorted, holding out his thin hands to the fire, his shoulder close enough to Caris that the young man could feel the wet cold that radiated from it as it steamed with the heat. "Don't you understand? In the state he is in now, he is anyone's tool."

From the windy yard outside Caris heard the sharp rattle of harness and the crunch of hooves on the gravel. Peelbone looked up, his cold eyes narrowing. As Pella walked past him he said, "Is that your carriage, my lady? It may be necessary to commandeer it on the business of the Church . . ."

"Not at all, not at all," the innkeeper said hastily, coming back to them, evidently mindful of the amount the Princess had paid. "There's a chaise your lordship can hire whenever you choose, though, as a wheelwright myself, I can tell you it won't take but a few hours to fix that axle . . ."

With great common sense, Caris thought, Pella did not reply or even remain to listen to this, but walked calmly out the inn door, slinging her massive tweed cloak about her shoulders as she went. Caris, buttoning his quilted coat and pulling up his hood, followed her out.

Joanna was waiting in the phaeton. The ostlers holding the horses' heads were shivering in their bulky coats and scarves; the wind had lessened, but still clawed the torch-flames into a jerky wildness of yellow light and darkness; spits of sleet still flew in the air. Caris knew the ice on the roads would be deadly. Still, driving at night here would be better than in the Glidden Valley. At least, there was no fog. He swung up to the seat and took the reins, Kyssha leaping up to snuggle near the heated brick, for which they had been charged extra, at his feet. His boot touched some unfamiliar piece of luggage as he did so. Looking down, he saw a bundle of bound-up cloth beside Joanna's backpack; a corner had pulled aside to show bright metal within.

"What the . . . ?"

"The innkeeper's wheelwright tools," she said matter-of-factly. "Your software's only as good as your hardware. One of the linchpins from the wheels of the spare chaise is in there, too. I replaced it with a stick whittled down from the handle of a kitchen spoon; with luck, it should last a couple of miles and break at least a wheel, if not Peelbone's neck. I suppose that's a case of replacing *hard*ware with *soft*ware. You'd better drive on. First and last, we've probably picked up at least a day."

"If a day will suffice," Caris said softly. "And if there's enough left of Antryg to save." He flicked the reins gently, picking out in the darkness the vague shape of the road. Beside him Joanna said nothing as they disappeared into the night.

CHAPTER VII

IN THE FEW HOURS OF SLEEP SHE HAD GOTTEN HUDDLED UNDER THE damp furs and rugs in the carriage, Joanna had dreamed. She had found herself again in a place she knew to be the Silent Tower, this time in a narrow and stinking room where the smoke of the chambers below collected in the darkness under the wheel-spoke rafters, a room chilly and damp as a pit, without fire, almost without light. She was trying to talk to a hunched, sobbing figure chained to the wall, whose crippled hands picked aimlessly at the vermin that crawled in his gray-shot beard and soiled rags. Vacant gray eyes squinted at her from behind a curtain of filthy gray hair. She had cried desperately, "Antryg, it's me!" and he had only mumbled, pointing off past her at some unseen vision of hypothetical saints. "Antryg, you have to help me! I can't defeat Suraklin alone!" For she sensed the Dark Mage to be somewhere near, listening in the gloom just beyond the turning of the stair.

But the figure had only whispered, "I tried to help—tried to help. I couldn't fight you all . . ." Awake, asleep, dead fifty years, she would have known his voice. It pierced her with grief for all the years they would never know, and she woke up sobbing, tears running down her face to mat in her tousled hair. Around her the hard gray hills loomed like granite under a sky milky with dawn. Pella was at the reins, the look on her face one of exhaustion that bordered on physical pain; Kyssha, in Joanna's lap, was anxiously licking her hand.

Joanna's first waking thought had been, *We have eighteen hours.*

But the dream lingered with her, like the smell of vomit, as she rode out to the Silent Tower in the afternoon gloom.

The wind had sunk to an indistinct mutter among the hills; the sky was low and threatening, but still. They had reached the Imperial Manor of Larkmoor shortly before noon, and the servants there had been considerably startled when their mistress, as drawn and haggard as her two shabby-looking friends, had ordered three horses saddled at once. "We don't know what we're going to find at the Tower or what's going to be needed," Pellicida said, shaking out the cinder-hued robes of a clerk in her bedchamber, while Joanna sorted through her forged papers. "After that string of accidents on the road, you know Peelbone's going to suspect a rescue attempt."

She seemed calm and matter-of-fact, for which Joanna was profoundly grateful. After organizing the journey and keeping her head fairly well on the road, Joanna found herself increasingly frightened in the face of the physical danger of what they had come to do. And beyond that, she was hideously conscious that rescuing Antryg—and we *will* rescue him! she told herself fiercely. We *will* succeed!—was only the prelude to the true task, the true danger.

The Silent Tower stood only a few miles from the ruins of Suraklin's Citadel. Joanna had never seen that, but it loomed like a darkness at the back of her thoughts, shrouding the evil secrets of its past and, beyond a doubt, Suraklin's computer, the most evil secret of them all.

Her head emerged from the stuffy wool of the clerk's robe in time to see Pella putting on a pair of sharply tailored black trousers. The gold-braided tunic and coat of the Regent's sasennan lay on the bed, beside a neat array of weaponry. "Two sasenna will look more official than one," Pella had explained, seeing her look of surprise. "Besides, I can escort you while you leave Caris to look after the horses—that way we won't have any trouble when he can't pass the Sigil of Darkness on the Tower door."

She spoke calmly, braiding her black hair flat against her skull, as some sasenna did in preference to cutting it off. But as she turned away Joanna glimpsed something in her eyes that troubled her then and caused her now, as they rode together over the bleak monochrome landscape toward the Tower, to steal worried glances back at her, trying to read what might be in that stern young face.

Fear Joanna would have understood—she was scared almost witless herself.

But why, for one second, had she glimpsed the wretchedness of some buried knowledge, the suppressed tear-glint of a secret pain?

"There it is," Caris said softly.

Involuntarily, Joanna drew rein. Through a notch in the hills ahead she could see it rise against the slaty sky, a finger raised in warning—windowless, weathered, dead to magic, and old beyond speaking—the Silent Tower.

He's got to be alive, she thought. *He's got to recover when we get the Sigil off him. Those forged passes have got to get us in there. The guards can't look at them too closely. He's got to be able to help us . . .*

Deliberately, Joanna took several deep breaths.

I am a clerk bearing orders from the Regent, she told herself, fixing the attitude in her mind. *I have every right to be doing what I'm doing, and the words* UP TO SOMETHING *are not blazoned across my forehead . . .*

"What's that?"

At the sharp wariness in Pella's voice, Joanna slewed around in her saddle. Silhouetted against the granite skyline, a small party of riders cantered away from the Tower.

"There!" Caris barked.

More men were visible, afoot this time, hurrying toward the Tower from across the barren hills. "Something's stirred them up."

Joanna swore.

"Do we turn back?" All Pella's grim coolness dissolved into anxiety. "They're liable to look more closely at the papers."

Caris, too, was looking at her uncertainly, and Joanna felt a twinge of irritation. This whole mess, she thought, came about because she was unable to make a correct decision.

She took another deep breath. "No. Those papers won't look any more convincing tomorrow, and Peelbone's on his way. We might be able to turn whatever's happening to our advantage." Without waiting for Caris to reply, she kicked her horse into a trot once more, hanging on grimly against the jolting pace as she rode up to the gate. Pella fell in at once behind her; Caris, rather unwillingly, brought up the rear.

The portcullis was open. A little knot of men in the quilted black coats of sasenna stood grouped there, gesturing as they argued; two of them wore the red robes of Church wizards, like those Joanna had seen at the time of Antryg's arrest. Past the darkness of the gatehouse passage, the courtyard was visible, alive with sasenna, running about, shouting, or fetching horses. A ferret-faced man came striding through the gate to meet them as they drew rein. With what she hoped was official hauteur, Joanna reached for the leather satchel of papers, but the man looked out past her at the two sasenna, and demanded, "Any luck?"

"Luck?" Caris looked baffled. With a flash of insight, Joanna remembered the Magus saying that the guards on the Tower were changed frequently. With their black quilted coats hiding the Regent's gold braid, the man thought them part of the Tower guard. Then he took a second look at the cut of their breeches, and frowned sharply.

"You're the Regent's, aren't you?"

Pella looked momentarily startled, as if trying to figure out how he had known she was the Regent's wife. Caris said, "Yes. We're here to . . ."

"Are his men joining the hunt?"

"Hunt?" said Joanna blankly.

The man spat, and it froze to a diamond of ice on the granite doorsill of the Tower. "For that damned sorcerer. He's escaped."

"He'll be making for Kymil." Joanna drew rein on the brink of a stream which cut the roadbed, black rainwaters rushing with silken silence down the narrow channel between ice and frozen weeds. Behind them, the Silent Tower was a truncated spike against the darkening sky. Cold wind stirred their cloaks, tugging at her blond hair where it strayed free of her hood. Soon it would be night.

"Are you mad?" Caris demanded. "It's the first place they'll look—the Witchfinders will be searching house to house."

"Tomorrow, maybe. They've got a lot of men, but not unlimited numbers. It's my bet that tonight they'll be concentrating on the hills themselves and on the roads north."

Caris considered the matter for a moment in silence. Joanna guessed he was recalling, too, Antryg's foxlike skill in lying low and doubling on his own tracks. Tricky, devious, more than a little crazy . . . All the fears she had felt for his life and his sanity, all her plans for rescuing him, had vanished in a sort of thunderclap of delight, and it had only been with difficulty that she had restrained herself from laughing aloud by the gates of the Tower. Caris, for his part, looked brooding and angry, as if he felt that Antryg had made a fool of them as well as of his captors—as indeed he had.

Finally he said, "He'll have to wait until it gets fully dark, I think. There are people in Kymil who will recognize him, even with those absurd spectacles that were given back to him, if he's still wearing them. It's beyond me how he plans to get into the city, but then I'm still trying to figure out how he got past the Sigil of Darkness on the doors of the Tower!"

He touched his heels to his horse's flanks and reined back toward the frozen Ponmarish and the city walls beyond. Joanna followed him, grimly reflecting that tomorrow she'd have a whole new set of aches to go with those acquired from four days of jouncing in the carriage. The last horse she'd ridden had been a riding-stable plug at the age of fifteen, and she was already sore.

As soon as they were well out of sight of the Tower, Pella had ridden back cross-country to the manor of Larkmoor. No further purpose was to be served, she said, by her staying with them to hunt for Antryg. The best thing she could do was to brief the servants with a cover story sufficient to divert the Witchfinders' inevitable questions about the movements of strangers in the district. While there was still enough left of the waning afternoon light, Caris, like every other of the several dozen sasenna at the Tower, had searched the grounds around the walls for tracks and had found none. The frozen sleet of last night had formed a brittle sheet over the dead grass, breaking like glass at a touch. The only prints were those of the sasenna of the Tower, searching like him without success.

"You don't think the story of his disappearance could be just a cover, do you?" Joanna asked worriedly as they left the road and swung north along the edge of the marshes. "The guards said he just vanished—one minute he was chained in his cell, the next minute he was gone. Even the manacles were still locked shut. Could he have been murdered quietly, and all this search be for the benefit of whichever member of the Council has been holding out against his death?"

"The Council's in hiding," Caris said briefly. "You can bet Bishop Herthe knew it the minute the last of them left Angelshand—the Bishop of Angelshand's hasu would have sent that news by scrying-crystal the same night. They could have slit Antryg's throat with impunity any time in the last week."

"Maybe they did," Joanna said softly.

"Then why make a fuss now? No, the Captain of the Tower was genuinely furious." Through his teeth, Caris added, "And I can't say that I blame him." He urged his horse down a treacherous slope to the first iron-hard sheet of ice where the marshes began, scanning the rotted snow, frozen mud, and brittle, black weed stems for the print of Antryg's feet.

"He was barefoot, they said, in the Tower," he went on after a moment, with a kind of grudging compassion in his voice. "He'd sometimes wrap rags around his feet for warmth, or the guards would do it for him when he forgot, but they said he didn't walk much toward the end. He knows these hills the way a rat knows the sewers—he lived here for eight years with Suraklin—but in his physical condition, he won't be able to get far. He'll need food, he'll need shelter, and he'll need them before night. It's coming on to sleet again. He'll never survive it."

He has to, Joanna thought desperately, fear for him swamping again her lingering sense of delight at his escape. *Somehow, he has to survive. We have to find him before the Witchfinders do, before the sasenna of the Church and the Council.* It crossed her mind to wonder whether he would hate her for what she had done to him. It might not keep him from working with her to accomplish Suraklin's defeat; she was too familiar with his conscientiousness, his quixotic sense of duty, to think he would reject her help or even be openly hostile. But she had betrayed him, given him over to the savage usages of the Inquisition and the slow torture of the Sigil of Darkness. And, rather typically of Antryg, she reflected with a grin, he had robbed her of the opportunity to display her contrition by a spectacular rescue.

At least he's alive, she thought, as the darkness closed round them and the wind began to moan among the hills. *Somewhere out there . . .*

The lingering daylight faded. Brutal cold settled in.

"My guess is he'll work his way around and come down from the north," Caris said softly, as they settled themselves in the lee side of a clump of naked alders on an islet in the marsh. Causeways led from the higher ground of the hills where they had hidden the horses to the tuft of ground where they sat, and thence to the city gates, a few hundred feet beyond. Around them stretched the marsh itself, the green fairyland of ponds and meres Joanna had crossed at the end of summer, now a solid lake of muddy gloom. Behind them, the wind throbbed shrilly over the hills. "They'll be watching the Angelshand road to the northeast, and the Stone Road that leads to the Tower itself, but this gate isn't much used. He'll have to come across the causeway—most of the marsh is frozen hard, but he'd be mad to risk a soaking in an ice bog."

"He is mad," Joanna said quietly. "And he's pretty desperate."

"He's mad but he's not stupid. If he got wet now, the cold would finish him long before daylight."

Joanna shuddered and tucked her gloved hands under her armpits in a vain attempt to warm them. The city gates were lit with torches and lamps, a promise of warmth and, she thought hungrily, food. The reflected orange glow showed up the cloud of her breath and brushed with fiery chiaroscuro the crumbling roof beams of the long line of trashy little shanties that crouched along the outside of the city wall on both sides of the causeway and its arched bridge.

"What are those?"

Caris followed her glance.

"Poor people live there in the summertime, fishing in the marshes for food. When the waters rise with the rains in winter, they're forced back into the town again. Most of those huts will be knee-deep."

"Could he be hiding in one of them?"

Caris leaned around the bare, coarse-barked trunk of the nearest alder to scan the dark line of pitiful dwellings. Then he settled back down at her side and whispered, "Someone thinks he might be."

Through the scaly trunks Joanna could see a line of black-clothed figures on the causeway. The glow from the gate beyond picked chips of light from the brass hardware of crossbows and pistols and caught the hard line of swords beneath dark, quilted coats. Church sasenna, she guessed, coming in from an unsuccessful search with the increasing cold of the night. One of them pointed down at the huts. "Have those been searched?"

And it seemed to her that her heart stopped.

The leader of the party cursed and gestured his men down the track toward the filthy, flooded little shelters. Her eyes on what were little more than black silhouettes, Joanna felt she was going to smother with anxiety, confusion, and overwhelming and impossible certainty.

"What is it?" Caris whispered, and she was aware that her hand had closed with convulsive strength on his wrist.

"Antryg," she whispered. "That was Antryg's voice."

"The *guard?*"

It sounded as impossible to her as it did to him, but she didn't take her eyes off the hut into which the tallest of the sasenna had vanished. It was close under the shadow of the bridge. She could see vague movements, men milling around, now and then caught in the gold lights from the gate. The tall man emerged briefly, wading through the half-frozen slime of marsh water and sewage to go on to another hut. Even at this distance, she could see that he walked with an odd, lithe arrogance, like a dancer.

"It can't be."

Her mind echoed it, over and over. *It can't be. It can't be.*

The sasenna reassembled. Somebody said, "Everybody here?" and there was a murmur of assent, though in the darkness, with that large a group, it would be impossible to tell. Scrambling in the slippery mud, they climbed the narrow track back to the causeway bridge.

Caris breathed, "They're one short."

"The hut there against the buttress. He never came out."

Caris was already checking the loads of the pistol he'd pulled from his sword sash. It was a local muzzle-loader rather than Suraklin's .45; in a stray glint of light from the gates, Joanna saw the runes of na'aar on the barrel. "He's got a crossbow," he said softly, and she remembered that, mageborn, Caris could see like a cat in the dark. "At this stage, he'll probably kill to protect himself." He rose to a crouch, glanced at the gate to make sure they were unobserved, then paused. "The fact that he's managed to escape from the Tower doesn't mean he isn't completely insane, you know."

The hut was low-roofed, half-fallen-in, a blot of darkness clinging like a dirty leech to one of the city wall's massive stone buttresses. It stood on higher ground than most, but getting there entailed wading through lakes of brown ooze which undoubtedly would have stunk, had it not been so bitterly cold. Joanna, her long clerk's robe hitched to her knees, was shivering, her toes numb in her boots and her thick woolen hose. Stalking ahead of her, Caris seemed not to notice. In the darkness, she could barely see him and certainly not see the ground; she slipped twice, nearly losing her hold on her ever-present backpack and the flashlight she had taken from it. The reflected glare from the torches at the gates overhead caught with a faint, citrous sheen on Caris' fair hair and the gold braiding of his coat as he paused before the darkness of the hut door. Then, before she could catch up with him, he stepped around the low doorpost, his pistol pointing into the blackness.

"Drop it," he said.

There was a long silence. Joanna paused, involuntarily frozen into stillness, waiting.

Then, slow and infinitely weary, Antryg's voice sounded within the hut. "Hello, Caris." There was the faint clatter and splat of something, presumably the crossbow, being tossed to the muddy ground. Joanna ran the last few slithery steps to Caris' side and shined the beam of her flashlight into the hut in time to see Antryg raise his hands in a gesture of surrender, his head bowed and a look on his face of utter exhaustion and the most total defeat she had ever seen.

He could have shot anyone, she realized, except Caris, who, in spite of everything, Antryg had never ceased to consider his friend.

The light flashed across the round lenses of his spectacles and he flinched; his hands, she saw now, in tattered, fingerless leather gloves, were shaking. He reached one of them out abruptly and leaned against the stone buttress for support; his face was cadaverously thin, bone-white against a frame of short, startlingly black curls; the hollows of his eyes were darkened still further with blue-brown smudges of exhaustion. After an instant, he raised his head again, squinting against the electric glare, and saw her.

Their eyes met. His expression did not change, but something in him seemed to settle into a kind of stillness, as if he were perfectly balanced between heartbeats on a razor's edge, awaiting the end of the world.

Caris shoved the pistol into his belt. "Suraklin's in Angelshand," he said quietly. "We're here to get you away."

Joanna said, "Antryg, I'm sorry."

She thought he was going to say something; but after the first sip of indrawn breath, he forcibly stopped himself. She saw the grief in his eyes, like a man pulling back his hand from that which he knows he must not grasp. In a conversational voice he began, "My dear Joanna . . ."

She took two strides forward and flung her arms around his waist.

In all her hesitant and approval-seeking life, she had never done such a thing, partly from fear of rejection and partly because it wasn't the sort of thing she did. Typically, she forgot to let go of either the backpack or the flashlight, so the ensuing embrace was lumpy and awkward, but of that she only became aware later. His arms crushed her against him, lifting her off her feet with his greater height; through layers of quilted coat and pilfered uniform, she could feel the desperate shudder of his breath. His ribs were like a washboard under her grip, and his pelvic bones like those of an old horse. For a time, she had the illogical sensation of wanting to lock their bones together, to meld his flesh into her body and never let him go, and the frantic strength of his embrace told her more than any words could have that her desire mirrored his own. Their mouths met. Had they been able to fuse then, truly lose their physical selves in one another's bodies, they would have done it. Joanna was aware that she was crying.

He set her down and pulled convulsively at the shabby muffler around his throat. Under it she saw by the dim glow of the flashlight the dark ring of the iron collar, harsh against the white flesh and edged with a mottled band of bruises and sores. "Get this thing off me," he said, breathless, and then, with a wry grin, "You don't happen to have a hacksaw about you, do you, my dear?"

Silently, Joanna dug into her backpack and produced one. He grinned like a pleased jack-o'-lantern, then seized her and kissed her again. "If this is all a hallucination," he said, his voice shaking slightly, "I'm going to be *very* disappointed in the morning."

He dropped to his knees, fumbling with the muffler; Joanna hitched the backpack up onto her shoulder and tucked the dirty green muffler between the iron and his neck. "Caris, can you hold the light for me . . . ?"

"No," said the sasennan briefly.

"Quite right," agreed Antryg, his voice blurred with the bending of his head. "Somebody has to keep watch. The noise may bring someone . . ."

"Maybe we could ride out first?" Caris suggested.

Antryg, who had taken the flashlight from Joanna and held it in one hand to light the collar, shook his head. "No. Just get rid of this thing."

It might not have prevented his escape, Joanna realized, but that didn't make the torment of wearing it any the less. It took surprisingly little time to cut through the soldered clasp—the iron had no kind of temper to it—and it made a hellish amount of noise. Joanna had broken two blades practicing before beginning her expedition and had brought several spares, but they weren't needed. The clasp broke apart as Caris whispered hoarsely, "Someone's coming!" Antryg stumbled to his feet, pulling the iron ring from his throat with hands that shook.

"Thank you," he gasped as Joanna shut off the flashlight. Amid the raw, scabbed flesh of his neck, a circular brown mark showed where the Sigil itself had touched, as if the skin had been burned with acid. Oddly enough, though he held the iron collar in his hands, Joanna had seen that he avoided contact with the Dead God's Seal.

"Hasu," Caris reported, ducking back in through the hut door. "Church dogs." He scooped up the crossbow from the mud and held it out to Antryg.

Antryg shook his head, pulled a board off the flimsy back wall and snaked his thin form through the gap.

Horrified, Caris gasped, "They can see us in the dark . . ."

"Of course they can." Antryg shoved the broken collar into his belt and made a dash toward the causeway.

Voices shouted behind him; they were evidently hasu who knew what Antryg looked like with his spectacles and without his beard. Joanna heard the *hrush* and whap of a crossbow bolt slamming into one of the nearby huts. Through gritted teeth, Caris snarled, "You're insane!" Antryg cut abruptly sideways between two crumbling board walls.

Through the gap in the back of the hut, Joanna watched him dash through the foot-deep standing water that flooded the ground hereabouts. She saw at once the reason that the water hadn't yet frozen—it trickled out of a sewer outfall just beneath the causeway bridge, a round stone pipe about four feet in diameter. It was, she realized, the way he had intended to enter the city.

On the other side of the hut, she heard the hasu splash by, running surely, unerringly in the dark. In the shadows of the causeway, it was difficult for her to see, but she caught the glimpse of Antryg's dark, spidery shape crouching for a moment before the outfall, and the moon-like flash of his spectacle lenses. Then he came sprinting back through the water, the black coat of the sasennan's uniform he wore billowing like a cloak behind him. He stumbled over some submerged irregularity of the ground, almost falling, but regained his balance and flung himself through the narrow opening in the wall through which Joanna had watched. She pulled the loose plank back over it as the two hasu came around the corner and dashed straight for the outfall pipe.

Beside her, Antryg was leaning against the wall, gasping for breath. His eyebrows stood out like india-ink against a face gone gray with fatigue; he was not, she realized, in any shape for this. In spite of the cold, his face was clammy with sweat, and the makeshift black dye in his hair ran in trickles down the high cheekbones and the dim shape of the scar left by the Regent's whip.

The two hasu jerked to a stop a few feet from the outfall. One of them reached forward hesitantly, then drew back his hand as if it had been burned. As one, they turned and pelted through the water for the little trail that led up to the causeway bridge, shouting for the guards . . .

"The Sigil of Darkness?" Joanna guessed, as the two small forms, their robes billowing suddenly red in the torchlight, ran with waving arms into the oven-mouth brightness of the city gates.

Antryg nodded, his old demented grin flickering through the lines of strain on his face. "Certainly superior to beavers, who are said to tear off certain of their bodily parts and throw them at pursuers to discourage the chase, though why it should do so has always escaped me. They're convinced I've gone through the outfall and are going to spend the rest of the night and all day tomorrow tearing apart the town. I hope whatever refuge you had planned for us *wasn't* in Kymil?" He was shivering violently with exhaustion, nerves, and cold. They were all soaked to the skin and the night was cruel.

She shook her head, "Larkmoor Manor." His brows dove together as he identified its name, then quirked upward, taking with them a whole ladder of forehead wrinkles. It was the first time she'd ever seen him put off-balance by anything she'd said. "We're guests of Pellicida of Senterwing."

"Good Heavens," he murmured, startled and bemused.

"The horses are at the end of the causeway . . ."

"Just a moment, my dear." And turning, he pushed aside the concealing boards. To Caris' utter horror, he dashed back across the open water to the outfall again.

As he came splashing back, Caris snapped, "You're not only mad, you're a fool! Every sasennan in town must be near the gates . . ."

"Nonsense." Antryg scraped the mud gingerly from the thing he held in his hand. "The Bishop had this made specially for me and it would be churlish to throw it away. Put this in your backpack, would you, my dear? We'll wrap it in lead when we get to safety . . ." He handed it to Joanna. It was the iron collar bearing the Sigil of Darkness.

They made their way back to the horses without further mishap, Antryg cheerfully directing the one group of sasenna they met on the causeway toward the town. Wet, cold, aching and exhausted almost to numbness, she scrambled up onto her horse behind Antryg, put her arms around his waist, and leaned her cheek against his bony back. She felt she could have gone to sleep that way and slept for days as the horses jogged into the windy darkness toward Larkmoor and what she knew would be only a relative and temporary safety.

One more subroutine successfully completed, she thought tiredly. They had rescued Antryg—or Antryg had rescued himself—alive, whole, and sane, or at least as sane as Antryg had ever been.

Now their troubles would really begin.

CHAPTER VIII

"So what was it that finally convinced you that I was telling the truth?"

Extravagantly gowned in a robe of plum-colored velvet that had originally been made for the Emperor Hieraldus, Antryg sat at one side of a small table laid for high tea, in the course of which he had made his appearance, interrupting his fellow conspirators. Though it was early yet in the afternoon, the drawing room lamps at Larkmoor Manor had been lit on sideboards of carved maple, the glow of them pale against the uncertain grayness of the stormy daylight outside. Now and then wind would sigh along the northern wall of the house, and Joanna, if she stood too near that wall, found it cold to her touch.

With the blackish dye washed out of it, Antryg's hair was far grayer than Joanna remembered, and with the loss of flesh the tracework of lines around his eyes and running back into his hair had deepened to gullies. In the daylight, he looked thinner and badly the worse for wear. The fur collar of the robe framed a three-inch band of sores and raw flesh around his neck above the too-prominent points of his collarbone; the big bones of his wrists, similarly wealed, stood out from the wasted flesh. Even so, his hands, cradling the creamy smoothness of an eggshell teacup, had all their old lightness; and behind the cracked spectacles, his gray eyes were daft as ever, but at peace.

"We've seen Suraklin," Joanna said quietly. "You were right. He needed an accomplice from my world, a programmer. No wonder you thought it was me. But he took over Gary, my—my boyfriend."

"Ah," Antryg said softly. "The one who got computers to do his stealing for him."

She nodded a little wearily, recalling the details of Gary's dealings with Suraklin, meticulously cataloged in the DARKMAGE files from the viewpoints of both seducer and seduced. Gary had never stood a chance.

For a moment she sat staring into her teacup, tracing the curves of its gilded handle with one fingertip. Then she took a deep breath, set it down, and plunged into a dispassionate account of her own belated conclusions and adventures, with Pella filling in, awkwardly but without omissions, her own experiences and suspicions of Cerdic's new Spiritual Advisor, the night at the gambling rooms, and the storm.

"The damn thing is that there's no proof," Joanna concluded. "It's only little things, nothing that can be pointed to. But these—these spells of deadness—are still taking place, though most people don't believe they're objective and not subjective. I'm starting to find that a little hard to believe."

"Are you?" Antryg said mildly. "Most people are firmly convinced there *is* a difference between objective and subjective reality and would find it extremely hard to believe otherwise. You're rather like someone looking down at a maze from the top, instead of wandering through it. There's really quite a nice maze at the Citadel of Wizards in the north, by the way. And since there's no proof of when any particular abomination appeared in this world, I suppose they're all credited to me whilst I was roving about loose at the end of the summer. I expect that, now I've escaped, the attempts on Pharos' life will start up again."

He set down his teacup and rubbed his fingers as if for warmth or to massage away some chronic ache. "I suppose there have been none since my capture? I didn't think so. Verisimilitude has always been Suraklin's strong point."

He glanced across the table at Caris, dressed in snuff-colored servant's livery and silently buttering and rebuttering a muffin which he clearly had no intention of eating. "I'm sorry, Caris," Antryg said softly.

The young man raised eyes like those of an injured wolf, ready to savage the hands extended to help him.

Antryg went on, "Suraklin destroyed a man we both loved very much —raped him of body and mind, used them for his own purposes, and threw him away when he was done. But the fact remains that I *was* the one who killed what was left."

Caris shook his head. Muffled and unwontedly low, he said, "If I'd found him the way the Emperor now is, I'd have done the same."

"I suppose Suraklin was counting on that—the fact that I couldn't stay long in that world and would never leave him there like that, helpless among strangers. But of course, whether I killed him or let him live, either way I'd have been blamed for it. Pella . . ." He looked across at the big girl, who sat quietly stroking Kyssha's head which lay on her velvet lap. "You were as much wronged by him as any of us, and it's worse, I suppose, since you just happened to be in the wrong place at the wrong time and married to the wrong person. Thank you for being good enough to help us. Caris, Joanna . . ." He turned simply to face them. "I do owe you my life. I wish I had a better way of thanking you than immediately hauling you both into greater danger with me, but I haven't. I'm sorry about Gary also," he added, turning to Joanna, who sat on the tapestried hassock at his side. "From the little I saw of him, he was never much of a man, but I suppose he was the best man he could be under the circumstances that made his life."

Joanna sighed, feeling as if she were seeing Gary clearly for the first time. "Not even that, I'm afraid." She reached out and laid her hand over his.

The night had been sleety and cold. In the late autumn dawnlight, Joanna had slipped out of the room Pella had given her, stealing down the silent corridor to the one where Antryg slept. A fire burned low in the grate there, its wickering the only sound but for the moan of the wind around the eaves and brief staccato of rain. Antryg had been in bed under a gray satin comforter, his hair close-curled still with the dampness of washing, profoundly asleep.

It was all Joanna had meant to do—to see him, to reaffirm to herself the fact that against all the odds in the world he was still alive. It had been her litany and her hope for two dreadful, endless months that she hadn't done the irrevocable and that somehow, somewhere, they would meet again.

Tomorrow or the day after, they would have to face Suraklin, break into whatever depths beneath his ancient Citadel housed his stolen computer, destroy him, or, as Caris said—as Joanna uneasily feared—die trying. Her thoughts flinched away from what would happen to her if she survived her own defeat as his prisoner.

But there in that still bedchamber of amber and gray, all of it seemed impossibly distant and very unreal. Yesterday she had been jolting miserably in Pella's phaeton, aching with fear and sleeplessness, feeling that the journey would never end. Tomorrow might see her, Caris, and Antryg dead, all hope and magic perished forever. Today, this morning, went no further than Antryg's preposterous profile against the bed linen, the whisper of his breathing and the spattering of wind and rain.

She had still been standing there, leaning one shoulder against the carved cherrywood bedpost, when his eyes had opened.

He had been sleeping again when she left. In fact, he had slept most of the day, and Joanna had the impression, looking now at the harsh lines around his eyes as he bent to refill his teacup from the ostentatiously garlanded pot, that he could have slept for the next twenty-four hours without trouble. He looked very tired.

Pella said gravely, "You know they're going to put the blame for all of it on you now—the storm, the abominations, and the failure of the harvest." She held a fragment of buttered muffin out to Kyssha, and the little dog accepted it with as much condescension as if she hadn't been watching every bite with tears of bogus starvation in her eyes. "If you could work enough magic in the Tower to escape, they'll figure you could work enough to do all that."

Antryg sighed. "I know. But, of course, I didn't escape by magic. I couldn't use magic—not in the Tower, not with the Sigil welded against my flesh."

"Then how did you get out of the chains?"

He shrugged. "Picked the locks. Three or four years ago, the Bishop went through some kind of scare and threatened to have me chained; the rings had been in the wall there for hundreds of years. As a precaution, I took apart some of the toys I used to spend my time making and fashioned about a dozen picklocks from the wires in them. I hid them in the cracks of the floor and the walls all around the rings, and down in other areas of the Tower when I could get to them. And since I couldn't pass the Sigil on the door, I pretty much had the freedom of the Tower in those days.

"I picked the locks of my chains fairly regularly, to pilfer things from the guardroom downstairs—the uniform coat and breeches, a razor to cut off my hair and beard, and an outer coat to hide the fact that I wasn't wearing any weapons. I used a razor to whittle a stick to make the right sword-line under my coat—if I'd actually stolen a sword, it would have been missed, and they'd have searched the place. I'd stuff everything up under the rafters when I wasn't working on it. With no windows the place was pretty dark, but of course I can see in the dark and none of the guards, not being mageborn, could."

"I'd been doing this for over a month—as soon as I got my hands working again, in fact. For weeks all I did was crouch in a corner, mumbling to myself while I grew my beard and worked at my fingers. The Inquisitors had dislocated most of them, but only four were actually broken. I think they'll always be a bit crooked now. I had to wrap them up twisted again so the guards would think I was still crippled and not watch me too closely."

Caris glanced up cynically from some private contemplation. "And you played mad for the same reason?"

"For a number of reasons," Antryg admitted, his long fingers moving unconsciously over the dark fur of the velvet robe's cuffs. "The important thing was to keep any of the guards from knowing how I really look. For one thing, I'm nearly six foot three. No matter how I was disguised, I wouldn't have got ten yards if anyone in the Tower had ever seen me when I wasn't hunched over and sitting down. It's why I had the visions of obscure saints."

"What?" Pella demanded, half-laughing. Joanna had forgotten to mention to her that conversations with Antryg were apt to contain several wildly disparate topics per sentence.

He regarded her with his mild, mad eyes, as if surprised she didn't see the connection. "Most Church sasenna are halfway to being monks. After two years in a monastery, I could describe saints that only other novices would recognize. Did you know Saint Kalwiddoes was supposed to have a metal nose? He allegedly lost the original for his faith; one calls upon him to cure sinus problems. Eventually I won enough sympathy among some of the Church guards to prod the Bishop into changing the lot every few weeks."

Caris sniffed disgustedly. "It was all a blind, then."

Antryg was silent for a moment. Then he said, "Not really." Outside the window, the bare trees that surrounded Larkmoor thrashed uneasily in the wind, their black branches clawing like witch fingers at the mottled sky. "There were times when it all came home to me—where I was, and what was happening outside . . . Moments of sanity, I suppose, when I realized the truth of my position and my prospects. But one can't pound on the walls and scream all the time.

"And I was so tired. The Sigil of Darkness not only eats a wizard's magic, it devours him through it. The thing was literally killing me by inches. I could barely eat; I couldn't sleep, and when I did finally pass out from sheer exhaustion, the dreams made me wish I hadn't." He sat silent again, his head bowed, the white light from the windows glancing across the round lenses of his spectacles like circles of cracked and dirty ice. He had, Joanna noticed, acquired a pair of earrings as well as the Emperor's robe, solitaire diamonds of well over two carats apiece which flickered when he looked up again. "I had to get that thing off me," he said simply.

"I had to break out. Even if no warrant of execution was ever issued, it was only a matter of time before I became too weak to do so."

"But the question is," Caris said suspiciously, "*how* did you break out? You say no wizard can pass the Seal of the Dead God. But it was on the door of the Tower as well. Even if you'd managed to disguise yourself as a guard, shave off your beard, cut your hair, and dye it, too—What did you use for dye, by the way?"

"Lampblack and dye soaked from the cover of a stolen book of scriptures. I'm told in Trembergil there's a root that will turn gray hair black permanently, if it's eaten, and Queen Darthirambis II once paid four elephants, ten lengths of second-quality silk, and two dancing boys for enough to cover the palm of her hand. The guards were forever stealing things from each other, the Church sasenna from the Council's and vice versa. No one noticed my thefts."

"But even if you managed to do all that," Caris said doggedly, "and went down among them with impunity, *how did you walk through the door of the Tower?*"

Antryg said nothing for a time, absentmindedly rubbing his fingers again. Joanna, glancing sideways at the round, brownish mark that seemed to have been burned into the galled skin of his throat, said softly, "Desensitization, wasn't it? They do that in my world as a cure for phobias."

A half smile flicked at the extravagant curve of his lips. "It was the one thing I was afraid of—that when it came down to the moment, I wouldn't be able to do it. And I almost couldn't. One never becomes desensitized—not to the Sigil of Darkness. Its hold never slacks. But I'd had it on me, welded against my flesh, for over two months. If I hadn't gone through that—if I didn't know that the alternative of walking past the Sigil on the door was enduring God knows how much longer of it before I finally died—I couldn't have done it. It took me about five minutes of standing there to work up my nerve as it was. But fortunately, I'd already roused the Tower with the news of my own disappearance, and the place was in such chaos that no one noticed."

He glanced over at Caris, half-apologetically, as if he sensed in the young man's folded arms and crossed knees his furious disapproval. The sasennan had come prepared to perform an heroic rescue and, like Joanna, still illogically felt slightly cheated. "Once I got through the door, I joined in the search while they ransacked the Tower and its grounds. I'd shoved my old robes and my cut-off hair and beard up into my hidey-hole under the rafters so the idea of disguise wouldn't occur to anyone. They thought they were looking for a barefoot and ragged cripple. Without my spectacles, I could see just well enough not to run into walls. Of course no sasennan wears spectacles. I'm told there have been those who've killed themselves as flawed when their eyes began to harden at fifty. Eventually I joined the parties going out to search the hills. Since they'd been changed so often, not only did no guard there remember what I'd looked like when I was brought in, before I grew my beard back, but they weren't able to identify each other by sight, either. After that . . ." He shrugged. "All that remained was to lose the other guards, put on my spectacles, slip into Kymil through the sewers, and pilfer a hacksaw. I had to wait until night, because in Kymil there are plenty of people who would recognize me—aside from the Church dogs, that is. But it's always easy to hide in a city."

He subsided back into his chair, the embroidered velvet settling around him like a royal mantle. Cradling his teacup once more in his big, deft hands, he stared into its henna depths as if he could read his own future there, as he had that of countless travelers on the Angelshand road to buy dinner for himself and his companions. And perhaps, thought Joanna worriedly, he could. At any rate, a small upright line twitched into existence between his brows, and he set the cup quickly aside.

She wondered what he'd seen there.

In time Caris broke the silence. "You know that was your last chance."

"Oh, yes." His deep voice was almost absentminded as his gray eyes flicked back to the young man's face. "By this time, there will be a mad-dog warrant out for me. If they find me now, they'll kill me out of hand. So this is quite literally our last chance to stop Suraklin—not merely to destroy his computer, which I'm positive is hidden beneath the ruins of his old Citadel at the node of the energy-lines, but to finish him." His lips pulled slightly in a smile again, but for one moment his eyes were quite sane—gazing, as he had said, when he spoke of his fits of screaming despair in the Tower, quite truthfully at his position and his prospects. Then he let it go, and the old, luminous madness of hope returned. "This time we'll just have to succeed."

"It came on very quickly, didn't it?"

Caris looked up, startled out of his own reflections, from his absent gazing at the slatey shadows of the doorway through which Antryg and Joanna had passed. Pella had been so silent that for a time he had felt he was alone with the wind-mutter and the ruins of the tea, but now he saw that the tall girl still sat on the pink silk settee where she had been during tea and the subsequent conference, the sleeping Kyssha cradled in her lap.

" 'Like a storm from out of the east,' " he quoted scripture, knowing without asking what the girl meant.

She smiled, half-amused, "Like the second fence of an in-and-out, really, that's hidden behind the first until your horse is just about on top of it."

He recognized the cant term. "Do you hunt?"

Ruefulness flickered in the fine hazel eyes. "Not really. I've always had too much sympathy for the fox, but the riding was the closest thing to flying I could get. It was another thing Mother and my aunt the Queen never approved of."

He returned her grin. "Along with being a sasennan."

"Well, Mother was terrified I'd get a cut on my face. When I was ten I wanted a scar like my cousin Tybal's in the worst way. I've been admiring yours all the way down from Angelshand," she added sincerely, and Caris touched the old slash on his cheekbone and laughed, picturing the very well-brought-up daughter of the Royal House of Senterwing trying to convince her horrified parents that she ought to have one.

She moved the stiff taffeta ruffles of her petticoat and underskirt with her toe, and the shining fabric whispered to itself against a lull in the wind outside. "I suppose putting all our energies into reaching here before the Witchfinder did and worrying how we were going to get Antryg out of the Tower . . . Is he always like that?"

"He was positively sedate, today," Caris said dourly, and Pella laughed again.

Then, soberly, she said, "I suppose it hid the real task."

"Not entirely." Caris' voice was very quiet. "But it made it possible not to think about it." It was the first time he had admitted, to himself or anyone else, that it was an event upon which he tried not to dwell.

"Do you think it's at the ruins of his Citadel?"

He sighed again and rose to his feet, Pella getting up too, Kyssha now tucked in her arms. "It has to be," he said. "I'm going to check the perimeter of the grounds before it gets dark. Would you like to come?"

It was something Caris had done at the posthouses where they had spent the nights or part of the nights, something, in fact, he did automatically when spending a night in an unfamiliar or potentially hostile place. It was a kind of patrol, an investigation of where things were and from what directions danger might or could come. At the posthouses, Pella had come with him on these rounds. He had welcomed this, partly because Pella, with her early training, would be the closest thing to a fighting ally he'd have if it came to trouble. In spite of her apparent clumsiness and absentmindedness in more domestic matters, the girl was silent, deft, and catlike on her feet.

But more than that, he had simply found himself glad of her company. In the gray times of deadness, it was good not to be alone; even outside of them, there had been times when he'd found his awareness of the upcoming battle with Suraklin, the knowledge that he would most likely die in it, more than he could hold at bay himself. He had broken his vows and had not even the strength of the Way of the Sasenna to comfort him. And in any case, he reminded himself, to seek comfort was not of the Way.

Pella slipped a smoke-colored cloak over her gold-beaded green gown; they moved like two shadows from the side door of the house to the nearest of the line of bare elm trees which surrounded Larkmoor on all sides, a windbreak against the cutting Sykerst gales. In the summer, the grass there was scythed close; now along the north and east sides, last week's dirty snow lay in a filthy and broken windrow, a frozen crust wide enough that it could not be leaped by a man. From the shelter of the trees, Caris squinted against the searing wind to study it for tracks, mindful that the sasenna of the Council and now the Witchfinder's men would be everywhere on the moor. But there was no sign of tracks, either on the crusted snow or on the iron-hard earth beyond.

They checked the outside of the stables, unobtrusively avoiding the notice of the grooms and coachmen, and moved on to the fodderbarn, out past the line of trees and commanding the best views both of the nearby hills and of the house. There were no tracks; Caris checked the small chips of wood which he had imbedded in the half-frozen mud of the threshold that morning and found them undisturbed. Pella stood out of the wind against the doorpost, wrapped in the thick folds of her cloak, her breath a blowing cloud of white against the dimness of the barn and the fading light from the moving sky.

"Would you do better to wait a day or two before going out to the Citadel?" she asked, and Caris glanced up from his study.

"We shouldn't have waited this long," he said bluntly. "Yes, we needed a day's rest; Antryg was at the end of his strength when we found him, and none of us in shape to do what we have to do. But two days, or three days, won't mend that. Suraklin's no fool. According to Joanna, Suraklin will be on the other side of the Void, in her world—or should be. But we have no guarantee of that. And every day that passes increases the chance that he'll come back and hear of Antryg's escape. We might—just might—be able to make it through whatever traps he's set up to guard his Citadel, for Joanna to poison his computer and then lay in wait there for him. But if he is there before us—if he knows that Antryg is coming—we'll stand no chance."

"That wasn't what I meant," Pella said apologetically and brushed a tendril of black hair from her face. "It's just that you might want to wait for better weather."

Caris stood up and grinned. "We'd be like three birds in a cellar, tucking our heads under our wings and waiting for sunrise. It's not going to be better until spring."

"Oh." Pella looked a little blankly out into that bitter landscape, her expression momentarily like that of a child who finds that coffee doesn't taste at all the way it smells.

Caris came over to stand beside her, shaking out the pleated linen ruffles of his shirt cuffs. After the relative shelter of the barn, the wind was stinging on his face, cutting like a knife through the coarse brownish wool of his livery. "I'm told people from the Sykerst miss it when they live in other lands," he remarked, shaking his head wonderingly. "They can keep it."

She glanced back at him. "Then you're not from here?"

He shook his head. "I was born in the Wheatlands, the black-earth country down on the Strebwell River. It's open country, but not like this—flat as your hand for miles, with deep black soil. Where there's water, the trees grow thick, in the marshes, and the bottomlands by the streams. It's a safe country—gentle. In the winter, Ratbane and I would wander for miles, with the full moon turning the snow luminous, as far as you can see to the edge of the sky, and the air so still you could hear a dog bark three villages away."

He stopped, his throat closing hard. It had been years since he'd thought of the country that was his home, years since he'd remembered the aching peace of those still nights.

"They wouldn't have let you ramble alone, would they?" he asked after a time.

Her smile warmed not only her great hazel eyes, but all the strong features of her face, the aquiline nose and the full-lipped mouth. "I wasn't supposed to," she said, "but I did. I used to sneak away and go bird shooting with my brothers and Cousin Tybal when we were staying in the country; sometimes I'd just go by myself. I enjoyed the clean skill of it—I like using things, tools, weapons—but more than that, I think I just liked to be alone and not have to worry about how I looked. And courts are so noisy." Her black brows pulled down over her nose, and a pain line like a pin scratch sprang into being between them. "It's as if people can't think of anything better to do with a summer evening and a garden than invite half the countryside to a garden party."

She was quiet for a moment, staring into the sunless distance, as if past the hills she could see the garden of which she spoke in the apple-green silence of a summer twilight. In her eyes, which were level with his own, Caris could see the silvery shine of tears. After a time she said, "If Suraklin succeeds in establishing this machine of his, that will all go away, won't it? No one will ever feel that—that magic—again."

"No," said Caris. Then, impulsively, "Will you come with us?"

She turned her head quickly; for one instant, he saw the leap of joy in her eyes, the warrior's eagerness for action. Then she looked away, so quickly her black hair made a sharp slithering over the collar of her cloak; he was close enough to her now that he could feel her tremble. "I can't."

"I'm sorry," Caris said instantly, realizing belatedly what he had asked. Only for a moment, it had seemed right, and the rightness had answered him from her eyes. "I shouldn't have . . ."

"It isn't that." Her eyes met his again. Now, clearly, he saw in them that haunted look he'd seen before in the last day or so of the journey and riding that afternoon in the hills—the despair of some unwanted certainty that could no longer be denied. "If it was just me, I would," she went on steadily. "It isn't that I want to fight to protect Pharos' life, though I know from what Gaire—Suraklin—was always hinting to me that he is in danger. He's a cruel man, vicious . . . I suppose I want to do this for—Rightness? Goodness? Do you believe in goodness?"

"I believe in evil," Caris said quietly. "And I believe that Suraklin has to be stopped." Here was another, he realized, who was more than a line fighter, more even than a campaign strategist like Joanna.

She looked away from him, her mouth flinching with an effort not to tremble. "It's just that I can't risk it." She went on, small and remote, as if trying to get quickly over pain or shame, "I think I'm carrying Pharos' child."

Anger hit Caris like a wave of night, disproportionate, illogical rage and revulsion, as if she had confessed to some filthy act. With an effort, he bit back words he knew would hurt her; she caught his arm as he whirled to storm through the door.

Her voice was desperate. "Caris . . ."

In the brittle light, tears shone on her face. He was breathing hard, the air cuttingly cold in his nostrils and lungs; everything in him was consumed with smothering heat. Confused, it flashed through his mind to wonder why this should be; the answer hit him like a thrown bucket of ice water, and in the next second, he saw that answer mirrored in her eyes.

It sobered him, the rage dissolving into horror and a grief he could not define. He felt as if he'd stumbled, accidently dropping and breaking something which he'd never known he had until it was gone, and which could never be replaced. In one instant the world was all changed from what it had been. Even then, he knew, there was no going back. Hoarsely, shakily, he stammered, "Pella, I can't do this."

She didn't need to ask what he meant. It was as if they had both fought the knowledge of it for days. "I know." Her greenish eyes met his, dark in the sweet-smelling gloom. "I know you need your hate to keep you strong—to keep you alive, maybe, when you go to the Citadel tomorrow. But—" She shivered suddenly, and looked away from him, struggling against tears that it was not the Way of the Sasenna to shed. Tiny and choked, she whispered, "But please don't hate me."

They stood at arm's length, facing one another in the darkness of the barn while the ashy light bled away outside. He felt a surge of hatred against Pharos for putting that fear into those fearless eyes. Then he stepped back to her and took her in his arms, willing himself desperately not to feel what he felt while she laid her head on his shoulder and cried.

"I had meant not to do this."

It was dark. Outside, the rain was falling, cold and steady now, with sudden splatterings where the wind flung it against the house wall in handfuls. A couple of candles burned at random out of the dozen or so on the desk and highboy. Antryg had lit them without getting up from the bed when the night began to close in.

"Does that mean you're going to press charges for rape?" Joanna looked up with feigned concern from the circle of his arms.

Antryg drew himself up, very much on his dignity, save for the wicked twinkle far back in his gray eyes. Then he sighed and let his head drop back to the pillow lace, his grip tightening around her shoulders. "It means that I don't want to make things more difficult for you than they already are."

"Well," Joanna said consideringly, "we're going out to Suraklin's Citadel tomorrow; we're going to have to get through whatever defenses he's set up around his computer and keep them at bay long enough for me to program the worm into the system. After we take care of that, we settle down and wait for him to show up—if he isn't there defending the thing already. I've got Suraklin after me, and you've got the Church, the Regent, the Council, and the Witchfinders after you, any of whom will be ready to nail me as your accomplice, plus any random abominations that happen to be around . . . It's hard to see how things *could* get more difficult, unless we get tangled up with invading aliens from another planet, or a crowd of peasants with torches. But I'll take your word for it."

He regarded her severely. "You know perfectly well what I mean."

"I know perfectly well that you're afraid I'll be hurt."

"Well, yes," he admitted, twining a tendril of her fair hair around one of his bony fingers and studying the resultant play of shadows thoughtfully. "But considering what we're up against, there's a good chance we're both going to be hurt and hurt badly. There isn't really anything either of us can do about that, except take the usual precautions and hope for the best. I have a general idea of what waits for us out at the Citadel, since I helped establish many of its original defenses, and it's not something I'd care to take any of my friends into. But I certainly can't deprogram the thing myself, and we need a warrior to watch both our backs. Neither you nor I has the option, as Caris and Pella do, of simply retreating."

"Caris won't retreat," she said softly. "Nor will Pella."

"No," he agreed. "They are souls who don't know the meaning of physical fear. But for them the danger isn't the same. Though I daresay Suraklin would use either of them as a tool, he wouldn't seek to establish the all-devouring grip on their minds that he did on Gary's—that he seeks to do on yours."

Joanna shivered, remembering the disjointed recollections of the Dark Mage's slow takeover, inscribed with clinical exactness by both prepetrator and victim in their separate files.

After a moment Antryg went on, "The whole time I was in the Tower, I was desperately frightened for you—frightened that Suraklin would get you under his influence somehow without your realizing what was happening until it was too late."

She was silent, drawing the soft, tatted pillow lace again and again through her small fingers. It was the screaming of his soul, Magister Magus had said, when the Sigil had touched his flesh, that she had heard in her dream . . . "You didn't hate me?"

The distant glow of the candles threw the long shadows of his lashes on his cheeks, as his gaze seemed to go out beyond those floating points of light. Then he looked down at her again. "I lived with Suraklin for eight years," he reminded her. "I grew to manhood in his household. I saw the kind of things he could manipulate people into doing." His jaw tightened momentarily, with shame and bitter anger. "Myself included.

No, I didn't hate you. Mind you," he added suddenly, "when I was trying to talk you into letting me go, I was angry enough to knock your head against the wall."

Joanna laughed, and for a time they did not talk. The candles burned down in fluted columns of white wax over the shelled sea goddesses of their holders. Distantly they heard a harpsichord being played somewhere in the rooms below and muffled voices, Caris' and Pella's. A servant's footfalls creaked on a distant backstair. The rain eased to a trickle. In the glowing jewelbox silence of the room, even the wickering of the fire seemed loud.

For all intents and purposes, Joanna thought, the future ended with tonight. This warmth, this silence, might be all that they would ever have.

Tomorrow she would do what she had feared all along she must—walk into the heart of Suraklin's power and put herself in the one place where he could most easily get her.

But like Antryg, standing trapped between the abomination of the Sigil on the Tower door and the knowledge that, if he did not face it, its twin would remain welded to his flesh, she knew she truly had no option. If Suraklin were not destroyed, sooner or later he would seek her.

As if he read her thoughts, Antryg said quietly, "If we manage to demolish the computer without getting ourselves killed, and if it's possible to do so safely, I want you and Caris to come back here tomorrow. I don't think your presence will help me against him . . ." He hesitated, as if debating within himself how much of the truth to speak, then sighed. "And I don't think I'll be able to protect you from him."

"I see," Joanna said softly and did. She reached up and touched his chest, her sun-browned hand dark against the marble whiteness of his skin. "That's why you didn't want to—to tie me more closely to you, to make me feel committed to you—to let me love you. You don't expect to survive meeting Suraklin, do you?"

His gray eyes, enormous without their protective lenses, avoided hers; the candlelight caught a facet of his diamond earrings, held steady for a moment, a burning point of many-colored light. Then he sighed, and looked back at her with a half-rueful grin. "Frankly, my dear, I don't see any way that I can."

CHAPTER IX

THOUGH SHE HAD TRAVELED THREE TIMES THROUGH THE HILLS OF the Sykerst, Joanna did not believe she had ever seen anything so desolate as the emptiness that surrounded what had once been the Citadel of Suraklin. Elsewhere the hills might be barren, the grass without life or color, combed like a dead dog's hair by the incessant winds, but at least the terrible silence had been broken by occasional signs of life. From Pella's carriage, she'd seen the start of rabbits in the thin clumps of naked birches which grew in the small pockets of soil in the bedrock; by the sluggish black streams near the Silent Tower, the prints of muskrat and weasel had latticed the half-frozen mud. At first sight a uniform pewter, the hills had a startling variation of color—mauves and sepias, the cobalt of shadow, and the occasional rich emerald of lichens clinging to the cold-cracked rocks.

Here there was nothing. In the wide dell with its scattered stringers of broken stone, its buckled pavements long veiled in a wind-flattened shroud of rotting weeds, and its crumbling pits and trenches like suppurating gray wounds, the only sound was the wind thrumming over stone and hissing in the dead grass. The jingle of the bridle-bits sounded very loud as the horses tossed their heads, made nervous by the silence, and the faint creak of Caris' sword belt as he turned suddenly at a noise that he hadn't really heard.

"That's very odd," Antryg murmured, frowning.

Caris looked quickly over his shoulder, then back in the direction of Antryg's gaze. "What is?" His quiet voice had an edge of fear to it. "I don't see anything amiss."

"Neither do I," the wizard said. "That's what's odd." He pushed his crazy schoolboy spectacles a little farther up on his long nose and dismounted with the light grace of a cavalryman. "Leave the horses here and follow me," he said softly. "It wouldn't do to get separated in this place." He turned to help Joanna down from her horse; the elderly blue roan, though the quietest Pella's stables had to offer, was sized for a woman of the Princess' height.

"We should split up," Caris said, his voice rough with nervousness. "You said yourself the spells you showed me this morning should keep Suraklin from scrying me out from afar. As long as Joanna keeps her backpack with the Sigil in it on her, he shouldn't be able to find her, either, protective wrapping or no protective wrapping. The Church knows whose pupil you were. They'll be expecting you to come back here. The hasu saw you beneath the walls of Kymil—they know you escaped dressed as a guard. If the Church sasenna see a search party sticking close together instead of spreading out . . ."

"Would you wander away from your friends to search Suraklin's Citadel?" Antryg inquired. "Particularly for an escaped renegade wizard who's known to be mad? Don't be obtuse." He turned away, a lanky figure in the crisp black-and-gold uniform of the Regent's sasenna, his sword—a real one now, not the whittled fake he'd worn in his earlier disguise—making the characteristic hard line under his long-skirted black greatcoat. "My only concern is that search parties came here yesterday and got caught in the place's defenses, whatever they are. You stay here," he added, suddenly turning back and catching his horse's bridle. He stroked the beast's forehead briefly. "And you," he added. His fingers brushed lightly the foreheads of the other two horses.

Ten yards away, Joanna looked back. The three animals stood grouped together, heads up, ears pricked, looking about them nervously, but they remained in place. She shook her head and followed Antryg along the broken, pitted ground.

From the hills above, riding down the track from the Silent Tower, the Citadel had been almost invisible—not as if a mist hid it, but as if Joanna's mind and eyes had simply skipped over that great, broken circle in the shallow dip in the hills. Caris had spoken of that effect, present even long after Suraklin's power had been rooted from the land. In the Dark Mage's heyday it was said men could ride straight through the gates and not notice where they were until the iron portals slammed shut behind them.

As they approached the remains of the outer walls, Joanna was conscious of the hammering the place had taken, the avalanche of power needed to destroy it so thoroughly. Huge sections of the ground had collapsed into the pits dug below, leaving vast, shallow subsidences half filled with rubble and knee-deep weeds. Chunks of stone the size of truck trailers scattered the landscape, half driven into the ground hundreds of yards from the nearest foundations. Weeds covered huge areas, a filthy carpet concealing treacherous breaks in the ground.

The rain had warmed the air, melting some of the stagnant brown ice where the land lay lowest. The surrounding hills sheltered the place from the wind. As they approached, cautious, ready for anything, Joanna was conscious of the nauseating foetor of decay that hung in the raw air.

Beside her, Antryg was tense, listening, it seemed, with senses beyond the human, sniffing the air with his long nose as if seeking some characteristic odor that would warn him when the first defenses closed in.

"Curious," she heard him mutter. "But logical, when you come to think of it. Too many people come near this place to advertise that there's something here worth guarding."

"And then again," Caris added softly, "I've heard it was Suraklin's way to lure and lull at the same time by an appearance of harmlessness, until it was too late to retreat."

Antryg rubbed one side of his nose. "Well, there is that," he admitted. "Though with two of us mageborn, I think we'll have some warning."

"And you think that will do us any good?"

The mad wizard grinned. "Oh, probably not. But the object isn't to retreat anyway, so we needn't worry about it."

Sourly, Caris touched the .45 and the brace of na-aar pistols shoved in his belt—his sword was naked already in his right hand—and followed them without further comment among the hushed decay of the ruins.

They had spread out a little, Antryg picking his way unerringly through the maze of broken, knee-high courses of stone which had once been walls, Joanna keeping uneasily close to his side and fighting the urge to hang onto his coat skirts. In one place she saw crumbled slabs of rusted ironwork half buried in black weeds and fallen stone. . . .

"That was the kitchen," Antryg explained quietly. "Those pits behind it are where the storerooms stood. I used to hide there when I'd displeased him. Not, of course, that anyone could hide from him for very long, but being mageborn myself helped." He paused, a frown buckling his forehead as he scanned what was now little more than a reef of shattered rubble, seeing it, Joanna knew, momentarily as it had been— gray, massive, turretted, toothed, the stronghold of the terrible old man he had so desperately feared and loved.

She said, very softly, "Do you miss him?"

He looked down at her, startled. His brows, reddish as his hair had long since ceased to be, pulled together for a moment. Then he said, "I've always missed him. Missed him as I first knew him, missed what I thought I had. Even when I realized I didn't—that in fact, the care he showed for me was only because he knew I'd respond to care . . . I don't know. I still wanted it. But after that, it was difficult to believe in anyone else's caring." He rubbed his hands in their shabby, fingerless gloves, an absentminded gesture as the cold bit into the damaged tendon and bone.

"It was all right, I thought—I could put up with the beatings, and the bloodlettings, the spells and rites I performed in the dark of the moon, the blackest kind of magic, things I knew were evil beyond description . . . I could put up with that if he loved me as he said he did. I'd had a rather unhappy childhood. I suppose I felt honored to be given that love, trusted with the emotions so powerful a mage never dared to show anyone else . . ." The long, sensitive mouth quirked slightly. "Rather like a trout feeling honored to be trusted with an angler's worm. Because none of them were real. They were only facsimiles, copied from what he had seen others sacrifice themselves for." He sighed and added wryly, "They were just copied dazzlingly well. He used to take my blood, to bring some of his—creations—to life. There was a time when I'd have let him take it all."

Around them the Citadel waited, wreathed in its uneasy silence. Joanna remembered that it was built on a node where the energy-tracks crossed, lines that would feed the life-forces of two worlds into its magically electrified heart. Perhaps that was what Antryg and Caris listened for, feeling the pulse of intangible forces along the unseen veins of the earth.

At length Antryg went on, as if speaking half to himself, "Salteris told me they made a bonfire of all his possessions, everything they could find —books, implements of magic, jewels, paintings. Beautiful things, things he had deeply loved. He lived very intensely, you know. Everything about him had a burning quality that drew you and fascinated you. He would get almost literally drunk on the beauty of a cup or a gem or the angle of the sunset light. The high you get from working magic, the fascination of watching people play their intricate social games—he loved them with a passion I don't believe he ever felt for another human being. But of course, human beings are more difficult to control than possessions."

"He managed," she remarked.

"Yes." Antryg sighed regretfully, his eyes returning to hers. "Yes, he did. It never surprised me that he wanted to live forever—that he would do almost anything rather than let that beauty go."

Was that why, Joanna wondered suddenly, Suraklin had chosen Antryg as his student, his slave, his victim? Because he, too, had that passionate delight in the mere drawing of breath? But it was not the same. There were things for which Antryg would cheerfully give up that brightly colored life, among them the thwarting of Suraklin's plans. Awkwardly, because she had never learned the right things to say, she reached out and took his hand and was rewarded with the fleet warmth of his smile.

"Antryg!" Caris' voice rang out sharply behind them. "Over here!"

The wizard swung around in a swirl of gold-braided black coat skirts. Caris stood on the lip of a shallow subsidence, blond hair flattened in a surge of wind, a look of shock and revulsion on his face. Joanna wondered briefly if his appearance might be some kind of trap, a lure set up by the Dark Mage's defenses; but after an almost imperceptible pause, Antryg put his arm around her shoulders and drew her along with him as he strode through the crunching weeds to see.

The thing that lay in the wide depression had been dead for weeks. When the wind fell briefly, the stench was terrible; Joanna drew back, nauseated, at the sight of the bloated, blackened face, orifices agape and filled with maggots and worms.

Antryg and Joanna exchanged a quick glance. Caris said softly, "An abomination. It must have come through the Void and walked straight into one of Suraklin's defenses." The track it had left in the weeds was still plain to see, the dead stems broken in a jagged swathe which began at the creature's body and ended, abruptly, less than a dozen feet away.

Cautiously, the wizard took a step forward and sank to one knee. "Fascinating," he said. "The maggots are dead."

Steeling herself, Joanna moved to his side. Both Antryg and Caris had been adamant that she not adopt the uniform of a sasennan, on the grounds that she'd never be able to maintain the imposture at close range —she was dressed in the breeches, shirt, and short crimson coat of one of the Regent's pages, the backpack on her back and the .38 shoved in one pocket. Her boots crackled in the brittle undergrowth as she hunkered down to look.

"They're tiny," she said after a moment. "They must have died the minute they began to feed." Her revulsion evaporated in academic puzzlement. "Look, there are dead flies on it, too."

She frowned at Antryg for a moment, then back at the carcass. "Could

—could Suraklin's defenses have done that? Killed even the maggots that fed on it after it was dead?"

Antryg raised his head and studied the gray skyline. Like a gunsite on the far hills, the last two stones of the line that stretched toward the Silent Tower notched the pale air. Directly opposite, to the east, a single menhir leaned like a weary drunk. Then he looked back at the unspeakable, rotting thing. "I wonder," he said softly.

"More likely this *is* one of Suraklin's defenses." With the tip of his sword Caris touched what was clearly a mouth at the end of a collapsed pinkish tube. Teeth like chisels stood out from the black gums.

"But in that case, what killed it?"

Caris shrugged. "Sasenna? Witchfinders? Peelbone was keeping an eye on the place before you ever escaped the first time. There's a lot of breakage in the weeds around here, but it's hard to say how old it is."

"Odd that he never ran into any defenses." Antryg stood up again, scanning the ash-colored tussocks of stone and earth around them, his gray eyes narrowed and uneasy behind his specs. "Very odd. Come along, my dear." He took Joanna's hand. "Caris, guard our backs if you will. Twelve feet was the usual distance between the trigger and the rear edge of the trap."

With these comforting words he began to pick his way cautiously back toward the ruins of what had been the main keep.

The outer walls of the Citadel keep had been well over fifteen feet thick. Their foundations formed a broken platform in whose splintered and riven cracks grew straggling weeds, now black and brittle as burned wires. From its edge, Joanna looked down into a chasm like an enormous open pit mine, a hundred and fifty feet across and easily as deep. Collapsed spills of rubble tracked its sides and made little heaps on the bottom around the brim of a silent tarn of standing water, enigmatically reflecting the silver sky. In places, fragments of old floors and vaulting clung to the stone sides of the pit, showing how many levels down the Citadel vaults had extended. Joanna counted seven of them. Beside her, Antryg was very silent.

"Had you ever come here since—since its destruction?"

He nodded. "Salteris and I came here—oh, years ago, when we traveled together. I didn't want to, but he insisted. I think he wanted to prove to me that Suraklin was truly dead—to exorcise the fear of him from my dreams. Ironic," he added, forcing lightness over the sudden flaw in his deep voice, "when you think of it."

Salteris' own experiences with the Dark Mage's Citadel couldn't have been anything he particularly wanted to relive, Joanna reflected, remembering the old Archmage's digitalized memories of what he had found there when he led the triumphant armies in. Yet he had come back to the place to help a frightened and half-demented youth readjust to the world, gently trying to lead him back to sanity. What had it been for Antryg to come into a room in the Silent Tower to greet someone who had cared that much for him and to see Suraklin looking at him from his eyes?

"I wish I could have known him," she said softly.

He glanced down at her with that same half-wary expression, like a nervous horse, afraid to trust. Then he sighed and put his hand briefly on her shoulder.

"There used to be a stairway over here," he said after a moment. "It was hidden behind a false niche near the hall fireplace and enough spells to darken the noonday sun. The wizards' army destroyed the top part of it but never found the rooms below. That's where it will be."

"What about the way you got us out when I first came?" Joanna asked. "An underground passageway . . ."

He shook his head. "That was a subsidiary hideout, connected to the main pits by miles of passage. I think Suraklin went straight there through the Void from Gary's—his mark was all over the room."

He took a step away along the brink of the huge pit, then hesitated. "I should leave you here," he said after a moment. "But I don't know what defenses will be in operation, or if there's a delay-trigger and it's already too late to escape. It's hard to believe Suraklin would leave it this late—unless he's down there himself, waiting . . ." He paused, and Joanna thought that, against his black coat collar with its gilded braid, he seemed very pale. It occurred to her that Suraklin's aim of killing Antryg might only have been a contingency plan if he could not take him—his first, chosen, and well-prepared victim—alive.

"The trouble is," Antryg went on, "I can't feel a thing amiss here, and that's making me very uneasy."

"It's making *you* uneasy?" Joanna said, with a shaky grin in spite of the uncomfortable slamming of her heart against her ribs.

He grinned back. "Stay close, and be ready to . . ." He stopped, his head coming up like a dog's that scents sudden peril. "Oh, pox."

"What is it?" Joanna whispered.

"The Witchfinders," he said softly. "Peelbone."

"Antryg . . ." Caris sprang lightly up to the top of the broken platform. "Can you hear it? Along the energytrack . . ."

"Peelbone, yes."

"Can you use some kind of spell . . . ?"

"They have hasu with them. Besides, apart from blowing a trumpet I can't think of a better way to let Suraklin know I'm here. Look, there they are . . ."

He pointed at the dark line of shapes on the colorless gray of the northern slopes. There was a red splash, like a drop of blood—a Church dog's robes. One thin gray form among them spurred his horse and began to canter down the slope.

"They must have been watching through a spyglass from a distance," Antryg said, catching Joanna's hand and hurrying along the top of the platform. "Peelbone knows me, of course. He was in charge of obtaining my—confession."

"Look!" Caris pointed to the western slopes above the Citadel; a dozen black forms could be seen riding down them. There was a thin glitter of drawn weapons in the heatless light.

"Where are Suraklin's defenses now when we need them?" Antryg wondered aloud.

"Should we split up?"

"Good heavens, no! Make for the pits . . ."

Caris skidded to a stop. "Are you mad? If the defenses are anywhere, they'll be . . ."

Clear and thin as the cracking of ice, Peelbone's voice rang across the broken Citadel. "Windrose!" He drew rein momentarily on the edge of the buckled pavement of what had been the court before the main keep, rising in his stirrups, his wispy gray hair streaming in the restless tweak of the wind. His hat had blown off; his eyes were hard and colorless as glass. "I should have known you would come here, back to the hold of your master!" The sasenna and the hasu behind him, galloping hard, had almost reached the edge of the pavement; the Witchfinder put spurs to his lathered horse and started across.

With a thin whine of steel Caris' sword was in his hand.

What happened then was almost totally without warning. In later nightmares Joanna saw it again in slow-motion and realized then that it was a thing she had dimly taken for a domed hummock of weed-covered stone which moved, bursting upward into the air as the horse trod on it in a flurrying scatter of dirt. But at the time it seemed as if it came from nowhere—as if suddenly it was hanging over the Witchfinder and his terrified mount, a huge, dustcolored thing like a monster jellyfish, slobbering tentacles dangling . . .

Adrenaline locked her lungs and circulatory system shut even before Peelbone began screaming. Sasenna were converging from all directions. Antryg grabbed Joanna's arm and made a run for the ragged spill of fallen stone and weeds that had been the head of the secret stair. From the tail of her eye Joanna saw Peelbone's horse running frenziedly in circles, the tentacles raking its flesh and almost wholly enveloping the shrieking, clawing man on its back as the floating body of the abomination lowered itself, like the canopy of a vast parachute, down over Peelbone's head.

She had no time to see more. Deep under the weeds were the broken rubble of old stairs. She clung to the brittle stems for balance as Antryg guided her down. Below the level of the pit edge, the weeds ended, leaving only a crumbling spiral of iced and treacherous gravel. Above her, she heard voices shouting, one scream riding over them. Dear God, she thought, how long will it take him to die?

Her feet slipped. She half fell, half rolled the last few yards, down what felt like a ladder of sharp and broken stone. Antryg pulled her to her feet and through a half-fallen archway like a skull's empty eyesocket, Caris panting and cursing at their heels. "What do you think you're . . . ?" the sasennan demanded hoarsely, as Antryg slipped his hand behind a shattered pilaster now barely distinguishable from its parent rock and cursed. He slid his sword scabbard clear of his sash, wedged it like a lever into the masonry and wrenched. Like the cries of some alien bird, the screams still drifted down to them, scarcely human anymore. A dark slot of ground opened in the grayer darkness.

Antryg thrust her unceremoniously through and was slipping after her when Caris grabbed his arm in a crushing hold. "You idiot . . . !"

"Oh, surely not!" the mad wizard protested. "Insane I may be, but not an idiot." With an easy movement of his elbow, he disengaged his arm from the baffled young man's grip. Dim daylight flicked along one spectacle rim, picked out the fracture in the glass and the facet of an earring. More soberly, he added, "They're never going to believe I didn't summon that thing. Most men would kill Peelbone for the things he did to me. And to Joanna," he added softly, touching her shoulder in the darkness. "And to you."

"And that's your reason for blundering straight into the heart of Suraklin's traps?" Caris' whisper was almost a scream of rage.

"Well, the odd thing is," Antryg murmured, "we don't seem to have sprung one." He slipped the scabbard casually back into his sash; Caris still held his, ready to draw and do battle. "We must needs have come here in any case, Caris. If it's a trap, it's a very good one. We might as well see the rest of it."

They moved forward, into a species of Hell in darkness. It was a darkness that chittered and whispered or, worse, simply seemed to watch them in waiting silence beyond the faint foxlight glow that Antryg called above his head. Twice he killed the light, quickly, and thrust his companions back against the wall; in the darkness, Joanna heard the slimy dragging noise that heaved itself slowly along the passageway and felt the clammy cold that seeped in the creature's wake. Against her arm, she felt Caris' muscles tighten in utter revulsion and horror. He was mageborn, she remembered. He could see in the dark.

Other things fled from the light, sometimes white, squamous shapes like naked and legless pigs, other times the more prosaic vermin of this world, swarming black roaches and rats that had clustered around rotting carrion of no shape known to her, whose putrefying stench poisoned the air. In one place Antryg whispered to them not to touch the bubbling orange mold that covered the whole side of one rock-hewn chamber. Snared in it, Joanna saw two or three other abominations of various sizes, all of them rotting, but none of them completely dead. There were rats and roaches there, too, gummed likewise in the putrid growth; by the faint, glittering radiance of Antryg's witchlight, she could see that several of the roaches were close to the size of dinner plates, and the rats displayed unspeakable mutations.

But throughout that darkness, no magic, no malice, and no trap touched its three invaders. It was a Hell untenanted, save by the abominations that crept, preying stupidly upon one another, through its arched stone passageways. Level by level Antryg led them deeper into the surviving corner of Suraklin's mazes, and nowhere did they find anything but the long-spent memories of his evil and power. Even the ghosts, it seemed, had been calcined away by the wizards' wrath.

"I don't understand," Joanna whispered.

They had come to the last, deepest chamber of all, a vast black cavern where a broken stone cover showed the inky waters of a stagnant well, and a round block of bluish stone, like an altar, crouched amid darkness that even Antryg's faint witchfire could not pierce. Beside her, Antryg stood, his full, oddly curving lips now tight and rather gray, as if the aura of the place, like a remembered smell, nauseated him. The blurred remains of a chalked circle were almost eradicated from the floor. Dark stains blotched the top of the altar block and tracked its sides. And that was all.

"This is it, isn't it?" Joanna asked softly.

Antryg nodded. Under a sudden sheen of sweat, all the muscles of his jaw rippled, like rope under strain, then eased again.

She looked hesitantly up at him, not liking the haunted horror in his eyes. "Do you—do you see something that I don't?"

"Only the past, my dear," he murmured. "Only the past." His breath blew out in a sigh; he turned to her, his eyes returning to the present once more. "Yes, this is where it should be, the centerpoint of Suraklin's power, the place where he—or I—performed his great magics."

"You?" The echoes of Caris' suspicious voice murmured back at them from the hard stone of the walls.

Antryg's eyes moved to the altar, then away. As if speaking of someone else, he said carefully, "You understand, there is a type of magic which can be drawn from certain—acts—which by then he was too old to perform himself." He looked around him. "This was the place of his power, and I should say, my friends, that we have all been well and truly taken in." At his small gesture, an explosion of light filled the room, bright and clear as a sodium lamp, digging like the eyes of God into every bleached, clean cranny of its hewn stone walls and flashing like diamonds in the obsidian waters of the pool. In all the space of that room there was nothing.

"But the abominations . . ." Caris began.

"They weren't guards," the mad wizard said quietly. "Half of them were herbivores, by the look of their snouts—even that thing at the top went for the man nearest it, God help his wretched soul, rather than for us, who were nearer the stair. We're on a node in the lines. Every time the Void is opened, gaps in it open for a short distance all around it—but when it is opened on a line, the whole line faults. Those poor things are mere blunderers-through, harmless . . ."

"*Harmless?*" echoed Caris indignantly.

"Comparatively harmless." The light around them faded again to the corpse-candle gleam above Antryg's head; he turned back to the stygian arch that led once more into the mazes and the hellish walk back to the outer air.

Caris strode after him. "Compared to *what?*"

Antryg shrugged. "Compared to what's going to happen when an intelligent one comes through."

They did not speak again until they had emerged from the pits, by which time darkness had fallen once more outside. From the protection of the passage, Antryg listened, stretching his senses out into the Citadel around them. The Church's sasenna had retreated, watching from the hills around. No one, no matter what his mission, was prepared to linger in the Dark Mage's fortress after the fall of night. They found Peelbone's horse lying half in a gravel pit, with the hacked and burned remains of the thing that had killed it. There was blood everywhere, soaking into the frozen weeds, and wide-strewn rags of clothing saturated with blood, acid, and slime. Elsewhere Caris found part of Peelbone's hand, most of the flesh eaten from the melted bone. Antryg looked somberly at it, rubbing his broken fingers in their shabby gloves, but said nothing.

It was only when they were on the hills again, having slipped through the scattered guards, that Joanna asked, "If Suraklin's headquarters isn't at his Citadel, where is it?"

"Elsewhere." Antryg sighed, and hunched his shoulders against the cold night. The horses had, of course, been confiscated by the Witchfinders when they had first surrounded the Citadel, and it was a long and tiring trek over the dark hills to Larkmoor once again. "And unfortunately, since now he'll be well and truly alerted to the fact that I'm at large and looking for it, I haven't the remotest idea where."

CHAPTER X

THEY LEFT LARKMOOR THE FOLLOWING NIGHT, TRAVELING NORTH on foot.

It was a bad time of year to be taking to the roads, and Caris knew it, worriedly eyeing Joanna's small, spare form as she stumped along through the bitter darkness at Antryg's side; it would be worse still away from the main roads. The Sykerst was a land unkind to men.

Antryg's escape coupled with Peelbone's death had roused the countryside around Kymil and set patrols along the Angelshand road. But deeper in-country, Antryg argued, among the isolated villages that sprouted wherever there was soil enough to support thin crops of rye, they would stand a better chance of making their way northward in safety.

"There's another node, a crossing of the energy-lines, on Tilrattin Island about twenty-five miles upriver from Angelshand," he had explained, when the four of them had sat around a picnic breakfast in the darkness of the deserted fodder barn at Larkmoor, following their return from the Citadel ruins. "Suraklin has to have established his computer at some node in the lines. That one has a lot to recommend it; it's on Prince Cerdic's land, for one thing . . ."

"And what do we do if it isn't Suraklin's headquarters, either?" Caris demanded, sitting in the mildewed straw at Pella's side, moodily stabbing his dagger into the floor. Reaction had set in on him. Having keyed himself for a death fight at the Citadel, he now felt empty, weary, and vaguely cheated. "Walk to the Citadel of Wizards in the taiga forests to check that one as well? And what if it isn't? What if it's somewhere on the other side of the world? Have you thought of that?"

"But we *do* know Suraklin's trying to take over control of the Empire," Joanna pointed out diffidently. "So it's a good guess that's where it is."

"I'm actually very taken with the notion of its being at the Citadel of Wizards," Antryg mused with a dreamy grin. "It is the next nearest node in the Empire. Lady Rosamund would have a seizure from sheer indignation. But going there wouldn't be necessary." He gestured with the muffin he was holding, his long legs folded tailor-wise under him and butter dripping on his gold-braided black cuffs. "By standing at a node in the lines when the computer comes up, I'll be able to feel the direction of the energy-flow and tell pretty well where it's going. I'd simply stay here eating your cook's excellent muffins, Pella, until I could do so from the Citadel node, only somehow I don't think that would be such a good idea."

Pella shook her head, missing the impish sparkle in his eyes. "They're going to be searching house to house," she said gravely. "I can keep my servants quiet about a chance visit, but not if you're still here."

So they had spent the day sleeping and quietly assembling provisions, and departed three or four hours after it grew dark. In that time Caris had seen seven or eight separate patrols on the hills, and two groups—one of Witchfinders, one of Church sasenna—came up to the manor itself, to ask questions. It would only be a matter of time, he thought, before the place was searched.

They traveled as physicians, Antryg wearing the old-fashioned, dull purple robes of a University doctor, torn and mended and stained with gin, Caris the cleaner, if threadbare, gown of a medical student. To his outfit Antryg had added his usual collection of the gimcrack beads of which he was so fond and the long-skirted olive coat of some nobleman's household cavalry, arguing that the hooded cloak of an academic was wholly inadequate; the worst of it was that he was right. Caris looked down his nose at the scarecrow appearance of his purported instructor, but shivered in the cutting wind.

For her part, Joanna was relegated to the rough, baggy trousers, sheepskin coat, and coarse woolen hood of the lowest type of servant, since she could pass herself as neither sasennan nor student.

"That should teach you to learn to read the wrong languages," Antryg chided loftily, steadying her over the gluey gray mud of the half-frozen potholes with effortless strength.

"Eat hot death, dog wizard."

"I fear," sighed the wizard, "that we shall all do that when—or if—we reach the inn at Plikey Wash this evening. The cooking there is notorious for miles around."

Joanna laughed, her breath a cloudly puff of silver in the cold.

In the event, none of them was obliged to endure the dubious hospitality of country inns. Raised in the populous Wheatlands, Caris had previously had little idea of the frightening isolation of the Sykerst and the knowledge that, if something went wrong, there was almost literally nowhere to turn for medical aid. For all his decrepit appearance and jangling beads, Antryg was welcomed in every village along their road, to tend illnesses, give advice, and often to repair injuries that had been left to fester all summer—injuries brought about by carelessness and exacerbated by the uncaring apathy of the dead times. Again and again, as Antryg examined mortifying flesh or bones set crookedly because they had been carelessly splinted or not splinted at all, Caris heard that tired refrain, ". . . don't know what I was thinking of, that day . . ."

And rather to Caris' surprise, the lunatic mage proved to be an excellent doctor as well.

"Won't the Council and the Witchfinders be able to trace you by your use of magic?" Caris asked quietly as the wizard bent over the bed of a small boy, counting the pulse in one fragile wrist. The lantern hanging on the rafters not far over their heads threw little light, but both men were mageborn and able to see in the dark.

"They would if I used magic for a cure, yes," Antryg replied. "But a fever like this can be brought down with ginger and elder; I asked Pella to put some up in the medical satchel she gave me. If they can keep it down until the ailment has run its course, the boy should be all right." He half lifted the child to a sitting position, and the boy's thin, gasping breath at once seemed easier. Caris folded the limp pillow and frowned. A glance around the loft where the child's bed stood yielded no sign of spare bedding—the family was a poor one—but after a moment he collected several sacks of peas and seed-corn from their lumpish white ranks along the far wall and stacked them up behind the little boy's shoulders, wadding the pillow in over them. Antryg eased the boy gently back.

"It's pneumonia, isn't it?" Caris asked, listening to the thick wheeze of the boy's breath. "But his mother said it was cowpox . . ."

"It probably started out as cowpox . . . Thank you, my dear." Joanna's head appeared above the crude ladder from the room downstairs. She set a steaming tin kettle down by the entry hole and scrambled up the last few rungs. "Pneumonia is a common complication, particularly in children. Elfdock steam should help clear up some of the congestion . . ."

"His mother asked me if you were going to bleed him." Joanna hunkered down beside the bed and looked worriedly at the dozing child. Three days on the road had not been kind to her; she looked worn and tired in her coarse smock and heavy boots, and the greasy yellow light picked out hollows under the pointy cheekbones.

"I hope you told her that I was." Antryg removed from his medical satchel several bleeding cups and dipped a little of the hot water up in one of them. From his boot he pulled his razor, flipped open the blade, and drew off one of the fingerless gloves that he wore indoors and out to keep some of the cold from the damaged tendons of his hands. Carefully he slit across one of the smaller veins of his wrist, and squeezed the blood into the water. "Astonishing what a mess even a little blood will make in any amount of water. Rinse that round all the bleeding cups, would you, my dear?"

"*Aren't* you going to bleed him?" Caris asked, shocked.

"Of course not. The boy needs his strength, but there's no point in having his mother fret."

Caris frowned, watching Antryg as he crushed up the dried elfdock and kindled his portable spirit lamp to raise the water to steaming again. "Doesn't bleeding bring down a fever, then?"

"Not in my experience. In fact, the only time I ever bleed a patient is if they are intent on getting out of bed too soon and doing something silly." He thoughtfully ran the razor blade back and forth through the spirit lamp's flame a few times, closed it, and returned it to his boot. "Remind me to mark the boy's back a little before we leave. Otherwise his mother will never believe me when I tell her to keep him sitting up and let him breathe steam."

From his coat pocket he took a tin flask of gin with which he doused the wound in his wrist; below the pushed-up edge of his sleeve, Caris saw the ragged trail of ancient slits and punctures that followed the vein back up his arm, broken here and there by the distinct scars of small and vicious teeth.

"You speak as if you were a physician at one time," he commented later, when they were once again on the endless, nameless road from one minute village to the next. That morning a farm cart had carried them a number of miles on their way before turning down a lane that was little more than a muddy slot in the broken and stony land. Around them, like the flanks of sleeping giants, the rolling land rose to rounded crests hundreds of feet high, barren, monotonous, and cold under a slate-hued sky.

Whitish outcroppings among the dead whin showed how close the granite lay beneath the thin veneer of topsoil; only by the gradual strengthening of the light above the cloud cover could Caris tell that it was nearly noon. The wind blew from the north, smelling of snow.

"Well, wizards do learn something about healing, though we're not allowed to practice it on anyone but one another, and I've passed myself off as a doctor often enough to learn some conventional medicine. The borderlands of midwifery and granny-magic are fairly wide, if shockingly inaccurate in places." He frowned thoughtfully at the young warrior from behind his cracked spectacles. "You don't do badly at it yourself."

Caris blushed a little. "Grandfather . . ." His tongue stalled momentarily on the name, hate and vengeance and grief clutching in him like a fist. But just as suddenly, he remembered Salteris himself, the real Salteris of his childhood, and the anger in him gave way like melting ice breaking. Hesitantly, he went on, "Grandfather taught me enough to help him, when I was a boy. It was more of a game for me, picking out this herb from that and remembering what each of them was good for. Grandmother was a midwife, too." He grinned reminiscently. "Even before I became sasenna, I was always getting into scrapes, so I started early learning how to care for cuts and broken bones, mostly my own."

He fell silent after that, for the memories hurt him in an odd way— vivid not only to the way the old man had looked, but to the smell of warm hay and herbs in his robes and the summer's heat on his skin. Caris thrust them aside, knowing that he could not afford to warm himself too much by those memories, as he could not afford to let too near to him all the dozens of small scenes of the last week that burned so clear now in his mind: the warm breath of the horses on his hands while he held their heads so Pella could gouge ice-balls out of their hooves; the lithe way she moved, like a big, splendid panther, as she mounted the footman's stand; the smoky-sweet timbre of her voice and the strength of her arms around his waist that afternoon in the barn. He had felt bitterly sorry for her, left behind to do nothing but wait and feel the child of an unwanted husband growing in her belly. During the last day between their return from the Citadel and setting forth to the Tilrattin node, he had avoided being alone with her, avoided any but the most perfunctory good-bye.

She had not sought him out. She had understood.

She had trained as sasennan, he thought, and smiled as he pictured what sparring with her would be like. She'd probably be a little slow, he guessed, but she'd have a forehand stroke like the blow of a timber beam. In the barn at Larkmoor she had said, "I know you need your hate . . ." When he had pursued Antryg through the darkness of the Void, he had known that, if he took his eyes from that flitting, tatterdemalion figure, he would be utterly lost. So it was now. Pella knew what he knew—that facing what he faced, to turn his gaze for one second on anything but the pure, sharp strength of his revenge would be a weakness that could be fatal to them all.

And in any case, any turning-aside from what he was now would be hopeless. Not only could he not afford to think of might-bes, but he knew that they could, in fact, never be. She was Pharos' wife and the mother of Pharos' child. As a recreant to his vows, Caris' life and soul were already forfeit. There was nothing for him but to accomplish his revenge and to die, as was the Way of the Sasenna to die, in the process.

Why then, in this gray journey, did he feel, not the grimness of one who seeks only vengeance and death, but a medley of strange and hurtful joys?

The joy of friendship, unlike the hard-edged and competitive friendships of the training-floor, with this woman Joanna, blunt, uncertain of herself, awkward, and oddly logical with the logic of the computers who for so many years had been her only friends. The joy that he had put aside and almost forgotten in his years of training to be a perfect weapon, the painful, puzzling joy of seeing the lives of others, the people of the villages through which they passed as well as Joanna and Antryg. The joy of a reawakened awareness of life, even now, on the threshold of winter's annual death and perhaps of a greater death to come—his own, his love's, the world's. The joy of watching the last dark stringers of geese hastening south high in the pewter air, of the warm smell of stables, or of Kyssha nuzzling at his hands. The odd joy he had felt, standing in the window embrasure, listening to Pella play the harpsichord, with the candlelight dancing off her over-embroidered sleeves.

For years, it seemed, he had seen all things in terms of the Way of the Sasenna, of defense and attack. Only now he saw them in terms of her—a heifer-calf in a stable where they were forced to spend one night, the way the mist clung to the low ground in the morning, and the sound of huntinghorns ringing across the hills the night it snowed. He wanted to crystalize those moments in molten glass, string them on a necklace, and carry them back to her. She, who so loved small beauties and simple things, would have wanted to know.

He knew what was happening and he fought it desperately. He could not, he told himself over and over again in the dark hours of the night, afford to let himself soften even a little, let alone fret himself with worrying over what would become of her, married to her spiteful and sadistic little lord.

By Antryg's very gentleness, he suspected that the wizard knew, and hated him for that knowledge, while silently thanking him for not speaking of it. And indeed, there was little anyone could have said.

Woven in and around these other joys and hurts there was the joy of finally, after so many years, touching and using magic, even the insignificant magics of healing that were all that lay within his scope. That was perhaps the greatest and certainly the most dangerous joy of all.

Caris pretended to himself sometimes that it was all in the interests, as Antryg said, of verisimilitude; he was supposed to be a medical student, after all. As a sasennan, he had learned the cleansing of wounds and the setting of bones, and there was, too, the vast, half-forgotten backlog picked up from his childhood fascination with the arts of his grandparents. From Antryg he learned a smattering of standard medical practice —to diagnose ailments from the different pulses of the body and from the colors of the whites of the eyes or of the tongue and the mucus. But threaded through this knowledge, like ribbon through bone, was the laying of spells upon the various herbs and salts to increase their efficacy and the sigils of healing to be written across the life-tracks of the body itself— matters not only outside the physician's knowledge, but outside the law, matters which interfered, however beneficently, with the ways of human-kind.

To work magic at all, Caris found, required a softening of the soul, a listening to all things in a manner different from a warrior's instinctive caution—a dropping of one's guard.

What appalled Caris was that he found it so easy.

"I shouldn't be doing this," he said quietly to Joanna one evening in the ill-lit sitting room of some isolated manor deep in the Sykerst. Their host, the local squire, and Antryg had gone upstairs to see to the squire's wife, a girl of seventeen, far gone in what looked like a very bad pregnancy. Joanna glanced curiously at the little card of parchment that lay before Caris and raised her eyebrows inquiringly. He had been practicing drawing the Sigil of Air—one of the easier ones—from memory, a sign to summon all the qualities of lightness, openness of the veins and heart and mind, and freedom of the soul. He saw the direction of her look and shook his head, pushing the Sign from him.

"I don't mean this, particularly," he said. "I mean . . ." He hesitated, feeling tripped by what he *did* mean—so much more than he was prepared to say.

"You mean dealing in life?" Joanna asked softly, "instead of dealing in death?"

He ran his fingers through his short-cropped blond hair, and avoided her eyes. Behind him, the wood shutters of the window quivered under a sharp blast of the sleety wind, the candleflames on the table before him starting nervously in their holders of Kymil porcelain. Like most small manors, this one was built largely of wood from the stands along the Sykerst rivers, exquisitely carved and fretted, but apt to creak. Around them the whole house seemed to be muttering to itself.

"No," he said evasively. "That is, I've been trained as a killer . . ."

"I didn't mean other peoples'," Joanna said, toying with the small parchment rectangle that lay between them. "I mean yours."

Caris was silent.

The girl's small fingers traced the lines of the Sigil, simple as a magic circle on the stiff, cream-colored card. There was no magic in it, for Caris lacked the ability to imbue what little he had in any inanimate thing; he had watched the mages drawing Sigils for years, for various purposes, from small to great, but this was the first time he had ever set out to memorize them for himself.

She went on, slowly, because speaking was no easier for her than it was for him: "Ever since I first met you in Suraklin's hideout you've been—been ready to die. Ready to kill for your cause, yes, but most of all ready to die for it."

"It is the Way of Sasenna," Caris said, "to be ready to die at the will of the one to whom you have sworn your vows."

"I know." She looked up, the glow of the several candles layering traceries of shadow across her dark eyes. "Since we left Larkmoor, I've had the feeling you're ready to live, but—it's as if you don't know how.

"I know about that," she continued uncertainly, after a silence broken by the creak of the house beams, and the distracted sobbing of the wind. "I don't know how either, really. This is the first time I've—I've felt like —I don't know, coming out and saying what I feel. To you. To Antryg. Pella and I did a lot of talking on the way down to Kymil; I don't know why that was easier for me, but it was. It's as if in caring for Antryg I care for other people more, too, and don't want to see them hurt. For so many years I've kind of—of had a lot of reasons for not giving time to people or not saying things to them. Silly things mostly, really simple stuff like, 'I'd like to know you better,' or 'I care about what happens to you.' I don't know what I was afraid they'd say back to me."

Caris turned his pen over in his hands for some moments, studying the shadow of the quills on the red-gold grain of the table. Then, with half a grin at her, he asked softly, "What were you afraid I'd say back to you?"

Her eyes warmed; he was a little surprised that he'd managed to say the right thing, but evidently he had, for she returned his smile.

Stammeringly, he added, "Thank you." He set the pen down and looked over at her in the amber and sepia gloom. "It isn't that I don't know how to live—or not just that, anyway. At this point, it would not only be useless for me to learn, but dangerous."

He thought she would contradict him, but she didn't, only listened in silence, her small hands folded, cold-chapped and so fragile against the coarse linen of her smock sleeves.

"After you shot that Witchfinder on the island near Devilsgate, I told you that sometimes you can't afford to think too much—remember?"

She nodded. He remembered the oppressive heat of the hay barn that night, his own impatience with listening to her stifled sobbing in the darkness, and his sharp jealousy at the thought that she had done the one thing he had trained for but had never actually done—killed a man in a fight. Two men, for that matter. The memory of that childish jealousy still embarrassed him.

"Do you want to learn?"

He looked away from her. To put it into words, he thought, even to deny it aloud, would make it too real for him to stand. "It isn't an option."

"We don't need a hero that bad."

He turned back. Small and unprepossessing in her crudely embroidered brown shirt, her feathery blond curls tied haphazardly back with a leather strap, and her brown eyes worried in their sketched fans of crow's-feet, she looked like a mouse in a cheese compared with Pella's splendid handsomeness. Joanna and Pella and Antryg were the only people who had cared about what he thought or felt since he had parted from Salteris in his thirteenth summer. That they did so still surprised him.

The thought of Salteris made him remember Suraklin, and he raised again that cold shield of obsession deliberately before his heart. He might hate it, but he could not afford to put it down. "You do," he told her quietly. "Believe me, you do."

The candleflames curtseyed suddenly in the rush of a draft as the door was opened; he could hear Squire Alport's lumbering tread retreat down the stairs to the first-floor hall as Antryg strode in, all his grubby tatters fluttering, absently rubbing at his gloved hands.

"How is she?"

The wizard's long mouth hardened. "Frightened," he said softly. "With far better cause than she knows."

Caris had seen the girl when Squire Alport had first offered them hospitality, presenting them to his bride of less than a year. Half her husband's age, her delicate, flaxen beauty was far too thin for her swollen belly. Everything Caris had learned from his midwife grandmother had made his stomach curl with dread at the sight of those too-hollow cheeks and those sunken eyes. Looking up now into Antryg's face, he saw the struggle there; as if everything had been spoken of before, he understood what the wizard was going to ask of him.

He had watched the wizard work minor magics for days, little healings such as granny-wives used, to nudge a bit of extra strength into weary hearts or to hinder the growth of proud flesh on a cleansed wound. Those bits of piseog were undetectable to the Council of Wizards, listening along the pulses of the earth for the whisper of Antryg's name—small things, that lay within Caris' rudimentary powers as well. But such things would never save that frightened girl's life.

Their eyes met and held. Even before Antryg spoke, Caris understood what he was going to be asked, what he had to be asked, and illogical rage surged up in him, a hot flood of anger at the taste of all the things that he would never have.

"You have no right to ask that of me," he said softly, even before Antryg opened his mouth. "I'm a killer, not a healer."

The wizard drew in a sip of breath and let it out. Deranged he might be, but he did not pretend not to understand. His flamboyant voice was low in the half dark. "Well, you're only the one masquerading as the other for the time being, I'll admit . . ."

"You need me for what I am." Caris' onyx eyes narrowed, blazing into the wizard's calm opal gaze. "Don't make it harder for me by showing me what I know I can never have."

The gray eyes did not waver. The fact that what Antryg wanted him to do was against the first law of the Council whose sworn weapon he was or the fact that it would make him an outlaw in the eyes of both Empire and Church was not spoken of. In a way, both sensed that it was not the issue, and neither pretended that it was. Gently, Antryg said, "I know it isn't fair to you . . ."

"Fair!" Caris' laugh was a harsh explosion, utterly without mirth. "Fair isn't even in it! If I don't learn whatever spell it is you want me to learn, to save her life—*if* I have the strength to use it . . ."

"You do," the mage said calmly.

The sureness in his voice stopped Caris for an instant with a split-second's leaping joy and then a rush of even more bitter rage.

"If I don't do this thing," he went on at last, "you will, won't you? You'll give yourself away to the Council by working magic to save her— give *us* away. Get yourself tracked and caught and killed, and never mind that Suraklin will go free—all to save the life of some half-educated petty noblewoman we don't even know?"

It was Antryg's turn to be silent. He stood for a moment, his big hands resting on the back of Joanna's chair, the flames of the two or three candles distorting even further the baroque shadows of his lips and nose. Around his neck and over the velvet collar of his patched green coat, his tawdry beads glittered sharply like a galaxy of trashy stars.

Then he said slowly, "I know that I should not—another of those great, awful laws that I can believe in at a distance. But I know myself well enough to—to doubt my own reliability at close range, with the life of another person in my hands."

"Reliability! That's rich!" Caris' voice shook with scorn as he turned away, the taste of the small magics he had learned warm in his mouth, and on his hands—things he knew he must not touch, for if he did, he would never want to return to being what he had been. He had been a good warrior, and a good warrior was what they needed. He knew he would never be even an adequate mage, useless against Suraklin's might. To work magic, to touch even the small power of which he was capable, would be like a drunkard's first taste of wine; it would be like lying naked in bed at Pella's side, knowing that he must not put a hand on her.

After a long moment, he turned back to where Antryg still stood silent in the candlelight. "You're such a damned sentimentalist you'd do it, wouldn't you?"

Antryg did not reply.

Disgusted with himself, furious with Antryg, Caris hooked one foot over the rungs of another of the carved chairs and thrust it in the wizard's direction. "I should have killed you in the Tower."

The spells were a deeper magic than Caris had ever before attempted, almost beyond his grasp; even shaping them in his mind, without putting his power into them, left him exhausted as after hard training. It was the discipline of his training that got him through, learning them as he would have learned a new sword form, and Antryg, trained as a sasennan himself, cast the lesson in those terms, the terms that Caris would unthinkingly understand.

Oddly, Caris trusted him. Antryg was clearly as mad as hatters got after years of breathing the mercury fumes of their trade, tricky, devious, and marked, far back in his soul, by all the dark abominations of Suraklin's magic.

Yet for reasons he did not fathom, Caris had felt drawn to the wizard from their first meeting and, though he knew he ought to guard himself, felt little hesitation in opening his soul to the scrutiny of those daft gray eyes.

Using the magic itself was like flying.

His power was slight, and nothing he or Antryg could ever do would increase its strength. But when the hemorrhaging started somewhere in the endless hell of the girl's childbirth, it took so little to reach in with his mind and close the ruptured vessels. Even that took all his concentration, to focus and transmit the healing light from his own palms to the small, sweaty, twisting ones so desperately clutching at him, summoning the vision of it by rote until sweat ran down his face like rainwater, repeating to himself everything Antryg had said, making himself see, making himself believe . . . But the power came.

Antryg's voice drifted away somewhere, with the girl's terrified sobs. The blood smell was everywhere, sweetish-sharp in his nostrils as it had been the first time he had killed a man—a thief, bound hand and foot to the big stake in the rear court of the training-hall; Caris still remembered the color of the man's eyes. Through the woman's hands he felt her spirit, feeble and summery and rather stupid, hopeless in the grip of unimagined pain. When he felt that of her living daughter, the shock of it nearly made him lose his grip on the inner chain of light at which he clutched so hard.

Then he heard the child crying.

After it was all over, on one of the terraced balconies on the lee-side of the house, heedless of the raw cold that had followed the sleety winds of the night, he put his forehead down on the wooden rail and wept as if his heart had been broken.

Joanna could hear the servants whispering in the hall when the household's single footman came into the sitting room with a tray of muffins. The lamps had been put out. Through the opened storm shutters and the double-paned windows, morning lay on a landscape, messy with patches of snow and sheets of water frozen into plates of gray steel. How Antryg could possibly have demanded breakfast was totally beyond her; after the truly appalling mess of childbirth, she thought queasily that she would never be able to eat again.

He was asleep on the divan now, only a tangle of gray curls and one crooked-knuckled hand in its shabby glove above the dull purple vastness of his patched cloak. Since she was supposed to be his servant, she took the tray from the footman and set it on the table near him, the table still littered with Caris' exercises in Sigil-making; she glimpsed one of the maids craning her neck to see in from the hall as the young servant closed the door.

So much, she thought wearily, *for traveling north unobtrusively.*

The events of the night seemed crowded and telescoped in her mind—the intentness in Caris' eyes as he drew the Sigils, and the bitterness in his voice, the stink of blood and her own nausea at the primal rawness of the birthing, the squire weeping as he knelt before Antryg, clutching his gloved hands. There should have been something faintly ludicrous about a fat, middle-aged man sobbing and jiggling awkwardly on his chubby knees, but there hadn't been. He had obviously never expected the girl he loved so desperately to survive.

She walked back to the divan, rested one hand on its scrollwork end, and looked down at the man sleeping there. The deep lines around his eyes aged him, as they had when he had worn the Sigil of Darkness; even in sleep he looked worried. Since his escape from the Tower, Joanna suspected that he was less resilient than he had been.

Voices rose in the hall downstairs. Tired as she was, it took Joanna a second to realize that there were far more of them than the small servant population of the house could account for and that their tread, clattering en masse up the wooden stairs, was far too numerous and heavy. Fear stabbed at her and she caught up her backpack from under the divan, fumbling the .38 from its pocket. Caris, where was Caris . . . ?

The door opened. Lithe and deadly in his dull purple robe, Caris stood framed against the brownish shadows of the hall. Beyond him, Joanna could see Squire Alport, like a fat brown bear in layers of heavy tweed. Massed around him were a dozen men and women in the coarse, bundly clothes of peasants, the damp sheepskin of their jackets steaming in the sudden warmth of the house after the cold outside. None of them were armed. Feeling a little silly, Joanna made a move to pocket the gun, then saw the look on Caris' face.

"What is it?" Behind her Antryg sat up and fumbled his spectacles on, to blink at the mob.

"These people heard about you from that woman whose son you cured of pneumonia back in Bel Gulch," Caris said quietly. "They want to talk to you about the spells of deadness, and the draining of life."

"They want to *talk* about them?" The wizard's huge gray eyes widened still further with surprise.

"You mean someone else has *finally* noticed that they all happen at the same time?" Joanna demanded.

"In a way." Caris' voice was carefully neutral. "They say they know what's causing them. It's at their village."

Joanna said, "WHAT?" and thought, panicked, *We're not ready for this yet* . . . Her eyes met Antryg's and saw in his that he, too, had been taken completely off-guard.

He turned back to Caris, and asked cautiously, "What is?"

Expressionless, the sasennan said, "The Dead God."

CHAPTER XI

"THEY'RE NOT LYING, ANTRYG." CARIS PAUSED AT THE TURN OF THE stairs, letting the squire lead the delegation down into the manor's big hall ahead of them. Through its open double doors, wan daylight filtered up to dispel some of the gloom on the landing, showing his face paler than usual against the dark of his eyebrows and his pleated robe. "I'm frightened myself."

"It has to be Suraklin." Joanna glanced worriedly up at the two men. "If he's established the computer *off* one of the nodes, off the energy-lines entirely . . ."

"Then it wouldn't work," Caris finished firmly.

"No, it wouldn't," Antryg agreed. "But for that reason it would be a splendid idea if it *could* be done—and, of course, all we're going on is guesses about what's happening, anyway. We haven't any more proof than anyone does."

There was an appalled silence, in which the muted scuffle of voices sounded below, and somewhere in the dim house rose the thready wail of the new baby. Hesitantly, Caris said, "Have we been wrong about *everything*? It can't *really* be the Dead God behind it all—can it?"

Antryg grinned. "Disconcerting, isn't it? Caris, for a man who doesn't even believe in the Old Faith, you're awfully worried about the return of something that supposedly never existed. I shall have to speak to the Archbishop of Angelshand about the general shakiness of religious training among the sasenna."

"Worried?" Caris retorted, his cheekbones staining red with annoyance. "I'm frightened, and if you had the brains God gave a chicken, you'd be frightened, too!"

The demented smile widened. "Oh, I am," he assured them cheerfully, "I am." In a swirl of patched coat skirts and robes he clattered down the stairs ahead of them and into the hall.

Caris' fine-cut nostrils flared and his upper lip seemed to lengthen. He started to follow, and Joanna caught his sleeve.

"It has to be Suraklin." She heard the uncertainty in her own voice.

"I agree." The young man threw a glance down at the brighter rectangle of the hall doorway, where Antryg could be seen, half a head taller than anyone else in the room, polishing on his shirt ruffle spectacles which had fogged slightly in the steam rising from their damp clothes. "They say the Dead God has been demanding his ancient sacrifices, ruling the town through terror. It's only superficially different from what Suraklin did for years in Kymil. A perfect setup."

Somewhere in the house, the baby's cries sounded again, sharp and demanding; there was the faint creak of floorboards, and the cries ceased in a contented gurgle. Looking up into Caris' face, Joanna saw for one moment in his eyes a look of such bitter yearning, such hopeless unhappiness, that she reached out with involuntary pity to touch his hand.

His dark eyes returned to her, briefly unmasked by the sound of the first life he had given instead of taken. Then his mouth twisted in a wry smile and he shook his head. With a warrior's deadly lightness, he strode down the remainder of the stairs to join Antryg in the hall.

Joanna followed, trying to collect and sort possibilities in her mind—how Suraklin could have organized the energy transfer away from the lines and how his power might be met. But this exercise in logical explanations was hideously evanescent; the tale told by the mayor of Far Wilden and her frightened delegation was bizarre, disquieting, and bore no resemblance to what she knew of Suraklin's calm methodology.

It had started, they said, with noises, knockings, and scratchings in the Church. The old priest claimed that the place smelled of death and of the coldness of the Dead God and had refused to enter. The young priest, sent out two years before from Angelshand and still filled with the arrogance of the seminary, had insisted upon performing as usual the services of the Holy Sun, the Sole God.

"It was known from the beginning what it was, then?" Antryg drooped back in the carved chair by the hearth, his hands in their shabby gloves folded across his middle, his eyelids half-lowered behind the cracked and mended lenses of his specs.

"Oh, yes, my lord." Greer, the mayor of Far Wilden, a tough, sun-browned woman in her forties, nodded. Her white linen chemise under an embroidered peasant bodice hung baggy over wide shoulders and the slack breasts of one who has lost weight quickly. Men and women, they all had that look, Joanna thought, sitting curled in silence on the plank floor at Antryg's side—the slight bagginess of jowls and necks and clothes that no longer fitted as they had. She had grown used to it, traveling through the Sykerst—that, and that crushed-in grayness of stress and uncertainty, of knowing there was something desperately wrong and not quite knowing what it was.

What she had not seen before was the shadow that seemed to haunt the depths of their eyes, the way they tended to stay away from windows, and the way they always seemed to be listening for some noise in the corridor outside. She felt obscurely glad that outside the heat-steamed glass of the windows lay daylight, dreary though it might be.

"We're true Believers, my lord," Greer went on diffidently, folding her big, brown hands, "good children of the light. But the Dead God is different."

Thoroughly orthodox in spite of his long association with the mages, Caris looked on the verge of indignant speech, but Antryg motioned him silent with one crooked forefinger. "I know," he said, his deep voice scarcely louder than the croon of the wind round the eaves. "It's a belief that sleeps in the ground. And the Dead God was never like the other gods."

"No, my lord," the woman said simply. "Old Father Del, he knew. But in Angelshand the Bishops and the Witchfinders, they don't like anything that can't be written in their holy books of the Sun. It's why they sent out poor Father Sweelum to tell us it isn't true, to make sure the Green Mass isn't said in the fields, and to knock down the standing-stones and put fences round the churchyards to keep the conjures out."

Her dark eyes narrowed as she studied the tall man who sat by the hearth, his faded purple robe hanging slack over his bony frame like a blanket on a picket fence, the firelight and daylight sparkling on the magpie treasure of glass beads around his shackle-galled neck. "There's talk you're a conjure, my lord. Lord Alport said his lady's life was despaired of, and over to Bel Gulch that boy . . ."

Antryg shook his head. "I have worked no magic," he said softly. "And in any case it would be unlawful for me to do so, even if I could. What became of poor Father Sweelum, who went into the Church to sing the hymns of the Unconquered Sun?"

Greer's full lips tightened; she sighed and shook her head. "It was only a matter of time," she said. "He went there two, three times, evening and morning—cursed Father Del for refusing to set foot over the threshold. It was the Dead God's eve; Sweelum went in to say services at sundown, though for three days there'd been no one to go into the Church to hear them. I was one of those who stood outside the door. We heard him scream, the first time in fear, the second time . . . I can't say, but I've never heard a human being scream like that in all my life. When we looked in, he was dead, lying halfway between the door and the altar, blood round his nose and ears, and the look on his face as if he'd seen into Hell itself."

"Was this before or after sunset?" Joanna asked worriedly, remembering the hot glare of the slanting light on the San Serano parking lot and crouching in the dimness behind the door, waiting for Gary to pass.

"Before, surely," Antryg murmured, and Greer nodded.

"He'd just gone in to sing the services. He always had them timed fine, the sun touching the horizon on the first word of the Farewell Hymn, and no fadiddling about waiting for it. The light fell nearly straight through the doors on his body when we opened them."

Joanna shot a troubled glance at Caris, sitting on the black sheepskin of the hearthrug, his back to the fieldstone chimney; he seemed lost in his own thoughts. "And how long before this had the noises started?"

Greer frowned, thinking back. One of the younger men of the delegation said, "Three days? Four days?"

There had been a Tiger missile program review during the week before the Dead God's eve. Gary—Suraklin—had worked late at San Serano every night. And in any case, the computer had been up and running intermittently weeks before. Joanna subsided, feeling as if pieces of a jigsaw puzzle had fallen out of her hands. Beside her, she could sense the tension in the line of Antryg's shoulders and see it in the way his bony hand lay on the chair's carved arm and in the tilt of his head.

After a moment Greer went on, "We—we went and fetched Father Del. We didn't go into the Church. The smell of it was something dreadful, rot and corruption and worse besides. It was pretty near dark when we opened the doors again." Her voice sank to a whisper, and she glanced involuntarily at the window, as if even in daylight she feared what she might see looking in. "He was standing up, my lord—Father Sweelum, with blood running down from his mouth and his dead eyes staring at nothing with the lolling of his head. He said, 'I am the Dead God. I have returned, as I said I would.' "

"Ah," murmured Antryg. *"When the last of a thousand candles burns out, the darkness will always return; though a thousand voices sing all the hymns of life, silence always waits upon the inevitable failing of their breath.* Yes."

From the corner of her eye, Joanna saw Caris, white-faced, sketch the sign of holiness on his forehead and lips.

"Entropy always wins," she said softly, and Antryg's fleeting gray gaze touched her.

"Precisely." His eyes returned to the peasants, clustered close now, like sheep who hear the howling of the wolf, though Joanna guessed they were probably the dozen most fearless men and women in the village. "What did he ask of you?"

He spoke gently and as if he already knew. There was a terrible silence. Then Greer spoke without meeting his eyes. "Life," she said, her words barely to be heard in the hush of the room. "Lives."

"Ah," Antryg breathed, like a man who sees some piece to a riddle, but his eyes, on Greer's downcast face, were filled with compassion and pity.

She raised her gaze to the wizard's, as if asking that he understand that no horror or accusation of his could equal what she had already felt toward herself. " He would have destroyed us, else."

"I know." Something in the sureness of his voice, the absolute understanding, made Joanna shiver, but it melted some of the woman's wretched self-hate.

"And he can," she said. "He can draw the life out of a man like a fox sucking an egg, then stand there in its rotting corpse, speaking out of its mouth. He can call down spells of death, of ruin—at least so he told Father Del and the town merchant, Pettin, who spoke with him in the Church. It's they who tell us his bidding, now."

"Aye," interpolated a younger man, stocky and bearded, who sat near the door. "It's not Del I mind, for all I think his brain's been turned. But that Pettin! Him and his sons and a bunch of their hired men keep guard on the Church, and do the Dead God's bidding, as he does theirs. Three of my sheep he's had, for his own use and none of the Dead God's."

There was an angry mutter of assent, and Antryg murmured, "Fascinating. But the Dead God has no use for beasts?"

That silence returned. They had sinned and knew it; Joanna wondered how many people they had given to the terrible thing in the Church and how those had been selected. Then an older man with short white braids said, "None. Only men. Once he asked for a child . . ." There was an awkward pause, as if all of them heard the echo of some mother's frantic cries. "It used to be every day. Then none for three, four days at a time. Now he's had three in three days again . . ."

Greer took a deep breath. "You have to come, lord doctor. In the name of God, of whatever gods you worship. The nights he comes out of the church and walks abroad are those nights like we've had all the summer, when it's like all the life goes out of the air, the ground—out of all of us. It's he who's been causing them all along. It's got to be! We'll hear him, lurching and staggering, and in the morning there's a trail of slime like a rotting beast was dragged over the ground, out to the Witchpath Stone and back. He's destroying the village and all the countryside around; they say he's drinking the life out of all the world."

"Why the hell would Suraklin be doing something like *that?*" Joanna demanded, when they were once more gathered in the small sitting room and Antryg was placidly consuming the now-cold muffins. "And it can't be Suraklin himself anyway—I *know* where he was on the Dead God's eve at sunset . . ."

"If it isn't Suraklin," Caris said firmly, "we cannot afford to turn aside from our task, much less risk getting ourselves killed on a side issue." He was pacing like a caged thing, his dull robes billowing about him, the short quiff of his blond hair falling into his eyes.

Antryg glanced up. "I'm not sure we can afford not to. Would you care for a muffin? Curious to think the gentry hereabouts import white flour from Kymil at twelve crowns the barrel to make muffins, solely because it's the correct thing to do, when rye-flour muffins are just as good." He licked the butter from his fingers and looked up at Caris, who had stopped, staring at him in openmouthed indignation.

"You are the most frivolous . . ." the sasennan began.

"Going to Far Wilden may not be frivolous—that is, if by frivolous you mean apt to pursue side issues. I hope that it will turn out to be frivolous, yes, for all our sakes. But I can't know until I've been there." He wiped his fingers on a corner of his coat and reached over to pinch loose one of the long stalactites of white wax which had dripped down from the side of a sitting room candle. Even at this hour of the morning, the sky outside was darkening with coming rain; servants were lighting the candles once again throughout the house. Antryg rolled the wax deftly into a ball with his long fingers, his gray eyes growing dreamy and distant. Then he pulled free one of the several pins he kept stuck through the frayed velvet lapel of his coat, and began scratching signs into the ball.

"I'm leaving you behind here, Caris," he said. "Put this *lipa* where you can see it. If it turns red, beg a horse from Squire Alport *at once* and ride for all you're worth to Far Wilden, but enter the town carefully once you get there. If it turns black . . ." He hesitated, the pin suddenly stilled, and his odd mouth set. Then he sighed, and handed Caris the tiny spell-ball. "If it turns black, I'm afraid you're going to have to deal with Suraklin yourself."

"Is it that important?" Joanna hunched her shoulders under the damp sheepskin of her coat and the weight of the backpack. The day was ending; the thin wind cut her like a knife. The utter weariness that seemed to have settled into her bones during the past week of continual walking dragged on her less than it had, but she still felt tired to death, as if she would never be warm or rested again. Not, she grinned to herself, that she wouldn't have enthusiastically jogged the fifteen miles back to Squire Alport's had Antryg said, *No, not really, let's go back.*

The spire of the haunted church was visible through a dip in the iron monotony of the hills. When the wind shifted, she could smell the village's familiar stinks—cow-byres, woodsmoke, and privies. It was growing dark. Her worry over Suraklin ebbed and she began to be scared.

"I'm afraid so, my dear." In the shadows of his cloak hood, little was visible of Antryg's face save the lenses of his spectacles, which caught the final pallor of the evening sky like luminous, insectile eyes. "I have a bad feeling about what's in that church. For all our sakes, I hope it has nothing to do with Suraklin, but I can't risk the chance that it might."

For the last five miles, the group of villagers had been very hushed and had seemed to huddle tighter together as they walked. Even Greer, who for most of the journey had kept up a stolid appearance of courage while she told them details of the hideous visitation, had fallen silent. Now they stood gazing at that silent spire in the distance, like a spike against an iron sky.

Hesitantly, Joanna said, "What *is* the Dead God, Antryg?"

In the tail of her eye, she caught the movement around her, like the rustle of wind in a grove, as the villagers all blessed themselves with the air of people no longer sure of the efficacy of a charm. Though Antryg was still looking out across the hills at the skeletal black spire, he must have heard the stirrings of their clothes, for, in the shadows of his hood, she saw his lips twitch briefly in an ironic smile.

"Not, as many people believe, the God of Death, the Lord of Gates, who was worshipped in the Green Masses held in the fields. The legends have become conflated in the years. The Dead God is the God of Being Dead—not even the 'God of,' but just Deadness. He is entropy, if you will. The final flickering-out of the last candle in darkness, the ending of all songs of hope for want of breath, the dying of the last blade of grass when all life has been leached from the soil—that is the Dead God. As you yourself said, entropy always wins."

A surge of wind caught his vast purple cloak and tossed it like a huge wing around him. In the twilight, his tall, thin form, with his deep voice and round, alien-looking eyes made him seem almost like something from a Danse Macabre himself.

"That is why the Dead God elected to die, you see. So that he would have it all in the end, even though it meant being nothing himself. He is the god of stasis, of stagnation, of the utmost death without even regenerative decay. No matter how much life the other gods created, say the legends, the Dead God died so that he would get it all in the end."

"Like a black dwarf star," Joanna murmured, "that is so dense that even light can't escape."

Antryg nodded.

She went on doubtfully, "So it can't really be the Dead God—can it? The Dead God—the true Dead God—wouldn't need something as petty as the village; he wouldn't need to make all those strange and senseless commands they talked about, like keeping everyone indoors on certain nights or bringing vats of blood to the Church or all those other things Greer told us about. All the Dead God would need to do is . . . wait."

"Precisely." The wizard shoved his hands into his coat pockets, and began to walk down the crooked and ice-slippery path toward the first wretched sod shanties of the town.

Her half-frozen buckskin boots sliding on the stony ground, Joanna hastened to catch up with his longer strides, and he slowed to wait for her. "Then what *is* in the Church?"

A thin stream of white breath escaped from the shadows. "I believe it's something I've been rather fearing all along," he said. "An abomination that has intelligence."

Without enthusiasm, Joanna said, "Hot damn."

"And I sincerely hope," he added cryptically, "that's all it is."

Joanna sighed. "I'm not even going to *ask* how the situation could be worse."

"Don't," Antryg advised.

In the village itself, the silence was almost palpable and had a watching quality that raised the hair on Joanna's nape. Even the occasional muttered comment among Greer and her people had ceased; they walked close together, always glancing back over their shoulders at the heavy darkness that seemed to clot between the lumpish buildings of sod and logs. The village sounds to which Joanna had grown used, the lowing of cattle and the grunting of backyard pigs, were absent; through the door of a byre, she caught a glimpse of a couple of goats, huddled head-down as if ill, their green eyes gleaming in the darkness. Before them the square bulk of the church, with its cluster of turrets and single emaciated spire, loomed black against a cinder sky.

Joanna shivered and drew closer yet to Antryg. She thought it was colder here than on the hills, in spite of the windbreak of the buildings. The foetor of decay hung over the town, clogging her throat like putrid dust. Antryg had pushed back his hood; in the wan twilight, his face looked strained and old.

"So you have returned, Greer." From the shadows of a round, stumpy building a dozen feet or so from the church itself—a baptistry, Joanna knew, having seen them near several village churches already—other shadows separated themselves. A torch was brought forth, and its jerking orange glare played over the faces of half a dozen men and women armed for the most part with the makeshift weaponry of farmers, though at least two held heavy but businesslike swords. The man who swaggered in their lead was one of the few Joanna had seen who had not lost flesh in the harshness of a failed harvest; tallish, red-haired, the cut-steel buttons of his middle-class coat strained across an undiminished paunch. He was unarmed, but a couple of his bullies walked with axes at his back. "That was stupid of you." Joanna noticed idly that one of his front teeth was gold, with a tiny chip of ruby set like a stray speck of beef in its center.

Greer drew in her breath for an angry reply. At that moment, however, Antryg forestalled her by breezing forward, gloved hands outstretched. "My dear Pettin," he cried affably, "you really must forgive her concern. Of course the Unnamed One wouldn't communicate all his plans to a mere subcreature such as her—how could you expect him to? But they serve also who only act as the Dark God guides, and I'm here now, so there's no harm done."

And, as Pettin the merchant gaped in speechless surprise and Greer stared at the wizard aghast, Joanna thought, *Antryg, you'd better make this work.*

Antryg shook hands briskly with the stunned town boss and flung a friendly arm around his shoulder. "Surely you don't think He . . ." He nodded toward the silent church ". . . would have let her out of the village unless to fulfill his will."

"Uh—" Pettin managed.

"Where's Del?"

Greer's gasp of rage, of betrayed fury, caught Joanna's attention like the rattle of a snake, and she turned in time to see the mayor twist an axe from the grip of the nearest of Pettin's guards. "Traitor!" Greer screamed. "You were its servant all along!" She strode forward, axe upraised, totally forgetting Joanna by her side until Joanna stuck out one booted foot and tripped her.

Joanna herself was a little surprised at the movielike patness of it. Even as a child, she had never dared to trip anyone deliberately and was astounded at how easy it was when the tripee had the momentum of rage. With a little more presence of mind, she supposed she could have dived in and got the axe away from her then and there, but didn't think that quickly; when she did, she decided to let Pettin's guards do that part—the axe looked damn sharp.

By the time Greer sprang to her feet again, covered in offal and mud, the guards were upon her.

"Stop it!" Antryg barked as one of them raised a fist to smash the infuriated woman across the face. Such was the authority of his deep voice that the man froze in midgesture. "Lock her up," he said coldly. "Don't hurt her." He glanced down at the totally discomposed Pettin by his side. "As you know, they must be untouched."

"Yes, my lord." Pettin clearly wasn't about to admit that nobody had communicated to him about *this*.

With a shrug that would have done credit to an Emperor, let alone the emissary of a god, Antryg shed the patched cloak from his shoulders. Joanna, with perfect timing, caught it and folded it over her arm. Casually, the wizard removed a club from the grasp of the guard nearest him and didn't even glance at it as its tip burst into flame. Pettin's bullies drew hastily back, murmuring and whispering; not a few made the signs against evil.

"Do as the god has bid you and keep everyone away from the doors," Antryg said. In the yellow glare of the new flames, Joanna could see the glitter of sweat on his face, but his voice was uncaringly arrogant. Magister Magus, Joanna recalled, had said he would have made the best charlatan in the business. "Obey my servant here as you would me until I come out." And he strode to the church steps as if he'd just closed escrow on the place.

"Liar!" As Antryg's foot hit the step, the doors slammed open; the rolling cloud of stench that swirled forth caught Joanna cold and she fought not to retch. With that stench, darkness seemed to pour out like smoke. The skinny old man framed in that vile and leaden darkness, Joanna saw at once, was completely mad.

Antryg ordered calmly, "Get out of my way, Father Del."

"Mountebank!" the old priest snarled. In the glare of Antryg's torch, drool gleamed on the old man's unshaven chin; by the black hollows of cheeks and eyes and the slack folds of filthy skin behind the ears, Joanna wondered, in the detached portion of her mind that wasn't sick with panic, if Father Del had eaten at all since the coming of the Dead God. *Not, living close to that smell, that anyone could . . .*

Antryg's voice was soothing, the deep notes played like an instrument against the shrillness of the lunatic's mind. "I am but a servant of the Unnamed One, as you are, who was once Del. He sent for me, and I came."

"Liar! Jackanapes!" Father Del advanced down the steps, leaning on a six-foot staff, heavy oak reinforced with plates of iron. Its iron tip grated on the stone. "Yes, he sent for you—it suited his purposes that you should come. He sees all, knows all. All things come at last to him! A mage, he says. Light shines through your flesh, he says, and the colors that halo you are not the colors of other men. You lie, he says." He stumbled a pace nearer, clutching at his staff with hands that shook as from palsy. At twenty feet, Joanna nearly gagged on the stench of his clothes.

Antryg did not move, but all around her Joanna sensed Pettin's men stir, hefting weapons in their hands. *If I run for it,* she thought, *it's an admission.* Adrenaline shot through her like gas to an engine racing in neutral.

"He smells your mind," Del's voice creaked. "Yours and this little girl's. You seek to destroy him. But he will have your flesh. Perhaps it will kill his long craving . . ."

Someone grabbed Joanna's wrist and she twisted the bone of it against the weak joint of her captor's thumb, at the same time slamming her full hundred and one pounds with her heel on the man's instep. The grip slacked. As hands snatched at her clothes, she plunged up the brick steps. At the same instant, the wizard thrust his torch at the priest's face and twisted the iron staff from his grip. Pettin's men surged up the steps at them, weapons flashing in the guttery light; Del's screaming, shrill as an angry hawk's, stabbed through Joanna's panic like the senseless sounds of nightmare.

With the hand that held the priest's iron-shod staff, Antryg thrust Joanna before him into the utter blackness beyond the great doors, and the doors thudded shut behind them.

CHAPTER XII

"HOLD THIS, PLEASE."

Antryg's calm voice was so quiet Joanna, stunned as much by terror as by the hideous stench and bone-freezing cold of the place, barely comprehended what he said. But she accepted the torch and the iron staff he shoved into her hands, even as the bolts outside the door were still scraping into place. The wizard was already down on his knees, a piece of chalk in his hand, sketching the wide arc of a circle on the stone floor around them. He must have practiced a lot, Joanna thought, as her panic drowned itself and left her feeling oddly cool; the circle was perfect to within a few degrees. Considering the bad light and the way her own hands were shaking, that in itself was astounding.

Around them, the pillared vestibule of the church was like a well filled up with evil, evil such as Joanna had never encountered—nauseating stink and gluey darkness pressing in on them, swamping the feeble torchlight. The cold here was intense, far more severe than outside, and she no longer questioned how the villagers had believed the assertion of the thing in the church that it was the singularity point of eternal death.

The chalk made soft crumbling sounds on the granite slabs of the floor. Straining her eyes into the aphotic depths beyond the carved and painted pillars—no two alike and all gaily colored like psychedelic barber poles—she heard the whispery hiss of the torch as it burned in her hands and the faint, quick creaking of Antryg's belt as he moved here and there, drawing out a five-point star within the double circle around them. He hadn't made the original ring quite big enough, and once the star was drawn there was only a square yard or so in its center for them to stand. Joanna had known Antryg long enough to know without being told not to step over the chalked lines.

Somewhere among the pillars, something was moving.

She heard it blunder against the wood with a fumbling hollow sound, heard a kind of wet slither that turned her stomach with a dozen gruesome implications. The smell was growing stronger, too, in spite of the killing cold—meat long rotten, the fetid excrement of fear, and something else, something she had smelled in the Void. *Don't panic,* she told herself, forcing herself to breathe slow and deep in spite of the appalling stench. *If you panic, you'll run, and there's nowhere to run to . . .* The cold was a living thing, malevolent, eating her bones. She wondered briefly whether she could scream long enough and loud enough to wake herself out of this nightmare and, if so, in what place she would wake.

Antryg stood up, his face clammy with sweat in the wavery yellow light. He took the iron-bound staff from her left hand, the torch from her right. His voice was calm and unstrained. "Joanna, get down and cover your head. It's psychokinetic; I think it'll try throwing things first. Don't try to move about to avoid me. I'll avoid you."

Joanna didn't even bother to try and guess how he knew it would be psychokinetic. She merely dropped to her knees, pulled off her backpack, tucked it beneath her—mostly to protect the worm-program disk—and assumed the position recommended by the California Public School System as effective protection against atomic bombs. Antryg carefully laid the torch down beside him on the floor and stood straddling her, the iron-bound staff in his hands. He'd kilted up his robe almost to his knees, and the rough wool brushed her back, weirdly comforting, as was the sight between her slitted eyelids of the brass rings of his boot harnesses. She clenched her hands more tightly over the back of her neck and tried to make herself small.

Somewhere in the blackness of the church beyond the pillars, she heard a knocking.

It was impossible to say where it originated or on what kind of surface. There were a few experimental taps, soft and strangely hollow-sounding, then suddenly a huge crashing like thunder or the slamming of some massive door. Heavier and faster the sounds came, iron boulders falling from some unguessable height to an iron floor, a vast fist beating a ringing wall—*It's only noise,* Joanna told herself, shutting her throat on a scream. *The same as the darkness is only darkness, the cold is only cold, the smell is only a smell . . .*

It wasn't. It wasn't.

Something flashed through the air with vicious force—metal; copper,

Joanna thought, glimpsing it from the corner of her eye. Antryg swiveled and smashed it with the end of his iron staff, sending it whirling, bouncing with a hideous clatter against the nearest pillar. Joanna saw it was an ewer, an altar vessel. Antryg whirled and batted again, catching a heavy piece of stone that had once been a sculpted cherub's head with a force that nearly snapped the staff in his hands. The next missile came in low and fast, aiming for his ankle. She gritted her teeth and turned her head away, but he caught that one, too. *Cricket as well as baseball,* she decided hysterically. At almost the same instant, she heard something connect against his other hip with vicious force and felt his knees give. The staff whined with an evil *swoosh* and she felt something strike him again and heard his grunt of pain.

Something glowing flashed between the pillars, swooping toward them with terrible speed. Fire, pale and flickering like ball lightning, streamers ribboning along the floor. Joanna flinched as it hit the outer magic circle, heard the faint crackle, and saw the flames dash, scattering around the perimeter before they vanished. Looking up, she saw Antryg's face set and grim, blood tracking down from a cut over his right eye and spreading everywhere as it mixed with the sweat pouring down his cheekbones. His gray hair formed a matted halo in the weak torchlight, broken by the diamond glitter of his earrings.

Another flicker of light, wan and corpsish, appeared among the pillars, its reflections slipping wormlike up the lines of gold leaf. Joanna shut her teeth hard as something came rushing and weaving among the dark forest of columns, glowing with a horrible radiance. Antryg half swung toward it as it broke against the outer circle, then turned back as something else lunged, dark from the darkness.

A tsunami of stench struck them first, overwhelming. Even the brief glimpse Joanna got of the thing was heart-shaking, a slobbering, half-melted travesty of a face whose fangs, she realized, were broken-off ribs thrusting out from the corners of the rotting jaw. Bone showed where the flesh of two of the arms was falling off; the other two were reaching to grab. *It's material. It can cross the circle,* she thought. She half rose to run, then dropped to her knees again. In front of her, Antryg braced himself, the staff balanced before him. Tall as he was, the thing topped him by over a head. *He'll never thrust it off* . . .

The thing—monster, demon, god of rot—was almost to the edge of the circle when Antryg snapped the staff around and thrust its end like a spear into the creature's belly. His long legs locked and his weight dropped to take the shock, the thing's whole momentum slamming into the one-inch circle of the pole's end. The iron ferrule punched through the rotten meat like an arrow, and an unspeakable fountain spewed out behind. With a violence that seemed to shake the floor, the thing fell just beyond the chalked line of the protective ring. It raised its head, fluid trickling from the working mouth. Then it dropped squishily and lay still. Antryg had to twist and level the rod to pull its dripping end free.

The silence in the church was more terrible than before. Under the fallen flesh of the face she half believed she saw the silvery gleam of an eye move. She sat up, cold and shaking all over. "Can you cut it to pieces with your sword?"

"I could," Antryg whispered softly. "But if you'll look at the way the muscles are rotting, you'll realize that it's psychokinesis that moves the whole thing, and the limbs probably don't have to be attached to the torso for it to control them. So on the whole, I think I'd rather not."

Joanna worked out the implications of that one and swallowed queasily.

Rather white around the mouth, sweat and blood tracking stickily down his face, Antryg stepped to the very edge of the circle. Like an image losing itself down a corridor of mirrors, the echoes of his deep voice chased one another away into the endless darkness of the columns. "Can you understand me?" he asked softly. "I'm not here to destroy you."

It was waiting, Joanna thought.

Something wet fell on Joanna's hand. Looking down, she saw a drop of blood. Another drop struck her, falling from the darkness above; then a pattering, hideous rain. Trails of it threaded their way down the bright paint of the columns and curled like ribbon across the floor. The smell of it, coppery-sweet and harsh, stung her nostrils. The dying torch smoked and sputtered in it; the darkness edged closer, like a ring of wolves.

"Speak to me if you can," Antryg said. "I can help you if you'll let me."

Slowly the monster's head moved, white sinews breaking through the slimy flesh of its neck. Joanna saw the chest rise and fall as if pressed like a bellows to force air through vocal cords that were all but gone.

"I—am—the—Dead—God." The glottal stickiness of timber made her flesh crawl, thinking of what caused it. "I drink the power that shines from men's flesh. All things are only lent to life, before they return to me. I am the Dead God."

Black fluid leaked from its mouth and from the hole in its gut as it swayed to a sitting position, head lolling gruesomely; fat droplets of slime hung from its wrists as it raised two of its arms; they elongated and finally dripped to the floor with a sticky splat. "The Dead God demands his due . . . transdimensional interface . . . I walk the boundless darkness in the pits of the world . . . universal field theory . . . xchi particles . . . structural shift at the ylem . . ."

"What?" whispered Antryg.

Joanna looked up at him, startled. "Don't you understand?" He shook his head, baffled. "Transdimensional interface?" She spoke the words in English, knowing that neither she nor Antryg had heard them in that language, though the Dead God had spoken, for the most part, in slurred and stammered Ferr.

He shook his head again. "You mean, you *do* get a translation through the spell of tongues? I mean, those words mean something to you?"

Joanna nodded quickly. The Dead God drew itself to its feet like a crumbling mountain, eyes gleaming slimily in the failing ruby light. "He's from another world, he's got to be."

Still holding the staff warily in hand, Antryg walked to the edge of the circle. "Look," he said, his deep voice echoing in the darkness, "I can help you. Send you back."

"A wizard," muttered the Dead God thickly. "Your power shines through your flesh. I will drink of your brain, your power will be mine. All power will be mine—psychokinesis at the molecular level—I am the Dead God . . ."

"I'm not getting through to him." His eyes never moved from the thing that had begun to lurch toward them, one staggering step at a time, huge arms outspread and broken claws bent to seize. Antryg's swollen knuckles shifted along the staff he held; his voice was low and rapid. "Do you have a weapon of any kind with you, my dear? I don't think the gun will do much good—my sword-scabbard, maybe, as a club. Remember it's only dead flesh . . ."

But Joanna frowned suddenly at the dark monster that loomed on the edge of the dying torchlight, her mind taken up with another question entirely. "You know, I bet it's a hardware problem," she said.

Any other companion in such adversity would have stared at her and said, *"What???"* in utter disbelief, but Antryg, who dealt completely in inconsequence himself, only said, "You mean with the physical bodies he's taken to make up what he is now?"

"Not the bodies—the brain." The stench was so terrible she could scarcely breathe, part of her mind screaming in panic, while another part, calm and calculating, worked out the logic of the situation. "Your software's only as good as your hardware."

"And he can't put his thoughts through the brains of the people he's taken," the wizard finished, his gray eyes lighting up like a truly mad scientist's on the verge of discovery.

"Yeah," Joanna breathed. "Only as far as brain chemistry is concerned, it isn't a simple binary—your hardware *is* your software. And his must be half-rotted anyway, even if he didn't get it from some not-very-bright priest and whatever town drunks or troublemakers the local sacrifice lottery decided the community could best spare. He's in there . . ."

"Poor bastard," Antryg whispered feelingly, and Joanna, looking at that filthy colossus of decay, felt a shudder of horror and pity. "But he can hear us."

"I'll bet he's only able to process information in terms of what was in those brains to begin with." She was on her feet now, her back to Antryg's; she slipped his scabbarded sword from his sash to hold like a baseball bat, knowing that her aim must be to strike, rather than to cut. The scabbard was lacquered wood and hard as iron, but it still felt like a hopelessly inadequate weapon in her small hands. "Look, we've got to get through to—to the original part of him, the part that still remembers what he used to be . . ."

"*If* he—or she—still remembers."

Joanna thought for a moment. Then, still keeping a wary eye on the creature that loomed in the darkness, she slid her makeshift weapon into her belt, dug quickly in a pocket of her backpack, and pulled out her Swiss Army knife. Kneeling beside Antryg's feet, she tapped the metal knuckle of the knife three times on the stone floor.

She paused, then tapped again, once, hard and small in the terrible stillness. "I saw this done in *Red Planet Mars,*" she explained breathlessly, and tapped again four times.

"Don't get it wrong," Antryg whispered, still standing braced only feet from the swaying form of the Dead God, his dripping staff held at the ready. "And pray the thing's a mathematician."

"I'm just praying the value of pi is the same in its dimension as it is in mine."

Pause, one. Pause, five . . .

"Hmm. Sticky if it's not."

Pause . . .

Then, hollow and terrible, vast as the slamming of some great iron door, the knocking came as before—nine times. A silence, like the black weight of the air after thunder. Then two knocks, blows that shook the walls. Silence. Six.

The silence stretched into an elastic eternity.

"Five," prompted Antryg softly, as Joanna, suddenly panic-stricken, blocked on the next number.

Tapping it out, she realized that to be a wizard, the ability to maintain the concentration for working a spell in any kind of bizarre emergency had to be the most vital of survival traits.

Three hollow booms answered her; five; eight . . .

"Can you make a Sigil?" she whispered.

"For what purpose?"

"Hardware. They're only giant chips, after all—patterns of lines encoding symbolic logic, like the synapses of the brain. If you can draw one, or some, or as many as you need, on the floor, and give him an alternative communications hardware to what he has . . . Would that work?"

"I haven't the faintest idea," he said, an expression of dazzled, scholarly delight in his face wholly at odds with the bruises and blood that marked it, the hell-pit darkness around them. "I'll need metal . . ."

"There's about fifty feet of copper wire in my backpack."

He hesitated. "And I'll have to step out of the pentacle." He had not taken his eyes from the thing before him; her shoulder to his side, Joanna could feel the swiftness of his breath.

She said seriously, "Not if you drew them real small." For one second he glanced down at her, protesting, then realized she was joking and grinned. His hand was perfectly steady as he gave her the staff. Having seen him whip and twirl it like a cheerleader's baton, she was startled by its weight.

"Don't let it rush you head-on," he cautioned softly. "It weighs three or four times what you do."

"Do you want your sword back?"

He shook his head, dug a piece of chalk from the pocket of his coat, and gingerly stepped across the protective points of the magic circle. There was a flicker of blue light, like tiny discharges of electricity, among the pillars. Then silence again, that terrible waiting. Crouched like a lion gauging its moment to spring, the Dead God edged forward as Antryg knelt and began forming the complex shapes of the Sigils on the floor.

The torch was going; in the darkness Joanna thought she saw the lines on the floor begin to glow with a cold, frosty light, but it illuminated little save the mad wizard's long nose and cracked spectacles and the wet gleam of the Dead God's eyes. It was aware of her, she knew, watching with the mind that seemed to fill the icy blackness around her—as if it knew that it was she who held all the weapons, she who was totally unsuited to use them. Her hands shaking, she braced the staff under one arm and dug into her backpack, pulling out the copper wire and one of the several candles stowed in a side pocket, which she lit from the end of the dying torch. The light wasn't much, but she knew Antryg could see in the dark. She felt the Dead God's glance shift toward her and hastily set the candle down, praying she wouldn't be panicked into stepping on it, then gripped the staff once again.

There was no sound but the crumbling slur of chalk on stone, and the swift lightness of Antryg's breath.

Watching the pattern of the Sigils take shape, Joanna recognized some from Caris' practice drawings: the Sigil of the Gate; the Sigil of the Single Eye; the Sigil of Strength; and the horned Sigil of Shadows which governs veiled and hidden things. Linking through them was the Sigil of Roads, that curious, oddball Seal which, like the Lost God who governed it, had no power in itself at all. Across the protective points of the circle she tossed Antryg the copper wire and duct tape, knowing from Caris' explanations that metal was necessary in their workings; and still the Dead God edged forward, slime tracking down the broken ends of his bone fangs, his hands with their hooked nails stirring hungrily, uneasily, at the ends of rotting arms.

When Antryg straightened up his face seemed very white in the ghostly glow of the Sigils under the stitchwork of tracked blood. Around him the Seals of those ancient gods lay in a lace of light, wire, and duct tape, seeming to float on the stone. He took a deep breath, walked forward, and held out his hand to the Dead God.

With a gluey snarl, the Dead God raised two of its hands; Antryg saw what was coming and ducked, but not quickly enough. Claws raking, they caught him a stunning blow, flinging him against the closest pillar, as if he'd been in truth the scarecrow he so often resembled; then the Dead God was upon him.

Not knowing what else to do, knowing she could never cross the distance between them in time, Joanna swung the iron staff and caught the pillar behind her with a crack like a gunshot. The Dead God's head swiveled horribly on its neck, one eye glaring, the other drooping sickeningly as the muscles that held it began to come loose. Picking up one of Antryg's discarded pieces of chalk, she stooped and marked the floor:

//////
//////
//
/////
//////

The Dead God stood for a long moment, staring down at the pattern of chalked lines. Then it turned to where Antryg still slumped at the base of the pillar. Closing one huge hand around his arm and another around the nape of his neck it hauled him to his feet. Their eyes held, the Dead God's glinting like a half-mad animal's, Antryg's calm and completely without fear. At length he took the rotting wristbones in his hands, and drew the thing toward the pattern of Sigils; it let him guide its hands to the points where metal and magic entwined, and left them there when Antryg rose and walked to the other end of the symbolic Road.

The wizard glanced down at Joanna's binary code. "What is it?"

"Planck's Constant."

"I'm sure Mrs. Planck is pleased to hear it." There was a note of strain in his voice, and she guessed by the way he moved that he'd cracked a rib against the pillar.

"If he's a scientist he'll recognize it. It's the ratio of energy to frequency of light and it occurs over and over again in physics. Like pi, it was a way to tell him that we knew he isn't the Dead God. That we knew who he is really."

Antryg knelt down near the Sigil of Shadow and touched the glowing latticework of wire and light. "Perhaps he needed reminding himself," he said softly and wiped the trickle of blood from the corner of his mouth. Joanna set down the staff and, shivering slightly, stepped across the psionic barrier of the pentacle to kneel at Antryg's side.

"I think you're going to need a technical consultant."

Behind the blood-fleckred glass, she saw the quick flare of concern in his eyes, but he couldn't deny the truth of what she said. After a hesitation, he took her hands, his long fingers and the leather of his gloves sticky with the gross corruption of the monster's touch, and guided them to the wan stringers of criss-crossing light. "I don't know how much you'll be able to hear," he cautioned softly. "If you feel him trying to get a grip on your mind, pull out at once. Don't try to help me. All right?"

Joanna nodded uneasily.

"Good girl." He drew a deep breath and flinched at the stab of his injured ribs, then seemed to settle in on himself, half closing his eyes, not working magic, Joanna thought, but drinking of the magic of the Sigils themselves.

Not being mageborn, she felt very little, only a kind of warmth where the light lay under her fingers. For a time she heard nothing; but glancing up in the dim amber reflection of the distant candle, she saw Antryg's lips move and realized that her own nervous observation of the Dead God in the darkness that surrounded them was blocking her concentration.

Great, she thought bitterly. *What a time to have to pick up meditation techniques.* But she had read enough to have some idea of what she must do. Perhaps the hardest thing was simply to close her eyes, to release all thought, all fear, and all planning of what she'd do if . . . to think of nothing . . .

Like the distant murmur of a metallic wind, she heard the Dead God's voice.

". . . The more lives I take, the greater my power will grow. I can drink the magic of your brain, Windrose—magic to keep this flesh from corrupting, magic to take, to hold. Why should I return to my own world, when with the powers of a god I can spread my will across the earth here?"

"I suppose you can." Antryg's voice seemed distant in the darkness, but perfectly conversational, no more ill-at-ease than if they shared a tankard of beer at some alehouse hearth. "Provided, that is, you're more than semiconscious and still able to take care of yourself. But I don't think you will be. Human psychic energy is really a rather poor substitute for what you eat in your own world, isn't it? Not to mention the air."

"This flesh tolerates the air."

"You're poisoning yourself and you know it—or you did know it when you tried to cut back on human sacrifices and when you tried all those other things—beef blood or walking out to the Witchpath Stone on the nights the energy ran along it."

Joanna felt, through the whispering whiteness of the Sigils' light, the bloody stir of the Dead God's anger. "The hunger grows," it whispered.

Diffidently, she put in, "That's common with food allergies."

"In my own world I was nothing," the god whispered. "A technician, a tracker of xchi particles for other men's research. Here, I have power."

"Only as long as you retain your consciousness," Antryg pointed out. "My magic will give you more power, yes. But it won't stop the clouding of your mind. At best, you'll become a random force, a psychic whirl-wind that grows with every human mind it devours until someone finally finds a way to destroy you as mad dogs are destroyed. At worst, you'll be controlled by others, as Pettin controls you now. I don't see another choice for you."

There was a rush, a surge, a blaze of light behind her eyes and half-drunken fury and hate slamming like a wave against her mind. Joanna jerked her hands free of Antryg's light touch and opened her eyes in time to see the wizard flinch aside with a cry. Though the Dead God had not moved, Joanna saw the fresh claw marks that scored Antryg's face and jaw, running with blood; as she watched, a second set gouged his neck;

the air rumbled with a sound of rage that seemed to come from nowhere, the foggy rage of the Dead God's half-polluted brain. Antryg bent under the blows, blood streaming from his face and neck, but never took his hands from the curving horns of the Sigil of Shadow.

The angry rumbling died.

Her heart hammering, Joanna could not bring herself to touch the Sigils again, but in time she heard Antryg whisper, "Where is the body that you came here in from your own world?"

The Dead God must have made some reply, for after a time the wizard breathed, "Since it has not corrupted in this world, were I to guide you back into it and back through the Void to a place where you could get help, would they be able to save you?"

An even longer silence followed; then Antryg, still half in his trance, smiled. "Yes," he murmured, like a distant echo of his conversations with Caris. "Mad, too. You no more know that I won't destroy you when you open your mind to me than I know that when I open mine to you, you won't simply devour it. Do you believe that you need my help?"

If he was sane he might, Joanna thought desperately. *If he wasn't fogged-out, half-poisoned with the psychic and metabolic garbage he's been ingesting for weeks . . . Don't do it, Antryg. Don't give him what he seeks . . .*

But Antryg took his hands from the Sigils, and climbed slowly, wincingly to his feet. The Dead God loomed over him in the shadows and held out two rotting hands to help him up; together the gawky wizard and the monster vanished into the black hole of the haunted darkness. The glow of light in the Sigils themselves faded, seeming to sink into the floor, leaving only a smudgy tracing of chalk and the tangled snakes of copper wire, glinting faintly in the flicker of the single candle at Joanna's side.

How long she sat alone in the darkness, Joanna wasn't sure afterward, her every nerve strained, listening for sounds in the utter silence of the distant crypt. The candle burned itself slowly down. Reaction was setting in, after a day's exhausting walk and only hours of sleep snatched at intervals in the endless childbirth of the squire's lady the night before. Weirdly enough, the blood that had rained down during the combat with the Dead God had vanished without a trace, though Joanna was at a loss to say when. She wondered whether it had, in fact, ever existed.

Antryg was alone in the crypt with the Dead God. That he had said nothing to her at their departure didn't surprise her; she suspected that he was channeling all his strength into maintaining some kind of psychic link with the Dead God's mind, some lifeline to that lost abomination's sanity that he dared not loose. The cold deepened. Joanna huddled into her sheepskin coat, watching the mist of her breath, gilded by the dim candle-gleam, and wondering how long she should give it.

Before doing what?

The great doors were bolted from the outside. In her heart she knew she'd wait a long time before she dared make her way through the sightless forest of the pillared vestibule down to those ghastly vaults alone.

The noise, when it came, nearly made her jump out of her skin with shock—the slamming scrape of the door bolts at her back, and a man's angry curse. Then the night air touched her face, close to freezing but almost warm compared to the icy stillness around her.

"Joanna?"

Torchlight fell across the floor over her in a gold bar, sparkling on Caris' blond hair and the blade of his drawn sword. He fell back with a gasp from the threshold. "What the . . ."

"Here!" She sprang to her feet and stumbled to him, her knees almost giving way with the cramp of long sitting; she was shaking all over as he caught her briefly in the circle of his arm. He wore his sword sash and dagger belt strapped over his scholar's robe; past his shoulder Joanna saw no one in the trough of darkness between church and baptistry save one man slumped unconscious at the bottom of the steps and the arm of another projecting from the shadows of the baptistry door. "Caris, we . . ."

"Where is he?" The young man held the torch aloft, looking swiftly around the vestibule, concern overriding for a moment both his nausea and his usual shield of aloof and bitter calm. "Is he . . . ?"

"He went down to the crypt with the Dead God," she said. "He was going to try to send the Dead God back, he said . . . Caris. You do care for him, don't you?" For the fear in his face was unmistakable and had little to do with being left to deal with Suraklin alone.

"He's the most maddening mooncalf I've ever had the misfortune to know," Caris retorted explosively, not answering the question. "If he's . . ."

He broke off and caught her arm. Around them the freezing darkness seemed shaken suddenly, like a curtain in a wind. Cold terror skated across Joanna's bones and she clutched tight to the coarse wool of Caris' sleeve. For an instant, the universe seemed to ripple into breathing nearness around them.

"The Void," Caris whispered.

Outside, thin and terrible as the death-cry of something that has long since ceased to be human, Father Del's wheezing voice could be heard, scaling up into a thin scream that ended as if dispersed upon the wind.

Joanna said softly, "He's gone."

Caris raised his torch again and, sword in hand, led the way into the black cave of the church.

After all that had gone before, what was in the sanctuary did not do more than make Joanna gag, but she heard Caris gasp and choke on the fumes that made the air there almost past breathing. From inhabiting the body of the luckless Father Sweelum, now an unrecognizable puddle in a black habit in a corner, the Dead God had used the flesh of his victims to fashion his own body. What was left over lay strewn across the altar, the chancel, the steps leading down to the crypt. Only the deathly cold which the Dead God had gathered about him to preserve his borrowed flesh intact saved the place from being more hideous than it already was. In the crypt, the swollen body of the Dead God lay, a huge sprawl of carrion, beside a stone niche that had once contained some local notable; dry bones lay heaped in a corner, still bundled in the dessicated shreds of gold-stitched winding sheet. In their place, stretched facedown upon the stone, lay Antryg, one arm extended, his fingers still twined with the Dead God's dissolving hand.

"Antryg . . ." She stepped forward; at the sound of her voice, and the touch of the torchlight, he flinched. Then his hand came up and groped for hers, seeking the touch of a human mind or perhaps only of living flesh. She barely even noticed what it was covered with as it closed convulsively around her arm.

He whispered, "Get me out of here."

On the outside steps of the church, Caris picked up Antryg's fallen cloak and put it carefully around his shoulders; Joanna dug into the wizard's coat pocket for his tin flask of gin, which he drank like a dying man receiving the elixir of life. Then with a shaky smile he handed it to her, and she decided after two swigs that there was a good deal to be said in favor of the vile stuff after all. Torches had begun to flicker around all sides of the square as dark forms emerged from the shadow—the merchant Pettin, looking white and scared and Greer the mayor, her face filled with concern and joy when she saw the three demon hunters gathered alive and more or less whole on the steps. Of Father Del Joanna never saw anything again.

"D'you suppose our welcome would extend to a cup of tea?" Antryg asked softly at last, when his hands had stopped shaking. He glanced up at Caris, the old impishness returning to his black-circled eyes. "You turned up with remarkable speed for a man we left back at Alport Hall."

"Don't be a fool," Caris said roughly. "I followed you here, of course." He sheathed his sword with a vicious click, but did not replace the scabbard in his sash. "The only delay was in putting Pettin's bullyboys out of the way."

Glancing around the square, Joanna identified only two of the merchant's hired men; of those two, one was nursing a closed eye and a lump the size of a pigeon's egg on his jaw, and the other was just pulling the remains of makeshift ropes off his wrists.

More gently, the sasennan added, "And you? Will the Council be able to track you through what you did here tonight?"

"I don't think so," Antryg replied and pushed the blood-tipped ends of his matted hair out of his face. "I did very little actual magic. Perhaps some, in the—the guiding of the Dead God's spirit back into his former body and back through the Void. Like the abominations we saw at Suraklin's Citadel, it was unable to breathe the air here, but for the same reason the organisms of decay here had taken no hold upon it. But the Sigils draw and transmit power of themselves. They are, as Joanna said, symbolic representations of the mind, in a way; they are fueled, like the teles relays, by the ambient magic all around us."

He frowned, as some other idea teased the back of his mind; his reddish brows pulled together, twisting the crusted claw marks that scored the side of his face.

Caris stood looking down at him for a moment in the uncertain dance of the torchlight. There was some of the sasennan's old exasperation in his face, tempered by understanding and pity. In a low voice, as if for the mage's ears alone, he said, "You know you can't keep it up."

Antryg glanced up at him swiftly, but there was no question in his eyes.

"It's only a matter of time before you get yourself backed into a corner where you must use your power or die."

The wizard looked as if he would have shed this remark with his usual lightness, but hesitated on his indrawn breath and then let it go. "I know," he said, so low that Joanna almost could not hear. He sat for a time, looking at the battered metal flask still clasped in his stained fingers, tiredness settling on him as if some sustaining inner cord had been suddenly cut.

"My greatest fear was that Suraklin would have heard of the Dead God, and gotten here before us," he went on quietly. "Whether the Dead God joined him as a willing partner or was overcome and dominated as his tool when his consciousness deteriorated with the pollution of those it subsumed, they would have been a terrible combination. The thing is . . ."

He stopped, his gray eyes staring out beyond the torchlight, beyond the darkness, looking, Joanna sensed, at some additional horror, some piece of the puzzle that had fallen into place. So he had looked, Joanna realized, when in the Prince Regent's carriage Pharos had spoken of what had become of his father.

"What?" she asked quickly.

He glanced down at her and shook his head, his eyes avoiding hers. "Nothing," he murmured. Then, "Do you think we could talk these people out of a cup of tea, some food, and a bed for the night? I'm chilled to the marrow and like to die of weariness."

But though Joanna, once they were in the bed of sheepskins and quilts in Greer's house, fell almost at once into heavy slumber unbroken even by nightmares, the last thing she saw was Antryg's open gray eyes staring into the darkness of the ceiling. Whatever it was that his encounter with the Dead God had told him or caused him to guess, she was aware that it did not let him sleep that night.

CHAPTER XIII

IN THE ENSUING THREE DAYS JOANNA TRIED TO GET ANTRYG TO talk about his interview with the Dead God, but found him silent and preoccupied. In Antryg's case silence, like sanity, was always a relative matter; on the road he chatted of the obscure customs of religious sects, the love lives of past Emperors, and the odder methods of divination; or he listened in absorbed silence to her explanations of computer hardware and the best methods of videotape piracy. But she sensed that, behind this gentle barrage of persiflage, he was worried and frightened.

They came out of the Sykerst and down into the lowland countries east of Angelshand, working their way through the brown valleys along the Glidden toward Tilrattin Island and the node in the energy-lines. She had come to understand that Antryg was not a particularly brave man. Like herself, he possessed far too vivid an imagination to contemplate the final confrontation with his ancient mentor with anything like Caris' single-minded fatalism. He had lived with fear for a long time. Then, too, Joanna realized uneasily, he was the only one of the four conspirators who truly knew what they were up against.

"As far as I can tell it looks like Suraklin knew what he was doing," she said diffidently one evening, looking up from the heap of photocopied programs on her lap in the feeble illumination of a couple of flickering candles. Antryg raised his head sharply from the makeshift pillow of his pack. She had seen the glint of the candlelight in his open eyes, staring up past the broken house beams that sheltered the abandoned cellar where they had made camp, studying the winter stars blazing above the naked trees.

As they had drawn nearer to their destination, they had avoided for the most part the farming villages; but, having left the brutal winds of the Sykerst behind them, this was less of a hardship. Here in the hedgerow country, too, it was far easier to find deserted barns or the ruins of old chapels or farms. Lord Alport and the villagers of Far Wilden had given them as much dried meat and the thick, heavily concentrated waybread as they could carry, so there was little need for them to seek out farmers who would spread word of strangers in the land.

Antryg rolled up onto one elbow and squinted myopically at her across the candles. "I'd certainly like to think so," he murmured, falling into the conversation, as was their habit now, in the middle, as if it were something they had discussed before. In the dim glow of the candles, his breath formed a little cloud; Joanna pulled her quilted blanket more tightly around her shoulders and brushed with her fingertips the papers that lay in her lap.

"As far as I can figure it without being a mage or a xeno-bio-psychochemist," she went on hesitantly, "the Dead God's problem stemmed from incompatible hardware-software interface—he'd put his consciousness into the physical brains of beings who were not of his species. I gather he was able to tap into human psychokinetic powers at will—which no humans but mages are able to do ordinarily—but he couldn't make the transfer until the human consciousness was absolutely gone—that is, till the poor yutz was dead. And I suspect he was doing it instinctively, rather than as a learned technique."

Antryg nodded. "More or less, yes."

"I don't think you need to worry that there will be a similar problem with Suraklin. I don't have anywhere near all the subroutines of person-ality transfer—I was just pulling them off the disk as fast as I could, and a lot of this stuff is total gibberish to me—but from what I've been able to tell from the ones I *can* understand, he's got all the personalities digita-lized down to the last detail. You're not going to get the kind of organic deterioration we did with the Dead God."

The wizard fished his spectacles out of their hiding place in his boot, which stood drying by the fire, and eased them carefully on over the narrow lines of bruises and Caris' stitching that marked the Dead God's final, furious attack. His coat, blanket, and cloak around his shoulders, he edged over to look down over Joanna's shoulder at the endless lines of the program.

"You haven't happened to come across any mention of *where* Surak-lin's put his computer, have you?"

"Not yet." Joanna wriggled her way under the corner of the cloak he held out to her—though still, the night was icy. "I've been looking for it, but you've got to remember there's *tons* of this stuff. The copy isn't all that hot, either. Toward the end there, I was just photoreducing it, doing a fast cut-and-paste job and having it copied again, double-sided to save space, without looking to see what it was. For that reason, a lot of it's barely legible, I had to bring as much as I could. And it isn't anywhere near the whole."

Antryg grinned ruefully and ran his thumb along the edge of the thick stack of unread papers. "That will teach me not to learn to read English."

She shrugged and smiled back. "Even if you could read English, you still couldn't read programming—the same way I can't understand the spells in here, even if they are in Fortran. At least, since Gary was doing most of the programming as Gary, the programs *are* in English—probably because Suraklin couldn't get a keyboard in those hearts-and-flowers you people use for an alphabet. I wonder what language he thinks in?"

She shivered suddenly and muttered, "Oh, damn," as the bitter, creeping grayness of depression whispered in like floodtide over her soul. Antryg's arm tightened around her, the warmth of it only a ghost, a memory that such things ought to bring her comfort rather than comfort itself. She bent her head wretchedly, steeling herself to endure what might be several hours, what might be the rest of a nightmare-laden night, or what might, she realized intellectually, be the beginning of forever. But she was too drained, too weary, to care.

She whispered, "I don't know how much more of this I can take."

Antryg sighed and rubbed her back with his big hand. "A great deal more, I'm afraid. Good parasites never kill their hosts." She gritted her teeth a little and rested her head on the bony hardness of his chest. She had never figured out how badly the energy drains affected him, though since they had become lovers, she suspected they did so more than he showed.

"Salteris—Suraklin—said something like that once," she commented dully. "That people grow accustomed—that in a few years no one will know what they're missing . . ."

Under her cheek, she felt him startle and raised her head to meet the hard, speculative glint in his eyes. "Did he?" Then his lips tightened and his long, narrow nostrils flared with the first real anger she had ever seen him display. He took a deep breath, almost forcibly releasing his hold on it, but there was still a kind of cold purposefulness in his face as he disengaged his arm from around her shoulders and began to dig through the capacious pockets of his great-coat. "Will you excuse me, my dear?"

Joanna nodded miserably, thinking, as he rose to his feet, *I should have known he didn't really love me . . .* and then stopped herself irritably from that old and, she knew, quite untrue train of thought. His decrepit robe nearly black in the starlight, Antryg climbed halfway up the fallen rubble and beams at the other side of the cellar and dug from his pocket an astrolabe he'd gotten from Pella.

"Suraklin thought like that, you know," he said, making a minute adjustment to the rete and sighting along the alidade at the North Star, high in the frosty sky. "He operated on the assumption that he was more intelligent than anyone else. For the most part he was right, of course, but it led to certain habits of thought. He could never be got to admit that there were things he did not understand."

He turned the astrolabe in his hand, manipulating the rule on the back. Joanna watched him without much curiosity, having seen him take sightings before in the uncertain glimmer of starlight. Now and then he would turn his head, his long nose silhouetted black against the Prussian blue of the sky as he scanned the horizon. Once he turned quickly at the sound of a sharp rustle in the blackened woods that were all around the ruined house, but it was only Caris, returning cold and wet from his nightly patrol. The young man scrambled down the decayed steps, cursing. "Now I can't even move through the woods without making noise! This is all your fault . . ."

"Nonsense." Antryg repocketed the astrolabe and slid lightly down from the beam to pull on his boots. "If my calculations are correct, the energy-line should lie about three miles southwest of us; there's something I have to check, now, while the energy's moving."

"You mean you could have sighted along it any time, anywhere, not on the node?" demanded Caris furiously. "We've come all this way . . ."

"Because I enjoy hundred-mile hikes in the dead of winter, yes." The wizard straightened up, shaking back his straggly gray curls; behind the spectacles Joanna saw the gleam of annoyance in his eyes.

Caris, who had drawn breath to say something else, let it out and looked away. "I'm sorry," he muttered. "It's just that . . ." He let the words trail off.

More gently, Antryg said, "I know." He held out his hand in its stained and ragged glove. "Joanna? Will you come with me? It isn't dangerous; but if what I fear is happening, it's better that I know."

They traversed the woods in silence. There was a village not far away —at one point Joanna could see the pinpricks of its lights across the stubble fields, like the dying glow in the heart of a burnt-out log—but on these cold and lifeless evenings there was little likelihood of anybody's being abroad so late. And it was not truly so late, Joanna thought, glancing at her watch in the starlight. Back in California, prime time television would barely have started. It was only here, in this bleak world, that the nights went on forever . . . here where she would be trapped . . .

She tried to shake off the depression, but knew it would do no good. Throughout the days of their journeying, the spells of deadness had become more frequent and longer, descending every few days as Suraklin completed, tested, and downloaded more and more of his programs. It was only a matter of time before he made his final transfer and, she suspected, not very much time at that. Her heart turned cold at the thought of it.

Our last chance, Antryg had said. At times like this, with her soul melting into a cold puddle of despair, she knew that she had no chance at all.

She felt nothing of the movement of the energy-line when they reached it, but Antryg evidently did. In the wet, brittle thickets of the woods he halted abruptly, looked this way and that in such thin starlight as filtered through the bare lattices of trees overhead, and turned west, holding Joanna's hand to help her over the rolling roughness of the ground. She'd forgotten to put on her mittens after repacking her backpack—laboriously rewrapping her Xeroxed files in plastic only because she'd made it a rule to do everything by the numbers when the depression was upon her —and her hands were almost numb save where his warmed them. She'd far rather have remained back in the cellar camp with Caris, but had come with Antryg, obscurely craving his company and now, in spite of herself, heartily resenting his preoccupied silence.

"Ah," he murmured at last. "Here we are."

Under a snarl of brown ferns and ivy stems a little standing-stone could be seen, like a child's coffin half embedded in the earth. The trees grew thick around the spot, sapling maple and elm; Antryg pulled off his gloves and waded through the dead underbrush, which rustled sharply as small animals darted away. He pulled loose handfuls of the stone's brittle shroud, baring the surface, then knelt before it, his spectacles gleaming in the cold starlight as he pressed his hands to the pitted rock. After a moment he leaned forward and touched his forehead to it, as if listening. Under his fingertips Joanna glimpsed the scratchwork shadows of traced Sigils and runes.

Shivering and weary, she folded her arms and bit back a number of smartass remarks. They stemmed, she was only too aware, from the gray exhaustion of her soul and her fear of that enormous woodland silence. What he could be seeking she could not imagine, but when he came back to her, she could see the anger in his movements, frustrated rage she had never seen in him before.

"Damn him," he whispered viciously, as they started back to camp. *"Damn* him. He may be the greatest mage in the world but he's a complete and utter fool . . ."

"What is it?" She had to hurry her steps to match his furious strides. Seeing this, he slowed immediately, offering her again a corner of his cloak for warmth. Beneath her encircling arm she could feel the jut of his ribs through several layers of coat and robe and the ripple of the muscle as they walked.

"It's difficult to explain . . ." He paused, looking down at her in the wan lace of star shadows. "No—it's difficult to *believe.* That is—you probably believe that objects are inanimate. So does Suraklin."

"Uh . . ." Joanna said, reminded once again that, in spite of his intelligence and charm and in spite of the fact that she loved him, Antryg was in fact several bricks shy of a load.

"Well," he said simply, "I don't. By the way, my dear—in your reading of the DARKMAGE files, did you ever find mention of where Suraklin hid the teles-balls that he collected over the years, the teles that he's now using to draw power—life-magic—down the energy-paths to convert to his computer's electricity?"

Joanna nodded, remembering one of those many cold little lists of facts that comprised all that was left of Suraklin's personality. "Something called the Bone Well?"

Antryg shuddered. "I was afraid of that. I can understand why no one wanted to look very closely there." She felt the shiver of his body against hers, and he started walking again, heading back to camp. In the starlight his face looked drawn and a little ill.

Glancing back, Joanna saw the little stone still standing like a stumpy dwarf. Pale against the back nets of ivy, the bald patch Antryg had torn seemed to glimmer in the darkness. Joanna could see no scratch on it, no mark of the faint web of signs that she had glimpsed beneath Antryg's hands.

It was, she realized, one of the first markers of the Devil's Road, the arrow-straight track that ran to Tilrattin Island and the crossing node of the lines.

Softly, she said, "Do you think he has them at Tilrattin Island? The teles-relay and the computer? Do you really think he'd put them that close to Angelshand?"

"He would, if he thought he could get the Archmage and the Council run out of that city—which of course he has done." He picked his way over the rocks that crossed a shallow stream, sluggish now with winter, the water like ink between beds of frozen mud lined with rims of ice. He held out a hand to Joanna; she noted, among the tracks on the bank, the small, deformed footmark of something unknown and hideous, a track that the marks of weasel and cony gave wide berth. "But from here, away from the node, I simply can't tell."

"In a way I hope they are there."

He glanced at her, his brows raised but no surprise in his eyes to hear her say it.

Stammering, she explained, "Time is on Suraklin's side. It isn't that I'm eager to face off with him, as Caris is. But if that computer's up and running when we get there—if Suraklin's already programmed himself into it—I don't know how much conscious control he'll have over his input."

"You mean he may simply spit it out."

Joanna grinned unwillingly at the anthropomorphic image. "Well, he can't, not physically. It's the trade-off he's made for virtual immortality and a limitless capacity for knowledge. He's at the mercy of his input. He can defend himself from a worm in the way computers fight human interference—with passwords and tricks and codes—but with enough time, and enough concentration, those *can* be worked through. The problem is that, with the teles relays in operation, such concentration is the first thing to go." She swallowed hard, frightened just to be saying it, thinking it and its implications. "If we get there while the computer's down, we're home free. But if that computer's on-line, I'm going to be making a *lot* of mistakes. And any delay's going to buy him time to bring up whatever second-line defenses he's got."

"I see." Antryg sighed and pushed up his spectacles to rub his eyes. "I *think* there's one last thing he needs to do before he goes 'on-line,' as you say—before he becomes his computer. But he may have done it already, whilst we were skulking about the Sykerst, pretending to be doctors. I wish I knew. I have a frightening feeling that time's getting very short."

He stopped, listening in the thin, starry darkness between the trees. Though one piece of woods still looked much like another, especially at night, Joanna thought she recognized the environs of the fallen cellar. She knew he was listening for any sound, any clue of danger. Still oppressed by the energy drain, physically weary and shivering with cold, she felt a flash of impatience and the urge to jerk on his sleeve and tell him not to bother. She forced herself silent until she felt, through his big hand in hers, his body relax, and they moved forward again.

She asked softly, "Is that what's been bothering you?"

He shook his head. "No. Since talking with the Dead God I've been uneasy about it, and feeling the energy-flow in the stone tonight I'm now sure; between his hardware and his software, with his input, once Suraklin enters his computer there is a very good chance that he'll be insane."

They reached Tilrattin Island two days later in the middle of a morning drowned in pearl-colored mist that limited visibility to a few feet. Moving cautiously through that clammy opal world, Joanna wondered if the fog itself were not some defense that Suraklin had thrown around his headquarters, but Caris shook his head. "It's always foggy in the river basin at this time of year."

"Convenient," Antryg murmured, pausing for the dozenth time since they'd entered the shaggy tangles of riverbank woods to listen. Though no countrywoman, Joanna remembered these woods at the end of summer with their myriad of bird calls, the hum of gnats above the boggy places, and the splash of fish in the streams. All was silence now, save for the muted clucking of the river itself, invisible in the fog. "Of course, tampering with the weather is very difficult to trace or even to detect, but if someone *is* watching from the island, all the fog rolling suddenly away so that we can see where we're headed is going to be a little hard to miss."

"Swell," Joanna muttered, tucking her mittened hands into her armpits for warmth. Beside her, Caris said nothing, but his narrowed dark eyes moved here and there about them, trying to pierce the milky vapors. Since the spell of deadness the night before last, the cold armor seemed to have risen around his heart again, black and impenetrable. He had resumed the loose black fighting garb of the sasenna and seemed glad to have put the distractions and the temptations of passing for a healer behind him with his purplish student's robe. When one is getting ready to die, she supposed, one can not think too much about living.

"Tilrattin and, in fact, all the woods between here and the Devil's Road have been shunned for centuries," Antryg went on after a moment. "If it's been anything near what it was like at Suraklin's Citadel, the concentration of abominations won't have improved its reputation any . . ."

"This is getting better and better." Joanna threw a nervous glance over her shoulder. They had, in fact, come across the carcass of one abomination and what Antryg took to be evidence of another—a fairly extensive grove of oak trees which within the last few weeks had been burned to their stumps, pulled down and fired until nothing remained.

"Still," the wizard continued, "I doubt we're going to encounter any traps until we set foot on the island itself. Suraklin wouldn't want to call attention to the place—not this close to Angelshand, not this close to the manor at Devilsgate."

"He has Cerdic fetching his shoes for him," Caris put in bitterly.

"That's only been since the end of September," Joanna reminded him. "He was setting up the computer before then—pity you didn't check Devilsgate for Suraklin's marks when we were there."

"I did," Antryg replied. "It was in the study, and quite old—twenty or thirty years—but it hadn't been reactivated; at least it hadn't then." He looked around him again, scanning the matte dove-colored mist, the flattened cutouts of the trees that faded back into pencil tracings, streaked here and there with rust. "But I don't feel anything and I don't hear anything, except . . ." He frowned, his gray eyes narrowing behind his specs. But he only said softly, "Come on."

Caris slipped his sword sheathe from its sash, holding it loosely in his left hand, his right held ready at his side. Stained and blotched with weather and patched with coarse brown and butternut fustians, the dull purples and greens of Antryg's coat and cloak seemed to blend uncannily with the fog as he moved away. Joanna followed, picking her way carefully over the carpet of frost-stiffened leaves.

They shed their packs at the edge of the river, with the exception of Joanna's ever-present backpack; the water was low, and a long series of crescent-shaped riffles like brown glass marked the ford. The island itself was invisible beyond a wall of fog. Caris cursed, and Antryg shook his head.

"Use the shielding spells I taught you," he breathed, pulling off his boots and hose and shivering as he kilted up the skirts of his long robe. "I'll whistle if it's safe." He drew his sword and began to pick his way gingerly down the ice of the bank. Over his shoulder he added softly, "If you hear a great deal of splashing, but no whistle, I suggest you look for another way across."

"Thanks," Caris said bitterly as the wizard vanished into the grayish wall of water and mist.

After what seemed like twenty minutes but which was, by Joanna's digital watch, less than five, the sound of the wizard's low whistle drifted across the smoky water. Feeling horribly like a character in a science fiction TV show ("Gee, the Captain's vanished utterly so we'd better beam down the second-in-command to exactly the same coordinates to see what happened to him!"), Joanna pulled off her boots and rolled up the legs of her trousers, gritted her teeth, and waded into the icy river .38 in hand.

But when the dark wall of the wooded bank materialized in the mists before her, only the solitary shape of Antryg was visible there. He was balanced on a rock above the water, still barefoot, she saw; he helped her up and ordered curtly, "Put your boots on." Thankful for this display of male chauvinism, she obeyed, then stood guard while he did the same. At Antryg's whistle, Caris appeared out of the fog a few moments later, shivering a little and tense as stretched rope. The fog seemed thicker here, as it naturally would, Joanna reminded herself, surrounded on all sides by water; the silence of the crowding black trees was frighteningly oppressive.

"The island's less than half a mile across," Antryg remarked softly. "If Suraklin's here, I suspect he knows by this time he's got company, so I think we can dispense with the element of surprise." As he spoke, Joanna felt upon her face the chilly brush of wind that seemed to come from nowhere, and gradually, gently, the fog began to drift and part. Over the water it remained thick, a rolling wall of white cobwebs, but before them trees emerged, scabby greenish elms and oaks whose coarse bark was nearly black with dampness, a wiry carpet of knee-deep sepia underbrush beneath their feet. Through the trees, startlingly close, rose the pale heads of the stone circle.

"Do you feel anything?" she whispered to Antryg, and he shook his head.

"Not from the knees down, anyway," he added ruefully. "There's no sign of a roof among the stones—he can't have left the thing in the open air. Let's have a look, but I suspect all we're going to find is a vacant lot." On that irreverent remark he moved off through the trees toward the damp, bluish stone giants, but he did not, she noticed, sheathe his sword.

The stone ring on Tilrattin Island was centuries empty, silent and overgrown with ivy and wild grape, but even so, something about it made the hair prickle on Joanna's nape. She had seen the menhirs that made up the Devil's Road, and the long tracks that crossed the Sykerst, some of them twelve and fifteen feet high—the bluestone monoliths of Tilrattin towered twenty feet high, dwarfing the humans who trod so warily beneath them. Standing within the innermost circle of trilithons, Joanna had the queer feeling that the ring was bigger than it was and that she stood in some huge courtyard surrounded by watching entities on the verge of speech. In its center, disturbingly reminiscent of that central chamber of Suraklin's power, a circular pool of water reflected the colorless sky.

"What was it?" she whispered, hardly daring to breathe. "What was it used for?"

"Many things." The frayed hem of his robe swishing wetly through the gray weeds, Antryg moved from stone to stone of the five great inner gates, passing his hands along their surfaces as he had that of the little menhir in the woods. Joanna thought she saw, ephemeral as the silver gleam of snail tracks in the daylight, the flicker of runes beneath his fingers. "Healing. At a node in the lines, a powerful mage could draw back life to the dying, back in the days when you wouldn't be killed yourself for doing so. Listening. Drawing on the strength of the stones themselves." His deep voice, always so flexible, had fallen to scarcely a whisper, as if he feared the stones themselves would hear. "They are ruinously old, Joanna. They pass power back and forth among themselves, like cells in a battery. They watch and they listen. They have seen so much that some of them are close to developing voices of their own."

"You mean they—they speak?" She followed him to one of the fallen stones of the outer of the three rings, crouched down as he knelt beside it in the dead bracken while Caris remained, forgotten, on one knee gazing into the mist-skimmed depths of the central pool.

"Not to us." The mad wizard pressed his palms to the pitted stone as he had to the menhir in the woods, bending his head down as if listening, until the long ends of his tangled gray hair brushed the damp rock. Light seemed to rise up through the stone, a wan foxfire galaxy of crossing lines —Sigils, runes, the marks of mages long dead, glowing palely for a few moments under the coarse winding sheet of lichen, then sinking back again into the stone's secret heart. "To one another." Antryg rose, and moved on to the next stone. "We don't concern them much, though it's still interesting to listen to what they have to say. It's a mistake many wizards make to believe that their spells have no long-term cumulative effect upon their surroundings . . . Caris!" He turned his head sharply. "Come away from there."

The young man looked up from the pool with a start. He got smoothly to his feet; his strides made barely a sound in the wet bracken.

More gently, the wizard asked, "What did you see there?"

Caris shook his head. "Nothing," he lied. He looked gray and sick.

Antryg tilted his head slightly to one side, studying him; the sasennan's brown eyes avoided his. After a moment Caris asked in a muffled voice, "They used that pool for divining the future, didn't they?"

Like the touch of black silk in the misty cold, Antryg said, "It took a great deal of power to get a true reading. It always does, with water. Most people just see lies, if they see anything at all."

The young man looked at him for a moment longer, an orthodox and unwilling pupil to this half-deranged mentor in his diamond earrings and scruffy cavalry coat. It seemed as if he would speak, but he only nodded and turned away. After a time he said, "Could Suraklin have his headquarters underground? Under the island?"

Antryg shook his head. "The digging would have been far too noticeable and too recent to have covered the signs. Suraklin's plan has been in preparation for some time, but the physical assembly of it—the computer, the teles-relay, and the conversion mechanism perfected by Narwahl Skipfrag—only took place in the last several months. No, we can only wait—there's a ruined chapel on the far bank of the river—until the next time the power relays come up. From here we can take a sighting along the lines . . . I can't believe it's at the Citadel of Wizards itself . . ."

Caris swung around, slamming the side of his fist into the nearest stone with a sudden explosion of pent violence. His dark eyes blazed, his voice shook with the strain of being released, once again, from the death-fight for which he must still hold himself ready. "And what then?" he almost shouted. "Take a month to journey through the taiga forest in the dead of winter and knock on the gates pretending to be wandering tinsmiths?"

Almost before the words were finished Antryg flung up one bent-fingered hand for silence. In the eerie hush Joanna could hear nothing but the distant mutter of the water beyond the trees, but Antryg and Caris both stood frozen, listening.

Caris breathed, "I don't . . ."

"Sasenna," Antryg murmured. "Mounted parties, big ones, on both sides of the river, by the sound of it—and coming this way."

The young man's face hardened, and his grip tightened over the sheath of his sword. "Then we've been betrayed."

CHAPTER XIV

JOANNA WHISPERED, "IT COULDN'T HAVE BEEN PELLA."

As Caris steadied her down the last few feet of rope, he could feel her shaking all over. Though he would rather have died than admit it, his own hands weren't too steady either. He wasn't sure whether the place Antryg had picked for concealment from the approaching troops wasn't worse than an open fight. It had certainly required far more nerve.

"Who else could it have been?" He wanted to shout the words, furious at her naïve trust and at his own. Though the energy-lines would have brought him warning long before they were anywhere in earshot, he strained his ears to catch any sound of the troop's return through the now-impenetrable blanket of fog that muffled the island. "They couldn't have us approaching—not in this fog—and we hid our tracks. Besides, they were on both banks of the stream. They knew we were here . . ."

"Did they?" The double line of rope that dangled against the clammy stone side of the nearest great trilithon shook, and Antryg shinnyed down neatly from the eiderdown masses of cloud-cover only a few feet above their heads.

The sasenna—several dozen of them, by the sound—had searched the circle and the entire island with unenthusiastic thoroughness, but it had never occurred to any of them to look above their heads, where the vast lintels of the trilithons loomed invisible on their twenty-foot supports. When Antryg had scrambled cautiously up a leaning stone and made that heart-stopping jump across to the nearest of the five monster gateways of the innermost circle, Caris had had to forcibly remind himself that the stones had been standing for thousands of years and were far too heavy and firmly set in the earth to be overbalanced by one man's weight. But climbing the rope and lying down at Joanna's side on the four-foot-wide stone lintel had turned his stomach, though in fact the lintel had been as firm as a floor. It was a four-foot jump to the next trilithon. He still didn't know how Antryg had gotten the nerve to do that.

Antryg drew on one end of the doubled rope, winding it neatly around his hands. "They searched the circle and the island, yes, but they're searching the woods as well—" His brisk movements paused, and he seemed to slide momentarily into something like a listening trance, "—out past the Devil's Road."

Caris half shut his eyes, trying to block from his mind his immediate surroundings—the dense, clinging fog and the iron-colored shapes of the looming stones—trying to hear out beyond the far banks of the river. He hadn't the power, but did not doubt for a moment that the mad sorcerer beside him did. "But they know we're somewhere in the land," he whispered. "They were expecting us, and they very nearly had us . . ."

"That doesn't mean it was Pella," Joanna responded coolly, falling into step with him as they began their cautious return to the ford. Her voice was very quiet in the deep hush of the fog-bound woods. "Don't think that because you want it so badly it has to be flawed, Caris."

He lengthened his stride, furious at this little mouse of a woman who had never done anything in her life, not caring that she couldn't keep up . . .

Her small hand seized the end of his sword sheathe, checking him. When he swung around on her in blazing wrath she continued, "That's what I did."

It stopped him. For a moment they stood in the dripping underbrush, brown eyes looking into brown, and Caris felt his quick anger cool to bitter slag as he understood that she was right. Hate himself though he might, he realized also that some perverse part of him had wanted it to be true. Then at least he would have been able to justify to himself turning his back on his greatest joy to walk into death.

She went on, "We weren't exactly inconspicuous traveling through the Sykerst. After programming in binary for months, Suraklin's got to be able to put two and two together . . ."

Caris shook his head, his whole soul hurting. What she said was true, he thought, but she had not seen what he had seen in the gray waters of the divining pool within the circle. He turned, and Joanna followed him more slowly down to where Antryg waited by the ford.

"She could have been tricked," he said, pulling off his boots. "We both know Suraklin is good at that kind of thing."

To that Joanna could make no possible reply. The fog was thicker now, summoned back by Antryg as easily as he had sent it earlier away. But listening through it, Caris could hear no sound from the riverbank, invisible beyond its white wall. He waded across, whistled softly, and stood shivering with cold and impatience until the thin little woman appeared wading out of the brown silk waters and mist.

He put on his boots as soon as Joanna had waded across to stand guard and located the packs where they had left them concealed. The long, thickly quilted coat of the Prince Regent's sasenna, left behind in anticipation of action in the circle, would cover the lack of insignia on his uniform while he asked information. With as many troopers as it would take to search the area Antryg claimed was under scrutiny, they shouldn't all know one another.

"Where are you going?" Joanna asked, shivering violently as she pulled on her boots while he stood guard.

"The manor," he replied. "Whatever's happening, they'll use that as headquarters. I can listen there . . ."

"Try to steal some food if you can," Antryg put in cheerfully, scrambling up the icy bank, looking for all the world as if he'd just been on a holiday outing, except for the sword unsheathed in his hand. "I'm deathly sick of waybread and hardtack."

His soul one well of black pain—at the possibility of betrayal, at what he had glimpsed in the pool—Caris fought the momentary urge to strike him. But in spite of Antryg's clownish gangliness, Caris had seen the wizard fight and wasn't entirely certain he'd even be able to land a blow.

"There's a ruined chapel on the far bank of the river, down about a mile and a half and inland four hundred and twenty strides or so, in a grove of laurels," the wizard went on. "If the sasenna are still searching the woods on that side of the river, we'll fall back to the little range of hills about ten miles north and wait for you on the hill on the west bank of the Spelding Stream. Two stones fifty feet from the camp mean it's safe by day—two fires if you don't get there till after dark. Whistle like a nightingale before you come in. All right?"

Caris nodded ungraciously. Whatever else might be said of the mad wizard—and a great deal certainly could—at least he understood a sasennan's evasion procedure. "I'll be there."

The crooked hand in its half-fingered glove sketched a sign in the air. "Good luck."

It was an old kitchen-magic spell Caris' grandmother had used to keep cakes from collapsing in the oven; coming at this moment, from one who had been the Dark Mage's pupil and was universally acknowledged as one of the greatest mages in the world, it cracked the wall of Caris' anger and grief and made him laugh in spite of himself. "Don't tell me you believe in that!"

The wizard grinned back. "Oh, I believe in everything." He threw the corner of his cloak around Joanna's shoulders; like ghosts the two of them faded into the fog.

During his earlier stay at Devilsgate Manor, Caris had made mental notes of the layout and approaches to the grounds. Naked with winter, the thin screens of trees and the little ornamental groves that dotted the gardens between the woods and the house walls of granite and rose-red brick offered little concealment. The gardens themselves lay like a peasant's patchwork of umbers and sepias within the spiky enclosures of knee-high box hedges, offering an almost uninterrupted field of vision from the silvery glass of the windows. Here on the higher ground, the river fog had thinned to a mere vaporish white cast to the sky.

Against the fallow, liver-colored earth, the uniforms of the men who moved through the garden beds stood out in harsh splashes—the black of sasenna, flashing with the glint of gold braid and the blood-crimson of the Prince Regent's personal guard.

In the woods beyond the stables, Caris folded up his spyglass and settled back against the warty bark of the elm beneath which he sat.

So the Regent was coming to Devilsgate.

That would explain the troops searching the woods for half a day's walk in any direction, whose sign Caris had crossed again and again on his way to the manor. Pharos was said to fear and suspect everyone and everything; Joanna's first, disastrous, encounter with the de facto ruler of the Empire of Ferryth had stemmed from the Regent's insistence upon having any house he entered searched and surrounded before he would set foot over the threshold.

But the old-fashioned manor was Cerdic's home, two days' journey from Angelshand. The Regent was certainly spiteful enough simply to take it away from his cousin on general principles; nevertheless, Caris felt uneasy. What he had seen in the divining well on Tilrattin Island still echoed in his mind, like the harsh, ambiguous note of an iron gong. At the time he had the impression that what he had seen was at Larkmoor, but he realized it could just as easily have been here. The thought turned him cold with anger and hopeless dread.

Was that what I saw? he wondered bleakly. *That he lied to her, deceived her?*

In his heart he hoped that it was. That was, in a way, the lesser of his fears.

Along the pale streak of road between the gray cutouts of the trees an outrider came cantering, his coat gaudy as outseason poppies against the colorless afternoon. Caris knew what his coming heralded. He rose cautiously to his feet, making sure he was out of clear sight of the house, and began his slow drift through the rim of the woods, edging along the knotted knees of tree roots where he could keep above the frost-stiff mats of leaves between, covering his tracks carefully where he could not. In another hour, he calculated, it would begin to get dark. That should offer some concealment as he crossed the vast brown spaces of the empty gardens toward the house itself.

A marble gazebo of the sort popular forty years ago stood amid the open lawns to the west of the house; through his spyglass Caris had glimpsed the gold flash of sleeve-braid in its trellised shadows and the glint of a watcher's glass. He approached the house from the stables on the east; with his own glass, he watched the point at which the half-mile drive from the main road cleared the trees. When at long last the dark bulk of the Prince Regent's carriage appeared, its lamps primrose in the gathering darkness, Caris folded up his glass, straightened his quilted coat, strode boldly across the open space between the woods and the stable, and thence along the drive to the house. Sasenna and guards from all quarters of the grounds were converging on the front of the house to greet their master. Those that saw Caris as he entered the kitchen quarters questioned him no more than they questioned one another. Unerringly, he passed along the halls to his chosen destination and place of concealment.

A fire had been kindled in the room that had been Prince Cerdic's study. The long curtains of crimson velvet had been drawn over the north-facing windows, cutting out the sight of the dark teeth of the Devil's Road against the dun-colored hills. Pharos hated the thought of being spied upon. Caris settled himself into a window embrasure, one of his dirks unsheathed in his hand.

He was prepared to wait for hours, if need be. But a servant came almost at once, lighting a holocaust of candles in every holder and sconce in the room—Pharos abhorred the darkness—and Caris felt a twinge of satisfaction that he had guessed aright. In a short while he heard the distant vibration of doors opening and closing and the rattle of the carriage teams being led around to the stables. Then, faint but approaching, high heels clicked on the parquet of the floor.

Caris had already arranged a small parting in the curtains, natural as a dark fold in the heavy velvet. Through it he saw a man enter from the shadows of the hall; from Joanna's description he must be the Regent's bodyguard Kanner, well over six and a half feet tall, scarred, ugly, and armed to the teeth. A former sasennan, Caris remembered, Kanner had been made deaf by a high fever and, instead of killing himself as sasenna did when they became physically flawed, he had recanted his vows to remain as Pharos' servant.

Immediately behind him walked a handsome, freshfaced boy of seventeen or so in white velvet and far too many pearls, and behind him, like a dainty flame of black and gold in the refulgent light, minced the Regent himself, Pharos Giraldus of the House of Destramor, pervert, sadist, and Pella's rightful husband and lord.

It was the first time Caris had seen him up close. His former glimpses had all been brief, and the last one—in the yard of the roadhouse on the way to Angelshand last summer—had been blurred by the changeable flicker of torchlight. This was the man who had legal power over Pellicida, Caris thought, feeling oddly cool—this doll-like, dainty, evil little creature with his painted eyes and bitten lips.

The boy in white was gazing around with wide eyes the color of ripe blueberries, his rouged mouth parted. He breathed, "Oh, my lord, it's beautiful. Thank you! Thank you."

Pharos smiled and reached up to pat the rosy cheek. "No more beautiful than you, my lovely Leynart. It was time my charming cousin Cerdic learned that, even though he's the biggest moneylender in Angelshand these days, the property of the Imperial House is mine to do with as I wish. If I wish to install you here for a year, ten years, or in perpetuity . . . you've certainly given me more pleasure than he ever did or is ever likely to."

The boy laughed and hugged him, the dark velvet curls mingling with the pomaded gold. Then he straightened up again—he topped the older man by a good five inches—and looked gravely down at the Regent, his hands resting on the bullion-stitched shoulders. "I wish I could travel with you."

"My pet," the Prince said, his rather shrill voice quiet, "you know that's not possible."

Leynart broke away from him, walked around the great desk of inlaid fruitwood to the pink marble mouth of the fireplace, close enough that, if Caris had reached out from his hiding place in the window, he could have touched a velvet sleeve. He extended his hands to the blaze, and the shape of them shone pinkly through the flawless lawn of his sleeve ruffle with the saffron glow. "Why not?" he demanded after a moment. "You know you can do anything you want. Who is she to object if you bring me with you?"

"She," said Pharos, folding his arms and regarding the boy inscrutably, "is my wife."

The scene he had glimpsed in the silver depths of the pool returned to Caris again, with cold and sinking dread, like the news of a cancer one has tried for months to tell oneself is indigestion. He felt no surprise, but only a grief that filled his body and hurt it to the marrow of his bones. As if it had been spoken aloud, he knew now where Pharos was bound, and why, and what it was that he had seen.

Leynart laughed, trying to be boyish and ingenuous and only sounding tinny. "I still think yours is the best description of her: one of those big black mares decked out to pull the processional cart on a peasant's saint's day. I still have nightmares thinking about that awful yellow riding habit . . ." The tone was of a familiar gambit, rallying for a response that he did not get.

"She's welcome to wear what she pleases," Pharos began impatiently.

"Not the lavender satin, surely!"

"I certainly don't have to look at her all the time. But I wasn't fooled by that tarradiddle about the cold. Her? Cold? Pah."

The young man shuddered with exaggerated delicacy. "What a bruiser! I'll bet she takes baths in rainwater straight out of the barrel! I can't think why you simply didn't take a crop to the slut when she slapped you."

"Can't you?" Pharos cocked his head a little, his pale eyes in their insomniac circles glinting oddly in the dancing light. "She would have taken it away from me and flogged the daylights out of me. A filthy little brute, that dog—but hers."

"As I am yours." Leynart turned from the fire and walked back to where the Prince still stood. Taking one lace-cuffed hand, he raised it to his lips. "You'd be welcome to torment any number of pets, for all of me. You know that."

"Yes," said the Prince softly. The boy's head was still bent over his hand, so Leynart did not see the glint of contempt in those pale eyes. "Yes, I know that." Pharos turned abruptly away and walked out of the narrow field of Caris' vision. By the sound of his voice, he was near the other window, close to the pedimented niches where the statues of the Old Gods clustered between Cedric's beloved books of occultism and quackery. Leynart stood where he had been, anxiety and apprehension in his face.

"I won't be at odds with her, Leynart," Pharos' voice said at last. "I need a child."

The boy laughed crudely. "Is that all? Since when has a man needed to ask permission to mount his own mare? I'm astounded you can even rise to such an occasion. I certainly couldn't."

Caris was aware of the pain in his palm from the crush of the dagger's hilt in his grip and forced himself to relax it. There was the faint slither of satin against lace, the muted creak of the corner of the desk taking the Prince's slight weight perched upon it. "They're trying to murder me, Leynart," that soft, edgy voice said. "All of them are plotting against me —Cerdic, Magister Magus, the Council of Wizards who wouldn't let me skin and slice Windrose when I had the chance to do it. Who's to say they weren't behind his escape? Or that the Bishop Herthe wasn't, with her sanctimonious whining? The only reason I married that musclebound Amazon was that Cerdic is my heir, and I won't have the country given over to a pack of superstitious dog wizards when I'm dead. But having married her, the least I can do is give her the respect due to my wife."

Tears gleamed suddenly in Leynart's cornflower eyes. Impulsively he strode out of Caris' line of sight, leaving only Kanner in view, standing impassively, arms folded, near the door. There was the swirling flounce of laces and silk as the boy flung himself to his knees. "So what do you think she's going to do?" his voice demanded, suddenly trembling. "Drive you out of her bed with a stick? She has to want a child as badly as you do, to make her someone at Court and not just the jumped-up provincial nobody she is! Your child for preference, to keep the family looks, but I'm sure anyone with blond hair will do! Pharos, I love you! I don't want anything from you except your love! If I don't have that, I swear I will die!"

Caris turned his face away, sickened, staring for a time out into the thin darkness beyond the windows' misted glass. Against a leaden sky, the Devil's Road was nearly invisible; the long stretch of open garden and lawn was lost in a lake of shadow, broken at the very edge of his sight by the gleaming white island of the gazebo's dome. He had no business here, he thought; no business hearing that spoiled child's hysterical sobs, or the dry swish of lace as, uncaring of his bodyguard's presence, Pharos stroked the dark, ruffled head.

Leynart wept, Caris knew, because he saw in Pharos' eyes the dawning of respect for his wife. And like Caris, he knew what that respect might become.

In the gray pool he had seen them together, Pharos and Pella, sitting side by side in talk while Kyssha slept on Pella's swollen lap. Pella's face had been grave, but in her eyes had been no fear, merely her matter-of-fact willingness to take people as she found them. Her husband's pale eyes, so shifty with everyone else, had been on her.

I will never have her, Caris thought, the desire for her consuming his flesh at the same time cold grief drowned his heart. When the sasenna had arrived to search the island, he had thought the scene was one of betrayal, but now he understood. In a way, for Pella to be tricked or forced into telling her husband of their whereabouts would have been preferable to what he now knew the scene had been. It was as it should be, he knew. He never could have had her anyway—neither her, nor magic, nor the brightly colored life that he sensed stirring like a perfumed carnival beyond the dark boundaries of his destiny. He wondered despairingly if it was a mark of love to wish that her husband would continue to hate her, so that she could be his, at least in his heart for the little that remained of his life. But having no experience of loving, he did not know.

"Antryg?" Joanna said softly and felt the movement of his pectoral muscles beneath her cheek as he turned his head. They had lain a long time in silence, twined together in a stone burial niche in the ruined chapel's wall. At some distance, in the center of the ruin, two small fires burned a few feet apart. The light of them filtered through the hanging curtain of brown vines, dappling Antryg's face in a moire of shadow and light. He'd put his spectacles back on, and fragments of red and orange skated across the cracked lens and glinted in the diamond of his earrings. "What *are* the long-range effects of magic upon inanimate objects?"

"I don't know." His mellow baritone was little more than a vibration in his chest against her ear. "In that, I'm like Suraklin, except that Suraklin always refused to believe that there were any at all. He has always discounted reasons for not doing what he seriously wanted to do."

"You said that the stones in the circle had voices, spoke to one another, because of all the magic that had been drawn through them over the years."

"Yes." His bony arm tightened around her shoulders under the pile of blankets, coats, and cloaks, as if to protect her against whatever lay beyond the black fog of the night. "Magic isn't a science, as the Council of Wizards claims it is, nor an art, as Suraklin always said. It's life itself. It imbues all things, and particularly those things it touches for long periods of time. I keep thinking about that poor scientist, playing the

Dead God in Far Wilden, gradually poisoning himself by the very thing that kept him alive. You're right, Joanna—software is only as good as the hardware it travels through. Suraklin believes that, because the teles-balls that make up the power-relays, and the stones along the energy-lines that convey the life-force to him, don't speak to him, there will never come a time when they might. But they do absorb magic. The teles-balls are practically indestructible, and some of them are older than any memory. There were two or three in Suraklin's collection that—frightened me. I don't like to think of them, lying hidden in the Bone Well beneath the Citadel with the black carrion strippings of half demons he called into existence and then imprisoned there because he couldn't quite kill them when he was done.

"Those teles, those stones, are now going to be in use constantly and have magic pouring through them twenty-four hours a day. It may all go as Suraklin believes it will for a year or two or ten—but how long will it be before those voices begin to bleed into Suraklin's mind, his self, locked in the computer and at the mercy of his input? All magic is balance, because all magic is individuated. When it all gets bound together into one giant interlocking web, *we have no idea what could happen.* Neither has Suraklin. But he's dangerous because he thinks that nothing will."

The travelers remained for three days in the ruined chapel on the north bank of the River Glidden, waiting for the next spell of deadness. The weather was cold, though not the brutal, piercing cold of the Sykerst; sheet ice broadened out from the banks, a film of it entirely covering the river between the shore and Tilrattin Island by night, only to crack away at midday. It was a still time, but desperately unrestful.

Antryg spent a good deal of his time in the stone circle and refused ever to get very far away from it. Though Caris knew he should have been concentrating his energies on honing his warrior's skills—on hunting the shy beasts of winter to sharpen his reflexes or on swordsmanship and shooting that he had perforce neglected during the days of steady walking—he found himself accompanying the wizard there. Hungrily, guiltily, as he had learned healing, he learned from him a little of the lore of the stones and that of the energy-trails, listening down the lines for the voices alive in the air. The wizard tried to instruct him, too, in the arts of divining and of seeing things far away. For two nights Caris sat near that tall, gangly figure bent over the fire, gazing into the embers with his spectacles throwing back the fulvous glow, watching the roads for the approach of danger or, indeed, of anyone or anything that might come upon them and spread word of their presence. The Regent had departed the morning after his arrival, and Antryg kept an eye on Leynart at Devilsgate. But the boy remained listless and seldom left the house.

Tormented by the knowledge that he should not be doing so, Caris tried to fan his own slight talents into sufficient strength to do the same. If the wizard guessed why, he did not say so, and Caris never admitted that what he wanted, as well as a glimpse of Pella, alone at Larkmoor, was to know where the Regent slept that night and how soon he would reach his wife's side.

The circle at the node of the lines was silent. The brown earth dreamed undisturbed under the mantle of coming winter. Joanna, thin and grubby as a shabby little wood-elf, alternated between reading Suraklin's incomprehensible files and checking and rechecking the contents of her backpack and the hardcopy, as she called it, of her own "worm" that she planned to feed into Suraklin's computer to destroy everything on its disks. Caris reflected bitterly that, like her, he should have been readying himself for the coming battle, not spending his time in pursuit of what would not help them and in any case could never be his.

Once in the night he slipped away from the chapel to wade the ice-skinned river and knelt in the circle's darkness at the side of the divining well. But its unfrozen waters showed him nothing, save the chilly blaze of the watching stars visible above the rising river fog, and he found that being in the circle alone troubled him. He was hideously conscious of the stones standing behind him in the cold starlight and prey to the uneasy sensation that as soon as he took his eyes off them they might move.

By day he was seized with a violent restlessness. Once or twice Antryg stripped out of his cloak and voluminous green coat and fenced with him, using trimmed saplings for swords instead of the razor-sharp weapons. Caris invariably felt himself worsted and cursed his sloth still further. At other times he merely patrolled the woods, as if by constant movement he could outwalk his burning awareness of how far Pharos must be on his journey and how soon he would be at Pella's side.

It was on one of these patrols that Caris heard the approach of the troops.

It was a clear evening and sharply cold; sound carried a great distance in the colorless ranks of the bare woods. Caris heard the strike of hooves first on the hard-frozen roadbed, and slipped quickly down into the concealment of the overgrown ditch at its side. It was only as the sounds came nearer and he realized that the troop must number nearly a hundred riders and a number of carriages that it came to him that something was fearfully wrong.

Antryg had had no warning of their approach. Yesterday he'd noted the presence of a peddler on the way to the village on the other side of Devilsgate, the passage of a wedding party from the village church. How could he possibly have missed an entourage of that size?

Baffled, Caris raised his head. White facings stood out on the unfamiliar black uniforms of fifty mounted sasenna, like floating bars of moonlight in the gathering gloom; they were followed by nearly as many household cavalry in emerald green. For the most part, the sasenna looked very young, newly fledged, newly sworn, tough and cold and trained to a hair. They surrounded a four-horse traveling coach, while several smaller vehicles with baggage brought up the rear.

He couldn't have missed it, Caris thought, baffled. *Yet why would he lie?*

The only place they could possibly have been heading was Devilsgate itself. Moving cross-country through the woods, Caris was at the big rose-red manor before them. Without Pharos' sasenna in the gardens, the place was far easier to slip into. The marble gazebo with its thin screen of trellises offered ample concealment and a good view, through the spyglass, of the front of the house; with luck Caris calculated that he could be away from the place by the time sasenna or guards were posted around the house or, at worst, pass himself off as one of them in his black coat in the evening gloom.

Leynart was on the steps of the manor, his primrose silk costume glimmering like a ghost in the dusk. He looked weary and haggard, as if he had found the last two days no easier than Caris had; in the dark frame of his curly hair the lines and hollows of his face showed through a careful application of concealing paint. The carriage drew to a stop. Through the glass, Caris could see it was drawn by a team of the showiest matched sorrels he had ever seen, the carriage itself ablaze with claret-red lacquer and gilt. The boy Leynart's haunted eyes brightened. He strode down the steps, his hands held out in welcome as the footmen opened the carriage doors.

A man stepped down from the carriage, and Caris realized instantly why Antryg had not had warning of their approach. It was difficult, he knew, for mages to divine the movements of other mages; even the slight spells that he was able to hold around himself would thwart any but a very powerful scryer. And though Magister Magus was generally spoken of as a charlatan, according to Antryg the dapper little gentleman whom the footmen now assisted down did, in fact, have true power.

Presumably, thought Caris dourly, he had been persuaded to use it in trade for being saved from the Witchfinders.

The footmen and Magister Magus bowed low as the second man stepped down from the carriage, and Leynart came forward to catch the lace-gloved hands in his own. Prince Cerdic was a good bit fatter than when Caris had seen him last and wore a suit of plum-colored velvet which must have cost more than the carriage and team combined. Leynart bent over his hands—though the Regent had taken Devilsgate and given it to his eromenos, it was obvious that, from that moment, the youth considered himself Cerdic's guest.

It took Caris a moment to realize who the third man must be. There was something vaguely familiar about his face; it was young, not yet thirty-five, yet settled already into hard and arrogant lines. His clothes were simple, a court suit of dark green and apricot, yet the Prince and Leynart both bowed deeply, and Leynart knelt on the icy gravel of the drive to kiss the man's hand. Perhaps it was the hair that jogged Caris' memory. It was shorter than anyone but sasenna and laborers wore it, yet familiar. He had seen it . . .

The man moved, gesturing toward the house. With a chill that was not quite anger nor yet quite dread, Caris remembered.

The face was the face of the man he had glimpsed through a darkened window, whining excuses to Joanna while the chaos of music and drinking went on at the party around the courtyard pool, long ago and in another universe. The face was the face of the hapless Gary Fairchild, but Caris recognized the gesture as typical of his grandfather.

He realized he was looking at Suraklin.

CHAPTER XV

"IT'S JUST THAT IT ISN'T FAIR!" LEYNART TURNED, THE SNOWY EM-
broidery that laced his coat skirts glittering like frost with the movement
of his caged pacing. With a passionate gesture, he strode back to the fire
where his guests sat, and his words became indistinct to Caris once again.

Caris had calculated that the boy's fulsome welcome of the Prince and
the two wizards would have given him time to take up his old hiding
place behind the study curtains, had he chosen to, but caution warned
him against it. It was one thing to spy upon the Regent, paranoid though
he might be. It was another to spy upon Suraklin. Instead, he had carefully jammed the sneck of the study door so it would sit slightly ajar and
had stationed himself in the disused alcove down the hall, listening for
the steps of the four men as they passed. It was his guess that they would
not risk the posting of a guard, for fear of the guard doing precisely what
he did—listening. But any passing servant in the dark corridor would not
know it.

Through the crack he could see more of the room itself than he had
before—dark-paneled in a fashion fifty years out of date, with a deeply
coffered ceiling and heavy antique chairs. Its shelves were crowded with
books whose titles Caris recognized from his days at the Mages' Yard—
tomes of wisdom and charlatanry ranked side by side. The resinous glow
of fire and candles mingled along the edges of the Five Mystical Forms
carved from polished hematite, objects of mathematical meditation
which had become semisacred to one of the more crackpot schools of dog
wizardry and gave a queer life to the statues of the twenty-one Old Gods,

lurking like watchers among the books of what had once been their faith. Most people these days did not even know their names.

Caris did. Aunt Min, possibly the oldest mage living and certainly the oldest at the Yard, was an Old Believer, though, like most of that discredited faith, she had only *chellim,* elaborately wrought slips of paper bearing the gods' names, pasted to the walls of her little room and now grubby with age and cooking grease. So he knew most of them, those silent watchers of diorite, hematite, malachite, and jade, who guarded shelf and mantle and whose eyes seemed to move with the shadow of Leynart's feverish stride.

Suraklin remained seated in one of the gilt chairs near the fire, arms propped before him, hands clasped on level with his chin, and forefingers extended to touch his lips. Caris had often seen his grandfather sit so, though not, when he thought of it, back in the days of his childhood. He wondered now how he could possibly have been so stupid as not to realize something was amiss even then. If nothing else, the mocking glint of irony in those brown eyes should have told him long ago that his grandfather had ceased to be grandfather.

But what, he wondered wearily, could he then have done?

Leynart's voice rose again, fighting for composure. "It isn't that I begrudge her position, please don't think that." His tone was that of a man trying to be just against his every inclination. "But she doesn't care for him. She can't. She only wants his affection for the status it will give her, to fulfill some petty, bourgeois moralities. She'll dull him, stultify him, make him miserable if he tries to please her . . ."

"I always thought," purred Suraklin, the very turn and inflection of his voice recognizable as accents Caris had heard in the Archmage's, "that a provincial moneygrubber's niece was hardly the proper choice for a man of Pharos' stature, even were she virtuous, which of course she is not."

Only years of training let Caris suppress the smothering heatwave of anger and stifle the harsh draw of his breath. Wizards had sharp ears and a sixth sense of danger—spying on them could be unbelievably perilous. His only hope was that Suraklin's mind was occupied with whatever scheme had brought him here and that the man was conceited enough to be at ease among these worshipful victims. The flame-flecked eyes did not even move Caris' way.

Pella had told him of her seduction by the wizard, though she was almost certain the child she carried was not his. For that, too, Caris hated the man. It occurred to him that he was within touching-distance of the end of his quest, only yards from the man he had sworn to kill. The butt of his pistol ground against his ribs; he had only to open the door . . .

Except, of course, that the pistol was not na-aar. With even an instant's warning, Suraklin could make it either misfire or blow up in his hand. The house was full of the Prince's sasenna and household guards; Caris doubted that he would get away; and even if he did, where would he run? The resulting dragnet would pull in Antryg and Joanna. Then, truly, all hope would be at an end.

All this passed through his mind in an eyeblink, as Suraklin went on, "No, Leynart, it isn't wrong to begrudge her the Prince's care. You aren't taking anything away from her, you know. All you want, truly, is his recognition of your love—which in fact your loyalty deserves." He moved his hand. Like a whipped hound eager for forgiveness, Magister Magus got hastily up from his unobtrusive seat in the shadows.

It was the change in Magus that hurt Caris most, hurt and angered him, as if he had seen cruelty to an animal or a child. When he had been the man's guest in Angelshand, he had despised Magus as a dog wizard who made his fortune while the mages at the Yard ate oatbread and worried about the leaks in their roofs. But the Magus had always dealt with him well, had taken care of Joanna when her presence under his roof had been a clear danger to him, and had helped her as much as he could. Seeing how the dapper little charlatan cringed when he approached his new master, Caris could guess how that fear had been instilled. Once Magus had been arrested, there had been no hope for him. Cerdic and his Spiritual Advisor were the only ones who could have saved him from the Inquisition—and Suraklin needed a slave who was a mage.

"I have prepared this for you." Suraklin held out his hand. Magus gave the wizard the box he carried, carved rosewood varnished like satin, then bowed and stepped back out of Caris' line of sight. The Dark Mage opened it; Leynart and Cerdic looked within.

"Wonderful!" Cerdic murmured ecstatically and reached into the box. "It's fresh! Roses like this don't even grow in Mellidane at this season . . ."

"Whoa!" Suraklin drew the box back, laughing. "Don't touch it, my lord, unless you look to become a good deal fonder of our Ley than you are now!"

The Prince withdrew his hand hastily and put a few feet between him and the youth for good measure. Leynart bridled at the promptness of the gesture, and the wizard laughed again.

"Of such stuff are bedroom farces made, my lord. It's a simple enough spell, but effective." A mocking gleam of amber danced catlike at the back of the brown eyes. "So have a care, Ley, unless you want suitors all over Kymil pounding down your door and snubbing poor Pella for no earthly reason whenever they see her. And incidentally, don't touch it yourself, until the moment comes when you lay it upon his Grace's pillow, where he shall sleep that night. Else all shall be for naught. Do you think you can do it?"

The youth nodded. His dark ringlets, plum-black in the firelight, swung against his cheeks. "If you can get me to Kymil, my lord Gaire, as you say you can, before his Grace arrives, his Grace's men will let me into his house."

"Trust me, my boy." The warm brown eyes smiled into the blue. "As I trust you." The wizard put out a hand and affectionately tucked a stray curl back into the dark mass of Leynart's hair. His voice was gentle. "I've never had the taste for boys—but now I understand it. You'll be in a position to wield a good deal of power, there on the steps of the throne, little lover. But I trust you'll do so wisely."

"I want no power," Leynart whispered, his cornflower eyes grave in their gilt and paint. "Only his love."

"Well spoken. And that you shall have."

So this, Caris thought sourly, was a love-spell—this harmless-sounding manipulation of the heart and the mind. To make Pharos snub his wife again and turn to this perfumed little catamite—to condemn Pella to lifelong humiliation . . .

Part of Caris wondered why he should be angry. The thought of Pharos touching Pella, kissing her—the thought of her lying in those thin, flabby arms—had kept him sleepless for two nights. He ought to be thanking the boy. But he knew his meeting with the Dark Mage was very near now, and he knew he would not survive it. It was not fair to want to be the only love she would ever have.

The Council was right, he thought, his whole body hurting with indecision and grief. Great and small, the affairs of humankind should be safe from meddling by those who had the power to do so. But in his mind he heard the cries of a newborn infant and felt the flash and throb of a tiny soul like primal fire, coming to life beneath his hands, and he did not know what he thought.

Leynart knelt to kiss Suraklin's hands. Beside the hearth, Cerdic was beaming like the bride's mother at a wedding, no doubt thinking, Caris reflected cynically, that with this one coup he had guaranteed himself Heir in the place of those that Pharos would not beget. Or perhaps he was merely sentimentally pleased to be helping his young friend. *Blind, fatuous fool.*

"Come." Suraklin shut the box and handed it to Leynart with a glance at the ormolu clock. "It's time. It must be before midnight, and there is something yet I must do here. Magus . . ."

Caris slipped quickly away as Suraklin and the Magus turned toward the door. With all the silence of his long training, he glided back to the alcove, waited till he heard them pass, then drifted, silent as river mist, through the dim halls and out of the house. Without Pharos' horror of the dark, Devilsgate was far less well lit than it had been; it proved an easy matter to conceal himself near the stableyard as grooms brought out three horses, their breath floating in clouds of steam in the yellow flare of the stable lamps.

Caris' mind felt shaken, torn as a hound's on a crossed scent. Everything else aside—Pella, the Regent, his doomed, frantic love—Suraklin was *here* at Devilsgate. Could Antryg have been wrong about the circle? *Was* the computer concealed somewhere underground, as Caris had guessed? For that matter, how close did it have to be to the actual node to drink the energy? As Antryg himself had said, all they had to go on was guesses and deduction. None of them, from start to finish, had one shred of actual proof. Antryg hadn't spoken or worked with Suraklin in twenty-seven years. How would he or Joanna know what was and was not possible?

Could the apparatus be concealed at Devilsgate itself?

Reflected lamplight splattered over the wet gravel of the stableyard. He heard voices and Cerdic's jolly laugh, then Suraklin's voice, firm and deep: "My lord, forgive me for making you play groom, but in truth I dare not trust another."

They came around the corner of the stables, flanked by a servant with a torch. Cerdic, heedless of that servant or the watching grooms, fell to one knee and kissed the wizard's hand. "Groom? I'll put my hand under your foot to boost you to the saddle, did it please you, my lord." Suraklin laughed, raised him to his feet, and clapped an affectionate hand on his shoulders while a footman hastened to sponge the yard mud from the Prince's velvet knee.

They were only facsimiles, Antryg had said, *copied from what he had seen others sacrifice themselves for . . . But they were copied dazzlingly well.*

Heart pounding, Caris flattened himself back in the shadows of the coach-house door to watch, wondering desperately what to do. Suraklin, Cerdic, and Leynart mounted. The Prince took from one of the grooms a closed lantern—to maintain the fiction, Caris thought, that Suraklin, or Gaire as he was called, couldn't call whatever light he wished or see in the dark. The three horses passed through the yard gate, their hooves crunching softly on the ice underfoot. Slipping from shadow to shadow, Caris glided in their wake. If he lost sight of the Dark Mage now, in all probability he'd never be able to locate him again—wizards were notoriously difficult to find. Yet he knew he was completely incapable of dealing with the wizard himself.

I'm only a warrior! he thought. *And out of practice, neglectful, indecisive of heart at that. I'm no match for him . . .*

Joanna had repeatedly asked, *Why me?* But she'd always been willing to take on Suraklin, the Inquisition, anyone . . .

Whatever happens, at least I can witness it to tell Antryg.

Soundless as a moth, he followed the bobbing gold splotch of lantern light across the vast gardens, into the woods, and along the narrow paths that led toward the dark stubble fields of the hedgerow country, and beyond that, the mist-shrouded river. The three men rode single file, Suraklin in the lead, the warm reflection of the lantern tipping his short brown curls and the fur collar of his greatcoat with gold. Cerdic, bringing up the rear and showing a surprisingly good seat on a horse, kept glancing behind him, though more, Caris thought, from nervousness about what people would say than from any real sense of being watched. Once they reached the woods, Caris kept easily out of sight, drifting from tree to stripped and rain-dark tree. Between Prince and wizard, Leynart said nothing, only clutched his precious spell-box to his chest and huddled deeper in this miniver cloak like a cold lapdog on a pillow. Overhead the clouds had grown thick; the scent of snow rode the wind.

The riders took a roundabout path, changing direction frequently, but at last Caris heard the muffled whisper of the river and dimly glimpsed the white heads of the stones above the dark branches.

The river was frozen nearly across; the horses' hooves broke through the thin ice, splashing loud in the black water of the ford. On the island, Suraklin and Leynart dismounted, handling the reins to Cerdic. Caris crouched in the shadows of a copse of birches, and the sable hem of the Prince's embroidered greatcoat all but brushed across his face as Cerdic rode back, lantern aloft now, still peering fearfully all around him. Suraklin, on the boulder where Antryg had stood, watched him for some moments, while Caris told himself firmly that he was sheltered in that direction from those darkness-piercing eyes.

To cross the ford—to follow them to the circle and see what Suraklin did there—Caris would have to break cover. By the stars it was nearing midnight. Suraklin had spoken of something which must be accomplished by then, and the roundabout way they had taken here had nearly doubled their time. Did the computer come alive at midnight? Caris wondered. And in that case, would Antryg be drawn to the circle and walk into his trap?

At last the wizard turned away, vanishing in the darkness almost at once. Still hugging his precious box to him, Leynard followed. There was a momentary blur of white stockings and hat-plumes in the underbrush, then nothing.

Should he wait? Caris wondered. For how long? Whatever it was they had gone to the circle to do . . .

He took a deep breath and stepped from his shelter.

Cold and crisp, a voice from the woods at his back said, "Take him."

Caris swung around, sword leaping as of its own will to his hand. Dark forms he would have taken oath had not been there seemed to rise from the ground all around him, shadowy shapes, glittering steel. He slashed at one and it melted before his blade, cut at another, water splashing icy in his boots as he leaped to avoid the return slash. Steel grated on steel; at least some of his attackers were of human flesh and not illusion. In the woods he thought he glimpsed a slender form, the black splotch of a Van Dyke beard on a white face. He thought, *Magister Magus,* as movement from the corner of his eye made him spin to meet an attack. As an axe whizzed toward his head and he raised his sword to parry he thought, *No sound of that one's boots in the water* . . .

But by then it was too late. His turning to defend against the illusion cost him the moment to parry the real warriors on his other side. He cursed himself as a halberd hooked his feet from beneath him. Something struck his head as he fell. He had no recollection of hitting the stony bank.

Fighting upward as if from black water, Caris thought, *Magus hid his men by spells. If I'd been a true mage, I'd have seen them—if I'd been a true sasennan I'd have been more careful* . . . Then he sank again into clouded dreams

He was in his grandfather's house in the Mages' Yard, in the narrow, low-raftered study; light from the diamond-paned window fell across Salteris' bald head where he sat before the dull black turrets of his tall desk. "Caris, please don't think ill of me, please don't run away," the old man was saying softly. "Why do you believe that I allowed Suraklin to share my body, share residence in my mind, without my consent? We are guest-friends, my son, not captor and captive. He has let me come with him into immortality. You have no idea of the capacity of the human mind—there is room here for us all. I am not dead, Caris . . . only my body that was finished anyway . . . Does the butterfly mourn the chrysalis? Come."

He held out his hands, thin and strong, the blue veins standing out in the white flesh. His brown eyes were dark and gentle, coffee-colored, like Caris' own, save for an amber gleam, like the spark of hidden coals, far back in their depths.

Caris backed away from him, confused. He missed the old man, missed him desperately, all the mourning he had held bottled inside for months welling to the surface in a surge of blinding pain. The magic pounded in his veins, the power to help and heal; a forbidden power, indulged in like unsanctioned killing.

As if he read his grandson's mind, the old man murmured, "Caris, I can help you. I, too, am a healer. I, too, cared for the sick in secret—we all did. It lies in the palms of your hands . . ."

Caris woke up sweating, smothered by a sense of panic. For an instant he thought he saw a silver scribble of light written on the wooden wall by the head of the bed where he lay, gleaming softly in the thin light of the foggy dawn. Then he blinked, and it was gone.

He lay back. His head ached, and his body felt chilled and shaken. A blanket covered him, thrown back by his restless tossings. His weapons were gone. By the slope of the ceiling, he guessed the room where he lay was in one of Devilsgate's attics; the single window was barred; when he rose and approached it, he found himself shrinking with loathing at the thought of touching the frame or the glass.

Fear-spells. Of course, he thought bitterly. Suraklin had known all the time he was being watched. He'd called Magus aside, given him time to set the trap at the ford by that drawn-out journey, set up this prison . . .

If they had taken him prisoner, he thought, it meant Suraklin had a use for him.

The thought turned his blood cold.

Or—*had* his dream been right? *Had* Suraklin found, instead of a selfish immortality that raped his victims of body and mind, a means of carrying them forward with him?

Caris shook his head, pushing the thought away as absurd. Why would Suraklin bother? He had already shown he would kill without compunction.

Yet within him, Caris was conscious of a nagging itch to talk to the Dark Mage, to ask him . . .

Ask him what? he demanded of himself in disgust. It was only Suraklin's influence, whispering to his mind. He wondered suddenly if this was how the wizard had lured Magus' mind to his, how he had lured Salteris'?

Antryg, Caris thought. *He'll know by now I'm missing. How long before he attempts to find me?*

Or has he already tried and been caught? His heart beat faster with dread.

A quick look around his prison served to tell him the room was utterly bare, barred, containing nothing but the bed on which he had lain, a covered latrine bucket, and a small table which bore a loaf of bread and a pitcher of water. Being at the top of the house, the room itself was fairly warm; outside he could see patches of new-fallen snow on the slaty roofs of the laundry and buttery wing. He touched the bread, found it fresh, that morning's. Hungrily, he broke a piece from it, then hesitated.

He set it down again and smelled the water in the pitcher. There was no scent of drug, but he remembered he was dealing with a wizard.

He had no experience with these sneakier tricks, the spells to deceive and sway the mind, for they were utterly illegal, unknown to the wizards he had served. Nevertheless he set both bread and water aside.

It was one of the longest days Caris had ever spent. The daylight was the livid yellow-brown of snow, which occasionally fell, thin as sifted flour, from a sky which seemed neither bright nor dark. His head ached. Not knowing how late in the morning it had been when he had come to, he found it even more difficult to estimate time. Sometimes he could hear movement in the house below him, the comings and goings of the Prince's sasenna, and now and then a servant's voice.

He wondered how long it would be, before Suraklin came up to see him.

When the draining deadness began, the leaden depression that told him that Suraklin's mechanical brain was in operation again, his captivity became a thousand times worse. Part of him thought bleakly, *So it is here. In the circle, or here in the house itself . . .* Most of him simply did not care. He was hungry and thirsty by that time; with the numbing of his mind he craved even the small activity of eating. The depression whispered to him that it didn't matter whether the food and drink were drugged or not—Suraklin would have him anyway. At last, unable to stand the temptation any more, he tore the bread in pieces, threw it in the latrine bucket, and poured the water from the pitcher out onto the floor.

They'd said that Antryg had spent a good deal of his time in the Tower pounding on the walls with his broken hands and screaming. Lying white-knuckled on the bed, Caris knew exactly how he had felt. *If this goes on . . .* he thought.

But it would go on. There was an increasing probability that it would go on, literally, forever. Antryg and Joanna would go to the circle to take their bearing and walk straight into Suraklin's trap.

Despair at their naïveté, at his own stupidity, and at the hopelessness of his fate drowned him like a velvet wave. They would be killed, he would be enslaved, Pella would be condemned to a living hell of mockery and derision, and what did it matter, anyway?

He slept, and Salteris sat on the foot of his cot and whispered to him in his dreams.

The sliding back of the door bolt was so soft that, had he been sleeping even normally—and he was, as all sasenna come to be, a light sleeper—he would not have heard it. But after the passing away of the grayness, his dreams had changed. The despair faded again into images of his grandfather, kindly, gentle, speaking of how they had all misunderstood Suraklin's intent, while that amber glint of mockery flickered somewhere in the coffee-dark eyes. Troubled, Caris tried to pull clear of the dream. Once he managed to open his eyes, and thought he saw again the wizard's mark gleaming on the wall near the bed in the semi-dark. But the dreams were strong, dragging him down like the sodden weight of river weeds. Dimly he wondered how long he would last.

But the slight whisper of slipping iron pierced his consciousness like the first drip of rain from a leaking roof. He was fully awake and poised to spring, a straight leap from bed to door, even as it opened and Antryg drifted through.

Caris aborted the leap half-made, but he could see his lunatic mentor had been ready for it. Antryg touched his lips, signaling silence, and beckoned with his huge gray eyes; outside the window the sky was deepening toward final dark. Within, lamps would be kindling.

"Hold your breath as we go through the main attic," Antryg whispered, and Caris nodded, not asking why. In the attic outside, a lamp had been lit, illuminating the table where two sasenna slept over a spread of cards. Four more had rolled, unconscious, from various hiding places. *A double-baited trap,* Caris thought as they moved swiftly through the hazy scrim of lamp smoke, pausing only long enough for Caris to collect a sword. *They were expecting a rescue. Suraklin didn't need me at all, except as bait.*

"An opium compound in the lamp-oil," the wizard breathed, as they descended the attic stairs, holding close to the wall so the risers did not creak. "Part of my medical satchel. The woods are simply stiff with sasenna—not the Regent's, either . . ."

"Cerdic's." Caris kept his voice to a subvocal wind-murmur as they glided along the upstairs hall. "How did you get in?"

"Thank goodness for the sins of bygone Emperors; there's a stair from the master bedroom to a passage that runs out to that marble gazebo. From the way the guards are positioned I think they're expecting me to fire the stables by way of diversion. Did you know the Empress Cha-nanda was credited with having forty-seven lovers during the time that her husband was keeping her prisoner here because of her debauchery? Here we are."

"Antryg, Suraklin's . . ."

Caris never afterward could decide what warned Antryg—whether it was natural caution or the magic that allows mages to see other mages in spite of cloaking spells. As his fingers touched the painted porcelain door handle the mad wizard suddenly turned, leaping aside as he thrust Caris back. The narrow corridor echoed with the whopping crash of a cross-bow, and the iron bolt came slamming from the shadows at the far end of the passage, punching through the door panels where Antryg's back had been an instant before. On second look—and Caris *knew* he had seen no one there a split moment before—Caris saw the figure at the turn of the hall near the stair, dapper in its full-skirted dark coat, the pale green eyes wide and gleaming like a cat's in the dark.

Antryg cried, "Magus, no!" as the little dog wizard threw the crossbow aside with a clash on the parquet floor and pulled a double-barreled pistol from his coat.

The Magus hesitated for an instant, grief and shame contorting his white face. He whispered, "I'm sorry, Antryg," and leveled the pistol at his friend's chest.

At the same moment Caris glimpsed a shadow on the staircase behind the Magus, a blurred impression of emerald velvet and straggly blond curls, Joanna in the uniform of one of Cerdic's pages . . . Even as the pistol cocked she had her arm up, and flung something with all her strength at the Magus' back.

Caris heard the tap of it, no louder than if she'd thrown a clot of horse dung, but the result was astounding. The Magus screamed as if she'd thrust a knife in his spine, flung up his arms, and in that one bought second Caris had covered the distance between them. The brief, tangled fight with illusion at the ford was in his mind, and the long agony of the day, as he grabbed a handful of superfine coat front; the hollow crack of the Magus' head hitting the paneling seemed to shake the house.

Downstairs men were shooting.

Antryg flung open the bedroom door. "Come on!"

Caris bent to scoop up whatever it was that Joanna had thrown, even as the girl reached for it; before his hand could touch it he jerked back, realization slamming him like the butt-end of a barge pole in the stomach —he almost threw up with shock. It was the Sigil of Darkness.

Joanna caught it up, shoving it back into its protective lead wrappings and into her backpack as she sprang over Magus' limp body and ran for the bedchamber door. As he followed her, Caris saw the stains of lamp-black on her velvet jacket sleeves—she must have disguised herself as a page to take up the poisoned lamp to the sasenna who lay in wait.

"He would have killed you . . ." She flung a last hurt look over her shoulder as Antryg yanked open the section of dark linenfold paneling near the head of the bed.

"Suraklin," Caris gasped. "He made the Magus a slave—they were all here together . . ."

"Suraklin was *here?!*" In the darkness of the little cubbyhole behind the panel, Antryg's gray eyes flared wide with shock. An instant later he was plunging down the narrow stair ahead of them into blackness, suffocatingly hot from the chimney against which it ran.

"But he couldn't be!" stammered Joanna. "The computer was up . . ."

"It has to be in the house." Caris' shoulder brushed the coarse plaster of the wall as they rounded a turn. "He was out at the circle last night; if you didn't trip over him taking a reading today, this is the only place it *could* be . . ."

Patched coat skirts swirling, Antryg stopped abruptly at the bottom of the stairs, caught Caris by the shoulder, and thrust him against the warm brick of the wall. In the frosty gleam of the witchlight that hung above his head his dilated eyes seemed almost silver. Soft as it was, his deep voice echoed against the close, earth-smelling arch of the low roof. "And did you speak to him?"

Caris shook his head. Even a few days ago he would have been furious at the implied mistrust; now he understood. "They—Suraklin and Leynart—had already gone to the circle on the island when Magus took me. I don't know what they were doing there, whether Suraklin wanted me for bait or to use me, whether he came back here or not . . ."

"Did you eat or drink anything," Antryg asked quietly, "whilst you were there?"

"No." Caris swallowed hard at the evil recollections. "There was bread and water. I threw them away. The room was marked—I had dreams . . ."

Antryg sighed. "So have we all." Turning, he led the way into the narrow, dirt-smelling tunnel that stretched away into darkness before them.

"But if Suraklin was here," Joanna protested, hitching her backpack up onto her shoulders and hurrying at his heels, "the computer *has* to be somewhere near, and not . . ."

"Not necessarily," the wizard said, striding ahead of them, his sheathed sword gripped sasenna-fashion in his left hand. "Theoretically it could be at any node in the lines. The lines—the energy-tracks—used to be called witchpaths, though few remember anymore how to use them. As it happens, Suraklin was one of the few. He could have walked from Kymil to the circle in a night, and walked back in another . . ."

"Kymil!" Leynart's words came back to him, with the glow of the study hearth and the glint of the forgotten gods' watching eyes. "Leynart said Suraklin could get him to Kymil before Pharos reached there. Suraklin gave him a love-charm, a rose . . ."

"Specializing in it these days, isn't he?" inquired Joanna viciously.

Bitterly, he said, "Of course it's to Cerdic's advantage to make sure the Regent has a boy and not a woman in his bed."

"Don't be naïve." Antryg paused at the foot of a steep stair, almost a ladder, his tangled gray curls tugged by the draft from the outer air. "That was a smallpox rose. It's a favorite trick of his. It will trigger an epidemic so virulent it will take out Pharos, Pella, Leynart, most of their household, and a sizable portion of the population of Kymil in the most innocent possible fashion, coincidentally leaving our clean-handed and horrified Cerdic with Regency over his imbecile uncle. When we hit the open air, make for the woods—with luck they'll all be converging on the house." The witchlight that illuminated the tunnel faded; Joanna, who could not see in darkness as Caris could, took a handful of the mage's patched and ragged cloak as they mounted the narrow twist of the hidden stair.

The gardens above them were alive with sasenna. For a moment they paused in the gazebo, like a miniature marble temple with its fluted columns and domed roof, the dancing rush of light from the guards' torches splashing over their faces through the lattice of last year's trellised vines. The woods were over a hundred yards away with no more cover than was offered by the knee-high brown hedges that defined the fallow beds. Caris felt his stomach sink.

"Don't run," murmured Antryg's deep, confident voice. "Stride as if you knew where you were going and make for the woods. With luck they'll take us for other sasenna . . ."

"Are you . . . ?" began Caris, and switched it to, "Not in those robes they won't."

"I'll have a cloaking spell over us—Joanna, you're going to have to keep up. Once someone notices there's something amiss, we can't get the illusion back."

"Sort of like being in love." She grinned wryly and gave her backpack an extra hitch.

"Less painful in the long run," he replied, with the swift flicker of a smile and, cloak swirling, strode down the pink marble steps and across the dark paths of the garden.

They made it less than thirty feet. "There!" shouted a voice. Turning his head, Caris saw Magister Magus come running from the house, twenty sasenna and guards at his heels. "Kill them!"

Antryg grabbed Joanna by the arm, leaped a knee-high hedge, and bolted across a brown sward, Caris running, naked sword in hand, at his heels. Around them in the darkness warriors were plunging out of the gloom, white markings dancing on their black uniforms, pale faces above the grass-green of Cerdic's household troops. Dim starlight flickered across drawn swords, pistol barrels dark with smoking and scratched with the signs of na-aar, the wicked barbed tips of crossbow bolts, closing around them like a tightening noose of razors. From the darkness of the woods far ahead Caris saw others emerging and knew they were trapped.

Seeing their way blocked, Antryg stumbled to a halt; as Caris took his stance beside him, sword in hands, he glanced back and saw the wizard's face in the darkness suddenly haggard and ill. The ring of sasenna was thirty yards away, closing, metal glittering in the moonlight. In Antryg's eyes was the despair of a man whom Fate has defeated against everything that he could do. Wretchedly, he whispered, "Oh, hell." Sheathing his sword, he thrust it into the sash at the waist of his threadbare green coat. "Hand me the flashlight, would you, Joanna?"

Caris, settling into fighting stance in the bitter knowledge of useless death, looked back at him and said, *"What?"*

As calmly as if he were back at the ruined chapel, Antryg was unscrewing the flashlight's bulb, tinkering with the cylinder's innards. In the advancing glare of the torches his eyes, behind their rounds of cracked glass, were invisible, but his mouth, usually flexible and silly as a rubber doll's, was suddenly hard and set.

There was a faint zap and hiss, the whiff of ozone as the batteries sparked . . .

And the spark leaped like tame lightning, tiny, vicious, living, between Antryg's forefinger and thumb.

He held it up before his eyes, the fey purplish light of it for a moment illuminating the lean, ridiculous nose, the tangled hair, the tawdry beads, and the claw-scarred cheekbones that seemed so delicate in that absurd face. Like a physical impact, realization hit Caris and understanding of what was going to happen.

Since he had first met Antryg, when he was a child of six, and later, when he had encountered the genial madman chatting of tortoise-shell rubbings and playing cat's cradle in the Silent Tower, he had known by reputation alone that he was a wizard. Though he had learned magic from him, he had never seen him display power of any kind, save in little things that he himself could do. Insensibly, he had come to think of him chiefly as a scatterbrained and devious lunatic, his maddening mentor, Joanna's lover, cheerfully pursuing a quixotic quest from which he could not hope to emerge alive.

He had almost forgotten that this man had been Suraklin's chosen student.

He remembered it now, as Antryg raised his hand, the spark still flickering, an inch and a half of baby lightning between thumb and finger.

Uncertain, the advancing sasenna slowed their rush. The wind caught Antryg's cloak and coat skirts in a batwing swirl, edged in that crackling glow. Caris, seeing that drawn face, the serene mouth, and the pain-filled, grief-haunted eyes, understood—it was a face of unhuman power, *the most powerful wizard in the world,* Salteris—Suraklin—had said, *including myself* . . .

A voice screamed, "Kill them!" and the ring closed.

Antryg's arm lashed down. As if he had a whip in his hand the lightning elongated, shattering out from his twisted fingers to smite the earth at his feet and show his face like a demented god's in the streaming mane of his gray hair. From the ground, the lightning sprang upward, vicious, living, swelling to a whirlwind in which Caris could see eyes, teeth, whips, claws, too bright to look upon in the exploding darkness. In a column of blinding fire it leaped from earth to sky, the sasenna still rushing toward them, as it was the Way of Sasenna to do, unflinching . . .

Whatever had taken shape within the lightning fell upon them, and the screaming began.

Blinded, shaken, shattered, Caris was aware of nothing else until a hand like an iron claw shut around his arm and he was nearly dragged off his feet by strength he never knew Antryg had. The wizard held Joanna by the other arm, dragging them both at a run within yards of the howling electric maelstrom, through the break in the lines of the sasenna it had caused, and across the huge darkness of the gardens, while the shrieks and cries behind them ripsawed the night. As he ran, Caris caught a glimpse of Antryg's face and saw it was like cut bone, a dead man's face; in his gray eyes was a terrible darkness over half a lifetime deep.

No one pursued them through the woods.

The ford was frozen, the river stilled. Snow lay thinly everywhere on the island, save upon the circle itself; their feet slipped in it as they climbed the graveled slope of the riverbank. Antryg stumbled as they reached the circle, as if all the strength had gone out of him, and leaned against the bluish granite of the outer ring, his face as gray as the stone. He whispered, "They never had a chance."

"Neither had we," Caris gritted through his teeth.

The wizard pressed his gloved hands together against his face, as if by doing so he could still their shaking; a spasm of shuddering wracked him, bowing his whole body. Behind the broken fingers Caris saw the hard glitter of tears.

More gently, he said, "It was them or us."

Antryg nodded, but his wretched sobbing did not cease. He had sinned, Caris knew, in the true sense of the word. Whether it had been necessary or not to protect them long enough to encompass Suraklin's defeat, the fact remained that he had turned his magic upon those unable to defend against it.

"An elemental?" Joanna asked softly, and Caris glanced back at her.

"How did you know?"

"They say Suraklin used to call them. I think he called one to destroy Narwahl Skipfrag, when Skipfrag caught him trying to remove his electrical experiments from his laboratory. From the look of it he used broken glass to clothe it, to make its substance."

Leaning against the stone, Antryg nodded and raised his head as if against the weight of some terrible yoke. "He could use anything," he murmured. "It was the only thing that would—would remain when we had left the area and that Magus couldn't brush aside." His breath blew from his lips in pale steam in the cold traces of glimmering moonlight that were able to pierce the clouds; he had taken off his spectacles. Tear tracks shone on his ravaged face. "They had no magic—most of them probably didn't even believe in it." He was shaking as if naked in a place of bitterest cold.

"You can't think about that," Caris said quietly.

Antryg shook his head, agreeing without the horror or the grief in his eyes abating one degree.

Joanna said softly, "They'll be coming after you now, won't they? The Council can find you . . ."

"Hence the circle." The wizard raised his head again and, with trembling fingers, pushed back the hair from his face. He looked spent, more weary than Caris had seen him except perhaps in the Tower after they'd put the Sigil of Darkness on him, all the colored fires of his absurd courage burned to ash by what he had done. "The other mages will guess I've used the wizard's path, but it will take them a while to guess where I've gone, and longer to follow. It's only a matter of time now, but then it has always been." He moved his shoulders against the cold slab, pushing himself to a standing position once again, his whole body moving slowly, achingly, like an old man's.

"Antryg, listen," Caris said quietly. "You and Joanna have to go to Suraklin's headquarters, wherever it is. I understand that—especially now, while he's in Kymil with Leynart. But Kymil is where I have to go. If what you say about the smallpox-rose is true, I have to stop Leynart before he delivers it. Does one have to be a mage to use the path? Would I have the power . . ."

"No," Antryg said simply. "But it doesn't matter. While the computer was up, Joanna and I came here to the circle and took a bearing along the line. The energy is flowing back to Kymil."

Caris stared at him, digesting this information, the implications sinking in . . . "But we went all through Suraklin's Citadel," he protested. "We looked—*You* looked. That's impossible."

"I know." Antryg replaced his spectacles on his nose, gingerly avoiding the healing wounds of the Dead God's claws. The ghost of his old lunatic grin brushed his lips. "But that's never prevented me from doing things before. Now come—it's growing late."

CHAPTER XVI

THE STRANGEST THING ABOUT TRAVELING THE WITCHPATH WAS that there seemed to be nothing strange about it. Though intensely cold, the night was clear. Only a layer of ground fog clung like white smoke about the feet of the menhirs as Antryg led his two companions across the circle and under one of the great trilithons, and Joanna, clinging apprehensively to Antryg's hand, shivered and looked around her, waiting for the magic to begin.

Only it did not begin. Antryg simply walked, holding her by the hand and Caris by the arm, along the aisle of broken menhirs. Beyond in the darkness Joanna could see the dark shapes of trees and the occasional patches of snow shining faintly through the gloom. A scrim of light clung like a thin frost about some of the stones nearest them; that was all. She wondered if Antryg would be able to overcome his revulsion at what he had done enough to work the magic that would carry them south. But looking up at him, she dared not speak. His face was set and very tired, his eyes seeming to look inward on some pit of haunted memory. The shimmer of the stones caught like starfire in his earrings, on the gimcrack tangle of his beads, and on the tears that still marked his face.

Give him time, she thought, wondering apprehensively how much time they had. *Give him time.*

It was only when they had been walking for twenty-five minutes by Joanna's digital watch and had still not reached the river—at best a hundred feet from the edge of the circle—that she understood. They were on the path already. The magic breathed so softly from the menhirs that neither she nor Caris could detect it. Only Antryg, walking silent between them, knew it was there.

"Can all wizards do this?" Caris asked quietly, and Antryg, at the request for specific information, seemed to rouse himself a little from the dreadful isolation in which he was trapped. "Or could they once?"

"Not all, no." The mage pushed up his spectacles to rub the smudgy circles weariness had painted beneath his eyes. "How to use them for travel was never knowledge held by more than a few, even in the old days before the Battle of Stellith. How they work, what they are, why journeys along them always take the length of the night, provided they are begun before midnight, why one doesn't sleep on the path, and can't do so, in fact, and why at certain seasons of the year they must not be traveled at all . . .

"There are legends, stories, conflicting accounts. I—I sense things about them, as I sense things about the Void, that I can't put into words. But I have no proof."

Joanna looked out beyond the line of light-edged monoliths and wondered where she would find herself if she stepped through one of those weedy gaps. She had, however, no intention of trying. Though the stones leaned tiredly, weatherworn and obviously ruinously old, nowhere did the lines gap, as she remembered them doing in the fields south of Devilsgate. She knew the lines did not run continuously clear to Kymil. Yet from the inside, the track was unbroken. Each stone along the way was individual, shaped and weathered to its own personality; each was cold and damp when she touched it, hard and real under her hand. Weeds grew thickly around them, stiff with frost. They bent and crackled under the brush of Antryg's heavy cape hem, and now and then Joanna could see in the frosted mud of the track other footprints, running on south ahead of them—the footprints of the Dark Mage.

They rested several times during the night, Joanna glad to be relieved of the weight of her backpack. By this time she had become inured to walking, though the cold troubled her; under her thick sheepskin coat, the velvet uniform of Cerdic's page was less warm than her coarse laborer's clothes had been. She felt shaken and depressed, the sight of Suraklin's footprints—Gary's footprints—disconcerting her unexpectedly, reminding her that soon they would meet. She tried not to think about that, about the possibility of defeat and enslavement, or about the possibility of her own death. Throughout the last few weeks, even trapped in the stinking Erebus of the Dead God's church, she had taken comfort in Antryg's presence. He had seldom used his power; but unlike Caris, she had always been conscious of its possibility and in her heart had never really believed in his defeat.

But though gradually the desperate tension of self-hate eased out of his body, she was conscious, through his gloved hand in hers, of his utter weariness. The power he had used to summon the elemental and to clothe it in lightning had left him spent and ill. Not knowing what to say, she only walked close to him, under the vast purple blanket of his cloak, her arm around his waist. After a moment, like a man seeking warmth, his arm tightened around her shoulders.

Freezing cold and nearly as black as the night they had just left, dawn found the three travelers at the nadir of the gaping pit that had been Suraklin's Citadel. Throughout the night Joanna had been prey to fears of what awaited them at the end of the witchpath, entertaining in her mind half a dozen hideous and mutually exclusive scenarios, from entrapment within the Citadel to cosmic rerouting to some distant point.

But when the mists faded around them as they stepped through the gap between the last two menhirs of the line, Joanna saw only the barren sides of the pit funneling up around her, calcined, charred in places, dangling with stiff black stringers of cold-killed vines. Above the vast circle of the pit's lips, the sky was the blackish yellow of an old bruise. The air smelled of snow and of the sickening carrion whiff from the rotting doorways all about the pit's sides. On the ground high above, the wind screamed over the stones. Even down here in relative shelter, it riffled the lead-colored waters of a vast pool of seepage that lay before their feet.

Antryg looked around him, exhausted and baffled, his tangled gray curls shifted by that cutting wind. "It has to be here," he said softly. "Somewhere—hidden so deep Suraklin wouldn't even need to guard the place for fear of drawing attention to it. It *has* to."

"We've been through every pit, every vault, every passage of the few that are left," Caris said, his voice quiet but hard as chipped flint, "and we have proven to ourselves that it *isn't*. If he makes anything like the same time we did, Pharos should be at Larkmoor tonight. Whether you go there or not, Antryg, I'm going to be there to intercept Leynart before he uses that charm of his to trigger a plague."

"Do that." Behind his spectacles, Antryg's eyes seemed to have darkened to smoke color with tiredness, but they studied the young warrior evenly, as if he, like Joanna, realized that, given a choice, Caris placed saving Pella's life above what might be his only chance for revenge upon the man who had murdered his grandfather. But neither commented on the final breaking of his obsession. There was a brittle, desperate quality about the young man now, like a sword blade bent to the snapping point.

Deep and soft as silk velvet, Antryg continued, "Joanna and I will stay here, search once again—there has to be something I've overlooked. If we find nothing . . ." He hesitated, absently rubbing his crooked hands, then went on, his tone carefully neutral, ". . . if nothing finds *us,* we'll sleep the night at the Silent Tower. In the weeks past, I've scried the place by magic. Since my escape, it's been abandoned. If you don't come I'll scry for you . . ." He paused again, as if his mind stumbled over the promise of that casual use of little magic, the muscles in his lean jaw jumping, as if he had carelessly brushed a raw wound. Then he took a deep breath and forced himself to go on. "Good luck."

"Thank you," Caris said quietly. He stood for a time longer, studying his sometime teacher. Joanna could see the hardness of his dark soul armor, an almost visible aura about that muscular, black-clothed form, but his eyes were not the eyes of the young man who had begun the journey north. He had made his choice, whether he articulated it to himself yet or not, that the saving of lives was preferable to the taking of them. "Go carefully, Antryg." His glance moved to Joanna, and he said, "Take care of him," and was rewarded with the ghost of her grin.

Joanna and Antryg watched him as he ascended the long, steep ruin of the old stair to the weed-curtained pit rim above. After his black uniform had vanished against the mottled sky, Antryg stood for some time, head bowed, listening intently while the cold deepened and the wind moved his stained cloak and the gray tousle of his hair. Then he sighed and took Joanna's hand. Together they began again to search the blasted ruin of what had once been his home.

"He'll be here in a few hours," Pella whispered.

"I know." Caris started to rise. "His men were everywhere outside the house."

Her hand on his bare shoulder drew him down again. The muted reflection of lantern light through the ladder hole in the floor snaked along the gilt braid of his coat sleeves, where the garment lay in a heap with Pella's plain brown riding dress. Here in the stable loft the warmth from the horses below collected, though the winds groaned outside; now and then they heard the muffled clunk of a hoof or the distant voices of the grooms cleaning tack at the far end of the stone-flagged passageway. But that was all. Kyssha dozed, Caris knew, like a dropped muff at the foot of the ladder. His arms locked more tightly around Pella's shoulders;

for a time he said nothing, only breathed the thick smell of the hay and the cardamom scent of her hair.

He would have been able to keep his distance from her, he thought, as he had resolved to do, had he only met her in the house. Their situation was impossible, and he knew it. No matter how much he hated the thought—and the hatred of it filled his flesh like slow-burning gunpowder in a flash wound—she was and always would be Pharos' wife. He had no right to come between them, particularly when he himself was very likely to die in the fight against Suraklin. His frantic love did not want to let this girl go, but fairness and caring told him that it would be monstrous to complicate whatever she and her husband would have with the torment of might-have-beens.

But he had found her, wrapped in her many-caped tweed coachman's cloak, silently patrolling the perimeter of the house as they had done together, and all his resolutions had come apart like soaked tissue paper at the first hesitant joining of their hands.

At last he whispered, "We'd better go back to the house. If Pharos is coming this afternoon, Leynart has to be ahead of him. You know none of the Prince's men will keep him out."

Pella nodded, but caught his hand as he moved to get up. She said softly, "I know. And I know we can't let Leynart succeed and unleash a plague, can't let Suraklin rule the country through Cerdic. It's all—the part of me that wants good rulership, the part of me that still wants to follow the Way of the Sasenna. But—there's a part of me that doesn't ever want anything but this."

He brought her hand up to his lips. "Joanna's right," he whispered. "These things have to be done one—one subroutine at a time." As he had hoped, her friend's logic made Pella laugh. "Then we'll see."

It was a lie, and he knew it. He knew now that there was no way he could go on living without her in his life.

But as they crossed the thin, hard snow toward the house, like a powdering of salt on the ground, he remembered the amber glint of Suraklin's eyes and knew also that there was very little likelihood that such a contingency would arise. And that, he thought, caught between his present bounding joy and the black emptiness of the future, was probably just as well.

The Regent's sasenna were in the house when Caris and Pella reached it, slipping quietly in through the kitchen quarters with Kyssha peering inquiringly from beneath the folds of Pella's capes. Caris said, "Is there a back stairs up to the state bedroom? Wearing this—" He touched his black-and-gold coat. "—was enough to get me close to the house, but if the captain gets a look at me, she'll know I'm not one of hers. It would only take one of the servants saying they saw me here with Antryg to destroy everything."

Pella nodded and set Kyssha down, then led the way to one of the several narrow back stairs which allowed servants access to the principal apartments to unobtrusively remove the chamber pots of their betters. As they climbed the enclosed flight, Caris was aware of the subdued turmoil in the house all around them; servants scurried to prepare a meal up to the Regent's exacting standards, and sasenna prowled quietly through the halls. In the great state bedroom, the curtains had been drawn and a forest fire of candles lit. Against the old-fashioned, gilt-edged paneling of the walls, the bed hangings of bronze and pink looked like columns of flowers, the embroidered coverlet like an autumn meadow. Standing before that symbol of dynastic duties, Pella's cheeks reddened as if scalded. Shakily, she began, "Caris . . ."

He put his fingers to her lips. "Don't." Then he took his hand away and put it behind his back, for the touch kindled in him an overwhelming desire to crush her in his arms, drag her to that imperial bed . . .

He looked away from her, confused and hating himself. Hesitantly, stammeringly, not sure that he should even be speaking the words aloud, lest he give them power, he went on, "It isn't that I don't want to help you, Pella. But I can't. I am—sasenna—or at least I was, before I went north. But my determination to follow the Way is leaving me—daily, hourly now, I can feel it going, dripping out of me like wine from a cracked cup. It used to be I could—could take a woman . . . And take her was all I'd do, and a woman was all she was. That's not the same with you. It shouldn't be this way—I shouldn't let it be this way—but it is. I should be out at the Citadel with Antryg and Joanna now, not here, trying to save you—trying to save Pharos . . ."

He was, he realized, asking for her help, as he had not asked help of anyone since he had taken his vows. It was not the Way to do so, not even in small things, physical things, let alone in things that truly mattered, things that were not supposed to matter . . .

Like an echo of his troubled thoughts, he saw Pella's training and her understanding in her eyes. "I know," she said softly. "I'm sorry. If I'd been a true ruler or even a true sasennan, I'd have sent you away myself." She smiled wryly across into his eyes, for they were nearly of a height; her black hair lay thick over the collar of her cloak, like coarse skeins of silk tangled with flecks of hay. Then abruptly she turned away, and preceded him out through the main door of the bedchamber, and into the darkness of the hall.

From the great stairwell, voices could be heard, muffled and distant from the front of the house, and the scurry of feet. A shadow was flung on the dark paneling of the walls—the hall lamps below had been kindled—and there was the quick creak of weight on the stairs. A servant's voice called, "My lady? His Grace's carriage is coming. Shall I send your maid up?"

In the reflected glow, Caris saw the girl's jaw tighten and put his hand on her shoulder. In a voice of forced calm she said, "I—I'd better get myself ready . . ." Her fingers strayed to her tousled hair, the rough tweed cloak still over her shoulders . . .

"We should get a guard in that room," Caris said quietly, like her, hardening himself to speak of commonplaces. "Remember that it won't be enough to find the smallpox-rose. If Leynart touches it he'll be infected, and anyone he touches, according to Antryg. He has to be stopped the moment he enters the room, before he even opens the . . ."

At Pella's heels, Kyssha suddenly raised her pointed muzzle, her feathered ears snapping in the direction of the state bedchamber, and she let out a shrill bark. Pella's eyes and Caris' met for one instant. Then they were both striding back down the hall.

The first thing Caris saw when he flung open the chamber door was the great bed, its coverlet now turned welcomingly back, a red rose lying like a great gout of blood upon the pillows. The second was Leynart, standing beside the embroidered curtains, his speedwell-blue eyes enormous with startlement and alarm. Caris strode forward toward him, calling back to Pella, "Get the tongs and throw that thing on the fire!"

The boy gasped with horror. "No!" He snatched up the rose to his chest and dived across the bed a moment before Caris reached him, plunging into the dark rectangle of the back stairs door and slamming it shut behind him. Caris jerked on the hidden handle, but the door held fast.

At the same moment Pella said sharply, "Listen!" Caris heard the grinding crunch of carriage wheels on the drive outside. He swore, gave the handle one final yank, and nearly overset himself when the inner catch gave way; then he was racing down that dark inner stair, hearing the clatter of high, jeweled heels rattling around the narrow turns ahead of him.

He'd be making for the drive. Caris heard the slam of the door at the bottom of the stairs and swore again, called to mind in midrun that the door did in fact open out into the kitchen, tucked his head and his arm, and hurled himself straight off the steps at it with all the momentum he could summon.

The panels burst but the frame of the door held firm, entangling Caris in a splintery web of shards. Swearing, he managed to get his arm through and fumble free the latch that held it. Behind the heat of his anger at the fatuous Leynart, he felt cold dread, remembering the small-pox epidemic that had swept Innkitar during his first year of training there, the stench of smoke and corpses and the quicklime burial-pits at the streetcorners. Pella could be gotten out of here, but many others would die, either of the disease or of being forced to take to the roads in winter.

The clatter of Leynart's heels on the stone floors of the kitchen quar-ters led him on, and Caris ran lightly, dodging through the big house, knowing the boy was infected already and that he must touch him, must seize him . . .

He heard the boy cry out, "My lord!" like a sob, and burst through the green servants' door into the hall, where Pharos stood among his sasenna and his guards, tiny, glittering, an evil, jeweled doll. His head snapped around at the sound of Leynart's voice, and Caris saw Pellicida beside him, half a head taller, like a crumpled-looking hoyden in her tweed cloak and plain gown with her hair in black handfuls over her shoulders.

Leynart halted for an instant, the poisoned rose still in his hand, as sasenna closed in on Caris from both sides. As his arms were seized and his sword wrenched from his hand, Caris shouted, "My lord, don't let him near you!" and Pharos' pale eyes narrowed.

His mouth trembling, Leynart's eyes darted from Caris to Pella again. "You'd like that, wouldn't you?" He almost spat the words. "You'd like even to take my gifts away from him and most of all the gift of my heart, which he's always had . . ." High heels clicking on the polished floor, he walked forward, like a golden image in his buttercup coat, the rose in his hand. His childlike blue eyes were on Pharos. "Please, my lord, if you must send me away, at least take this, to remember me . . ."

"It's poisoned, Leynart," said Pella quietly.

The boy stopped, his eyes slitting. "You're lying, you frumpy bitch."

But she was sasennan now, not a girl uncertain of Court usages, and the insult slid off her without breaking her serene battle calm. "I wish it were a lie," she said in her deep, husky voice, "because I don't want to see you hurt. But you were tricked. Cerdic was tricked. The rose is imbued with a spell to cause smallpox."

There was a sharp stir, a murmur and a drawing back of Pharos' red-clothed retainers. Pharos himself blanched and backed hastily toward the door.

"You believe her!" Leynart's eyes flooded with tears of rage. "You'd cast me off on her say so!" He whirled on Pella. "If it is you'll never live to have him!" he cried, and flung himself at the girl.

In the split second of confusion, Caris kicked the ankle of the man on his right, jabbing back with his elbow to break his balance, and whirled to snap kick his other captor in the gut. He shouted "NO!" and sprang at Leynart, hands reaching, knowing there was no way he could stop the boy.

In a single fluid movement, Pella had her heavy tweed cloak free of her shoulders and tossed it over Leynart's head. The boy let out a shriek of rage and clawed at the thick fabric as Pella stepped aside, holding a corner of the cloak to further entangle him; the next second Caris caught the muffled figure and foot-swept him to the floor. Leynart ceased struggling almost at once. Under the stifling layers of capes, Caris could feel the slim body shaken with sobs, through which the boy gasped, "Liars! Liars!"

From the safety of the door, the Regent said, "Take him away. Let him be confined in one of the best bedrooms . . ."

"I'd suggest the state bedroom, your Grace," Pella said quietly. "It was where he put the rose originally for you to find."

Other sasenna helped Leynart to his feet, taking care not to touch more than the entangling folds of Pella's cloak. The boy shook his head free, raven curls matted around his face, and tears of bitter frustration tracking the powder on his face with streaks of melting blue. As they led him to the door, he braced his feet and looked back at Pharos, who still hovered in the doorway behind his bodyguards. "My lord, if it's true, I knew nothing of it," he choked. "I—I only wanted your love. You have to believe that."

"If it is true," Pharos said with unwonted gentleness, "I fear that the reason will not much matter, my Ley. If it was false . . ." His pale eyes slid sidelong to Pella close beside Caris. The calm of battle was wearing off her and embarrassment taking over; her brownish skin stained with a blotchy red blush. But she met the Regent's eyes squarely, a warrior, not a confused Princess trying to make herself something she was not.

After a long moment, Pharos asked, "Do you hate me, child?" He spoke as if there was no one else in the room.

"I don't know," Pella said frankly. "You're the ruler and my husband . . . and generally, I *don't* hate people. Even if I did," she added honestly, "I wouldn't say so in public." Then she blushed even hotter, realizing the gaucherie of comparing her own manners with his.

But after a quick flicker of irritation, the Regent's sinful eyes smiled. "Then I shall take an opportunity to ask you the question in private, my little Princess." And as he stepped forward to kiss her hand, Caris faded silently out of the room.

"It has to be there," said Antryg quietly, raising his chin from his elbows, which were crossed over his knees. He had been sitting in much the same folded-up position in one of the crude wooden chairs in the watchroom of the Silent Tower when Joanna had fallen asleep beside the hearth—hours ago, by the grayish quality of the light. That he'd gotten up in that time she knew; the fire had been replenished, and his cloak lay over her like a dilapidated purple horse blanket. But she hadn't heard him. Weariness that she had carried all the way north crushed her, far more than a few hours' sleep would dispel. Like the bitter cold, it had eaten into her bones, and she wondered if she would ever recover from it.

They had found nothing in the Citadel ruins, nothing but the abominations, hiding deep in the dead ends of such of the underground labyrinth as had survived the wizards' wrath and the attenuated dreams of an evil long calcined to nothing. Not even the Church's sasenna watched the place now; they had long deserted the Silent Tower to the darkness of its memories. And so at last, as the day grew colder with the turning of noon and a thin, dry snow began to fall, they had come to the Silent Tower, the only shelter in all the bitter hills.

"All the signs point to it," Antryg went on. "It isn't just that the energy of the lines was flowing to the south to Kymil—dammit, Joanna, it's the only place it *could* have been flowing! I felt it, I knew it was going there! It's other things as well."

She sat up under his cloak, pulling the thick wool around her shoulders, though the watchroom, built into the thickness of the wall off the arched passage of the tower gate, was warm now. On the hearth she saw a tin teakettle and a big pewter tankard which had evidently been pressed into service as a teapot; an earthenware cup rested on the table near Antryg's chair, though no steam rose now from its long-cold contents. He had refused to enter the Tower itself. Though the Sigil of Darkness had weeks since been removed from its door and taken back to the Bishop's treasure house, the walls of the Tower were still thick with spells that prevented the working of magic—thick too, she thought, with evil memories.

Throughout the day, Antryg had been silent. In his eyes she still saw the darkness of the garden at Devilsgate and the blinding refulgence of the elemental springing to life, clothed in the lightning he'd given it to destroy those whose only defense was metal swords. The memory lay on him like the brown scar left by the Sigil of Darkness that marked his throat among his tattered shirt ruffles, but it was a pain that it would take more than a carbide hacksaw to remove.

He went on, "It's the logical place for it, you know. Yes, the Church has watched it from a distance, but seldom closely, I'll wager. Everyone else would have shunned it. And though there were abominations near the Tilrattin node in the north, they weren't anything near as plentiful as there."

"That's because the woods wouldn't concentrate them like the pits did," Joanna pointed out.

"Even given that," he insisted, "there are still more—many times more. I never felt—easy—going to look for it elsewhere. Everything points to the old Citadel. It *has* to be there. I know it. I feel it."

Joanna pushed aside her backpack, which she'd been using for a pillow, and poked at the rock-hard jerky and waybread Antryg had dug from what remained of the guardroom stores. "That's neither here nor there," she said reasonably. "We've looked twice, and it's *not.*"

"Neither here nor there," the wizard repeated ironically, leaning back in his rickety chair and hugging his knees again. "From here to Tilrattin and back—from your world to mine—neither here nor there . . ." He paused, his gray eyes suddenly sharpening behind his spectacles; then he sat up straight, unfolding his long legs to the floor. "Neither here nor there!"

His eyes met Joanna's. For a time the silence in the guardroom was so intent that the silken *whump* of the log crumbling in the hearth sounded loud and individual beneath the chaotic drone of the wind in the passage of the gates outside. Doubtfully, Joanna said, "A—a vest-pocket dimension?"

His eyes widened. "You know of such things?"

"They're in all the comic books."

"Actually, a sort of enclave between universes, like a bubble in the fabric of the Void. They sometimes occur, but they're fairly short-lived because the movement of the Void pulls them apart. But now that I think of it, your universe and mine have been in phase for a long time, and certainly energy is being drained from both."

"Could he make something like that? Or find it?"

"Found, probably, and is shielding in some fashion to keep the dimensions together indefinitely and to keep me from being aware of it." He leaned forward, and the grief that had haunted him for the last twenty-four hours faded from his eyes in the daft glow of a theorist's enthusiasm. "You see, I'm the only person I know who can 'cast through' the Void— see things on the other side, touch its fabric with my mind. Suraklin never could; though he can cross it at will, he has no sense of how the Void operates. It is actually a rather specialized field of knowledge. Many wizards have them, some of them completely useless, like the ability to summon frogs or sculpt the wind. But all the same . . ."

"Could you find it?"

He shook his head. "That's the trouble. Before I can see through the spells of unseeing that guard it, I'd need to know what it looked like, know its shape and boundaries, even as I have to know what the Gate to it looks like before I can see it. And, of course, such things exist only in Suraklin's mind."

Joanna looked up at him, feeling inside her such a blaze of illumination that she wondered her flesh didn't glow. Her voice was not quite steady as she said, "No they don't." With shaking fingers, she reached out and touched her grubby backpack. "If he's programming it, he can't do it in patterns—only linearly. And I've found graphics programs in here, mathematical equations that translate into three-dimensional shapes—or four-dimensional ones. The human mind can't really picture a four-dimensional shape, but a computer doesn't give a damn whether a thing is supposed to be able to exist or not . . ."

"Rather like wizards," Antryg mused, "or madmen. Are all computers insane?"

Joanna hesitated, disturbed by the question for reasons she'd preferred not to examine, and the wizard went on, "Can you graph those equations? Give me a picture of it?"

She nodded, shivering all over with suppressed excitement. "It's really only reverse engineering. I'll need graph paper."

"There's paper in the Tower. Lines can be drawn on it."

"It'll take a hell of a long time. If I'd known I'd have brought my calculator . . ."

"I had a set of calculating bones—little slips of ivory about the size of your finger with numbers on them. They're probably still up there. A mathematician in Mellidane showed me how to use them. They work very quickly."

He got to his feet, collected his cloak from around her shoulders, and started for the watchroom door. Then he stopped, came back to her, and seized her in a fierce hug of mingled joy and desperation, his face pressed against her hair. Her arms went around his waist, being careful of the rib he'd cracked during his encounter with the Dead God. For a long moment, they stood so, while she thought, *This is going to be it. We're really going to have to deal with Suraklin this time.* The thought left her weak with dread.

Then he was gone, striding across the courtyard in the failing light with all his old gawky insouciance, the snowy wind whipping his cloak and coat skirts into lunatic billows about his thin form and fraying at his long gray hair. Watching him go, Joanna felt a stab of grief and the burn of tears behind her eyes; for all his height, his loose-limbed strength, and his scatterbrained cheerfulness, it came to her how fragile he seemed. She understood, suddenly, Suraklin's obsessive desire to preserve the things in his life as they were, to hold to those joys no matter who else suffered for them, and to keep the taste of them on the tongue, so they would not slide away into the fast-flowing darkness of time. She forced the feeling down, telling herself, *One thing at a time.* Caris was right. There were some times when it did not pay to think too much.

Shaken inside, she sat down by the hearth again and began digging through the DARKMAGE files for the four-dimensional equations whose significance she hadn't understood and whose importance, at the time, had seemed to her to be neither here nor there.

It was long past dark when Caris returned to the Silent Tower. Had he not been mageborn and able to see in the dark, he doubted he could have found it at all, for not even stars pierced the black sheet of clouds that covered the sky from horizon to horizon. To his mage's sight, the Tower loomed queerly against the ebon backdrop, black within black, utterly untouched by light. The wind had risen, driving the hard little pellets of snow like a sandstorm against his cheeks; the cold ate through his tunic, jacket, and cloak as if he had worn nothing but a thin shirt of cotton lawn. Nevertheless, he circled the Tower twice, observing the ground and the walls, seeking for a sign. It was only when he climbed the rear wall with the hook and line of the standard sasenna's equipment which he'd gotten from Pella that he saw the blue glow of witchlight from the watchroom's slit windows and the faint shiver of heat above the chimney, before the wind whirled the smoke away.

If they were here, he thought, they had not found Suraklin at the Citadel after all. His heart turned sick inside him. Another time of search, then; how many more weeks of forcing himself to be what he no longer was, of warming himself at a revenge that had grown cold, and of waiting to die?

But it would have been worse, he knew, to have returned and found them not there.

His feet made no more noise than did his shadow as he crossed the court. He stood in a lee angle of the gatehouse passage and listened until he heard Antryg's deep, beautiful voice before slipping up to the door.

Before he could raise his hand to knock, he heard Antryg say within, "Ah, there's Caris." There was the scrape of a chair, and the door opened to the cool brilliance of witchlight and the warmth of the fire. Caris reflected that there were times when he wanted to hit the wizard up alongside the head with the hilt of his sword.

He said dully, "It's done. I got there in time—Leynart's under guard, and they know about the rose."

Joanna looked up from the vast graph spread across the table—a bed-sheet, in fact, ruled with penciled lines, on which she was marking dots in the midst of half a dozen wax scribbling tablets that were covered with mathematical formulae in the spiky little numbers her people used. "And Pella?"

"She's gone back to Pharos." Caris stripped off his cloak and jacket and folded himself up beside the hearth, his arms crossed before his chest. There was hard bread and dried beef there. He realized he hadn't eaten all day, save for a few mouthfuls of bread and ham Pella had stolen for him from the kitchen, but didn't care.

Joanna set down her pencil, startled and aghast. "Pharos . . ."

Roughly, Caris said, "It doesn't matter. It's better. There was nothing for us."

Except joy, he thought, leaning his forehead against the stones of the hearth and closing his eyes, feeling the warmth of the fire like the brush of Pella's fingers on the lids. *Except joy.*

Behind him, Antryg said quietly, "We've found Suraklin."

"Good," Caris mumbled. He lay down and drew his cloak over him. *At least,* he thought, *it will then be over.*

And on that thought he slept.

He was wakened by grief, dull and uncaring, beyond even the effort of tears. Pella was gone, and it seemed to him that even his pursuit of Suraklin was futile, a waste of his time, a fool's errand. Opening his eyes he saw wet grayish light seeping through the watchroom windows that let into the courtyard, making the small chamber seem dim and frowsty, with its stink of old smoke and wet clothes. The vast graph spread over the table was now covered with arcane lines and symbols, with scribbled marginal calculations half-hidden by tablets, by the disgorged contents of Joanna's precious backpack, and by Antryg's little ivory calculating bones. Under the grubby curtain of her straggling blond hair, Joanna's face looked thin and old, as it had by the candle light of the pos-tinghouses on their journey south, ravaged by lack of sleep and weari-ness, the sharpness of her cheekbones and chin emphasizing the awkward nose and the shrew lines around her eyes. She was looking at the strange magic watch that was strapped to her wrist. Antryg, sitting on the bench beside her, seemed strangely subdued.

She said quietly, "It's nine in the morning."

The wizard glanced across at her, his fingers, as if idling away from his conscious thought, beginning to make a corral of his mathematical ivory bones. "There have been daylight spells before."

"Not on weekdays. This is Tuesday, Antryg; if Suraklin was still being Gary, he'd have to be at work. He needed to stay working so he could program on the San Serano computer. The fact that he isn't means he's done with that."

The sleep cleared from Caris' mind, but left it still muzzy, as if he were half-drunk. He realized that his depression and grief were not solely his own. "You mean he's gone into his computer." He sat up, scrubbing his fingers through his cropped blond hair, wondering why it didn't matter to him that they had lost their race with the Dark Mage.

Joanna nodded. "I think so." She began folding up her papers, mechanically, as she always did, like a task she was forcing herself to perform. Her eyes were dull; she looked beaten, wretched, and badly scared. "I hate to say it, guys—but I think the system just went on-line for keeps."

CHAPTER XVII

UNDER A CUT-STEEL MORNING SKY, WHAT WAS LEFT OF THE CITADEL of Suraklin lay cold and bleak, the puddles of slush frozen, and skiffs of hard, powdery snow blowing restlessly over ground barren now of any living thing. Save for those ghostly flurries, even the snow did not lie here, though it blotched the hills all around with white. Joanna, hugging Antryg's patched purple cloak around her, wondered if Hell would look like this after Judgment Day—inhabitants gone, Devil destroyed, even the glamour of evil burned out of it, leaving nothing but a few lines of stones that stank of forgotten corruptions.

Beside her, Antryg looked ghastly in the dun-colored light. "Can you feel it?" he whispered.

Joanna nodded, though she was not certain what it was that she did feel. Her mind felt clouded, dulled with the now-familiar uncaring depression of the energy drain; but added to that was a hideous sense of wrongness, as if she might extend her hand and push it inadvertently through the structure of the universe itself.

"He's weakened the whole fabric," Antryg said softly. "The enclave is being maintained from moment to moment now by the computer's power, by the energy relays. It's unstable; where it touches, this universe is unstable as well." He spoke barely above a whisper, as if he feared that too loud a sound would shatter the very semblance of reality around them. Wind stirred his hair and swirled the long skirts of his coat; a foot from him, Joanna felt none.

Something caught her eye, and she whirled, her heart in her throat.

She thought she had seen something near one of the old pits, scraggly with wet stones and frozen slush, but there was nothing . . . or . . .

Try as she would, she could not focus her eyes on the place. It was like a puzzle with pieces missing, though she could not describe what was preventing her from seeing the spaces in between.

"Yes," Antryg murmured. "There are abominations here."

"Let's get this over." In spite of the day's freezing wind, a rime of sweat glittered on Caris' face. His long sword flashed naked in his hand, cold in the daylight like a living thing; it was his eyes that seemed dead.

"It will be in the pits." There was no doubt now in Antryg's deep voice. "In the bottommost room, at the center of his ancient power. It's fairly easy to see something invisible, if you know what you're looking for, have a picture of it, as the graphic program delineated it. My dear . . ."

For an instant Joanna seriously considered giving Antryg a quick rundown on how to input programs from floppies to mainframe, then stopped herself. Experience had taught her that whatever could go wrong with a computer would, even ones that didn't house the corroding souls of dead wizards. Though her own soul felt dead within her, she knew intellectually that she still loved this man and that he'd need her help. After several nights of little or no sleep, he looked like ten miles of bad road; if he felt anywhere near as bad as she did, he would, she told herself, need all the help he could get.

Trying to keep the whimper of fear out of her voice, she said, "Once I program the worm in, we'll have five or ten minutes. That's how long it would take that program to wipe the whole Cray at San Serano—ops, systems, everything."

"All right." He was glancing all around him as he spoke, his long nose pointing like a nervous dog's, the diamonds in his earlobes flashing like nuggets of dirty ice. "That will give us time to get out before the enclave itself collapses. Presumably, you can't tell which programs will be the first to be devoured, so there is the chance that we—won't make it out."

Joanna swallowed. During the spells of deadness, she always felt anxious—the anxiety now had intensified to a wretched sense of almost-panic in which she wanted only to do whatever she had to do *quickly* and then run away, run to safety . . . She said in a tiny voice, "You mean—die?"

His gray eyes were somber, looking down into hers. "I don't know—but probably not. There's a good chance," he added carefully, "that, though the enclave will seal up once the power goes down, Suraklin won't die. He will only exist in the enclave, unable to touch either of our worlds again, but . . . his consciousness may remain."

Joanna whispered, "Oh, swell." *No Exit,* she thought: the Sartre play about the damned sealed into a room with those who understood them all too well, for all eternity.

"So when you get your program input, I suggest you run like hell. It's certainly what I'll be doing."

She thought, *I'll never make it.* Antryg, with his longer legs, might. The door would close between them, and she would be Gary's—Suraklin's—forever . . .

With the hideous sensation of plunging down a limitless elevator to nowhere, she stumbled after Antryg and Caris toward the brink of the monster pit.

"Antryg . . ." Caris whispered, his voice fading to nothing.

Antryg turned his head, to follow the young man's eyes. A ragged stringer of ground mist whirled aside, and Suraklin stood before them at the head of the broken stair.

Joanna's throat felt as if it had been shut with a valve.

Whatever else Suraklin was now, he was not Gary anymore.

It was Gary's body, Gary's jeans and jacket and Nikes under the black cloak of a Council wizard. Even the face, she supposed, was still Gary's, though the expression had changed it so completely that she was no longer certain she would recognize the man she had once made love to, years ago on a hot Los Angeles night. There was nothing left of that slightly vapid, good-natured selfishness, amoral and greedy without being actively offensive to anyone. Nothing left at all. The lines of the cheeks and around the brown eyes with their queer golden luster were the lines of age, age infused by driving will and a single overmastering purpose.

Suraklin smiled, like something wound with a key. "Antreges." His voice, nothing like Gary's now, softened the hard g of Antryg's name into a diminutive, the name of the boy he had known. "Like the windrose on a map, you point in all the directions of the wind—but I did suspect you'd finally point your way back here, to your home, to me. Babe . . ." His eyes touched Joanna, the nickname turning her stomach. "Do you think, if I can make a roulette wheel stop on red or summon lightning, I can't degauss a disk? You're just not thinking, babe . . ." As Joanna gasped, sickened with shock, the brown eyes moved to Caris, the inflection of the voice shifting again. "My son."

The sasennan began, "You dare . . ."

At the same instant, Antryg whirled utterly without warning, caught

Joanna by the shoulders, and flung her to the ground. Lightning seared up like a blue-white snake striking from the earth as he dived on top of her. Caris, his breath and attention momentarily diverted in anger, wasn't so quick. The lightning flung him a dozen feet, its earsplitting crack drowning his final cry. It was over before Antryg had time to react. Her face in the dust, her nostrils filled with ozone and the stink of burned flesh, Joanna was still nearly blinded by an explosion of light that seemed to ignite the very air. She felt Antryg spring to his feet and wisely stayed where she was; his coat skirt brushed her face briefly and that soft, flexible voice whispered, "Get under cover and keep hold of the backpack." Then he was gone, his footsteps thudding through the ground in her ear.

Even faced with death, the effect of the energy drain made her want to stop and argue—the backpack was too heavy, the disk it contained was now useless, Suraklin had said so . . .

Do it by the numbers, she told herself fiercely. They'd been standing near a shallow subsidence. She rolled over and over, nearly blinded through her shut eyelids. The ground dropped away beneath her and broken masonry dug into her ribs through her heavy coat as she skidded down. The searing white glare seemed to sicken and purple; raising her head a little, she could see Suraklin with his head down, squinting against the light. Antryg, sword in hand, was within thirty feet of him by the time the Dark Mage could see enough to use the implement he had whipped out from beneath his cloak.

Quite sensibly, somewhere along the line, Suraklin had acquired a submachine gun.

Joanna had to clamp her hands over her mouth to keep from screaming. Antryg flung himself down, sliding and rolling, his sword screaming in a steel arc toward Suraklin's ankles. Bullets stitched the dust in front of him. He jerked and twisted like a cat flung in water, diving for the minimal cover of a broken wall; the glaring, unnatural light faded as he let the spell slip from his mind. It had served its purpose, but he had been just too late.

"Really, my dear," Suraklin said, amused. "You used to be quicker than that."

"Old age comes to us all." Antryg was moving already, flattened to the single broken course of stones, though Joanna thought his voice still seemed to come from where he had first gone to ground. He'd done voice-throwing, she remembered, as one of his dog-wizard tricks to earn supper when they'd first traveled the post road from Kymil to Angelshand during the summer. Behind the truncated wall, there wasn't much of anyplace to go, but already she could see the dead weeds around the place begin to smoke and wither as if under blasting heat.

"Not to me, my love. Never to me."

Antryg had reached the limit of the wall. He lay crushed to the ground, to keep from Suraklin's line of sight; Joanna could see blood black on the dull green of his coat sleeve, the sweat of concentration beading his face. "No," he said. "Nor youth, either, nor warmth, nor cold. Don't you understand yet what you've done to yourself?"

The snout of the gun never wavered from the wall. The bare ground was blackening there, the dead weeds starting to smoke inches from Antryg's feet. A counterspell, Joanna guessed, held the burning at bay, but for how long?

"Indeed I do. What you see is only what our little Joanna would call a waldo, operated by my mind at a distance. Now that I've taken steps to put Pharos out of the way for good, I'll have plenty of them. Cerdic will see to that. But the mind is not in any of them. I have made myself immortal."

"You have made yourself like the Dead God."

Suraklin's brows came together, his voice sharp. "Nonsense!"

"The Dead God isn't immortal," Antryg pressed. "The Dead God is dead. Without feeling, without caring, even for himself—without changing. More stagnant than the very stones, which transmute from rock to air and sand. What do you have, Suraklin, that makes you want to continue? As a computer, as a metal thing of electricity and knowledge, what do you want? *Are* you Suraklin anymore? Or have you become like Joanna's Xerographs, a fourth-generation copy of what you once were, with each copy a little less legible than the last, a little more mixed in with other peoples' minds? What is deathlessness on those terms?"

Around her, Joanna was conscious of the smell of dust, rising from the ground as if blown by imperceptible wind. She fought to stifle a choke, but found the air increasingly thick with it, grayish, stifling, clogging her breathing and burning her eyes. A gust of wind cleared it a little. Through it, she saw Antryg's face taut with concentration, fighting the spell of the dust's suffocation. The heat around the wall was still intense; she could feel it, even at this distance, on the unsteady wind. A computer is capable of millions of operations per second; she wondered how many subroutines constituted a spell, and how many spells could be maintained by a computer as opposed to a man.

"I was in the Silent Tower for years, Suraklin," Antryg went on. "I risked death to win my freedom. But you have walled yourself into a tower from which there is no escaping."

Suraklin laughed. "Are you tired, my love? You're older than I am, now . . . Trying to talk me into surrender, when you know you cannot defeat me by magic? I suggest you save your breath—I can outlast you, you know. Entropy always wins. I will still be here, waiting for you, when your concentration begins to crack from starvation or weariness— just how many spells *can* you hold off? Shall we see?"

Antryg's hand moved, flinched as if with sudden cramp; Joanna saw his face contort with pain. The wind faltered, the dust almost suffocating her. A moment later something stirred in the thick grayness, like a whirl-wind rising from a slush pool between the buckled pavement of the old court, droplets of slime shivering into the air, half-forming into the shape she recalled from the electric darkness of the Devilsgate garden. The countering wind died. Through a curtain of silt, she saw Antryg gather himself together for a rush that would take him under the muzzle of the waiting gun.

Then she saw Caris move. His face was white where it wasn't smeared with mud, twisted with pain, but the hand that held his .45 was com-pletely steady. Suraklin turned his head in the same instant that Antryg yelled, "NO!" With a shattering crack of flame the gun blew up in Caris' hand.

Caris screamed, doubling his body over the ruined bone and bleeding flesh; Antryg was already moving. One sword stroke severed Suraklin's right hand where it held the Beretta's trigger before the Dark Mage could bring the gun back to bear on him. At the same moment, Antryg backfisted the Dark Mage across the face with his other hand, sending him staggering back. Suraklin swung around, as if blood weren't pouring from the stump of his right arm and his shattered nose, and with the heavy lock of the gun, still clutched by the left handgrip, cracked Antryg across the temple.

Antryg fell to his knees, a yard from the edge of the chasm that had been the Citadel vaults. Before he could raise his sword again, Suraklin swept the spouting stump of his arm through the air, and the blood itself whirled—red, hideous, multiplying—into the form of an elemental that plunged down on Antryg in a reeking wave.

White light stabbed like a laser beam from Antryg's bony fingers as he sprang back. The elemental dissolved before it in a torrent of flying gore, even as the pit edge gave and crumbled under Antryg's boots. He tried to catch himself, but Suraklin was upon him, wreathed now in fire, his single hand weighted with the gun flashing through the air to crack like an iron club on the side of Antryg's skull.

Antryg clutched at the brittle weeds on the edge as he went over; then even his shabby half-gloved hand slithered from sight.

Blood streaming from his severed arm, Suraklin stood looking down into the pit. "That was very foolish, my darling," he said. Joanna's heart lurched into beating again—Antryg had to be holding onto some projection, some ledge, not too far down the abyss. He was alive—and just for the moment she wasn't going to have to cope with the Dark Mage alone.

Suraklin's back was to her. She could hear Caris still moaning faintly where he lay among the broken, weed-grown pavements, remembered his scream as the gun exploded in his hand and thought detachedly, *Thank God I decided against explosives.* Had that been a general spell, she wondered as she dug the .38 and the Sigil of Darkness from her backpack, or only against Caris, because Suraklin had seen him? She was shaking so badly she could barely tear the Sigil's lead wrappings free or hold the gun straight. One shot, she knew, was all she'd get, if she got that much. After that, she reflected in weirdly wry terror, he could not help but notice her.

The Dark Mage hitched the submachine gun under his arm, switching his left hand from the grip to the trigger. "Killing this body won't do you any good, you see."

Joanna braced the .38 in both hands, straightened her elbows and took time to align the sights as carefully as she had done during her few practice sessions; she pressed the round lead plaque of the Sigil tight against the lock as well as she could while keeping her fingers clear of the cylinder flash. It seemed to take forever; blood and terror pounded in her head, an almost palpable roaring noise that she was certain Suraklin had to hear. The first night Gary had kissed her flitted briefly through her mind, and her elation that for the first time in her life someone found her desirable.

Suraklin—Gary—braced his weapon under his arm, to aim down. "There's plenty of time left before it bleeds to death to . . ."

Here goes nothing, Joanna thought, and squeezed the trigger.

She saw the explosion of bone and hair and brain shatter outward as the automaton that had been first Gary, and then Suraklin, bowed forward and fell into the pit.

Dust still hung heavy in the air as she stumbled to the edge, still clutching her backpack and the gun. She sensed a shifting somewhere in it, not far off, and remembered that there were abominations about, drawn to the smell of blood. *Caris,* she thought desperately, but did not swerve aside to where the dying sasennan lay.

Blood was puddled everywhere on the lip of the pit, steaming faintly in the cold air. Her head ached with the weight of the drained weariness that clutched her soul. Her hands, as she fumbled at the pocket of her backpack for the nylon rope, seemed to belong to someone else. And what, after all, she wondered bleakly, would it matter? Suraklin had been right. Killing him—killing Gary, or what was left of Gary—had done no good. The disk was wiped, and she knew that, while the computer was running, she'd never be able to maneuver through the long and complicated process of putting together another worm.

And the computer would run forever.

Tears of despair nearly blinded her as she peered down. There was no dust below the level of the ground. She could see Antryg clearly, pressed flat to what had once been the wall of some vaulted room. One hand gripped about three inches of what had been ceiling molding; the other spread out over a sharply sloping piece of stone that offered little if any purchase. One boot toe was wedged into the remains of a broken capital. Below his heels gaped a hundred and fifty feet of straight nothing, with Gary's body lying smashed like a road-kill at the bottom.

Her hands shaking, she made a loop in one end of the rope and stumbled back four or five feet to wrap the other end around the nearest broken rocks. Things were moving in the dust, converging on them—abominations, she thought, for they lacked the deadly speed of elementals. But that, she knew, would come soon. Antryg's over-stretched concentration couldn't keep them at bay forever. She had killed the Dark Mage's last body, but he was far from dead.

Antryg came scrambling, gasping, up the rope, crushed her in one fast hug, and planted a kiss on her sweat-soaked hair, even as he was dragging her toward the matted weeds which hid the broken stair. "Caris . . ." she began, and he shook his head.

"There's nothing to be done," he said hoarsely. "We have a few moments now when Suraklin can't see us, when he must marshall his influence on the minds of whatever he can—the abominations, for a guess—to stop us. Before he does . . ."

"But it's no good!" She balked, her feet sliding on the ice that had turned the broken rubble of the hidden stair to treacherous glass. "Antryg, Suraklin was right! It wouldn't take anything to demagnetize the disk; you can do it by leaving one too near the telephone! There's nothing we can do in there!"

He stopped on the slippery track below her, looking up; in spite of its coating of dust and grime, his face seemed suddenly very white in the frame of his unruly hair. "Are you positive it's blanked?"

She shook her head, the stringers of her wet hair trailing against her numbed cheeks. "But it's Suraklin's logical move."

He took a deep breath, as if bracing himself, then nodded. Sweat tracked down through the dust on his face, and Joanna realized that, dead though Suraklin's latest body might be, his magic still lived, pressing against Antryg's hard-held counterspells with the relentless patience of a computer. It was only a matter of time, she thought, until the human wizard tired, and then . . .

He said, "All right. Give me your backpack and get as far away from here as you can. If this deadness doesn't end, it will mean I've failed. Find the other wizards of the Council, tell them everything, make them believe you. If it does, find them anyway . . ."

"What about you?"

His gray eyes shifted away from hers, behind their cracked rounds of glass, then returned, after a moment. "Whatever happens, my life is forfeit," he said quietly, his long fingers closing around the dirty webbing straps of the backpack. "If it wasn't when I broke out of the Tower, it has been from the moment I summoned the elemental to hold Cerdic's warriors at bay. I don't know whether I'll succeed or fail, but once I go into that enclave, I won't be coming out."

She heard it as if from some great distance, her soul numbed by exhaustion, terror, and the leaden ache of the energy drain. He started to move off down the ruined stair again, and she tightened her grip on the packstraps, holding him back. "What are you going to do?"

"Put the Sigil of Darkness where the teles-relay feeds into the electrical converter. It will break the flow of the magic and seal off the enclave."

"With you in it," Joanna said. "Imprisoned alone with Suraklin, forever." It had, she realized, been his backup plan from the first.

He looked away again, his face contorting with momentary pain. "I can't think about that now, Joanna," he said softly. Desperation shivered in his deep voice. "Now let me go. We've wasted too much time already —every second he'll be rallying new defenses, and I don't know how long I'll be able to hold them at bay. Can't you feel the spells around us now? It'll be worse within the dimensional enclave. If my concentration breaks, we'll both go up like touchwood."

"And the minute your fingers touch the Sigil," she returned, "all your defenses will vanish anyway, won't they?" Cold panic and the scorch of adrenaline stifling her, she drew the backpack from his hands and slung its familiar weight once more onto her shoulder. "Let's get this over with."

The entrance to Suraklin's enclave opened directly above the black pool in the stone chamber of his ancient power. Joanna couldn't see it at all until Antryg reached out over the water and touched it; then it flared into smoky life in the darkness, more like an optical illusion, a trick of mirrors and light, than a real gateway. The burning, unnatural glare of the witchlight that he'd called added to the sense of surreality. Through the clotted darkness of the labyrinths they had heard the lumbering, slurping tread of abominations, closing on the place, tracking them by the scent of their blood, and only the searing radiance of all the light that Antryg could summon had held them at bay. His sword was gone, lost somewhere in the frozen, weedy rubble of the pit where it had fallen when he'd gone over the cliff edge; with the abominations gathering and Antryg's face growing grayer and grayer from the strain of the tireless spells bearing down upon him, there had been no time to search. Even maintaining the light, Joanna sensed, was taxing him, draining his strength like a cut artery. His hand was shaking as he sketched a glowing sign on the wall of the underground chamber.

"When I tell you to run," he said, "run for this. Don't distract me, don't interrupt me—do exactly as I command. All right?"

She nodded, the fear in her growing, swelling—fear, and the sense that there was something she was forgetting, some detail knocking at the back of her mind . . .

He sprang lightly to the threshold of the gate, his boots resting on the glowing surface that seemed to be no more than a projection in the air. Her heart beating heavily, positive she was going to end up falling through into the accursed pool, Joanna reached across, twined her small fingers in the bone and grubby leather of his hand, and jumped.

It was deathly cold within Suraklin's enclave. This didn't surprise Joanna, in view of the physical preferences of computers, but it depressed her further and weighted her down with a physical exhaustion, as if her very body were unable to produce enough heat, enough life, to keep her going. There was a noise there, too, a kind of whispering hum that tugged oddly at her attention. She sensed the presence all around them of unseen forces, the shift of the stone walls—or were they stone?—in the darkness that stopped the moment she turned her head, and the tingle on her skin that made her wonder in terror what would happen if Antryg's concentration on his protective spells broke. Once she smelled a burning, a spot of itching on her thigh that swelled suddenly to searing heat. In numb panic, she pressed her hand over it as hard as she could, not daring to speak for fear of distracting Antryg's mind and making things worse; in a moment the heat passed. *We'll both go up like touchwood,* he had said, and panic sweat rolled down her sides under the dirty sheepskin of her coat and the green velvet jacket underneath.

Then the darkness opened out before them. It swallowed the beam of Joanna's repowered flashlight, which she'd turned on to save Antryg's strength; a vast chasm stretched in all directions, colder than the bitterest of the Sykerst nights. Faint and bluish, a glow rose from the double ring of globes on the floor, some of them no larger than a good-sized grapefruit, others the size of soccer balls; around and between them, like a monster web of brass, glass, and scribbled Sigils of Light, lay the apparatus Dr. Narwahl Skipfrag had invented for converting the ambient energy of life into electricity. The wires spread like weed runners along the floor, interspersed with Sigils and marks written in light, so that the web seemed to sink into the physical fiber of the place itself. Joanna had a sense of those veins of power fanning out over the walls and ceiling of the place, if there were any, hidden in the darkness. And eerily like the trilithons on Tilrattin Island, in the center rose the tripart bulk of what Joanna recognized from articles as an experimental fiber-optic superconductor Cray Three, undoubtedly the one which was rumored to have dropped out of sight early in the year from the Alta Clara Research labs —harder to steal than the 250-odd microcomputers necessary to make up a parallel-process Cube, but far easier to program. Like a vast monolith behind it rose the biggest power conditioner Joanna had ever seen.

Joanna whispered, "Damn!"

"What is it, my dear?"

The whispering in her mind was growing stronger, and with it was the sense of a half-guessed pattern, like an optical illusion of negative space— do you see a lamp, or do you see two faces?

And whose faces?

"It's a UPS—an Uninterrupted Power Source—a backup battery. It means that, even when we pull the plug, the computer itself will be up for at least a day, maybe more. We'll be able to get out . . ."

"But his spells will continue. And he'll be able to summon reinforcements."

Joanna walked forward, her heart slamming against her ribs, loathe to step across the teles-ring. Wan and blue, their sickly light was worse than darkness; as she passed between them, she felt a cold sense of evil, as if she heard the tittering whisper of laughter in the darkness beyond the reach of any light. Her mouth dry, she whispered, "I'm going to check the disk. You start pulling the leads out that connect the power conditioner with the spare battery packs—those small boxes stacked beyond it.

They're to give it still more running-time if the power goes down. Just unfasten the clips and pull the plugs out . . ."

Antryg moved to obey, his flowing robe and longskirted coat incongruous against the hard-edged metal and plastic, his face set now and lined with intolerable strain. Near the chair before the computer's central monitor, a single teles sat in its copper housing, the focal point of the vast spiderweb of wires and leads. It was by no means the largest; Joanna could have closed her two hands over it, had she dared. But nothing in the world could have induced her to touch the thing. She didn't know why she felt that it was aware of her, watching her; old, far older than Suraklin, it was far more evil—and alive.

Her hands were shaking as she pulled the flat disk box from her backpack. She dropped it twice before she got it open, sweat streaming down her face in spite of the intense cold. And all the while in the back of her mind, that whispering suspicion nagged at her, the feeling of being faced with a quadratic equation, with two solutions . . .

She managed to get the disk in the drive, trying not to think about the process of bringing it up, and let her hands go through the motions automatically.

The disk was blank.

Resolutely, aware that the computer was Suraklin and might be lying about it, she tapped through the entry sequence, but the machine made no sound.

Then, before her eyes in the darkness of the screen, the green words formed up:

WELCOME, JOANNA.
I HAVE WAITED A LONG TIME FOR HIM TO BRING YOU TO ME.

Rage hit her like a falling wall. Betrayal, grief, horror, realization, and fury at herself for not seeing that she had been led all along, tricked into coming to this single place that she had most feared, deceived into walking into Suraklin's hands at last. Hate exploded in her as she swung around in her chair, her hand diving blindly for her backpack, coming up with the .38.

He had been Suraklin's servant from the first.

The crash of the gun was like thunder in the vast darkness. The bullet took Antryg in the side, knocking him back against the power conditioner—Joanna had not paused to take aim, and the kick jerked her aim awry. He raised his head, the sulfurous glow of the teles turning his spectacles to opaque rounds of gold and glinting in the star-fracture of the left lens. She braced herself carefully for a second shot, aiming for his forehead in the spiral strings of his blood-tipped hair. He had used her, used her . . .

She never knew what he shouted at her. Her name, she thought, and some other word, a spell-word that sliced through the calm fog in her mind like thrown ice water. At the same moment, she felt the burning scorch of fire on her hair, her back, and her arms. He stumbled to his feet, caught her, and held her, smothering the heat between her skin and her coat, pressing her to him, heedless of the gun wedged between their bodies.

After a moment the heat faded again. She brought up her hand from his side and saw her fingers covered in blood.

She began to shake uncontrollably. "Antryg, I'm sorry," she sobbed. "I'm sorry—it was a spell—Suraklin's spell—"

"Don't!" he whispered desperately. His breath came as if he fought for every lungful, his face chalk-white with shock and strain. "Don't say anything. I understand. Put the Sigil in place and let's get out of here. Someone's coming; he's summoned help, and we have to stop them before they get here . . ."

"Who . . ." she began dazedly.

"Never mind that!" Behind his specs, his eyes were frantic.

Her hands shaking, Joanna tore open the velcro pocket of her backpack, fumbled with the lead shielding in which the Sigil was wrapped. She felt an increasing reluctance to touch the central teles under which she knew she must place it, a distaste for the whole project—she would be killing the last vestiges of Suraklin, Salteris, the Regent's father, Gary . . . It was murder . . .

So was your trying to shoot Antryg, she reminded herself disgustedly. *And Caris, dying up at the top of the cliff* . . . Antryg made a swift gesture toward her, swiftly repressed; looking up she saw the strain on his face and the sweat tracking down through the grime and blood, and realized that in his mind, too, Suraklin was whispering.

Her fingers shrinking from the task, she swiftly pushed the teles aside in its copper bed and slid the Sigil of Darkness into place.

The breaking of the energy drain was like the snapping of a metal band encircling her brain. She felt almost shocked, once more aware of the bone-numbing cold, of the danger in which they stood, and the smell of gunpowder and of Antryg's blood. The bluish gleam of the teles-balls died, and the scribbled light of the runes on the floor faded. Only the red and green lights of the Cray gleamed, baleful stars in the darkness, picking out Antryg's nose and lips and spectacles and winking in the haphazard collection of tuppenny beads and Imperial jewels around his neck. The drone of the UPS kicking in filled the black emptiness around them, broken by the shrill hooting of the alarm. At the same time, she felt the power all around her grow; the crackle of inchoate hatred in the darkness was held at bay only by Antryg's failing spells. Heat seemed to whisper, inches from her flesh.

"How long?" he breathed as they stumbled through the darkness, back toward the beckoning glimmer of his mark.

She shook her head. "A battery that size can keep a computer going for about a day." She felt him shiver and knew he'd never hold out that long. "But he'll be drawing energy from it for his spells to keep the enclave open for his repair crew, whoever they are, to get in—and to destroy you."

Antryg managed a crooked grin. "Added incentive for my death, I see." He was leaning on her, the sleeve of his coat warm and scratchy on her frozen face, permeated with the smells of sulfur and blood. Joanna realized Suraklin would never have needed an added incentive—Antryg was the only wizard who would have been able to hold out this long against the defense-spells. No wonder Suraklin had tried at every opportunity to have him killed.

"I don't know how much that takes, but I'd guess an awful lot." She cocked an ear back, listening to the alarm hooters. Was it her imagination, she wondered, or were they more frequent than before? "With all the spare battery packs disconnected—maybe an hour?"

He shuddered again at the endless length of time. "Unless he can break me first."

The inner chamber of the Citadel, beyond the Gate of the enclave, was crawling with abominations. Pausing on the insubstantial threshold above the pool, Joanna heard them and smelled them in the foul darkness, and all her innards seemed to contract with dread. She whispered queasily, "Can you summon light?"

Antryg shook his head. "Not now," he breathed. "Joanna, I can't. He's in my mind, tearing at it with his spells . . ."

"Okay. Don't worry about it." She unslung the backpack from her shoulder and found her flashlight. Its feeble beam glanced off the obsidian waters beneath their feet and caught the glitter of slime, the flash of mismated eyes. The beam shook as it traveled over them: fat things like monster slugs with foul, dripping snouts; something like a daddy longlegs skittering nervously near the wall; bloated, mutant rats; and things that must once have been cockroaches before some effect of the Void had changed them. She clenched her teeth hard, trying not to make a noise.

Beyond them, the door into the sightless mazes of the vaults stood open, and she could sense movement in the darkness beyond.

"We've got to close it," Antryg whispered desperately. "Block it, barricade it . . ."

Behind them, the grating rumble of the backup battery echoed like a bass thunder; the alarms were hooting faster. If nothing else, thought Joanna, they had to get out of the gateway before it collapsed . . .

"Here goes nothing." She pulled open her backpack, removed the first of the DARKMAGE files, and wadded the photocopied pages into a ball. *Thank God,* she thought obliquely, *I brought lots of matches . . .* The abominations shrank back from the fire when she tossed it among them. She lit five more crumpled balls and flung them, some to one side, some to the other.

"Screw the sheets into torches." Antryg was already doing so as he spoke. "If we can make it to the door . . ."

"We really have to bar it with us on *this* side of it?"

"Believe me, Joanna," he said softly, "I guarantee you it's preferable."

She didn't believe him until they reached the door—ancient, dusty, thick wood strapped and reinforced with iron on the inside and sheeted with copper on the outside. It was hung perfectly on steel hinges and it would swing with a touch. For a moment Joanna stood in the black arch, listening, and heard the footsteps in the passage beyond. They were slow and dragging; once she heard the thud of a body falling against a wall, and the clash of a dropped weapon, then a scrabbling noise as it picked itself up again.

She looked up at the tall wizard beside her, her revulsion stark upon her face.

"Bolt it," said Antryg softly. "Suraklin's magic will still be in his flesh."

Behind them, the abominations closed in. Joanna formed a barrier of wadded paper, crumpling and lighting all the DARKMAGE files, the pounds of paper she'd lugged on her back for hundreds of miles, the last details of the lives of two wizards, an Imperial Prince, and a computer programmer—the final records of their existence. From the enclave gate, still hanging, glimmering, above the pool, the tempo of the alarms had increased, shrieking, desperate, calling help, blocked on the very edge of immortality. All through the horrible shadows of the room the abominations stirred, prowling back and forth, the rats' eyes gleaming, outsize chisel teeth bared. Listening behind her, Joanna imagined she could hear the approaching footfalls in the hall, stumbling, slurring. Leaning against the door beside her, Antryg looked gray and drawn, his eyes shut, reaming the last strength, the last magic, from the marrow of his bones.

The blow on the door, when it came, seemed to shake the very stone from which the vaults were cut. Antryg flinched, but turned a little, to press his face and hands to the iron-bound wood, his eyes shut and his face twisted with pain. Joanna heard a sharp hissing behind her, smelled damp smoke, and swung around to see a trickle of water from the pool snaking toward the flickering line of her barrier blazes. That was impossible, she thought, terrified, as the abominations moved forward with the lessening of the fire—the floor sloped up . . .

She pulled more paper from her backpack, twisted it into another torch and lit it. Gritting her teeth, she strode toward the slobbering, pulsing things on the other side of the light, lashing at them with the torch.

The water was indeed seeping up from the pool. Wider, thicker streams of it, like black slime, flowed up the slope of the floor toward their feet, dousing another one of her little fires. Another blow fell on the door, and she saw, close to Antryg's head, the solid oak timbers heave and crack. Antryg himself seemed hardly to notice; he appeared to be almost in a trance, except for the gasping of his breath and the desperate contortion of his face. Grimly, Joanna stuck the torch into a crack in the wall and twisted another one, then caught at the first as it fell—she could have sworn it had been firmly wedged. With quick-blazing fire in each hand, she swung at the abominations. One of the rats, the size of a dog and grossly fat, hissed at her; for a hideous second, she thought it would leap, but it backed away, its twisted face a nightmare.

Another blow drove a shard of the copper sheathing through the door and made the strapping jerk and pull in the wood. It was Gary out there, Joanna thought as she swung again at a tentacled thing like a groping black wart that edged toward them. Gary with the top of his head blown off, Gary with his nose a bloody mash, Gary with nothing in his eyes but Suraklin's will . . .

Antryg made a small sound of pain. At the same instant, Joanna herself felt a stab of sickness, deep in her guts, the burning wrench like poisoned heat. From the enclave, the alarms were screaming, thick and fast now, louder and louder, like a heartbeat skipping out of its rhythm, spiraling up into the danger zone. Blackness swam in front of her eyes, and pain and nausea twisted at her guts as she pulled another handful of paper out, lit it with shaking hands from the last, and swung it at the things that waited greedily in the ankle-deep waters of the flooded floor.

The pounding on the door seemed eerily to pick up the tempo of the alarms, faster, more urgent, more desperate. Antryg cried out again, blood tracking down from the corner of his mouth as his counterspells began to crack under the inexorable pressure of the computer's strength. The alarms scaled up, blending into a single, screaming note. Beneath the screaming, Joanna could hear voices, like the wicker of colorless flame. Some of them were thin, unformed whispers of minds that had never been human; others were terrifyingly familiar . . .

Babe, you're coming out to my place this weekend, aren't you? I've got four new games for the computer, some good beer . . . new jet system for the Jacuzzi . . .

You must do as you think best, my son, but I think you would be a better healer than a fighter . . .

My father won't hear of it, but if you say Suraklin really is a danger, my lord Archmage, then I am behind you with all the support I can raise . . .

And far back of them all, half obliterated by those random snatches of memory, an old man's voice, high and harsh and terrible, whispered, *You were my only love . . . my only love. Of course I can still love . . . I can still feel . . . I can still taste the wine of life . . . It's all in the programs and will be forever. I still live . . .*

The silence falling was like a blow over the head with a club. For an instant Joanna wondered, *What now?* and turned to look back toward the shimmering gate of the enclave and the distant glitter of the red computer lights that were like evil stars in some impossible darkness. But the lights were gone. With a tired gurgle, the water around her feet had already begun to slither away toward the well again; the abominations, sniffing and hissing, backed further from the crude bundles of burning paper still in her hands. A moment later, like smoke dispersing, the dark gate faded away.

Antryg's voice was no more than a thread. "Entropy always wins," he murmured. With hands that would barely close, he shoved back the door bolts. Neither of them looked at what lay across the threshold as they began their stumbling ascent once more to the light.

CHAPTER XVIII

THEY FOUND CARIS LYING WHERE HE HAD FALLEN, TWENTY FEET OR so from the lip of the chasm, a broken black shape in a pool of blood. Joanna knelt beside him and felt his face and his remaining hand, searching against hope for some sign of life. She had thought all emotion wrung out of her by the ordeal in the vaults, but now realized that that had only been the result of the energy drain. Now tears collected in her eyes—for Caris and for the fact that she had left him to die without a backward glance.

It had, of course, been what he would have done—what it was the Way of the Sasenna to do.

The short winter day had passed noon. The sky was a low sheet of steel-colored billows, like the undersurface of murky water; the air smelled of snow.

She heard the crunch of Antryg's boots on the hard frost behind her. Glancing up, she saw he'd retrieved his cloak from the subsidence where she'd rolled wearing it. In the daylight he looked ghastly, his haggard face tracked with runnels of blood through the sweat-matted dust, and spreading stains of it dark on his left sleeve and side. He moved stiffly, slowly, like an old man. His crooked hands shook as he covered Caris with the cloak.

"We'll have to get word to Pella," Joanna said dully.

"I'm sure the wizards will do that." Antryg knelt beside her and pushed back the short-cropped fair hair from the young man's still face. "They'll be here very soon now."

The thought of the effort flight would entail turned her stomach, but she said, "We'd better go." She started to get to her feet, then gasped with startled pain. Under her coat and jacket, half her back was burned and beginning to throb. She gritted her teeth, fighting the tears and the wave of faintness that came over her at the pain. It was nothing, she knew, to what Antryg was going through or to what Caris must have gone through, raising himself for that final shot. "We've got a lead on them—with any luck they'll think you and Suraklin destroyed each other . . ."

Something changed in the air, some shock—blast—impact—as if the reverse side of the universe had been kicked by a giant foot. The air as well as the ground seemed to shudder with a noise that Joanna was not entirely certain was not solely in her own skull, the crying of voices in a dream. She caught Antryg's shoulder in fear. Dust rose in a white column from the abyss that had been the Citadel vaults, slowly mushrooming into the freezing air, then slowly dispersing.

"The enclave," Antryg said softly. In the ashy daylight, his face looked as deathly as that of the boy at whose side he still knelt. "He's used the last of whatever power was left to him to implode it completely—to destroy himself. So he did remember, after all."

Through the pain in her back and her grief over Caris, it was hard to think, but Joanna said, "Remember what?"

"Why he wanted to live forever." Tears made a shining track through the grime on either side of his beaky nose. "The operative word in that phrase is not 'forever,' but 'live.' And living is not only listening to songs, but singing them; not only possessing the wine in bottles, but tasting it in the company of those you love. Part of the beauty of a sunset is the way its colors change and intensify as it fades to night. Maybe he did realize at last that he was only the copy of a copy, a series of subroutines condemned to an eternity of Read Only . . ." He sighed and pushed up his specs to wipe his eyes with the back of his glove. "Or maybe, like me, he simply couldn't abide the thought of being locked up once again."

She looked down at his face, half hidden by his hair, and the grief that haunted his gray eyes. "You still loved him, didn't you?"

A smile flicked at the corners of his mouth. "Oh, not actively anymore. But I, too, remember." He sighed and stopped himself sharply, pressing his hand to his side where her bullet had grazed.

Gently he raised Caris' right arm, the burnt chunk of the gun-butt dropping from the two remaining fingers. Blood oozed stickily from the wound.

Through a blur of exhausted tears, Joanna scanned the barren hills. The iron-colored earth was streaked with snow beneath a leaden sky. Cold wind stirred the singed ends of her hair. Though the landscape was utterly desolate, she had the uneasy feeling of being watched. She said, "We'd better go. The wizards will be here soon."

"I know." He folded Caris' hands on the young man's breast, and laid his own on top of them, the long, crooked fingers stained with blood. "I can feel them seeking me with their minds, seeking my magic. But here at the node of the lines, there is one more magic that it's possible for me to perform." He sat for a moment, gathering the remains of his concentration and his exhausted powers through the staggering weight of pain and weariness. Joanna did not understand what he meant, until his eyes slipped shut and his head bowed, and she realized he had gone into a healing trance.

She stood for a long time at his side, her throat hurting, half-sick with her own pain and exhaustion. Then slowly, painfully, she sat down again on the gray earth. Despite the thick sheepskin of her coat, the quilted velvet page's jacket, and the lace-trimmed shirt beneath, she felt cold to the marrow of her bones. Tears burning at her eyes, she leaned her head against Antryg's shoulder and tucked her chilled fingers for warmth around his arm. The wind spat snow at them from the surrounding hills and groaned among the charred bones of the Citadel all around.

After nearly an hour of silence, Joanna saw Caris' eyelids move, his ribcage rise, sink, and, after a long moment, rise again.

After two hours, with the darkness beginning to thicken in the louring sky, she was wakened from a half doze of sheer weariness by the strike of hooves on stone. She raised her head to see the ring of mounted sasenna who surrounded them, halberds and spears glittering like metal teeth in the failing light. Half a dozen horses stood apart in a group, the black robes of their riders whirling like storm-clouds in the sleety wind. At their head sat Lady Rosamund, her face like stone and her green eyes pitiless as jade.

"It's odd, you know," Antryg said quietly, steam blurring his spectacles as he poured bubbling water from the kettle into a cracked earthenware teapot. "The two places I've lived longest in my life—really the only two places where I've stayed long enough to qualify as 'home'—have been Suraklin's Citadel and here in the Silent Tower. Would you care for some tea?" he inquired of the pair of red-robed Church wizards who sat stiffly watching him by the door. Both of them glared and the older of the two, a woman, made the sign against evil.

Antryg sighed, wincing a little at the pinch in his cracked rib, and replaced the kettle on the narrow hearth. He handed Joanna a cup of tea with a rueful smile. "In any case, they can't put the Sigil of Darkness back on me." He rubbed absently at the brown mark on his throat. "Have you heard how Caris is?"

Joanna shook her head. The sheer mass and darkness of the Silent Tower oppressed her. Curiously, though the wizards, both Church and Council, who kept guard over her solitary cell on the lower level of the Tower, treated her far better than the Witchfinders had when she had been their prisoner, she found herself far more frightened. Perhaps this was because, when she had been a prisoner of the Witchfinders, she had known Antryg, and Caris, and Magister Magus, were still free and capable of helping her escape, as indeed they had done. She was now without options.

Then, too, she thought, watching Antryg's tall shadow move across the smoke-stained granite of the ceiling vaults, her sense of utter hopelessness might simply stem from exhaustion, the physical reaction to pain and overexertion, and to the repeated emotional shocks of the previous day. Upon being locked into her cell in the Tower, she had fallen almost immediately asleep, in spite of her wretched conviction that Antryg might very well be dead by the time she woke up. Looking at the weariness that seemed to have ground its way indelibly into the deep lines of his face, she wondered if he had done the same.

"I know he's at Larkmoor," she said in a small voice. "And that they say he'll live."

He took the battered and mended chair at her side, and his long, swollen-jointed fingers automatically sought hers. The room in which the Council had imprisoned him was his old study, crammed with his books, his astronomical instruments, and his mechanical toys. In shadow at the far end, Joanna glimpsed a narrow cot, heaped with a haphazard collection of furs and faded quilts. It did not look as if it had been slept on.

"He'll live," Antryg repeated softly and sighed again. "Now I wonder why they said that?"

"Because there are certain members of the Council who insisted upon it."

Both of them looked up quickly at the sound of that cold, sweet voice from the doorway. Lady Rosamund stood there, framed in darkness, immaculate as ever, the red-purple stole that marked her position in the Council sparkling faintly in the fire's reflected light. The Church wizards bowed to her and stepped past her through the door, though Joanna sensed they were in the narrow stairway still, listening for the slightest rise in her voice to summon them back.

"And because in your latest confession, you swear that he was injured in trying to apprehend you for your attempt upon the Regent's life. Or didn't you read it this time?"

"No," Antryg admitted, with a ghost of his old airiness, at which her Ladyship's pink mouth tightened disapprovingly. "I didn't think there would be much point." He looked down and met Joanna's frightened glance. "They didn't hurt me," he added, seeing the way her eyes darted to his hands, as if to see what new injuries those threadbare half-gloves might conceal. "But I told them I'd sign anything, as long as it contained a clause saying that I had forced you to help me by means of my spells, and that you were not responsible for what you did. At least they didn't have to tie the pen in my fingers this time."

Joanna opened her mouth protestingly, his image in the firelight and shadows suddenly blurring with her tears. He put out a hand and brushed her tangled blond hair.

"Joanna, there was never a shred of proof that things were as we said they were. Even the DARKMAGE files are gone now."

Crushed and miserable, she looked away. After a moment, he gathered her in his long, bony arms, holding her against him, the fabric of his shabby purple doctor's robe and the ruffled shirt he wore beneath it soft and scratchy as an animal's pelt against her cheek. She wondered what had happened to her, whether it was the pain and shock of her burns in spite of the wizards' treatment of them or whether she was simply too weary to go on fighting. She seemed to have come to the end of her subroutines. For the first time, she understood that she, too, stood in danger of imprisonment or execution in this world—that she, too, faced punishment as Antryg's accomplice. But she felt only exhaustion, her mind too tired to grope for the next possible course of action. It was very odd, she thought detachedly, only to sit here in the strong ring of his arms, comfortable in the single present moment, and let events take their course into a black and hopeless future.

Past her shoulder, she heard Lady Rosamund say, "Minhyrdin has gone to Larkmoor, with Issay Bel-Caire, to deliver your confession to the Regent and to ask for clemency for the girl. Whether that perverted mad dog will grant it or not, I cannot say; but beyond a doubt, before they return, the Regent's messenger will arrive with the orders concerning the manner of your death."

Joanna felt Antryg shiver, but he only murmured, "Thank you." A moment later she heard the two Church wizards reenter and the whisper of the Lady's black robes as she passed down the stairs.

* * *

"Why did you let me live?"

Caris was a little surprised at the weakness of his own voice. Once the words were spoken, he doubted they had carried as far as the carved armchair between his bed and the window, through which the bare trees of the windbreak could be seen clawing the dun-colored sky. But the old lady who slumped there like a bag of black wool raised her head, the thin light catching silvery on the cap of her hair. The steady click of her ever-present knitting did not stop.

"Tush, boy," was all she said.

"Whatever you told the Regent, you know I broke my vows," Caris went on, finding every word an effort against the lassitude of weakness and drugs. "I may have turned my back on the Way of the Sasenna, but I know what it means. They say a sasennan who breaks his vows, for whatever reason seems good, proves nothing about that reason, but only that he is a man who will break his vows. And then," he added, moving his bandaged hand on the coverlet, and wincing against the stab of the dulled pain, "I don't imagine the Council had much use for broken sword blades. No one does."

"Nonsense." The old lady gave her knitting a tweak to clear its tangled strands and glanced sidelong at him with those faded blue eyes. "All things have their uses—even broken sword blades. Was your reason so good?"

"I thought so."

Partly from weakness and partly from his bitter self-recrimination, he spoke half to himself, barely audible, and perhaps the old lady did not hear, for she lapsed back into fussing with her knitting like any old granny by her hearth, muttering to herself as she did. "I knew him," Caris heard that thin, wavery old voice mumble. "Not well, but I knew him—no one really knew him well but that poor boy of his. And I knew your grandfather and the Emperor, that was the Prince then, and so handsome. I talked to Antryg when he signed all those papers they wanted him to sign last night—meddler, oathbreaker, and mad, yes, completely mad. But I knew them all." Her weak blue glance flicked to him, suddenly disconcertingly bright. "You do as I say, little son. You get well . . ."

"For what?" he burst out desperately. "To live as a cripple? I was no good as a wizard, and now as a weapon, too, I am flawed . . ."

"Then be just a man." She seemed to forget that her yarn had become tangled in her too-long black sleeves and resumed the steady clacking of her needles, her little white head bent over them, her face in the crossed lights of the window and the fireplace nearby like a very wrinkled apple at the bottom of the winter barrel. "Is it so hard?"

Caris said softly, "Yes."

"*Are* you sasennan of the Council?"

There were times when Aunt Min reminded Caris of the old weapons riddle among the sasenna—that hatpins could also draw blood. After long silence he stammered, "I vowed to be so, to the end of my life. But I don't know."

She made no reply to that. Caris realized the clicking of the needles had stilled and, turning his head on the pillow, saw that she had fallen asleep.

For a long time he lay still, staring at the play of honey-colored firelight on the red cedar of the rafters overhead. He felt as if his life had been laid down on the coverlet beside his remaining hand, and that it was now his choice as to whether he would pick it up again.

The numbness of his soul, cracking these long weeks, had broken like spring ice, and pain welled through like a dark fluid—the pain of a child whose soul will not bow to the responsible rhythms of seedtime and harvest, no matter how he loves them and those who try to teach them to him, the pain of a youth whose inner magic is simply not strong enough to make him a mage. At the age of sixteen he had vowed away that pain, the pain of choosing and of wanting. As a result, he was aware now that he had little experience of either.

Tears leaked from his eyes, hot on his temples—not the stifled, hurtful tears of anguish shed at his grandfather's murder, but tears of weariness and of deeper grief that leached from his soul poisons of which he had long been unaware. As a sasennan, it was expected of him that he refuse to continue as a cripple in his life—he who, like a fighting-dog, had been trained for nothing else.

And yet . . .

As if a door had been opened, he seemed to smell again the fragile sweetness of the dried herbs in Antryg's medical pouch that had been left behind, with so many other things, in the chapel on the north bank of the Glidden. The kinesthetic memory of sifting salts and powders together came back to him and Antryg's deep voice, speaking of the qualities of certain plants—ground holly for rheumatism, slippery elm for disorders of the bowels, the white berries of mistletoe for bleeding. He recalled the way his hands had warmed when the healing light passed from them into the body of another and the shattering touch of a newborn child's mind on his . . .

He was not aware that he had slept until he began to wake again, floating, it seemed, a few inches beneath the surface of dreams, aware that the firelight had deepened to amber with the turning of the afternoon light. He was aware of the small warmth of Kyssha lying curled against his side, her nose under what was left of his bandaged hand, and of the strength of Pella's fingers over his own. From somewhere in the room, he heard the rustle of silk taffeta and Pharos' voice saying softly, "I thought I should find you here."

The hand over his flinched, but did not release its hold.

"I just thought you ought to know, my little Princess, that Leynart has indeed fallen ill with smallpox. The mage Bel-Caire is with him. So it seems you did save my life."

He heard her take in breath to answer, then hesitate for a moment, as if not sure what to say to those inscrutable blue eyes. Then she spoke, her deep voice like an alto flute in the gloom. "I'm sorry Ley is ill."

Pharos sniffed. There was the muted click of high heels on the parquet of the floor—Caris remembered, half-dreaming, that the Regent walked very quietly—and the overwhelming waft of orris-root perfume. "Tedious little bitch. I expect if he survives, his looks will be gone, though I'll see he gets some reward for his devotion."

Pella's voice was angry. "He only did it for love of you."

"Let himself be made a dupe? Tried to work magic on me that he didn't understand, on the bare word of someone he didn't know that it was for his own good and mine, and not my heir's? That silken rat you call a dog has more brains—more courage, too."

"That's still no cause to be cruel."

"As far as I've ever been able to ascertain, my little—Pellicida . . ." Caris heard him change his form of address to her and knew that, again, he had met her eyes. ". . . the world has never had any cause to be cruel to me or to you. But I think we've both suffered a certain amount of pain anyway. I'm sorry," he added, his voice halting on the words. "You did not have to save my life. I pay Kanner to do things like that. Hurting the weak is a habit with me—a bad one, like biting my fingernails. I'll try not to do it to you again. You had at least one good reason to wish me dead— was this young man another?"

"No." Pella's hand closed more tightly around Caris' fingers, and he heard the slide of her hair over her satin shoulders as she bowed her head. "Neither of us wished you dead."

"Ah." The way she had spoken the word "us" was, even to Caris' ears, unmistakable. "I thought I did not recognize him as one of my men, in spite of the uniform." There was a slight, undefinable shift in the harsh voice. "They say you're with child. Is this true?"

Again he heard the dry slither of her hair.

"Mine?"

"Yes."

Caris opened his eyes, to see those two forms silhouetted in the amber light, Pharos standing like some pretty doll in black and gold, two white fingers emerging from an explosion of sable lace to rest lightly beneath Pella's chin. The girl was gazing up into his face, her green eyes unwavering, looking very young and yet very calm, as she had in the clash with Leynart—the face of a sasennan who is also a queen.

Pharos' mouth twitched in a wry expression. "A pity, in a way," he said at last. "A madman, a credulous fool, and an idiot are no advertisement for a dynasty, whatever our respective families might say. I am not good myself, any more than I am a man for women, but I do know goodness when I see it—and I know that the good are often happy as well."

There was a long pause as he studied her, this girl whose spirit he had never been able to break, and the scorn in his eyes with which he looked upon a hostile world seemed to abate, as it had abated a little in the study at Devilsgate.

"Well," he said at last, "God knows I have little use for a woman, except to bear me an heir, and you seem to be fulfilling that part of what strikes me as a rather agricultural custom. So I will ask of you only that you raise my child and whatever other children you may happen to bear, with a sense of responsibility for the Empire and whatever happiness you can manage to give them as well." Picking up her other hand, he kissed it, turned in a great rustling of black silk ribbons, and walked toward the door.

Pella rose, holding out her hand. "Pharos . . ."

He paused, looking back. "Yes, Pellicida?"

"What about Antryg and Joanna?"

The Regent hesitated for a long moment, the old vindictive paranoia gleaming once more in his pale blue eyes. "They betrayed me," he said at last, with soft and vicious finality in his voice. "Both of them."

"They were trying . . ."

"We have Windrose's confession," Pharos cut her off, his shrill voice suddenly harsh. "That same document exonerates your friend here . . ." The diamonds of his rings glittered sharply around the great, cut hematite in the middle, live stars circling a dead one, as he gestured to Caris. Then, he went on quietly, as a ruler explaining a decision to a counsellor he trusts, "You must have known there was never hope for his reprieve.

The messenger has already left for the Silent Tower. Sentence on them both will be carried out tomorrow."

"Both?" protested Pella. "Joanna . . ."

The small hand waved aside her fear. "Oh, never fret. It isn't your affair . . ." Pella started to rise, and Pharos went on hastily, "Of course, nothing fatal will be done to her—banishment—imprisonment . . ." But Caris saw his pale eyes shift from hers as he turned toward the door and heard the careless evasiveness of the voice. Caris knew that Pharos lied.

Even through the thick walls of the Silent Tower, Joanna heard the stormwinds rise, groaning in the wheel-spoke rafters overhead. As Antryg had said, even in the summertime, the Tower was icy cold; now in the dead of winter, the wind slipped like black snakes through the barred and hidden ventilation slits to drain the warmth of the room. She and Antryg had sat for a long time before the fire, sharing his scruffy cloak and one of the quilts from the bed, while the two hasu watching them shivered slightly, having indignantly refused Antryg's offers of other blankets.

They had talked, of California, of Mellidane, of Antryg's village of Velskonoe on the edge of the taiga forest deep in the Sykerst, whence Suraklin had taken him as a child, of Star Wars and the different types of magic, and of the possibility of Joanna's imprisonment for a greater or lesser time in this world.

"I tried to do what was best," Antryg said softly, his breath stirring the ends of her hair on top of her head. "Unfortunately, it's something I've never been terribly good at. I couldn't leave Caris; and if I'd simply sent you away, you wouldn't have gotten far before the wizards caught you anyway. There were still abominations about, too."

"And I wouldn't have gone." She raised her cheek from his chest long enough to push clear one of his trashy glass necklaces, then settled it back again.

"Oh, Joanna." He sighed, and tightened his arms around her shoulders. "I did want to keep you out of it, as much as I could. It isn't the first time my friends have been hurt through my meddling. It's just that I needed you too much . . ."

"Hey, they always said computer consultant was a high-demand field."

He laughed softly and looked down into her face. "That wasn't what I meant."

She knew it hadn't been and felt her throat tighten again with tears. But all she said was, "I knew the job was dirty when I took it." She wondered, feeling the hardness of muscle and rib through the baggy folds of the robe beneath her cheek, how long they would keep her prisoner here, and if she would ever make it back to California. Her old life seemed very strange and distant to her. The thought of being here alone made her feel weak and frightened, but it was totally peripheral to that blacker grief she resolutely refused to contemplate, the knowledge that Antryg was going to die.

She had fought it as a rearguard action for so many months that at times it seemed completely unreal, and his perfectly genuine cheerfulness tricked her mind away from it still further. But she'd seen it in the eyes of the Church dogs and heard it in the whispers of the mages who guarded her cell. Antryg was going to die and, in all probability, die tomorrow.

After tomorrow, she would never see him again.

Except, perhaps, in dreams.

In the darkness of the twisted stairwell, Joanna heard the moan of the wind and then the Lady Rosamund's voice, raised in indignation, "Don't be absurd! The Regent has no intention of letting her go and you know it!"

Then she heard old Minhyrdin the Fair's creaky little wheeze, coming closer with the scuffle of her laborious feet. "Nonsense. What know you of the Regent's plans—or care?" The two women, lady and crone, appeared in the darkness of the doorway. With an impatient sign, the Lady Rosamund dismissed the two guards. Aunt Min peered up at the elegant Lady with a shrewd old eye and added, "Or *do* you care what Pharos thinks?"

"Of course not!" her Ladyship retorted hotly. "But simply to go against his orders . . ."

"His orders have not yet arrived," the old lady pointed out blandly, turning her head a little, because of the stooping of her bent back, to look up at Lady Rosamund. "How are we to know his intention? His messenger has been delayed by the storm." Aunt Min's black robe was wet through and her cloak, patched, shabbier even than Antryg's, was covered with flakes of melting snow and ice. She was drawing off her knitted red and green mittens and getting the ends of her muffler tangled in her eternal knitting, which, clotted with ice, was still in its basket under her arm.

Lady Rosamund's eyes narrowed suspiciously. "When I scried the skies this morning, I saw no trace of a coming storm."

Antryg smiled graciously from his seat beside the hearth and chipped in, "Well, these things come with practice." Joanna almost stifled, trying not to laugh at the way the Lady's green eyes flared with rage.

Unperturbed, Aunt Min continued, "But since we have received no orders, run along now and fetch what I asked you."

"We have no right . . ."

The withered little ancient drew herself with some effort to her full height—an inch or so less than Joanna's five-foot-barely. And Joanna, looking at that old, seamed face in its thin tatter of white hair, suddenly understood why she had once been called Minhyrdin the Fair by all. In a voice totally unlike her usual vague mumbling, she said, "*I* am the Archmage. *I* have the right." Then she dropped her knitting and bent laboriously to pick it up, dropping the needles as she did so. She fumbled for them. The Lady Rosamund bent to help her, and Aunt Min waved her fussily away. "Oh, let it be, Rosie! Now run along and do as I asked."

Stiffly, her Ladyship straightened up and strode with an indignant billow of black robes into the darkness of the stair. Joanna and Antryg both got to their feet and went to help Aunt Min, Archmage of the Council of Wizards, collect her scattered belongings.

"Thank you," the old lady said, shoving the sodden tangle of wool haphazardly back into her basket and sticking the needles into it at random. "Thank you, my dears." She had to twist her spine to look up at Antryg's great height. She reached out to pat his big, crooked-fingered hand. "You always were a good boy."

He smiled down at her and held out his hand to help her to a chair. "No," he said, with genuine regret. "But I always did want to be. I never thanked you for speaking out for me at the end of summer when they brought me back here . . ."

"Only to escape again." She shook her head, clicking her tongue pettishly, as if at a child's scrapes. "I knew him, you see—knew Suraklin. I knew them all."

"I remember." Antryg smiled. "In fact I remember you taking a broom-handle to him, the one time you were at the Citadel . . . at the time I was shocked to death, of course."

The old lady chuckled, her pale eyes warming briefly with a trace of their old color. Then she sobered and said, "It cannot be so again."

"I know," Antryg said quietly. The brown mark left by the Sigil of Darkness showed up more darkly against the whiteness of his face. "Just please get Joanna out of here."

"Since we have received no orders from the Regent concerning the girl Joanna," the old lady said, "though we have no jurisdiction over her, as Archmage I think it best that she be taken back to the place where we came through the Void, the shed marked with Suraklin's marks."

Joanna felt Antryg's long fingers close tightly around hers; then he said, "Thank you."

She was looking up into his face as he glanced past Aunt Min to the shadow of the door and saw what was left of the color there drain away. Her glance flicked after his. Lady Rosamund stood there, silent and disapproving, in her hands a cup made of gold and horn.

Aunt Min looked, too, and nodded her little head. "Set it down, dear, set it down," she instructed, making vague little gestures toward the table and dropping her knitting again. Automatically Antryg stooped to retrieve it, then straightened up again as the old lady continued, "And be careful of it, Rosie—it's poison, you know."

Her Ladyship's beautiful mouth flexed with disapproval as she turned and stalked from the room once again. Aunt Min plucked her knitting needles from Antryg's yielding hand and said, "You know there is nothing we can do for you. The original sentence of death is still in effect."

Joanna remembered Antryg's airy recital—*hanged, broken, skinned, and sliced* . . . At the time, that day-long public torture had seemed so far away.

Antryg whispered, "I know."

The old lady added, "I am sorry."

Antryg nodded and patted her tiny hand where it curled around his own.

Joanna caught his sleeve, her mind refusing to take it in. It seemed to her that the warmth and the color of the afternoon was still on her and the taste of the deep and nebulous joy of mingled friendship and love. She had the helpless, protesting sense of being suddenly forced to leave a party long before it was over, of losing something which had been, and should have been, part of her for years.

Aunt Min touched her arm. "You had better come along, my dear. The storm won't be a long one." She said it with a serene knowledge that was almost comical, but for the circumstances. "There is no knowing when the messenger will come and then, of course, whatever orders he bears must take effect."

Joanna shook her head, her mind a blank of darkness and grief. Antryg folded her gently into his arms and bent his tall height to press his mouth to hers. Her hands tightened over the patched robe and tangled in the long gray hair. For a moment, it was as if she were trying to memorize, once for all, the sinewy movement of the loose-jointed frame, the magpie sparkle of beads and diamonds, cracked spectacles, and those wide, intent gray eyes, and the brocaded flamboyance of his deep voice.

Then he murmured, "Good-bye, my love." The word he used in the language of Ferr was the equivalent of *Adieu,*—to God—the long good-bye from which there is no returning.

Aunt Min took her hand and led her into the narrow darkness of the stair, where she saw that Lady Rosamund waited. As they escorted her down, to lead her far enough away from the Tower so that no chance weakening of the veil between worlds within the Tower itself would permit Antryg again to escape, she looked back at the gold rectangle of the door.

Through it she saw Antryg standing beside the table, the cup between his hands, his face like chalk in the firelight. As she watched, pulling against the Archmage's coaxing, she saw him raise the cup to his lips, drain it, and set it down, his fingers shaking uncontrollably. Then he walked back to his bed, lay down in the shadows, and turned his face to the wall.

CHAPTER XIX

IT WAS JANUARY, AND LATE-BLOWING SANTA ANA WINDS FLOWED over Los Angeles like a river of silk. After weeks of winter in the Sykerst, the balmy desert warmth was even more disorienting to Joanna, the crystal magic of the air adding to her sense of separation from this world to which she had returned, as well as from that which she had left. That was another thing, she reflected detachedly as she stepped through the double-glass doors of the Building Six lobby and looked out across the tepid twilight of the nearly empty parking lot, that they never mentioned in tales of adventure—the sheer amount of cleaning-up the participants had to do afterward and the gut-wrenching period of letdown.

Antryg was dead.

She was young enough never to have lost anyone close to her in her life —certainly not someone as close as he had been. She felt stunned and empty, not only of him but of everything. She had not imagined it possible to miss someone that much.

As she descended the shallow concrete steps, she thought to herself that she had not realized in the fall how lucky she'd had it. There was a good deal to be said, after all, for fear of Suraklin, terror of crossing the Void again alone, obsessive paranoia, and her frantic mantra that Antryg was not—could not be—dead. At least it had kept her busy. There had been almost no time to think or to feel.

Now there was.

During the Santa Anas it was as if Los Angeles had never heard the word "smog." All around the low concrete bunkers of San Serano, the hills seemed to have crept nearer during the day, vast, rounded cutouts of matte cobalt cardboard against a periwinkle sky. The wind lifted strands of her hair like a sensual ghost; the air was milky against her bare arms. Weeks of freezing, she reflected, did have the one advantage of making her temporarily proof against all but the chilliest evenings. She hitched her massive purse with its dangling tassels and rabbit skins more firmly onto her shoulder, still kinesthetically missing the familiar weight of the backpack. When it brushed the bandages over the worst of the burns she flinched, though after four days the pain had dulled to no worse than a really bad sunburn.

It was after six o'clock, and most of San Serano's employees had braved their way onto the freeway an hour ago. Joanna had stayed, as she had stayed late the last two nights. Part of it was catching up on the horrible volume of work left undone at her departure, but a great deal of it stemmed from her unwillingness to face the emptiness that waited for her at home.

The snow would be deep around Larkmoor now. Aunt Min had assured her that it was possible now for Caris and Pella to be together. She wondered how Pella was, whether they were happy and how Caris was adjusting to the new life that had been Antryg's final gift to him. She wondered, too, whether Magister Magus had recovered from his slavery to Suraklin, whether Cerdic had helped him regain his ostentatious house, and whether Marquises and Countesses again clustered to his pink-and-black drawing room, waiting to pay him lavish sums to tell them what they wanted to hear.

She would never know, of course. It was as if they, too, were dead. Sometimes in these last three days her loneliness had seemed to fill the earth.

Most of the time it seemed as if Ruth believed her. From the gas station near San Serano, she had phoned Ruth to come and pick her up. All the way back to Van Nuys, her friend had not said much, but had looked at her sidelong, where she had sat slumped in the corner of the front seat in her grubby green velvet knee breeches, squalid peasant boots and tattered, lace-ruffled shirt. She must, she knew, have looked very different, besides being much thinner and having three inches of her hair singed off. That first evening Ruth had treated her with a care very much at odds with her usual breeziness and did not dismiss what she said.

Wherever she had been, thought Joanna wearily, she at least must look as if she'd been *someplace*. As ever, she had no proof.

She'd gotten something of the same reaction from her colleagues at work who saw her and a great deal of sympathy regarding her fictitious sister-in-law's three-month bout with terminal cancer. Most, though not all, respected her flat request not to talk about it.

Slowly she began reacclimating herself to driving a car, gauging traffic speed, taking showers, and having noise around her virtually all the time. It was odd to have possessions again, odd not to be always on the move, and odd not to be terrified of capture half the time.

But it all felt hollow and strange, as if it, and not the past three months, had happened to someone else.

Antryg was dead.

Gary was dead, too, of course, she thought, feeling the residual heat of the pavement radiating softly against her sandaled feet as she crossed the parking lot. But it wasn't Gary's voice she remembered, lying awake at night.

I'll get over this, she told herself, fighting the wave of grief that threatened to swamp her. *It won't always be this bad.*

She didn't believe it. She felt a flash of sympathy for Suraklin. It wouldn't be too bad, she thought, simply to program herself into a computer and forget what it was like to feel.

She raised her head, scanning the parking lot for her blue Mustang. It sat in solitary splendor beneath one of the tall lamps which, like a network of artificial moons, cast primrose light against a luminous blue dusk.

Someone was sitting cross-legged on the hood of her car.

She stopped, regretting the absence of her hammer and reflecting that miscellaneous weirdos were things she hadn't had to put up with on the other side of the Void. But after Suraklin and the Inquisition, she found the thought of minor hassles of this kind far less frightening than she once had. Then he turned his head.

She saw the flash of round spectacle lenses, the gleam of a silver-foil rock concert logo on his baggy t-shirt. As every drop of blood in her veins transubstantiated painfully into straight adrenaline, she thought, *Supposition A cannot be true.* And then: *Whoever it is, I'll kill him for doing this to me.*

She crossed what seemed like twenty acres of black pavement, first quickly, her heart squeezed like a fist inside her, then slower and slower as she came near the spot.

He unfolded long, jeans-clad legs and scrambled to his feet. The lamp overhead sparkled on the cracked spectacle lens, the diamond earrings snagged in the curly tangle of gray hair, and the strands of gimcrack beads. Even at this distance, she saw there was a bandage on the bare arm where Suraklin's bullet had grazed.

"Joanna?"

Her arms crushed him in a hug before she remembered he had a cracked rib—she could feel the stiffness of the dressing under his t-shirt. If it was a dream, she thought obliquely as his arms closed painfully around her burned back, it was an awfully accurate one . . . His embrace lifted her off her feet.

When they'd finished the first hundred-year kiss, he managed to say, "Look, I swear I won't be a burden to you—unemployed wizards can *always* find work . . ."

She dragged his mouth down to hers again, the familiar awkwardness of their mismatched heights convincing her finally that it couldn't be a dream. She must have caught him on his cracked rib again because his convulsive grip suddenly relaxed. "I'm sorry," he gasped. "I forgot about your back . . ." He looked around at the empty parking lot. "Did they make you stay on after everyone else left as punishment for desertion?"

He must, she realized, have been sitting on the hood of the Mustang for an hour at least, watching the sun go down. He was wearing only the jeans, boots, and t-shirt he'd had on when she'd first met him, but didn't seem chilled—like her, he had come from a place of bitterest cold.

"No. I had some things to finish . . ." She paused in the midst of her usual excuse, then said, "That's not really true. I just didn't want to go home to be alone."

"Ah," he said softly. For a few minutes they didn't speak, only stood wrapped in one another, as they had done under his grubby cloak in the Sykerst, silent and content.

After she quit crying Joanna said, "I guess I shouldn't be surprised."

"It's flattering of you to say so, my dear. I'm speechless with astonishment that I'm not dead."

Her arm tightened briefly around his waist. "You've never been speechless in your life," she said, with unkind accuracy. "Don't tell me the Council miscalculated the distance they had to be away from the Tower when they opened the Void to send me through?"

He shook his head. "No. It was—rather unlikely. A *deus ex machina,* so to speak." He sounded a little shaken, as if it still puzzled him, not only the manner of his escape, but that he had escaped at all.

"Don't tell me Cerdic came through at the last minute? Or Aunt Min?"

He grinned, and shook his head again. "Though I wouldn't swear Aunt Min was as asleep as she seemed to be when she was allegedly keeping the deathwatch over me. She seldom is, you know." He rubbed his hands absently, as if trying to massage some old ache from the swollen joints. "No, it was quite literally a *deus ex machina.*" For a moment he was silent, as if still trying to puzzle it out. At last he said, "It was the Dead God who saved me."

A technician, thought Joanna. A scientist. She remembered the rotting tower of borrowed flesh and bones, the gluey, freezing darkness of the haunted church, and the poltergeist knocking, hammering out the numbers of pi. She wondered whether the thing he had built out of the bodies of others had been meant to resemble his true physical form.

Lamplight snaked along Antryg's spectacles as he turned his head. "Universal structural theory was his specialty, you know. In fact that was why he got trapped on our side of the Void to begin with, because he was investigating the Gate that was opened, rather than running away from it like a sensible person. After having crossed the Void twice— through and back—he knew of its existence and was doing experiments with it. He picked up the heavy disturbances on his instruments when Suraklin destroyed the enclave and was focused on that area when the Council sent you through. Since he had telepathically touched your mind as well as mine through the Sigil net he recognized you; and he realized you were being sent through under guard and against your will. Having located you, he was able to backtrack the mages to their starting point and locate me."

He fell quiet again, staring out into the Prussian-blue darkness, as if through it he could look into some other, deeper night. The lamplight overhead glinted on his earrings, and among the trashy finery around his neck Joanna recognized the necklaces given to him by Pella and earlier by Pharos, delicate as Fabergé work among dimestore beads.

"I had already taken the poison," he said softly, as if to himself. "Considering what was in Pharos' warrant, the Council was doing me the greatest favor they could. The Dead God—he told me his name, which is really only an identification sequence—was working on a machine to open Gates in the Void, but it was only in the experimental stages. He ran a considerable risk coming to get me at all. If Aunt Min had been awake, she could have stopped him easily, trapped him on that side of the Void, and destroyed him. But she wasn't or didn't seem to be."

I knew them both, the old Archmage had said. Aside from Antryg, Aunt Min was probably the only person living who had known both Suraklin and Salteris well.

Joanna reached across and put her hand over his. "Are you all right?" Her voice sounded smaller than she had meant, her thoughts on that silent stone room and Antryg lying there alone.

He brought his other hand around to cover hers, the big, crooked bones of it reassuring. "A little surprised at the Dead God. I hardly suspected him of that kind of sentimentality, or honor, or whatever it was that motivated him. I was nearly unconscious when he fetched me through to his own world and then I was ill for days, living on artificial air while he got the poison out of my system. And then I came here."

He put an arm around her shoulders and drew her mouth once more to his. In the midst of the kiss he added absently, "You know, you really *are* going to have to do something about your height . . .

"I promise I won't be a burden on you any longer than it takes me to find something to do for money and my own place to live," he went on after a few moments. "I can tend bar—read tea-leaves—heave coal . . ."

"There hasn't been a coal heater in Los Angeles since before World War II."

"Another promising career blighted. You have to give them numbers to tell them apart?" He dubiously regarded the car as Joanna unlocked the passenger-side door, then clambered in and pulled the door shut behind him. Joanna got in, gave him a brief lecture on the operation of the windows, started the engine, and, blithely disregarding the white lines, roared off across the parking lot, out the gate, and down Lost Canyon Road.

She braked where the road crested the hill above the Ventura Freeway. Full dark had come, warm and magic; the electric wind had fallen; and in the dry, brilliant air, the San Fernando Valley lay before them in a glittering carpet, with the outlying blaze of the greater city of lights in the distance. Beside her, Antryg was silent, gazing out across the jewel-box glory of the world in which he would now live as an exile.

Quietly, she said, "Your magic is gone, isn't it? You have no power in this world."

"Probably not." Against the reflection of the light, his face was only a dark profile of extravagant nose, shining steel spectacle rim, and a point of light caught in the beads at his throat. "Considering the uses to which I put my magic in the past, that may be for the best, at least for a time. Later . . ." He shrugged. "Is later. Right now I'm only glad that there is a later—or even that there is a now. And in fact, that's really all there ever is."

" 'Had I world enough, and time,' " Joanna quoted softly, wanting nothing more than that moment, the velvet voice in the darkness, the liquid warmth of the night, and the miles of flame-sprinkled blackness stretching out to the encircling hills that hemmed a flame-sprinkled sky.

His lenses flashed as he turned his head; his deep voice was rueful in the dark. "All those weeks you were in my world, under my protection, I never fully appreciated how uncomfortable it must have been for you to be that dependent on someone."

Joanna nodded, her small hands resting on the worn plastic of the steering wheel as she gazed out into the night. "Well, let me warn you, dog wizard, now that you're in *my* world under *my* protection, I intend to take advantage of you to the fullest."

She couldn't see in the dark, but she sensed his grin. "Oh, good . . . What do people here eat? And will you teach me how to drive one of these things?"

She shuddered as she put the car in gear and headed down the hill toward the freeway. "That will be all I need . . . We'll talk about it later. In the meantime, let me explain to you about tacos . . ."

ABOUT THE AUTHOR

At various times in her life, Barbara Hambly has been a high-school teacher, a model, a waitress, a technical editor, a professional graduate student, an all-night clerk at a liquor store, a karate instructor. Born in San Diego, she grew up in Southern California, with the exception of one high-school semester spent in New South Wales, Australia. Her interest in fantasy began with reading *The Wizard of Oz* at an early age and has continued ever since.

She attended the University of California, Riverside, specializing in medieval history. In connection with this, she spent a year at the University of Bordeaux in the south of France and worked as a teaching and research assistant at UC Riverside, eventually earning a Master's Degree in the subject. At the university, she also became involved in karate, making Black Belt in 1978 and competing in several national-level tournaments.

Barbara Hambly now lives in Los Angeles, California.